Kings Row

Kings Row

Henry Bellamann

Introduction by Rachael Price

Hastings College Press | Hastings, Nebraska

Production and Proofreading
Taylor Lipinski
Jora Jackson-Brown

ISBN-13: 978-1-942885-84-9

Note on the text: This edition has been reset from the 1942 Simon and Schuster edition. Original spelling and grammatical conventions have been maintained, except in the case of publishing errors in that edition. The original punctuation has been maintained but updated using modern conventions (e.g., eliminating spaces around dashes).

Introduction

Rachael Price

Perhaps the most enduring cultural artifact of Henry Bellamann's 1940 bestseller *Kings Row* is a scene from Sam Wood's 1942 film adaptation, in which Ronald Reagan, as Drake McHugh, awakens one morning after a terrible accident to find that his legs have been amputated and shouts "Where's the rest of me?!" Reagan himself was apparently so taken with this line (and with the sexually adventurous McHugh, which he considered his "biggest and best role") that he actually titled his 1965 autobiography *Where's the Rest of Me?*, a move that serves to underscore the connection between *Kings Row* and Ronald Reagan in the public eye (Wills 26). It is more than a little ironic that such an important figure in the history of American conservatism would come to be associated with Bellamann's story, because, as this introduction will detail, *Kings Row* undermines considerably the sentiments of American exceptionalism that Reagan himself made famous with the regular invocation of John Winthrop's "city on a hill" metaphor.

As was the case with the literary movement often labeled "the revolt from the village," which hit its high point about twenty years before the publication of *Kings Row* and was a clear influence on Bellamann's novel, the main way in which the text undermines these American ideals is by questioning the supremacy of its small towns, which themselves were long considered to be the foundation of the young nation. In his 1966 publication *As a City Upon a Hill: The Town in American History*, historian Page Smith uses the term specifically to refer to Winthrop's actual audience at the time who were, as he writes, members of a "covenanted community," a precursor to the village that, he argues, is the core building block of America.

Kings Row represents, in many ways, a logical outgrowth of the modernist "revolt from the village" movement and its success shows the ways in which what began as questioning and experimentation in the early twentieth century became an established paradigm shift in popular perceptions of small-town America by 1940. As was the case with its thematic successor, Grace Metalious's 1956 blockbuster *Peyton Place*, *Kings Row* struck a chord with readers in repressive small towns across the country. While several scholars, most notably the late Jay Miles Karr, have established the connections between the fictional Kings Row and the real-life Fulton, Missouri (Bellamann's own hometown), readers recognized their own hometowns as a swiftly urbanizing nation reassessed its worship of pastoralism. Bellamann himself emphasized this point in a 1940 interview with the *St. Louis Post-Dispatch*:

To show the fallacy of trying to decide that the story is of Fulton, Clarksville, Richmond, or any other place I have lived, one of the guests at this [the Ansonia] hotel stopped me the other day and said: "Mr. Bellamann, I have read your book and as I went along I wrote in the real names of the people you were telling about. The town is ----," and he named a small town in New York State of which I had never heard. (Goldstein 63)

And yet, while the success of *Kings Row* was indicative of a cultural sea change in the 1940s, it was out of print for many years and largely forgotten. Furthermore, it has been conspicuously absent from the literary canon. As was the case with *Peyton Place* nearly a generation later, its treatment of controversial issues garnered a reputation for salaciousness, an element that aided book sales but also hindered its staying power, relegating it to the realm of the potboiler. A careful reexamination, though, reveals a novel that is not only thoughtfully written but also provides an important cultural touchstone in the legacy of the American small town. A contemporary reading reveals a sensitive portrayal of a small town and real issues of the day as they affected citizens of Kings Row, particularly the outsiders and the most marginalized voices in the community.

Indeed, by focusing the narrative on the "outsiders" of the community, Bellamann erodes these characters' very outsider status, thereby shifting the reader's focus away from hegemonic definitions and experiences of small-town America. In his 1940 *New York Times* review of the novel, editor and critic Harold Strauss notes that "The publishers say that the theme is the hatred of nonconformity and that the town of Kings Row brutally crushes and throws aside those who do not measure down to its warped standards. But half a dozen characters live in bold and admitted nonconformity" (89). In foregrounding these nonhegemonic narratives alongside more conventional depictions of rural America, Bellamann renders the town of Kings Row as a kind of interstitial space between convention and progress.

To understand this delicate balance that Bellamann invoked, it is, of course, necessary to hearken back to the influence of "revolt" itself. His early writings make many references to it. In fact, in the Henry and Katherine Bellamann Collection at the University of Mississippi, there exists an early draft of Kings Row in the form of first-person poetic monologues in the style of Edgar Lee Masters's *The Spoon River Anthology* (1915). Jay Miles Karr adds that, "On a certain page, his handwritten Kings Row notes break off, and he lists the landmarks of the small town novel: 'Sherwood Anderson, Spoon River, Dreiser, Lewis, Twain'" (xi). As someone who left his own small Midwestern town as a young adult, Bellamann certainly fits the pattern of a member of the movement. Like these authors, the town he presents us in his fiction serves not as an outright backwater, but as a complicated locale within which we can assess the problems with the pastoral ideal of small-town America. In one of the more overtly philosophical passages of the novel, *Kings Row*'s Catholic priest Father Donovan takes a walk along the outskirts of the town:

> He had walked today along his favorite way. Up the creek for a mile, then through the woods, and out where the hayfields and slanting meadows were ablaze now with late fall flowers. The Spanish nettle, rich gold of a lingering summer, was fading. The goldenrod plumes waved handsomely. The stately joe-pye held its rose-purple plumes high in every corner. Father Donovan stood leaning against an old rail fence. He plucked sprays of Indian paintbrush and stroked his fingers with the silky clusters. A breeze set the whole field of yellow blossoms to running madly. How gay they were! A world of little people in festival. Father Donovan wished he could raise his hands and give them a blessing.
>
> They were happy and good—these flowers. And when you looked closely they were all different. Each one had its own face. He smiled down into the crowd of them about his knees. Some of them had a comic look, some were serious, but none of them was sad.
>
> He raised his head, and shaded his eyes with his hand as he gazed for a long time at the roofs of Kings Row, just showing here and there through the trees. If one could see all of the people of the town gathered together like this they would look alike, too, just as the black-eyed nettle flowers did. But, like these wild-blooming things, they too were different when you looked close. Each one different—some gay, some thoughtful, but, alas! a great many of them sad. (324)

Here, Bellamann uses the metaphor of the nettle flowers to illustrate the danger of failing to see past a town's conformist surface. The text does not paint a uniformly negative picture of the town or its inhabitants, but instead pushes for a greater understanding and acceptance of the town's more marginal characters (and, thus, textually rebels against the town's act of marginalization).

This rebellion against conformity certainly echoes larger sentiments of modernism. While the novel itself appeared in 1940, the storyline unfolds over the course of about 20 years, from 1890 until approximately 1910. This chronological discrepancy is important for two key ideas relating to the broader movement of modernism. For one thing, the text's look back at the past calls to mind Raymond Williams's famous "escalator" into history, a metaphor he invokes to illustrate the conflation of the rural with the past in the modern era. This chronological setting clashes with modernist mantra of "Make it new" and thus illustrates the more "backward" (both chronologically and metaphorically) nature of the small town in relation to the city. The year 1890 also marks a crucial turning point in American, and more specifically Midwestern, history. While the year 1920 marked the first United States Census that showed more people living in urban areas than in rural ones, the year 1890 set an important precedent for this later milestone, in the form of what came to be known as the death of the frontier, when the Superintendent of the Census famously remarked that "Up to and including 1880 the country had a frontier of settlement, but at present the unsettled area has been so broken into by isolated bodies of settlement that there can hardly be said to be a frontier line. In the discussion of its extent, its westward movement, etc., it cannot, therefore, any longer have a place in the census reports" (qtd in Turner 1). We cannot overlook this particular juncture when assessing portrayals of the American small town. If we view literary portrayals of rural America as largely bucolic and pastoral in the nineteenth century, we cannot separate such feelings from the romance of the American frontier. Those who revolted against such a village were not only questioning what it meant to be rural, but what it meant to be American.

Such questioning is key in the development of *Kings Row*. As a town in the center of the United States, Kings Row is portrayed as a place entrenched in the difficulties of the death of the frontier; we find Kings Row, during the setting of the novel, at an important juncture in the history of this very death. Kings Row itself was, obviously, part of the frontier, as Colonel Skeffington, a prestigious lawyer and a symbolic elder statesman, remembers fondly. Skeffington, who had come to Kings Row from distant Virginia, associates his early attraction to Kings Row to its "wild" frontier qualities: "He loved [Kings Row]—always had. Loved it when he first saw it sixty years ago. It was like home then—like the lovely Shenandoah Valley, but wilder, and that wildness had appealed to him then.... The people ... Made a state, a real state, out of a raw territory" (334). Here the depiction of "making" a state from "raw" and "wild" territory posits Kings Row as a kind of liminal space; it is wild, but part of the appeal of that very wildness is to craft one's own civilization from it. The frontier Kings Row is not just a pastoral paradise, but a blank slate upon which to model a new society. The text makes it clear, though, that Kings Row no longer carries the possibilities of the frontier. Skeffington himself, despite the fact that he "always had" loved the town, echoes the idea of the death of the frontier when he insists that "'Pioneer times are over—past and gone'" (258). In this same conversation, longtime resident Tom Carr, a bereaved widow who is about to leave Kings Row, tells Skeffington that he plans to leave for "'out West,'" adding that he "'always meant to go on further out. Just got stuck here'" (258). This statement refers to the now apparently outdated idea that perhaps the frontier that Tom had so desired as a young man can be realized with a move further West. It also reiterates the precarious nature of the Midwestern (i.e., not quite Western) small town at the turn of the twentieth century. Kings Row is no longer part of the mythic frontier; it is just a place along the way wherein one can become "stuck."

Though the idea of revolting from the village might conjure up images of the supremacy of the city, as opposed to the country, Bellamann makes it clear that part of the problem is that, with the loss of the frontier, Kings Row is not country enough. A typewritten synopsis of the story, which accompanies an early draft of the novel in Bellamann's papers at the University of Mississippi, tells us that Kings Row "is, in its basic structure, the story of a town in the Middle West covering a period of significant change (1890–1920) when such towns lost their individual character with the disappearance of the 'second wave' pioneers, and merged into standardized imitations of small cities with the consequent loss of much that made them interesting." Like so many other "revolt" authors, Bellamann does not present the city as a panacea; part of the problem with Kings Row is that it looks too far beyond its country past and tries too hard to be like the city. Thus, while the text embraces much of modernism's style and ideals, it is also apprehensive of the encroaching uniformity that accompanies this period of modernity.

This middle position of Kings Row, both geographically and chronologically, ironically robs it of its liminality to a large extent. The Midwest of the popular imagination is not the urbane East, nor is it the frontier West. It is simply a middle ground. Among the stereotypes that Bellamann (and his modernist predecessors) was rebuffing was a kind of universal conflation of the Midwest with the pastoral. Here I use "pastoral" to signal not the wild, untamed frontier but the peaceful, tame countryside that is frequently invoked in popular rhetoric to this day. James R. Shortridge links this conflation back to the turn of the twentieth century, which was not only the immediate aftermath of the "death of the frontier" but also, as he notes, the time of "the emergence of the Middle West as a regional name," thus reiterating the connection between the death of the wild frontier and the emergence of the American Midwest as a more middle-ground pastoral space. Shortridge goes on to explain that "The two concepts—pastoralism and Middle West—which initially were similar in several respects, rapidly intertwined and soon became virtually synonymous" (28). William Barillas, in *The Midwestern Pastoral*, explains that

> The Midwest is the nation's middlescape, its "heartland," a regional label that associates geographical centrality with a defining role in national identity and emotional responses to place. Not only books but paintings, films, and other media have reinforced this image of farms, bucolic woods and streams, and small towns populated by plain-speaking, upright citizens. The Midwest, according to pastoral myth, is what America thinks itself to be (4).

With this in mind, it is important to note that the key figures of the "revolt" were all from the Midwest, thus making their revelations all the more shocking. While a great deal of literature dealing with similar themes was emerging from the American South during this time, it was not popularly viewed as the kind of affront that was, say, *Main Street,* because of the very "Othering" of the U.S. South that was so important in constructing post–Civil War American identity. While the South functions as the nation's "Other," as demonstrated by Leigh Anne Duck in *The Nation's Region: Southern Modernism, Segregation, and U.S. Nationalism,* the Midwest stands in for the nation as a whole.

Bellamann pushes back against this pastoral view from the very beginning of *Kings Row,* in opening paragraphs that describe the physical landscape of the town:

> Spring came late in the year 1890, so it came more violently, and the fullness of its burgeoning heightened the seasonal disturbance that made unquiet in the blood.
>
> On this particular day, the twenty-eighth of April, the vast sky seemed vaster than ever—wider, bluer, higher. Continents of white clouds moved slowly from west to east, casting immense drifts of blue over the landscape which seemed alternately to expand and to shrink as sunlight and shadow followed in deliberate procession.
>
> The green distances of the land were gashed and scarred with wandering roads, lumpy and deep-rutted from the heavy wheels that had groaned and strained through the winter mud. These roads came from the outlying regions, springing up, like casual streams, marking themselves more and more deeply in the soil as they moved between rail fences, widening as they wound toward the county seat. Scattered in their beginnings, they drew nearer to each other, converged and straightened as they approached the town.
>
> They were like the strands of a gigantic web, weaving and knitting closer and closer until they reached a center—Kings Row, the county seat. "A good town," everyone said. "A good, clean town. A good town to live in, and a good place to raise your children" (1).

Here he invokes this physicality in a manner reminiscent of the bucolic ideal of rural America, but amidst these invocations of nature he inserts images of destruction; the beginning of spring is not marked by blossoms in bloom, but it comes "violently," marks a "seasonal disturbance," and makes "unquiet in the blood." This uncomfortable juxtaposition of springtime and violence brings in mind another set of opening lines, those of T.S. Eliot's "The Waste Land": "April is the cruellest month, breeding / Lilacs out of the dead land, mixing / Memory and desire, stirring / Dull roots with spring rain" (545). Such a reference reinforces *Kings Row*'s ties to the experimental stylings of modernism. Note also that the green landscape is "gashed and scarred" with roads that are "lumpy and deep-rutted from the heavy wheels that had groaned and strained through the winter mud." An earlier draft makes the influence of modernism even more apparent as it commingles sexuality in the midst of all of this violence, adding that "when Spring came down the great valley it did not come with maiden shyness as in southern climates, but with the whoop and clamor of conquest" (2). The endorsements of a "good, clean town" and "a good place to raise your children" make no mention of anything specific to the town itself, and thus come off as mere empty platitudes; even today, communities that most don't see as particularly exciting are said to be a "good place to raise children." This is certainly not a bucolic paradise. Rather, Bellamann uses the rhetoric of the pastoral to dismantle the movement's own viability. The gashing roads even suggest the threat of encroaching urbanization, showing us that it is not only the large cities whose landscapes have been disturbed. In other words, the novel's description of the landscape suggests that true pastoralism involves land completely untouched by urbanization of either the big city or the small town and, in this way, romanticizes the old notion of the American frontier.

And yet, while this geography is critical to the novel's meaning, it is the characters who impart the greatest importance. Karr writes that "*Kings Row* is a novel with a humanitarian social purpose behind it. The quintessential point of the huge complex example is social tolerance" (xxiii). The main way in which Bellamann constructs this particular motif is through his continued foregrounding of the town's nonconformists. Setting a pattern that *Peyton Place* would later famously replicate, the novel tells the story of myriad characters, focusing especially on a small group of characters who begin the novel as children and grow to adulthood in the titular small town. In the first chapter, as the narrative wends its way from the outskirts of the town to the main thoroughfares, it settles on the schoolhouse, "where Miss Sally Venable held sway over some sixty children ranging in age from ten to fourteen" (3). The text then introduces the reader to several of the novel's most prominent characters via the ruminations of Miss Venable, whose thoughts appear to focus on the ways in which each child is different from the others; thus each of these characters is textually "othered" from the very beginning.

The first child that her thoughts introduce is twelve-year-old Jamie Wakefield; according to her observations, he is "[t]oo pretty for a boy," with other children referring to him as a "sissy" (4, 5). This thought reinforces what R.W. Connell labels "hegemonic masculinity," which she defines as "the masculinity that occupies the hegemonic position in a given pattern of gender relations" via the assumption that one must look a certain way (a way that is not considered "sissy") to be considered "a boy" (76). The character's opposition to such norms becomes even more apparent as he matures; even though the 1940 novel dared not show us the word in print, Jamie Wakefield is clearly a gay character. Bellamann's typewritten synopsis refers to the character as "a born homosexual," a description that not only helps to completely

clarify the character's sexual identity but also displays progressive thinking in
Bellamann's assertion that someone can be born gay, an idea more humanizing
than theories of "inversion" popular at the time.

Though Jamie is a relatively minor character in the narrative, the text
continually reinforces his nonconformity via his interactions with more
prominent characters. About five years after his introduction in the classroom
of Sally Venable, Jamie takes an evening stroll with his friend Parris Mitchell,
and Parris ruminates on the ways in which Jamie is different from other
teenage boys in town: "He liked Jamie. Yes; he was sure about that. But why
was he always a little embarrassed about it? The other boys didn't seem to
dislike Jamie—they, well, they merely seemed to push him aside somewhat.
They called him girly names. Certainly, he was girlish, but he was really all
right" (89). In addition to his gender variance, Jamie goes on to confide in
Parris about myriad other ways in which he fails to fit in with the life that
is expected of him in Kings Row. He speaks of his determination to make a
living as a poet, despite his family's insistence that he work at his father's bank.
The scene culminates with Jamie's sexual identity coming into clear focus as
he makes a sexual advance toward Parris: "Jamie had strange hands … His
fingers left a tingle where they touched.… Jamie leaned forward and kissed
him on the mouth. Parris was too amazed to move, too amazed to think.…
He was not too clearly aware of anything for a while except Jamie's caresses
and his flattering hands which carried both violence and appeasement in their
touch" (93). And yet, while the town as a whole rejects him on some level,
the character of Parris reacts to the situation with a much more nuanced and
understanding approach. He does not invoke the homophobia often associated
with hegemonic masculinity; not only does he not dislike the experience but, as
we see via syntactical choices such as fingers that "left a tingle" and "flattering
hands," he does enjoy it on some level. The fact that Parris associates his
friend's touch with both "violence and appeasement" illustrates the Freudian
rejection of sexual binaries that was a part of the burgeoning modernism that so
informed Bellamann's writing. Through the protagonist's approval of Jamie, the
text as a whole presents him as a sympathetic character. And yet such sympathy
takes on the mantle of the novel's aforementioned plea for social tolerance. As
Jamie grows into an adult and ends up taking a job at his father's bank, he feels
forced to blunt his individuality and laments the fact that, while he may be able
to quietly go about his life in Kings Row, he can never be his authentic self.
Jamie acknowledges this conundrum inwardly, as he laments that "It seemed
so arbitrary, and heartless, and impersonal. Some were included in the approval
of the arranged mass, some were left outside.… He himself was, certainly"
(294). In foregrounding the narrative of one of these self-described outsiders,
Bellamann builds a textual case for the inclusion of marginalized voices.

Back in the schoolroom of the text's early pages, Miss Venable's attention
drifts to another outsider, one with a fate even more tragic than Jamie's:

Cassandra Tower. She thinks of Cassandra as "the prettiest girl in town," noting the romantic attention she is already attracting from her male peers (4). And yet, while one might think that such positive attention would equate to popularity in the world of Kings Row, Miss Venable can tell that there is something different about Cassandra, or "Cassie," as others often call her; she notices the ways in which she does not give school her full attention: "Cassandra was looking elsewhere. She had not moved, but her eyes drooped a little, and her face wore a look of sly secretiveness. She ran her hands through her short coppery curls with a gesture that was curiously troubled" (5). This juxtaposition between outward beauty and inward secrets characterizes Cassandra for her entire existence in the novel.

This sense of secrecy hovers not just around Cassandra, but around her family as well. Her father, Dr. Alexander Q. Tower, is ostensibly a physician, but the text notes that "So far as anyone knew, Dr. Tower had never had a patient" (24). He spends most of his time shuttered away in his house, while his wife spends all her time there as well, often sitting at the front window in what appears to be a catatonic state: "For several years now, Mrs. Tower could be seen every day, sitting inside her living-room window. She never seemed to occupy herself in any way with fancy work or knitting. She simply sat there hour after hour, apparently taking no notice of people passing in the street nor, as far as anyone could tell, of anything in the room" (25). Such unusual behavior not only suggests deeper troubles in young Cassie's life, but also prejudices townspeople against her; one can see such attitudes early on in the novel, when Parris is the only classmate who shows up to her birthday party. Shortly thereafter Dr. Tower removes her from public school to educate her himself, only exacerbating her isolation from the community.

The text does not revisit Cassie's story until Book Two, about five years after the story's beginning, when Parris, who wants to be a doctor, finds himself under the tutelage of Dr. Tower. Though he visits the family residence on a regular basis, he rarely sees Cassie or her mother until one evening when he returns to the doctor's study to retrieve a notebook after the doctor himself has left for an unexplained trip to St. Louis. He finds Cassie there in the room, and their conversation soon evolves into a sexual encounter. For the next several months, they meet in numerous encounters, with Cassie taking the lead in furthering their sexual relationship. In attempt to describe the nature of their relationship to his playboy friend Drake McHugh, Parris surmises that she might possibly have what he terms "nymphomania." While this term for female hypersexuality reflects Parris's (and the novel's) ongoing interest in sexual modernity, it is also problematic by contemporary standards because of its particularly gendered approach to sexual pathology. Carol Groneman, tracing the history of the term, explains that "Nymphomania is variously described as too much coitus ... too much desire, and too much masturbation. Simultaneously, it was seen as a symptom, a cause, and a disease in its own right. Its etiologies, symptoms, and treatments often overlapped with those of erotomania, hysteria, hystero-epilepsy, and ovariomania" (340). This association with now-discarded female pathologies like hysteria and ovariomania underscore these problematic associations in the novel.

And yet, while the story of Kings Row is presented from a largely male perspective, the text offers numerous attempts to reject hegemonic masculinity and a more nuanced understanding of sexuality from multiple perspectives. While Parris does characterize Cassie's behavior as possibly pathological in nature, he admits that he often expresses a similar enthusiasm in sexual matters, telling Drake, "'I guess I'm kind of the same way ... far as she's concerned, anyway'" (164). He continues his relationship with her, even as Cassie's home life appears to become ever more isolated. First her mother dies under mysterious circumstances, and shortly thereafter she arrives at Drake's house to visit Parris, and begs her young lover to take her with him to Vienna, where he will be studying medicine (in keeping with the novel's strong Freudian overtones). When he rebuffs her, she leaves abruptly, and Parris tries to rationalize her behavior by referring to it as a "'hysterical outbreak'" (226).

The reader soon learns that Cassie's story was not just mysterious, but tragic, as that very night Dr. Tower kills his young daughter in a murder-suicide. Soon afterwards, Parris learns, by looking through Tower's private writings, that the doctor had been sexually abusing his daughter since childhood, and surmises that he killed his daughter as a result of the growing independence she had developed during her relationship with Parris himself. As he explains to Drake, "'I think she must have tried at last to break away, or he must have lost his hold on her, or control over her'" (252). While this particular storyline certainly added to the novel's salacious reputation, Bellamann presents Cassie's plight in an unsensational manner, focusing on the tragedy and trauma of the experience. As Parris tries to come to grips with this information, he feels not only intense grief and guilt for not helping Cassie, but also anger at the fact that his academic mentor was a narcissist who thought he could get away with imprisoning and abusing his own child indefinitely.

This knowledge also adds an element of explanation of Cassie's sexual behavior. Reading her experience through a modern lens, one can surmise that what Parris considered possible "nymphomania" or "hysteria" could instead have been explained as behaviors resulting from sexual trauma. A study by Perera et al (2009) found strong indications that "young adults who were sexually abused during childhood and who grew up in poor family environments were more likely than others to develop sexual sensation seeking and sexually compulsive tendencies" (140). Bellamann presents the story of Cassie as an outsider whose family life obviously does not meet the expected ideals of a "good, clean town" like Kings Row. And yet, in telling Cassie's story, even if only through the eyes of a male protagonist, the novel creates awareness of child sexual abuse as a real problem that must be addressed and that can happen anywhere, even in a wealthy family in small-town America.

The next character introduced by Sally Venable's interior monologue is the one who is ostensibly the most normal in the eyes of the town: Drake McHugh. Indeed, Bellamann portrays Drake from the very beginning as almost an exemplar of hegemonic masculinity. In that early classroom scene, we meet him as someone who seemingly meets the gender norms of King Row; yet, as with Cassie, the text hints that there is more to his character than meets the eye: "Drake was watching Cassandra now, his long faun eyes glinting a little under his brows that grew shaggily together over the bridge of his arched nose. Drake, robust, deep-chested, hair always falling into his eyes. 'A regular boy,' most people said, but Sally Venable was not so sure of that" (5). His leering at Cassandra suggests a budding interest in sexual matters, an interest that intensifies as he matures. He brags of his numerous sexual encounters to Parris, often invoking the names of his two favorite paramours, sisters Poppy and Jinny Ross; after his guardians die and leave him their house, he becomes even more transparent about his conquests: "'All this time I've been taking Poppy Ross out to Moore's tobacco barn! I just kind of forgot that I'm my own boss and live in my own house! Say, I'm going to get her to come up there—her and Jinny. Hot-choo, Parris, we can have a time right in my own house'" (123). Parris sees Drake's sexual enthusiasm as something exciting, as opposed to what he sees as the possibly pathological female sexuality of Cassie, which furthers Drake's attitude as a kind of hypermasculine bravado. And yet the town still marks Drake as an outsider, because he does not go out of his way to hide his frequent premarital encounters, bringing the Ross sisters to his own house. His courtship of Louise Gordon, the daughter of the town's most prominent physician, ends after her parents discover open evidence of such encounters. His reaction suggests that it is not his behavior *per se* that is out of character for the townspeople, but rather his openness about it: "'All the old busybodies in this town sit around and talk about me. Just 'cause I'm out in the open about what I do'" (196). His open brand of sexuality has landed him in the realm of the outsiders.

Drake continues to defy hegemonic expectations in his eventual choice of a partner, a woman of lower social class named Randy Monaghan. After Parris leaves for Vienna, Drake and Randy begin an affair that, while having a sexual component, is about more than just sex. It is not a masculine conquest, but a mutually satisfying relationship; as Randy explains, "'Listen, Drake, when a girl acts the way I do about you, she means it. It's because I want to, because I like you better than anybody in the world'" (280). This egalitarian dynamic flourishes even more after the president of the Farmers

Exchange Bank steals Drake's inheritance and flees the country. This shift in fortune causes him to get a job as a railroad section man, and it is there that he meets with a terrible accident that results in the loss of his legs. While the town whispers that Dr. Gordon, Louise's father, amputated his legs on purpose, the salacious element of the tale becomes secondary to the strength that Drake displays despite his reversal of fortune. Instead of fading slowly and helplessly from the narrative, Drake goes on to a second act in life, one marked by but not destroyed by his disability. He and Randy end up marrying and achieve a degree of financial success with local real estate. He learns to depend on his wife for help, but this shift in power is not tragic. It is a necessary and viable way to navigate their married life. Bellamann makes a note of this shift via a symbolic tableau right after Randy agrees to marry the newly disabled Drake: "Drake raised his arms and clutched the head of the bed. Then he turned his face to the wall again, but one hand reached out for hers. He held it so tight she winced, but she held perfectly still … It seemed to Randy that all of the balances of life were slowly turning in the singing silence of the little room" (356–357). Through Drake's story as an outsider in the world of Kings Row, Bellamann's textual quest for social tolerance extends to those with disabilities.

Circling around all of these other local iconoclasts is Parris Mitchell, whom the reader also meets in Miss Venable's classroom. He, too, is an outsider, though the text suggests from the very beginning that Parris is othered not because of lack of proper behavior, but by, in a sense, too much proper behavior:

Parris Mitchell was her pet. It was a tribute to the just conduct of her teaching that not one of her pupils suspected this partiality—least of all Parris himself. The boy was different in every way. Perhaps it was because he lived with that curious foreign grandmother, Madame von Eln. Dr. Axel Berdorff, pastor of the German Lutheran church, said that Parris spoke French and German better than he did English. Miss Venable remembered that even two years ago he spoke with an accent. The other children used to laugh sometimes. But the accent had disappeared, leaving his speech oddly precise.

He looked foreign, she thought. Stocky and broad-shouldered. Vitality showed in his warm coloring and in the heavy eyebrows arched high over large hazel eyes. His hair, too, was as thick as plush. A slight shadow showed on his upper lip, although he was only twelve. He had a quickness of motion that bespoke Latin blood. The rippling motion of his hands, for example. Maybe that was because he played the piano. He was the only boy in Kings Row who studied music. Dr. Berdorff, who taught him, said he was talented. (6)

Parris, the teacher's pet, does well in school, is a talented musician, speaks multiple languages, and demonstrates maturity for his age. In many places, these traits might be considered assets, but in the world of Kings Row they mark him as a foreigner, a literal outsider. Raised by his European grandmother, he later travels to Europe to complete his schooling, and this creates a kind of worldliness that distinguishes him from the majority of the other characters. Leslie Jean Campbell notes that even the name "Parris Mitchell" suggests a kind of European/American hybridity (13).

Thus it makes it makes sense that those who do not fit into the established social fabric of Kings Row seek out the company of someone who is both part of the community and distant from it at the same time. Over the course of the novel, Parris develops friendships with nearly all of these outsiders, often taking on a kind of mentor role to others as he himself navigates the difficulties of coming of age in small-town America. This role intensifies after he returns from Vienna and takes a post at Kings Row's own state hospital, known colloquially as the asylum, where he works as a psychiatrist, thereby adding an important professional layer to his already keen powers of observation and analysis. If the novel itself is a plea for social tolerance, then Parris Mitchell is its mouthpiece, as it is largely through his interactions with various characters that the voices and experiences of the marginalized citizens of Kings Row are amplified.

While much of the publicity of the day focused on the scandal that lay beneath the façade of a small town, reading Bellamann's magnum opus in the twenty-first century shows a much more complex picture than a one-sided "revolt" against Midwestern pastoralism. It is through the narrative web of the town's outsiders that we learn what Kings Row really is when you take everyone into account. At the novel's end, Parris reflects on his experience as it relates to the town, realizing that the experiences of Kings Row are the experiences of people everywhere: "Kings Row was only a link in a moving chain. Kings Row was only a small unit in a diverse and fluctuating world. His discontents had grown out of imagining that his work had anything to do with Kings Row. It was only an infinitesimal part of the world's work. He … was not Parris Mitchell of Kings Row, but Parris Mitchell of the world" (501). With such a perspective, we can realize that the issues that Kings Row deals with cannot be hidden away beneath a pastoral mirage; they are issues that we must face as humans. According to filmmaker Lenny Pinna, "By looking both back and forward from near mid-century, Bellamann seems to have bridged the universality of the human condition in America throughout the 20th Century, which at this moment seems even more relevant today. Surprisingly, we find ourselves deeply divided as a country struggling with competing desires of going backwards or forwards as a society." *Kings Row* teaches us that we can go forward, if we take the time to appreciate the differences of all the "wild-blooming flowers" among us.

Works Cited

Barillas, William. *The Midwestern Pastoral: Place and Landscape in Literature of the American Heartland.* Athens: Ohio University Press, 2006.

Bellamann, Henry. *Kings Row.* Fulton, Missouri: Kingdom House, 1981.

Bellamann, Henry. *Kings Row.* N.d. MS. Henry and Katherine Bellamann Collection, University of Mississippi.

Bellamann, Henry. *Kings Row.* Hastings, Nebraska: Hastings College Press, 2022.

Campbell, Leslie Jean. "Henry Bellamann's *Kings Row*: A Re-evaluation of a Forgotten Bestseller." Thesis, University of Mississippi, 1982.

Connell, R.W. *Masculinities.* Berkeley: University of California Press, 2005.

Duck, Leigh Anne. *The Nation's Region: Southern Modernism, Segregation, and U.S. Nationalism.* Athens: University of Georgia Press, 2006.

Eliot, T.S. "The Waste Land." *The Norton Anthology of English Literature.* M.H. Abrams, general ed. New York: W.W. Norton and Company, 1979, pp. 2295–2308.

Goldstein, Alvin H. "Missouri Author and His Disputed Best Seller." *St. Louis Post-Dispatch*, 3 November 1940, p. 63.

Groneman, Carol. "Nymphomania and the Freudians." *Psychoanalytic Quarterly*, vol. 67, no. 1, 1998, pp. 187–188.

Karr, Jay Miles. Introduction. *Kings Row.* By Henry Bellamann. 1940. Fulton, Missouri: Kingdom House, 1981.

Kings Row. Dir. Sam Wood. Perf. Ronald Reagan, Ann Sheridan, Robert Cummings, and Claude Rains. Warner Bros., 1942.

Perera, B., Reece, M., Monaghan, P., Billingham, R., and Finn, P. "Childhood Characteristics and Personal Dispositions to Sexually Compulsive Behavior Among Young Adults." *Sexual Addiction and Compulsivity*, vol. 16, 2009, pp. 131–145.

Pinna, Lenny. Personal Interview. 9 December 2020.

Shortridge, James R. "The Emergence of 'Middle West' as an American Regional Label." *Annals of the Association of American Geographers*, vol. 74, no. 2, June 1984, 209–220.

Smith, Page. *As a City Upon a Hill: The Town in American History.* New York: Alfred A. Knopf, 1966.

Strauss, Harold. "The Tale of a Western Town; Henry Bellamann's 'Kings Row' Is an Eventful, Swift-Paced Novel, Full of the Sap of Life." *New York Times*, 14 April 1940, p. 89.

Turner, Frederick Jackson. *The Frontier in American History.* New York: Henry Holt and Company, 1920.

Williams, Raymond. *The Country and the City.* New York: Oxford University Press, 1973.

Wills, Garry. *Reagan's America: Innocents at Home.* New York: Penguin Books, 2000.

Rachael Price is an Associate Professor of English at Abraham Baldwin Agricultural College. Her research interests include modernism, regionalism, and portrayals of small towns in American literature. Her work has appeared in *Contemporary Literary Criticism, Critical Regionalism, The North Carolina Literary Review,* and *MidAmerica.*

The town of Kings Row does not exist.
The characters are imaginary.

Kings Row resembles many towns of the
period, but this is neither a picture
of an actual place, nor is the story
the reporting of the lives or
behavior of living persons.

Book One

1

Spring came late in the year 1890, so it came more violently, and the fullness of its burgeoning heightened the seasonal disturbance that made unquiet in the blood.

On this particular day, the twenty-eighth of April, the vast sky seemed vaster than ever—wider, bluer, higher. Continents of white clouds moved slowly from west to east, casting immense drifts of blue over the landscape which seemed alternately to expand and to shrink as sunlight and shadow followed in deliberate procession.

The green distances of the land were gashed and scarred with wandering roads, lumpy and deep-rutted from the heavy wheels that had groaned and strained through the winter mud. These roads came from the outlying regions, springing up, like casual streams, marking themselves more and more deeply in the soil as they moved between rail fences, widening as they wound toward the county seat. Scattered in their beginnings, they drew nearer to each other, converged and straightened as they approached the town.

They were like the strands of a gigantic web, weaving and knitting closer and closer until they reached a center—Kings Row, the county seat. "A good town," everyone said. "A good, clean town. A good town to live in, and a good place to raise your children."

In the sagging center of this web of roads Kings Row presented an attractive picture as one drove in from the country. Elms, oaks, and maples arose in billows of early summer green. The white steeple of the Methodist church, the gilt weather vane of the Baptist, and the slender slate-covered spire of the Presbyterian thrust high. In the center arose the glistening dome of the courthouse. A few mansard roofs and an occasional turret broke through the leaves. Outside the comfortable shade a straggle of unconsidered Negro shacks and tumble-down houses of poor whites lay like back-yard debris.

In the first glimpse of the town, if one happened to approach it from the west, one saw the public-school building—Kings Row's special pride. It stood on a rise of ground and looked down on Town Creek, where that noisy little stream bent itself around the west and south of the city limits. It was a red brick building, luxuriantly Gothic—a bewildering arrangement of gables, battlements, and towers. The tall narrow windows, sharply pointed like those of a church, were divided into many irregularly shaped panes. In late afternoons, when the towers and windows caught the level flow of waning light, it was as picturesque as an old castle.

On an adjoining rise stood Aberdeen College, the Presbyterian school for boys. It was less imposing than its neighbor, the public school, but most people thought its classic Corinthian portico impressive in spite of the mansard roof and square, iron-railed tower that surmounted it. Aberdeen College stood in a wide grove of beautiful elms.

The principal streets of the town had lately been macadamized. Formerly the stifling clouds of dust in summer and the quagmires of winter made these streets as bad as country roads. The new macadam was dazzling in the blaze of hot sun, but it was neat.

The old brick sidewalks, uneven after many years, were mossy and cool under the shade trees. The houses stood back from the street, and the lawns were dotted with flower beds which would shortly glow with verbenas, geraniums, and "foliage plants."

To the east of town the State Asylum for the Insane expanded its many wings through ample grounds. At night, with its hundreds of windows gleaming through the high trees, it had a palatial and festive air.

Kings Row was no frontier town with raw newness upon it. It had successfully simulated the mellowness and established ways of older towns East and South—towns remembered in the affections of the early builders. Kings Row was, in fact, an odd but not incongruous blend of characteristics to be found in trim New England villages and more casual towns of the deep South.

A mid-afternoon drowsiness lay over Kings Row. Here and there in the residential sections some belated gardeners raked leaves and burned heaps of dead vines, the columns of blue smoke rising straight, and whitening as they thinned and drifted.

The business streets were deserted. There were no farm teams at the hitching posts about the courthouse, no knots of men gathered at street corners or in saloons. The country was busy launching a season, and the life of Kings Row came from the farms.

In the courthouse yard, a few men sat under the trees with chairs tilted back. Some, declaring that summer had come and that such heat was unseasonable, had taken off their coats.

"It's not healthy," they declared. "There'll be a lot of sickness if this keeps up."

A wagonload of lumber passed, the creaking of harness and the squeak of dry axles noticeably loud in the quiet street. The eyes of the loafing group followed it idly as it turned and passed out of sight along West Street.

"Jim Miller's building a new barn out to his place," someone remarked.

"Old one burned down, didn't it?"

"Yep; last of February."

"He's late buildin'."

"Had to borrow some money and old man Long over to the Home Savings Bank wouldn't let him have it no sooner."

"Miller's a good farmer."

"You'd think Mr. Long would let Jim Miller have a loan all right."

"Long always wants good security."

"Yes. Guess that's right, too."

"Maybe so. Long's a hard man, though."

"Got to be. Other people's money."

"Yes. That's right."

The subject seemed to be exhausted. Nothing else passed; conversation died.

The wagon made its deliberate way along West Street. Streets had borne names for years in Kings Row, but it was only lately that people had begun using them. Miles Jackson, editor of the *Gazette*, had started the fashion in the weekly paper. Some thought it sounded too pretentious for a town of four thousand people.

"Kings Row's trying to be tony, like Fielding."

"It's as good as Fielding any day."

"Yes, but Fielding's a lot bigger."

"Don't make no difference."

The lumber wagon had reached the hill where the road sloped down to the bridge across Town Creek. Ray Barber, the driver, awoke from pleasant meditations as the heavy load gained unwonted speed on the descent. He jerked the lines. "Whoa, God damn it, where you think you're goin'?"

Ray's voice carried easily through the open windows of the schoolroom where Miss Sally Venable held sway over some sixty children ranging in age from ten to fourteen. Several boys giggled. One or two bolder girls grinned across aisles toward the boys' side of the room in appreciation of Ray's vocabulary, but most of the girls pretended not to hear.

Miss Sally rapped on her desk with a brass-bound ruler, and stretched her abnormally long fingers out in a gesture of admonition. Miss Sally was tired and she had broken schedule to devote the last hour of the day to reading. She was a veteran teacher and much a law unto herself. The reading was entrusted to two or three of the better readers, and Miss Sally had settled into a wandering reverie behind her desk until aroused by Ray Barber's passing. She wrinkled her long nose fastidiously.

"Disgusting!" she remarked to the room. "Go ahead, Lizzie."

Lizzie, the proudly self-conscious reader, feigned not to understand the interruption, and continued with an increased elegance of delivery.

Miss Sally, whose sense of humor was seldom far submerged, passed a hand over her face and smoothed away the derisive smile that lurked in her deeply seamed features. That smile was her strongest weapon of discipline.

There was not a pupil in her room who did not dread it far more than the superintendent's switches. She sank back in her chair and shut out the sound of Lizzie Morris' mincing pronunciation. Her prominent brown eyes roved the room, resting for brief instants on first one face and then another. Her charges were intent on the story and remained unaware of her quick scrutinies.

Sally Venable was not an ordinary woman. She was intelligent, and the sardonic cast of her features indicated that her observations of the world were rewarding. She liked her children and she had been teaching long enough to see a generation grow up. She never lost interest in old pupils, and the knowledge so acquired lent more than common zest to her speculations about those who sat before her this afternoon. She knew practically everybody. She knew the homes of these children, and their present fortunes, so she found interest in imagining their probable destinies.

She stirred in her chair and sniffed audibly. The windows were open—those tall, narrow church windows, but they afforded poor ventilation. The room smelled abominably. Sweaty bodies, most of them infrequently washed; winter clothes that had seen a hard season; the harsh odor of small boys verging on adolescence—she closed her eyes for an instant and thought of the hour of dismissal, still thirty minutes away. When she glanced up again she saw Jamie Wakefield looking at her. Almost she could believe he wore a look of concern—of sympathy, even. She nodded at him, and the boy flashed back his quick, brilliant smile.

"He's pretty, that boy," she thought. "Too pretty for a boy. But all the Wakefields are good-looking."

Jamie's attention had returned to the reading, and Sally Venable watched the play of expression on his mobile features. He was affecting, now, a sort of disdain—a precocious expression for a boy of twelve—that pursed his full red lips and narrowed his wide over-bright eyes. His hair, soft and black, swept back picturesquely from his wide blue-veined forehead with its exquisitely traced brows.

"I wish they'd dress him differently. That ruffled collar now—"

That very ruffled collar spread out over his blue jacket did get Jamie into trouble sometimes. Boys called him "sissy," but he never resented it and usually this proved a good defense.

He was interested now in spite of himself. He had forgotten that Miss Venable was looking at him and his lips parted in a halfsmile—an enchanting smile.

"He looks like a girl—like a girl in love," his teacher thought. "He's as beautiful as Cassandra Tower."

Cassandra Tower was the prettiest girl in town. Boys were beginning to be interested in Cassandra. Only yesterday Miss Venable had noticed a legend chalked on the walk: "Drake McHugh loves Cassandra Tower."

Miss Venable grinned. Those inscriptions multiplied in the spring of the year.

"Yes," she agreed, "Drake McHugh *would* be in love with Cassandra."

Drake was watching Cassandra now, his long faun eyes glinting a little under his brows that grew shaggily together over the bridge of his arched nose. Drake, robust, deep-chested, hair always falling into his eyes. "A regular boy," most people said, but Sally Venable was not so sure of that. He was open and frank, but his mouth was a trifle loose for so young a boy. It was likely to go slack and sensual in a few years, unless—

She sighed a little. Was there really anything in that word "unless"? Wasn't it determined? She veered from the philosophical consideration. She would take him in hand next week.

Drake gave up his fruitless ogling of Cassandra Tower. That lovely creature was far away on an island with the Swiss Robinsons. Cassandra's oval face remained as ivory-cool and pale as always, although her eyes were excited. Odd eyes—very odd.

She always had that startled look, distended pupils, a strained look about her nostrils, her thin curved lips compressed.

Miss Sally tapped the desk. "That will do, Lizzie; we'll let Jamie read for the rest of the period."

Jamie flushed. He was pleased. He knew that he read exceptionally well.

The children rustled and stirred while Jamie walked to the reading stand. Drake McHugh was trying to attract Cassandra's attention again, but Cassandra was looking elsewhere. She had not moved, but her eyes drooped a little, and her face wore a look of sly secretiveness. She ran her hands through her short coppery curls with a gesture that was curiously troubled. Then she gave her whole attention to the reading. As she leaned forward, pressing against the desk, her dress strained across her bosom, revealing unexpected curves beneath. Drake McHugh was watching her again but he did not see this. His eyes were on her long legs in their shimmery silk stockings. Cassandra was the only girl in school who wore silk stockings.

Miss Venable's keen eyes missed nothing. "Well," she muttered. "The forward little devil." She shrugged her bony shoulders in her worn blue velvet blouse. "Still—Drake's about fourteen, and big for his age. I guess it's to be expected."

Drake McHugh leaned forward and whispered something to Parris Mitchell who occupied the desk in front of him. Parris gave an impatient wriggle but glanced quickly at Cassandra's legs. Her short dress lay above her knees, and between a blue frilled garter and the lace edging of her drawers there was a glimpse of pink flesh.

A slight flush warmed Parris Mitchell's downy face.

Miss Venable made a slight sound—tch! tch! but no one heard her.

Parris Mitchell was her pet. It was a tribute to the just conduct of her teaching that not one of her pupils suspected this partiality—least of all Parris himself. The boy was different in every way. Perhaps it was because he lived with that curious foreign grandmother, Madame von Eln. Dr. Axel Berdorff, pastor of the German Lutheran church, said that Parris spoke French and German better than he did English. Miss Venable remembered that even two years ago he spoke with an accent. The other children used to laugh sometimes. But the accent had disappeared, leaving his speech oddly precise.

He looked foreign, she thought. Stocky and broad-shouldered. Vitality showed in his warm coloring and in the heavy eyebrows arched high over large hazel eyes. His hair, too, was as thick as plush. A slight shadow showed on his upper lip, although he was only twelve. He had a quickness of motion that bespoke Latin blood. That rippling motion of his hands, for example. Maybe that was because he played the piano. He was the only boy in Kings Row who studied music. Dr. Berdorff, who taught him, said he was talented.

He stole another quick, fleeting look at Cassandra, and his flush deepened. He fidgeted and thrust angrily with his elbow at Drake who was whispering again.

Randy Monaghan, two seats back of Cassandra, had her attention derailed by the movements of the two boys. She leaned forward and looked under Cassandra's desk. A grin, shrewd and a little coarse, widened her mouth. Randy Monaghan knew many things that boys talked about. She played more with boys than with girls, and liked them better. Round-figured and muscular, strong legs in heavy stockings, stubby hands, and two thick plaits of chestnut hair—she was a picture of energy and aggressiveness. Randy was common, but with a frank and engaging commonness.

She made a low sibilant sound. Both Drake and Parris looked back. Thrusting her knee from under the desk, she snapped her red elastic garter and grinned again.

Vera Lichinsky, a child of Polish Jews, looked wonderingly. This seemed naughty, but it didn't appear to have any sense to it. Her brother, lean and eager Amos, was looking at Randy, too. She must ask Amos about Randy. Her slow gray eyes returned to the reader, but she was thinking of something else—her violin lesson after school. Carefully, methodically, she began to go over her exercises in her mind. The effort knotted her broad, calm brow and gave her the look of a troubled old woman. At that moment she resembled her grandmother, who lived above the Lichinsky jewelry store and always wore a shawl over her head. No one ever spoke to old Mrs. Lichinsky because she understood no English.

Miss Venable drew in her chin and screwed her head to one side to look at the gold chatelaine watch she wore pinned to her blouse. Thank heaven, only ten minutes more and she could go home and change to cooler clothes.

2

This same afternoon Father Aloysius Donovan came out of his little church on Walnut Street and walked south toward the business part of town.

Father Donovan was what Mariah Shane, the janitress of the church, called "black Irish." A tall man, worn to gauntness, his massive bones stuck out and rendered shapeless the fit of his cheap clerical clothes. He had fervent brown eyes and coarse black hair that grew low to a peak on his brow. His jaw and chin were always blue. His large, patient hands were tufted with wiry hairs, and he had a strong masculine smell about him. He was well loved by his tiny congregation, but he had not in the ten years he had been in Kings Row ever completely won their confidence. His wide mouth, squarish, like the mouths of many orators and actors, was markedly humorous, a shade derisive, even. It was his mouth that made the members of his church a trifle uncomfortable. It seemed to say that he knew more than they guessed, and that what he knew was comical. It was the last thing he would have suspected—this racial trick of feature—for he was in reality a most earnest man.

"He's a grand face," Mariah Shane declared. And, indeed, he had. His features were large and rather handsome—his nose was as bold as a jutting rock—but it was an earthy face with a simple earthiness, neither gross nor sensual. An earthiness as good as that of a kindly soil which covers hard rocks. That look of goodness was, perhaps, the nearest approach to a look of spirituality possible for a man of Father Donovan's age and nature, and it betokened as much of spirituality as would be practicable or useful in his particular setting. The bishop knew this, recognized it, and was well content to have Father Donovan in Kings Row.

Priests being in no wise different from other men, Father Donovan was restless this warm April day. After a morning of severe mental exercise he had eaten his midday meal and swung off for a long hard walk.

Mariah Shane finished sweeping the vestibule of the church and stood leaning on her broom, watching the good man heaving himself along the sunny side of Walnut Street. Father Donovan always walked as though he were struggling with an invisible adversary.

Mariah had been the janitress of little St. Peter's for many years. She was big-boned like the priest himself, and vigorous. She also kept house for the father and made his place neat.

She passed her hand across her mouth, which twitched as she half talked to herself.

An acquaintance stopped, and Mariah came out to the white picket fence. They exchanged opinions on the weather and agreed that it was a difficult season.

"My wool drawers itch me so I'm halfways on fire, but I'm afeared to take 'em off. It's awful easy to catch cold this time of year, it being that changeable you can't guess what it'll be like before dark, an' a cold is hard to get rid of in the spring."

The neighbor nodded.

Mariah continued. "I told Father Donovan this morning to be careful. I didn't say nothing more. I'm afeared he'll change too early, but I can't mention it, of course."

Both women looked down the street where the black figure of the priest rocked along over the uneven walk.

"There's a good man if there ever was one," Mariah said softly. "You know, Nellie, I'm gettin' to be an old woman, but I've still got me eyes, and I can still see a speck o' dust from here to yonder, and a good many things besides. It's hard to be good in this world, I know that for myself. I've never had a dime to give to the Church, so I just thought I'd give what I had to give in sweepin' and dustin'. The blessed Virgin, being female, like meself, would be like to know just how much it's worth. But that's not what I was goin' to say. I guess we've got no right to think about a priest being like anybody else, but there must be times when that's so, all the same. It's a lonely life, Nellie, an awful lonely life. Havin' a house that never is a home—oh, I know, I suppose it's right since that's the way it is, but—" she paused and gave a sort of snorting chuckle. "Do you know what I've thought sometimes? I've thought maybe there ought to be a special kind of heaven for a priest—a heaven like Father Donovan says the heathen black Mohammedans all think is waitin' for them on the other side!"

She winked broadly, involving half of her face in the grimace of implication. Nellie laughed and slapped Mariah on the arm. "You old divil, you ought to be ashamed!"

"But ain't it the truth?"

Nellie laughed again. "I've got to be gettin' on." She paused after a few steps. "There's a lot of dandelions comin' up in there. You ought to gather a mess of greens for the father. It's good for the stomach this time of year."

"I will that, Nellie. It'll be up and big enough by next week."

Father Donovan continued on his way, his lively eyes taking note of all activities. It was seldom that anyone spoke to him because few outside of his congregation knew him well enough to speak. In this Protestant town a Roman Catholic priest was almost outside the pale, and actually, in the minds of most people, a somewhat sinister figure. There were always tales about the Catholic Church plotting this and that. Some of the more ignorant subscribed to anti-Catholic papers and believed the lurid stories they read of arsenals concealed in the churches, of clerical immorality, and other still wilder stories. One heard occasionally, from Baptist or Methodist pulpits, tirades against Popery. There were few individuals in Kings Row belonging to Protestant denominations who had ever been inside the little church in Walnut Street.

The priest knew of this and accepted it as one of the minor, but inescapable, trials of life. He was a warmly human man, and a very lonely one.

He had no one to talk to—certainly no one of his own intellectual stature. He would have enjoyed a little consideration. That was it. He had once read something about that very thing. One did not always crave love, or admiration, or any other more active kind of tribute, but one did wish for the consideration of one's fellow men. He was unconsidered and he knew it—as unconsidered, he thought ruefully, as the Negroes or those foreign families who came to work in the coal mines and clay pits about Kings Row.

He turned into Union Street, the town's principal thoroughfare, and passed the courthouse where the little group of men sat in their shirt sleeves. It would have been pleasant, Father Donovan reflected, to join them, to talk of town affairs, of crops, of local politics, of the new project to gravel the road to Camperville, but he knew he would not be welcome. He had tried it a few times. Men fell silent and looked at him curiously, glancing away quickly if he caught their eyes—as though they did not wish to have him surprise their thoughts and opinions. It made them uncomfortable, and it made him uncomfortable. He had acquired the habit of side streets. When he did come on Union or Federal Streets where the stores were he assumed a stern and preoccupied air as though hurrying on to pressing engagements. Even at such times his eye was watchful for any chance welcome. If such an event occurred—sometimes Lawyer Skeffington stopped to talk to him—his face would light, and he would shake hands too long and too warmly. The other person would be embarrassed by the unexpected fervor of the response and would fall into awkward silence. Father Donovan was quick to sense the change. Hurt and puzzled, he, too, would become inarticulate and with a hasty excuse hurry on, setting his face again in its look of concentration upon important matters. Sometimes the muscles of his jaw ached from the effort of holding this expression until he had once more reached his accustomed back streets.

Matt Fuller, owner of the feed store, cut himself a liberal chew of tobacco. "There goes that Catholic priest. Looks like he's in a hurry. Where you reckon he's goin'?"

"Maybe some of his Irish crowd is dyin' and he's hurrying to give 'em a passport to Saint Peter. Can't none of them Catholics git in without a pass from the priest?"

The men laughed, Ricks Darden was quick at that kind of thing.

"And then after they're gone," Ricks continued, "he has to pray them out of purgatory. So much an inch. I heard of one of them Catholic families once that paid for fifteen years to git their old man out of purgatory. They got tired of payin' and they asked the priest how much further the old man had to go. He told 'em their Pa was all out but one heel. The oldest boy told him, 'Look here, if Pop's that near out, he can jump out. Damned if I'm goin' to pay any more!'"

A hearty laugh greeted this story. All of them had heard Ricks Darden tell it a hundred times. It was always funny.

"Fact!" said Ricks. "I bet that old Donovan's got a mattress full of money right now."

"No. He has to give it to the Pope."

"Bet he don't give the Pope all of it."

"Don't see what use he's got for money, or any of them priests, for that matter. They can't do nothin'."

Ricks winked. "Donovan goes to St. Louis once or twice a year. Don't nobody know whether you're a priest or a dry-goods drummer once you get there."

They turned their heads to get another look at Father Donovan hurrying on toward the lower end of town.

"Besides," said Matt Fuller, "I've seen this here Donovan a-prowlin' round the streets down around old Julie Ann Martin's away after midnight when ever'body's at home in bed."

"What was you doin' around Julie Ann's that time o' night, Matt?"

The roar of laughter echoed in the pillared portico and startled the pigeons flying around and around with muted protests. Father Donovan heard the laughter as he crossed the street below the courthouse. It sounded pleasant, he thought. He realized that it had been a long time since he had laughed with anyone.

The priest had come to Jake Bloomfield's tannery. Jake was at the door of the detached little box of a room he called his office.

The men greeted each other cordially. There was a strange bond of sympathy and understanding between the two—the alien Jew and the no less alien Catholic priest.

Father Donovan felt better as he passed on. He had from even this one moment of friendly exchange a sense of release. His severe lines of concentration relaxed, and an added spring came into his step.

The streets in the south end of Kings Row were irregular. They had grown from old cowpaths, perhaps, and had never been straightened. Many Negroes lived along the creek. The acrid, smoky smell of their houses hung heavy in the streets. Pickaninnies sat on the cool damp ground, making playhouses of sticks and pieces of old china and glass. Now and then Father Donovan paused and spoke to them, but they looked at him with round liquid black eyes and did not answer. They did not know what to make of this strange white man. Their elders squatting on doorsteps looked on stolidly, almost with hostility. They knew who he was and they shared to a considerable degree the feelings of the town. A priest—a man without a woman—that was an unaccountable kind of man.

He crossed the rickety footbridge and climbed the steep hillside beyond. He made his way slowly up the slope, wiping his face from time to time with a large yellow bandanna handkerchief.

Presently he came to a clearing and sat down on a rock. He fanned himself with his heavy felt hat. Little rivulets of perspiration tickled his neck, and the heavy beading of moisture on his hands stung slightly as it dried.

He sat for half an hour looking out through the wide-spaced branches of a sycamore at the town of Kings Row as it lay piled up on the long gradual rise to the north. It reminded him of pictures he had seen of towns in the Holy Land. He could just see the modest little steeple of St. Peter's at the upper reach of the slope. A few more days and the leaves would open to their full and obscure the view.

He sank back to a more comfortable position and gave himself up gradually to the spell of the day.

The alarming beauty of April filled the woods. The afternoon sunlight flooded the tops of the highest trees. The long levels of light touched the young green and the bright gold with a curious unreality. It was like—what was it like? Something haunted and teased in the back of his brain. Yes, yes—it was like the backgrounds he had seen in old pictures. It seemed a world apart— that upper sea of light that appeared to flow straight from horizon to horizon. Something untroubled by the turmoil and striving of the earth beneath it— something pure, eternal, apocalyptic.

Birds arose from the depths of the trees, glinted sudden bronze, and flung themselves in long curves, like aerial skaters. Their thin notes dropped down into the shadows where the earth seemed to rustle and whisper. Minute whirrings, tiny harmonies of insects, water chuckling suddenly out of the hillside, and hiding in dead grass—these and the indefinable sense of a fullness of life, invisible, but everywhere, underground, in the trees, overhead in the air, filled all the spaces of the wood.

Father Donovan shifted his position and took a book from his pocket, but he did not read. He sighed deeply, and sniffed. The air was warm and damp. Yesterday's rains had stirred a thousand smells—fresh smells of leaves so young they still showed the crinkles of the bud, cool woody smells of the earliest flowers, green rooty smells, and the nostalgic smell of dead leaves sinking back into the soil.

He yielded to an almost sensuous abandon. His contemplation of the day became a kind of lively participation.

Already, he noticed, the Judas tree was dropping its faded blossoms. By tomorrow, or the next day, all of the haw trees would be white. Overnight they would come. Indistinguishable now in the tangle of undergrowth they would appear suddenly—like Annunciation angels. The woods would be peopled with them.

Needles of new grass thrust everywhere through the broken and tangled mat of dead stems. He could see the secret way of tiny rivulets on the slopes. They showed plainly by an intenser line of green that thinned on either side. Like the canals on Mars, he thought, happy in the allusion.

In the somehow *full* silence of the afternoon the voices of these multitudinous threads of water rose and filled the air with a delicate clamor.

Father Donovan sighed again, plaintively, as he glanced at the close-printed page. Saint Francis' *Little Flowers*. He could understand that mystical saint today. He felt a little that he, too, could stand up, here and now, and preach to these birds. He closed the book and returned it to his pocket. Probably Saint Francis never felt exactly as he felt now. He remembered that this feeling for nature was a modern one. Perhaps a very old one, he amended—some sort of paganism that might even be dangerous.

He turned his mind resolutely to thought of his morning's reading. He had been hard at it this past winter going through some of the old theologians—the great Church Fathers. Curious things they thought about sometimes. Strange discussions. *How many angels can stand on a needle's point?* That, now ...

He recalled a lecture he had heard in St. Louis last year. A young man talking about new kinds of mathematics, fourth dimensions and the like. He had understood very little of it, but he had enjoyed it in the same way he enjoyed music. It gave a spread to the imagination. With that kind of confusion of time and space, maybe the old disputations were not so abstruse and useless as they seemed. Like these new geometries—many parallels through a single point, like many lives passing together through a point of time— parallel and yet disparate—each passing this ever-crucial instant of present and moving on to the infinite, intent and determined by God alone knew what forces—each toward its separate destiny.

He smiled, a little shamefacedly—he could not grasp the new mathematics— he, bound to this visible earth he loved so much, could not free his mind from the old, familiar Euclidean space, but he believed it, somehow. It was consonant with one's ideas of an infinite God, the infinite power of Deity, and that sense of the infinite which he could always feel in the finite moment.

How many angels can stand on a needle's point? He felt an expansion of spirit. Infinite angels—he could almost see them—infinite angels, *dancing* on a needle's point!

He had been staring, unseeing, at the town. His vision cleared suddenly and the streets and houses swam once more into focus. He thought of his little flock of parishioners, of their lives, of all the lives of all the people in Kings Row—in the state—in the world! Infinite lives swinging upon this instant— this needle point of time. He could see them balancing in elaborate and ever- changing figures, leaning upon each other, crossing and weaving, attracting, repelling, but always bound together by links of invisible chains—parts of an eternally shifting but foreordained pattern from whose laws and compulsions no man, wherever he might be, could ever be loosed.

He saw the designs dissolve and form again—break into confusion only to resolve themselves into conclusions of harmony and satisfaction. It was a picture of life—this dance of angels on a needle's point—a picture of the world—a symbol of the way of this town of Kings Row now lying before him in the bright sun of an April day. Those souls—there in houses, on the streets, traveling toward the town or away from it—were all a part of the pattern, all touched by its influence, interdependent, and exerting each upon all others, and all upon each individual, the most amazing forces.

"I'm not being so original, at that," he said softly, but the idea of his dancing angels pleased him. He made a mystical vision of it as he let his imagination shine on it, and a mood of ecstasy came over him.

The hands of Miss Venable's watch pointed to four. She tapped on the desk, and instantly the room buzzed.

"Quiet, quiet! Clear your desks."

The buzz became a clatter.

"Monitors, pass."

Hats were distributed quickly by boys and girls who were appointed weekly to this privilege as a reward for good behavior. Miss Venable often wondered why it was considered a privilege.

Peyton Graves, a quiet boy in school, but a noisy one outside, slapped each hat down on the desk in front of its owner as he moved rapidly up the aisle. "Here's your louse-cage," he remarked softly to each one. He adroitly avoided the kicks aimed at his shins and reached the safety of the last desk in a mild glow of triumph.

"Position!"

The children sat upright.

"Turn!"

Heels clomped into the aisles.

"Rise!"

Scuffling and scraping of feet.

"Pass!"

Their departure was thunderous.

Miss Venable fetched a long tremulous breath of relief. She walked to the window and watched the dispersing crowd. In the hall she could hear the hollow thumping of the upper grades descending the stairs. Shouts of the boys mingled with the shrill chatter of the girls. She thrust her hands into the heavy waves of her crimped black hair as if to relieve her brow of its oppressive weight. She took in gulps of the warm soft air.

She felt that she was too tired to move from the window. Leaning her head against the frame, she gazed absently at the milling groups which began to break up into smaller groups and pairs. Here and there an occasional child walked alone—hurrying home or loitering and scuffing the loose gravel of the playground in a wistful sort of fashion. Miss Venable was sometimes given to half-philosophical meditations on life and society as she saw it through her pupils. She could see the forces of society at work this moment as the children fell apart from the hurly-burly at the main entrance to the building. The prescribed social lines of the town fell upon them the moment they left the democracy of the classroom. The children of rich parents, the "nice" children, the poor children, and the children who rested under the fatal classification defined by other children as "tacky"—they were all like so many helpless pieces thrown out from a common center by some centrifugal force that sent them severally and separately on predestined ways. Already their feet were set on roads that led them farther and farther apart. "It's strange," she thought, "how quickly they feel it themselves, and how effectively it works. They seem to know it and to accept it. I guess that's a mercy."

There was one individual in that noisy crowd who felt something of this, and who thought about it. That was Parris Mitchell.

Parris was, in his own dark way, a thoughtful boy. He was standing a little apart and was dreamily half thinking, half feeling something of Miss Venable's thought. It was quite vague in his mind—little more than a sort of wonder. But he was aware of a marked difference that took place in the relationships all about him as soon as they came out from school. Inside they were all—well, kind of alike. If you knew your lessons and didn't make too much noise, you were what Miss Sally called a "good scholar." If you were a bad scholar, things got pretty difficult sometimes. But outside—here, everything was different. How was it that inside the schoolroom you felt a certain way about Dodd McLean, and outside another way entirely? Dodd was stupid. He made wrong answers and he couldn't read well. You were a little embarrassed for him, and when he was called on to recite you kept your eyes on your book so he wouldn't think you noticed. Out here on the playground Dodd was almost a hero. He played games well, he was the strongest boy in his class, and he possessed a fascinating fund of horrible knowledge. It wasn't nice to listen, but you did. You didn't want to be a sissy—besides, it was interesting.

It seemed, as he thought about it, to have something to do with that feeling of embarrassment. Inside you were embarrassed by different things. Out here you felt easy and comfortable with some of the boys and girls and a little strange with others. It was very puzzling. But there were so many things that puzzled one, and teased in one's head. You couldn't bother too much about them. He supposed he'd understand a lot more when he grew up. It must be very, very nice to be grown up. He was always thinking about it. It would be jolly, he said—Parris said *jolie:* he thought it meant the same thing.

"C'mon, Parris. What you standin' there for?"

"Nothing," he answered vaguely, giving the second syllable of the word a slight stress.

It was Peyton Graves calling—the quiet Peyton now transformed into a leaping, shouting Indian. "Well, c'mon. I've got some new stamps. Amos and Vic'r comin' over to my house."

"I can't. I have to go home."

"Aw, what for? C'mon."

"I can't."

"Well, come tomorrow. I got some I'll trade you."

"All right. Maybe."

Two or three girls were standing near, talking with their heads close together. He wondered why they always acted that way—as if they had secrets. Vera Lichinsky was one of them. She caught sight of him.

"You going down to Professor Berdorff's for your music lesson?" She called the Reverend Doctor Berdorff "Professor" because her father did. No, not today."

"Why?"

"'Cause."

"Well, 'cause why? It's your regular day, ain't it?"

"It's my birthday."

"Oh." She looked slightly mystified. Nothing ever interfered with her violin lessons. She couldn't see what a birthday had to do with it.

"I've got a new Bach piece." Vera made it sound important.

"Have you?"

"Yes. It's not very pretty."

"I have a new Bach piece, too."

"What is it?"

"It's an *Invention*."

"What's that?"

"I don't know. It's a piece."

"Is it pretty?"

"No."

"Is it hard?"

"Yes. It's in four flats."

"I've had pieces in all the keys. Long time ago. Ain't you?"

"No."

"Well, I've got to go." She turned with an air of serious decision. She did not look back.

"Hello, Parris." Cassandra Tower hung back from the other girls who were walking away, their heads still close together.

Parris blushed. He remembered the way he had looked at her legs in school. He wondered if she could have noticed. Probably not. She'd be mad if she had.

"Hello, Cassie."

"Do you like Vera Lichinsky?"

"I—I don't know."

"You don't know?"

"Well, I don't know. I guess I like her all right."

"I don't."

There seemed to be nothing to reply to this.

"I don't like her, or Amos." Cassandra was emphatic.

Parris was silent.

"What makes you like Vera?"

"I don't."

"You said you did. Just now you said you did."

"I said I liked her all right."

"You silly, what's the difference?"

"I mean I don't like her *specially*."

"Oh." Cassandra smiled. "I heard you say today's your birthday. How old are you?"

"Twelve."

"I'm thirteen. Why don't you have a party?"

"I don't know."

"I'm going to have a party next Saturday."

"Are you?"

"Yes. I'm going to invite you."

"I'd like to come."

"Will your grandmother let you?"

"Of course."

"All right. I'll send you an invitation."

Parris stared a little. Invitations were something grown people used for parties.

"Good-by, Parris."

"'By, Cassie."

She walked backward for a little way, smiling. Parris smiled, too. She turned and ran until she caught up with her companions.

The playground was empty now. He walked slowly toward the stile which mounted the tall fence surrounding the school grounds. He did not see a little girl who stood outside watching him through the gap in the boards. She was smaller than Parris, and rather poorly dressed in a faded calico dress. Her stockings were lumpy where long winter underwear was carelessly stuffed into them. She was extremely blonde, and an expression of sweetness—half angelic, half sensuous—gave her a somewhat enigmatic charm. As Parris descended the stile, she swung into step with him. He had not seen her until she appeared beside him.

"Hello, Renée."

"Hello."

They proceeded without further speech along the road toward Parris' home. Renée lived on the von Eln place. Her father, Sven Gyllinson, was the overseer of the nurseries owned by Parris' grandmother. Renée and Parris had played together since they were babies. She was only a few months younger than Parris, but she was a grade behind him in school. Seemingly, they took no notice of each other now. Parris was thinking of other matters. When he picked up a rock and threw it, she threw one also with ridiculously similar gestures. If he swung his book strap from one shoulder to the other, she did, too. If he stopped to watch a bird in a treetop, she tilted her head back and looked. She matched her step to his with assiduous care. Apparently she wished nothing but his company. He, in turn, paid scant attention to her. He was used to Renée. She was always "tagging" along—always had been as long as he could remember. No one teased him about her. Some of the boys had tried that and met with a fury in him that was as astonishing as it was inexplicable. Renée was a "tacky" child, but her father worked for Parris' grandmother, so they decided maybe he had to look out for her. After a while no one paid any attention to the odd companionship. Parris liked Renée very much, but he didn't think about her often, except in vacation times.

As they neared home Renée spoke. "I'll be glad when school's out, won't you?"

"Yes."

"I'll be *awful* glad. We'll go swimmin' then, won't we?"

"Uh huh," he answered indifferently.

"Up in our own pond?"

"Uh huh."

He opened the wicket gate and stood aside for her to pass through. She turned into a lane that led to the overseer's cottage.

"Good-by, Parris."

"'By, Renée."

3

Parris Mitchell's mother had died when he was born, his father less than a year later. Since then he had been cared for by his maternal grandmother. She adored him, and he adored her. Doubtless she spoiled him in some ways, but she had trained him to the observance of an old-fashioned, Old World courtesy that made him somewhat conspicuous. Because of this he appeared older than he was, and sometimes a shade theatrical. Children, for the most part, thought him a bit queer, but adults approved of him.

His grandmother, Marie Arnaut von Eln, was wholly French. Her family came originally from Lorraine. She had been twice married, the second time to a wandering German aristocrat who had come to America to make a fortune. He did not make a fortune, but after various enterprises had bought lands at Kings Row because of some fancied similarity of the soil to that of his native German province. He built a house of foreign fashion, laid out elaborate grounds, and planted extensive vineyards. He manufactured sufficient wine to drink himself to death, and left his widow with debts and unpaid taxes far beyond the value of the land.

Marie von Eln was a resourceful woman. She employed French and German labor and turned the vineyards into a nursery. It had prospered, and she was now, twenty years after her husband's death, accounted a wealthy woman. Not so rich as the Sansomes, or the Skeffingtons, or the St. Georges, but more than comfortable.

Kings Row had never known quite what to make of her. She was a "foreigner," but obviously did not fit into the usual categories of what were always derogatorily referred to as "the foreign elements." She had the bearing and manner of an aristocrat, and her sense of humor was of the kind that often made the women of Kings Row uncomfortable. One could never be sure what it was that amused her. Everybody knew her, and everybody called her "Madame."

She was slight and quick of movement. She had black hair, threaded with gray, a high Roman nose, and extremely delicate hands. Her face was lined with innumerable thin crisscross wrinkles—like the cracks in an old glaze—but her high cheeks, faintly rose, were apple-smooth. Her dark blue eyes under the heavy bands of her almost masculine brows were deeply set in tragic shadows. Their grave expression was partly due to affliction: Madame was almost blind. She habitually wore a few fine diamonds set in black enamel.

Madame von Eln spoke French or German by preference. She emphasized, underscored, and generally illumined her discourse with graphic movements of hands, shoulders, and eyebrows.

Parris bore a striking resemblance to her.

She was waiting now for him to come home from school. Laying aside the thick reading glass, she thrust a sheaf of papers into a drawer and closed it. She patted the waves over her ears, gave a twist to the taffeta bow at her throat, and waited. She smiled a little. It was almost a smile of coquetry. Her quick ears had caught the sound of running steps on the lower terrace.

"*Bon soir, grand'mère.*" He held her very tight and kissed her four times on each smooth cheek. He rubbed his face against her hair. "*Ma belle grand'mère!*"

"*Mon enfant.*" She held him off and put up her lorgnettes. "*Tu es fatigué?*"

"*Moi? Non. Pas du tout.*"

"*Mais, elle est ennuyante, cette Venable, n'est-ce-pas?*"

He laughed. She liked the trick he had of keeping his short square teeth tight together when he laughed.

"*Mademoiselle Sally? Jamais. Elle est drôle!*"

"*Drôle?*" She nodded. "*Ah, oui, c'est bien possible.*" There was a shade of malice in her smile. "*Oui, c'est bien possible!*" Then, in English, "You are hungry?"

"Of course."

Madame called, "Anna!"

A short fat maid appeared so quickly that one suspected that she had been waiting at the door.

"*Anna, dass Kind hat Hunger.*"

The maid smiled broadly. "*Was willst du—Milch, Brod—eine Pastete?*"

"*Was für Pastete gibt es, Anna?*"

"*Kirsch—ganz frisch.*"

The trilingual discussion continued without anyone being aware of the shifts from one tongue to another. Parris decided on the cherry pie, and Anna left the room with a loud rustle of starched petticoats.

Madame turned to her desk again. "Go with Anna, please, Parris. I have more work."

He started to speak, checked the words, and went softly out.

Madame von Eln's house was as individual as she was herself. The plastered walls of the big square rooms were whitewashed. Bright rag carpets covered the floors and gay prints hung at the windows. There were rows of potted plants in all of the deep windows. The furniture was nearly all of sycamore, made in the cabinet shops of the asylum for the insane. All of the pieces were massive and plain. There were patchwork quilts on the beds and some rather garish religious prints. There were none of the knickknacks common to most houses. People exclaimed when they saw it, "Quaint! Charming!"

Madame always shrugged indifferently. "Peasant style," she said. "It is comfortable and convenient."

Lately Parris had realized the difference between his home and other houses. Home was comfortable and he loved it, but he thought red velvet curtains and flowery Brussels carpets very elegant. Sometimes he wondered if his grandmother was less rich than he had supposed.

One thing he was self-conscious about. His grandmother smoked cigarettes. He had seen country women smoke pipes, and it seemed quite the same. Once he had asked her not to smoke when he had visitors. He had been disconcerted and mystified beyond measure by her laughter. But she respected his wishes, and he never mentioned it again.

After the cherry pie he went directly to his piano practice. The square rosewood piano was old, and the keys were yellow, but it was in good tune. Very slowly, very carefully, counting aloud as he practiced, he attacked the Bach piece "in four flats." Fifteen minutes passed—half an hour. He began again at the beginning for the tenth time when his grandmother came to the door.

"What is this that you play?"

"It is an *Invention.*"

"Indeed. Is that something important?"

"Herr Berdorff says so."

"It is extremely ugly. It must be frightful to learn such a thing! Come with me—it is enough of this—this *Invention* as you call it—and it is your birthday. I have a present for you."

Parris lay in bed listening to the little sounds of the night. He was very happy. It had been a beautiful evening, and his present—all those books! His *"belle, belle, belle grand'mère!"* It would be nice when vacation came and he could stay at home. But in thinking of that he felt a tightening in his chest. He had heard Anna say that Madame was growing old. Anna said he should never wish time away. Old! Someday his grandmother would die—sooner than other boys' mothers who were much younger. He had had another grandmother, but she had died a long time ago. Terror seized him. He took the edge of the quilt between his teeth so he wouldn't cry, but it was no use—he was already crying. His throat felt like stone.

"No, no, no! *Le bon Dieu* would never permit that. He remembered once that his grandmother had shrugged her shoulders contemptuously at something Anna said about trusting the good God. Was it—was it possible that his grandmother knew something she had never told him—that perhaps—perhaps there wasn't a *bon Dieu* at all, just as he had found out when he was a very little boy that there was no Santa Claus and no real giants?

He turned his face down into the pillow and pulled the covering over his head.

4

Union Street was the town's principal business street. It ran north and south and passed the imposing west front of the courthouse, which occupied the center square of the town. Federal Street, next in importance, ran east and west and lay on the north side of the square. West of Union was Walnut Street; east of it was Cedar. On these four streets, within a few blocks of the courthouse square, was the best residence section of the town.

At the northern end of Union Street stood Thurston St. George's red brick house. Thurston St. George was very old and very rich. He owned innumerable tracts of land and was greatly respected. The St. George house was the largest in town.

At the western extremity of Federal Street Aberdeen College lifted its pillared portico and looked straight across the town to the insane asylum whose white galleries and many-windowed façades gleamed through the trees three quarters of a mile away.

These were social boundaries. Every step away from these clearly marked precincts took one a step downward in the well-defined and perfectly understood social order of Kings Row.

Wealth and occupation were the determining factors. Lawyers, doctors, bankers, landowners, and the more important merchants made up the first families. To be sure, even this restricted category was crossed by lines of religious denominations. The Presbyterian was the "high-toned" church. The Campbellite ranked second, though a good many newcomers had somehow become enrolled there. The Baptist and Methodist graded equally, but certainly much lower than the first two.

Of course there was the Catholic church, but that didn't figure in any way. The little German church didn't either, though children of good families went to its pastor for music lessons.

There were some people who wondered just what was excluded from social groups by the rigidly kept conventions. There wasn't really any kind of formal social activity. Sunday drives and evening visits were about all anyone did. Wedding invitations overflowed the lines, and funerals were free to all. But somehow the tall narrow-windowed houses of the elite kept a fiction of exclusiveness and maintained a sort of prestige. All of this was the sole concern of womenfolk. The men of the town met democratically.

The very heart of the inmost circle was represented by the family of Thurston St. George. They were Virginians and maintained a comfortable formality in their mode of life. "Old Thurston," as everyone called him, was a massively built man, bearded as a patriarch and with a fine, mild face. Every day that weather permitted he rode about his scattered farms on a fat white horse. A small Negro boy always rode behind him and in the summer carried a huge cotton umbrella to shelter his master. At each gate the old man took the umbrella and the boy dismounted to open the gate and close it again. The pickaninny also took down a panel of rail fence and laid it up again as they went from field to field. Such a tour of inspection, always conducted at a majestic pace, took the whole of one day. The next day they visited another farm.

Thurston had a brother, Macmillan St. George. A tactful silence prevailed in society concerning Macmillan and his affairs.

Thurston was always well dressed. In winter he wore black broadcloth cut to a fashion at least forty years old. In summer he wore shiny alpaca. But Macmillan dressed like a farmer. He wore blue hickory shirts and high boots. Twenty years earlier he had built a handsome brick house on Federal Street, where he lived alone with a mulatto housekeeper named Fanny. Fanny had one daughter, a strikingly pretty quadroon child of twelve who was the image of Thurston's granddaughter Hester. The girl was named Melissa and was enrolled in the colored school as Melissa St. George. Every afternoon she sat on the front porch with Macmillan, studying her lessons. Sometimes he took her books and heard her spelling, or listened as she stumbled through the pages of her fourth reader. If any of Macmillan's friends stopped in for a chat, she quietly gathered her books together and went into the house. She was as neat and well dressed as any white child in the town.

For a time it had required the full strength of the Thurston St. George respectability to withstand this assault on propriety. But the utter imperturbability of Macmillan St. George and his really formidable wealth eventually silenced all whispering. Nowadays no one mentioned the matter at all. Macmillan never visited at the home of Thurston—or anywhere else, for that matter—and none of the women of Thurston's family were ever seen to enter Macmillan's door.

The St. Georges, with the Sansomes, the Curleys, the Gordons, and the Skeffingtons made up a strong and influential social stronghold. They were sometimes referred to irreverently by lesser people as the "Big Five."

Young Hart Sansome was the mayor. Lucius Curley was president of the Burton County Bank, and Dr. Gordon was the town's leading physician.

Colonel Isaac Skeffington was a lawyer—"the best defense lawyer in the state." Everyone knew Ike Skeffington, most people liked him, and a good many were genuinely afraid of his caustic tongue.

"Colonel" was probably a courtesy title. No one remembered how he came by it, and no one ever asked. He was a tall, gaunt man with a fiery red beard that spread its splendors to his lowest vest button. He wore a frock coat the year around and, save in the hottest weather, a tall silk hat. He carried a heavy gold-headed cane and walked with a slight limp. No one ever saw him out of the courtroom without a cigar. He smoked a special brand, made for him at Packer's Tobacco Factory from tobacco grown in the county, A dark smoke-stained spot marked the location of his mouth. Miles Jackson, the editor of the *Gazette*, said that wasn't due to smoke but to the Colonel's brimstone vocabulary, which had singed his whiskers brown. Jackson and Skeffington were close friends. It was probable that these two men knew more about the life of Kings Row and the people in it than anyone else.

The Colonel had built his house with the back toward Federal Street. He said he didn't want all of the damned riffraff of the town walking by in the afternoon looking at him when he took off his shoes and sat with his feet on the porch railing. People said: "Just like Colonel Ike—does everything wrong end to. He'll die standing up and be buried upside down, like as not."

Skeffington walked through his vegetable garden one morning, and came out on the sidewalk. He stopped and took off his tall hat with a near flourish.

"Good morning, Marie, good morning, ma'am. How are you this fine morning?"

A basket phaeton, its cream-colored fringes swaying to the jog trot of a small plump horse, came to a halt. Madame von Eln greeted the Colonel cordially. He gave Parris' leg a vigorous pinch.

"How are you, sonny?"

Parris disliked being called "sonny," but he smiled. Colonel Skeffington, he knew, was one of his grandmother's cherished friends.

"Very well, sir, thank you, Colonel Skeffington."

"Fine boy you're raising, Marie. He's got manners. What are you going to make out of him?"

"Well, he wants to be a doctor."

"Doctor? Doctor, hey! What for, my boy?"

"I think I'd like it—sir."

"Nonsense. Working around with stinking pills and stuff. Have to get up in the middle of the night and go out to Godforsaken places because some old fool's got a bellyache."

Madame laughed aloud. "It's a good profession, Isaac."

"Stuff! Make him a lawyer. He ought to be a smart one. You're smart, his daddy was smart, and his granddaddy Mitchell was smart."

"Well, we'll see. Will you ride downtown with us? Plenty of room."

"Thank you, ma'am, I'm going the other way."

The old lawyer walked slowly up Walnut Street. His great beard flashed and sparkled in the sun, and the clouds of smoke from his cigar gave him the appearance of a walking conflagration.

In the middle of the next block he squinted narrowly at a dingy house set in the midst of tangled shrubbery and swarming vines. The place was neglected and in bad repair. The narrow porch roof sagged like the back of an old work horse, and the floors of the side galleries were greenish with moss and damp.

A girl with copper-colored curls was standing at the decrepit gate. The Colonel bowed gravely. "Good morning, sissy."

She looked at him without smiling. After a moment's hesitation she replied, "My name is Cassandra."

"Oh, ho! Is that so? You are Dr. Tower's little girl?"

"Yes. Yes—sir." She spoke with a certain reluctance, and Colonel Skeffington's small brown eyes twinkled. "And how is the good Dr. Tower today?"

She eyed him with open suspicion. "Very well, sir."

"That's good. Fine crop of curly hair you've got, miss, fine color—like mine." He removed his hat and shook his long straight locks. "Redheads have got spunk and character. Don't you ever forget it. Fine people—redheads."

She smiled a little—a wan, uncertain smile that flickered quickly away.

He bowed again, with an exaggerated politeness, and clicked his cane briskly on the soft brick walk.

"Likely-looking gal," he said to himself.

Dr. Tower came out on the front porch as Colonel Skeffington walked away.

"Cassandra!"

"Yes, sir."

"Come in the house."

"Yes, sir."

The child hurried back to the house. Her father stood waiting until she came in, then closed the door.

5

Dr. Alexander Q. Tower had lived in Kings Row for eight years. No one was quite sure where he had come from. It was generally understood in the beginning that he came from somewhere "back East." Such arrivals were few in Kings Row professional ranks. Usually, if a new doctor or lawyer moved in, it was only after looking over the field and consulting with the banks and businessmen. Dr. Tower had settled here without any preliminaries. He bought the old Price place on Walnut Street. This house had been vacant for ten years and was in a run-down state. He bought new furniture but made few repairs on the house. His wife and five-year-old daughter arrived a few weeks later.

There was a semi-detached wing to the house, and on this he hung his shingle: DR. ALEXANDER Q. TOWER, PHYSICIAN AND SURGEON.

A few women called. They found Mrs. Tower a quiet, well-bred lady, but singularly uncommunicative. The Towers made vague references to various places of residence, but nothing of their previous history was clear. Mrs. Tower returned none of the calls and no further advances were made by the town.

So far as anyone knew, Dr. Tower had never had a patient. After a while the office rooms remained shuttered, and Dr. Tower was seen less and less frequently. He sent a Negro boy for his mail, and he was known to order a great many books through Brighton's Bookstore. Strange books, too, some of them in French and German.

It was said on the authority of Lucius Curley, the banker, that Dr. Tower was "well fixed"—the regulation phrase describing anyone of ample means. It was also known that he drew regular drafts on a bank in Philadelphia. But why he chose to live in Kings Row no one knew. Many people said that he must have run away from something.

He was a tall man, slender and fastidiously dressed. His large brilliant eyes seemed unnaturally alive and observant in contrast to his pallor and masklike absence of expression. He appeared preoccupied or distrait, but he invariably returned greetings with a grave courtesy. One noticed his slender, beautifully kept hands—quick, nervous hands. Somehow he gave the contradictory impression of being dead to the world about him but keenly—even painfully—aware of some other world inside. It was a strange impression, and an uncomfortable one.

Everyone heard that he had fitted up a long room at the back of the house—a room which had been the nursery of the numerous Price children—

as a sort of laboratory. Bottles and curious apparatus and hundreds of books, it was said. But there was no guessing what he might be studying or working at. "Making experiments," people said and let it go at that.

Dr. Tower was the town mystery, and however little ground there was for speculation, there was never any lack of whispered wonder and comment.

For several years now, Mrs. Tower could be seen every day, sitting inside her living-room window. She never seemed to occupy herself in any way with fancywork or knitting. She simply sat there hour after hour, apparently taking no notice of people passing in the street nor, as far as anyone could tell, of anything in the room.

Colonel Skeffington often said that she looked as if she were afraid. "She's listening for something," he remarked to his friend, Miles Jackson. "If that woman doesn't end up in the lunatic asylum over there, I'll be surprised.... I wonder what in the hell that 'Q' in his name stands for."

Several days after Cassandra had mentioned her party to Parris, some thirty-five children received invitations. The list with a few exceptions indicated a lively awareness of the town's carefully drawn social lines.

Louise Gordon showed her invitation to her mother. Louise was the only child of Dr. Henry Gordon. Mrs. Gordon was a social power. She was the wife of the leading physician—and doctors knew all there was to know of their patients' family affairs. Mrs. Gordon had a thin, pious face. She was indefatigable in church work and took her social position seriously.

Her features seemed to congeal when she read the formally worded note. She looked narrowly at Louise. "Do you like Cassandra, dear?" she asked softly.

The question seemed to foreshadow and to frame the answer.

"Well, n-no," Louise replied.

Mrs. Gordon folded the invitation and replaced it in the envelope. She handed it back to Louise with a gesture that placed it among childish considerations.

"I think, then, I would prefer you didn't go," she said.

"Oh, but Mother—all—everybody's going. She sent out lots and lots of invitations. I do want to go."

"I don't think you'd better—"

"Oh, Mother!" Louise's protest verged on a wail.

Mrs. Gordon smiled. She had a peculiar smile. "Why don't you have a party of your own?"

"Honestly? Could I? But I want to go to Cassandra's party, too. Why can't I? Then I could invite her."

"You could have your party at the same time," Mrs. Gordon suggested.

"You mean Saturday afternoon? But everybody's going to Cassandra's."

"Oh, I dare say there will be a lot of children who won't be going. You can find out. Suppose you use your father's telephone. You can ask them this afternoon. I'm sure you can have quite a nice party without going to Cassandra Tower's house."

All of that week there was much buzzing on the playground about the two parties. Girls whispered together in little groups and boys asked each other self-consciously, "Which party you goin' to?"

The usual answer was: "I don't know, yet. Which one you goin' to?"

Very quickly there was a tension in the normally casual relationship of various children. It was somehow understood that a kind of rivalry lay behind the important question.

Louise Gordon was busy with her lists. She was certain of some fifteen or so of Cassandra's guests. Her mother had undertaken to extend some of the invitations in her behalf. She had suggested more than once during the course of her chats with parents how desirable it really was to have normal, healthy children meet and enjoy themselves under cheerful and normal conditions. "Conditions we fully understand, you know."

Louise spoke to Parris the first day after her mother's decision. "I want you to come to my party, Parris. Saturday. We're going to have lots of fun."

"I can't, Louise. I told Cassandra I'd come to her house."

"Oh, pshaw. Why can't you come?"

"I told you," he explained patiently. "She asked me first."

"I don't think that makes any difference if you really *want* to go somewhere."

Parris stared uncomprehendingly. It was clear that Louise hadn't heard what he had said. He began all over again.

"But Louise, I got Cassandra's invitation first, and I cept—cept—I accepted it. Anyhow she asked me before—"

Louise interrupted him with a toss of her head that sent her two brown plaits flying. "Oh, well, if you don't want to come, it's all right, of course."

"I—listen, Louise—" But Louise was signaling Garvin Adams.

"Oh-h, Garvin. I been wanting to see you. Listen ..."

Cassandra Tower gave no sign. Seemingly she was unaware of the unwonted excitement. By Friday it was apparent that Louise had gained some valuable desertions.

"Garvin Adams is going to Louise's." Garvin was a popular boy. His father owned a lot of the store buildings on Federal Street, and other boys respected this.

Opinion and inclination had been swaying for two or three days. Boys had begun to notice Cassandra more and more, and this was the first chance they had had to see her at home. But gradually it seemed indeed that *everybody* was going to Louise's. The vacillating ones leaned with the majority.

Friday afternoon Louise Gordon with two or three satellites passed Cassandra after school.

"Hello, Cassandra," Louise said sweetly.

"Hello," Cassandra answered indifferently.

Louise and her friends skipped gaily ahead, looking back once or twice and breaking into irrepressible giggles.

6

There were only five guests in the Tower parlor when Parris arrived. They did not represent "leading families," but neither Cassandra nor Parris knew that. Cassandra looked very pretty in a much-ruffled white dress, but she seemed bewildered.

"I don't know why everybody's so late," she said to Parris. "I invited ever and ever so many."

Parris blushed and looked away. Cassandra didn't really seem to understand. She must certainly have heard of the other party.

"Oh, well," he said casually, "you know how awful busy everybody is on Saturdays. Come on, let's play something. What do you want to play, Cassie?"

She looked very solemnly at him. "I don't know. What do you play at parties?"

"Oh—croquet, or—or just anything."

"I haven't got a croquet set. Maybe they'd like to play crokinole."

"All right—let's ..."

The party was a failure. Only one more guest came—Pearl Houston who lived up on Berry Street. Parris remembered that someone said the Houstons weren't very nice—Mr. Houston worked in a dairy—but he didn't know about that. Anyway, this was a party, and you had to have a good time.

The games weren't very successful, either, but there was a huge amount of ice cream and many colored cakes.

He saw Dr. and Mrs. Tower talking quietly together. Dr. Tower was speaking very rapidly and Mrs. Tower said "sh-h" when Parris came into the hall. He repeated polite party speeches to them and Dr. Tower bowed gravely. Mrs. Tower smiled. Parris liked her.

"Thank you," she said gently in response to his formality. "I hope you'll come again."

"I certainly will," he said heartily. "If—if I may," he added. Cassandra looked cross by this time. She was almost snappy when he said good-by.

The Gordon party was in full swing when he passed. There was a gay, fluttering marquee on the croquet ground, and everyone was noisy.

Drake McHugh caught sight of Parris and shouted, "C'mon, Parris, c'mon in."

Parris shook his head and walked on. He heard Louise say, "Oh, let him alone. We don't want him."

Parris decided that Louise had been very mean to give this party the same day as Cassandra's. He believed she must have done it "on purpose."

At the end of the next week the school principal received a note from
Dr. Tower saying that he was withdrawing Cassandra from school. "I shall
henceforth undertake my daughter's education myself," it concluded.

7

After what seemed an interminable spring season, vacation came at last.
Parris and Renée ran nearly all the way home. This afternoon was different,
somehow, from other afternoons—it was larger, brighter, gayer. And tomorrow
there would be no school. Ahead lay an infinity of days when there would be
no school. Immense days, with long, long mornings and longer afternoons.
There were ten thousand things to do. The reopening of school was too far
away to cast even the faintest shadow on the splendor of these days which were
all one's own to do with as one wished.

The great sweeps of orchard back of the house were in full bloom.

"Let's go look at the apple trees, Renée. Come on, hurry up."

"All right," she answered meekly, matching her step to his as best she could.

He dashed about the orchards like something mad, gathering the low
branches into his arms and making loud inhalations as if he tried to breathe
them into himself.

"Aren't they bee-eautiful, Renée? Prettier'n last year."

"Uh huh," she replied, dutifully smelling as loud as she could in imitation
of his ecstasy.

The months of May and June were rapturously happy. The days were all
blue and gold and none of them failed of novelty or excitement. July came in
hot and dry.

They walked one afternoon through the groves of young evergreens that
stood on the farthest outskirts of the place. Beyond, there was only woods.

It was cool-looking in the long alleys of green and the air smelled good; but
it was very hot, and swarms of black gnats buzzed about their faces, making
thin, whining sounds like the singing of tiny wires.

They came presently upon a small green pond with spruces and cedars
planted in a wide circle about it. The sharp points of the young trees were
perfectly mirrored on the still surface.

"Ooh, looky—the pond! We ain't been here this summer, have we?" Renée
ran ahead.

Parris walked slowly about the edge of the pond. A few green frogs hopped
from the banks into the water with a loud plunking sound. The wide ripples
sent a wave through the reflections, weaving them into fantastic shapes.

"Look, Renée. It's like a wind in the water."

Renée looked. "Uh huh," she said indifferently. She stooped and splashed
water with her hand. "It's warm," she said.

"Is it? Let me see." Parris dipped his hand and flung a few drops at her. "It is warm. Warm enough to go in swimming, I guess."

Without any comment Renée pulled her dress over her head and flung it under the apple tree.

"Unbutton my back, Parris, I can't reach." She slipped the buttons of her short muslin drawers which were attached to the waist Parris was unbuttoning. She stepped out of the skimpy garment and waded in.

"Ooh—it's not so warm on the bottom." She hunched herself together and shivered.

"You have to go in gradual," he reminded her. He was out of his clothes now and was dabbling a foot in the shallows. "Feels kind of cool to your feet."

"Let's get some blackberries first," Renée suggested. "Over there by the fence."

"*Ouch,*" she exclaimed. "They scratch."

She examined her wounds. "That one hurts."

"Put some mud on it," he recommended.

"Here," she said. "Here are some big scratches ... We look like Adam and Eve in your picture Bible," she added casually.

They were used to each other. They had been swimming here for what seemed many, many summers.

"Adam and Eve had leaves on. Don't you remember, Renée?"

"Uh huh. Let's get some and put 'em on."

"There aren't any fig leaves."

"Why do we have to have fig leaves?"

"That's what Adam and Eve wore."

"How do you know?"

"I know."

"Well, grape leaves'll do. There's some on that wild grapevine."

"Where?"

"Right there on the other side of the fence."

Parris made a painful crossing of the rail fence.

"Watch out for poison oak—'n snakes!" she warned.

"I am watching out." He returned presently with a handful of leaves.

"How'll we put them on?" Renée demanded practically.

Parris looked at them quizzically. "I don't know."

"In the pictures they was just stuck on."

"Well, you can't do that."

"Maybe they had glue."

"Maybe."

Suddenly he laughed. He punched a hole in a large leaf and affixed it by a simple but not exactly modest device.

Renée laughed very loud. She bent over, crossing her arms on her stomach, and danced with mirth. "Oh, my, that's funny! But it looks nasty. Anyhow, I can't do that."

"Try some mud. Maybe it'll stick," he suggested.

They ran laughing to the pond. Parris lost his leaf as he ran into the water.

"Ouch! You're splashing me. It's cold."

The leaves were forgotten, and for an hour they laughed and splashed and shouted in their own little special Eden.

"Let's get out. I'm getting cold," Parris suggested.

"All right. I got to dry my hair anyhow so Mama won't know I've been in swimmin'. She'd take a switch to me, I guess."

"Would she?"

"I 'spect so."

He thought a minute. "Yes; I guess she would. Here, I'll help you unbraid it."

She flung her bright hair about and sat on the grassy bank with hands clasped about her knees. "I'm awful glad we don't have to go to school."

"Uh huh, so'm I."

"Let's go in swimmin' again tomorrow."

"All right."

"Would your grandma *get you* if she knew?"

"I don't know."

"I guess we'd better not tell anybody." She nodded her head wisely to the words.

"No; I guess we'd better not."

Of course she was a girl and he was a boy, and, somehow, that made a difference. That, too, they understood somewhat. Other children at school, older children, had furnished a good deal of enlightenment during the past two years. It was all sort of curious, but not especially interesting. They had believed all of these stories at once—they seemed reasonable stories, but that was all there was to it. It had nothing to do with them.

Renée talked about these subjects last summer. She pointed at her navel—she called it her "belly button"—and said: "When you get a baby it comes out right here."

Parris nodded. He thought she was mistaken, but it didn't make any difference. They said no more about it.

She swished her hair from side to side to dry it quickly. Parris decided she was a very pretty girl—prettier than anybody—prettier, even, than Cassandra Tower. Of course he'd never seen Cassie with her clothes off. Funny how much prettier Renée was when she was naked. He thought it might be because she didn't have very nice clothes.

He liked Renée. Better than any girl—or boy, either. "You're my best friend, Renée," he said impulsively.

She turned her wide blue eyes slowly. A pleased look parted her lips—the inside of her mouth was stained almost purple from the blackberries.

"Am I? Honestly?"

"Yes, you are. I like you better'n anybody."

"You're my best friend, too. I like you best of anybody—exceptin' of course Papa and Mama," she said contentedly. "C'mon, let's put on our clothes! It's getting late."

They dressed hurriedly, and went slowly homeward, talking a kittle—drifting carelessly in their walk.

8

Parris watched his grandmother rather anxiously on Sunday mornings. If she planned to go to church she always gave orders at breakfast for the surrey. He hoped, on this particular Sunday morning, that she would decide not to go. It was very hot. Sundays in summer seemed hotter than other days. Not that he minded. He really never thought much about it, but others were always mentioning the weather. This morning when he thought of the long church service he realized what they meant by the heat being disagreeable. Ordinarily he liked going to church. He liked to see people.

Madame von Eln put down her coffee cup and folded her napkin. "Anna, tell Uncle Henry to have the carriage ready at half-past ten."

"Yes, Madame."

Madame smiled absently at her grandson. He waited. Perhaps she would suggest that he stay at home. But she went slowly upstairs and he sighed a little as he went out on the terrace. It was nice this morning. The flower beds had a droopy look. The grass was dry and yellow; withered leaves showed on the hollyhocks. There was a special smell about this time of year. He remembered it. A hot spicy smell. Geraniums and verbenas.

He walked about slowly. The chickens were already slipping into shady spots, scratching places in the soft soil, lying on their sides to absorb the cool. From the upper orchard he could hear the dry, metallic rasp of the guineas.

The sky was a smoky blue—almost the color of hydrangeas—where the spruce plantings lifted a thousand blue spear points above the slope.

It was all very still. Warm smells came from the kitchen—Sunday smells of apple and cinnamon. He sighed again. It would be fun to call Renée and build a dam in the little creek. Much more fun certainly than putting on a clean white waist and a starched collar and going to church. He wondered if he had a fresh linen suit, or if he would have to wear the blue one. The blue one would be pretty hot. Most boys of his age didn't wear coats in summer, but he would have to. His grandmother was very strict about that.

He went reluctantly into the house and upstairs to his room.

The surrey stood shining in the sun. Uncle Henry, his chocolate face wrinkled into Sunday decorum, sat on the front seat. He wore a blue-and-white-striped seersucker coat and a wide-brimmed straw hat. The horse stamped impatiently and switched his tail at the flies. He had a red cord fly net thrown over him, but it was not much help. The net was pretty, though. There were even pieces with little tassels at the tips that fitted over the horse's ears.

Madame came down, crackling in her black taffeta dress. She was wearing her onyx-and-diamond earrings and a large brooch at her throat. It had belonged to her grandmother, she said. Under a round glass lid in the back was a tiny plait of blond hair. "It was my grandmother's hair, when she was a child—your great-great grandmother, Parris." But Parris could not imagine anybody young living such a long time ago.

This morning he looked appreciatively at his grandmother. She looked very fine, he thought, with her tight shiny black kid gloves, and the little spray of jet trimming that twinkled on her bonnet. He particularly liked that Sunday bonnet. It was no more than a broad band of jet that tied under the chin with long lace streamers. From the exact center an ornament, like a tiny tree, stood up and shook with every motion of her head. Her hair waved smoothly to a high knot in the back which was fastened with a tall comb that had a row of silver balls on the edge. He thought it looked like a crown, and that it made his grandmother look like a queen.

She carried a small lace parasol, and wore long-handled tortoiseshell lorgnettes on a thin gold chain.

"Are you ready, Parris?"

"Yes, ma'am."

"Come here, let me see." She passed her hand over his hair, already brushed to a mirror smoothness. "Didn't you have a white collar to go with a white waist?"

"No, ma'am. I couldn't find one. This one's all right." The stiffly starched collar had broad stripes of blue. "It's pretty tight," he added.

"It looks nice, though. Come now, or we'll be late."

Uncle Henry swung his whip smartly, and the wheels crunched softly through the deep sand of the driveway. Parris leaned out to watch the fine sand follow the rim of the wheels and fall away like smoke. He began to like the drive. The fringe of the surrey top swung in quick waves. It had a festive look.

The second church bell was ringing from the Presbyterian tower when they turned into Federal Street. Services would begin in fifteen minutes. The Methodist bell joined in presently. It wasn't so nice a bell—the Presbyterian bell was deeper and richer. Then the Baptist bell began, too. People on the wide walks quickened their steps. The sounds clashed overhead, buggies rolled by in a cloud of dust, and Parris felt a rising excitement. Uncle Henry drove to the stone carriage block in front of the church, and Madame stepped out and shook the dust from her skirts. Parris took her hand so she wouldn't stumble going down the three narrow steps to the sidewalk. She never wore her glasses when she went to church and depended on him somewhat.

A number of men stood on the little lawn before the church. Several of them lifted their hats and spoke. Parris could see that they liked his grandmother from the respectful tone of the greetings. That was because she was an awfully important person, of course, the *owner* of the Burton County Nurseries, and a woman of affairs. He had once heard her called that, and although its meaning was not clear, he knew that it was complimentary. He was glad, after all, that he had come to church today.

The inside of the Presbyterian church was most pleasant. It was very high, and tall slender windows of colored glass reached far up to the curved ceiling behind the graceful sweep of gallery. The windows were open today, and puffs of warm air came in.

The ushers thumped softly down the red-carpeted aisles, and Sunday silks rustled and creaked. Delicious breaths of perfume floated from the Amory twins who sat directly in front of Parris and his grandmother. Mr. and Mrs. Curley also occupied that pew. Mr. Curley deposited his silk hat under the pew. Parris was interested in the white satin lining gathered to a circular disk in the crown. Mrs. Curley wore a wine-colored silk dress so tight that it was a wonder she could get into it. The silk clung to the creases in her fat arms. The shields under the arms were clearly outlined, and there was a damp half-circle on her back just above the corset line. It spread slowly like the rising of a large dark moon. Mrs. Curley turned and smiled a subdued greeting to Madame von Eln, and the old banker turned also and bowed gravely sidewise.

Parris caught sight of Drake McHugh across the aisle with his aunt and uncle, Mrs. Livingstone and the Major. Drake leaned forward and made eager, unintelligible signs, but his aunt tapped on his knee with her gloved fingers and he subsided.

On the far side of the church, in the little-used north section of seats, Parris saw a gleam of copper curls under the floppy brim of a brown straw hat. He was surprised. It was Cassandra and her mother. He couldn't remember ever having seen them at church before.

More people came into the pew, and he was crowded to a corner. He felt very hot and tugged at his collar.

The church had a smell unlike any other place. A bit musty, but pleasant at the same time. Now it was enhanced by little currents of varied scents— colognes that smelled like roses and lilacs and lilies of the valley. He decided that he liked perfumes, and wondered why his grandmother never used them.

The choir was settling self-consciously into their seats, and Miss Ludie Vance was taking her place at the organ. An uncomfortable hush followed, and fans redoubled their agitation.

The service seemed interminable. Parris knew that Dr. Mackay preached exactly an hour, and he felt at the beginning of the sermon that he could not possibly bear it. Maybe he would get sick. That would be terrible. Everyone would look at him. He swallowed hard at the thought and wriggled desperately. He was sticking to the seat. Maybe the seat of his linen pants

would be wet from perspiration and people would think—oh, dear, why didn't
he beg off from church today?

His thoughts wandered from one dreadful possibility to another. Church
was oppressing him now. He thought of funerals. He had attended a funeral
last year—Billy Churchill who had been in his grade at school. He remembered
old Hector Godbold, the undertaker, wheeling the coffin in at the north door
and out at the south. Someone everybody in this church would die, and Hector
Godbold, bald and queer-looking, would wheel them through those doors.
His grandmother, too. He gasped and swallowed and looked at her fearfully.
She smiled vaguely at him. He resumed his gloomy reverie—someday he, too,
would die—Renée would die.... Maybe he and Renée would build that dam
this afternoon. He thought of the delicious feeling of water running over his
bare feet, of sitting on one of those big mossy rocks under the bridge, of ...

He was startled by a stir and rustle. It sounded as loud as thunder. He
opened his eyes. Then he flushed very red and sat looking into the depths of
Mr. Curley's silk hat. He hoped no one had seen him asleep.

Miss Ludie began the prelude to the last hymn. She missed some notes
and made hideous discords. Parris nudged his grandmother, but she appeared
not to notice. His foot was asleep—it felt like wood, but like wood with lots
of ants crawling on it. Maybe he felt like that all over when he was asleep but
didn't know it.

The congregation, at a signal from Dr. Mackay, arose. The singing increased
in volume. Cautiously he felt of the seat of his pants. It was damp but it wasn't
really wet. He felt relieved and sang a few lines of the hymn.

The church seemed fuller now than it was before the sermon. The whole
congregation bowed and the lovely words of the benediction faded into a
whispering cadence across their heads ... *In the name of the Father, the Son, and
the Holy Ghost, Amen.*

There was an instant buzz. Mrs. Curley turned with an everyday smile and
spoke. Mr. Curley tugged at the seat of his trousers. Parris guessed he had stuck
to the seat, too.

Drake McHugh was squeezing through the outgoing crowd. "Parris!" The
sibilant sound carried sharply. "Hist! Wait a minute outside, will you? I want to
see you. Oh, good morn—good day, Madame. Uncle Rhodes and Aunt Mamie
said could Parris stay in town and eat dinner with us and stay this afternoon?
Will you, Parris? Can he, Madame?"

"Why certainly, if you want him to."

Drake gave Parris a hearty nudge in the ribs. "C'mon."

"Wait a minute," Madame interrupted. "I'd like to say good morning to
Major Livingstone and your aunt. Where are they?"

"Right there, standing in the aisle."

The group walked slowly out of church. "Now send him home if he bothers
you," Madame smiled at the Livingstones. "Be a good boy, Parris. You'll have

to walk out home this afternoon—Uncle Henry won't be there to come for you. Don't get too hot now. Stay in the shade." She mounted the carriage block and turned to where she thought Drake was standing. "You must come out and play with Parris someday soon." She could not see that she was speaking directly to Major Livingstone. Drake giggled, but Parris gave him a violent push. "She's nearly blind—she couldn't see," he said. Drake looked at him curiously. Parris was not looking at him and his voice sounded strange and sort of faraway. "Oh," Drake said. "I didn't know that. Well, c'mon, let's go."

The Livingstones lived near the Presbyterian church. Parris thought this must be very convenient and pleasant, but Drake did not regard it as an advantage.

Drake McHugh was an orphan, too, and lived with his aunt and uncle, both of whom were as old as Madame von Eln. Drake said that when he was twenty-one he would inherit his money. Uncle Rhodes, he said, was his "gardeen" now. The Livingstones were very strict and very religious. Parris had heard people say it was too bad that Drake had to grow up without parents. He could not imagine why they said this. He had no parents either and he was very happy. He often thought that it would be very strange to have a father and mother. He was sure he could never have loved either of them as much as he loved his grandmother. It would have been too bad, he decided, for her not to have had him all to herself. She would have been very lonely, he was sure. Sometimes he looked at the photographs of his mother in the blue velvet album but he couldn't tell much about it. It gave him a very strange feeling—not lonesome, but sort of sad. He wanted to say the word "mama," as Renée did to her mother, but it stuck in his throat. It was just a photograph. The picture of his father he decidedly did not like.

Mrs. Livingstone went directly upstairs when they came into the house. She came down again shortly in a cool-looking thin dress.

"Won't you take off your coat, Parris? You must be very warm."

"No'm, thank you. I'd rather not."

She looked surprised but did not urge him.

Sunday dinners did not vary much in Kings Row homes. It was customary to make it the largest and heaviest meal of the week, Mrs. Livingstone had the reputation of "setting a good table."

Today there was soup—large steaming plates served from a huge china tureen. There followed roast chicken, mashed potatoes, dressing and gravy, cold ham, beets and peas and creamed onions. A fresh plate of hot biscuits appeared every four or five minutes. Mrs. Livingstone served side dishes of sweet pickled peaches and preserved watermelon rind.

Parris and Drake ate until their clothes felt tight before the double dessert of peach cobbler and cocoanut cake arrived. Parris was miserably uncomfortable. He missed the cool salads and the iced tea he was accustomed to at home. The high-backed plush chair stung through his clothes, but he tried not to squirm or to scratch when anyone was looking.

After dinner Mrs. Livingstone retired for a nap, and the Major sat on the front porch smoking.

"C'mon, Parris, let's go down in the back lot where it's shady."

They sat on the grass, somewhat stunned with food, but making the effort at conversation which seemed always somewhat difficult on Sunday visits.

"Gee, I hate Sunday, don't you?" Drake threw a stick at a tall mullein stalk.

"Why?"

"You can't do nothing."

"Why not? What do you want to do?"

"Anything."

"Well, what let's do?"

"Gee, they won't let me do nothing on Sunday." Drake seemed surprised that Parris shouldn't know this.

"Why not?"

"'Cause it's Sunday. Does your grandma let you play on Sunday?"

"Of course!"

"Same as any other day?"

"Of course she does. She doesn't care what I do. I mean, of course—"

"Gee! They won't let me do one thing. Of course I slip off, but they don't know it."

"You mean your uncle and aunt won't let you play because it's Sunday?"

"Sure. It's wrong to do anything on Sunday. It's a sin—they say it is, anyhow. I don't see how it can hurt anything just to play."

"Me, neither. I'm glad my grandmother lets me play."

"Gosh, you're lucky, boy."

"I guess I am."

"Well, Aunt Mamie's gone to sleep. Uncle Rhodes'll be asleep pretty soon. Then we can slip off."

"Won't they get after you?"

"They won't know anything about it."

Parris considered this. "Where you going to?"

"Oh, I don't know. Anywhere."

"Well, I guess it isn't any harm just going somewhere."

"'Course 'tain't. Gee, Parris, you're funny."

"How?"

"You always talk so proper."

Parris blushed. "It's the only way I can talk, Drake. You know I have to think when I speak English, and I guess it just goes kind of slow."

"Gosh, that's so. You do talk some other language, don't you?"

"Two of them."

"Two?"

"German and French."

"Darn, but that's funny."

"I don't think it's funny. I always did."

"It's funny for an American boy to be talking any other kind of talk but American."

Parris scraped at the ground with his heel. "Does—does it sound sissy, Drake, the way I talk?"

"N-no—it don't sound sissy exactly. It just sounds like you're tryin' to be awful proper—kinder like you're *puttin' on.*"

"Well, I ain't."

"Now, that's more like it—when you say 'ain't.'"

"But 'ain't' ain't—isn't really right."

"I don't care. Sounds better."

"I wouldn't like to sound like a sissy—like Jamie Wakefield—"

"Say—ain't he the big sissy, though? I'd like to take his pants down and see if he *is* a boy."

Parris laughed, but it was a halfhearted laugh. He wanted Drake to like him. Drake was pretty nice, and there wasn't anything sissy about *him.* He felt a little twinge of disloyalty somewhere inside when he laughed at Jamie. He liked Jamie, too. He supposed Jamie couldn't help being sissy. Still, he was funny.

Drake jumped up. "Let's go."

"All right. Where?"

"Let's go down to the depot. I guess we'll find some of those lower-end-of-town kids and we can do something. They're tough as hell, too," Drake added admiringly.

The streets were deserted. A few people sat out on shady porches and rocked slowly as they wielded large palm-leaf fans. The heat danced dizzily over the white dust. Far down the street the houses and trees quivered in broken outlines.

They walked on the shady side of the street and hurried from time to time through occasional stretches of sun where trees were missing.

"I guess this is the hottest day I ever saw." Drake stopped and wiped his face on his sleeve. A deep flush made his freckles stand out larger and darker than ever.

"I'd like to go swimming." Parris sounded almost wistful.

"So'd I, but the closest swimmin' hole is way down the creek. Too far, I guess."

"We got a pond out home."

"That's pretty far, too. I got to get back before supper or I'd catch it hot and heavy. I tell you—let's go down to the Elroy's icehouse. We can play in there an' it's cool as everything. Gus Elroy's got a trapeze, and flyin' rings an' par'llel bars fixed up like a regular gymnasium."

"All right, come on then. Let's go fast."

They crossed to Walnut Street and hurried toward the south end of town.

There was no one at the depot, or near it. Kings Row had no Sunday trains. The boxcars stood huge and solid-looking, as though nothing could ever move them. Everything lay baking in the pitiless sun. A keen, acrid smell, compounded of grease, overdry pine wood, and heated metal stung the nostrils. It was very dirty and rusty-looking. The yards, purplish with cinders, the cars with scarred red paint, the tarred and graveled roof of the depot and the tool houses—everything had a disused look. The immobility seemed permanent. Only the edges of the car wheels, unbearably bright and burning to the eye, suggested that yesterday there was activity here, and that tomorrow it would begin again.

The unfamiliar odors aroused a sort of excitement in Parris—a sense of not quite safe adventure which verged on uneasiness. Drake seemed more at home in these surroundings. He made knowing remarks, mentioning easily and carelessly the names of engineers and firemen, brakemen and flagmen. Parris was impressed. He felt very young and inexperienced.

They walked along the tracks toward the Elroy icehouse. Long rows of empty cars stood on the siding. The worn flanges of the wheels caught the sun and made a succession of diminishing arcs down the line. They looked like rows of drawn and glittering scimitars.

Drake picked up a thin iron rod and tapped the wheels as they passed. He read the lettering on the cars and recited the long railroad names they stood for. It sounded highly romantic.

"Chesapeake and Ohio."

"Chicago and Alton."

"Chicago and Northwestern."

"Mobile and Ohio."

"Illinois Central."

"Baltimore and Ohio."

"Wabash—that's a fine railroad! They run the fastest trains in the state."

Parris regarded the freight car with respect. He could imagine those wheels singing along endless lines of steel rails across vast reaches of strange country, past farms and houses he had never seen, and through towns whose names were in his geography book. He could see the weeds and grass along the track bending in the cyclone of speed that roared over them.

"Look, there's one from 'way out West. Denver and Rio Grande. I bet that's a good railroad, don't you?"

"I bet so, too."

"I wish we lived on a main line. This ain't nothin' but a branch. You ought to see the flyers go through Camperville. Some of 'em don't even stop there.

Great big engines with three drive wheels on each side! You've been to St. Louis, ain't you?"

Parris nodded. "Two times."

"Did you ride the Wabash or the Chicago and Alton?"

"I don't know which it was."

"Did you go by Rhode House?"

"Yes, I remember that."

"It was the Chicago and Alton. The Wabash is better."

They came to the end of the line of cars. Drake walked backward and squinted along the rails.

"Hello, Drake! Hello, Parris!"

They looked around for the voice.

"Up here—on the fence."

It was Randy Monaghan hanging over the tall fence at the top of the embankment.

Drake answered gaily. "Hello, there. What you doin' up there?"

"This is where I live. What you all doin'?"

"Nothin', just walkin'."

"What you doin' way down here, Parris?"

"I just came with Drake."

Drake spoke quickly. "We're goin' down to Elroy's icehouse."

"What for?"

"Nothin' much. Swing on the rings maybe.

"Jake ain't down there."

"How do you know?"

"Seen him and a whole gang of boys goin' out towards Nichols Pond. Guess they went swimmin'."

"Well, I guess we'll go to the icehouse anyhow. Jake won't care."

"It's cool down there."

"Why don't you come, too?"

Randy was evidently waiting for the invitation. She looked back over her shoulder.

"All right," she called softly. "You go on. I'll catch up with you."

Drake and Parris walked slowly. "Why didn't she come right along with us?" Parris asked.

Drake looked at him and grinned. "'Fraid of her old man, I guess."

"Why?"

"Say, you don't know much, do you? I guess her old man knows better'n to let Randy go round with these tough kids down here. She's kinder tough, too. I bet she can give as good as they can send. You ought to hear her cuss."

They had come in sight of the icehouse—a long, low structure, half wood and half stone, with a high-gabled roof. It stood at the edge of what was called the Railroad Pond, a body of water that supplied the railroad tanks.

They opened a heavy door and jumped down on a great pile of sawdust. The air was damp and cool. It was dark, too, after the glare. Long streaks of sunlight cut across the high space from a small window in the west gable.

"Gee, most of the ice is gone. See how low it's gettin'?" Drake seized the two rings and swung far out from the tall heap. He let go and landed on his feet, half burying himself in the loose dry sawdust.

Someone banged on the door. "Let me in! Drake!"

"It's Randy. Push on the door." The door swung out, letting in a great gust of hot air. Randy climbed over the high sill and dropped down. She rolled over and over.

"Gosh darn! Look at me. Sawdust all over me."

"You got to know how to jump on sawdust."

"Shoot. I just slipped." She removed her shoes and peeled off her long black stockings. "There. That feels better. Ain't it cool?"

She struggled up to the rings which swung from the rafters. "Can you skin the cat?"

"Sure!" Drake scoffed. "But I bet you can't."

She executed the feat, her stout legs cutting her hold neatly, and landed upright.

"Pretty good."

"I can do the double roll on the par'llel bars, too."

"Bet you can't."

"Don't think I could do it very good with my Sunday clothes on, though."

"Take 'em off," Drake suggested with a wink at Parris. "Nobody here but us."

"Well, you look outside and see if anybody's comin'."

Drake reconnoitered. "No one round anywhere. Go ahead."

She flipped her dress over her head and hung it carefully on a projecting plank. Her frilled and starched white petticoat followed. She stood up, round and stocky in waist and drawers.

"That's better. Now watch me."

She swung up on the parallel bars with ease and flung herself through the double roll.

"Doggone," Drake exclaimed. "Where'd you learn to do it?"

"Jake Elroy showed me. He can do a lot of things. Come on, Parris, you try."

"I don't think I could do that right away. I guess I'd have to practice. I can skin the cat, though."

"Let's see you. Take off your shoes and stockings and your coat. What you so dressed up for?"

Parris' first effort was not successful. He fell on his back with a thump. It knocked the breath out of him. Randy laughed. "You got to bring yourself up better, then shoot your legs down quick. Looky." She repeated the performance. "C'mon now, try it again."

With her encouragement and advice Parris made rapid progress, but the double roll was beyond him.

"Your pants are too tight. Take 'em off, why don't you?"

Parris flushed. "I haven't got anything on under them."

Randy shouted with laughter and slapped her knees.

"Well, I don't care, but maybe you can do it anyway. Try again." She considered his effort seriously. "You could do it pretty soon. I'm tired now. Let's set down and rest."

Drake found a roll of building paper on the ledge. "Spread this out and you can lay down."

The trio dropped down panting. Randy stood on her head as a final gesture. "Gee, I'm glad we came down here. Feels good to be cool."

Drake rolled over and whispered something in her ear. She put her foot in his side and thrust him away. He rolled down the slope laughing. She laughed, too, but her face was very red.

"You shut your old dirty mouth."

Parris thought she did not look angry, despite her words.

Drake grinned impishly and brushed sawdust from his hair. "Well," he said airily, "Parris don't know much. You could 'nitiate him." He pronounced the unfamiliar word "knee-shade."

Randy looked sidewise at Parris. "You shut up, you old fool," she replied to Drake.

Drake flung himself back in the sawdust and laughed. "You ain't mad. You're just pretendin'."

"'Course I ain't mad, but I ain't goin' to do it."

"All right, don't then."

"I ain't."

An awkward silence fell. Drake tried one or two swings on the flying rings, but it was a halfhearted activity.

Randy arose. "I better be goin'. I'll get Hail Columbia if they catch me out here with you all."

Parris was somehow pleased at this. It gave the afternoon an additional zest. He didn't know why, exactly, but the cool shadowy icehouse seemed like a sort of secret meeting place. Randy dressed quickly.

"Drake, you or Parris will have to help me up to the door, an' then I'll pull you up."

Drake lifted her, but she couldn't reach the sill. He let her down again. "Gosh, you're heavy."

"Catch me lower down so you can lift me up higher."

Drake grasped her around the knees. "Hold stiff now." This time she reached the sill and pulled herself up.

"Now, you all come on. I'll yank you up."

They retraced their way along the railroad track. Randy walked along the rail, balancing herself from time to time by a touch on Parris' shoulder. He felt quite happy when she did this and stayed carefully in easy reach.

Drake walked on the other rail, flapping his arms with a great show. "It's hard to walk fast and not fall off," he explained. "Say," he said, "I bet you're Jake Elroy's girl."

"I am not any such." She made the denial without any apparent rancor.

"I bet if *he'd* a-said to you what I said back there in the icehouse, you wouldn't a-kicked *him* in the ribs."

"You're a liar, Drake McHugh," she replied calmly.

Drake laughed and lost his balance. "All the same, he told me something 'bout you."

"What?"

"'Bout you and him."

"It was a lie if he said it."

"Honest?"

"'Course it was. Wasn't it, Parris?"

"I don't know. What did he say?"

Both Randy and Drake lost their balance this time.

"I told you Parris didn't know much of anything, didn't I?"

"I guess he knows enough to know you're tellin' lies. Anyway," she added, "I think Parris is nice."

Parris turned fiery red.

Randy ran up the embankment. "'By, you all."

"I'm comin' down this way again sometimes," Drake said. Parris thought there seemed to be some sort of special meaning to the words.

"All right," she answered carelessly. "It's a free country, I guess."

Parris trudged toward home. He was tired and his feet felt heavy. It had been a very long day—like a whole week. The sunlight was beginning to slant now. He hastened his pace a little. It must be nearly suppertime. He realized that he was hungry.

He felt strangely happy. Nothing much ever happened at home. One day was like another. Today had been different—this afternoon he had entered on a wider experience. Drake seemed to know so much, and to understand and be familiar with many things that he vaguely guessed about. He felt that he was a closer friend of Drake's than he had ever been before. It would be exciting to see him often. And Randy, too. He had never imagined she would be so amusing. He thought of Renée with a sudden stab of contrition. He hadn't thought of her all day, and she was certainly his best friend. It might be best not to tell her about Randy. Renée had such a queer way of looking at him when he told her about anyone else. He thought, too, that he wouldn't talk to Drake about Renée. It was all right for Drake to joke the way he did with

Randy, but he wouldn't like him to talk that way to Renée. Renée was so quiet, and it would hurt her feelings, maybe.

It gave him a very pleasant sensation to think about Renée as his best friend—his very best friend. Randy was like a boy—sort of. He remembered the way she looked when she swung from the rings. He knew that Renée made him feel—another kind of way entirely. He supposed it was because he liked her so much better.

9

The whole of Kings Row lay on a gentle slope that lifted gradually from the creek on the south to the straggle of Negro quarters that edged the northern boundary of the town with a disreputable fringe of shacks and haphazard lanes. On the northwest the land dropped suddenly down a steep incline. There, at the foot of the hill, was a stretch of level ground perhaps a quarter of a mile square which was the site of Jinktown.

No one knew why it was called Jinktown. Long ago a few foreigners bought tiny lots there and built neat little brick-and-stone houses. It was a village in miniature. The few narrow streets were laid out at precise right angles, and the trim little houses were set in narrow plots of ground bright in summer with ordered rows of hollyhocks and other common flowers. It was a picturesque spectacle viewed from the top of the hill—like a doll village, almost. Years earlier Jinktown had been quite respectable, though it had always been made up of poor people. Of late some of the Dutch and Bohemian residents had grown more prosperous and had moved away. A lower order moved in. It was still charming and quaint, but Negroes were beginning to build their nondescript cabins around it, and it had lost, on close view, something of its original neatness. No one went to look at it any more from the top of the hill as they used to do. It had once been one of the odd sights of the town. But it was still called Jinktown, and Jinktowners were defined and set apart from other people.

Benny Singer and his mother lived in the smallest of the Jinktown cottages—two rooms, one of them hardly more than a lean-to. The house and the paling fence were painted bright blue.

Benny was a big, gangling boy of sixteen, with enormous pale gray eyes and a pasty complexion. He was good-natured and, in his awkward fashion, kind. Benny was a halfwit, but his mother was thankful that he was obedient and affectionate.

Mrs. Singer was a widow. She supported herself and Benny by taking in washing and doing odd jobs of house cleaning. She was a cheerful woman.

She was thinking about Benny this morning. It was the beginning of September and the first day of school. She had seen to it that he washed his neck and ears well and combed his hair, wetting it liberally from the washpan and flattening it close to his big round head. He had a new blue shirt, and she thought he looked very nice as he set out for school. She had heard people refer to Benny as an idiot. He wasn't, of course, she thought with a faint resentment—he was slow in his books, that was all. She had never been quick in school either—just couldn't seem to get things through her head—arithmetic and the like, and maps. She never had been able to make head or tail of maps. Benny was slow—he'd catch up sometime, she had no doubt, and if he didn't, she couldn't see that it would make much difference. He'd have to get a job somewhere and work, and like as not wouldn't have any use for book learning at all.

It was still hot, and extremely dry. The sycamores in the yard—even the trees in Jinktown were small—cast a thin and spotted shade. They were shedding, too. It had been a very dry summer. The moon-vine on the front porch was dead now—just a snarl of dry, brown stems. The zinnias, though, down each side of the narrow brick walk, were bright and pert-looking. Mrs. Singer took off her quilted gingham sunbonnet and fanned her flushed face. Her scanty hair escaped the hard little knot at the back of her head and fell outward in long strands like yellow grass. She hoped Benny would get along all right this year in school. He was having to stay in the same grade again. This was the fourth year he had failed to be promoted. But that, too, was all right. He'd know his books thoroughly before he went on to harder ones. If he were only a little bit quicker with figures he might get a job clerking in a grocery store or something like that. She sat there on her low doorstep thinking. It would be pretty fine if Benny *could* do something like that. In time—when she was old—he could support her. There might come a day when she would no longer take in washing. Washing was downright hard work. Of course Benny helped a good deal. He carried the heavy baskets of freshly ironed clothes home to her customers. That was a big help.

She fanned slowly. Benny's lop-eared hound came uncertainly around the corner of the house. He hung his head meekly and his eyes beseeched her for some sort of reassurance. He advanced diffidently, a step at a time. Finally he curled at her feet, licked himself, and waited. She scratched his back with her foot, and he stretched out flat with a long, ecstatic sigh. Drops of sweat gathered on her seamed neck. She wiped them away and rubbed her moist hand on her old green calico skirt. A faraway look came into her faded eyes. She was dreaming daring and ambitious dreams for Benny.

Benny was hurrying up the long winding path toward school. The first bell had already rung, and he was afraid he might be late. He had never been tardy in his life, nor had he ever missed a day's attendance, but he was always afraid he might be late someday. Every quarter his report card read: *Times Tardy ... None. Attendance ... Perfect.* His mother always exhibited those items to her neighbors with great pride.

He labored up the hill. Benny walked with a slight roll as though his head were too heavy for his body. He was not exactly comfortable in his mind. He was trying to remember something. He couldn't be sure what it was, but something—something he wanted to get straight in his head. It was very hard to do. Whenever he tried to think about something or to remember, the whole thing seemed to shiver and dissolve. He couldn't seem to get hold of what he wanted. One thing after another floated through his head—glimpses that worried and tantalized him.

He was very glad he was going to school. He liked to be with the boys. Lots of times they wouldn't let him play games. They pushed him away and told him he didn't have any sense, but if he stayed around they usually let him join in some sort of way.

He remembered other times when they stood around him in circles and said things he couldn't understand. It frightened him to remember those times. Sometimes they said things about his mammy taking in washing, but that didn't seem to have any sense to it. He knew she did.

Of all the boys in school he believed he liked Drake McHugh best. Drake was very friendly. Drake never pushed him out of a game or said things he couldn't understand. Once Drake had given him a pocketknife. He had kept it for a long time on the shelf in the front room. He had been afraid he might lose it, but now he carried it all the time. It was a very fine knife with a deerhorn handle and four blades.

All at once he slowed his walk. He remembered now what it was he was trying to think about. He stopped and looked back toward home. A cloud darkened his happy mood. Almost he wished he didn't have to go to school. He hadn't been promoted last year and he'd have to stay in the same class with the very young kids. Most of the boys would go on to another room this year and he'd have to stay with Miss Venable again. He half resented this—Miss Venable ought to have promoted him. He'd been in her room four years.

Benny was ashamed. The more he thought of it the more he felt that somehow he hadn't been treated right. "'Tain't fair," he said. "'Tain't fair."

When he came in sight of the playground he forgot all about it. Lots and lots of the kids were there already. He hurried. He paused on top of the stile and looked at the boys running about.

They caught sight of him. Fulmer Green shouted, "Looky! There's Benny. C'mon. Ol' crazy Ben!" He winked, screwing his mouth to one side so that his teeth showed all the way back. "C'mon."

A crowd gathered around the stile. A few of the boys said "hello," but mostly they stood laughing and nudging each other with their elbows. Their grins were derisive, but Benny did not know that. Their eyes were eager for some chance to make fun of him—waiting for him to say something silly, but he did not know it. They pushed closer—it was the pack gathering—sensing a victim, but he knew nothing of packs or their ways. Benny was glad to be back at school where there were so many friendly faces, where there was so much noise and jollity.

He stepped down from the stile. "Hello, everybody," he said happily.

10

The next two years were not exactly pleasant ones for Parris. School itself was less interesting. He had a new teacher, Miss Martha Colt. None of the children liked her. Whippings were frequent, and other punishments which were out of all proportion to the offenses. The children were quick to recognize her bad temper and unfairness, and it brought out in them a determination "to get the best of Miss Colt." Parris escaped her displeasures, but most of the boys did not. Day after day they left school, their legs covered with a crisscross of long red welts. Some of them exhibited their injuries with pride.

Fulmer Green, one of the "tough boys from the lower end of town," fully expressed the sentiment and attitude of all of them. "She kin cut the blood outa me if she wants to, but I'll get even with her, darned old fool."

It was not school that weighed heaviest on Parris. He could not say what it was. It seemed to be inside of him—some stirring, some restlessness, some urge which made him say again and again: "I don't feel good." His grandmother thought he might need a tonic but forgot to do anything about it. He roamed the place more than usual, summer and winter. He read a great deal—impatiently. Sometimes he sat and dreamed, vague, half-shaped dreams like those pictures beggars make in India by sifting colored dust on still water. But always something moved and shook the outlines and broke the visions into confusion.

He had grown considerably but he filled out well as he gained in height and retained his rather rounded and sturdy figure. The shadow on his lip was more pronounced. Drake McHugh said he would have to shave next year. Drake already boasted the possession of a razor of his own.

Parris was not unaware of the physical changes in himself or unobservant of the changes in others. But almost without noticing it he and his friends began to think of themselves as an older crowd. The children in Miss Venable's room seemed very young. Drake, who was nearly sixteen, kept his friendship with Parris, who found the association flattering. Both of them assumed grown-up and superior airs to boys of twelve or thirteen.

Only his friendship for Renée remained unchanged. She still waited for him after school and walked home with him, but she talked more now than she used to—mostly about the other girls and what they said. Parris paid scant attention to her conversation and sometimes did not listen at all. She never seemed to notice his distraction, and was content to chatter on in her husky little voice. She had an odd trick of ending all of her sentences with a rising inflection as though she were asking a question, but she never waited for an answer. Sometimes she, too, was silent and they walked nearly all of the way without speaking. She was still his shadow, but less his double in action. Even he noticed that. She was less of a tomboy now in her walk and behavior—more girlish. He realized that she was really very pretty. Other people spoke of it. She didn't look so babyish. Her face still kept its endearing heart shape, but her chin was more rounded, and she was almost as tall as he.

When Parris talked she listened with close attention but asked few questions. She was not really intelligent and had very little curiosity about things she could not readily understand.

She particularly liked to come and sit with him while he practiced the piano. She sat very straight in a high-backed velvet chair and listened with rapt attention, but she was immediately distrait if he stopped to explain why this or that passage was so hard to do. There were a few pieces she liked especially. When he played them her lips parted and her breath came quickly. Parris thought she looked like an angel at such times, but she was really looking slightly vacant. She wore much the same expression when she was eating. Her enjoyment of music was purely sensuous. When it was finished she thought no more about it.

On his fourteenth birthday Parris had his usual birthday supper with a cake and candles. Renée was his only guest. It wasn't really convenient for children to come out from town in the evening, especially on a schoolday. Renée gave him three handkerchiefs with crooked initials worked in the corners. She had made them herself.

After supper Anna, the stout German maid, gave him fourteen playful spanks—one for each year—and another to grow on.

"It's after eight, Parris," Madame reminded him. "You'd better walk down to Renée's house with her. It's moonlight. You're not afraid to come back by yourself, are you?"

He flushed. His grandmother didn't seem to realize he was fourteen and would have to shave next year. "Of course not," he answered impatiently.

As they went down the terrace steps Renée took his hand, and they walked on, swinging their clasped hands between them.

"I guess I ought to give you fourteen licks, too, like Anna did."

He laughed, but the laugh died quickly and his throat tightened. He swallowed. "I'd rather you'd kiss me," he said.

"All right," she said readily. "I'll kiss you fourteen times." She placed her hands on his shoulders and kissed him on the mouth, counting each time…. "Twelve … thirteen … fourteen … and a big one to grow on." She hugged him tight around the neck and made a humorous little grunt with the effort. He returned the embrace awkwardly and they stood for a moment a little breathless. The moon shone full on her face. Her moist red lips were parted, and she had her familiar look of listening to music.

"That's the best birthday present I ever had," he said. The gallantry of his speech surprised him, but he was pleased to have said it "I—I love you, Renée."

"Honestly, do you?"

"You bet. I guess you're my girl."

"I like to be your girl. I guess you're my sweetheart, too."

"Let's be sweethearts forever, Renée, you and me."

"All right."

"Cross your heart?" he demanded.

"… And hope to die," she replied.

"Good night, Renée."

"Good night. I had a nice time."

"So did I."

"Well, see you tomorrow, Parris."

"Remember what you promised?"

"Of course."

"You won't forget?"

She shook her head. "Never."

"Good night, then."

"G'night." Her voice trailed the words softly. He watched her go up the short walk to her door, her bright hair looking more silver than gold in the moonlight.

A few days later when they were coming home from school they overtook Willy Macintosh. He was walking slowly, absently kicking a stone ahead of him. He looked very solemn.

"What's the matter, Willy?" Parris asked.

"Nothin'."

"Goodness," Renée said, "you look like you been crying."

"I ain't."

"Well, you look like it."

"My pa is awful sick." He blurted the words, and tears stood in his brown eyes.

"What's the matter with him?"

"He's got sores on his leg."

"Oh." Renée's tone conveyed the idea that this was nothing much.

"They're bad sores," Willy explained.

"What kind of sores?"

"They're ulcers."

"What are ulcers?"

"I don't know. They're terrible bad though. He's going to have an operation today."

"Oh, my goodness!"

"Uh huh." Willy was apparently relieved that he had convinced them of the seriousness of the case. "Dr. Gordon's there now, I guess."

They walked slowly, keeping step with Willy, who delayed as much as possible. When they came to the crossroads where the big white Macintosh house stood in a grove of trees they saw a buggy standing at the gate. Two big bay horses pawed the ground impatiently.

"That's Dr. Gordon's buggy," Willy said as if to prove his story. "I guess he's performin' the operation."

The children stared curiously at the windows of an upper room where white curtains were looped back from the windows and the shades rolled high.

"Well, Willy, I hope your papa'll—" Renée's speech was cut short by a dreadful sound. A long-drawn cry came from those open windows. It was more like the howl of a dog. It mounted and mounted as though it would never stop, then broke into several short, quick sobs and died in a long moan. Renée turned pale and caught Parris by the arm. The cry came again—louder than before—rising and ending in a fearful shout.

Willy whimpered and ran back a few steps. His face was working with terror.

"Good gracious, Willy," Renée spoke in a loud whisper, "didn't Dr. Gordon give your father chloroform?"

"I—I heard Mama say he c-couldn't take chloroform because he's got heart disease."

"Good gracious me! Parris, didn't you think they *had* to give people chloroform for an operation?"

The terrible yells began again. Willy threw his books into the ditch beside the road. His face was crimson, and he was crying aloud. He clenched his fat dirty hands and rubbed his eyes violently. Then he began to run toward the house. "He's got to quit that," he sobbed. "He's got to quit that. I'll—I'll kill that old durn fool doctor."

Parris and Renée watched Willy as he dashed up the walk and flung himself at the front door. He wrenched and pulled at the door, but it was locked. He ran around toward the kitchen door crying, "He's got to quit that—I'll kill him—I'll kill him."

"Come on, Parris, let's go home. I'm scared. I never heard a man cry and holler before, did you?"

They hardly spoke but walked as fast as they could.

The next day at school they were told that Willy's father had died. Parris overheard Miss Colt say to Miss Venable that Mr. Macintosh had died from shock. He wondered just what that meant. It was a long time before Parris could forget the sounds he had heard that afternoon. Whenever he saw Dr. Gordon dashing along the road behind his two high-spirited bays, he was reminded of it, and always he was divided between two feelings—one, a sort of terror of the man who cut people with knives, and the other an excited admiration. He wondered, as he watched Dr. Gordon pass in a cloud of dust, if he were hurrying to another operation. But it must be wonderful to be a doctor, anyhow, he decided. He imagined Dr. Gordon working and fighting to save somebody's life. Dr. Gordon must be a very fine doctor. Everybody said so. The more he thought about it the more certain he was that he wanted to be a doctor; but he often wondered if he could really cut people open and sew them up—especially if they had heart disease and couldn't have chloroform.

One thing, however, he was certain of. *He was afraid of Dr. Henry Gordon.*

1 1

Madame von Eln decided that spring to make a visit to friends in St. Louis and then to go on to Philadelphia where she had a few relatives.

"I think I'll take you with me, Parris. You'll like visiting the cities, though I suspect my relatives are dull. God knows they were dull enough the last time I saw them, and I'm sure time hasn't improved them. Still, they *are* relatives. I suppose you ought to know them. I won't live always and you should know your kinspeople."

Parris was excited beyond measure. He had never made a long trip and he loved riding on trains. Madame decided they would leave the first week in June. Parris told Renée about it and became eloquent about the wonders of Philadelphia. He had heard his grandmother talk at length about it, although he remembered suddenly that she was always somewhat sarcastic at the same time.

Renée was not excited. She kept her eyes on his face as if waiting for him to say something different from what he *was* saying.

"Why, what's the matter?" he asked finally.

"Nothing. Why?"

"You look so funny."

She kept silent.

"Aren't you glad I'm going to get to go on a trip?"

She shook her head. "I'll be lonesome," she said simply.

He was instantly contrite. "Aw, Renée, honest, will you miss me?"

"Of course."

"I'll bring you something when I come back."

"What?" She asked the question listlessly.

"I don't know. Something nice. What do you want?"

"Anything you want to bring me."

"All right. I'll keep looking for something for you."

"I know I'll like it—whatever you bring."

They began to talk of other matters. Neither of them had ever spoken about the night of his birthday. Parris had not forgotten it. He had thought of it several times, but he remembered it more as a mere corroboration of the simple fact that Renée was his sweetheart.

She came to the house to say good-by to him the morning of his departure. She looked at the valises as Uncle Henry carried them to the surrey and piled them on the front seat, but her face was expressionless.

Madame counted the innumerable parcels and re-counted them. "*Bien!* I suppose that is all. Almost I wish I had not begun this, but I suppose we must go through with it, eh, Parris?"

Parris looked at her in amazement. It was incomprehensible that she should not look forward to the excitement and novelty.

"Now, then, we go." She turned to Renée. "I wish you were coming, too, my child. I don't know why I didn't think of it. You would have been company for each other while I talk with my dreadful family." She leaned over and touched her lips to Renée's cheek. "Be a good girl. Come, Parris."

Parris grabbed Renée roughly by the arm and kissed her. She received the caress passively.

At the big gate he looked back and waved. She was standing on the terrace. Very slowly she raised her arm above her head and waved back with a childish flapping motion.

The summer was well advanced when Parris and his grandmother returned. Parris was astonished at the appearance of the place. It looked so rough and unkempt.

He hurried at once to see Renée, with the package he had brought her. His grandmother had spent the whole of one morning shopping with him in an enormous store, and had made the selections herself.

Renée looked taller than he had remembered her.

"You've grown since I left, Renée. Look how tall you are!"

Gudrun, Renée's mother, laughed. "I guess she don' grow so much in six weeks!"

"Gosh, is it just six weeks? Seems like I've been gone a year."

"It seems long to me, too." Renée sounded formal.

"Look, I brought you something. My grandmother helped me pick 'em out. She said she hoped you'd like them. I hope so, too."

Renée looked at her mother, then at Parris. She drew her shoulders up with a little giggle of pleasure. "I can't wait, Mama. Quick, let's look."

"Take them in the other room and open them there."

There was a box containing a dozen hair ribbons, all different colors.

"Oh, Parris, they're beautiful!"

"They're nice, nice—ver-ry," Gudrun agreed with her broad smile.

Renée rustled the papers ecstatically. "Let's see what else. Goodness, I'll have enough hair ribbons to last me a whole year! What's in this long box, Parris?"

"Look and see."

It was a parasol, pink silk inside and white lace ruffles on the outside. Renée gasped.

"See," Parris explained. "It's got a crook handle so's you can carry it on your arm—like this."

"It's the prettiest one I ever did see."

"Och—" her mother warned. "Don't open it in the house. Bad luck!"

Renée laughed and twirled it over her head, making the lace ruffles stand out in little rippling waves.

There was a box covered with tiny iridescent shells. "To keep little things in," Parris explained, handing it to her.

"Now—I've saved the biggest box for last. I can't guess what *that* is."

She unwrapped the package and lifted the layers of tissue paper. "Oh— look, look! It's a green silk dress."

She took it out and held it up against herself. Parris felt his face burn with pleasure. He had never seen Renée so excited.

The dress was an intricacy of insertions, ruffles, braid loops, and tiny buttons.

"That's a pretty dress, sure enough," said Gudrun. "Parris, you tell your gran'ma we thank her ever so much. Renée, you got to go right away and thank Madame yourself."

"Of course, I will; but Parris brought it to me, too."

"Yes, yes, of course. It's awful nice. Did you have a good time, Parris?"

"Yes'm. Wonderful."

"And Madame, she is well, yes?"

"Quite well, thank you."

"I want to try it on, can I, Mama, right now?"

"Couldn't you wait?"

"No, I got to see how it looks."

Renée snatched at the hem of her short gingham dress.

"My goodness, Renée," her mother expostulated, laughing. "You ain't goin' to undress right here before Parris?" But Renée's dress went flying toward a chair. "My goodness, look at the child. Here, let me help you. It's all pinned up. Be careful now!"

"Look, Parris. It fits exactly right." She turned around two or three times. "It's lovely," she said softly—almost under her breath.

Parris and Renée fell quickly into their accustomed summer pastimes. They waded in the creek, climbed trees, hunted berries, and got themselves thoroughly sunburned.

One stifling afternoon they went up through the spruce planting and down on the other side. It was the way to the pond—their "secret lake," as they always called it. They went without discussing their destination. Ordinarily they understood each other so well that words were unnecessary. They simply drifted here or there by unspoken agreement.

This day did not differ from any other day, but they found themselves loitering through the long emerald lanes as though some intangible reluctance slowed their steps. It was very still among the rows of evergreens. The hot air hung motionless. An occasional bumblebee zoomed up before them and shot away, leaving a thinning trail of sound behind him.

They came to the pond, and Renée sat down on the bank. She took off one shoe and stocking and dipped her toes in the water.

"It's warm," she said.

"Of course," he answered. "Look how hot it is today."

She leaned back and threw the shoe and stocking toward the shade of a wide low-hanging apple tree. She took off the other shoe and rolled the stocking into it. It followed the first. Stretching out both feet, she paddled them quickly, sending the little waves flying across the still surface.

Very slowly Parris removed his shoes and stockings. Both sat for some time without saying a word.

"Well, going in?" he asked. His voice sounded a little strange in his own ears—thick, as though he had a cold.

She nodded. "In a minute."

Parris looked sidewise at her. She was watching the water splash about her feet, apparently unaware of him.

"Want me to help you undress?"

She shook her head.

"Do you remember how I used to have to unbutton your waist in the back?"

"Uh huh. I don't wear that kind now."

He sat silent for a few moments, throwing small clods into the water.

"Gee, Renée, it's hot here in the sun. Let's undress under the trees."

She arose without a word. The branches of the big crab-apple tree swept the ground on all sides.

"Lots of crab apples this year," he said. "Look how they pull the limbs down. Clear to the ground."

"Uh huh, lots of them."

He held the branches aside, and she stooped to enter the canopied space beneath.

"Isn't this nice? Look, like a tent."

She nodded.

"What's the matter, Renée?"

"Nothing."

"Why don't you talk?"

"I don't know. Why?"

It was strange. He had never felt like this before. He could not imagine what was the matter with him.

"Gee, I feel funny, Renée. Don't you?"

She turned her eyes slowly toward him. "Yes, I guess I do. Maybe we'd better go back."

He was surprised. "Don't you want to go in swimming?"

She hesitated a moment, then she nodded. "I guess so," she said. Her voice sounded strange, too—hoarse.

"I think I'll hang my clothes up on this old dead limb here," he said with an effort to be casual.

She glanced at the limb. "Looks like a good place."

He rolled his shirt over his head and hung it up. In a moment he was undressed. Instinctively he turned his back. He did not look at her. He pretended an interest in a small caterpillar laboring along one of the knotty branches.

"Ready?" he asked turning around. She was undressed and was sitting down.

"In a minute. I—I want to rest just a minute."

"Good idea," he agreed, sitting down beside her. "You don't want to go in when you're hot. Gives you cramps."

She broke off tufts of grass and covered her toes. He began pulling grass, too, heaping it on her feet until they were hidden under little green mounds. He pulled some more and scattered it over her.

"That tickles." She smiled, looking directly at him for the first time.

He seized a handful and held it out, letting it trickle through his fingers on her back.

"Ouch, ugh, it feels like bugs!" She clasped her arms about herself and rolled over.

In a moment they were lying side by side talking with something of their accustomed ease. Renée tried to reach a low-hanging branch with her foot. She caught a twig between her toes and swung it back and forth. He reached with his foot and tried to capture it from her.

After a few moments they lay quite still. Parris could hear the quick spring of grasshoppers outside in the tall grass. Renée was so quiet he thought she must be asleep. He raised himself on one elbow and looked at her. Her eyes were wide open. Suddenly his heart pounded—suffocatingly. The green world seemed to rush at him. The illusion made him dizzy. His thoughts flew back and forth in his head.

He leaned over her. "Renée!" he said in a harsh whisper.

She looked at him. Her eyes were wide and black in the shadow of the leaves.

"Renée!" he repeated.

She drew her chin in and caught her lower lip with her little pointed teeth.

"*You know?*" he asked almost inaudibly.

She nodded slowly, her eyes fixed on his face.

"Do you want to?" he asked.

She drew her breath sharply, and turned her head quickly to one side.

"Renée." Parris did not recognize his own speech—or the words.

They seemed to say themselves.

She turned her head back again with the same quick motion. There was question in her look.

"I don't know," she said.

He moved closer and pressed his cheek against hers. Her soft skin was flaming.

"Do you want to?" he repeated.

He felt her nod against his cheek. "*Yes.*" She turned her face as far away as she could, but her arms went around his neck.

The world of green leaves and grass and blue sky seemed once more to rush toward him, over him, past him—and to recede suddenly into a deathly silence. He scarcely knew what he did, but he knew with an amazing clarity how Drake McHugh's talk had prepared him for this moment. He felt her soft, yielding body stiffen with surprise—he felt her try to thrust him away from her, but he knew he could not help her, or spare her in any way—he heard her cry and felt the resistance go out of her. Then her arms tightened around his neck, pressing his face hard into the cool sweet grass.

The deep gold tide of afternoon covered them. They lay side by side without speaking. He felt her shiver from time to time—a long shiver that seemed to shake her from head to foot.

"Renée!"

"What?" she whispered.

"Are you mad at me?"

"Of course not."

He reached for her hand and held it. Her fingers were cold.

There was a rustle in the shrubbery back of them. Renée leapt to her feet and cowered against the tree.

"Parris, there was somebody in those bushes—somebody watching us."

He scrambled to his feet and stood close to her, holding her arms tight. "How do you know? Did you see anybody?"

"I saw somebody—I don't know who it was—oh—" she began to cry.

"It was just some one of the hands. They've been thinning out trees up that way." He pointed across the pond.

"He saw us; I bet he did. What'll we do?"

"But listen, Renée, maybe he didn't—maybe he couldn't see in here through all these leaves."

"I—I think it was that awful Gus Metzger—it looked like him."

"Oh, gee!"

"Quick, let's get dressed."

They threw their clothes on and scrambled through the branches into the sunlight.

"Come on, Renée, let's go."

"No." She thought a minute. "I tell you what let's do. You stay here, and I'll go first. You come on after a while. But you wait a *good* while. Maybe it'll look like we wasn't up here together."

"I better go with you."

"You do like I tell you. You wait."

Before he could argue further, she ran. He watched her blue dress fluttering down the long alley between the trees. Once she turned and looked back, raised her arm. She waved; then she walked on slowly out of sight.

He stood by the edge of the pond for what seemed an interminable time. Twice he started to go, but he remembered her words, "wait a *good* while." Maybe she knew best.

The sun dropped lower and long shadows reached across the pond, darkening its bright surface. Overhead a little flock of swallows circled and dipped, appearing now black and now a rusty brown, as the light caught them.

He decided he might go now. It must be all of an hour.

He went slowly down the same way she had gone. He thought first he had best go home some roundabout way, but he felt that he must see her—pass her house. Maybe she would come to the door and give him a look—some sign of reassurance.

When he came in sight of the little cottage he was surprised. The doors were shut and the shades were drawn. He felt a sense of relief. Maybe her father and mother were away from home. He was about to pass when he heard voices. He stopped and listened. They were angry voices. It was Sven—Gudrun, too. A wild alarm shot through him. Without thinking he ran up the walk to the door. He could hear Sven cursing, and Gudrun saying something very loud. They were speaking Swedish, though, and he could not understand. Sven began to shout. Through it he heard a little wail that almost stopped his heart. *Renée!*

He went close to the door and called her name. There was no answer. He called again. There was a thud on the door as though someone had been thrown against it. Then he heard a dreadful sound. It was the unmistakable swish of a heavy leather strap. He heard it strike flesh and heard Renée's piercing scream. He hurled himself against the door and shouted.

"Sven! Sven Gyllinson—*Sven—Sven ...*"

But Sven did not hear. Sven was cursing louder than ever. The sharp slap of the strap came faster and faster. Renée's screams ran together in a continued stream of sound. Still the murderous blows went on and on. The screams changed. They were suddenly hoarse—like the cries of an animal.

Parris whirled and leaned his back against the door. He flung his arms straight on either side to keep from falling. He looked up where a few clouds seemed to hang motionless. "Dear God—dear God—dear God—don't—don't let—"

Suddenly the terrible crying sank to a shaking moan and stopped, but the hideous swish of the strap went on—steadily—relentlessly.

Parris felt himself turn icy cold. He knew he was going to be sick. He felt himself sliding against the rough weatherboards and threw out his hands as he saw the ground slanting sharply toward his face.

12

It was almost dark when he opened his eyes. He remembered at once where he was and what had happened. He crawled a few paces and listened. The house was silent. *Had they killed her?* His breath shook out of him in gasps. He felt terribly ill. *Tomorrow*—he'd tell his grandmother about Sven. They'd take Renée away from him. *Tomorrow*—he couldn't do anything now. He must hurry home before he was sick again. *Tomorrow*—Sven—the dirty, horrible, monstrous, terrible dog—*tomorrow!* He could not keep to the path. It kept swinging out from under him—slipping to one side—slithering from under his feet.... He tore his hands in the rose trellis.

He stumbled up the steps of the terrace. He heard Anna's startled exclamation as he stepped into the blinding lamplight, and then his grandmother saying, "*Nom de Dieu! Anna, vite, de l'eau....*"

They undressed him and put him to bed. He felt a little better, but the bed rolled under him. Madame hung over him anxiously.

"Child, what is the matter? What happened?"

He wanted to tell her. He would have told everything, but he didn't know the right words. How could he say it—to her? He turned his head from side to side. "I don't—know. I fell down. I guess I got sick—" Waves of nausea swept up and over him when he tried to speak again.

Madame spoke quietly to Anna. "Tell Uncle Henry to hitch up the buggy and get Dr. Gordon—quickly."

Dr. Gordon came, but Parris could not see him clearly. He heard questions, and tried to answer. Faces without bodies attached to them seemed to float over the bed. They came close, and enormous eyes looked at him. He tried to get away but could not. He tried hard to think. He said Renée— Renée—Renée, over and over. What was happening to her? Maybe she was still lying on the floor behind that locked door. Maybe she was lying in bed—all bloody. He screamed and pushed at Dr. Gordon's face. Then he felt someone hold his hands and force him back on the pillow. He knew he was falling through the pillow—through the bed—through the floor—down a long shining tunnel that dwindled away and away to a tiny shimmering point. He was rushing violently toward that minute spark at the end of the slippery tunnel....

13

Evening light filled the room. Parris tried to open his eyes wider, but the
lids were very heavy. Everything looked wavey—it was like looking through
glass that streamed with rain. Maybe it was raining. He strained hard to see.
No—that was sunshine. It was very still. It must be late in the afternoon.
Afternoon ... Then he must have slept all day. Goodness! He tried to lift his
head but it stuck to the pillow. He tried to raise his hand but it would not
move. It seemed weighted. What *was* the matter? He knew he ought to get
up—there was something he ought to see about. Was it school? No, no—this
was summertime—he didn't have to go to school. But there was something—
something. What was it? Something dreadful he had to do, or see about. He
could almost think of it. It—whatever it was—slid nearer—something terrible.
He was afraid now to think. The effort tired him. He didn't believe he had ever
been so tired. He would have to go to sleep again ... maybe when he woke up
he could remember. He closed his eyes....

When he awoke it was dark outside. There was a shaded light in the corner,
and someone was in the big rocking chair. He tried to turn his head to see who
it was. It must be Anna.

"Anna!" He could hardly hear himself—such a funny weak croak he made!

"*Gott, Parris, bist du wach?*" Anna ran to the door. "*Madame, bitte komm'!*"

In a moment his grandmother leaned over him. "Parris," she said very
softly.

"Yes." He tried to move.

"You must lie very still. Don't talk."

"Why?"

"S-sh! Not now, tomorrow you can talk, perhaps." She slipped her arm
under his pillow and raised him a little. "Try to drink this."

The glass clinked against his teeth, and something very queer-tasting
ran into his mouth. Some of it ran out again, and Anna wiped it away
with a napkin. After a little he felt sleepy ... something he must remember,
though—something he must tell his grandmother. He would remember—
tomorrow.

He waked and slept and waked again but never for very long. Then one
morning the objects in the room were steadier and clearer, but the inside of his
head was heavy as lead. His temples seemed to spread out like balloons—then
he floated for a moment until the heaviness returned and thrust his head down
hard into the pillow.

He lay half awake and tried once more to think. A wagon rattled along the
drive below the terrace. *He heard a whip crack.* A quick little cry escaped his
lips. That was it! *Renée!*

His grandmother was instantly beside the bed. "Parris, what is it?"

"Where's Renée?"

"Renée?"

"Yes, where is she?"

"She's not here just now, dear. Try to lie still."

He wailed a little. *"But where is she?"*

Madame laid one of her wrinkled little hands on his. "Renée has gone away, Parris."

"Gone? Gone away? *Where?*"

"Well, I don't know, dear. Her father moved away somewhere."

All of the breath went out of him. Madame was wearing her thick-lensed glasses and saw how he sank back on the bed.

"That's all right, Parris. I daresay she'll come back sometime. You mustn't mind that."

His face drew up, but he couldn't cry. "Oh, oh!" he said weakly.

"Why, Parris! Were you so fond of your little friend as all that?"

He noticed that she said "were." The word seemed to close a door—a great, heavy, iron door. Renée was gone. He knew he would never see her again. He felt his stomach shake, but his eyes were quite dry.

"Parris! My darling child—you mustn't. I'll try to send for Renée if you'll be very quiet and not worry."

He knew she could not. Never, never, never, never, never! He held on somehow to her hand, but his fingers were like paper.

"Have I been awful sick?"

"You've been quite sick, yes."

"A long time?"

"Yes, Parris—now be quiet."

"What time is it?"

"Why—I don't know, child. Almost seven, I suppose."

"I mean—no, no—I mean what time this week?"

"Oh—it's Sunday."

"Goodness! Why, I got sick last Tuesday, didn't I?"

"Longer than that, dear. It's the middle of August."

"*The—middle—of—August?*" He whispered the words. "Have I been—"

"You've been unconscious for weeks, Parris. You see now how very sick you have been, and how careful you'll have to be."

"What's the matter with me?"

"You've had fever—a very bad fever."

He was silent for a few minutes. He turned his head very slowly on the pillow and looked out of the window. "When—when did she go away?"

"What? Oh! The Gyllinsons left just the day after you took sick."

"Why?"

"Well, Sven told me he had the offer of better wages and he'd have to go. I hated to lose him. He was a good manager."

"Did Renée—did—" He couldn't frame the question; he feared the answer.

"I didn't see Renée, Parris. Anna said she came to the kitchen door that morning. She thought Renée seemed very frightened—maybe because she heard you were so sick. She ran away again very quickly. Sven made up his mind very suddenly. It seemed queer. Certainly it is the first time I've ever known him to do anything in a hurry."

"Was she all right?"

"Renée, you mean? Why, I guess so, Parris. Anna said she seemed sorry to go, and very sorry to hear you were ill, but the doctor was here, and we were all busy looking after you. You were really very ill that day."

Parris had shifted his position and watched his grandmother's face narrowly. It was certain that she knew nothing of the events of that terrible afternoon.

"Where did they go?"

"I don't know, dear. I don't think Sven told anyone. He packed up in a hurry and went off. I think down toward the Ozark Mountains, somewhere. Now don't talk any more. Try to go to sleep. You'll be getting strong soon, now."

His convalescence was slow and tedious. Gradually he learned to take a few steps, and then to walk without leaning on Anna. His head had been shaved and now it was covered with a thick soft stubble—like black velvet. He was very thin, and his bones stuck out. Seeing himself in the mirror, he thought he looked like the scarecrow in Amos Miller's garden.

It was a long time before he could bring himself to so much as look toward the Gyllinson cottage. It stood empty and close shuttered. The sight of it struck him with an almost physical impact.

He would think now—go over that day again. In spite of the ache and soreness of his heart, he remembered it all—made himself think of it. Something between pain and an unbearable pleasure made him a little sick. He wanted to lie down and cry when he thought of Renée and what had happened to her. He blamed himself. He could hear again her voice saying, *"Maybe we'd better go back."*

If only they *had* gone back as she had suggested. And yet—something, some obstinate feeling in his flesh refused that regret. It was hateful to think that she had suffered, and for him. But he knew they could not help it—either of them. That—that which happened just had to happen. Even now, weak as he was, a strange imperious thrill ran along his nerves, tightened them, made them respond again to the recollection of her as she sat in the dappled shade under the tree. She was so white, and sweet. Where the quivering spots of sunshine fell through the leaves and touched her she was all silvery—

He decided he could not wait any longer. He must go to her house, walk around the yard where she used to be, maybe look through the windows. He went slowly down the rough stone steps.

"Where are you going, Parris?" His grandmother called from an upper window.

"Just going to take a little walk."

"Well, you must carry an umbrella over you. The sun is warm today. Take that old black one in the hall. Don't stay out long."

"Yes'm."

He went a bit unsteadily across the wide stretch of dry grass, holding the big black-silk umbrella over his head.

The cottage yard was weedy and overgrown. The late summer rains had washed the sand from the walk that led to the door, and heaps of trash had blown into corners of the porch. Pieces of paper and old rags lay about, testifying to the haste of Sven's packing and departure. It was unbearably desolate—and so still!

He walked around the house. The back yard was cluttered with pieces of lumber. An overturned chicken coop lay on the ground near the kitchen door. A barrel stood at the door of the smokehouse. His eye caught a glimpse of something green through a wide crack between the staves. He went idly, unthinkingly, to see what it was.

The barrel was filled with debris—broken china and some rusted cans, but underneath was something green—something familiar. He pulled at it. It was the dress he had brought Renée from Philadelphia—torn to shreds and thrust in among the odds and ends of trash. He turned the barrel to one side to see better. There was the parasol, too, its white crook handle snapped off short. Pieces of the shell box, and a crumple of colored ribbons!

The sight of his presents, thus contemptuously and angrily discarded, struck him as nothing else had—not even Renée's departure—with the utter completeness of his loss. They wouldn't even let her keep the pretty things he had given her—the things she had liked so much! The ugly, dirty *awful* people—the *dogs*. Rage shook him. If God would just help him, he'd hunt for her sometime—he'd take her away from them. Then he began to cry, a broken whimper that puffed out his lips and hurt his throat. He leaned against the barrel and held to the rim with both hands while tears ran down his face and dripped into the barrel. The drops fell on the soiled and crumpled silk and made round, dark spots. He cried with long hoarse sounds, weakly, hopelessly—filled with despair and a harsh pressing realization of his own helplessness. When he could cry no more he sat down and leaned his face against the splintery wood. He pushed hard against it in a desperate effort to relieve the ache and pain in his throat and breast.

After a while he arose, and mechanically sorted out the fragments and scraps of Renée's treasures. He found a broken china doll at the bottom of the barrel. He remembered it. She used to play with it a long, long time ago. He made a little heap of his ruined gifts and added to it everything he could find that had belonged to her.

There was an old hoe leaning against the garden fence. With that he dug a deep hole in a corner of the yard by the snowball bushes, and carefully buried the shabby bundle. Then he opened the umbrella, held it between him and the sun, and trudged home without looking back.

He wished he had died when he was sick. He wished he could die—right now.

14

"I guess Uncle Henry could hitch up and take me to school next week, couldn't he?" Parris asked the question a bit diffidently one morning at breakfast. "I guess I couldn't walk that far yet?"

Madame folded her napkin carefully, placed it beside her plate, and hunted in her reticule for her glasses before she replied.

"You're not going to school this year, Parris."

"Wha-at?" His eyes opened very wide with astonishment.

"You won't be strong enough to start next week, and I have decided to get a tutor for you this winter. You can study at home."

"Oh, goodness!" The tone of his voice dropped a little. It was mixed with dismay. School was really not bad. He had been looking forward to seeing everybody again. It was pretty lonesome at home.

"Besides," Madame continued, "you need study in German and French that you don't get at school."

"But what for? I can talk all right—"

"Not really correctly, Parris. You must learn to read both languages easily, and to write them. You'll be glad someday. You make mistakes."

"Oh, dear. I don't know—"

"I'll arrange at Aberdeen College to get a nice young man to come here and hear your lessons. You can study at home, and I'm sure you will make better progress anyway. Of course you can go on with your piano lessons if you want to."

Parris knew that tone in his grandmother's voice. It was settled. He sighed. "All right," he said.

He went restlessly about the house that day, scuffing and shuffling his feet and making a considerable number of small noises.

"Heavens, Parris. What's gotten into you today? Couldn't you make less noise?" Madame demanded finally.

"Yes'm," he answered meekly.

He went slowly upstairs and stood at the hall window that looked out on the gently rising landscape. Beyond the green rows of the nursery plantings wide yellow fields tilted upward. One of the St. George farms adjoined Madame von Eln's land. He drummed on the glass. It was going to be pretty bad not to go to school. If he lived in town, it wouldn't be so lonesome, but out here in the winter—

"*Grand'mère,*" he called presently.

"Yes, what is it?"

"I see Mr. Thurston St. George coming across his pasture. I bet he's coming down here."

"Is he riding?"

"Yes'm. Toby's laying down the rail fence for him now."

"Well, come down and tell Anna to prepare a pitcher of lemonade. It's warm this afternoon."

"Yes'm." He stood for a moment watching the familiar spectacle. Mr. St. George sat motionless on his huge horse, holding a vast cotton umbrella. It was as big as a tent. Presently the rails of the zigzag fence were laid aside and the old horse walked sedately through and stopped. Mr. St. George sat as grandly as a sultan on an elephant and waited until little black Toby replaced the panel of rails. Toby remounted, took charge of the umbrella, and they got under way again, with the effect of a procession.

Parris clattered down the uncarpeted back stairs to apprise Anna of the visit. He liked Mr. St. George.

Half an hour later the old man dismounted at the foot of the terrace and came up the steps with a sort of heavy alacrity. He took off his high-crowned straw hat and bowed to Madame, who had come out to greet him.

"Howdy, Marie, howdy, ma'am."

"Well, it's very nice to see you, Thurston. I hope you're well."

"Thank you. I don't need to ask how you are. It's warmer than usual this September, don't you think so? I notice your young trees up there next my place are looking a little peaked."

"Yes, it is hot, and dry."

"I wonder if I could trouble you for a glass of water, ma'am?"

"Why, certainly. Parris, tell Anna to bring some lemonade."

"Oh, so that's your grandson back there!" Mr. St. George affected surprise. "I'd never have known you, boy. You've shot up so fast. Been sick, I hear."

"Yes, sir."

"What's the matter?"

Madame interrupted. "It seems to have been a spell of brain fever."

"Brain fever, eh? That's no good. Been studying too hard, sonny?"

"I—I don't think so, sir."

"Parris—the lemonade."

"No, now, ma'am. Water'll do very nicely. Don't trouble."

"It's no trouble, Thurston. It's already made."

"Oh, well then. In that case it will be very agreeable. I wonder if your man could give my horse some water, or Toby could do it himself."

"Not at all. Parris, tell Uncle Henry to water Mr. St. George's horse, and—
Parris!"

"Yes'm."

"Call Toby and give him some lemonade."

"Thank you, ma'am, you are very kind. Toby always remembers your
lemonade."

Parris was back in a few minutes and sat a little way off to listen. Mr. St.
George fascinated him—he was so big. Thurston St. George just missed being
a giant. His great frame and enormous beard, his broad feet and thick legs were
all on heroic scale. His hands were well shaped and well cared for. Parris thought
they looked like hands seen through his grandmother's big reading glass.

The talk ran on easily. They discussed crops and retailed the small news of
the countryside.

"Money is awful tight this year."

"It always seems to be," Madame responded.

"Worse than usual, Madame."

They spoke of the cashier of the County Savings Bank being in trouble.

"Money's the root of all evil," Mr. St. George said holding out his glass.

Madame laughed. "I don't believe that—neither do you, or you wouldn't
have spent your life making so much."

"That's what Holy Writ says, ma'am."

"No, it doesn't."

"Yeh? How's that? Heard that all my life."

"Heard wrong, too, Thurston. The Bible says, 'The *love* of money is the
root of all evil.'"

"Well, now, is that so? Amounts to the same thing in the end, I guess." He
shook his glass, making a pleasant tinkle of ice. "By the way, Marie, I hear you
lost your overseer."

"Yes, I did. I was sorry to lose him, too. He had a way with plants and trees."

"Where did he go?"

"Off somewhere. I don't know."

"H'm. Got anybody to take his place?"

"Not yet."

"D'you know old Tom Carr?"

"Torn Carr? No, I don't believe I do."

"Tom Carr—lives 'way out north of town. Rents a little place of mine and
works at the Stillman Flour Mill."

"Oh, yes. Big bushy head of white hair? I've seen him."

"Believe he'd be a good man for you."

"But isn't he pretty old?"

"Not as old as he looks. He's spry as a cricket. I hear he's had some
experience along your line."

"Well, I might talk to him."

"Tell you what. I'm riding out that way tomorrow. I'll send him around. I'd like to see him get a good place. Surely you remember the Carrs! They used to live in the Fuller place."

"Don't recall them, Thurston."

"Long time ago. They came here from New York state. Had some money. Started off in big style—horses, carriage, everything. He tried trading in real estate. Lost it all. Wife went crazy—she's been in the asylum here twice, but he keeps her at home now and looks after her himself. He's a good man. Just didn't have a knack of getting on somehow."

"Um—send him to see me."

"It'd be a mercy, ma'am, if you could take him. He's educated—not the regular run at all. His wife was quite a highflier, I imagine. I heard she was a graduate of Vassar College back there, but she's crazy as a loon now. Got dropsy, too. Fat as an elephant."

"Dangerous, do you think? I wouldn't want to have—"

"Oh, no, no! Not at all. Just sits and sings. Too fat to move."

"Heavens. I'll be glad if I can help the poor man. What a life that must be!"

"Terrible, terrible. But I never heard a word of complaint out of Tom Carr all the years I've known him. He's as cheerful as Santa Claus."

"Looks like Santa Claus, too, if I'm thinking of the same man."

"That's Tom Carr, all right! There's nobody else in the county looks like him. Well, thank you, ma'am, I'll be going along now. Good afternoon. Good day, sonny. Watch out you don't study too hard!"

Toby led the horse to the terrace wall, and Mr. St. George dropped into the saddle. He unfurled the umbrella and handed it back to the inky boy already perched behind him. Majestically, they returned the way they had come.

The fires of Indian summer burned on every hill, and the nostalgic odors of autumn filled the air. It was the most stirring of all seasons in this region.

Age-old instincts stirred in the blood. Older men and women sat and watched the procession of colors veiled in the grape-blue haze that hung like a mysterious presence in the distance. Younger folks wandered over the hills, possessed with a restlessness they could not define. It was unlike the heady disturbance of spring; it was more like some primitive instinct of the chase— tamed now to a nervous wandering in unaccustomed places.

One warmish day a crowd of boys swarmed down the hill after school, shouting the relief of their escape from the stuffy classrooms. It was Fulmer Green's "gang." Fulmer Green had won through to undisputed leadership after two years of bullying fights and the commission of such minor depredations as gained him the admiration and adherence of his kind. Fulmer was a broad-shouldered, muscular boy, good-looking, rather, though his hair grew low on his brow and his small bright blue eyes were a shade too close together. His

father had made money the past two years on some road-building contracts
and had bought the Mason Thill place on Union Street. His mother, ambitious
for a better standing in Kings Row now that she had moved "uptown," tried to
break Fulmer's old associations. So far she was unsuccessful.

The boys swooped down the hill and passed through the tiny streets of
Jinktown.

"Looky!" Fulmer Green pointed to the blue cottage at the end of the street.
"That's where ol' crazy Ben lives." He picked up a rock and threw it in a long
easy curve. It landed with a loud thump on the rotten shingles. A little puff of
dust marked the accuracy of the shot, and Mrs. Singer's chickens gave loud,
startled cackles. The boys shouted gleefully.

"C'mon, let 'em have some more." A shower of rocks clattered on the low
roof, making the splinters of dry wood fly in every direction.

Mrs. Singer came out on the front step. "Get on with you! What do you
mean throwing rocks around here? You're going to hurt somebody first thing
you know."

The boys did not answer. They grinned and shuffled a shade uneasily. Mrs.
Singer went into the house and closed the door. A heavy clod shattered against
the panels, and yells of laughter greeted Fulmer Green's daring and spirited
answer.

"C'mon," he commanded, looking back at the house as they passed. "Ol'
slut—talkin' to us like that. Who does she think *she* is, anyhow? Crazy, that's
what she is. People like that ain't got no business livin' round Kings Row,
nohow."

There was a murmur of agreement. One of the bolder boys sent another
rock banging against the side of the house. Mrs. Singer appeared once more.
"Go on, now," she called. "You quit that, or I'll have the law on you."

Fulmer stood in the road facing her squarely. "Aw, you shut up," he said.

"Go on, go on. If you don't behave yourselves, I'll sick the dog on you!" She
closed the door once more.

"Did you hear that?" Fulmer demanded. "Goin' to sick her ol' dog on us, is
she? I guess we got a perfick right to be out here in a public street. I guess my
pa'd show her, crazy ol' fool."

They shuffled on a few steps, looking back darkly at the house. Fulmer felt
he had not acquitted himself very gallantly as a leader.

"I'll tell you," he said. "Let's give her ol' house one good rockin', then we'll
run."

A hail of stones fell on and around the house. A few windowpanes shattered
with loud crashes. At that moment Benny, returning from a neighbor's, ran
down the road and yelled at the top of his voice. "Stop that, stop throwin'
rocks at our house, you dirty ol'—dirty ol' *snoozers,* you!"

The stones whizzed so close to his head he had to dodge. He ran quickly
around the house and reappeared with an old rusty pitchfork. Holding it ahead

of him, he charged straight at his tormentors. They stood ground for only a moment and then ran. Benny chased them well out of Jinktown, and came back wiping the sweat from his face with his sleeve. "Dirty ol' snoozers!" he muttered.

A week later Drake McHugh came to see Parris after school. "Did you hear about Benny Singer?"

"No, what?"

"He had a kind of fight over there in Jinktown with Fulmer Green's gang. They rocked Benny's house and he got after 'em with a big pitchfork. He pretty near got some of 'em, too. Guess he'd have killed 'em."

"Goodness, I never saw Benny fight, did you?"

"No, but he went for 'em that time. Fulmer told his daddy, and they had Benny arrested."

"Sure enough? Did they put him in jail?"

"Just one night. Mr. Green said he ought to be sent to a reform school, but Colonel Skeffington was on Benny's side—he got him off. But they bound Benny's mother over to keep the peace."

"What's that mean?"

"I don't know exactly. Just a kind of a *warnin'*, I guess."

"Fulmer Green is kind of low-down, I think, don't you?"

"Sure he is. He's a stinker."

Parris told his grandmother the story that evening after supper.

The next day he and Madame met Mrs. Green in the Burton County Bank.

"How do you do, Madame von Eln!" Mrs. Green extended her hand, but Madame did not see it. Mrs. Green flushed.

"How do you do," Madame replied.

"And how is Parris? I heard he'd been very sick."

"Yes. He's quite well now."

"But he's not in school, is he?"

"No. He is studying with tutors."

"My, my, you don't say so! Well, I think school is good for boys. The associations—"

"Are not always desirable," Madame interrupted sharply.

"Well, no, of course not. That is true," Mrs. Green swallowed audibly. "I suppose you heard about Fulmer?"

"Your son?" Madame said politely.

"Yes, yes, of course; my boy Fulmer. Parris knows him. He nearly got killed by that crazy Singer boy."

"I hadn't heard *that*." Madame's emphasis on the word escaped Mrs. Green's attention.

"Yes, yes, indeed. I told Mr. Green that boy ought to be in the reform school."

"Which one?" Madame's voice was like a thin trickle of ice water.

Mrs. Green stared. "That Benny Singer—that's who I'm talking about. He's dangerous. Or else he ought to be in the asylum."

"I heard some boys had broken the windows in the Singer house and that Ben was protecting his home."

Mrs. Green's eyes opened very wide. "Well," she said, "I guess you can hear most anything."

"So it appears," said Madame crisply. She bowed slightly and walked away.

Mrs. Green looked after her with narrowed eyes. "Why—why, the stuck-up old—*old foreigner*," she said softly.

They met Colonel Skeffington on the bank steps.

"Good morning, Marie, how are you this fine day?" The Colonel extended his left hand to Parris, who shook it gravely.

"Very well, Colonel Skeffington."

"Mighty fine weather we've been having."

"Too dry, Colonel. I've been needing rain on my place."

"That so? Can't please everybody about the weather, though. How's the boy?"

"Parris is all right, I believe."

"Hear you're keeping him out of school."

"Yes, I'm going to have a tutor for him this winter."

"Fine idea, too, Marie, a mighty fine idea. Public school's full of ruffians like that Green youngster—Rodney Green's boy. You send your boy to public school and they rub against all kinds. That's democracy for you! Damned if I believe in it—not that kind, anyhow. Suppose you know Rodney Green's bought the old Thill place up on Union Street."

"So I heard."

"Yes. Moved in already. All the Thills dead and gone. I bet they'd turn in their graves if they knew Rod Green was in their house. White trash, that's what they are, white trash!"

"Are they going to do anything about the Singer boy, Colonel?"

"Not now. But somebody will aggravate that boy until he does something desperate. 'Twon't be his fault, but they'll blame him, and he'll be in serious trouble."

"Don't you think it would be a good idea to get some sort of employment for him—out of the way somewhere? I hear he really can't learn in school."

"It would be a good idea, ma'am, and a mighty sensible one. I'll ride around to Jinktown some of these mornings and have a talk with his mother about it. I don't suppose you could take him on your place, could you?"

"I've got more help of that kind than I can use, but if you can't find anything else, let me know. I suppose I could pay him a little something if he's willing—not much, though."

I'd like to send that infernal young Green scamp to a reform school."

Madame laughed. "Mrs. Green just suggested to me that Ben Singer ought to be there—or in the asylum."

Colonel Skeffington flared red above his shining beard. He brought his cane down with a loud thwack on the stone step. "There you are now! Did you ever notice, Marie, in this town how everybody's always ready to send somebody else to the asylum? It's a fact. First thing occurs to them."

Madame smiled. "It does seem to crop up in conversation a good deal."

"Certainly it does, certainly. Do you know, I think it's a bad thing to have a lunatic asylum in a town. Keeps it in everybody's mind. I think a lot of people go crazy just because the building stands out there at the end of Federal Street. It's too confounded convenient." He chuckled and clawed his beard. "What's more, if you'd turn all the lunatics out and put the rest of us in there, I doubt if you could tell any difference."

"Oh, Colonel—"

"It's the living truth. Look what the world's coming to—just look at the infernal thing! Well—good day. I'll see about Ben Singer right away."

"Oh, by the way, Colonel. Do you know Tom Carr?"

"Yes, yes, indeed."

"Well, Thurston St. George suggested I try him for overseer. I lost my man—a Swede—a good man, too."

"Now, let me see. Surely, ma'am, I do believe old Tom might be just what you want. He's got a crazy wife, though, if that makes any difference."

"I know. Thurston told me."

"Tom Carr's a fine man. Don't come any better."

"Thank you. I'm going to talk to him."

Colonel Skeffington bowed deeply and turned to go. Then he took off his hat again. "I still think the Greens are trash." He chuckled.

"You're a cynical old sinner, Colonel."

"Not cynical, ma'am, just a sinner. Had a happy career at it, too." He laughed and hobbled up the steps.

"Don't pay any attention to what Colonel Skeffington says, Parris. He's a good man, a very good man. I wish there were more like him."

Tom Carr moved into the overseer's cottage the following week. Time was oppressively heavy on Parris these days when his lessons were finished. He went down to watch the men unload the household stuff. There was very little of it. Mr. Carr was the most extraordinary-looking apparition Parris had ever seen. A cyclone of snow-white hair and whiskers enveloped his massive head. Parris thought he looked as though somebody had dropped a stone in his face and splashed the whiskers in all directions. Only his eyes showed—the brownest, merriest, kindest eyes imaginable. When he spoke his voice boomed. Parris had been heavyhearted at sight of the house; it was the first time he had been

near it since that day he had made the little grave under the snowball bush. He
glanced furtively in that direction. A faint rise in the ground showed where the
mound had been.

Mr. Carr was so lively and said so many funny things that Parris laughed.
He realized he hadn't laughed much in a long time.

The last thing taken from the wagon was an old square piano with an
extremely scarred and battered case.

"Oh, you've got a piano!" Parris exclaimed. "Do you play?"

"No, my wife plays. It was her piano when she was a girl. I brought it out
from the East with us. Years ago." He added the last two words a bit sadly.

"I have to practice every day."

Mr. Carr finished adjusting the pedals after it was set up. He opened it.
"Let's hear you play a little, son."

Parris sat down and ran his fingers lightly over the ancient yellow keys.
A crazy jangle greeted his ears. He drew back, startled, but tried to conceal
his surprise. He tried once more. The piano was so badly out of tune that it
was impossible to tell anything about the sounds that came out of it. It was a
nightmare of hideous discords.

Parris looked up with some embarrassment. "It's pretty badly out of tune. I
guess it got shook up a lot hauling it down here."

"Out of tune? Is that so? I'll have to ask Lucy about that. She never said
there was anything wrong with it. I had it all fixed up once—about twenty years
ago. Well, well, we'll see about it. I got to go get Lucy now. I guess everything's
as much in place as I can get it today. I'll see you later, Johnny; you must come
down often and play for Lucy. She's always been a great lover of music."

Parris grinned. It was going to be fine to have Mr. Carr around. "But my
name is Parris, Mr. Carr."

"Parris? That so? Well, I think I'll call you Johnny for short. Easier, too. 'By."

"Good-by, sir."

Decidedly Mr. Carr was a very different sort of person from Sven
Gyllinson. The thought of Sven made him "go goose flesh" all over. His eyes
filled with tears, but he dashed them away. He wondered where Renée was and
what she was doing this very minute. There was such a lump in his throat that
he could hardly breathe. He went out on the road and skipped rocks in the
creek for a long time.

Mr. Carr drove out of the gate in a rickety two-wheeled cart. His gray horse
was so old and poor that its bones stood out in sharp crags all over. It had a
comical jouncing gait as though it moved up and down more than it trotted
forward. A little stepladder with two carpeted steps swung from the back of the
cart. Parris wondered what it could be doing there, and what it was used for.

It was nearly dark when the horse and cart came in sight again, creaking
and creeping along the sandy road. In it was the fattest woman Parris had ever
seen. The cart sagged on one side until the springs buckled.

Lucy Carr wore a dress trimmed with many colors. Innumerable strings of beads lay about her neck, and many cheap rings shone on her tiny hands—deformed-looking, helpless little hands—so tiny that they seemed like doll hands attached to her enormous arms. She wore a large round hat perched precariously on a lopsided bunch of false curls. It was trimmed on either side with a tuft of curving feathers. Parris thought they looked like ordinary rooster-tail feathers.

The cart rolled into the back yard. Tom Carr hopped out gaily, detached the little ladder, and set it close to the wheel. "Now, then, sweetheart, here we are. Give me your hands. Upsadaisy!" He heaved and strained; the little cart joggled dangerously. Parris watched, his eyes popping with astonishment. Lucy came up from the seat at last and surged down the steps. Her feet were as tiny as her hands. They almost disappeared in the rolls of fat that lay about her ankles.

"Whew! Well, we made it, honey."

Lucy wheezed noisily. She said "Ha!" once or twice, and then "Ho! Ho! Ho!"

"Lucy, my love, this is Mrs. von Eln's grandson. Name's Johnny."

All at once Lucy became very gay. She took a tottering step forward and held out her hand. She nodded her head with a certain graciousness. There was in the slight and elegant inclination of her bonnet something of an air. Like something in a play, or an old-fashioned picture in a book,

"Come now, darling, we must get in and have a look. Got to get some supper for you. Is Papa's baby hungry?"

She leaned so heavily on Tom Carr that he almost carried her. At the door she turned her ponderous weight slowly. She gasped out some words. "Glad, Johnny, glad." Then she said "Ha!" and as she squeezed through the door, "Ho! Ho! Ho!"

On the way home Parris met Uncle Henry carrying a large basket.

"What you got in there, Uncle Henry?"

"Got some suppah for Mistah Cah' and Mis' Cah'. Yo' gramma sont 'em. She say hurry up, de suppah settin' on de table gittin' cold."

Tom Carr had proved to be a valuable man. Madame was delighted. Parris went to see the Carrs two or three times a week. Lucy always made him play for her. He had learned to go through the motion of playing on the wrecked piano. She always listened seriously and thanked him. Sometimes she struggled to the piano and played for him. Her little hands flew back and forth across the keys in obedience to some automatic memory. The sounds were as mad as Lucy Carr herself. Some days she was not so well, and could see no one. At such times passers-by heard her thumping diabolic music from the piano and singing old songs at the top of her voice.

Mr. Carr talked once or twice of Lucy to Madame von Eln. "She was a pretty girl, Mrs. von Eln, and a happy girl. A proud girl, too. When we ran

out of money it seemed she just couldn't stand the snubs she got here in Kings
Row. She was as well-born as anybody, and, as I said, proud. I guess she just
couldn't stand it," he repeated. "She just went out of her head. Then she was
happy. I made up my mind she should stay happy. I kept her with me as much
as I could. Twice she got so bad I had to send her to the asylum, but I took
her home again as soon as she was better. I decided I'd just do the best I could.
You know, she's like a child. I had to put rockers under her bed—like a cradle.
Every night of the world I sing to her and rock her to sleep."

Madame von Eln stared.

"Yes'm; I know it sounds like I'm crazy, too, but I know how to humor
her. The thing is to keep her from getting excited. Of course, I wouldn't like
anybody to know what I just told you about the cradle-bed and all, but Parris
has seen it. He knows all about it, don't you, Johnny? Lucy likes your boy, Mrs.
von Eln. I've never seen her take to anyone so before."

Madame shook her head sadly as she watched the white-headed old man
trudging home. She passed her fingers slowly across her eyes.

"*Dieu!*" she said. "*La vie! Comme c'est affreuse!*"

Almost every day Uncle Henry went down the slope carrying a covered
basket to Tom Carr's door.

A strange friendship sprang up between Lucy Carr and Parris. It had begun
a few days after the Carrs arrived. Old Tom saw Parris and hailed him,

"Hey, Johnny!"

"Yes, sir."

"Are you busy right now?"

"No, sir."

"Well, Lucy's been asking about you. Wants to see you."

"Me?"

"Yep. Took a fancy to you right off. Tell you what you do. Go down and
see her. Let her talk to you for a little while. She gets pretty lonesome, you
know. Don't be afraid, son, she won't hurt you. Wouldn't hurt a fly—my Lucy
wouldn't. Likes to talk, though."

Parris went reluctantly. He *was* afraid. Well, maybe not afraid, exactly, he
thought, but he felt queer anyway.

Lucy Carr sat in a huge armchair by the window. Old Tom had rigged
up an elaborate system of cords and pulleys with handles in easy reach of the
chair. She could open and close windows or doors, lower shades, or open and
close the stove door without moving from her chair. Actually she could not get
about the house without assistance. She sat looking out of the window all day,
waiting for Tom Carr to come home at mealtimes.

"Ha!" she exclaimed at sight of Parris. "Ha! Glad, Johnny, glad!" She wasted
no words. Each syllable cost her asthmatic lungs an effort. Nevertheless, she
managed to talk a good deal. And she talked well. She told stories of her

girlhood, of travel, of funny people she had seen. She roared with laughter, purpling and gasping and strangling through involved narratives. She beat on the arms of her chair to recover breath, quivering and shaking her semiliquid bulk until it seemed she must burst.

Listening to her was like looking through a lattice. Her short, broken sentences shattered the continuity of her stories, but somehow they pieced together. Somehow one perceived a gay and amusing mind that functioned in a fragmentary, fluttering sort of fashion.

She was always glad to see him. She always said, "Ha! Glad, Johnny, glad," and then, "Ho! Ho! Ho!"

The mind of Lucy Carr was like something flying in dizzy circles. It darted in and out of the darkness that encompassed her, that pressed always closer as though waiting to engulf her. Parris felt sometimes that if he could only seize her flickering attention and fasten it down, she would suddenly become herself. But that bright spot of lucidity and sanity was now here, now there, hovering for a moment and then gone from sight. It was kin to the flight of a dragonfly, so sudden, so quick and unpredictable.

Her helplessness appealed to his sympathy. He aided in many small ways, but most of all he talked. He discovered the kind of news that interested her and learned to tell it bit by bit. She could not follow a long story.

One day in the late spring Tom Carr came up on the terrace. "I guess I'll have to take tomorrow off, ma'am."

"All right, Tom. No trouble, I hope?"

"No, no. I'm going to the circus."

"Oh!"

"I used to take Lucy to the circus—whenever one came along. She liked it tremendously and talked about it for weeks. I thought maybe she'd enjoy it. It's been years since she's even been to town."

"Why, certainly. Go right ahead. I hope she does enjoy it."

Parris and his grandmother drove into town the next day. She agreed to see the parade, but he would have to go to the circus with some of his friends.

They hitched the horse on a side square and walked to Union Street. They met August Kummer who owned the bakery shop and ice-cream parlor opposite the courthouse.

"Tell you what you do. You go up and sit on my upstairs porch. You can see goot and you won't be crowded so."

"Thank you, August, I think we will. I don't like being pushed about."

"It's awful—these country jakes," he growled. "Like cattle."

The parade, an hour late, moved grandly up the street, the heavy cages grinding and crunching on the hard gravel. Parris felt that he was a little too old to show too much pleasure, but he really found it rather thrilling.

The long procession ended with a leaping crowd of clowns.

"That's all," said Madame, sighing with relief. "Let's go. We'll have some lunch downstairs."

"No, wait, there's something else. Look at all that crowd. What is it?"

Laughing and shouting boys, black and white, were crowding about some last feature of the parade that had gotten behind. They watched its approach curiously.

"Oh—oh—look! Oh, it's the Carrs!"

Tom and Lucy Carr with their bony old horse and cart were moving slowly up the street surrounded by a howling mob. Tom was making furious efforts to escape the crowd, but Lucy, her feathers tossing and all her finery glittering in the sun, was enjoying herself. She waved her arms and shouted and jounced up and down with glee.

"Oh, look, *grand'mère*. They think the Carrs are part of the parade."

"*Nom de dieu!* What shall we do, Parris? This is terrible. She'll kill herself with excitement. Oh, how dreadful!"

The frantic old man managed at last to turn into Federal Street. The crowd stopped but waved and cheered. Lucy waved, too, and shouted as loud as she could.

Parris hurried as they went downstairs.

"What's the matter, Parris? Where are you going?"

"I think I'll go home with you. I don't believe I want to go to the circus."

"Aren't you feeling well?"

"I'm all right. I just don't want to go."

Tom Carr had put Lucy to bed when Parris and his grandmother reached home. He asked to have Uncle Henry fetch the doctor. Dr. Gordon came about the middle of the afternoon and gave Lucy a sleeping powder.

"Excitement," he said. "She'll probably be all right by tomorrow."

Late that afternoon Parris went down to the little house and tiptoed into the front room. Lucy Carr lay on the bed, and Tom was rocking her gently, crooning in his deep bass voice.

Lucy saw him. "Look, honey, it's Johnny. Glad, Johnny."

Parris sat down on the edge of a chair and waited. She closed her eyes and slept for a while. Her breathing was louder than he had ever heard it, though she always struggled to get air. From time to time a loud strangled breath came and went roughly. It sounded like the turn of a rusty wheel.

"Is she better?" he asked.

"Yes—much better."

Lucy opened her eyes after a while. They seemed to roll loosely in her head. "Johnny, play," she gasped.

"Please," Tom Carr begged.

Parris sat down and began to play. The weird sounds jingled and crackled under his fingers. He turned around and spoke over his shoulder. "Won't this make her awful nervous?"

She heard, and her voice came shrill: "Play, Johnny!"

He played on and on. He heard her breath come more and more slowly, but he thought the awful cranking sound was more frequent.

"I don't know any more pieces, Mr. Carr," he whispered.

"Play the same ones. She likes it. She's getting quieter, Johnny."

The afternoon light faded, and the still spring twilight came on gradually. Still Parris played on and on. He thought Lucy must be falling asleep. He could scarcely hear her. The insane witches' music that came from the piano was beginning to make his head ache. He dropped his chin on his chest and played more softly. The sounds were ghastlier than ever—like the chattering of ghouls and devils, he thought. The creak of the rockers on the floor slowed and stopped.

Tom Carr laid a hand on his shoulder. "That will do now. Thank you, Johnny."

Parris saw that the sheet covered Lucy's face. The old man pushed him gently toward the door.

"Is she asleep, Mr. Carr?"

Tom Carr shook his head. "She's dead. Will you tell your grandmother, please? And—thank you again, Johnny."

The hot summer months dragged slowly. Parris was lonelier than he had ever been. His grandmother seemed preoccupied. She talked less than usual. He realized that she was not looking well Old Tom went silently about his work. Parris saw Drake McHugh only three or four times. Once he found himself saying aloud: "I'm not having a good time. I'm not having a good time at all." He stopped, surprised, and laughed a bit uncertainly. He was embarrassed to have been talking to himself.

Parris had never thought much about God. When he did, it was with a certain uneasiness. He had always supposed there was God—somewhere.

The death of Lucy Carr made him think about it more definitely than he ever had before. It seemed to him if there was a God, who looked after everything and everybody, that events were strangely ordered. Things didn't seem right—or fair. He thought about Renée and the memory was stony hard in his breast. *That* wasn't right, or fair, either. He was bitterly resentful.

He began to recall as much as he could of what he had heard at church. There was no help there, certainly. The very thought of it bounced back at him—hard, hard, and uncomforting.

One day he went to see Drake. It turned out to be a pleasant visit. They had a lot of fun. Toward evening they walked up Walnut Street.

"Have you ever been inside a Catholic church?" Drake asked.

Parris shook his head.

"Let's go in there and look around. I never have, either. It's open all the time."

The little church seemed very odd indeed with its pictures and its altar glittering with unfamiliar objects. The dim glow of a small red lamp swung from the ceiling gave Parris a strange feeling. As they became accustomed to the gloom, they saw Father Donovan at the altar rail. He was kneeling.

Drake nudged Parris. "Look!"

Parris nodded.

The dark figure was motionless—seemingly lost to all awareness of anybody or anything.

They tiptoed out again.

"Parris! Was he worshiping an idol?"

"I don't know. Just praying, I guess."

They began to talk of other matters.

Parris walked up the long shadowy avenue toward the house. The lamps were already lighted. The happy mood of the day had gone. He felt that his familiar world had changed. It was aloof. It had drawn away from him a little, as though it looked at him, considered him, weighed him.

He rushed his hand across his eyes with a gesture he had borrowed from his grandmother. It was not a childish gesture.

Book Two

1

Sam Winters leaned on the short-handled, wooden-toothed rake he had been using, and mopped the sweatband of his heavy felt hat. The late September sun slanted through the tall trees of the Old South Cemetery and touched the white marble and gray sandstone monuments with dusty gilt. The trees billowed upward like pillars of cloud. The ground was strewn with colored leaves. The stretch of sward just cleared of them was emerald fresh and bright—all the glistening blades combed one way. Swales of brilliant leaves lay to left and right like the heaping of fabulous treasures.

Sam Winters was as oblivious of this prodigal fall beauty as the headstones clustering about him. Just now he was watching John Farrel. "Old John" was nearing eighty and was wobbly about the knees. As he teetered along he peered sideways with a look of eager curiosity. His interest in the Old South Cemetery was rather morbid. Most of his associates and acquaintances lay under the grass that waved liquidly across the wide area.

Old John came here often. He liked to remind himself of departed friends. Also he liked to remind himself that he was still aboveground. Walking beside the graves of the men he had known and talked with emphasized the life that still moved slowly through his ancient veins. He could see, and breathe, and feel. *They* were still and dead—boxed up and buried—insensate and rotting.

He came here two or three times each week. These visits gave him the keenest pleasure he knew. From time to time he would cover his mouth with his dry old hand to hide an expression of triumph. Then he would look cautiously about. He had a superstitious fear that some invisible power might observe this joy and take instant vengeance. Behind his hand he silently smacked his wet lips and forbore to smile.

Sam Winters missed little of this. His eyes narrowed with a sly but unrancorous amusement.

"Hi, John!"

"Oh, oh! How are you, Sam? Didn't see you."

"Pickin' out a place for yourself, John? Thought you'd a-done that long ago. You'll be needin' it one of these days."

Farrel's eyes winked rapidly with anger. "Ain't picked out a place, an' I ain't goin' to. Leave that for somebody else to do—" he hesitated and added under his breath, "when the time comes."

But Sam heard the muttered words. "Oh, the time'll come all right. I'll be digging a hole for you some cold winter mornin'."

"Not you, Sam Winters! Lay you money I'll outlive you. I've outlived a heap of 'em now—a heap of 'em."

"Well, you won't outlive everybody."

"Ever'body's got his time. No use worryin' till it comes."

"That's right, that's right." Sam spoke conciliatingly. "Still," he went on with a covert shine in his cool blue eyes, "there's some like that fellow there." He pointed at Farrel's feet. The old man looked down quickly.

"What you mean, Sam?"

"That fellow whose grave you're standin' on."

Farrel made a violent side step that almost threw him off balance. "What about him? Whose grave is it?"

"Morris Reagan. Recollect him?"

"Morris Reagan? Reagan—Reagan. No, no. Who was Morris Reagan?"

"Fellow got in a shootin' scrape down at Faulter's saloon. He shot Dorsey Sims. He was hung. I hung him myself—let's see—twelve years ago the sixteenth of December. Well—he didn't have to wait for his time. Judge Golden set the time fer him, an' I did the job. Neat job, too."

He made a gesture that ended with a swish and slap. "Just like that! You could a-heard his neck crack a hundred yards away. Never knew what hit him. I buried him right there next day—at the county's expense."

Sam raked a few leaves from the low unmarked mound, and tamped down an irregularity in the sod.

John Farrel walked away as fast as he could, and Sam resumed his work.

Peter McGurney, who kept the general store at Federal and Walnut Streets, once remarked: "Sam Winters does have the damnedest jobs I ever heard of." Which was true. Sam had been the deputy sheriff of Burton County for many years. As such he was the official hangman. Sometimes he was summoned to neighboring counties for executions. He said he had hanged twenty men and one woman.

If some tramp was run over in the railroad yard, it was Sam who collected the remains. If a Negro was lynched, Sam cut down the body and buried it.

"By God, I can do anything," he boasted.

"Remember Tom Shirly? He killed a woman down in the Westbrook bottoms. Mob got after him but I beat 'em to him with the bloodhounds. Stood 'em off, too. I took Tom to jail. Fed him for six months before the trial and afterward while he was waiting to get hung. I hung him, too; buried him, and a year later dug him up—what was left of him—and sent him to his folks down in Indian Territory. Hell, there ain't nothing I can't do."

Between more spectacular jobs Sam took care of the Old South Cemetery and acted as a sort of handy man at the insane asylum. He was assigned to the morgue there.

Sam looked as though he might be made out of some particularly durable kind of leather. His face was splotched with large areas of red and brown. He said the brown spots were freckles that had "run." It was not a cruel, nor even a callous face. It was simply a face that had never registered feeling of any kind. It was easy to believe that he had never experienced feeling. What he had to do he did directly and indifferently. He acted as simply and as immediately as gravitation.

He lived alone in a tiny house at the edge of the cemetery and took his meals at Mrs. Monaghan's boardinghouse. No one knew anything about his more intimate habits. He kept busy at his strange jobs, and talked but little. He had no real thoughts—only recollections.

The morning chill vanished. Sam squinted at the sun. Must be about eleven o'clock, he decided. He thrust the handle of the rake into the soft soil and set it firmly upright. Then he sat down on a wide flat tomb and fanned himself with his hat. Absently, he noted the brickwork supporting the moss-covered slab. Scratching the ancient lichens from the lettering, he read: JOHN LOVE, DIED JULY 10, 1780. Sam did not think of the long century of days and seasons that had passed over this forgotten grave or wonder about the man whose name it bore. He thought the brickwork was a good job—"A damn good job," he said aloud. "They knew how to do things in the old days." His sharp eyes appraised this and that burial plot with a certain grim matter-of-factness that came from a sure knowledge of the state of things underground as well as above.

"Guess I'll go get a glass of beer."

He walked heavily toward the stile, pausing now and then to scan some headstone that looked out of plumb.

"Mis' Sheeley's leaning way over a'ready. Ain't been there a year." Sam called each stone by the name of the person beneath. He considered the Greenway family plot near the gate. "H'm." He shook his head. "They ought to clean the old man up a little. You can't make out a word of that readin' any more. That sandstone goes quicker'n one of them thirty-dollar coffins."

He crossed the stile with stiff, mechanical steps. His movements might have reminded an observer of a badly made, animated effigy. As he passed the Bascom house he touched his hat brim to Mrs. Evelina Bascom who was sitting on the porch.

"Good mornin', ma'am."

"Good mornin', Sam."

She watched him idly for a moment and resumed her morning snack. She was eating thin strips of bread and butter. The thumb was missing from Evelina's left hand, and she held the pieces of bread between her index and middle fingers, as men hold a cigar. This gesture imparted to her quiet little repast an air of rakish festivity. Her eyes still followed Sam Winters.

"Old buzzard," she said to herself.

Finishing the bread and butter, she wiped her mouth on the back of her hand, and the back of her hand on her blue-checked apron. Balancing the empty plate on the slanting porch rail, she rocked with a sort of idle vigor. Her farsighted gaze traveled between the houses on the other side of the street, across the town creek where a dazzle of light shuttled briskly, over the rise and along the south road toward the open country. But her mind outran her vision. She was thinking of the rough river hills which lay in that direction, and the shaggy slopes of scrub oak which marked the beginning of poorer land. That was what the whole country looked like when she came West with her father. That was—Lord, Lord!—that was away back in eighteen twenty-something. She wasn't certain about the date just now. Anyway, all of seventy years ago, maybe seventy-five—yes, it had been seventy-five years. She was eighty-one now, and she had been six when Pa brought her there.

Kings Row was already a town then. She wondered why it was that those long-gone days seemed now to have been much like this bright sunny one. True, she could remember the winters. Cold—terribly cold, but more days like this one. There couldn't have been more early fall then than any other time. But time was so different—much slower, and not broken up into such little bits as now, each one hurrying after the other like pieces of ice on the creek in a March freshet. There had been only seasons then. Great wide seasons—long arcs of time that stood over one like high heaven itself. Now it was different. There were too many events—Fourth of July celebrations, political rallies, county fairs, college commencements, and the like. Left a body downright breathless keeping up with them. Broke up time into too many pieces—small, hurrying pieces, rushing to catch something that was always ahead. Spoiled any kind of thinking. Spoiled people, too. People used to be big—like the place and the time. They didn't move too fast. There had been a kind of peace that went with those great stretches of blue time arching over the seasons. Yes, people were big then, like Pa, like Thurston St. George, like Mason Thill, dead now, poor soul, and—yes, like herself, too. She felt crowded. People talked so much and about too many things. They didn't finish one subject by half before they were already talking about something else. They nicked up time—that's what they did—nicked it up into little pieces. One little piece for this and another little piece for that. Made themselves little, too, to fit into the pieces. That's what made the days seem so short, and—so little. Now the world was just like a crazy quilt. Nobody could say a crazy quilt was restful, either.

Big things happened back there. When she was a child Pa still talked about the British and 1812. Then there was the Mexican War, but nobody heard much about that. And the gold rush. Her two youngest boys went out; but they weren't lucky. Brought back mighty little. The ring she wore had been made out of gold they found. She guessed that was about all, too. Then the Civil War with first one side and then the other burning the town. Pa preached on Sundays, and played the fiddle whenever a few young people could get together. She smiled, remembering the Saturday night he had played all night while the Rebs burned his church to the ground. Everybody thought it was a good joke on Pa. Next day he preached in Gilkey's tobacco barn. After the war people didn't want them because they had come from the North. Bushwhackers shot at Pa now and then. But they had stayed on.

She remembered the James boys. They had made quite a bit of excitement. There were contradictory tales about the Jameses. From what she had heard of Jesse he seemed a likable kind of a man. If she'd been a young woman she'd have liked to marry Jesse James.

Nothing like those things happened now. Whole business tamed down.

She peered at the sky. H'm. Eleven, or a quarter past. She arose, picked up the plate which had warmed in the sun, and walked firmly into the house.

In the narrow hall she passed beneath the portrait of her husband. She seldom noticed it, but today it caught her attention for a moment. He had been a good man. Many people had come to sit and talk with her after he died. They thought she must be lonesome. But she hadn't been. She had felt like a free horse in a pasture.

On the back porch she surveyed her little garden patch. She took a short spade from a covered box.

"I think I'll bank up some of that fall cabbage for the winter. We'll be having frost the first thing we know."

The thought of Sam Winters crossed her mind again. She grunted. "That Sam Winters!" The tone expelled some unpleasantness with it. He was associated in some way with the hidden and secret and disagreeable necessities of living. She supposed there had to be people like Sam. Life and living had a good many nasty incidents. Death had some pretty bad things about it. Birth was messy—for that matter, the whole getting of children wasn't any too nice to think about.

Sam Winters, now. He was a pretty good example of the way nature worked. Yes—there had to be people like that. Just as she had to have a privy down at the end of her garden. Life had front porches, and privies. Sam belonged at the lower end of the garden. She believed the Bible said something about all this, but she couldn't recollect just what it was. The Bible, though, had something to say about most everything. "It's right wonderful that way," she concluded.

In the meantime Sam continued on his way toward Faulter's saloon. Old Farrel had gone the opposite direction. He was out at the edge of town now where the open country began. He had walked fast and was breathing hard. He worked his jaws, and tiny bubbles of saliva glistened in the corners of his mouth. He, too, was thinking of Sam Winters, and hating him. He was really afraid of Sam. Sam represented something indifferent, implacable, and inevitable. He meant death, and gravedigging, and burial, but he wouldn't admit either the words or the images to his consciousness. He only knew that he disliked Sam more than he disliked anyone.

He thought Sam's mouth looked like the rough, hard edge of a milk crock.

Father Donovan coming up from the lower end of town passed Sam just where the row of Lombardy poplars began in front of Mr. Foy's house. They spoke: Sam with a sort of hard reserve—he didn't like priests; Father Donovan with another kind of reserve—he didn't like Sam. "He does some bad things—some very bad things."

Sam walked on.

In the stillness of this September noon, his passing sent out a little slanting wave on either side of him, breaking the secret calm of the hour the way a water creature breaks the surface of a quiet lake. The waves sped out on either side, widening, and perhaps rolling more as they widened. Father Donovan felt that he could see those waves. They touched people and moved them, disturbed them, set them to doing this or that, set them to thinking or feeling something they would not otherwise have thought or felt. On the surface of the imaginary lake in Father Donovan's vision clusters of leaves moved, shifted, changed relations. Here in the three-dimensional mirror of this hour, people moved like the little yellow leaves of his fancy. Shifts were made. New patterns formed. A dance changed time—and figure. Infinite angels on a needle's point—infinite angels again....

The priest stumbled a little where a root had lifted a flagstone in front of Lafe King's gate. His lips twitched in the beginning of a wry smile. His visions and his fancies were always being broken by some trivial awkwardness. It was a good thing, he supposed. There was no telling, otherwise, where his imagination might carry him.

Isaac Skeffington eased into the one comfortable chair gracing the office of Miles Jackson. The Colonel's angled bones made him cautious about chairs. His eyes, old and a bit rheumy behind double glasses, glinted with malice. Jackson, milder of face than the Colonel, smiled.

"What's on your mind, Ike?"

"Not a thing. Just thinking, though, as I came around the square. This damn town's changing so I hardly know it."

"The city administration would be pleased to hear that 'old inhabitant' notes signs of progress."

Skeffington spat. "Progress! Hell. Sansome's a young squirt. Every time we get a new mayor in Kings Row he thinks he has to tear up something to show how earnest he is. Look at those sidewalks on Union Street! What they call it!—granitoid. Hell of a name, anyhow. Looks ugly; hurts your feet; imitation of something or other. You know, Miles, that's what we're coming to. Characteristic of the times. Every damn thing is an imitation of something else.

Galvanized-iron false fronts on the new store buildings—sanded to make them look like stone. Posh!"

"I hear Sansome wants to cut down the trees around the Square."

Skeffington glared. "What for?"

"He claims Kings Row looks like a village. Says we ought to imitate Camperville and some of the places that size.…"

"We are a village. Got village ways—village minds. We're country people! Anything wrong with that?"

"Well, Ike, I guess Sansome would say you aren't *exactly* in line with progress."

Jackson always declared Skeffington's whiskers grew redder with his face when he was in a rage.

"Progress! You're not progressing unless you're going somewhere that's a good place to go to. Oh, hell—let's don't talk about it. I'll have a fit someday over that infernal young fool Hart Sansome, and I don't want to pay him that much of a compliment."

"We stumble a lot; but I wouldn't be surprised if we didn't get somewhere with it."

"You don't believe any such stuff. You're too smart—at least. I've always thought so. We're no better off than we were when this town was a trading post. Old stock had the right ideas. We haven't improved on 'em. Don't grow that kind any more either, Jackson. You know that. Take all the old stock in the county—the old men, old women, too—look at 'em. Got anything to beat 'em, or to match 'em, even, coming up with the young ones?"

"Hart Sansome says—"

"Sansome's a pissant."

Jackson laughed. "I see there's going to be a job for Sam Winters in Camperville. They found that young fellow guilty over there last week."

"So I heard. Well, he was. Guilty as hell; no doubt about it." Skeffington picked up his hat and smoothed it. "I saw Sam a little while ago. He was passing the time of day with that priest Donovan. God, this world makes me laugh! Donovan spending his life trying to teach faith to a handful of ignorant Irish and foreigners, and Sam standing around waiting for the chance to break their necks with a rope. Hell of a thing for a man to do, when you come to think of it. I don't know anything that'll give me goose bumps quicker than seeing Sam Winters sitting in the back of the courtroom during a murder trial."

"Turkey buzzard, eh?"

"Worse. I swear I don't believe Sam can keep his eyes off a man's neck any more than Shoemaker Schwartz can keep from looking at your shoes. Ever notice?"

"Every man to his trade?"

"Father Donovan and Sam Winters! One of 'em trying to pull a few souls into a heaven he believes in, and the other ready to kick 'em to hell for a fee of twenty-five dollars."

"Is that what the county pays Sam for a hanging?"

"Yep. Twenty-five dollars. By God, we ought to make it thirty just to be dramatic."

The talk dwindled. Skeffington smoked, and Jackson, tilted back in his swivel chair, stared out of the window. The bright fall trees seemed to gild the air. The courthouse clock struck the afternoon hours. The mellow rings of sound dropped down and swung outward over the town, settling here and there like slow golden quoits encircling a stake.

Jackson spoke after a long silence, quite as though he spoke to himself. "Often wondered about Winters. How does a man get to be like that?"

"Born that way."

"I don't believe it. There's always a story somewhere."

"Pish-posh, Jackson! Newspaper point of view."

"There's always a story, Ike, and where there's one story there are two—two sides."

"Um—maybe."

"Fact. And both of 'em true."

Skeffington nodded, but not in agreement. It was merely a sign that he was saying nothing for the moment.

"Think of these files, Ike, and the old stories. There's the story we print—"

"Which mostly isn't true."

"Which mostly is a polite outline for anybody to fill in that wants to. Then there's the real story."

He paused to fill a charred corncob pipe and light it. "Nobody knows the true story. As far as that goes—the truth of anything—there are only points of view." The pipe drew badly and required probing. Jackson kept some broom straws in his desk drawer for the purpose.

The sunlight poured through the flyspecked window and emphasized the dingy disorder of the room. The two men talked on, glossing each other's remarks, checking and rechecking details of buried scandals, romances, and tragedies—stories that came again into lively existence through the foreshortened memories of men growing old.

They had a talent for homely philosophy, and the happy gift of appreciating platitudes. Their conversational coinage was worn smooth with long use, but they had a sensitive knowledge of its basic values. They played their verbal duos with acknowledgment of the dignity of human communication. Talk for these two friends was one of the ways of life. Their daily use of the plain and local flavors of language was unself-conscious, but it had, nevertheless, something of the nature of a personal testament.

There was always a great weaving of talk in Kings Row. Over and back and across, the strands fell and interlaced. Town talk was town history. Year after year it was selected, and fitted together, and colored by the town's composite mind and personality.

Father Donovan often thought of this. He pictured the great talk, in which he had so little part, as an invisible shape of the town itself, a sort of hovering ghost of the past, or again as a shell having only the form of the life that created it—a shell sounding with illusory echoes.

One Sunday morning this image broke into his consciousness while he was preaching. Old thoughts and ideas did this from time to time, sometimes causing his discourse to take sudden and amazing turns. His small gathering of faithful listeners, understanding little enough of what he said at any time, were fortunately undisturbed by these excursions into the byways of the father's fancy. This fine Sunday morning the little church was a cool grotto still fresh against the pressing warmth of a delayed Indian summer. Bees sounded outside the windows among the gay yellow flowers Mariah Shane had planted close to the church wall. They stood straight and still, a few belated blossoms, looking for all the world, Miss Mariah thought, as she noticed them, like curious children peering over the window ledges. Father Donovan's voice buzzed deep in his throat—somewhat like the buzz of the bees themselves, God bless him! Miss Mariah murmured a pious phrase and brought her wandering mind firmly to attention.

She knew that look which was coming now into the eyes of the fervent speaker. He's not in this world at all now, not at all, she thought.

Father Donovan was saying: "Strive as we may with the present, it is constantly being destroyed even in its moments of realization. We build, moment by moment, living only on an infinitely small needle point of time and consciousness. Moment by moment as we live and build, the life and the structure of the life of those moments are swept into a past which is recoverable and tenable only through the medium of memory."

"Memory ... memory ..." Miss Mariah said the words almost audibly. "Memory. It's a beautiful word.... My father, and my mother, and my two sisters who went to heaven...." She lowered her head a little, her stiff old fingers made the sign of the cross, and her lips moved. The priest's voice came from far away....

"It is an illusion that the present moment is the sum of all our past successions of moments. It is only that the present moment is colored by all that has gone before, standing for its own instant of consciousness in the long increasing shadow cast forward by the past."

His voice rose a little in pitch. His congregation was quite lost to him now, but they felt a sense of tragedy in the sound of the strange words he spoke— words as incomprehensible as the Latin phrases of the Mass.

"We have no home in the present because it is too fleeting—vanishing segment by segment, as it comes, with incalculable swiftness.

"We have, equally, no home in the future because the future is a vast and mysterious and unpredictable complex of chance combinations. Any accident of fate, any slightest interference of our own will, and the whole kaleidoscope of possible destinies shifts in a bewildering haze of possibilities."

Father Donovan was looking out of the window now as though his mind sought some conclusion far beyond the visible. He spoke softly.

"Our real home is in the past, in the silent place of memory—itself a shadow, and ourselves but shadows moving amid the uncertain ghosts of imperfectly remembered events."

Almost by some other sense than sight he was aware of Miss Mariah lifting her face, half startled, at the word "ghosts." He caught his breath sharply. He had been talking out of the back room of his mind again—and being all flowery, too—an esthetic as well as a theological error. Was he not safe from the Devil, even in his own pulpit?

The listeners settled again into the warm drowse of sermon-time. The words which fell now on their ears were the familiar ones of admonition, exhortation, and reproof.

Miss Mariah sighed. I wish he'd gone on about the ghosts, she thought, it sounded beautiful.

2

Benny Singer was happy. Whenever he went to town on errands for Tom Carr, he went without shrinking from encounters with his old tormentors. He saw them, of course.

"Hey, Benny! Look, kids, here's old crazy Benny!"

He didn't mind being called "crazy Benny." Not now. He laughed and shouted and waved greetings. Anything that anybody said seemed kind and jovial. He had a job. He worked for Madame, and Tom Carr was his friend. He was *paid* for working. There was not a cloud in Benny's sky.

Tom Carr said Benny had "green fingers." Young plants seemed to feel the good will in Benny's touch.

"He has a way with growing things, ma'am," Tom reported. "He understands them, and I declare I believe his plants *know* him."

Old Tom almost winked at Madame von Eln. "He talks to them, you know."

To such praise and goodness of heart Benny responded as his plants responded to sun and rain. He was beyond the reach of anything Fulmer Green and Fulmer's gang could do.

Sometimes Parris followed Tom and Benny as they went about the varied work of the nursery. Tom's talk was interesting most times, and there was something about Benny that touched him a little. It was exactly the way he had been touched by Lucy Carr. He wasn't quite comfortable with Benny, however; it disturbed him to feel that Benny didn't always understand simple words.

Parris remembered how he used to feel that Lucy's mind darted here and there with no seeming attachment to anything. Benny's mind didn't do that. No; Benny's mind sort of—well, sort of *staggered* ... the way a chicken staggers and tries to run, after its head is cut off. He shivered a little at the unpleasant picture, and looked sideways at Benny. It wasn't a very nice way to think about anyone, he felt.

Once or twice Tom Carr talked to Parris about Benny. "He's a little like Lucy, sometimes. I guess I got so used to Lucy's ways that I kind of understand Benny. You know, Johnny, people that are a little off that way are just like a string of beads that's come undone. The beads roll around any which-a-way. If there was some way of getting them on the string again, they'd be all right. Looks like there'd be some way of doing it. Doctors do some right wonderful things when it comes to cutting people open and sewing them up again, but they're not so far along with people's brains."

Parris half listened. He had heard Tom say all of this so many times.

"You know, Johnny, what I'd do if I was you?" The old man's sharp eyes shadowed with the gravity of his feelings. "I'd study that if I was you."

"Be a doctor for—for—" He didn't like to say "crazy people" to Tom.

"Yes, sir, Johnny, for crazy people. May be that nobody's found out much about it yet, but it seems to me it would be a grand thing to study."

Parris thought about the asylum and the way it smelled. He was sure he wouldn't like to be a doctor for crazy people.

"People like Benny, and—like Lucy. Not real crazy, you know, Johnny, just off a little. If there was just some way of holding them together again …

Tom went on with his work as he talked, and Parris stood with his hands in his pockets, hoping the old man would change the subject. He was pretty sure now that he would like to be a doctor. His grandmother had spoken of it, too. But he thought he'd rather drive two fiery bay horses like Dr. Gordon and go around saving people's lives. Suddenly he recalled that day Dr. Gordon operated on Willy Macintosh's father. He remembered the terrible yells that came from that upper window, and Willy's wild face as he tugged at the front door and cried, "I'll kill him, I'll kill him!" Perspiration wet his upper lip as he thought of it. He didn't believe he could cut at a man who yelled like that. He kicked a small white stone out of the way. He couldn't think of anything he'd really like to do, except just to live here on this place forever.

It seemed that everybody talked to him about what he would do when he grew up. He shrugged impatiently, but a kind of weight lay on him that he couldn't shake off. Why couldn't they let him alone? He walked a few steps and kicked the white pebble again. He supposed he'd *have* to think about it. What *would* he like to do? Of all the things in the world, what would he like most to do? He looked across Thurston St. George's farm. A distant undulation toward the prairie country showed an edge of blue above the yellow field. He made a face and grinned.

Goodness, he thought, I like to look at things; I like to look at everything, but I can't think of anything else in the whole world I really like to do. I guess it'd be kind of hard to make a living out of that!

He realized that he loved this place—this, right here, the ground, the crisscross pattern the wiry grass made, the shiny red stems of vines, the dusky blue coat on winterberries.

Tom Carr broke in on his reverie.

"Want to come along, Johnny? We're going over that way." He pointed toward the evergreen plantings.

From where he stood Parris could see a gleam of water through the trees. A sudden cold tightness gripped him. The pond … Renée …all that terrible time.…

"Parris! Want to come with us?"

"No, I guess not. No. I got to go on home now."

He felt that he might cry if he didn't go away by himself. He started at a dogtrot toward home.

Halfway down the slope he stopped where a clearing opened to a wide view of the warm, drowsy landscape. It was very pleasant to look at, he decided. The tightness across his chest let go, and he felt better. This—all of this was home. The faded green flecked with gold leaves, the obscuring blue against the far rise of the land to the south, the trembling loops of the creek passing now and again half out of sight beneath the thin-leaved birches, the big rusty stone house with its mossy roof there in the heavy billow of bright yellow maples. It was familiar and comfortable. He sighed happily—his own place in the world!

But even in that instant a small unease returned. A presentiment ruffled his content as a shiver of wind ruffles a poplar tree, lifting the quiet leaves in a thousand tiny signals of alarm. In just that way a multitudinous tingle of apprehension touched all of his nerves.

He knew what the feeling was, and what it came from. He had felt like this a good many times lately. Other boys had parents who were not so old as his grandmother. They had brothers and sisters and relatives. He had only his grandmother. What would happen when—when—? He couldn't say the word even to himself. Then—all of this would be gone somehow. Where would he go? What would he do? His face worked slightly, but he did not cry. He looked across the field and then up toward the sky. If one could, maybe, pray about it. He looked down again quickly with a sudden expression of violent resentment. Once—once, a long time ago, in a moment of terrible trouble he had prayed. He had looked up at that very sky and begged—*begged* for help. His mouth set. *No:* he would not ask again. If they—he vaguely visioned rows of saints and angels like those in the old Doré Bible—if they couldn't, or wouldn't, help when you needed them as much as he needed help for Renée that time—why, they could just—just … Just what? He asked himself the question. The shining row of wings and the robed saints showed transparent as glass. He knew all at once that he didn't believe in them. They weren't there at all. They never had been there.

He was shocked at himself. Good gracious! Was he an infidel? Tom Carr had said just last week that Isaac Skeffington was an infidel. Probably he wasn't exactly an infidel because he wouldn't go around talking about it as Mr. Skeffington did. Perhaps that made a difference.

At the bottom of the hill he looked back at the spruce and poplar plantings rising row above row, like soldiers standing, and waiting. That look of waiting that lay now over the whole place oppressed him. Everything was waiting for something to happen. He was certain that when it came it would be something terrifying and disastrous.

3

"I wish I had something to do!"

It was a plaint heard frequently from Parris these days.

"Why don't you go to see your friends sometimes?" It did not occur to Madame von Eln that he missed school.

Parris seldom replied to this. The truth was that he felt like an outsider when he saw other boys, and he saw that they felt the same way. All except Drake McHugh, who was always the same, and—and Jamie Wakefield. It was odd, he realized, how his mind always seemed to stumble when he thought of Jamie Wakefield—just as though he didn't really want to think about him. He tried hard to think just what it was, as he had tried before, but he couldn't make up his mind—not quite. He liked Jamie. Yes; he was sure about that. But why was he always a little embarrassed about it? The other boys didn't seem to dislike Jamie—they, well, they merely seemed to push him aside somewhat. They called him girly names. Certainly, he was girlish, but he was really all right. Anyway, he thought a bit ruefully, Jamie was actually the only one who wanted to be his friend.

One evening Parris stayed in town rather late. He liked the streets at evening; and the strange look of familiar places in the changing light gave him a sense of adventure.

He was walking slowly up Walnut Street trying to make up his mind to go home. This was supper hour in Kings Row, and the streets were deserted. He walked more slowly. Might as well go home, he decided.

Upper Walnut Street was without a sidewalk, and a wide path of fine white dust took its place. Parris kicked little puffs ahead of him as he wavered from side to side.

"Hello, Parris."

Jamie Wakefield's slightly muffled voice startled him.

"Oh, I didn't hear you coming. Hello."

Jamie was a little out of breath. "Where you going?"

"Nowhere. Home, I guess."

"What for?"

"No place else to go, I guess."

"Let's walk a while."

"Looks like that's what we are doing."

"Aw, Parris."

Parris looked at Jamie with a little surprise. Jamie seemed so anxious about something.

"What's the matter, Jamie?"

"Nothing. I just wish you wouldn't go home yet."

"All right. What let's do?"

Jamie's face flushed. More like a girl than ever, Parris thought.

"Let's walk over to the college campus. It's pretty over there."

"Kind of dark and lonesome at night, though."

"It's not night yet. Besides, there is a full moon. It'll be coming up later."

"All right."

Parris felt a bit puzzled. Jamie seemed so ridiculously happy over nothing. He chattered all the way out to the Aberdeen campus. Parris could hardly put in a word, but he was pleased somehow. He was glad to be with Jamie— grateful that Jamie wanted to be with him. Jamie's fluent color came and went with the excitement of his talk, and Parris found himself more interested in Jamie's face than in what he said.

Goodness, he thought, he is good-looking. He's prettier than Cassie Tower. And then some small sense of trouble came over him. The way Jamie walked, almost sideways, looking up as he talked, reminded him of Renée.

Jamie saw the slight change of expression in Parris' face. "What's the matter?"

"With me? Nothing. Why?"

"You looked sort of funny—just for a second."

"Nothing's the matter with me." He threw his arm across Jamie's shoulder in a sudden rush of warmth. Very shyly Jamie put his arm around Parris, and they walked slowly through the deep grass, thrusting the fall of yellow leaves aside and leaving a dark trail behind them as they went.

They came out on a broad walk that stretched along the edge of a steep decline.

"Sunset Walk," said Jamie.

"Is that the name of it? This walk?"

"That's what I call it. I just named it myself."

"Oh! I thought I never had heard it called that. It's pretty up here, though."

"It's beautiful I—I come here lots of times."

"What for?"

"To see the sunsets."

"That's a funny thing to do. Can't you see the sunset anywhere?"

"Not good. You can see all around the country from here. It's beautiful. You come up here with me sometime—I'll show you."

"All right."

"Let's sit down here." Jamie veered toward a low wooden bench. His voice sounded suddenly husky as he spoke. That breathless quality struck Parris as being a little odd—and familiar. It reminded him of something, he couldn't recall just what, but something troubling and unhappy. What was it?

Jamie snuggled close, and Parris stretched his arm along the back of the bench.

"Seems cold when you sit down, doesn't it?"

Parris didn't answer. He was still trying to remember something.

"Doesn't it, Parris?"

"Yeh? Oh, yes, a little. Not much."

They sat for a while without talking.

"Look!" Jamie pointed to a faraway house that stood on the very crest of the long western rise. It stood sharp and white against the stained-glass blue of the sky.

"The moon's coming up back of us." Jamie almost whispered the words. "It catches that house first thing. Look, Parris, it's like a wonderful enchanted country. I guess Italy must look like that—you know, with white villas and all."

It was not yet dark, but a deep stillness seemed to settle over the world. Both boys began to talk in half-hushed voices.

Jamie took Parris' hand between his own. Parris was slightly embarrassed again, but the gesture was rather warming. Jamie certainly had curious ways. He couldn't imagine holding hands with Drake McHugh, for instance, or Willy Macintosh. The thought increased his discomfort, but the feeling passed. He decided that maybe he liked Jamie's ways, after all. Jamie was just different, but he was all right.

"You know what I want to be, Parris?"

"What?"

"A poet!"

"A poet?"

Jamie nodded, rubbing his head against Parris' shoulder.

Parris considered this idea for a moment. "Well, but Jamie—how do you get to be a poet?"

"You write poetry."

"Can you write poetry?"

Jamie nodded again, more shyly.

"How did you learn?"

Jamie sat up and a little quiver of excitement came into his voice.

"Listen, Parris, do you know Bob Callicott?"

"You mean Mr. Callicott that's an editor, or something in the *Gazette* office?"

"Yes, Mr. R. E. Callicott, he's the one. I—he lets me call him Bob, though."

Parris was a little astonished at this. Jamie spoke quickly. The huskiness was gone from his voice now. "Haven't you ever seen the poems he prints in the *Gazette*—most every week?"

"I guess I've seen them. I never did read any of them, though."

"You've got to read them, Parris. They're beautiful."

"You mean they're sure-enough poetry—like Shakespeare—and Milton?"

"I guess they're not much like Shakespeare, or Milton, but they're good. They're different." Jamie hesitated. "They're *lyric* poems."

"Say, you know all about poetry, don't you? What's lyric poetry?"

"Well, I can show you some. I've got a whole book. They're short, not like long plays—and things."

"Well, ain't—isn't it awfully hard to think up rhymes and all those things?"

"Not as hard as meter."

"What's that?"

"Don't you know what meter is? It's the way you count the feet—I mean, you got to have so many syllables and accents in a line."

"Sa-ay. Jamie! Do you mean that the poets, Shakespeare and all of them, had to count up how many words, or syllables, or whatever it is, they put in every line?"

"Of course they did. And there are a whole lot of different kinds of meter with different accents."

"Is it like *time* in music?"

"It's just exactly like it."

"It sounds like it would be hard to do!"

"Sometimes it is. Well, what I started to say a while ago was 'that Bob Callicott helps me. He told me all about meter and stanzas and how you scan—"

"Scan?"

Jamie shrugged impatiently. "How to count feet and accents. Don't your tutors teach you anything? I think Bob is a fine poet. It's just that nobody appreciates him. He thinks it's the greatest thing in the world to be a poet."

Parris nodded gravely.

"And I do, too," Jamie added. "Say, you know he plays the violin. Why don't you come along with me to his house sometime? You could play accompaniments."

"All right. I guess I'd like to." Parris spoke with a sudden enthusiasm. "Yes, I would like to. But listen, Jamie, will your father let you be a poet?"

Jamie sank back. "That's going to be the trouble, I expect. He keeps saying I got to go to work in the bank when I get through school and college and everything."

"Can't you work in the bank and be a poet, too?"

"I don't know. I don't want to work in the bank."

"Oh!"

"What are you going to be, Parris?"

"A doctor, I guess."

"That's wonderful."

"Do you think so?"

"Don't you? Don't you want to be?"

"I don't know. I guess so. You have to be something."

Jamie sat up again. "Let's always be good friends, Parris, and tell each other how we feel about everything."

Parris smiled. Jamie was really very nice. "All right."

"Will you, honestly?"

"Of course."

"I think friendship is a wonderful thing, don't you?"

"Why—I guess so. I guess I never did think much about it."

"Gee, Parris!"

Jamie's face wore a rapt look. Parris thought again that Jamie was better-looking than anyone he knew. He was like velvet.

Parris slipped forward and leaned his head on the back of the bench. He felt lazy and comfortable. He was going to like Jamie a whole lot better than he ever had. He knew that.

They sat for a long time without speaking. Jamie unfastened Parris' wristband and slipped his hand into the sleeve. Parris was a little startled by the sensation. Jamie had strange hands—small, and plump for so slight a boy. His fingers left a tingle where they touched. But Parris felt puzzled about something, he didn't know just what. He kept trying to think his way through entangling and conflicting ideas, when—without warning—Jamie leaned forward and kissed him on the mouth. Parris was too amazed to move, too amazed to think. He felt as if a gust of flame swept him from head to foot. He was not too clearly aware of anything for a while except Jamie's caresses and his flattering hands which carried both violence and appeasement in their touch.

Finally he pushed Jamie away and stood up.

"Come on, let's go."

"Aw, why, Parris?"

"I've got to go home."

"No, you don't."

"Yes, I do."

"Do you want to go home?"

"Yes."

Jamie did not reply to this. Parris could feel a hurt in the silence.

"Parris!" Jamie's voice was husky again.

"What?"

"Are you mad at me?"

Parris swallowed hard. Something rushed at his brain out of the nerveless warmth and strengthlessness that had enveloped him and all of his senses as in a sleepy haze. That phrase! *"Are you mad at me?"* He could hear himself saying it—that terrible, terrible afternoon. He sat down quickly on the bench, glad that Jamie couldn't see that he was about to cry.

This ... this ... no, he didn't want to think about it. In spite of all that happened to Renée and to himself following discovery, he could never feel sorry for the happening itself. He had shut it away and there it was, like those colored pictures sealed in glass which lay on the center table in the parlor at home. But this—this had nearly broken through.

"Parris! Are you—?"

"Please don't say that again! Please!"

"Why, what's the matter?"

"Nothing. Let's go home."

"Won't you come up here with me again, ever?" Jamie's real distress touched Parris. But he felt better. He wanted to hit Jamie. He realized that it was the first time he had ever wanted to hit anyone—not for this night but for a strange ugly trail that Jamie was breaking across an area in his memory he had thought inviolable.

"Is that why you wanted me to be friends with you?" Parris was surprised at the hard cruelty in his own voice.

"Oh, Parris. Of course not."

Parris walked fast, and Jamie hurried to keep up with him. They reached Federal Street without speaking.

"Please, Parris, don't be—"

"Oh, shut up!"

Jamie whimpered and turned away. He began to run. Parris watched him disappear.

On the way home he picked up a stick and cut viciously at the goldenrod beside the road.

"Darned fool!" he kept saying as he lopped the dusty blossom heads from their stems. "Darned fool! Darned fool!"

Parris did not sleep well. He watched the moonlight lying watery green against the straight white curtains at his windows, falling in a broken rectangle on the floor and creeping along the sides of his bed. It felt like a presence, and his imagination invested it with all sorts of sinister qualities.

Jamie ... Jamie ... little fool! He tried to hate Jamie, but that didn't come off very well.

He couldn't keep Renée out of his thoughts. Over and over he saw her, and remembered her. When she was very young—in the faded skimpy little dresses she wore to school. Later in the green dress he had brought her from Philadelphia, and as they walked that fateful day toward their "secret lake." He was near to crying, but he thought of Drake. He was sure Drake wouldn't cry about a girl. But Renée, and everything about Renée, was different—entirely different.

It was Renée who troubled him most tonight. It seemed, as he thought of what had happened (and he could not keep from thinking about it), that Jamie had done something to Renée.

Acute embarrassment struck him again and again. He felt hot, and threw the covers aside. Then he sneezed and replaced the blanket.

He began to dramatize his sleeplessness. Older people often spoke of troubled and wakeful nights. He felt that he had entered into the company of grown-up suffering. There was a surprising comfort in this, and he was interested in the thought. But grown-up troubles were very real, and somewhat fantastic. A whole world of intolerable possibilities loomed in that direction. He considered several of the more picturesque varieties, but others less desirable intruded. Troubles of the world of older people were terrifying.

A lot of things could happen. He visualized catastrophes he had heard discussed, events and consequences having no relation to the immediate cause of these wakeful hours. The stories he had heard of fugitives and prisons magnified and merged, reappeared in new combinations, lost reality and loomed as illogical specters of half-waking, half-sleep.

He started and pulled the covers over his head. The dark was protective and comforting. He felt that now at last—in this smothering secrecy—he could cry. He tried screwing up his face, but no tears came. Presently he was asleep.

4

The next day Parris found it difficult to revive any real sense of the preceding night. He could not perfectly believe in its reality, or recapture the trouble of mind that had beset him after he had gone to bed. He wandered about the gardens and the nursery plantations in a rather pleasant vagueness.

The weather was still fine. The yellow maples and hickories were thinning a little at the top. Against the deep reds and yellows the evergreens took on an unexpected freshness. The distant lines of the familiar landscape were dim and strange in the deepening blue haze.

Parris went through the spruce and cedars, past the little pond, to a small rise where an outcropping of rocky ledge was topped by a growth of birches. The leaves were scant now, but those which still held were like flakes of pure gold. There was another kind of tree, too, still green with a sharp, springlike green.

Parris sat cross-legged in the tufted, wiry grass. He could see the pond now. It looked unearthly still. It made him think of graveyards and pictures of places you could never go to because they no longer existed. There it lay, just down the slope, but he felt as if he could not possibly go to it. He knew that all he had to do was walk down the slope and he could stand on the bank and throw clods into the water. He could—and still he couldn't.

He wrinkled his brow and squinted. He couldn't go there—he couldn't go there—because—because of a lot of days and nights and weeks and months. That's what it was. All of that time—two long years of time shutting in and shutting down on another time that he was trying to remember into life again. But—once more a certainty of irrecoverable loss struck at him as it had that day when his grandmother said Renée had gone away. He could not reach the place—his lake, his and Renée's "secret lake," was back there—away back there, and down there at the end of all those days and nights.

He lay down and stared up through the trees. The light hurt his eyes, and he turned over on his side. It was warm and very still. Last night's loss of sleep made him drowsy. He could hear a faraway crow sounding his half-warning, half-jeering call. There was another sound, too—a subdued, swishing whisper. Parris was uncertain if it was inside or outside of his head, but it might be, he thought, all of the sounds of the whole countryside sort of mixed and passing on out of the world.

Jamie Wakefield said—oh, Jamie again!—darn it!—couldn't he get rid of Jamie, and stop thinking about him? He pulled handfuls of grass and threw it up in the air, watching it scatter and fall again. Poor old Jamie—he had acted so—so scared. Little fool!

His resentment against Jamie was less violent today. After all, he was just as much to blame if anybody had to be blamed. He wasn't sure it was a question of blame. Jamie—well, Jamie was just different, that was all. He did seem kind of like a girl, sure enough—as Drake McHugh said. Now if Jamie were really a girl ... that thought crossed another which he must not let himself think. Jamie was—yes, he was really beautiful, and he made you like him just for that. And that was strange—Parris couldn't exactly make sense of it. Beautiful in the way a girl is beautiful, and that always made you feel you had to do something about it.... He flounced about and lay face down, shutting his eyes in the crook of his arm. He pressed his face hard against his rough sleeve, and his breath came back hot and damp against his face. He shut his eyes tight. Pictures shaped in the reddish pulsing dark—rather meaningless pictures—Drake and Jamie, and over and over, Renée—and again, Jamie and Cassie Tower. He came wide-awake and stirred. Cassie Tower ... what was she doing here with Drake and Jamie—and with Renée?

The sun was warm on his neck and back, but the ground was cool. He turned over again and covered his face with his cap. The pictures faded for a moment and sounds floated back. The crow was still calling from the same place—still impudent and assured. The dull clunk of a cowbell came from the lower woods. That would be Reddy down by the creek. A thinner sound of turkey bells—a sort of glinting tink-tink came from near by. Parris could imagine the cautious, inquiring heads of the gobblers thrust up from the tall grass back of the cedars.

He stirred a little—the humps in the ground seemed to grow harder. After a while he sat up and groaned. He wished he had someone to talk to. Not Tom Carr, or Benny who couldn't understand much, or even Drake who laughed too readily when you were trying to be serious, or maybe—no, not Jamie either.... If Renée were here! He took a quick short breath—the bright silvery image of Renée confused for an instant with that of Cassandra....

"I've got to think about something now." He said the words aloud, but he scarcely heard the sound of his own voice.

He said them again, more softly: "I've got to think about something now."

But he was not thinking. All of his senses were in a warm confusion. What he heard, and saw, and felt were all one—something his mind was doing of itself—half eager, half reluctant—a forward thrust of imagination into a disquieting new world. A secret urgency lay behind this almost furtive exploration.

Parris bit hard on his lip to quiet the conflict of misgiving and excitement that shook his nerves.

"I don't feel good," he muttered.

Madame von Eln sat on the terrace that same afternoon talking with Dr. Gordon and Colonel Skeffington.

Upstairs, Anna and another maid stood looking down at the three. Anna shook her head. "When a body sends for a doctor and a lawyer at the same time—" She left off.

"Do you think Madame is worse—or something?"

Anna began to cry silently. "She looks worse every day. Nobody else notices because they see her every day, and because she's so quick and bright about everything, but I notice. I notice everything. I've been with her too long not to notice."

The younger maid turned and peered through the curtain. "My goodness, oh, my goodness!" she said.

"You see, Colonel," Madame was saying. "I must be sure that I arrange everything. The boy has no one—no one in the world but me."

Colonel Skeffington folded and unfolded his gold-rimmed glasses. "I always thought you had a lot of kin in the East?"

"Oh, I have—in Philadelphia. I don't like them, Colonel." She smiled rather gaily, and the Colonel nodded. "They really are quite distant and I hardly think would interest themselves much in Parris. I want to do the best I can for him with what I have. He—he's all I have, too."

"Yes, yes. Of course. You know, Madame, if anything should happen to you—unexpectedly—"

"It wouldn't be unexpected, now, Isaac."

"Well, well, now. I never believe the worst until it has happened. What I was going to say is this: if—if your grandson finds himself alone, he can come to me any time, for as long as he wants to. Got a big house, plenty of room. Fine boy he is. Rather make a lawyer of him, though, than a doctor." He slapped Dr. Gordon on the knee, but he did not smile.

"Thank you, Isaac. I know your generous heart. I—I think Parris leans to medicine as much as to anything—except, maybe music."

"Music!" The Colonel dismissed that. This time Dr. Gordon laughed a little with his habitual quick intake of breath.

Madame nodded. "I don't take that inclination seriously, Isaac. I have him study because I think it will keep him from being lonely sometime, maybe."

"Yes, I see, I see." Skeffington slipped his glasses on again and looked at his notes. He twisted his beard into long Assyrian curls. "It's a good property, and with the money in the bank he can get a good education, but—"

"But what?" She leaned forward in her chair.

"Not more than that. But he'll be fixed to earn his living."

She sighed. "It will have to do. But I do think it is urgent that we make definite plans quickly."

Colonel Skeffington looked hard at her. "I have to be blunt, Marie. How much time do you think you have?"

Madame looked at Dr. Gordon. The doctor did not answer at once. His overbright eyes searched Madame's face.

"Well, Henry?" Skeffington snapped the words out at Dr. Gordon.

"Madame has a year, maybe two—two at best."

The Colonel's face showed hard red patches as it always did when he was moved or excited. He looked steadily at Madame for a moment.

"I don't believe it," he said. "I don't believe a word of it, but we'll act as if Gordon knows what he's talking about, which I very much doubt. You don't look it, Madame, you don't look it at all."

But Colonel Skeffington was not telling the truth. He was sure Dr. Gordon was right. Madame's face had a chalky look, and she was frightfully thin.

"Parris, you say, has made good progress with his tutors?" Dr. Gordon asked the question in a sudden matter-of-fact tone.

"Excellent, Doctor. His tutors say he is far ahead of the high-school classes."

"Then we must put him in Aberdeen, at once. But it will save time if he reads medicine with someone for a couple of years. Then he can take examinations and save much time."

Skeffington nodded. "Good idea. Now, if it had been law, he could have read with me. I'd have taught him a lot of things not in the books."

Madame laughed dryly. "I've heard you know a lot of such things."

"You bet your life I do. But who can the boy read with, Gordon—you?"

"I haven't time."

"But there's nobody else." Madame's tone was anxious.

Skeffington and Madame waited quietly. The three of them sitting there in this quiet terrace garden, with the dimming October sunshine over them, made a curious picture. These were to them familiar procedures. Without hush, or awe, without sentimentality, or obliquity, they were arranging the sequences of death and life. They were not unaware of the gravity of these matters, but they were unaware of their dignity in dealing with them.

Quietly, simply, almost casually, they were setting another act in the drama of their lives. Perhaps Skeffington alone, with his lively sense of the dramatic, was appreciative of the scene. He cut his eye in Dr. Gordon's direction.

"Well, Henry?"

"I'm going to make a suggestion—" Dr. Gordon hesitated. "I'm going to make a suggestion you may not approve. But there is one man who could do more for him in such a way than anyone I know." He hesitated again.

"In Kings Row?" Skeffington was impatient.

"Yes. Dr. Tower."

Both Madame von Eln and Colonel Skeffington started. Madame repeated the name incredulously. Dr. Gordon compressed his lips and nodded firmly. "Yes, ma'am. He's a brilliant man—most able. He's a hard student. Far ahead of any of us. Knows all the new things. He would certainly be the man."

"I didn't know you knew Dr. Tower very well—I mean to say, any better than the rest of us, and that's just not at all." Skeffington was curious.

"I've talked with him very often. He's able—most able."

"But, would he take Parris?" Madame was immediately practical.

Dr. Gordon thought a moment. "I believe he would. It would give him a new interest. I'd be very happy to speak to him myself about it."

"Would you really be so kind, Doctor?"

"Certainly, ma'am. Happy to do it. I can tell you that Dr. Tower is a whole medical college by himself."

Skeffington reached for his hat. "Are there any other details, ma'am, you think of?"

"Well, if you think now it's best to arrange for the bank rather than some one person to be guardian—"

Skeffington interrupted. "Anyone you'd want would be older than you— likelier to die than you are. The Burton County Bank will take care of him all right. They're good men in there."

"All right. There is one more thing—and I'd like this to be clearly put in my will. As soon as practicable, I want Parris to go to Vienna for his medical training."

Skeffington put his hat down again. "Vienna? Why?"

"Doctor Gordon will tell you, Isaac, that Vienna is the best place in the world to study medicine."

"But a foreign country, Madame—"

"Parris is halfway a foreigner—at least, most people think so. He understands and speaks German. He won't be handicapped by the language."

"Well—"

"As you see," she went on quickly. "There's money enough for just about that long a time, and that kind of education, and a little over, maybe, if everything turns out all right, to set him up in practice."

"Well—"

"Will you see that this is in the papers and that it will be carried out?"

"Yes, Madame, I will, if you—and Gordon here—think that's best."

Doctor Gordon stood up. "I have to hurry away, Madame. I'll see you next week." He turned to the Colonel. "Madame has a good plan there. Wish I could have gone to Vienna when I was a student. It'll give her grandson an immense advantage when he starts his practice."

Madame rose and walked to the terrace steps with the two men.

"Good day, ma'am."

"Good day, and thank you, both of you. I'll see Dr. MacLaughlin tomorrow about Aberdeen. The rest—" she suddenly sounded tired "—the rest I leave to you."

Skeffington swept his shiny hat in a wide arc. "You can depend on us, ma'am."

Madame inclined her head formally.

"Good day, and thank you again."

She watched the Doctor's buggy until it passed the gate and rolled out of sight among the trees along the creek drive. She drew her shawl about her shoulders. The west had clouded over, and the air was chill.

It would soon be winter.

5

Parris was dismayed when he heard that he was to go to Aberdeen College. Sudden changes invariably gave him a stirred up feeling inside that was highly unpleasant. He realized that his grandmother was much given to sudden changes. They seemed to please her and to excite her with the liveliest sense of accomplishment. She always announced a new plan with great vivacity and seemed to expect happy responses from all sides. Then she forgot about it and was likely to be absent-minded or indifferent until she thought of something else.

For the first time in his life Parris was near to being critical and resentful of his grandmother's arrangements. He felt that he should have been consulted or at least told while the plan was being made. He didn't really want to go to Aberdeen. The session had already begun, and the students were strange young men much older than he. He dreaded the ordeal of beginning.

But Aberdeen turned out to be far pleasanter than he could have hoped. Learning new things proved to be unexpectedly entertaining.

Parris did not know that he was regarded by the other students as something of a prodigy. They also thought him conceited and standoffish, so he made no friends. Outside of the classrooms, Aberdeen made but little impression on him. His reading with Dr. Tower was a different matter. Dr. Tower was bitterly contemptuous of Aberdeen and its teaching, and Parris was naturally influenced by this. It contributed to his detachment at school. He spent three afternoons each week with Dr. Tower. They were hours of excitement and revelation.

He never forgot that first afternoon when Cassandra answered his ring at the door. The hall was dark and had a disused look and smell. All the doors were closed, and Cassie spoke in a half whisper. She pointed to the end of the hall.

"Down there—the last door."

Parris stood looking at her. She was much prettier than he had remembered her to be.

"How have you been, Cassie? I haven't seen you in an awfully long time."

"I'm all right." She looked at him steadily, her eyes very large and bright. She pointed again toward the study.

"Down there," she repeated and turned away.

Parris walked the length of the dim passage and rapped softly on the door.

"Come in, come in."

The voice was something of a surprise. It was deep and musical.

Parris entered. The room was bright and cheerful. A whole row of windows looked out on the side lawn. The rest of the room was lined with books. Tables were covered with them. Many lay on the floor.

"How do you do, sir."

Doctor Tower nodded. He did not speak at once. His eyes, exactly like Cassie's, Parris thought, seemed nevertheless somewhat unseeing as though his attention was still held elsewhere. He closed his book and put it down.

"Hereafter, you may come around to the study door. It won't be necessary to come through the house."

Parris felt his face flame. The simple statement seemed to carry not only a rebuke but some sort of obscure threat.

"Sit down."

"Thank you, sir."

Here in his study, with the sunlight touching his heavy mahogany-colored hair, Dr. Tower looked younger than Parris had expected. The doctor had the appearance of being "dressed up." Also he had an air that was not easy for Parris to define, but which he knew was unlike that of other men. He wondered what it was. Distinction, yes; but also something quietly and intensely alive, maybe a shade menacing.

"You want to be a doctor?"

"Yes, sir."

"A good one, or just one of these country quacks?"

"I want to be a very good one, like—"

Doctor Tower waited with a distinctly malicious smile on his pale face. "Like whom?"

Parris blushed again. "Like those you read about."

"Where?"

"In books."

"What books?"

This time Parris smiled. "I got into it that time, sir, didn't I? I guess I mean the—the legendary sort of doctor."

Doctor Tower smiled, too—differently this time, at the unexpected word.

"I hear your grandmother proposes sending you to Vienna."

"Yes, sir."

"Extraordinary."

"Sir?"

"I mean she must be extraordinary herself."

"She's quite wonderful," Parris said quietly, and Dr. Tower nodded gravely. Then he began to talk. Parris could not follow all of it, but he listened as he had never listened before. Part of the time he forgot to think of what the Doctor was actually saying in, the brilliant and bewildering play of words. Some of it sounded a good deal like the "lyric poetry" Jamie was always talking about.

Parris felt enormously important as he listened. Dr. Tower had the air of taking him into a quite special confidence. Parris was giving his most concentrated attention now, but he was giving something else, too, and that was a sudden and violent loyalty. He was sufficiently analytic to know that this was partly a loyalty to a point of view and a method, but also very largely a loyalty to a man.

Dr. Tower turned abruptly in his chair. "You aren't having psychology at Aberdeen, are you?"

"No, sir."

"Good. Don't take it."

"Very well, sir."

"You're at music, too, I hear."

"Yes, sir."

"With Berdorff?"

"Yes, sir."

"Good. One of the best disciplines in the world. Bach?"

"Yes, sir."

"Beethoven and Mozart?"

"Not much Mozart."

"Why?"

"I like Beethoven better."

"A youthful taste. You will change."

Parris did not answer. Again the Doctor's words carried a seeming rebuke. "You can read German, Gordon says."

"Yes, sir."

"Really read it, or just able to understand a few fairy tales?"

"I don't know. I guess I haven't tried anything very hard."

"And French?"

"Not as much as German."

"All right. You seem to have something to go on. You wouldn't be here if you didn't. Gordon says a good word for you. I'll see you on Friday."

"Thank you, sir. I enjoyed the afternoon very much."

"Yes? Well—" Dr. Tower seemed slightly embarrassed for an instant at Parris' old-fashioned manner.

"You may go out this way. If you follow the drive, you'll come out on Cherry Street."

It sounded like a command.

Parris could not sleep that night. He was more deeply excited than he had ever been in his life. For the first time there were intimations of authentic communication between his world—which had been until this very day the world of children—and the adult world which had always moved a little mysteriously either to the side or above him.

He thought about Drake and Jamie and felt that he had suddenly left them far behind concerned with things no longer important to him.

A door was opening, and he was unbearably impatient to pass through.

In the months that followed he saw very little of either Jamie or Drake.

Once he did go with Jamie to see Robert Callicott. Jamie was fluttery but touching in his eagerness. He wanted each of them to know how superior the other was.

Parris decided Robert Callicott looked like a scared cat. He was incredibly tall and thin, his fingers were in constant motion and curved as if he were trying to hold some object too large to grasp, and his pale blue eyes were popped with a look of perpetual inquiry.

"Jamie here tells me you like poetry."

Parris gulped at this. "I don't know if I do or not. I like to hear him talk about it."

Callicott laughed heartily. "There are a lot of people in your boat, son. You play piano, though?"

"Yes, sir."

Callicott leaped to his feet and opened his violin case. "Seldom have a chance to have an accompanist." He threw music about on top of the big square piano. "Study with Berdorff, I hear."

"Yes, sir."

"God, that must be terrible! Don't let him ruin you. Cut and dried. Doesn't know the first thing of what music is about."

Parris was utterly shocked at this, but had no chance to reply. Callicott continued to toss sheets of music right and left. "All those Germans," he went on, "all alike. Military, strict—'in time now, one, two, three'—God! Music is the wind, it's clouds and free running waters—improvisation—the troubadours—the pulse of a sudden love song blown down a road in Provence! You can't chain music to a metronome any more than you can hitch a flying cloud to—to an oxcart. Here—can you play this, do you think? It's Sarasate."

Parris turned the pages. "Looks pretty hard, but I'll try it."

"Right. Just follow the violin. If you don't get all the notes, don't mind. Keep with me—get into the feel of it. Gypsies now—wild clouds scudding across the moon—free! Above everything else, free!" He tuned the violin as he talked.

"Now then, my boy—forget Berdorff."

Parris was startled by the sudden and violent onslaught. He couldn't read that quickly—in fact, he couldn't tell where Callicott was at all.

"What's the matter?"

"I don't seem to get it very well."

"Well, now, look—here, like this—" Callicott pointed with his bow at the piano score, sang with a mighty roar, and stamped his foot.

"Let's try again."

It went better, but Parris discovered that the violinist had no regard for the printed page. Maybe he was playing the right notes, but he played with a grand disregard for time. It *was*, he thought, surprisingly like clouds scudding in the wind.

"Now this—Wieniawski—a little stricter in this, maybe."

But Callicott's notion of comparative strictness carried a wide margin of license. They played on and on. Callicott was obviously enchanted, not really with his own playing, but with something quite outside of the music—something that he was experiencing while the music sounded.

After an hour, Parris began to adjust himself to the racing, loitering, unordered playing. It was a kind of playing *with* music, but well, it wasn't really music, he was sure of that, but he also was not sure why he thought so.

Callicott's talk was like his playing—sudden, rapid, flying this way and that like a distracted bird.

"Now, you play for me. What do you like best?"

"I think I like Beethoven better than any composer."

"Um—you do? Berdorff, probably. Beethoven's always beating on a locked door, running up hill and down again—too self-righteous, too. How about Chopin? Greatest artist of them all. Deeper, too, than most people think. Do you play Chopin?"

Callicott leaned across the piano and listened heavily. His eyes were slightly bloodshot now, and he smelled strongly of whisky.

"Isn't he wonderful?" Jamie's voice shook.

Parris looked doubtful. "I don't know if he is or not."

"Why, Parris, he is wonderful. He's a poet, and he sees things a poet's way. He doesn't care for money, or success, or fame, or—or anything like that. He just loves beautiful things."

"Well—I don't—"

"Oh, Parris. You've just got to understand him and like him. I'm like that, too. I expect you'll laugh at me, but I know I'm a poet. I'm sure."

"Don't you want to be famous, and make money, and everything?"

"No. I don't care. I want to write poetry, and I want them to let me alone— at home, I mean."

"What do they do to you?"

"They're after me all the time!"

Jamie's face began to work. "They're going to make me go to a business college, and learn shorthand and typewriting, and book-keeping and all that terrible stuff. I can't stand it! I won't do it!' I'll—"

"What?" Parris tried to speak quietly and naturally, but he was embarrassed.

"I guess I won't run away. I'm too big a coward to do anything. But I'll kill myself."

"Oh, you won't either. Listen, Jamie, I've been reading a lot about poets and writers in my literature classes in school. An awful lot of them—"

"I know what you are going to say. They had dull jobs, but they wrote anyhow."

"Yes, that's true."

"Well, I can't. It would kill me. Look at Robert."

"What's the matter with him?"

"What's the *matter* with him?"

"Yes, he can write all he wants to, can't he?"

"Oh, Parris, I thought you'd understand!"

The first visit to Robert Callicott disturbed Parris. The next week he decided he would talk to Herr Berdorff. Vera Lichinsky was finishing her violin lesson when he arrived. He slipped quietly into the pastor's study and listened. Herr Berdorff nodded but he did not speak. Vera was playing an unaccompanied Bach sonata. Again and again Herr Berdorff shook his great head. He spoke in a tumultuous mixture of German and English.

"No, no!" he shouted. "Strict! Strict! You do not have to make the expression. All the expression is already in the notes if you play correct. You and your sloppy Polish temperament! You make such a *Traurigkeit* over nothing, such a—such a *to-do* for a simple cadence. Listen, such a making of expression you cannot in Bach. On the page he has said it. Play that and no more. Fine tone, and in time, but this whining with your fiddle—Polish, that's

what it is, Polish, complaining always about everything all the way up to *Gott!*
Now, once more, simple—keep the excitement *oudt....*"

Vera listened with passionate attention. Her round eyes were fixed on
her teacher's face as if she were drawing the words from him. Never for a
second did she lose a kind of detachment. There was nothing personal in this
denunciation of the Polish temperament. She was used to that. It was merely
an inferiority, like her weak fourth finger, a handicap to be overcome. On that
score she was completely insensitive.

"So. Iss better. Now, for Saturday ..."

Herr Berdorff was smiling. His rages were merely a part of his teaching
method. He turned to Parris. "She does well, this *Kindchen*. In two years more
she goes to Berlin, and her teacher will say: 'This Berdorff—this country
preacher, he iss no clodhopper.'"

Vera departed in a sort of meager glow. She seemed to be a really colorless
child, blindly obedient, humorless, and pathetically in earnest. She practiced
endless hours, and had no recreations. But there was a subtle transformation
in her when she played. One felt that this was not so much Vera herself as
something or someone from long ago speaking out at last—inheritance,
maybe—poetry and disaster, injury and defeat—a thin thread burning under
the generations like the survival of fire under heavy falls of leaves, breaking out
at last in a clear and luminous flame.

She and her violin seemed to belong together. Even unmusical observers
saw this and were moved. Berdorff was an excellent teacher and Vera's playing
was better than anyone, except Berdorff himself, knew.

"I want to ask you some questions, Herr Berdorff, if you please?"

"*Ja*, what now? Go ahead."

Parris related the story of his visit to Robert Callicott. At the first mention
of Callicott's name, Herr Berdorff turned an apoplectic red.

"*Ach*, that—that—"

Parris waited until the sputtering subsided. Finally, after many exclamations
and interruptions from the *Herr Doktor,* he managed somehow to pose his
questions about what Callicott called "the way of music."

Berdorff's eyes glittered behind his gold-rimmed glasses. He controlled
himself with a ludicrously righteous effort that was more violent than an
explosion. He wagged his head.

"It iss a good thing that you ask me this, because this man with, his
Pfuscherei knows nothing—nothing! He comes one time here to me and wants
to play with me. He plays everything like a drunken gypsy—" Berdorff laughed
bitterly. "Like a drunken gypsy, sure enough, it wass. Of music—real music, he
knows nothing. Now, mark me, Parris, music like any art iss first of all—*order.*"

Parris listened intently. Herr Berdorff was a giant of a man. His thick
black hair shook in every direction, and his eyes, magnified behind shining
lenses, sparkled and burned with intensity. He inclined his great frame forward

and tapped Parris' knee as he talked. His extreme sincerity and earnestness reminded Parris of the thunderous German sermons he had heard in the little Lutheran church. He was impressed, far more deeply than he had been by Robert Callicott's rhapsodic outbursts. Still—a little corner of his mind held stubbornly to some phrases of Callicott's talk. Maybe, a little—a little here and there—maybe Callicott could have little bits of right that even Herr Berdorff didn't know. But this—his mind came back hard and sharp to attention—this must be right. It sounded so—so dignified, so sure—like that Bach sonata Vera played—like the firm, sure heaven in its perfect curve over the earth.

"Is Chopin a very great composer?" Parris edged the question in.

Herr Berdorff glared, expelled his breath contemptuously, and laughed as at a child's question.

"Beethoven iss the greatest composer," he said simply.

"And Mozart, is he a great composer, too?"

Berdorff laid his finger beside his nose. "Now—Mozart. Mozart iss—well, he is a German composer, and already that iss something. Of course he iss a great composer, more *lieblich* than Bach, but always there iss something a little too childlike in Mozart...."

And so the afternoon ran on. Berdorff talking with the hungry eagerness of a learned man who has been long without understanding companionship. Parris listening with the flattered anxiety of a newcomer to adult experience.

And so, too, there were resolving about Parris, and in his mind the collisions and conflicts of his growing and contradictory work.

He found that he was altogether happy in this bewildering expansion and change. Only ... there was a lack: he needed someone to share it. Drake couldn't, and Jamie didn't want to. He had no one.

In midwinter Drake's Uncle Rhodes died, and his aunt had a stroke shortly afterward. Plans were being made to close the house and to remove Mrs. Livingstone to a sanitarium.

"What are you going to do?" Parris asked when Drake told him about it.

Drake looked a little forlorn under a thin bravado.

"I guess they'll send me to live at Mrs. Searcy's boardinghouse."

"Oh."

Drake tried to appear casual. "I'll be my own boss then, and I can do as I please."

"Haven't you got any kinfolks?"

"Yes, I guess so. I bet none of them would want *me* around though. Say, it will feel pretty funny not to have a home any more. I expect I'll like it though."

Parris couldn't think of anything to say. The two boys walked slowly out Federal Street. Today, faced with the imminence of a new kind of life, Drake looked much older than Parris. His freckles had thinned as he grew up, and just now he looked a little pale. The thick lashes shadowing his dark gray eyes, his overfull lips, and his look of extreme vitality still gave him an air of strength and sensuality almost animal. But it was an attractive air. His gaze was direct, and his wide smile was frank and quick. He seemed much more open and straightforward than Parris whose play of expression was subtler, and more fleeting. Unless Parris was actually smiling he looked troubled—a look that was often mistaken for bad humor.

"Say, Parris, you and I are mighty near in the same fix. Did you ever think of that?"

"How do you mean?"

"No father or mother, either one of us, no close kin. When your grandma dies you'll be all by yourself in the world, too."

"Yes, I know that."

Parris' head went down and he slid his hands deeper into his pockets.

Drake continued more cheerfully. "I'll have forty thousand dollars when I'm twenty-one."

"Will you, sure enough?"

"Sure; and nobody to say anything about the way I spend it. I guess you'll have more'n that, won't you, when your grandma dies?"

"I don't know. I never thought about it."

"Sure you will. I heard Uncle Rhodes say your place out there was worth a lot of money. It's got a mortgage on it, though, did you know that?"

"I've heard my grandmother say something about it."

"'Tain't much, though. When the place is sold, you can pay it off and have a lot left. It's nothing. You know people borrow money to make improvements and things like that."

"How did you know about it?"

"Oh, I don't know. Everybody knows everything about everybody's business in this town."

"Well, I don't."

"You're a peculiar kind of a kid, anyhow, Parris."

"How, Drake? I wish you'd tell me."

"I don't know, just peculiar. I like you all right, though. You know that." This was unusual from Drake.

"You know, Parris, what I think I'll do?"

"What?"

"Soon's I get my money I think I'll buy an interest in something or other and work hard, and in a couple of years get married."

Parris was stunned for a moment. Getting married was something he never had thought about. He looked respectfully at Drake.

"Sure enough, Drake?"

"Yep. Got the girl picked out, too."

"Who? Cassie Tower?"

"Lord, no. Her old man won't let you get in a mile of her. I'll tell you, but keep this to yourself—"

"Of course."

"Louise Gordon!"

"Oh."

"What's the matter? Don't you like her?"

"Why, of course, I guess I do. I don't know her any more. Ever since I dropped out of school I don't know many people."

"That's so, I guess. You do kind of live to yourself, don't you?"

"It isn't because I want to."

"Is that why you go around with Jamie Wakefield all the time?"

"I don't. I don't see him once a month."

"He's always talking about you."

"Is he? I guess I like Jamie all right."

"Aw, Jamie's all right. A little sissy, but that don't hurt anybody."

Parris glanced quickly at Drake to see if there was any meaning behind this offhand remark. But Drake's face showed nothing.

"I go with Jamie to see Robert Callicott every once in a while."

"Yeh. You told me that before Christmas. How you like him?"

"All right. He's interesting."

"Interesting, eh? That sounds just like you. Say, do you know about Robert Callicott and Ludie Sims?"

"That Mrs. Sims that drives the pony carriage?"

"Yes. Lives out on the State Road. Well, Bob Callicott goes out there all the time."

"What for?"

Drake laughed. "Well, what do you think for?"

"I don't know."

"Jiminy crickets, Parris! Ludie Sims' husband takes care of the asylum greenhouses. He ain't home much."

Parris couldn't think of anything to say about this. He had to make an abrupt mental adjustment to this new aspect of Robert Callicott. He had no doubt of the correctness of Drake's information. Drake was usually right, and he didn't bother to tell lies.

"Say, Parris, listen. You know the Ross girls—live next to McGurney's store? Well, listen now …"

A familiar expression came into Drake's face, somewhat the look of a gleeful faun. There was contagion in that expression, and in the ribald comment that ran with it. Parris laughed. When he was with Drake his own life seemed dull and childish. Drake had adventures, real adventures. A mood of recklessness answered to the recital of them, and Parris felt his throat tighten as he listened. He knew that later he would draw back through sheer timidity from any share in these wild plans, but just now he was ready to go anywhere and try anything with Drake.

He brought the conversation back to Mrs. Sims. His curiosity had been stirred because of Robert Callicott.

"Drake, is she—a—a regular?—"

"No, I don't think so. Just likes to have some fun like everybody else. She's good-looking for an old married woman. I wouldn't mind going after her myself."

This time Parris was really horrified. The thought was actually embarrassing. Drake saw that it was. He gave Parris a sounding thump on the back.

"You're a fool sometimes, kid. Don't miss all the good times. You go around with me, and I'll show you something. I want to try everything before I get married and settle down. Say, how about Cassie Tower? How did you happen to mention her a while ago?"

"I just happened to think of her."

"You go there all the time, don't you, to see her old man?"

"I never see her any more, though—just once in a while."

"That's the prettiest girl around here. Gee, wouldn't I like to take her out some night."

"I thought you said you were in love with Louise."

"Oh—I guess I'll marry Louise. That's different." Drake's tone changed, and somehow forbade further inquiry in that direction.

"Why don't you go after old Cass yourself? I think she used to like you a whole lot."

"I don't know."

"You're a funny kid, Parris. First thing you know you're going to be like Jamie Wakefield. Say, did he ever try to get funny with you?"

"How do you mean?" But Parris' question was hesitant as if he were afraid of the answer. Drake looked keenly at him, and Parris felt a slow red burning his face. Drake roared.

"I see you know all about him. Did he get you to go up to Sunset Walk with him?"

Parris' eyes opened very wide with astonishment. Drake flung his arm over Parris' shoulder and mimicked Jamie's slightly lingering speech. "Oh, Parris, look at the moonlight! It looks like Italy, and that house away off there is a villa. Isn't it romantic?"

Parris laughed, too, but a bit reluctantly. Drake was half serious again. "Better watch out for him, though. Too much of Jamie ain't good for anybody."

"I really like Jamie, though, Drake—a lot better than I did at first."

"Oh, he's all right. Just crazy in his pants, that's all. Gosh, ain't he a pretty boy when you come to think of it? He kind of gets me some way or other. If he was a girl I'd go for him—or her—or whatever it would be! Say—it's a hell of a funny thing about Jamie. You don't know how to take him, do you?"

Parris nodded. He knew that his face was still flaming. Drake thwacked him again. "Don't let old Jamie bother you. All of us know about Jamie. Now, listen, 'bout Poppy and Jinny Ross—what do you say?"

"Oh, I don't know, Drake!"

Drake's dancing eyes turned serious again. "Look a-here, kid. Ain't you never—?"

Drake stopped as he saw the flush fade suddenly in Parris' face. "What's the matter with you? You're all white around the mouth. Sick?"

Parris shook his head. "No. I'm all right, I guess. I've got to go on home, though."

"Aw, say—did what I say make you mad or something?"

"No, of course not."

"Well, then—what I asked you—did you? Ever?"

Parris tried to be casual. "Oh, of course I have."

Drake laughed. "Count on *you!*"

Parris tried to grin, tried to be offhand and easy. Drake went on persistently. "I'm going to see the Ross girls. They're hot stuff. I'll fix it up for us some night."

"You'll let me know?" The words came with some difficulty and sounded weak.

"Sure, sure." Drake was hearty and frank as if this were the most ordinary agreement in the world. He punched Parris once or twice. "Oh, boy," he said. "Oh, boy!"

"So long, Drake."

"S'long, kid." He turned and went quickly back along the street, whistling very loud.

Parris pulled his muffler tighter and buttoned his overcoat across his throat. He hadn't realized how cold the wind was, but a slight perspiration stood on his brow.

A thick scurry of gray-blue clouds was coming up, and a strong wind poured over the rim of the western rise toward the prairies. From beyond that rim the wind blew straight across a thousand miles of level snow. Parris stopped, as he always did, at the beginning of the long sloping road that passed the Aberdeen campus, to look at the wide landscape spread out before him. The snowy fields and hills were taking on a bluish shade in the early twilight; the lines of fences, the clusters of small wooden buildings about each home, were blots of black. His imagination quickened a little at the familiar picture. He used to think of it as looking like northern countries of Europe in the Middle Ages, or Russia, maybe. Today he was less fanciful. It looked like itself, and nothing more. That was the Macintosh barn, the corncrib, the smokehouse, the tool shelter. Everything seemed to shrink, too. The steady light burning there to the northwest was in the Davis kitchen. It was less than a mile away. The road, cut into a deep crisscross of ruts and ridges, curved out past the Yancey farm, past Robert Callicott's home, and on—to Camperville and Fielding. He thought of a silly sentence he used to say: "The long winding road that led through the frozen wastes to Riga." He used to repeat this again and again as he looked at rough country roads in the winter. He didn't know where the sentence came from, or if he had made it up. In summer he changed it to say: "That led straight to the heart of Auvergne." He was uncertain where Auvergne might be—whether it was in France or Spain. These sentences used to be magical. Jamie would understand why he said them.

He turned the collar of his ulster high about his face and walked backward for a few steps to avoid the wind that cut his face. The muffler about his chin was wet from his breath.

He was exceedingly uncomfortable but still he did not hurry his steps. These winter evenings outside of the town had a sort of grandeur about them. He was on lower ground now, and the wind lost some of its violence. He could hear it roar overhead. The top branches of the trees were flung tumultuously back and forth. Parris began to dramatize himself now. "A lonely figure ..." He shaped the words with his lips and half said them. "A lonely figure, wrapped from head to foot in a heavy greatcoat ..." "Greatcoat"—that was nice: no one said "greatcoat" nowadays. "... Wrapped in a heavy greatcoat, moved slowly along the deserted road." He suited his steps to the picture in his mind. "Who was he? Where was he going?" It was a game he had played a thousand times, but today the enchantment of a complete make-believe refused to materialize. He made a face. He was really too grown up even to try such childish tricks. It was just the same old road home—the same familiar landscape. Summer and winter. He tried to recall exactly what it looked like in summer. For an instant everything spun around in his head, the way the earth and sky seemed to spin when you turn a somerset. He recalled something else, too, as he made the season whirl— the picture of Renée as she used to trot along this road with him on the way home from school. The recollection shot through him like a physical pain. Renée, shabby and little, and something else that squeezed his chest at the thought of her. Just her sweet way of not doing or saying much of anything, maybe. He remembered so much and the pictures rushed at him so fast that he felt breathless.

He turned around and walked backward again—a fine drive of sleet had begun and it stung his face like fire ... she was somewhere—right now. At this very minute, somewhere in the world. She was talking, or studying her lessons, or helping her mother, or laughing—would she be laughing, maybe? Could she be somewhere laughing while he was thinking so hard about her, and remembering, and feeling so terrible? He tried hard to separate the many mental pictures of her—to see her as she stood in the moonlight that night of his birthday supper, and said: "I like to be your girl. I guess you're my sweetheart, too." She was such a baby. That was when he was fourteen. She was—he stopped, startled by a new thought. Why! He was seventeen now, and—Renée was *sixteen!* That meant she was a big girl—growing up, tall, maybe, like Cassandra. Oh, gee!—he hadn't thought of that. In all of this time it had never occurred to him that Renée could ever change. Maybe she was prettier than ever, maybe she didn't think about him any more. Maybe she had a sweetheart. No: he couldn't face that thought. He knew she thought about him just as he thought about her.... "*Let's be sweethearts forever, Renée, you and me ...all right ... cross your heart? ...*"

Parris forgot the sleet whipping across his face. He could hear her soft half-whisper—"*... and hope to die.*"

No—no—no: she wouldn't forget, she *couldn't!*

The wind was increasing, the sleet was mixed with snow. It was thickening fast. "I guess we're going to have a blizzard, maybe." Parris said the words aloud. He was actually loitering: sometimes he stopped and frowned hard; then he walked sidewise or backward to shelter his face. But he was wholly lost in his thinking.

Renée! What was he to do about it? He'd have to find her someday. Someday, when he had money of his own. And then—Drake's startling phrase crossed his mind. And then—why then, he might get married. A kind of dismay swooped at him. Would he ever find her? He was sure Drake could help him when the time came. Drake was adventurous and practical. But, maybe—no, he was not so sure about Drake. He was not sure what Drake would think of Renée. The children at school used to call her a "tacky" child. He remembered the time he had slapped Billy Morris for saying it ... a fierce loyalty fired up in him suddenly. What did he care what anybody said or thought about anything?

It was getting dark now. He walked faster. Sometimes he leaned so hard against the wind that he stumbled into the shallow ditch. He held his head down as far as he could and hurried. As soon as he crossed the narrow footbridge over the creek it would be easier going. The double row of great birches along the drive that bent about his grandmother's place sheltered one a little. They seemed always to break the force of the powerful northwest winds. The trees twisted and cracked tonight, but beneath their interlacing branches it was calmer. He would soon be at home now.

As he edged up the long slippery terrace steps he thought of Drake's disquieting remark: "*You and I are mighty near in the same fix.*"

This solid house and these secure acres of ground—they could pass away and belong to someone else. Drake had so casually said: "*When the place is sold.*" It would be his when his grandmother died. Maybe he wouldn't let them sell it. Maybe he'd just keep it and try to run it as she did. But then he wouldn't be able to be a doctor, and he had to be a doctor. She wanted him to be, and of course he would do as she wished.

He took a deep breath and shook himself. His "greatcoat" was white with snow. "Gee!" he muttered. "I wonder what's going to become of me."

Madame von Eln sat by the fire. It was late, and Parris had gone upstairs to study. She knew that Anna was in the kitchen waiting for her to go to bed. Usually she felt a little uncomfortable when she kept anyone waiting. She made a little gesture of annoyance. Tonight Anna would have to be patient.

The room was warm, though the fire was low now. The sound of the wind rose and fell in long sighs and howls. Madame wanted to think. She shook her head. No, she didn't want to think. She only wanted to sit there and remember. There hadn't been much time in her life for such a luxury—there was no real time for it now, but here, at this moment, when there was nothing else to do, she could indulge herself. Again she shook her head with a little air of self-admonition. Remembering would be a doubtful luxury. There was little to enjoy, even in retrospect, in that past.

Madame kept up a lively play of expression as she half directed her thoughts. Sometimes she made the beginnings of gestures. Her fingers moved and tiny fires danced from her diamond rings. Her face reflected now an amused ruefulness. No: even as an old lady she could not enjoy any of the orthodox pleasures and pastimes of age. To sit by the fire and dream—no, not yet. Never, perhaps. Quite surely, never. There was still too much to do.

She tried very hard to be reminiscent, but it was not successful. Certain pictures, clear enough, perhaps, but unrelated one to another, were all that she could summon up from her youth. The present had always been too pressing with its immediate and practical problems. She had no talent for remembering.

The uneventful years of her girlhood; a first marriage and the birth of Parris' mother; the second marriage to the picturesque but unstable Franz von Eln; von Eln's crazy project of establishing a German wine-making colony in this western state; his death; her own first struggle; the ensuing poverty; the practical help and advice of Thurston St. George, Mason Thill, and others; the deaths of Parris' father and mother—how many deaths one counted in a lifetime!—and these happiest years of all her life with Parris to watch over. The broken reflections flickered in her unwilling recollection. Now—this time—this day was more important, and more interesting.

People had praised her for courage and marveled at her successes. She deserved little credit for those, she was sure. Help, encouragement, the labors of others, and—luck. She had never been courageous. She knew this. She had merely refused to look backward. She had refused equally to look too far forward. Now she was forced to think about a future—not her own (there was too little of that left to bother much about), but Parris' future which was of utmost concern to her.

Her face drew in on itself a little more as she went over her various plans and arrangements. Her fingers played restlessly. She wouldn't like anyone to know how little courage she had had—how little courage she had now.

She had always been afraid—of first one thing and then another. Now she was afraid that she would be unable to make adequate provision for the one person in the world she loved. She was afraid of something else, too; but she could make sure that no one would find out about it. She was afraid of pain, and she was afraid of death. Not of what lay beyond—she knew there was nothing there—but of the processes of dissolution. She had come through many practical difficulties, but she had always had help. She had met a good many dark days, but her secret strength had been something of a falsity. She lived through such bleak times by not thinking much about them. Most of the anticipated catastrophes never arrived, and those which did befall were usually different from expectations. But pain could not be shared. Death she would have to meet alone.

She wondered a little just why she so much wanted to live. Parris? Yes, of course. Because he loved her, but more because she loved him. She thought of him and smiled. Then she dozed ... yes, and because she liked to see the wind moving the tops of the maple trees ...

She waked—the fire was very low, and the room was chilly. She had never liked the dark, or the cold. For just a moment she turned her head sideways and whimpered against the quilted cushion....

She called Anna.

"Yes, Madame. You are ready for bed now, yes?"

"No, Anna. I have to think. Fix the fire."

"Think? Madame! You are going to think at this time of night?"

Madame laughed—a slightly rising cadence of her habitual gaiety. "Don't you ever think, Anna?"

"Me, Madame? I think all the time." Anna laid the logs on the coals and sat back on her heels. "Me, I always think."

"What about?"

Anna looked bewildered, and slightly annoyed. She made a widely inclusive gesture. "Everything, Madame."

"About the future—about what's going to become of you?"

Anna frowned. She assumed a puzzled air. "What could become of me? I stay with you, I take care of you until—" She bit her lip sharply.

"Until when, Anna?"

"Always, Madame," she concluded simply.

"Anna, you are good. I haven't deserved to have anyone be so good to me—"

Anna's face screwed up in a rather ludicrous effort not to cry.

"Now Anna, I don't want you to cry. I don't like to see people cry. You know that."

Anna turned to the fire and raked the ashes from beneath the grate. "Yes, Madame."

"Well, now, Anna, I was just wondering what *would* become of you when—when I'm not here any more?"

"Oh, Madame—"

"Let's don't be silly, Anna. You have been here with me for thirty-two years. It's time, if ever, that we can talk without being—well, like this."

"Very well, Madame. What do you wish to say?"

"Have you any money, Anna?"

"Yes, Madame. I have saved everything. I—I shall—should be able to take care of myself."

"Good. You were always sensible. I shan't leave a great deal, and there is Parris' education. Sit down, Anna."

Anna drew a hassock near the fire. She looked practical now. Affairs—managing—these were matters she understood. Madame's eyes twinkled. Anna had exactly her Monday-morning house-cleaning look.

"Madame, who will look after Parris?"

Madame drew her shoulders together a little as though a chill draft struck her. "He will have to look after himself, Anna. He's a good boy—I suppose."

"Parris is a good boy." Anna spoke with undoubting emphasis.

Madame laughed again. The rising note was more apparent this time.

Madame was more comfortable when she could talk to someone. Thinking was difficult.

"I hope so, Anna, I hope so. I think he is some kind of a gentleman. I shouldn't expect him to be an angel—or want him to be."

Anna ignored this. "Madame, you do not expect him to be alone—for a long time yet." She was not quite able to keep the question out of her voice.

Madame answered as though it had been a question. "I don't know, Anna. No one can tell. I shan't live very long—maybe a year or so."

Anna started from her seat. "*Gott*—"

Madame held up her hand. "I'm nearly seventy, Anna, and I have—oh, so many things wrong with me. It seems, Anna, that nothing inside of me is working very well any more. It's a question which will stop first and make an end."

"Has Dr. Gordon said—?"

"He gives me one year, or two."

"I don't believe it."

Madame shrugged. "Perhaps we need not believe him; but we shall have to plan and act as if we did."

"Yes, I suppose that is prudent." Suddenly Anna was near to tears again. "What can I do for you, Madame, quickly?"

"Nothing, Anna. Just go on as if everything were the same as always. I don't want Parris to be disturbed—"

"He doesn't know about this?"

"He must not know, Anna. We must be as gay as possible, plan things, and appear to be happy. His studies—I want him to do very well. Now, go to bed."

"You are not going to bed yourself?"

"Not yet."

"Then I will wait." She arose and smoothed her apron. "I'll just set some bread. Might as well bake tomorrow."

Madame smiled affectionately at Anna, whose broad kind face had resumed its accustomed tranquility. They understood each other well. It would not be necessary to say any more on the subject.

Anna moved with decision. "I think I'll make salt-rising this time."

The fire crackled and the room was alive with the moving light. Madame felt much better. She held up her thin brown hands toward the flame. The glow rimmed each finger with a line of transparent red. She felt for her glasses and put them on. She seemed absorbed in studying her hands—like a child. The veins stood in clear relief. Odd. The pattern was slightly different on the two hands. She had never noticed that! She pressed hard on one hand with the fingers of the other. Four white spots showed on the warm olive skin. They showed white for a long time. Very slowly the blood crept back, but she could still see the spots, a little paler than the surrounding area. Probably a sign of something, or a symptom. Probably not a very good sign, either, she thought. All signs are bad in the shadow of disaster.

She continued to play with her fingers, but she no longer saw them. She was beginning to wonder about Parris. Her own phrase—"He is a good boy—I suppose"—came back to mind. What did she really know about this boy who was the central idol of her heart? Very little, really. He had good manners, a quick and responsive sympathy, and a good mind. "I suppose," she spoke the words aloud. Oh, of course, of course he had a good mind! She had been reassured on that point by everyone.

But what was he like, deeper down than the surface? What did he dream of, look forward to? What did he desire?

The answers to these questions—these all-important questions—would not come from Parris or from her observation of him. Her own training had given him an exterior that communicated little, for all its seemingly expressive vivacity. Now, as she thought of it, she realized that he was far less vivacious than he used to be. Growing up, becoming a young man— adolescence. Adolescence. She didn't remember that anyone used that word when she was young. She couldn't recall just when she first knew exactly what it meant. People said it—Dr. Gordon and Dr. Tower—as though it covered a whole world of mysterious things. Now what, really, was mysterious about it? She tried to remember her own growing up. Growing up. You simply became more like older people, thought less childishly, and became interested in the opposite sex. Rather silly, too, about that time. And full of curiosity. But she had married early, and the mysteries were of short duration.

Parris was less lively. He talked a good deal but less gaily. He was—she hunted for a description—he was darker. Yes: that described him exactly. She wondered why. She must observe him a bit more closely. Maybe she had been neglecting him a little. He came and went as he pleased. She was vaguely disturbed to realize that she didn't know much about his friends, or where he went.

She would try to understand him better. Where she would find her answer—that was another matter. Not in Parris, she thought again, no; not in herself, because they were quite unlike. She tried to recall her daughter, Parris' mother. A slight shade crossed her face. She realized that it had been a long time since she had thought of Marian. The curious expression on Madame's face deepened. It seemed part reluctance—reluctance to think of her daughter at all, part pity and regret. She had never understood Marian very well. Marian had been like her erratic young father—hardheaded, rebellious, but with little of his quick changefulness and ready affection. She had never really liked Marian much. That was doubtless unnatural. Madame moved petulantly in her chair. A child was an accident. There was no more reason for loving a child than there was for a child loving a parent. So often children did not love parents. No, she hadn't really liked Marian. As for Marian's father—wasn't it strange that she remembered his characteristics so well but couldn't recall exactly how he had looked?

Obviously, she wouldn't be able to understand Parris through his mother. Parris' father, Sumter Mitchell—what an attractive boy he had been! A simple, forthright person—pretty much what people called "typically American," whatever it was that they meant by that. Anyway, he must have given Parris good qualities—more solid ones, she had no doubt, than Parris had from her own blood.

It might have been better if Parris could have had less of her own "foreign" ways, and more of the Mitchell manner. She knew that people commented on her bearing and conduct and thought her peculiar and alien. That was silly. Her family had been in America long before the Revolution. Languages had simply been a tradition of the family. She wondered if speaking foreign languages gave one foreign ways. Maybe, to some extent. She gesticulated, and most people didn't. Parris did, too. Then, of course, Franz von Eln had really been a foreigner. She found this hard to realize now. He had been an interesting person with his extreme enthusiasms and wild schemes. Yes; she had loved Franz von Eln, but he had been pretty difficult in those last years. Drank too much and, like most Germans, was quick-tempered and belligerent when he was drunk. Life, even with all of its practical difficulties, had been better after his death. It was inconsistent, of course, the way she leaned this way and that for help, and yet had to keep a certain independence in order to be happy.

Too close trammels of any kind irked her—more than irked her, she thought. They made her crazy. Parris, maybe, had something of that in him. Well, she had left a wide circle of freedom about him—mental elbowroom, just as she demanded, and had to have, for herself. He had been happier because of that, she was sure.

She had tried to keep that circle cleared of the very elements and factors which had crowded and cramped her own early years—those elements ... she brought herself to a mental standstill for a moment. Why ... yes, it was true. That crowding in on her by family and relatives, that continuous invasion of herself—it was that which had pushed her into her precipitate first marriage. She hadn't escaped, however. She had merely exchanged one kind of mental clutter for another. Then her second marriage—oh, dear, that had been a life! ... She had had to achieve her mental elbowroom, achieve it and hold it. She hoped she had been tactful, and wise, in these matters with Parris—she who had never been really wise in anything.

... And she had taught him good manners. From the first she had been determined to hold her own small fortress against the thoughtless crudity of this Western World. She had determined to live here that she might be independent and escape return to stuffy relatives, but she had been equally determined not to become too close-woven a part of the kind of life she observed about her. The older men—almost pioneers, they had been— Thurston St. George, Isaac Skeffington, and the others—had been more nearly her kind She hadn't liked the women—still didn't like them, and the women of Kings Row had not liked her. That attitude had changed for the greater part. She had been respected at last, and held the respect, but in earning respect she had lost feminine friendships. Not that she had ever cared! All she wanted was to be left alone. Men were superior to women, anyway. Men like Thurston St. George and Isaac Skeffington kept their Eastern manner much better than their wives had. They were better company. She quirked an eyebrow and smiled. She quite simply preferred men. And that was the way it should be.

But Parris ... she brought her wandering attention back with an effort. She must look the whole question of Parris' rearing full in the face. She wanted most eagerly to reassure herself.

I'm not fooling myself even now, she thought. I'm just trying to be pleasant to myself. She moved her lips, following inaudibly the words of her thinking.

Her threatened ills she forgot for the moment. She was not sure, anyway, just what the threats were. Doctors were vague, always,, and used words she didn't understand. She never asked about anything she didn't understand, fearing it might prove embarrassing. She had never been able to discuss ailments and organs freely, not even with the doctor. Now she realized that her knowledge of her own interior geography was extremely sketchy. Just as well, she decided—she'd think about it if she knew. Anyway, it was Dr. Gordon's business. At this illogical conclusion, she arose, and went to the kitchen. Anna had "set" the bread, and was spreading a white cloth over the huge crock. She placed it on a chair near the open oven door, adjusted the damper of the big wood stove, and picked up the lamp.

She smiled at Madame. She had worked away the force of her initial dismay, and presented now her ordinary and restored face. Madame smiled, too.

"Ready, Madame, yes?"

"Yes, Anna. I am tired."

"Good. We will go to bed."

Anna laid her firm, shiny hand under Madame's elbow, and the two women went slowly up the stairs.

Parris came to his door frowning against the light of the unshaded lamp Anna carried. Madame shook her head. "You are up late."

"So are you, both of you."

"You are studying at this time of night?"

"I'm up late every night, *Grand'mère*—you know that."

"I saw those new books. So thick and so heavy. Do you have to read all of them?"

He laughed and walked toward her room with her. "I guess those books are just a beginning."

"Don't work too hard. I believe you look pale. Do you think he is pale, Anna?"

"I think Parris is all right, Madame."

"Well, well. But you must get your sleep. Good night."

He kissed her on both cheeks. "Good night. Good night, Anna." He sighed as he returned to his room. He was tired. There was so much to do every day. Work at Aberdeen was not easy, Dr. Tower demanded that he cover a lot of ground; and his music—he didn't want to neglect practice.

He walked to the mirror and looked closely. Maybe he was a little pale. He tried several serious expressions to see which was best. He was really growing up now. His talks with Herr Berdorff and his reading with Doctor Tower gave him a new sense of importance. He tried another face before the mirror—a serious one. That was a pretty good one, he decided—he must remember how it felt so that he could assume it at any time. He hoped he would meet Cassandra on the street some day. He would put on that look and bow very gravely as if he were deeply abstracted. He seldom saw her but she, more than Drake ever had, made him self-conscious and uncertain. He practiced the bow and the greeting for a moment, and turned again to his worktable. The book was thick and heavy, as Madame had said, and the old-fashioned type was small and spiteful. He turned the pages, looking at the hundreds of them to be read, and sighed again as he rested his head on his hand. The assumed expression of gravity faded, and his face looked more like that of a little boy than he would have believed possible.

Parris worked hard throughout the winter. He felt that he had moved completely into a new world. He did indeed look thin and a little pale by April.

Dr. Tower, who consistently maintained an impersonal attitude toward his pupil, noticed the changes.

"Better ease up on your work a little, young man."

"Oh, I'm quite all right, sir."

"You don't look it. Leave your notebooks today and get out somewhere. Why don't you walk? Look up some of your friends—"

Dr. Tower's quick eye caught the slight change of expression on Parris' face.

"What's the matter, boy? Don't want to go out?"

"I don't think so. I walk to and from home every day, often twice. It's quite a way."

"Need to see some other boys—rowdy around a little. Do you good."

Parris looked straight into Dr. Tower's eyes for a moment. There was a barely perceptible softening of the Doctor's hard, bright gaze.

"What is it?" Then he added jocularly: "Have you no friends?"

Parris did not smile. "No, sir," he said simply.

Dr. Tower flushed a little, whether with embarrassment or annoyance at the turn of the conversation, Parris did not know. He added quickly: "I'm awfully busy, you know, with everything outside of my schoolwork."

"Yes, yes, I know. Won't hurt you to work hard. You'll realize the benefits quickly enough. Even a little loneliness won't hurt you to speak of."

Dr. Tower looked out of the window. "You get used to it."

Parris did not reply to this. Dr. Tower looked back after a moment and went on, almost angrily: "Anyway, there is nobody around here for you. You seem to have a mind—hope I'm not mistaken about it: I'd hate to waste my time. You wouldn't get much from a lot of oafs."

"I used to have some pretty good friends." There was a kind of protest in his voice. "I guess I haven't now. I don't get to see them often enough."

"Well—you ought not to live too much to yourself." Dr. Tower spoke more gently. "Go on out today and look up somebody. Knock around a little." He slapped the notebooks on the table. "Forget this and your piano for a couple of days, cut classes, get some air."

"All right, sir, I will. Thank you."

He walked down the drive that skirted the Towers' front yard. Cassandra was on the porch. He waved gaily to her, and she lifted her hand in an awkward, childish response. It did not occur to him to stop and talk to her. He looked back when he reached the street. She had dropped her book in her lap and was still looking at him. He waved again. This time she merely nodded and turned quickly to her reading.

Parris looked up and down the street. The trees were nearly in full leaf. Only a powdery sprinkle of sun dotted the soft brick walk. There were smells in the air, damp, warm smells, and a thin acrid hint of old leaves rotting in corners and under shrubbery. He felt very lighthearted and happy. It was Monday and Drake might be at home. He turned into Federal Street and walked toward Drake's house. He turned again. Union Street was even prettier than Walnut. The wide-arching maples were pink and green, and the top twigs glinted like silver. The lawns were green, and freshly mounded flower beds showed rows and circles of young plants, some of them still limp and spindly from their transplanting.

It was early afternoon, and Union Street in the residence section was deserted. Later a few surreys, pony carriages, and buggies would pass on afternoon drives.

As he came in sight of the Livingstone house he saw Drake coming out of the drive. He had Molly, a fat old mare belonging to Mrs. Livingstone, hitched to a shiny new buggy.

"Hey! Hey, Drake!"

Drake was about to turn in the other direction, when he heard him. He stopped. "Why you old country stick-in-the-mud! Where have you been all of this time? I haven't seen you all winter. Hop in."

"Where you going?"

"Nowhere. Just trying the new buggy. How you like it?"

"Fine. Brand-new?"

"Yep. I'm going to buy a good-looking horse, too. I can't drive this old stack of bones with a new buggy."

Parris laughed. "I'd say her bones were pretty well out of sight."

"Say, how you been? What all you been doing?"

Parris took a deep breath. "Oh, working hard."

"You look like you been sick."

"No. I'm all right."

"Why aren't you in school today?"

"No classes today. Dr. Tower sent me out, said I needed—said I needed to see you."

"Aw, now!"

"Almost. Said I better go out and see some of my friends."

"Let's go to the country. How about it?" Drake looked pleased.

"Fine. Let's. I'd like to. If I hadn't found you I'd have had to go home."

"Why?"

"Because I haven't any other friends."

"Aw, stuff." Drake jeered. He slapped Parris on the leg. "Let's drive out past the asylum and on out the State Road."

"All right. Suits me."

Parris settled back. The new buggy had rubber tires and rolled softly along the macadamized street.

"How's Louise, Drake?"

Drake grinned. "Fine. How's Cassie?"

"I don't know."

"Say! Do you mean to sit there and tell me you ain't done anything about her yet?"

"Well," Parris felt that he ought to justify himself somehow for something—he was not quite sure for what. He swallowed hard. "Well, I don't ever see her."

"Well, why *don't* you see her?"

"Dr. Tower makes me use the side door, and I just don't see her."

"I bet I'd find a way. Say boy, Cassie Tower is—well—well, I'd see her in spite of her old man. Hell! What does he do, keep her locked up?"

"I see her on the porch once in a while, but I'm kind of afraid to stop."

"If you don't go and get things in this world, boy, you don't get anything."

Parris flushed, and Drake gave him a terrific nudge. "You never did come with me to see the Ross gals. I took them and Dudley Wright down to Whaley Pond just last week on a picnic." He nudged Parris again. "Hot-choo, boy!"

"Are they—did you—?"

"Sure, of course. Gave each one of them two dollars afterwards."

"Oh. Then they're—" Parris flamed with embarrassment that he found it so difficult to say plain words even to Drake. But Drake hardly noticed his hesitation.

"Chippies? No, not exactly. I guess they wouldn't play around with just anybody. Kind of particular, maybe, but not so much so that it gives you any trouble." He laughed and the warm color rose under his freckles. Drake looked happy today.

"I saw your house was closed, Drake. You at Mrs. Searcy's now?"

"Yep. I've been there three months. Just take my meals. Still sleep at the house, though."

"All by yourself? Pretty lonesome, isn't it?"

"I don't notice it now." He turned suddenly. "Gee, if I ain't the darndest dumb fool! I guess it's just habit or something like that. You know, I never was allowed to do much of anything around home, Aunt Mamie and Uncle Rhodes used to be so doggone strict. You know what? All this time I've been taking Poppy Ross out to Moore's tobacco barn! I just kind of forgot that I'm my own boss and live in my own house! Say, I'm going to get her to come up there— her and Jinny. Hot-choo, Parris, we can have us a time right in my own house." He slapped the reins on Molly's sleek round back. "Get up there, Molly. Gee, ain't I the darndest dumb fool, though, you ever heard of in your life?"

Parris did not answer, but Drake was shiny-eyed with plans. "Say, you know what I'm going to do? I'm going to see if I can't stay on in the house. Maybe the bank will let me do that. I could even rent out one side of it, maybe, and keep my own place. That would be a whole lot better than having a room at Mrs. Searcy's."

"It would be better," Parris agreed.

Drake whacked Parris' leg again. "A hell of a lot better than Moore's tobacco barn, too!"

As Drake talked Parris felt his spirits rise. There was a contagion in Drake's exuberance. A tension of excitement arose in his throat. He talked, too, more and more freely. It was a fine feeling to have a friend—an especially fine feeling to discover that Drake was really his friend as much now as ever. He jounced about in his seat like a small boy, forgetting all about the grave poses he had planned to try out on the first comer.

The day was perfect. The grounds and vegetable gardens of the asylum were green and well tended. Colors everywhere were fresh and pure.

Drake had lowered the buggy top, and the April sun was warm on their backs.

"Look a-yonder!" Drake pointed down a side street.

"What?" Parris leaned forward to look.

"Ain't that Jamie's friend, Bob Callicott?"

"Um. Yes. I guess it is. Why?"

"You know what? He's going to see Ludie Sims!"

"Aw. How do you know?"

"She lives right down there. The white house at the corner."

"Well, maybe he isn't going there."

"Sure he is. Now would you believe it? Right in broad daylight. Say, he don't care what he does, does he?" There was a note of admiration in Drake's voice. He pulled Molly to a stop.

"Look!" Drake pointed with the buggy whip. Robert Callicott stopped at the Sims house and opened the picket gate. There was something accustomed about the way he crossed the yard and took the porch steps, two at a time. He did not knock but entered the house and closed the door behind him.

Drake grinned. He flicked Molly harder with the new red-tasseled whip. Molly responded with an acceleration of vertical action—a great show of trotting, but with no perceptible increase of speed. Drake settled back in the seat. "No use trying to hurry Molly, I guess. I got to get me a horse. Trots like a sewing machine, don't she?"

The harness jingled with Molly's valiant efforts, the wheels made a pleasant grinding sound in the sandy road, the sun warmed more and more.

Parris gazed with lively delight at every detail of this unfamiliar place. There were a hundred shades of green, from a thin veiling of brilliant emerald in the slow-budding oaks to the quivering full leaf of the poplars and maples. He looked back toward the town: it was already half obscured by the spring green.

"Gee, I feel good."

Drake laughed. "Maybe you got a little sap in you, after all."

Parris frowned a little. "I've been working pretty hard this winter, Drake."

"Sure, I know you have. That's what I'm talking about. You can't keep your face in a book all the time. You got to get out and have some fun."

"I guess I'm kind of peculiar, Drake. I don't know very well just how to have fun. You know—I live way out there and I don't see anybody—I mean in my free time. At school—well, I guess I don't get on very well with the fellows at college."

"Yeh, I heard about it."

"You did?" Parris sat up straight. "What did you hear, Drake? About me? Honest?"

"Sure. Madison Geer said you were stuck up and conceited."

Parris flushed darkly. "Oh!" he said rather weakly.

"Sure," Drake went on cheerfully. "That's what they all think. I told Mad you were not any such thing. I guess he don't like you much."

"Well—well, you know it's not so."

"Of course I know. It's all right. What in the hell do you care, kid?"

"I do care, somehow."

"You come around with me. I'll fix you up with them."

"I haven't got much time to do anything, you know."

"Take some time. Hell—you don't work all night, do you? We'll get us some gals."

Parris swallowed hard. He half wished Drake wouldn't talk about girls, and half wished he could talk about them himself with Drake's offhandedness. The lump of excitement in his throat persisted.

"Maybe the Ross girls wouldn't like me." He tried to sound casual.

"Sure they will, sure they'll like you. You're all right, kid. You're—well I guess girls think you're good-looking, and all."

"Aw, foot."

Drake laughed easily—his shade of embarrassment passed. "Of course they do. I've heard plenty of them say so."

"Sure enough?"

"Hell, yes. Jinny Ross'll go for you like a brush fire. She's hot. So's Poppy." Some of Parris' reserve slipped away. "I bet I'd be scared, Drake."

"Scared? Say, I thought you told me you—you—*had.*"

He stopped as he saw the high color fade from Parris' face.

"I have."

"Well, then, what in time makes you look like that?"

"Something kind of terrible, Drake. I don't—"

"Say, I bet you got caught and somebody lammed hell out of you." He chuckled, but rather uncomfortably, and urged Molly to renewed exertions. "I don't want to know anything about it if you don't want to tell me, kid. Keep your troubles to yourself. All I want to know is, do you want to have some fun with Jinny Ross, or not?"

Parris pulled himself together, and steadied himself before he spoke. "Of course. Why not?—sometime." He thought he sounded quite natural.

Drake changed the subject. "Parris, are you sure enough going to Europe to study?"

"Yes."

"Whyn't you go to St. Louis or somewhere in America? You're an American."

"I don't know. It's my grandmother's idea, I guess. The medical schools in Vienna are the finest in the world, though."

"Is that so? Well, now. Say, I bet they've got pretty girls over there. Seems to me I heard Uncle Rhodes say something about it. He went over there one time—didn't take Aunt Mamie with him, either. Seen Jamie lately?"

"'Bout a couple of weeks ago. Went with him to see Robert Callicott."

"Parris, d'you reckon there's some kind of funny business going on between Bob Callicott and Jamie?"

Parris opened his eyes very wide. "Why—why, do you mean? Oh, gee, no! Robert Callicott is a *man*."

Drake lifted his head and yelped. "Doggoned if you ain't the regular little innocent, sometimes."

Parris was deeply shocked—perhaps more startled and astonished than shocked. It never really occurred to him that adults were really interested in the curiosities and urges of young people. There was in his mind still a marked and impassable division between children and grownups. He realized with a jar of revelation that he thought of himself as being a child, and that he thought of Robert Callicott as a "grown man," concerned with the serious affairs of the older world. He realized, too, that he had somehow thought of everything relating to sex and sexual concerns as a sort of childish frivolity—a kind of secret and still fascinating game. It was all a little like his and Renée's "secret lake."

A faint wonder tinged his mind at this moment. He had really felt that keeping all such matters secret from adults was more because of the childish nature of sex than because of any moral implications.

The faint wonderment passed away, and he seemed a little foolish to himself that he hadn't thought more clearly. No—he readjusted the idea—he just hadn't thought much at all—it had merely been a feeling. He knew better, of course, but he had kept himself in a childish category. He shaped his lips to form the word. "Category"—it was quite a fine word. He went on with his thought. But he wasn't really a child any more. That thought, that self-classification, had been one of the barriers separating him from Drake. Drake assumed adulthood, and therefore belonged in that world. That world of older people—he began to see new facts dimly—didn't really differ so much from the world he had always lived in as he had believed. He—himself—and Renée; Drake and Poppy Ross; Robert Callicott and Ludie Sims.

A hot surge of refusal met this easy sequence. No: no matter what anyone else in the whole world might think, or feel, or do, he and Renée and their "secret lake" stood forever apart, set in a world of—he hunted for a word, and Jamie's lisping voice came to mind—set in a "world of beauty." That's what Jamie would say, probably, and that defined it well. Parris pressed his lips tight together. Yes: the words made it almost noble. Set in a world of beauty, and sealed away forever from anyone's curiosity or meddling. Drake and Poppy Ross; Robert Callicott and Ludie Sims—if there was to be any kind of linking of himself to that group, there would have to be someone else. Renée's name just wouldn't go in with the others. Jinny Ross! He didn't know her, but of course he had seen her lots of times. The palms of his hands were wet. He tried not to attract Drake's attention when he wiped them on his handkerchief. Drake was whistling softly, squinting across the sunny fields. Jinny Ross. It was a sign, he thought, that he had passed over, a little, at least, into Drake's world that he could think of Jinny Ross without a feeling of disloyalty to Renée. Renée, who was growing up by now, and maybe not thinking of him at all. That other Renée—the one he was really thinking about and remembering—she was there in that world of beauty, set apart and sealed forever from any kind of intrusion.

He dwelt on the thought of Renée for a moment and made a picture of her—bright and shining like a tracery on glass, but transparent, and very still.

He tried hard to recall his familiar images of her, with her silver-gold hair that always seemed to float on currents of light, her faded print dresses, always too short, the lift of her rounded thighs against her too tight skirts—he could summon everything back today except her face. It persisted in eluding him in almost the silly way she used to have of hiding behind trees and around corners. He could catch a gleam of light, of color, but her look, the tilt of her head, the shape of her smile—these he could not recapture. They were like reflections in the water. Something came between, something broke up the pictures whose fragments lingered even while they seemed to be running away. Maybe, he thought—and he was pleased with what he considered the brilliancy and poetry of the thought—maybe it was like trying to see a picture in the water, and what was always in the way was himself. Just what he felt that might signify he did not stop to think about, or to analyze; but vaguely, something dark, maybe a feeling of disloyalty, maybe the lasting memory of grief, shadowed the moment. He moved uneasily in the seat, and stole another look at Drake. Drake was apparently pleasantly, if idly, occupied with his own thoughts. Parris suspected Drake didn't really think very much—just let his mind browse as it wished. Drake was all right; Drake understood him mighty well, he decided; he'd better stick pretty close to Drake. It wouldn't do not to have any friends at all. It was fine of Drake to speak up for him to Madison Geer.

Parris' eyelids dropped a little in a characteristic look of tenderness. Through the lashes he saw Drake's face more clearly. Attractive, warm—an easy face, each feature seemed to flow freely into the next. There were no jars, no collisions of expression. It was all one all over. A harmonious face—Parris was inordinately pleased today with his words—but, he amended justly, a rather loose face. There wasn't a single sharp line. Lately he had been noticing faces and thinking of them. Dr. Tower had talked a lot about facial structures, contours, and expressions. He had linked it up with diagnosis. Parris realized that now, just as when Dr. Tower had been talking about it, he was more interested in the picturesque application of the ideas to people he knew than he was in the more scientific implications.

He shrugged the momentary self-admonition away. He wanted to think about Drake right now as a friend. He wanted to like him, and he knew that he did like him wholeheartedly. Drake glanced sideways at him and gave him a quick, absent-minded grin and wink. He was obviously ambling along some easy path of thought of his own. The wide, devil-may-care grin relaxed. The look of a half-smile lay over his entire face, though the lips had grown serious. It was a look so free of untoward elements, so single in an elemental enjoyment of the actual moment, that it touched on beauty. Parris knew that he had never felt so drawn to Drake as at this moment. He wished there were some way he could show it, but he knew that any such effort would result in discomfort for both of them.

"What you say, Parris, we go on down to Gallatin Springs?"

"All right."

"It's about three more miles—a big trip for old Molly, but we'll let her take her time coming back."

"Suits me."

Drake swished the whip over Molly's head. She turned her ears as he clucked vigorously and exhorted her to lengthen her stride. Her response was amiable but ineffective. "Let her walk, the old son-of-a-gun. Bet she never ran a step in her life. Aw, get up, Molly, for time's sake move a little bit! Oh, all right, take it easy, don't overstrain yourself! It'll be dark when we get back. You don't have to be home any special time, do you, Parris?"

"Me? No."

"Your grandma expect you to supper?"

"She won't be worried if I'm not there."

Molly's jouncing gait had an almost hypnotic effect. It was hard to keep the eye from resting on some shining buckle or patent-leather trimming of the harness which rose and fell with her pace. Parris began to feel sleepy. A thin hum sounded in his imagination like the singing of a wire in the wind. After a while he began to see behind his half-closed lids something like a luminous thread stretching on and on ahead of them. It moved and whined faintly, and little figures ran and danced along the silvery transparent line. They were like the people he knew: Drake, himself, Louise Gordon, Willy Macintosh, Cassandra, and over and over again tiny images of Renée, like a long screen of linked paper dolls. The figures fell about and postured and grimaced. They seemed not to like him. He felt that they were vaguely hostile, that they were laughing at him, making gestures at him, talking about him. A hundred little Renées running hand in hand, bending forward and backward like paper in the wind, but keeping time to a small chiming sound, a steady rhythmic tinkle. All the little Renées bent now this way, now that, as if convulsed with laughter. He began to feel uncomfortable and lonely. He wanted to call out to them, but they seemed very far away....

"Hey, sit up." Drake pushed him with his elbow. "Darned if you didn't go to sleep."

"I—I guess I did. I was even dreaming."

"Gosh, I nearly went oft myself. I think old Molly's been asleep for half an hour. Go on, Molly, for Pete's sake." He swished the whip again, sharply across her ears, but the lash never touched her. "No use hitting the old turtle, I guess. She wouldn't know what you meant. She was Aunt Mamie's pet, you know."

"I remember."

"Aunt Mamie was awful good in some ways."

"Do you miss them a terrible lot, Drake?"

Drake looked hard at Molly's ears. "Sometimes. They were strict, but they did the best they could, I guess."

"I'm sorry, Drake."

"Oh, I'm all right. I guess you and me had better stick together a little bit, Parris. Good gosh, you got to have somebody."

"We will; you bet."

"I want to get married and all that kind of thing someday, but I want to have all the good time I can first. But—well, you get kind of tired even having a good time."

"I expect so." Parris slipped back into the awkward feeling of childish inexperience again. He didn't know what to say exactly. He wasn't even sure what Drake meant by a "good time."

"Madison Geer and all that crowd, Jesse Alexander and Babe Fuller and the rest of 'em, get drunk a lot, but I swear, Parris, I don't like that much. I like the way a drink tastes—but I hate to be dizzy."

"Gee, you know I never did have a drink."

"Well, no use taking one either, kid. I expect to stay off drinking. Don't do you any good. Now, girls—that's another question. You can go around lifting all the petticoats you want to and you're all right afterward—you know, you feel light as a feather. I guess it does you good. If it ain't too often, I mean."

Parris nodded and tried to look judicious. "Um, yes, I expect so."

Drake chuckled. "You sounded just like a doctor then. You know, I expect you'll be a good doctor. Wouldn't surprise me at all."

"Well, darn your old skin. I expect to be. And you'll be coming into my office, and I'll say, 'Better not lift so many petticoats; old man, it's telling on you.'"

Both of them laughed, but Drake sobered quickly. "I guess I won't be doing anything like that by that time. I'll be having kids, and all. I'm going to have my good time first, and settle down."

"It's awfully hard to think of you ever being any different from what you are right now."

Drake looked very serious. "You know, Parris, I wouldn't tell this to another soul on earth, 'cause I know everybody thinks I'm kind of wild and that I run around an awful lot, and that I ain't steady. But I'm going to surprise some people around this old town. I'm going to settle down hard when I do settle, and," he cut a quick sidewise look at Parris, "I'm going to make Louise proud of me."

A sudden shy silence fell on both of them. Drake spoke quickly, and louder than was necessary, to lessen the embarrassment of this sudden confidence. "I wouldn't tell anybody else that, though, you can bet."

"Of course, I understand that all right, Drake. Say, you're sure enough in love with her?"

"Well, I guess that's what you call it." He smiled now, at ease again.

"Does she know it?"

"Gosh, I've told her often enough. She ought to know it by this time."

"Is she in love with you, too? Now, I mean."

"I don't know. You can't tell anything about Louise."

"Well, of course she is. If she wasn't I expect you'd know that in a hurry."

Drake blinked at this unexpected perspicacity.

"Say, I guess that's right. I never thought about that. Gee—get up there, Molly, for Christ's sake. We don't want to spend our lives out here—no, sir, I never thought of that! How d'you happen to think about it?"

Parris waved his hand with a wise little gesture of deprecation. It implied a wide knowledge of the ways of women of which this was the merest sample.

"Parris, you know Preston Hill out there west of town?"

"Yes, of course. Why?"

"I want to buy it."

"Good gracious, Drake! What for? It's just a hill."

"Kings Row has got to grow, hasn't it? That's the best direction for it to go. Wouldn't that be a good place to build houses—you know, looking down across the creek there, and away out over the country?"

Parris was mightily impressed. "Why, that's wonderful! You'd make a lot of money, wouldn't you, and be rich?" His voice sounded a little wistful.

"If you had some money you could come in with me. It belongs to the old Wilhite estate."

"I never will have any money, I guess, except to study medicine."

"Well, doctors make a pile of money. Wouldn't it be the darndest thing if we, you and me, could build houses for ourselves out there, right next to each other?"

"Listen, Drake—" Parris wriggled about and pulled one foot under him. He rested one arm along the back of the buggy seat and gesticulated in his odd foreign fashion with the other. The talk ran on into details. It seemed to them at that moment that life was clear and straight ahead of them and pleasant. It required nothing but choice. They would do this, or that, thus or so. They wondered once or twice why older people always spoke of the difficulties of life. But, of course, in olden times everything was different. There really wasn't much use in paying attention to old people. They didn't understand that the world had changed now, and that things were easier and simpler.

"Whoa, Molly. Look, Parris, we're at Gallatin Springs already. I guess this old land turtle covers ground faster than we thought. Shall we go on down?"

"Let's look a little while first."

The level farm land dropped suddenly in a wide arc to a meandering creek. The descent was sudden and steep. A broad valley lay blue and dreaming in the spring sunshine. Following the creek, the hazy river hills began. Great white clouds lifted dome above shining dome in the sky, which seemed to take on new immensity as the view widened. Slow-winged buzzards circled high above the hills. Sometimes they seemed to hang motionless, poised against the high currents of wind from the south.

"Sky seems 'bout twice as big out here, don't it?" Drake waved an arm largely.

"Yes. I always imagine it must be like this in Switzerland or in the Rocky Mountains."

"I'd like to travel someday and see a lot of places."

"I would, too."

"You're going to."

"Oh, yes, I forgot."

"Let's get out and sit here. Believe I'll unhitch Molly and let her eat some grass."

Parris walked to the edge of the sharp decline. The treetops billowed suddenly down and away into the valley with a curious dizzying effect. He sat down on a large flat rock and waited for Drake. The rock was soft and crumbly and filled with small fossil shells.

Drake came presently, looking backward at Molly who stood idly looking about.

"I think the old idiot's enjoying the view. Hope she doesn't take a notion to fall down this hill."

Parris crumbled the stone and laid out some small shells. "Look, Drake, this was the bottom of a sea once."

"Huh? What do you mean?"

"Haven't you ever seen these shells?"

"Yes, lots of times."

"Well, what did you think they were?"

"Gosh, I don't know. Never thought about 'em at all."

"They're fossils."

"Yes?"

"Left over from some other age—millions and millions of years ago."

"Are you fooling?"

"No, sure. That's what they are."

"Well, I'll be darned. Millions of years, eh?"

"Oh, fiddle, you know that."

Drake looked curiously at Parris for a moment, then he let his gaze drift away to the hills. "I don't know much of anything, Parris. I'm not smart like you are. You think about things."

Parris choked uncomfortably. His next words came with difficulty. "Oh, stuff."

"That's the honest truth. I never think about anything unless someone makes me. I never could figure out anything much for myself. I guess I never even wanted to, and I guess that's just exactly the difference between a smart person and somebody that ain't. You'll get on, Parris, and make something out of yourself. I'll always be in Kings Row, and unless I can use a little common sense—well, I guess anything could happen to somebody like me."

This sudden change of mood almost frightened Parris. It sounded so old— really old, this time. He looked so troubled that Drake laughed and slapped him on the back. "You're all right, kid, you are all right with me. I bet you don't even care whether I'm smart or not."

Parris did not smile. He scarcely trusted his voice. For some reason which he did not understand very well, he felt close to tears. He looked straight at Drake. "You're just as smart as anybody, Drake McHugh. Don't you ever think any different. I—I just happened to know about—about those darn old fossils because Dr. Hitchcock talked about them in class one day—about these down here on Gallatin Hill, I mean."

"Well, what you so worked up about?"

"Did you think I was trying to show off?"

"Naw! For time's sake, Parris, I was just telling you that I don't know much. It's the God's truth, too, I don't."

"You know a lot of things I don't know."

"Maybe. I bet I could get one of these country girls into the hayloft while you'd still be talking about the weather."

Parris grinned happily. This was better.

"Useful information, too, kid. Never know when you can use it. Comes in handy all over. Now—fossils: if you begin talking to a little gal about fossils, you've got such a long way to go before you get to the point."

Parris chucked the handful of tiny fossils at Drake, who rolled over into the grass.

"Um! I guess after all I do know a few things, Parris."

"You can teach me a lot, I know that."

"And I'm going to, boy; I certainly am going to." He laid his floppy plaid cap half over his face to shade his eyes from the sun. He talked lazily, moving his lips as little as possible. Parris lay on his side and rested on one elbow. He pulled the tender young grass, rolling it into loose balls and flipping them away. Squinting through half-closed lids, he tried to follow the course of the meandering creek which appeared and disappeared among the willow thickets and finally bent out of sight in the blur and confusion of distance. There was not a sound. The countryside was as silent as the sky above it. It might have been that primeval world Parris was talking about when he said "millions of years ago."

Down in the valley the lights on the water began to deepen from blue to purple. Masses of shadows from the slow-moving clouds lay like islands against the green hillsides. Imperceptibly, the brilliant sunshine softened—a subtle altering from silver to a pale gold.

Parris watched the shifting light and changing color. He forgot Drake. It was as though he felt the vast swing of the earth under him as it turned silently away from the sun.

Drake peered out from under the peak of his cap. "What you thinking about?"

Parris gestured vaguely toward the valley, and Drake sat up. He looked steadily at it for a long minute, twirling his cap on his finger, and nodded slowly. "Yeh." He nodded again more emphatically. "Sometimes I wish I could live out like this away from everybody. Come on, we got to be going. It'll be dark before we get back to town."

All of the next day, and the next, Parris went about in a pleasantly unthinking haze of mind. He did not read, and he did not particularly want to see anyone. He went for long walks, following the winding little creek into the country, searching out the sheltered places where the spring delayed, and where the first buds were just now breaking. The sunnier slopes and hilltops were already an unbroken, waving green.

That one afternoon with Drake had relieved the whole feeling of loneliness which had weighed on him for weeks. He thought of Drake, happily, but he did not want to see him—not just now. He thought of Jamie, too, but again he was sure that he would rather be alone. It was strange, now that he paused to compare one with the other, how much he liked Jamie and Drake, but how completely they seemed to exist in separate spheres of his own mind. Where all of his easy, simple affections were concerned—there was Drake. He could talk to Drake about his work, his hopes and plans, and about a good many of his everyday little troubles. But now, at this moment, when he leaned down to look at the design of a frail lemon-green plant outlined against the dark soil of a moist bank, he thought of Jamie. Jamie would know how strangely beautiful it was, how dreamlike the perfection of each thin line. Jamie would talk for a moment with a rush of warm feeling, and then fall suddenly silent as a deep blush darkened his face with embarrassment. It was always necessary to pick up the conversation quickly or Jamie would prolong his shy spell and presently go away.

Parris pulled his ear meditatively. Drake on one hand, Jamie on the other—they looked in opposite directions. They did not even see or hear the same things. He did not stop to ask why he saw and heard with both of them. His analysis stopped just short of that speculation. Beyond that point he proceeded on the guidance of his affections. He saw Drake's profile with the warm glow that always shone behind the freckles, the lazy look of his dark eyes that seemed to drift from one object to the other, the half-laugh that followed immediately any seriousness of his own. There was another look, too, which Parris always saw when he thought of Drake. A sudden darkening of his eyes, and something that was more a look of tension than a change of expression. It gave Drake an instant air of going somewhere. That look belonged to any mention of Poppy Ross—or, almost any girl.

In complete contrast to this gay, understandable picture of Drake he saw Jamie—Jamie was uneasy, and secret. Parris hunted for words—Jamie could be likable and sweet. He could also be sulky, and sultry and brooding—and, well, just too uncomfortable to be good company.

Parris was amazed to discover that he had tears in his eyes. He didn't really know why. Drake and Jamie—he liked them more from this moment of thinking about them than he ever had. He could even tell Jamie about it, but not Drake. He was sorry for Drake, but he was sorrier for Jamie. He decided not to try to understand the feeling. Thinking along in the dark of one's own mind was really hard work. He guessed some people didn't try to think very much—Drake, for instance, and some others thought themselves into trouble, as he was sure Jamie did. What about himself? He didn't know.

He remembered Lucy Carr. Maybe Lucy thought herself into trouble, too—thought herself on and on, out into very lonesome and faraway and cold places such as there must be up above the world and beyond the usual places of the mind. Maybe she got so far out she lost her way, or was frightened, or couldn't call to anyone, or—or something like that. Perhaps people ought to hold fast to something when they set out on a thinking expedition—have some sort of tether so they could pull themselves back. He was rather sure that people such as Drake ought not to think too much. Why—Drake would get lost if he tried to go too far, and Jamie—well, it might be that Jamie was lost right now. Certainly he seemed to stay pretty far away. Jamie's thoughts and ideas were strange and curious, sometimes like words out of an unknown language or faces from an utterly alien land. He frowned and pulled his ear again. Something puzzled him just at this point. It was this: most everyone liked Jamie and said he was a smart boy and what a pity other boys were not like him. Older people held him as a model. But not many people said a good word for Drake McHugh. They said he was "wild." They gave to that simple word many shades of meaning.

He recalled now what Dr. Tower had said last week about intuition. He had been captivated by that talk. It was one of the times when Dr. Tower sounded a good deal like Jamie's poetry. Dr. Tower had placed strong reliance on intuition, if one had a mind that worked clearly and well, on the—now, what was it he had said?—oh, yes—on the normal planes of consciousness. If so, then all of one's unnoticed observations might be correctly assorted and appraised by the mind without one's being aware of just how a conclusion was reached. But, in such cases, it might be relied on.

Parris remembered exactly how he had been impressed that afternoon with Dr. Tower and with himself. He had felt extremely intellectual as Dr. Tower's talk grew more and more abstract. He shrugged slightly. He guessed he had actually felt pretty conceited when he came right down to it. He'd remember that. Gee, Dr. Tower would skin him alive if he got conceited. But—oh, yes, Drake and Jamie. This brought him back to them. People thought certain ways about them, and he disagreed with them. He knew now that he was somehow on sure ground. His intuition said no to everything people thought. It wasn't, he told himself, because of any goody-good notions, either. As for that, people didn't know all about Jamie. But that—all of that still wasn't what made the difference. It was something or other about being headed in a certain direction. It was—it was because Drake was on a certain kind of road and Jamie was on a totally different kind. He realized that this wasn't very good thinking and that it was like something out of a sermon. He wondered if his intuition was reliable. Had his secret observations come to a secret but correct conclusion somewhere in the back of his head?

He believed so, and he believed he could trust those conclusions. But he liked Jamie in spite of anything—he liked Jamie very much.

He wrinkled his brow and stared hard at the moving water. The afternoon was warm and still. The creek made a little chorus of cool sounds. Here and there the rusty yellow stones broke up the stream into a dozen noisy rivulets which flowed together again in clear brown pools, the bubbles turning around and around and winking themselves out as the water stilled. Parris sat down on a low ledge where he could watch the reflections as they wavered and straightened, then broke and wavered and straightened again. The simple sound of running, gurgling water was not so simple as he listened. His eyes, half closed against the minute points of dazzling reflections, accepted only a kaleidoscopic shuttling of prismatic color. He felt the sun on his face and hands and an occasional breath of cooler air that arose from the surface of the stream. The tiresome movement of thought came nearly to rest. There was nothing but the awareness and the perception of his senses—the silken warmth of the sun, the meaningless circling of color against his eyes, and the sleepy murmur of water.

He stirred after a while. The rock was hurting his elbow. He sat up and rubbed his eyes. A low bank of dull blue clouds lay across the west. It might rain soon. He arose, a little stiffly, and brushed the leaf stems and sand from his clothes. He felt an increasing restlessness as though something forgotten tugged at his attention for remembrance.

After supper he remembered his notebooks. He had left them in Dr. Tower's study the afternoon he began his unorthodox holiday. He would have to walk into town for them. Maybe he would look up Drake tonight. A tingle of excitement ran along his nerves like a thin edge of fire. He recalled Drake's promises—Poppy and Jinny Ross! He stopped. No: he would not go to see Drake. Somehow the prospect of such an adventure excited him so acutely that he felt he could not bear to face it. He would think about it some other time.

He turned the lamp higher and looked closely at himself in the mirror. He brushed his thick black hair experimentally and decided he liked the old way best. He tried his plaid cap at a rakish angle, suddenly changed it for a dark blue one. He flung a light topcoat around his shoulders and with an appreciative look at the effect in the mirror went out, scuffing along the hall in small-boy fashion and clattering noisily down the back steps.

He paused on the terrace. The sky was darkening fast. He thought he heard a faint tremolo of thunder from the southwest, but he was not sure. Anyway, he had to have the notebooks. He took a short cut through the long rows of poplar plantings, whistling a quick staccato air in time to his hurrying step.

It was quite dark when he reached Cherry Street. He decided to go in the back way—Dr. Tower would likely be in the study. As he neared the house he saw the reading lamp was lighted and that the study door stood open on the side porch.

As he was about to step onto the low porch floor, he saw to his surprise that it was Cassandra and not Dr. Tower who sat in the deep chair under the green-shaded light. She had flung herself sideways in the chair, and her long slim legs were crossed over the low tufted armrest. She held her book at the top, like a child, and her free hand slowly twisted and untwisted strands of her brilliant coppery hair.

Parris knocked lightly on a porch column. She looked up quickly.

"Hello, Cassandra. It's me—Parris. Didn't want to scare you."

"Why, hello." She arose and dropped her book face down in the chair. "Come in?" The words were distinctly question, and not invitation.

"Well, I—I just came after my notebooks. I left them here Tuesday."

"Oh. Come on in. I guess you know where they are."

Parris dropped his cap and coat on a chair. "I've been playing hookey."

"From father?"

"No. He put me up to it. Said I needed to rest."

"Oh."

"But I got to get back to work now."

"Do you work pretty hard?"

"Yes, I guess so."

"Sit down?" The question was less apparent this time. Possibly, just possibly, the tone of invitation was present.

"Thanks. I'd like to. Is your father in?"

"He's in St. Louis."

"Sure enough? When did he go?"

"Yesterday. Unexpectedly. He won't be back until next Tuesday."

"Oh."

"He said tell you when you came back he'd be ready to see you on Wednesday."

"Wednesday. Oh. All right."

Parris felt himself grow a little ill at ease under her steady scrutiny. He really hadn't had a good look at her for a long time, and he had forgotten how lovely she was. He felt his heart beat a little faster and his breath come quick and short. She was as tall as he, round and soft-looking. Her skin was amazingly white and her mouth vividly red. The unexpected maturity of her figure struck him sharply. Her green foulard dress was an old one, and fitted tightly. Her breast rose and fell quickly as though straining against it. Parris looked away.

"Well, I guess I'll hurry on."

"Why?" Her long green eyes were steady now. They looked straight at him. He replaced the notebooks and looked at her in some surprise.

"Do you have to go?" she continued.

"Why—no. Can—may I stay awhile?"

"Sit down. No, over here—on the couch. It's comfortable."

She sat down and pulled a pillow behind her head. She seemed perfectly at ease now.

"I—why, do you know, Cassie, I haven't seen you to talk to you, really, in a long, long time?"

"Yes, I know."

"Well, I hope—"

She cut in suddenly. "It will probably be the only time."

He flushed. "Well—why, Cassie?"

"I can't see anyone. You don't have to ask questions to understand that, do you?"

Parris didn't know what to say. He felt as though he had been snubbed by a much older person.

"Well—my goodness, Cassie, I don't know. I guess maybe I want to ask you why, but if you don't want to tell me, or don't want to see me any more—"

"I said I couldn't see anyone."

He faced her squarely. "Your father won't let you?"

"I told you you didn't have to ask questions."

"Oh. All right."

"Don't get your feelings hurt. Don't ask questions. Let's just talk."

"All right. What about?"

She laughed—simply and naturally. Some severe constraint disappeared with it. "Oh, anything. Tell me what you do all the time."

"I just read and study and practice. That's all."

"Do you still study music?"

"Yes."

"Well, I just read and study, so you're ahead of me."

They talked a little feverishly, and a little jerkily. Parris watched her closely and tried to follow the rapid changes of her mood. One moment she seemed to be as he always remembered her, the next she seemed strange and different. She seemed then to look at him from a distance—exactly the way older people sometimes did. Then he floundered and stammered and lost his words. Suddenly she would return and laugh, and the conversational going was easier again.

A flick of lightning threw her face into high relief and intensified the lambent green of her eyes.

"My goodness, but you are pretty, Cassandra!"

She smiled a thin little smile.

"Honest you are—you're prettier than you ever have been, and you always were the prettiest girl in this town."

She leaned forward and gave his wrist a quick squeeze, "Thank you, Mr. Mitchell." Her hand lingered for a moment on his, and he leaned over and kissed it.

"Silly!" But her voice trailed over the word ever so slightly.

Again that painful excitement clutched at his throat. Outside a few large drops of rain spattered against the porch floor.

"I—I guess I'd better go."

"Oh, I'm sorry." She stood up—so close that he felt a little wave of warmth from her. Without hesitation he put his arms around her and kissed her. He felt her lips part slowly under his own as she crushed herself against him.

There was another flash of lightning and an instant roll of heavy thunder. She twisted herself free and stood quite still. Her eyes had gone black. Only the thinnest line of green circled the pupil.

"Are you scared—of the lightning?" Parris hardly recognized his own voice, it was so husky and breathless.

"No," she said roughly. She seemed to be listening. The thunder rolled again, heavier and nearer. Cassandra crossed the room and opened the door into the long center hall. Then she closed it and locked it. She stood still, apparently stiff with embarrassment or fright. She stared hard and long straight at Parris. Her face was near to breaking up. Her lips quivered. Then suddenly, as if completely satisfied at what she saw in his face, she crossed to the lamp, turned the light low, and blew it out. Parris felt her coming toward him in the dark.

"Come over—*here*." Her voice had the same unnatural roughness—almost a note of anger in it, as she pushed him back on the couch.

The storm was coming with a rush. Cassandra lowered the shades and closed the door. In just a few minutes the room became hot and close. In the flashes of lightning he saw her fling the shining green dress across a chair. A white slip followed. Then she stepped out of a fluffy circle of frills that lay around her feet. She stood for a second in a sudden blaze from outside— slender and white. The sight of her swept him like a fire. Then she dropped beside him, and her deft fingers loosened his tie.

"Quick," she said. "Take them off—everything."

Outside, the night roared in fury, but neither of them heard it.

Parris did not know how long they were there. Time passed, but no awareness of it reached him. Cassandra lay curled dose against him. Her breathing was slow and even. He wondered if she were asleep.

"Cassie."

"Yes."

"Are you asleep?"

"No, silly."

"What time you reckon it is?"

"I don't know."

"Is there a clock in here?"

"No."

"You think it might be pretty near morning?"

"I guess not."

"It's stopped raining."

"Yes."

"Maybe I better go now."

"Maybe." She laid her arm across his bare chest. "Pretty soon."

"But maybe it's morning, or will be pretty soon, and somebody might see me leaving here."

"That's so."

"I guess I better dress."

"It's still dark."

"I know it is—now."

"Wait a little."

He sank back. "I love you, Cassie."

"No, you don't, Parris. But that's all right." She laughed noiselessly. "You don't have to say that. You think I'm a terrible girl—and bad. You're trying to make me feel better. Don't—don't try. It's all right."

"But I mean it."

"No, you don't."

"I—"

"Hush." She raised herself on one elbow. He could see her dimly. Her hair fell against his face. The strange unaccustomed presence of her soft body, the gusty intoxication of her touch seemed utterly unreal. It might all be a dream. He—here in Dr. Tower's house—with Cassandra.

"Cassie."

"What?"

"It isn't a dream, is it? You are here, and I am, too?"

"Yes, silly."

"You love me, don't you, Cassie?"

"I don't know, Parris." Her voice squeaked slightly as it slipped from control. "I don't know."

"Cassie, you do—you do."

"I said I didn't know. I don't—"

"Oh—but you do—you must."

"Why?"

"Because—because of this."

The queer angry tone returned to her voice. "That hasn't got anything to do with it. You'd play with any girl."

"Why, Cassie!" He sounded so hurt that she laid her fingers across his lips. He took them away.

"Listen now, Cassie."

"All right, what?"

"Someday I want you to marry me."

She was quite silent and held so still that he said it again. She pressed close to him but did not answer.

"Cassie."

"Yes."

"Will you?"

"Oh, Parris, there isn't any answer for that—now."

"But why?"

"Because you don't really want to. You're sweet. You think you ought to say that."

"I mean it! How do you know what I think? I've got to study and be a doctor and it will be a long time—"

She smothered the rest of the sentence with her hand. When he took it away she leaned her face hard against his. He felt her grow taut as she held him tighter and tighter.

He whispered in her ear.

"Yes," she said. "Then you've got to go."

Parris opened the door and shivered when the drenched night air struck his flushed face. It seemed cold, and he fastened his coat tight about his throat. He stood for a moment before going out.

"Good night, darling."

"'Night."

"When—?"

She interrupted. "Maybe never."

"Listen, Cassie, I've got to see you."

"Maybe. Maybe I can think of a way. But you'd better go now, Parris, sure enough. It feels late."

He shivered again. "It feels early."

"Listen!" The deep bell of the town clock struck slowly—four times.

"Goodness, Cassie, it's four o'clock! It'll be daybreak before I can get home!"

"What'll you do?"

"I don't know. But you'll catch cold standing there with nothing on."

"I'm all right."

"I know what I'll do."

"What?"

"I'm going over to Drake McHugh's. Then I'll say I was with him all night."

"That's a good idea."

"Good night, then. I want to kiss you again though."

"All right. Maybe I love you—I don't know." She giggled. "Those buttons are cold. You'd better hurry. Somebody *might* see you leaving here. I believe it's getting lighter now."

"All right. Good night."

"Good night."

The sound of his step on the drive startled him. It was a cinder drive. He had never noticed how it crunched under foot in daytime. He ran into a low-hanging branch, and a shower of drops soaked his light coat. The wet leaves swished noisily. He felt panicky. If he could just reach the street without being seen he would be safe. Then no one could tell *where* he had been. His steps seemed to crunch louder than ever. He stepped aside and into a puddle that covered his ankles. A few more steps and he would be on the sidewalk. "The blessed haven of Walnut Street," he muttered dramatically to himself.

He breathed a sigh of relief. Cassie was right. It was getting light. He looked up. The sky was almost clear. A few gray feathery clouds scudded rapidly eastward. His heart leaped to his throat again; his steps on the granitoid sidewalks were louder than on the drive. He walked beside the smooth blocks on the slippery bank. In spite of the chill, his forehead was wet with sweat. He went as fast as he could, but watchfully. It simply wouldn't do for anyone to see him. But the streets were empty. Kings Row was sound asleep.

The thinning clouds were turning pink overhead when he knocked at the side door of the Livingstone house. He knocked two or three times. At last Drake's voice answered, thick with sleep.

"Say! Who's out there?" Parris thought Drake sounded just a little frightened.

"It's me, Drake. Parris."

Drake flung the door open, blinking and incredulous. "Well, for Christ's sake, what are you doing around here this time of night?"

"Let me in, quick, Drake. It's getting light, and I don't want anybody to see me."

"Come on in then. What's up?"

"I've been somewhere, and—and it's too late for me to go home without somebody seeing me."

Drake shook the hair out of his eyes. "Been somewhere?" he asked stupidly.

"Yes—I've been somewhere."

"Well, I guess I can see that, all right. That's good ... I guess you *have* been somewhere! Say, are you crazy, you galoot?"

"No, I don't guess I am."

"Take off that wet coat."

Parris had a violent shivering fit. He didn't know if it was from the cold, or relief.

"Say, I'll get you a cup of coffee. Won't take a minute. I just got to heat it up."

Parris had taken off his shoes and socks and was rubbing his feet with a handkerchief when Drake returned. "Here. Drink it now. I'll get you a towel. I—I kinda guess you better tell me what's happened, Parris."

"I just want to stay here. I'll telephone out home in the morning and say I stayed here all night."

"All right, all right. Only I want to be sure you're not in trouble, kid."

"I'm not in trouble, Drake. I'm all right."

"Where have you been, Parris? Better tell me."

"I stayed all night with Cassie Tower." He was astonished to find how easy it had been to say it, now that it was actually said. He set the empty cup on the table and looked rather blandly at Drake. Drake's eyes were popping.

"Well for Christ's sake! You—you spent the night with Cassie Tower! Just like that. You spent the night with Cassie Tower. And I was going to take you around and show you the ropes! For Christ's sake! Say, are you still cold?"

"N-no. I think I've got a chill, though."

"Come on and get into bed."

Drake yanked at Parris' clothes, helped him to bed, and threw an extra blanket over him. The shivering subsided quickly.

"I think I'm sleepy now, Drake."

Drake threw his head back and roared. "Well I guess you've got a right to be—for time's sake! Go on to sleep, but move over. I've got to sleep with you— if you don't mind the change, Mr. Mitchell."

Parris laughed a little. What a wonderful friend Drake McHugh really was! You could tell him anything and he understood you. He was lucky to have such a friend—awfully lucky.

He drew the blanket about his ears, and rolled closer to Drake. The chill was gone and the tension of his nerves lessened, A subtle exultation pervaded his mind. Cassandra! A flash of recollection struck across his drowsy thinking. She had said Dr. Tower would be in St. Louis until Tuesday. Then he could see her again—tonight, maybe, and tomorrow night—and the next!

He opened his eyes very wide. It was daylight now. A silvery bar showed between the lowered blind and the window sill. The cheeping of many birds reached his attention—a multitude of tiny pointed sounds. He covered his head with the pillow. He thought of Cassie. Then everything swam together and he thought: I'm going to sleep. An image of Cassie floated into his waning consciousness and came to rest. Slim and white and delicious. His recognition of her presence in his mind flooded his nerves with a faint tingling excitement. No tremor of unease shook the dreaming picture, no slightest premonition of possible disaster, no stir of conscience. He sank deeper and deeper into a sleepy warmth.... A sense of innocent well-being pervaded him as his breathing evened: he looked like a child as the flush of sleep mounted in his cheeks.

Spring in Kings Row was never more than a brief prelude to summer. The leaves unfolded and there was a week or two of balmy warmth, then a sudden onslaught of blistering heat. The idlers who hung about stoves in the back quarters of stores came out and took their accustomed places on the courthouse lawn. Down at the southwest corner nearest to McKeown's saloon a shirtsleeved group gathered shortly after the morning mail came in. By eleven the assembly was complete. A few sat in chairs brought across the street from Burkhalter's hardware store. Others sat on the ground and whittled, or leaned against the trees. They were the habitually idle. Their wives kept boardinghouses, or took in washing. One or two owned small shares in coal mines or clay pits and lived somehow on a meager income. They were the top layer of this lower-order gossip shop.

On the west porch of the courthouse was another group. County officials, lawyers with near-by offices, and hangers-on of the town's administration. This was the upper order. They were witness, jury, and judge of any happenings in the town or county. Any event at all was reported, considered in the light of their memory's history, and passed on to its probable outcome. Ignorance and wisdom, tolerance and prejudice, detachment and malice, met here in amiable conflict. The verbal dissection of character, of event and motive, went on like a story continued from day to day.

"Say, I hear old man Tod Irving down at Little Fork passed on."

"Old man Irving dead?"

"Yep."

"I hadn't heard about it."

"His son-in-law was in to the bank this morning."

"What was the matter with him?"

"Some kind of kidney trouble, Alf said."

"That his son-in-law, Alf?"

"Yep. Alf Barker."

"Oh, yes. I recollect him now. Married Tod Irving's oldest girl."

"No. Second one. Caroline was the oldest. She's married to a man up in Madison County."

"That's right."

"There's still one girl at home. Bertha. Kept house for the old man."

"Kidney trouble, you say."

"Alf said the doctors couldn't quite make out what all was the matter."

"How old was Tod Irving?"

"'Bout seventy, I'd say."

"No. Seventy-two."

"Sure enough. Older'n I am."

"Yep. Seventy-two last July."

"Well, well! Seventy-two. Looked right hearty, too, last time I saw him."

"Yep. He'd a-been seventy-three if he'd a lived till the third day of July."

"Well, I recollect when Tod Irving was a young man. He bought that place down to Little Fork from my grandfather."

"Is that so?"

"Yes, sir. In the spring of—now, let me see—I think it was the spring of '51 or '52, I can't be quite sure which, but it was one or the other."

"Well, well."

"Yes, sir—bought it from my grandfather. It was a good farm."

"It's a fine farm right now."

"Guess the old man was pretty well fixed, wasn't he?"

"I expect so. He never spent anything. Everybody said he was pretty close."

"I wouldn't say he was close: he lived well, built him a good house, always had good stock and wagons. No, he wasn't what you'd call close, but he never throwed nothing away."

"Reckon they'll sell the place?"

"I don't think so. He's got a boy, you know."

"Is that Fred Irving—the one that's got a place out close to Williamsport?"

"That's the one. Same one. Fred's his name."

"He's got a right nice little place there."

"Not as good as his pappy's place, though."

"Reckon he'll try to run both places."

"Well, I guess the girls would have something to say about that. They might want to sell and get their part out of it."

"Farm land's down now. Bad time to sell. It'd be better for Fred to sell his place and run the other."

"Farming's bad enough when you're farming for yourself, but when you've got a passel of people who's got a say-so in what you're doing, 'tain't much go."

"That's right. Better be your own boss."

"I expect Bertha Irving could purt near run that place herself."

"I ain't never seen a woman yet that could run a farm right."

"That's so."

"I don't see why Caroline Irving and her husband wouldn't want to come home and take over the place."

"What's her husband do?"

"He's got a feed store at McAlpin."

"He might could do it."

"What's his name?"

"Warder. I think it's Marvin Warder. They call him 'Fiddler Warder,' though. Plays the fiddle."

"Any kin to Dr. Warder at Camperville?"

"Brother."

"You don't say so? Brother, eh?"

"Yep. He's got another brother that's an eye doctor in St. Louis. They say *he's* a big man."

"Caroline Irving married into a tony crowd, didn't she?" "Marvin Warder ain't so tony. Keeps a feed store."

"I know, but I've heard 'bout that Dr. Warder in St. Louis. They say he won't look at you for less'n twenty-five dollars."

"I'd hate to have him look at me every day!"

"Yes, sir. Fact. They say the waiting room in his office is always full."

"Twenty-five dollars every time, too, eh?"

"Well, you know, when something gets wrong with a body's eyes they'll pay anything. Nobody wants to go blind."

"Yes, I guess that's so."

"Well, now, 'bout this Marvin Warder. How's it happen he ain't something like that? You say he runs a feed store?"

"I heard he just wasn't much force. Always playing the fiddle. You know how it is."

"Yep. Like this here Bob Callicott Miles Jackson's got on the *Gazette*."

"Something like that, I guess."

"He ain't much good."

"Jackson says he's all right."

"On a newspaper, maybe."

"Say, does he still run after that Sims woman?"

The speaker's voice dropped to a confidential pitch. All leaned forward to hear.

"They tell me he's out to her house two or three times a week."

"You don't say so?"

"Yes, sir. Regular."

"What's her husband think about it?"

"Don't nobody know. Brock Sims weighs two hundred and could kill an ox with his fist. Guess nobody wants to ask him any questions."

"Don't he know nothing about it?"

"Well, that's what's kind of funny. Bob Callicott goes there in broad daylight, just like you or me would walk into our own house. Goes there on Sunday sometimes when Sims is there himself."

"Well, I'll be damned. If I caught anybody hanging round my old woman—"

"Ain't Bob Callicott afraid of Brock Sims?"

"Don't look like it."

"What you reckon she sees in Bob Callicott? He looks like a scarecrow to me."

"You never can tell 'bout women."

"That's so, too."

A new speaker interrupted. "I guess you all ain't heard the news about Mis' Sims."

"What's that?"

"She was operated on by Dr. Gordon last week."

"Is that so? What for?"

"I don't know exactly. Something about her ear, I heard."

"Oh."

"Pretty serious, though."

"How's that?"

"Well, I hear the operation went through all right, but they say half her face is all paralyzed."

"What you reckon could have been the matter?"

"Ain't got no idea whatever. But my wife told me her face had all kind of swung around on one side. Mouth's way off over here. You know exactly like that man from St. Stephen, what's his name? Aw, you know who I mean: Alvin Keller—that's the name, Alvin Keller. Comes up to Kings Row on circus days and fair week. Never see him till next circus comes around. Well, he's got a paralyzed face, too. Recollect?"

"Gosh, yes. I hate to look at him. Face all slewed round toward one ear."

"That's it. That's the man. Well, they say Mis' Sims is just like that."

"Lord, that's terrible, ain't it?"

"Yes, 'tis."

"Can't Doc Gordon do anything for it?"

"Not for that. Once you're paralyzed anywhere, there ain't nothing they can do about it. You're that way for life."

"That's so. Ain't nothing you can do."

"'Bout Mis' Sims, you all know there's been talk about her for years and years. It used to be old Judge Roseborough himself was always calling on her."

"I never heard about that."

"It was years ago. Shortly after she was first married to Brock Sims."

"Well, what in the hell's wrong out there?"

"I don't know. Nobody knows."

"You reckon something's wrong with Brock—you know, like that there Vincent boy, the one that never did have any whiskers?"

"Brock Sims' got whiskers!"

"Yeh, I know. But when a woman looks around like that right after she's married."

"I guess some women are like that."

"Just can't satisfy 'em."

"That, or they just like a change. I bet you like a change yourself, sometimes."

There was loud laughter and a great slapping of thighs.

"But to come back, you say Mis' Sims is pretty likely to stay; that way?"

"Sure. Dr. Gordon saved her life though, I guess."

"She was bad off."

"She must have been or they wouldn't a-operated."

"Yeh, guess so."

"There's been men going to see that woman off and on for years. As I said, Judge Roseborough was the first one. You recollect him, don't you? Big, fine-looking man. Very dressy, he was, too. When Judge Roseborough died they tell me Mis' Sims went to the funeral and up at the graveyard she took on like she was one of the family. They say Judge Roseborough's wife never got over that. Moved away shortly after, and never has come back here again."

"I guess half the time we don't know what's going on right in our own town."

"'Twasn't long after the Judge died when she took up with a Mr. van der Luke. Smart fellow, sold reapers and other farm machinery. Made his headquarters at the hotel here. He run around with her for more'n a year. Took her out buggy-riding. People said they seen them away down as far as Phillips' Crossing many a time. He'd take her to supper Saturday nights at the hotel. Bold as brass, both of 'em. Then he went away. Was transferred to some other territory, or something. I never heard of him again. Then there was that young Dr. Hand—one of the asylum doctors."

"Oh, I recall him well. Good-looking fellow, too."

"Sure. She picked 'em good-looking until she took up with Bob Callicott. He was the last one."

"She ain't *dead* yet."

"Might as well be, if she looks like they say she does."

"Maybe 'taint her face Bob Callicott goes out there for!"

The roars and guffaws echoed around the square once more.

"Some folks say faces ain't got anything to do with it."

"All I say is, give me a pretty face to go along with everything else."

"That's me, too."

"You know I always thought Mis' Sims was a mighty good-looking woman."

"She was. But there'll be others. There always is."

"Some of 'em in this town going the same way right now."

"Wouldn't be surprised." This time the tone of casual gossip gave way to one of eager curiosity.

"You fellows know them two little Ross gals?"

"Live on Cherry Street, just above McGurney's store there?"

"Them's the ones I'm talking about Well, they tell me can't nobody teach them kids anything. They know everything."

"They're older'n kids, though. Must be sixteen or seventeen."

"Just about that age. Prettier'n a picture, 'specially the younger one."

"I see one or the other of 'em flying round pretty often with that McHugh boy from up on Union Street."

"Drake McHugh?"

"Yeh.

"Um-m! He won't do her any good. B'longs to the upper crust."

"Well, he's always picking her up and going out the St. Stephens Road. 'Long about dark, too."

"That's the way they go when they get started."

"His uncle, Mr. Rhodes Livingstone, was a high-stepper himself."

"That's what I've heard, too."

"Guess the boy takes after him."

"Say, didn't old man Livingstone leave that boy a pile of money?"

"He left him some, but mostly his own daddy left him a regular fortune in trust."

"Won't ever have to work a lick, eh?"

"Not less'n he wants to. He can take it easy all his life."

"He won't have money long if he starts out with rubber-tired buggies and fast girls."

"That's the truth. One thing leads to another."

"I've seen it a heap of times."

"So've I. Time and time again."

Up on the courthouse porch there was more talk. It was more quietly spoken. It was framed in more graceful phrases. Sometimes it was indirect. Occasionally it was old-fashioned, a shade formal, even elegant. But the tenor was the same.

The slow hours passed. The slow talk marked the time without excitement, making the verbal pattern of the town in full consonance with the varied emotional shadings of the varied beings who acted parts, and of those who watched. Old men died, and the even talk went on appraising, condemning, summing up. The good and bad deeds, the exploits, the qualities of the subjects, were set in terse and homely phrases and became the very fabric of all the county's legend, the very coinage of human evaluations. Young men came into action and were watched from every side with zealous attention. The transitions from generation to generation were so gradual and so smoothly joined that no one noticed them at all. Life presented the familiar illusion of a continuous and unbroken stream.

Violence, and shock, and the sudden shearing of vital courses took place in the secrecy of individual minds. Kings Row in all of its externals was in no way different from the appearance of the world anywhere, any time. Life seemed to be lived in a low key and at a creeping tempo. Only a few—Miles Jackson, Isaac Skeffington, Father Donovan—saw below the surface. Occasionally their remarks stirred their listeners to an unease and unrest they did not understand.

Parris was practicing. It was really too hot to practice comfortably, but just lately his study with Herr Berdorff had taken a surprising turn, and he was interested.

Herr Berdorff had stopped him one morning in the midst of a Clementi study. Parris could tell by his heavy breathing that Berdorff was excited about something. "Look now," he said. "We begin somethings. No more of this Clementi and Czerny. It iss now enough of these, and this little watchfulness of each finger. You have learned good, most good. Lissten to me now. The real playing of the piano iss big, very big. It iss under *streng*—strict control, always. It sounds free, but always the player knows how far, how loud, how free. We do now some big Beethoven and, yes, if you will, somethings, too, of Chopin. Those are somethings—

"We work now for the big line, the big effect. *Heroisch*. You understand? *Olympisch*. Beethoven—like Moses, like the ancient prophets, like the great Greeks. You understand? You read? You know what I say? Yes. I think maybe you are really intelligent. Now. You see here. I show you a little how this goes. My fingers are maybe too thick when I don't practice. But, later—"

Herr Berdorff puffed and perspired. Sometimes he snorted. He shouted explanations above the roar of the piano. "You see? You hear? From here we go direct—like an eagle when he flies—to there. *Aber* direct. No wiggling with *Kleinigkeiten*. There iss no time—no *room* for such. Little peoples make little effects, little phrases. No! No! It iss the tramp of a hero—a giant. And the tone, mind you—for this great Beethoven—the tone. Never sweet—never. *Fein, ja, kernig*. I tell you—when you go home, you read. You have a German Bible?"

"Yes, sir."

"You read Isaiah. Out loud you read it. And listen with your mind. What kind of tone? You listen and you hear something like Beethoven maybe. It iss no way to teach you, but maybe you, too, have the imagination as much as

I think. For you maybe I don't have to say somethings about Isaiah and the Greeks. Maybe I do. You are a boy and you cannot read everythings at once. Lissten, again—"

Parris thought Herr Berdorff looked pleased at the next lesson. He felt that he had understood much of what the earnest German preacher had said. *Heroisch*. Yes; not unlike Herr Berdorff himself. Something sound, and simple, under the rolling German speech that poured through the lesson like a torrent.

He wiped his face and his hands, and began again. As exact as possible, he told himself, but remembering "We start *here*, we go direct to *there*." His piano did not yield the thunders of the Professor's big Steinweg. He arched his fingers firmly, set them over the chords, and lunged with the weight of his body. A string broke and curled and danced with a wild jangle inside the lid.

"Oh, damn it!" That meant calling old Hans Wickermann. He would potter for two whole days making the repair.

"Parris! Parris, please!"

"Yes, Anna, what is it?"

"Someone calls you on the telephone. It sounds like somebody almost is crying. What do you think, maybe, is?"

"Crying?" A stab of fear thrust at him. Cassie! Something had happened to Cassie. He picked up the receiver.

"Hello!"

"Hello, Parris. Is that you?" It was Jamie Wakefield. He sounded tearful.

"Yes. What's the matter?"

"Oh, Parris! Haven't you heard?"

"Heard what? What are you talking about, Jamie? What's happened?"

"Bob!"

"Mr. Callicott? Well, what about him?"

"Parris, he's dead!"

"Oh, gee, Jamie! I'm awfully sorry. Don't cry. Tell me what happened."

"He—he had typhoid fever. I went out to see him. I—I didn't think he was so sick. He—he died yesterday afternoon."

"Gee, I'm sorry, Jamie. You lost a good friend, didn't you?"

"Just about all I've got in the world, Parris. He understood me so!"

Parris repressed a smile, feeling it would show in his voice. "Gee, I'm sorry."

"Listen, Parris. I want you to do something for me."

"Why, of course, Jamie. What?"

"I want you to go to the funeral with me this afternoon."

"Where is it?" Parris couldn't keep a shade of dismay out of his voice. He didn't want to go.

"At the Presbyterian church, at three o'clock. Parris, you just got to go with me."

"All right, Jamie—if you want me to specially, I'll go."

"You don't want to go, do you?"

"What difference does that make? I guess I don't like to go to funerals, maybe. I never have been to but two or three. They make me feel bad."

"You got to go with me. I couldn't bear to go by myself. Of course nobody here at home would go with me. Everybody in this town was so down on Bob, and now he's dead." Jamie wailed.

"Well, hold on, Jamie. You got to be fair. Mr. Callicott didn't die because people were down on him, as you say. He died of typhoid fever."

"All right. You'll go with me, won't you?"

"Yes."

"Will you meet me somewhere?"

"Did you say three o'clock?"

"Yes."

"What'd they pick the hottest hour in the day for to have the funeral?"

"How can you think about anything like that?"

"Well, it's hot, isn't it?"

"You come by here, why don't you? You can cool off first, and then we'll go together."

"All right. I'll be there 'bout half-past two."

"Thank you, Parris."

"Oh, fiddle. You don't have to thank me. I'll be there."

The interior of the Presbyterian church seemed very dark and cool in contrast to the white afternoon outside. The north windows were open and one caught a view of the sunlight quivering across the Livingstone yard.

There were not more than twenty people in the church. They sat in the unnatural hush preceding a funeral. Now and then someone whispered softly to a neighbor. A few fans fluttered.

Jamie shrank back toward the vestibule. "I—I don't want anybody to see me, Parris. I—can't keep from crying. Honest, I try not to. Let's go up in the gallery. Nobody'll see us up there."

Parris liked the suggestion. Jamie's face was red and splotchy, and he sniffed frequently behind his handkerchief.

"Come on."

They went up the narrow stairs to the wide shadowy gallery that circled the auditorium. It had a musty smell. It was warmer here, too, than downstairs. They went cautiously down the irregular aisle steps to a front seat. Both started violently when the big bell in the south tower boomed.

"I guess the funeral's pretty near here when they begin tolling the bell, isn't it?" Parris' voice was unsteady. Jamie nodded. He was crying again and could not speak. At each muffled stroke of the bell Jamie winced as though he had been struck.

"Look, Jamie. Isn't that Herr Berdorff at the organ?"

Jamie nodded again and blew his nose. "Yes, Mr. Jackson down at the *Gazette* office got him to play instead of Mrs. van Meter because she doesn't play very well. The family kind of thought since B-Bob was a musician they ought to have a professor play at his funeral."

"Where's the choir?"

"There isn't going to be any singing. Mr. Jackson told old Mr. Callicott that Bob didn't want any singing at his funeral, so there's going to be just some playing, nothing else."

"That's sort of original, isn't it?"

"It seems all right."

There was a stir in the little group downstairs and a craning of necks. The funeral procession was drawing up beside the church.

Parris could see the glitter of Herr Berdorff's glasses in the gloomy recess where the organ console stood, as "the professor" bent to examine the stops. The bell tolled once more and the sound died away in a fading pulse of vibrations. Parris visualized the sound as slanting golden rings that rocked and swayed about the trembling bell in the tower.

He nearly jumped from his seat as the organ crashed suddenly in a fortissimo chord that seemed to shake the whole church. The chord thrilled and quivered and sank and rose again. Another outcry from the full organ struck the two boys with the effect of a blow. Jamie was wide-eyed with astonishment. Parris thought of what Herr Berdorff had said: "The tread of a giant."

The music circled closer and closer, and subsided to an almost imperceptible sigh. Very slowly it swung into a march so desolate that Jamie began to cry again. Parris had never heard anyone play the organ well; he listened with a growing emotion. Presently his face was wet with tears. Herr Berdorff played for several minutes. The music lost the tone of wildness and grew calmer. An unexpected modulation to a major key came like unexpected sunlight Parris recognized the Bach chorale that followed, with its whispered closing cadence.

His attention wandered as the minister read and spoke conventional phrases. He came back suddenly when he heard the words, "tribute from one close to him," and the name, "Mr. Miles Jackson."

Everyone stirred and sat up. Miles Jackson rose from a front pew and walked to the head of the coffin. He faced the auditorium which had gradually filled during the music, and laid his hand on the black cloth of the casket.

Everyone waited. A few people looked about inquiringly. This was certainly an unusual proceeding.

Miles Jackson rocked back and forth on his toes for a moment. He was not an impressive figure. His white linen suit was rather shapeless and his tie was too loosely tied. He removed his hand from the coffin and thrust it deep in his trousers pocket. Usually Miles Jackson forgot to button his pants. Parris looked nervously, but all was well today.

"We have come here today to honor a man." His voice sounded thin and high-pitched—a little rasping. A sarcastic sound, Parris thought.

"In this person was gathered together a constellation of gifts and qualities which constituted the personality of Robert Callicott. Maybe this constellation of qualities, flowing through countless ages of time, and assembling in the mind and character of this man—maybe this constellation of qualities made up his soul. I say, maybe: I don't know.

"I don't know if Robert Callicott admitted the existence of the soul. What he thought about such matters he kept to himself. I don't know what he thought about religion, or salvation, or immortality. But I know what he thought about beauty."

Jackson paused and again laid his hand on the coffin. He tilted his head sideways almost as if he were examining the quality of the black cloth under his fingers.

He looked back at his audience. His thick white eyebrows pointed forward like threatening horns.

"This town didn't think much of Robert Callicott."

An instant rustle greeted this sentence—the quick concerted intake of the breath of surprise.

"This town," he repeated, "didn't think much of Robert Callicott. This town didn't know him. Robert Callicott was a poet.

"I don't know how good a poet he was. Time may tell. Maybe not. His work may be forgotten with him. No one can tell. But being a poet doesn't consist solely of writing poetry. It is, first of all, a way of seeing, a way of knowing, and a way of life.

"This universe was not conceived in beauty. It was conceived in tragedy and travail. It evolved, and continues to be, only in the throes of desperate struggle. Pain, and ugliness, and brute force rule it.

"In the midst of that continuous hurricane of destruction and death there are born from time to time men who resolve this disorder. They create another vision from the fire and dust of disaster. They are poets, and musicians, and artists. That is their answer to the ugliness of the world. They do not ask to be understood. They do not even ask to be liked. But without them we should find the universe an intolerable habitation. They lessen its terrors, and ameliorate the eternal torture of its unanswered and unanswerable questions. They are a gallant company. They go singing down the highways of the world, and the echoes of their words comfort us when they have passed. To that small company—that company of God's own elect—Robert Callicott belonged.

"I have said that I do not know what Robert Callicott thought about immortality. I only know what I think about it. Scientists tell us that if you drop a stone into the ocean the widening waves will pass on and on to the remotest shore, and that they will then return, traveling forever back and forth as long as the sea shall stand. I believe that. I think our preachers ought to preach sermons about that scientific truth.

"In some such way as that Robert Callicott will return to us from the farthest coasts of eternity."

Jackson had been looking over the heads of his listeners. His gaze came back now. He touched the coffin again. He spoke his concluding sentence in a half-voice as though he were speaking to himself.

"Many angels visited this man while he lived: the kindest one was the angel of death."

The speaker looked directly at his listeners. He took his hand from his pocket and passed it across his face. He opened his mouth to say something further, changed his mind, and sat down.

... The minister was reading again, and praying. The music began its regretful murmur, and the congregation rose as Hector Godbold wheeled the coffin toward the south door.

"Listen, Parris, I'm not going to the cemetery. I—I just can't go. I can't go out looking like this."

"Well, stop crying."

"I can't, Parris. Please, Parris."

"Please what?"

Jamie lay down on the hard cushion of the narrow pew. He buried his face in his wet handkerchief.

"Here, take my handkerchief."

Jamie reached for it without looking up. "Thanks."

"Come on, Jamie. Everybody's gone out of the church."

"I don't care. I tell you what you do. You go on and just leave me here a little while. I'll come on out after a while. I—I've got to stop crying first."

"Aw—I'll stay with you."

"No. You go on. I'll stop easier if you're not here."

"Oh, quit that, Jamie. You got to behave yourself now, and stop crying."

"I will—pretty soon. Please go on without me."

"You want me to, sure enough?"

"Yes."

"'By, kid. Don't stay here too long."

Jamie shook his head but crouched lower in the seat.

Parris stumbled up the steps again. He stopped at the last row of pews, a little startled to see a woman sitting there, and suddenly a little uneasy, wondering if he and Jamie had been observed. She was heavily veiled and Parris saw that she was crying. He wondered for a moment who she was and why she was hiding in this far corner of the church. He was about to speak as he passed, when he saw in the half-light that she was hideously disfigured. Her features were terribly drawn to one side. She gave the grotesque effect of crying on one side of her face.

He was acutely embarrassed, and hurried down the stairs as fast as he could.

The funeral procession was under way, and the bell was tolling again. The sound seemed less mellow now. It was as harsh and hard as the sound of iron striking on iron.

Isaac Skeffington and Miles Jackson were getting into the Skeffington carriage as Parris turned into the shady side street.

"Well, Miles, that kind of talk won't build up your subscription lists much."

"I don't give one half a god-damn," Jackson answered. "Gimme a match."

Sam Winters stooped over Robert Callicott's grave in the late afternoon sunlight, patting the mound into shape with a narrow spade.

"Tall feller, wan't he?" he said to his assistant. "Danged if that grave don't look ten feet long. There, I guess that's all right. There'll be a little fixin' up to do tomorrow. I'll be around here. Let's go."

Mrs. Emma Bascom sat on her front porch finishing the last of her narrow strips of bread and butter. She scraped the sugar from the bottom of her iced-tea glass and smacked her lips with relish.

Sam Winters passed her gate. He tipped his hat.

"Howdy, ma'am."

"Howdy, Sam." She salvaged the slice of lemon and popped it into her mouth. "Old buzzard," she muttered. "I hope I outlive him. I'll be dogged if I want *him* shovelin' the last dirt in my face."

Book Three

1

Dr. Tower handed a small German pamphlet to Parris. "This may interest you."

Parris turned the pages rather listlessly. The type was bad.

"It is new—and important."

"Shall I take it with me?"

"I should like to see what you get out of it. It is along the lines of the newer investigations we've been talking about."

Dr. Tower watched Parris keenly. Parris was unaware of the rather professional scrutiny. He leaned his head on his hand, and his thick black hair tumbled across his brow, puckered a little just now, as he scanned the close print.

"I saw your grandmother yesterday."

Parris looked up, somewhat startled. It was unlike Dr. Tower to speak of anything in the slightest degree personal.

"Yes, sir? She drives most afternoons if the weather is good."

"I thought she was not looking well."

A quick alarm shot through Parris.

"She—she isn't quite well."

"Is she under a doctor's care now?"

"Well, she sees Dr. Gordon from time to time. I don't know if you'd say she is exactly under his care."

Dr. Tower tapped his teeth with the eraser of a pencil. He looked out of the window and back at Parris without moving his head.

"I hope you won't misunderstand my question, but have you any idea what's wrong?"

Parris laid the book down. "No, I haven't really. I believe—well, sir, I just hadn't thought it could be anything serious. She's rather—rather lively all the time."

"She doesn't look well."

The peculiar emphasis this time really frightened Parris. "Do you think there is something—"

Dr. Tower interrupted brusquely. "I don't think anything about it. I'm not your grandmother's physician."

Parris flushed darkly. "I beg your pardon."

"I guess maybe I should say the same thing. Have you any relatives, Parris?"

"None at all. Only some very distant ones—that my grandmother doesn't like much."

The doctor smiled. "I daresay. Most people have such connections. No near relatives at all? That's rather unusual, isn't it?"

"Perhaps so. I guess I never thought much about it. I'm just used to the idea. My father and mother were both only children."

"So you have no uncles or aunts?"

"And no cousins."

"Naturally. H'm. You'll be quite alone when—quite alone someday."

"Yes, sir."

"It could have its advantages, I imagine."

"I expect it could be pretty lonesome, too."

"Have your father and mother been dead a long time?"

"My mother died shortly after I was born, and my father just a few months later."

"You were lucky to have this grandmother."

"You bet I was. Certainly."

"Very devoted to her, aren't you?"

Parris didn't answer. His lips were quivering.

"Now listen, Parris. I want to give you just a very little bit of advice. It—it has to be very confidential."

"Yes, sir." The words came breathlessly. Parris felt his heart beat quickly and heavily.

"Did you ever hear of Dr. Ladd in St. Louis?"

"Dr. Emmett Ladd?"

"Yes."

"Yes, sir. He's a great surgeon, isn't he?"

"A very fine surgeon, indeed. Ever hear of Dr. Everett? Dr. John Everett?"

"No, sir."

"Good diagnostician."

"I see."

"Do you think you could in any way persuade Madame von Eln to go to St. Louis to consult them?"

The color faded slowly from Parris' face, his eyes darkened, and his words came huskily. "I don't know how I could do it. I don't think she'd pay any attention to me. She'd want to know what made me think of it."

"Yes, yes. Doubtless. Is Skeffington her lawyer?"

"Yes, sir."

"Good friend of the family?"

"I think so."

"Could you talk to him?"

"Maybe. Or—could you do it for me?"

"No." The reply was curt and cold.

Parris shrank sensitively from the cutting tone. "I guess I'm being kind of awkward this afternoon, sir, but, gee, Dr. Tower, I'm scared. I—Ive been scared all this winter. I didn't know why. It was just—just instinctive."

"H'm, yes, I see. I think you're going to be a good doctor, Parris. Now let me see."

"I'd like to ask you a question, sir, but I expect you wouldn't want to answer it."

"Well, fire away. What is it?"

"Isn't Dr. Gordon a good doctor?"

Dr. Tower looked steadily at Parris for a moment. "Not a very tactful question, young man, nor a very ethical one for a young doctor-to-be to ask." He smiled, and Parris smiled, too, rather wanly. "But I must say that so far as I know Dr. Gordon knows his business."

"Oh, gee, I'm glad to hear you say that."

"You trust my judgment, do you?"

"Oh, absolutely. I know you know."

"Maybe you're a fool, Parris Mitchell."

"No, sir, I don't think I am—not about this. I know you always know what you're talking about."

Dr. Tower colored a little, a very little. Parris stared. Dr. Tower was always so cool and detached, so remote and cold, that this slight show of emotion took on an aspect of exaggeration.

"I'm curious to know why you think so. You're flattering, but it may not be a very intelligent conclusion of yours."

"Well, sir, there are some things you just *know*."

"Instinct?"

"Yes, sir. I guess so." Parris moved forward in his chair. He forgot the distant formality that usually characterized his talks with Dr. Tower. "You remember that little book of Friedlander's that you had me read last month. He said a lot about unconscious observations and how we sometimes add up a long sum of this kind of observations and come to conclusions that are quite right without knowing how we got them."

"Yes."

"Well," Parris smiled frankly, "it's like that."

Dr. Tower looked grave. He did not smile, and an odd, faraway expression, almost a look of inattention, came into his eyes.

Parris went on. "There are some of the teachers over at Aberdeen I feel that way about. Dr. Vance for one."

"Physics?"

"Yes, sir. And Dr. Purdy."

"Mathematics?"

Parris nodded. "But, Dr. McLaughlin—"

Dr. Tower waited a moment. "What about Dr. McLaughlin?"

"I don't think he knows much about some of the things he talks about in ethics class, and I don't think he believes them, anyway."

Dr. Tower laughed.

Parris continued. "But I know you believe what you say—"

"Whether it's so or not?"

"I wasn't going to say that."

"Well, keep your mind open. You're going to see and learn a lot of new things in your life. We're on the brink—the very brink of important discoveries. You'll see. And—I guess, even at the risk of paying myself a compliment, I'd advise you to trust your instincts as you call them—your intuitions. Sometimes intuitions are a good corrective for the natural astigmatisms of human perceptions."

"Yes, sir. About my grandmother, now—"

"You'll have to think of some way. It may not be important for her to consult anyone. I can't mix into it in any way."

"I see. Oh, gee! I didn't think of that!"

"What?"

"Anna!"

"Who is Anna?"

"She's a maid, but more like a companion to my grandmother. She scolds and bosses everybody. She's awfully goodhearted—awfully good to both of us."

"Could you talk to her, you think?"

"Yes, sir. And she'd worry my grandmother into doing anything she'd want her to do. She just wouldn't let her alone until she did it if it was for her own good."

Dr. Tower smiled again. "I *think* I follow you. It may be a good idea. Now, mind, leave me out of it. I spoke in confidence."

"Of course, certainly, and thank you a lot."

"By the way, I understood when you first came here that the plan was to send you to Vienna."

"Yes, sir."

"Is that still the plan?"

"Why, yes, sir."

"I don't mean to be inquisitive. I am only interested in the way I work with you. Has, er—has your grandmother made such arrangements?"

"Well, sir, she did tell me that there would be money enough for me to do this, if that is what you mean."

"I only wished to be assured that you wouldn't be disappointed in any way."

"She told me that the bank would be—I guess you say act as guardian and see that I got my medical education."

"I see. Your grandmother seems to be most intelligent. All that seems very good. Then, when you are a doctor, what?"

"How do you mean?"

"It takes money to set up in practice—and while you are waiting for patients."

"I guess there'll be enough for that, too. You know what I want to do?"

"No. What?"

"I want to be a doctor out at the asylum."

"Here—in Kings Row?"

"Yes, sir."

"What put that idea into your head?"

"Tom Carr."

"Who is he?"

"A man who works on our place."

"Indeed. You seem to have a number of influences."

Parris flushed again. It annoyed him that he couldn't control it. He felt his cheeks grow hotter as Dr. Tower's sarcastic tone took full effect. He felt a wave of something like anger, too, as he thought of that tone being directed at old Tom Carr. He spoke up with an almost defiant loyalty. "Tom Carr is a very unusual man."

"I have no doubt. Suppose you tell me about him."

Parris related the story of Lucy Carr and her death, and explained the way he had felt, even at the outset of his acquaintance with her, that there should be some way to seize her flitting mind and hold it still. Dr. Tower listened without a word of comment.

"And there's another thing, too—somebody else."

"All right. Tell me the whole story."

Parris told Dr. Tower of Benny Singer and of old Tom Carr's theories about curing him, or at least helping him. He finished, a little disconcerted by Dr. Tower's silence. The doctor pushed the papers aside.

"I owe you some kind of an apology."

"What for?"

"Well, if you don't know, all right. I apologize just the same. It's all right, Parris, it's all right. You ought to be a fine doctor. There's just one thing I feel a little dubious about."

Parris waited.

"It's your idea of coming back here to Kings Row."

"Well. Tom Carr was the first one to suggest it, and then I kind of mentioned it to my grandmother, and she spoke right away to Colonel Skeffington, and he spoke to Dr. Nolan out at the asylum."

"Is he the new head out there?"

"Yes, sir."

"D'you ever meet him?"

"Yes, sir. Colonel Skeffington took me out riding with him one day and stopped by there to speak to Dr. Nolan. He introduced me, but I could see he had talked about me beforehand."

Dr. Tower laughed once more. "I dare say. I dare say. Well, you seem to have friends paving the way for you. It's just—"

"It is a fine asylum, isn't it?"

"Oh, I suppose so, I suppose so. Any one of them is a good place for the young doctor. It's just—"

"Just what, sir?"

"'Young eagles should nest far from home.' Ever hear that?"

"No, sir."

"It's a good saying. There's a curious rivalry between the old and the young. It's everywhere, but it's keener, and it's more ruthless and more cruel in the home nest, so to speak."

"I—I guess I don't understand that very well."

"No; you couldn't, but it is a fact. However, we don't have to settle all those problems today. They'll doubtless take care of themselves when the time comes. I want to tell you, though, that you are fortunate in a lot of ways."

"I know it, Dr. Tower. I know I'm fortunate to be reading with you, sir."

Dr. Tower inclined his head gravely. He did not smile, nor was his look deprecating. "Thank you," he said simply.

Parris looked away quickly as he felt his color rise again. For the first time some conflicting emotions struck hard across each other's way. Dr. Tower had never before relaxed his distant detachment. Parris had always admired and respected the doctor's mind and had kept a curious loyalty—curious because it was so remote from any affection or any emotional coloring. Today Dr. Tower, by his concern for Madame von Eln and for Parris' future, had touched a new chord. The response was instant—and uncomfortable. Parris felt guilty.

He had seen Cassandra several times this year—"whenever she could slip away," as she said. He had never felt any unease of conscience about it. Those meetings with Cassandra were in a world apart. Once Dr. Tower had used the phrase "We live in multiple worlds many of which are solitary and strange to all others," and he had found himself making immediate application of the figure to himself and Cassandra. As Drake would have said, and did, in fact, say several times, it was their own business.

Just now he was less certain about that. He hadn't been troubled by that word "slipping." He hadn't associated it with sneaking. But now the two words came into sudden collision, and he shrank in his chair.

Cassandra! He could not precisely say to himself how he felt about her. He had always been quite clear about his feelings for other people. His likes and dislikes, his attractions and gravitations, fell into easily recognizable categories. He knew exactly how he felt about Renée—still. He knew how he felt about Drake, and Jamie, and almost anyone he knew well. But, Cassie. That was a different relationship. She made him uncomfortable sometimes, and sometimes she almost terrified him. She was so wild, so violent, so—so furious. Once she had come to meet him at Drake's house—well, he had felt that night that maybe he didn't want to see her again. He understood now what she had said that first night in this very study—he glanced sideways at the couch—right there. She had been right. He was not in love with her—not exactly. He didn't know what to call it. It was a fascination of some kind that came back again and again with unflagging force. Her amazing loveliness, her almost embarrassing frankness, her crazy abandon, and—he sorted out words carefully—yes, her wearying intensity. She tried him so—not physically so much as some other way—psychically, maybe. She was a kind of excitement that he dreaded, but which he found he wished for, too.

He was equally sure that Cassie was not in love with him. Again he supplemented the thought—not exactly. He thought it likely that she felt about him much as he did about her. It was all kind of crazy. He tried to tell Drake about it. Drake merely whistled and said, "Hot-choo!" Drake clearly had no conception of the nature of the relationship. To Drake it wasn't a relationship at all as Parris saw it, it was merely a bit of luck of which he was openly envious.

Parris had thought often of the danger of discovery. Drake discounted his fears, and Cassie ignored them. Just now he was once more aware of the disastrous consequences that might follow if Dr. Tower so much as suspected anything. There was a quality of threat about the man that was not comfortable to contemplate. Parris shrugged but not with disdain. It was an atavistic gesture. Many long-gone generations of realistic Gallic ancestors facing wreck and ruin contributed to it. Dr. Tower had been watching Parris with interest. He was amused now.

"Daydreaming?"

Parris started. "Oh, I beg your pardon! Yes, I guess I was."

"Well, from that shrug which was certainly years older than you are, you must have made up your mind to make the best of it."

Parris tried to smile, but the essay was not successful.

The doctor continued in a rather bantering tone. "Let the Devil take the hindmost, eh?"

This was getting too near the mark. Parris grinned a bit sheepishly, but he felt daring and adventurous. "Guess I'll have to."

"It's not too bad a philosophy sometimes." Dr. Tower seemed to forget the subject. He looked absently at Parris, who was buckling a strap around his books. "I'll see you on Thursday this week. Is that right?"

"Yes, sir."

Parris hurried toward home. He was nearly at the end of Federal Street when Drake overtook him. Drake had gotten rid of old Molly, and the new chestnut horse was smart-looking and high-spirited.

"Hop in. I'll drive you home."

"Fine. Going my way, anyhow?"

"Yep. 'Sides, I got something for you."

"Oh." Parris' exclamation was dull and disinterested.

"Is that the way you receive a note from your sweetheart?"

"She's not, and you know it."

"Well, I'd say Cassie is something or other pretty important to you."

"Let's see the note."

Drake gave it to him. "In my box this morning."

Parris read the few lines hurriedly. "Oh, gee!" He sounded dismayed.

"What's the matter?"

"She wants to see me at your house tonight."

"Don't you want to?"

"No."

"Say, what's the matter with you?"

"I just can't see her tonight."

"What's the matter with that gal, anyhow?"

"Oh, she's all right, Drake."

"Likes you, eh?"

"I guess so."

"Hot, eh?"

"Nymphomania, maybe."

"What in hell's that?"

"What Cassie's got."

"Say, is that a disease?"

"Not exactly."

"Oh! Just hot, you mean?"

"More'n that."

"Gee!"

"I guess I'm kind of the same way, Drake. Far as she's concerned, anyway."

"Like her, eh?"

"Yes. Just terribly much, sometimes. Then, sometimes—"

"I know, kid, I know all about it. That's Poppy Ross, too. Same way. Sometimes I'd—I'd—well I could bite her to pieces. Then next day I wish she'd let me alone."

Parris grinned. "Not what I mean, exactly. Cassie—gee, I feel terrible talking about her like this, Drake—you know I wouldn't to anybody else. I guess I'd hardly talk to you even if it wasn't that you know all about us, anyway."

"It's all right, kid."

"She's pretty nice, Drake."

"Yeh. Kind of top layer, ain't she?"

"Yes."

"Funny she keeps after you. Generally nice girls—you know what I mean, I think Cassie's nice all right, but—generally—"

"Oh, you don't have to be so careful what you say."

"Well, I mean nice girls generally ain't so anxious."

"It hasn't got anything to do with nice girls—or—or the other kind."

"You think everybody feels the same way?"

"Different degrees, Drake."

"I see. I don't believe that, kid. The easy gals are a lot more fun, but the easy ones are not—not what I said just now—they're not top layer."

"How do you know?"

"I know all kinds."

Parris laughed. "Might be different kinds of manners—like table manners, you know."

"Say, you're smart. That might be right, too. Parris, you're getting to be a regular—er—philosopher."

"No, I'm not. I've learned a lot from Dr. Tower, though. He's more intelligent than all of Aberdeen College put together."

"Is that so. Smart, eh? He always looked sort of crazy to me, a little bit somehow."

"He's not."

"No? Well, something's funny as hell about that house. And old Cass—you just now said yourself ..."

"Well, darn it, Drake, that's not *crazy*."

"You said it was—what did you call it?"

"Nymphomania. Well, it's just kind of outside normal. A condition, maybe—like running a high fever."

"Say, you dummy, that's what I said—hot. Didn't I? Ain't that what I said?"

"All right, all right. But I can't see her tonight."

"You're a fool, kid. Better take everything you can get while you can get it."

"I can't be there tonight."

"Another gal somewhere?"

"No. Of course not."

"Well, don't bite me. No reason why you shouldn't have a dozen if you want 'em."

"What'll I do?"

"'Bout what?"

"About Cassie. She'll be coming to your house tonight. I haven't got any way to let her know."

"I could just tell her you couldn't come."

"Would you do that, Drake? And see that she gets back home all right, by Cherry Street?"

"Of course. Or—" Drake grinned broadly.

"What?"

"I could do a little looking after her myself, if she's—if she's running such a high fever!"

A queer feeling struck Parris. It was like a cold pain in his middle. He didn't know what to make of the feeling.

Drake chuckled and slapped Parris on die leg. "Oh, ho! Feel different when you think about anybody else snooking up to old Cass, eh?"

"Gee, Drake!"

"Sure, I know how you feel. Only you didn't know till just now how you felt yourself, did you?"

"I'm not in love with Cassie, Drake."

"How you know?"

"I—I just know."

"Haven't got another gal you're not telling me about?"

"No. Of course not. I guess I'd tell you anything."

"Of course. I bet you would, too. You better come on back with me and take care of your own gal. You can telephone home and let 'em know you're staying with me."

"It's my grandmother I'm worried about, Drake."

"She sick?"

"She's not well. I got sort of worried about her today."

"Well, you're not her doctor—not yet. What you going to do about it tonight? Better come on back with me."

Parris thought about it. He wanted to go back.

"What time is Cass coming over?"

"About eleven or twelve, I guess, whenever she thinks it's safe to leave the house."

"She's nervy, ain't she? Gosh, if her old man'd catch her!"

"I talked to her about it. I got awfully scared for her, but I can't do anything with her."

"Well, what do you say, kid? Here we are. Want to come on back with me, or not?"

"I tell you, Drake. I'll have supper at home. I—I got to talk to Anna about my grandmother. Then if I feel better, I'll come on later."

"And if you don't?"

"I'll telephone you."

"What you want me to tell Cassie?"

"Tell her the truth. Tell her my grandmother is sick and I'm worried and can't come."

"Bet she'll be mad."

"Well, let her."

"You'll feel different 'bout tomorrow."

"Maybe."

Anna listened carefully to Parris. She controlled her face and answered him calmly, remembering Madame's warning.

"To tell you the truth, Parris, Madame did see Dr. Ladd."

"When? She hasn't been to St. Louis."

"Dr. Ladd came to Kings Row to see Mrs. Fuller that time she was so sick. They had some other big doctors here, too, for a—a—"

"Consultation?"

"Yes, that's it."

"And she saw Dr. Ladd then?"

"Yes. Dr. Gordon thought she ought, too. There's no use denying she ain't been so well, but she's better. Don't you think she looks better?"

"No."

"Madame's not so young, Parris, and little things get wrong with you when you get older. But you shouldn't worry now. You work hard and don't worry. I look after her the best I can."

"Yes, I know you do. You're mighty good to—to both of us, Anna."

"Ah, pshaw, now. Nonsense! Run on and don't worry."

"Where is *Grand'mère* now?"

"She's lying down. She said she wanted to nap. I guess you better not wake her up."

He felt mightily relieved. "All right. I guess I just got a little worried when Dr. Tower said he thought she didn't look so well."

"She's had a little cold, you know. That pulls a body down, too. Look, Parris. The cookies are done. I guess you're getting to be a young man, though. Maybe you don't care about fresh, warm cookies no more?"

Parris grinned. "And a glass of milk!"

"Good. I get it right away."

"I've got to telephone, too. I'll be right back."

He ran through the hall to the telephone. He put his hand on the bells and turned the little crank.

"Number two hundred and six, please."

Drake answered.

"Listen, Drake. I—I'll be in tonight. I guess I was a little foolish this afternoon."

"All right, you old kickapoo, come on. You ought to have come with me and you wouldn't have had to walk."

"I don't mind. I feel better now. I guess I'll have supper here at home. See you 'bout eight."

"I'll be back from supper myself by that time. If I ain't, the key's under the step. Say—you don't mind if I sort of step out early and leave you, do you?"

"Of course not. Poppy?"

"How'd you guess?"

It was not yet spring, but there was a feeling of spring in the air. Indefinable at first, and subtle. Day by day it became more noticeable. The touch of the

wind was less harsh. Steps on the walk were slower. The normal staccato of
speech, even, changed. Parris noticed the curious lyric drag that came into the
sound of passing conversations.

Parris was invaded by the strangest discomfort he had ever known. He was
unable to analyze it, but he knew it was more acute and arose from deeper
sources than the normal unrest of spring. Its very elusiveness added to the
sensation of unease. He roamed the place from end to end. He found it harder
and harder to stay indoors. As soon as he sat down to work he thought of some
corner of a field, some stretch of windy slope, some tree, even, that he felt he
must see at once.

Madame von Eln observed his restlessness. So did Anna.

"Anna, what is the matter with Parris? He seems unlike himself these days."

"Yes, Madame, I have been watching him. Always on the go. He no sooner
comes in than he goes out again."

"Where does he go?"

"That's what's funny, Madame."

"Funny?"

"Strange, maybe, you say. He never goes anywhere."

"Anna, he must go somewhere. Anywhere is somewhere."

"He doesn't go anywhere, Madame."

"Where is he now?"

"He's right up there on the side of the hill."

Madame arose and walked slowly to the window. Anna watched her with
troubled eyes.

"Where is it? I can't see, of course. I don't know why I look."

"Up there at the beginning of the orchard. He's standing there looking at a
tree."

"A tree? Looking at a tree, did you say?"

"Yes, Madame."

"Well, what for? One doesn't look at a tree. At least not when one is a
young man. Anna, why is he looking at a tree?"

"Madame, I do not know. To tell you the truth, he has been behaving a
little strangely."

"Anna, are you suggesting that my grandson is maybe a little peculiar in the
head?"

Anna laughed. "No, Madame, no, no. But he looks at stones, too."

"At what?"

"Stones, Madame, just stones."

"Stones?"

"You know, Madame, just rocks."

Madame resumed her seat, and Anna spread the brilliant peacock afghan
over her feet. Madame put on her thick-lensed glasses and looked at Anna with
lively amusement.

"Anna, is it possible that you are quite—quite—?"

"Oh, yes, Madame. I'm not crazy one bit. But I tell you Parris looks at things."

"Anna, I understand you less and less each minute. Of course he looks at things. How could he avoid looking at things? Come now, what are you talking about?"

Anna took a deep breath and wrapped her hands stubbornly in her checked gingham apron. It was a stand-pat gesture that Madame knew well. Anna could argue for days over the smallest trifles.

"It is just as I say, Madame. All the time he goes out. He comes in, then he goes out. Then he looks at things."

Madame began to laugh. Her thin shoulders shook. "Anna, you are a true Alsatian. Tell me in your own way. Go on. Parris goes out—then, he looks at things."

"Yes, Madame."

"Well?"

"It is peculiar. It is very absent-minded. He walks all over the place; he looks at the sky and at the ground and at the trees. He picks up a stone—yes, just like I said, a mere stone—and stares at it as if it were strange, then drops it and picks up another. He feels of twigs and fingers the evergreens, and—and— *looks at things.*"

"Heaven help us, maybe he's turning poet."

"No, Madame."

"What? How do you know?"

'What did you say? Turning into what?"

"A poet."

"Oh." Anna regarded Madame with open suspicion. Sometimes Madame made fun of her for a long time before she found it out.

"Anna, maybe there is a girl!"

"I don't think so."

"How would you know?"

"He doesn't write letters."

"What has that to do with it?"

"You know as well as I do that when there is a girl one writes letters."

"Maybe he doesn't have to write—maybe he sees her."

"There would be letters. When a young man—when there is a girl—I mean young men behave that way."

"Which way. Look at things, or write letters?"

"They write letters—all the time. They may see the girl, but come at once home and write letters. I have seen it often."

"Anna, you are romancing. You have read this. You have been here in this house with me for thirty-three years and—and you don't know what young men do."

"I think there is no girl."

"Well, maybe you would know. What is the matter with this young gentleman, then?"

"I think he is in love—"

"But you said—"

"Oh, not with a girl, Madame, but here—with this place."

"I have no idea what you are talking about."

"It is this. I think Parris feels something. I think he does not know what it is. I think he feels change. I think he is afraid something is to happen and he does not understand. Oh, Madame, you know I have watched him grow every day of his life. I *feel*, in here, sometimes just what he feels. I think he cannot help but see that you are not well—"

"You have told him?"

"No, Madame. But he asked me. I reassured him. He thought you should see Dr. Ladd, and maybe Dr. Everett, too—in St. Louis."

"How is that? Anna, what would he know of them? Who told him?"

"I have told him nothing at all, Madame. Naturally, he sees you—you do not look so well—"

Madame held up her hand. "Dr. Tower!"

"What? What do you say?"

"I met Dr. Tower a few weeks ago in the bank and spoke with him for a few minutes. Anna—it is in my face! They can see! Everybody can see! Then Parris must know."

"No, Madame. I reassured him—as you wished. I told him nothing."

Madame was silent for several minutes. Anna kept her hands tightly twisted in her apron.

"You were saying, Anna, that he is in love with this place."

"Yes, of course. It is home. Madame, I remember it well, when I knew I was to leave my home forever, I could not see it enough. I looked at every bush, every little leaf. I even—" Her voice shook slightly. "I even—oh, it was foolish, but I brought with me a large stone from the garden wall I carried it in my satchel all the way from the old country. I kept it for many years. I could not part with it. I felt that I still had a little piece of my own home. It was on my bureau, Madame, for years."

"I see." Madame spoke gently. "You have it still?"

"No, Madame. It fell one night—on my toe. Do you remember once I had a broken toe? Then I threw it away."

Madame von Eln smiled, but Anna did not see it.

"It is like that, Madame, with Parris."

"Perhaps you are right, Anna. I suppose there is nothing we can do."

Anna's diagnosis of Parris' state of mind was correct. Her observation was a neat compound of native peasant shrewdness and affectionate intuition. Parris was apprehensive and miserable for precisely the reasons she had named.

Throughout the winter faint premonitions had disturbed him. They were at first nothing more than undefined intimations. They gave him the odd feeling that somewhere, somehow, disaster already existed.

Just here was a side of Parris that no one knew. He was not clearly aware of it himself. It was a side of his nature that had been developed through the more or less solitary years of his childhood—from long wanderings alone about fields and woods, and from solitary contemplations of the minutest details of every aspect of the countryside. It was a kind of shy sensitivity, such as small animals possess. It was an acute awareness of appearances and movements and of change. Like those watchful small creatures, he received impressions and alarms as by some special sense. Sometimes he felt that he could perceive tremors in the air of some distant passing or of steps behind the hill. He really tried to ignore and to laugh away such fancies. But in some way they registered in places of his mind or in phases of his nature over which he had little conscious control. A few times he made distinct efforts to understand himself in this obscure relation to the simple reality in which he lived. He half visualized some aperture of his mind open to a special direction—like a high turret window opening to a distant and unique view.

Whatever the signals might actually mean—these vague warnings from the mysterious watcher at an equally mysterious watchtower—he was, against all common sense and reason, responding with something like actual fear. It was this that sent him on the half-contemplative, half-agitated excursions that Anna had reported to Madame.

Parris was more at loss to understand his own feeling than he had ever been in his life. He could make no sense of his own impulses. He only knew that he was—no, he was not afraid. It was not fear, he told himself. What was there to be afraid of? It was more like dread. Here he was on surer ground. His grandmother! She was not well. It was evident now. But even there he closed his thinking to the thrust of an obvious conclusion. Maybe he was just sort of stirred up, knowing the day was near when he must go away to study—to be gone a long time. But he would come back. Maybe, even, Madame would go to Vienna with him. He did not ask himself why he had never spoken to her of this. Again his attention and his half-directed musing veered away from the subject. He would return, of course, after studying—after he was a doctor, and—and maybe live here again. An echo, a mere overtone of what Drake had said, "when the place is sold," came back and sent a quick wave of dismay through him. It was physical, this dismay. He had an impulse to run when he felt it—somewhere, away from something, to some place of security.

This state of mind persisted. It expressed itself over and over in the same way—not flight, really, but motion. He must go, he felt, here and there over every familiar foot of ground. He found himself looking with a new concentration at every common object. He did exactly what Anna had said he did. He looked at things. He stared at trees; he held leaves and grass between his fingers, sensing them to some curious extremity as if to know them utterly; he examined stones, one after another. "I'm making a geography of every inch of the place," he said to himself.

Parris was doing something much more profound than making a geography of a place. He was compounding the record of his own odd and solitary way of life—the way his deepest self had gone on quests so secret and so obscure that he had scarcely been conscious of them. During those years when children make the acquaintance of each other, learn ways of speech and games, and acquire habits of community, he had been learning something quite different. He had been learning the innumerable faces of a few acres of simple earth. He hadn't been a conscious nature lover. He knew very few birds by name, fewer plants. He knew these phases of the natural world only through aspects which had no names. Almost it was a collection of appearances. And now, in the aroused regions of his nerves, he found these nameless aspects, these appearances, to have a suddenly enhanced value, an increased importance. He hurried to look at them again—and again—and again.

All at once he felt that human beings, and language, and the long, tiresome story of many books, were of no significance to him.

He liked especially the upper slopes and hillsides which laid the country for several miles around, mapwise, before him. A favorite spot was the outcropping ledge where he lay that day after his now almost forgotten encounter with Jamie. He went there often, leaning against the slender birch trees and looking with a kind of consuming dreaminess at the design of roads and fences and ordered plantings. He seldom watched the sky. In a way, he thought, he loved the look of the sky best of all. But he stubbornly resisted looking up at it. He knew why. There had been a time when he had looked up there, asking for help, expecting it, demanding it. He would not so much as look back there again. He thought this through one afternoon. It was a silly way to feel. It was really an admission that he still half believed something was there. He was trying to retaliate—to strike back at something which didn't exist. One couldn't do that. There wasn't even a way to ignore what had never been. He lifted his head and looked at the great white clouds moving steadily eastward.

He turned again and studied the curling brown bark of the birches. The spot was thick with the wiry growth of buckberry bushes. Later they would be covered with knotty clusters of hard rose-colored berries. They had a quite special color. He couldn't think of anything else which had precisely that shade of lavender rose. And there was that thorny vine lacing itself from branch to branch of the low trees. He had always called it King Solomon's vine until Jamie told him it wasn't. He had forgotten what Jamie called it. No matter. It was the way it looked that was important It had a—a cryptic look, as if it might be some kind of rare medicine or as if it might be a talisman. It might have been sacred to some old religion or witchcraft. It decidedly had a hands-off look about it.

Slowly, tree by tree, shrub by shrub—detail by detail, he was memorizing every step of what had been one time his playground and was now become his thinking-ground. He thought with a degree of surprise that he had grown here, just as these rooted things had grown. Out of this soil, from this air, under this sun! He wanted to reach out and gather these fresh green things into his arms. They were the—the—they were the *people* he knew best!

The urgency to know them perfectly, beyond any chance of forgetting, returned in strength. Once he had accomplished this—this task of learning them all by heart, he would be safe from accident and bereavement.

As he searched and looked and learned, there settled in his memory and in his thinking a store of something that he recognized as poetry. It was the same kind of poetry Jamie talked about, the same quality Herr Berdorff talked about, and related, not very clearly, to something which was emerging from Dr. Tower's constant talk of the subconscious where, as Parris himself realized, were stores of puzzling and unorganized feelings.

He kept recalling that phrase of Dr. Tower's: "We live in multiple worlds." It and its attendant corollaries of thought played like a fugue through his fancy. *Multiple worlds:* sometimes one inside of another, like the spheres of Ptolemaic cosmogony—encasing again a smaller world, each one complete and occupied with its own motion, and direction, and content; and, he thought, many persons in many worlds. He was, he felt certain, as many different personalities as he had worlds to live in. No: not just different facets and varying phases of himself, but different selves. It was not that one side of him was revealed to Drake, another to his grandmother, and yet another to Dr. Tower. It was that he, Parris Mitchell, functioned differently in these several presences.

Nor, he continued, musing more and more slowly as his drifting awareness colored with emotion, was there question of one of these selves and its own special world being more real than another. There was only question of importance, and nearness, and constancy.

If any one of these ways of living meant more than another just now, it was this private world in which he walked and observed almost every day—this world of little, familiar, simple details. Again he was half regretful that he knew so little of the habits, and names even, of this friendly, leafy company. Only aspects, though in those illimitable changes lay the meanings which were at certain hours the farthest reaches of eloquence and persuasion that he had ever known. Not even music could say so much, and so instantly. Music played in the single dimension of time: these spoke simultaneously and infinitely in a single indivisible instant.

Curious, very curious, he thought, twisting long strands of grass around his fingers—neither music nor poetry seemed to mean quite so much when he was hearing or reading, as they did in recollection. The memory of music, for instance, seemed richer than music itself. Perhaps because you were set free in memory from that tantalizing and changeless pace of time. You could have the full meaning of anything all at once by remembering it—a kind of triumph, wasn't it? over time which seemed such an enemy of happiness.

Parris slowly and sometimes patiently threaded the *ABC* of philosophy, recognizing the easy signposts of mysticism, and trying with the best conscience he possessed to keep clear of that constant, haunting threat of emotion that so quickly and easily jumbled the clear design of thought. He was following as imitatively as possible the harder precepts of Dr. Tower and the violent intellectual rectitude of Herr Berdorff. They were hard masters, both of them. The lush growth of what had seemed to be thinking, during these just past years of his adolescence, fell before the withering integrity of their instruction. The passage of their criticism left a mental landscape that was often rather bleak of prospect, but granitic in outline. Parris shrugged with a gesture of rueful fatalism. So it was, this landscape of his mind. It could not very well be changed, nor would he wish it to be. Sometimes there was scant comfort, and no shelter at all in such a scene, but its horizons led to clear infinity.

Today, for the first time since—since that dreadful day, he walked boldly down through the evergreen groves toward the pond. The young trees had grown surprisingly in these four years. The branches reached across the space between rows and touched. He pushed them aside and presently came out on the little clearing about the "secret lake." His heartbeat quickened uncomfortably. He choked a little. He walked to the edge and dipped his hand in the still water.

"It would be too cold to go in," he said aloud. He was glad that it wasn't warmer, but he couldn't imagine why. He looked around quickly. The feeling that he was not alone was so strong that he almost heard her quick little breathing—the way she breathed when she was excited.

He turned and went quickly to the apple tree. The young leaves covered the branches. There were the red stubby beginnings of apples where the blossoms had been. He parted the branches hurriedly and stepped into the tentlike interior. He felt that he must do this and get it over with as quickly as possible. He put his back to the trunk and laid his arms along the two large drooping limbs. He wanted to talk to her. He wished to say some words aloud to her. He felt that he must: it would be some sort of explanation, some sort of expiation, maybe, some mysterious way of sending one more message back to her, there where she must be. He saw her now, clearly once more.

"Renée, my darling. I love you. I didn't know then how much. I know now."

At the sound of the words which startled him back into the present, all sense of her presence was gone. He glimpsed, for an instant only, the flutter of her blue dress, down the long avenue of spruces. She had turned that day and had raised her arm, and waved.

… Jamie said "forever" was a melodramatic word. Jamie was wrong. It was a tragic word. He had never really used it, or even thought of it before. It was a horrible word. It stood there—there at the end of that long avenue like—like a black angel.

He came out from the shelter of the tree and stood looking down the green alley. He thought maybe he ought to go home that way, retrace the steps of that afternoon as—well, as a sort of memorial, a carrying-out of the idea he had had a while ago—making it a kind of payment of an incalculable debt. But he felt that he could not quite do that—not yet. He would not be able to pass the little house where Tom Carr lived. The front door might be closed, and he knew he could not bear to see it.

"Renée," he murmured again, but he did not try too hard to recall the sharp vision he had just had of her. Nor did he stop to think of her in actuality, as she must be somewhere now—at this instant. He did not even know that he consciously directed himself away from that thought. Only a faint stir of unease warned him away. He had gone simply and wholly back to another day. It was like remembering music—all at once, the whole sweetness, and best of it without the weariness of sequence. He looked about him once more. Maybe, he thought, he might never come here again. It might be that he wouldn't want to—ever. It might be best that way.

This short walk down the slope, through the evergreens, and to the pond with the lone apple tree beside it, marked some kind of a period. He wanted to think of it as epoch, but that was a pretty big word. But it had—he fumbled among many words—it had sealed something, ended something. Perhaps in all the many walks he had taken in this direction he had been tending to this place, but had never before been able to complete the journey. Now that it was done, and he had actually set foot on the crumbly bank of the tiny pond and had actually stood under the apple tree, he wouldn't have to do it again. It completed a circle—that was it—a circle. And back there was a whole piece of his life, a complete part of himself. He would go on to something else now. Two worlds had overlapped and merged this afternoon—his nature world where he had always been alone, and another, almost chimerical world, where childish ecstasy and a too swift pain and disillusionment mingled unhappily.

He sighed. Maybe this kind of mulling things over, and trying so clumsily to think and to classify and to make periods and define words and worlds— maybe this was all a trite and familiar phase of human experience. Maybe these virtuous processes of sorting the wilderness were things everyone knew. He didn't much want to believe that. It was somehow a little comforting to think of his troubles as being strange and unique.

He threw a small stone toward the pond. It struck the water and skipped two or three times, breaking the quiet surface into small circles of confusion which collided and crossed each other, leaving a chatter of color where the still reflection had been.

His mood broke, and he turned toward home. He walked rapidly. He had a lot of work to do tonight.

Parris remembered how often his grandmother spoke of time passing, and of the surprising speed of its passage. When he was very young he had been mystified each time she said it. Time, he felt, did not pass quickly—it did not pass at all: it stood still, and he himself made a slow and exasperating journey through it. Now, suddenly, he felt something different about time. It was as though the great static present gathered itself together and arose and spread vast invisible wings, or sail, and got slowly under way. Certainly—as he stood still to think about it—there was an actual sense of motion in all the world about him and above him. A phrase he had once heard came back to him with some new impact: "a sound of going in the tops of the mulberry trees." He couldn't recall just where he had heard it. Perhaps it came from the Bible—he wasn't sure; but it curiously expressed his feeling of this moment.

Time had begun to pass. It wouldn't ever stop now. It would *go* every day, faster and faster. A stirring, unhappy, frightening thought.

Aberdeen College ended its college year with the usual dull and repetitious ceremonies held during what always seemed the hottest week of the year. Parris avoided most of the events.

A week later Madame von Eln left for St. Louis. She reassured Parris. It was to be only a week or ten days in a hospital for observation. Anna accompanied her, and Parris yielded to Drake's insistence on a camping trip. They went to the little town of St. Stephens, an old river port, and camped in the hills. Drake was a capable and resourceful camper, and Parris lay about on the sunny slopes watching the changing aspects of the great river. He realized, perhaps as never before, how much he loved this region and how deeply he felt a part of its nature. Here in the river hills was a wider landscape, a larger view. The hills wore a look of eternity no less impressive than that of the sky. All day long the lights played on the currents of the yellow river, and purple shadows marked the drift of clouds overhead. The buzzards hung nearly motionless in the sky and seemed to emphasize the dreaming slowness of time. Parris forgot the vague, disturbing premonitions of the past few months. On the way back to Kings Row he felt happier than he had in a long time.

His grandmother had returned to Kings Row the day before and was in bed—resting, she said. But Parris was not satisfied with her superficial gaiety. She looked less well than when she left.

He went to Anna. "You've got to tell me! How is she? What did the doctors say?"

"Nothing new. I must tell you, Madame is not well. I guess you know that since you're going to be a doctor. She needs rest now, and she mustn't be worried about anything for a while. Just go on as if everything were as usual,

Parris. It's the best thing you can do for her just now. Don't let her think you are worried about her."

"You're not telling me everything, Anna."

"Run along now, Parris. I'll tell you if there is any danger."

Parris went moodily to town. He had half a mind to go to Dr. Gordon and ask him for the whole truth. But he felt young and shy when he thought of it. Dr. Gordon would look through him with that disconcerting way he had, and maybe tell him to mind his business.

He was crossing the courthouse yard when he met Colonel Skeffington. They exchanged greetings, and the Colonel met Parris' odd, old-fashioned courtesy with extreme gravity. The fact was that Skeffington was delighted with Parris' manner. It wasn't quite natural for a boy, he decided, but he liked it. It was a reflection of the way he had been reared himself. It was a sign of a tradition that ought to be kept alive. He asked about Madame, and sent stately messages. Parris was about to ask him if he could find out from Dr. Gordon about the real state of his grandmother's illness, when the Colonel said: "You've been up to Dr. Tower's since you got back?"

"I'm going today."

"You know about his wife, of course?"

"No. Mrs. Tower? What about her?"

"Died."

"Mrs. Tower died! Why, I didn't know it. Oh, gee, it'll seem terrible I didn't know, won't it?"

"No. That's all right. You were away in the woods somewhere. You can explain that."

"Dr. Tower knew I was going away. I didn't know Mrs. Tower was sick."

"Nor did anybody else. How long since you've seen Mrs. Tower, son?"

Parris thought. "Why—you know it's kind of curious, Colonel Skeffington. I never see anyone there except Dr. Tower. I go in the side door always."

"Don't even see that good-looking daughter?"

"Very seldom." Parris colored, and Skeffington noticed it. He laughed.

"But you notice her when you see her, I bet."

Parris grinned. "Couldn't help it, could I?"

"Right, my boy, right! Always keep an eye for a pretty girl. Very stimulating, very stimulating, indeed. Kind of a—a gauge, too. You can tell how you feel. But now, about Mrs. Tower. You haven't seen her in a long time, eh?"

"Come to think of it, Colonel Skeffington, I don't believe I've seen her since—since 'way last fall."

The Colonel nodded vigorously, as if in confirmation of something he already knew. He peered at Parris, his eyes like two knife points under his heavy bristly brows. "Not even sitting at that front window, like she always did, eh?"

"No, sir. I haven't seen her at all."

"Dr. Tower said nothing about her?"

"Oh, no. He never mentioned his—his family to me. Never."

"Well. It seems a little peculiar, somehow, don't know just how."

"When was the funeral?"

"Next day. Very next afternoon. Buried her up in the new cemetery. Funeral at the house. They *did* have a preacher. That surprised me—a little. But you know what, son?"

"What?"

"Nobody went to the funeral!"

"Oh, gee! That's terrible, isn't it?"

"Nobody felt like they ought to, I guess. No one knew the Towers."

"Nobody there at all?"

"Well, well, I say nobody. There were the pallbearers. Hector Godbold selected them. Dr. Gordon was there. I went myself, but there weren't any womenfolks at all. Dr. Tower looked like he might be at any kind of meeting; and that girl didn't even have on a black dress!"

The old man was enjoying his gossip, and Parris encouraged him. "That was strange, too, wasn't it?"

"Very unusual, son, I'd say. Maybe didn't have one—young girls don't, and there wasn't much time, but you know you can always buy a black dress."

"Yes, sir."

"I got the idea she didn't even think about it—nor the Doctor. Damn curious."

"What was the matter with Mrs. Tower?"

"Nobody knew she was sick at all, not at all. All at once she's dead. I think Gordon was there, maybe. He's on speaking terms with Tower, but he's so damned close-mouthed. Won't tell you anything—not a thing."

"Well, I must go up there right away."

"If you notice anything curious, son—" Colonel Skeffington stopped, just a shade embarrassed by his own sentence.

"Yes, sir?" Parris waited.

"Well—well—well. I'd keep my eyes open around that place."

Parris found Dr. Tower reading. He appeared as calm and unperturbed as always. He closed his book and kept his finger at his place as he nodded gravely in response to Parris' rather breathless greeting.

"I just heard a few minutes ago about Mrs. Tower. I'm very sorry."

Dr. Tower looked as if he were not really listening. He inclined his head again.

Parris stammered a little, and continued: "I was away, you know. My grandmother was away, too, in St. Louis, or you would have heard from us."

"Thank you. How is your grandmother?"

"I don't know exactly. She's in bed. I—I hope you understand about not having any word from us, sir."

"Certainly, certainly." Dr. Tower spoke impatiently.

"I'd like to say so to—to Cassandra, too, if I may."

Dr. Tower looked very straight at Parris. His gaze frosted ever so slightly, but he replied in a somewhat gentler tone. "I shall be very glad to tell Cassandra. Thank you."

An awkward silence fell between the two. Parris fumbled with some papers. Dr. Tower continued to look at him, but more absently than before. "Parris, I like your good manners. You are a credit to your grandmother, and I hope you appreciate exactly what she has done for you. You are the only young man I've seen in Kings Row who isn't a bumpkin."

Parris flushed darkly this time. "My grandmother is pretty fine, sir. She certainly is. But—but, really—"

"Madame von Eln came to see me just before she went to St. Louis."

"Oh, did she? I didn't know that."

"She wanted first of all to know about your progress."

"I see." Parris was puzzled by this. It seemed unlike Madame.

"She particularly wanted to know if you'd be ready to go to Vienna in September."

"This coming September? This fall? "

"Yes. Certainly."

"Why, she didn't say anything to me about it."

Dr. Tower answered dryly. "Probably not."

"Well, what did you say to that?"

"I said that you were not fully prepared, but that I thought with this summer of hard work, and some letters of explanation to the authorities there, we could arrange it."

Parris' breath went out of him. He filled with an inexplicable dismay.

"Oh." His tone was dreary.

"What's the matter?"

"Well, you see, Dr. Tower. *Grand'mère* treats me as if I were a child. She doesn't tell me anything she plans to do. I just—just sort of feel like she ought to have told me."

"Don't be silly. She doubtless will. She is a most sensible woman. No use agitating you about all sorts of things."

"What do you mean, Dr. Tower?" His usual quick alarm showed in his voice.

Dr. Tower hesitated. "Well—I mean, generally. I'm not referring to this, or to any special instance."

"Oh."

"You'll have to do some stiff reading."

Parris sighed. "All right. Do you suppose—did she say anything about going with me?"

The doctor stared this time. "No, nothing at all." He spoke almost kindly. "I'm sure that would be rather a severe undertaking for her—at her age."

"She's not so old. But I guess she's pretty sick."

"Parris, I undertook this work with you with decided misgivings. I guess it's fair to you to tell you that it has been a pleasure."

Parris blushed. He was curiously touched, and couldn't think of anything to say.

"Thank you."

"I hope that when you get into your work in Vienna you'll find that—all of this has been a help. I've done the best I could for you. Some of it has been inadequate, some of it has been—*is* in advance of any institutional study you could have gotten anywhere. I think some of it will prove useful. But don't be fooled by Vienna, just because it's Vienna. There are old fogies, and crazy experimenters, too, in that city. It's important that you develop some kind of point of view, a way of judging and estimating things that will help you keep on an even keel."

Parris settled back in his chair. Whenever Dr. Tower started like this he was in for a long, but usually happy, digression.

"You know, Parris, it's getting harder and harder to have a point of view. It's getting harder and harder to keep a nice mental balance." He paused and looked out of the window. "It's been becoming steadily more difficult for the past six hundred years."

He looked keenly at Parris. "You had medieval history this year at school, didn't you?"

"Yes, sir."

"Pretty good?"

"I—I guess so. I read a lot outside the text."

"Interest you?"

"I think so. Well, yes—yes, it did."

"Not too much, I gather."

"Professor Perry was very fond of the textbook and its exact words!"

Dr. Tower smiled. "Oh, I see. Yes, I dare say. I've seen Perry, passed him on the street. Don't know him, of course. He looked—well, just what you said: fond of his textbook."

Encouraged by this successful comment on the professor he really disliked, he added: "He likes dates, too." Dr. Tower didn't hear this.

"It's too bad. You must pay some attention to the twelfth and thirteenth centuries. Man's discomfort, his real discomfort in this world, began not long after that."

"But I thought—"

"I know what you thought. Perry probably reminded you that we have soap and macadamized roads, and dentistry and such things, didn't he?"

"Well—yes."

"Negligible factors. In the thirteenth century man was more comfortable and more at home in the world—in the universe—than he is now. He had a place there, and he was important. He *thought* so. And then Galileo and a lot of other fellows with brains in their heads came along and spoiled all that."

Parris tried to look intelligent and appreciative, but he was not following what the doctor was driving at.

"I mean this. Remember that the European man of the thirteenth century, the Italian particularly, lived in a simplified order. Don't confuse your thinking now with a lot of petty wars, or the way the whole thing didn't seem to work at times. I'm not talking about the political man any more than I'm talking about the physiological man, or the economic man. I'm talking about man in relation to his universe in the big sense. Listen now, this has a direct bearing on your professional future. I'll show you in a minute what I mean. In the thirteenth century men lived under one empire."

Parris frowned.

"One empire. The Holy Roman Empire. It had hardly more than a kind of mystical existence, I'll grant you, but there it was, and they believed in it. One empire. One church. One religion. One head to it. The blackest villain believed in that religion and that church. He could devise tortures and send out an underling to stab an enemy at night, but he yelled for the church when he thought he was going to die. He believed in something. It was more than a belief: he simply knew it was so. Such a faith—a faith that passes over into absolute knowledge—is a tonic, physical and mental."

Tower smiled that rare smile of his that was so unexpected a blend of humor and camaraderie. "You know, worry and doubt give you a bellyache. Your thirteenth-century man didn't have worries and doubts—not about the very biggest things. Deep down in his mind, or nerves, or wherever peace is finally resident in us, he was as still and calm as the deeps of the ocean.

"He had the awfully comfortable feeling that God would take care of his soul and the universe, and that given a good sharp dagger and some stout henchmen he could take care of his troublesome neighbors himself, and help out God at the same time with certain heretics he knew of."

Dr. Tower wagged his head. "Must have been a real joy to crack the skull of some man you didn't like, and know that it was for the greater glory of God."

Parris tried to visualize Dr. Tower cracking a skull but couldn't do it. He could more easily see him issuing orders to those stout henchmen to do the cracking, and then turning absently to other more pressing affairs.

"Then, too, there was just one language of culture. Learning and scholarship rode confidently on it. Think of what that meant, my boy. Less confusion of thought because of the different natures of languages. Latin said what it had to say, completely and clearly. It was the greatest kind of freemasonry. Men knew each other as scholars and gentlemen by that speech.

"Now think again. One empire, one church, one language of learning. But there was one more factor—the most important one of all. Know what it was?" Dr. Tower did not wait for an answer. "Remember the cosmogony of the time?"

Parris nodded.

"That was it, Parris, that was it. The earth was the fixed center of infinity, and all around it was the rest of the universe in a purely subservient capacity. Stars, moon—whole shooting-match waiting on this regal child of God's fondest fancy—the noble earth, imperial heir of heaven. And outside of it, in a kind of glorious high noon, sat God himself, watching, and seeing to it that nothing went wrong with the works, and that nothing irremediable should happen to the darling of His eternal day—man! Wonderful, wasn't it?"

Parris moved forward in his chair.

"And then, as I said, along came those troublesome fellows who talked about another kind of physical universe. It dislocated God, and greatly dislocated man, and shook the relationship between the two. The vanity of man couldn't stand it, and the church knew better than to let it go on. There was the ever-useful rack, and other devices of enlightenment and persuasion.

"I think the church was right. Maybe from the wrong motives. The church saw its power threatened—and it was threatened—and as always in such cases acted quickly. But what was really threatened was the happiness and peace of mind of all mankind."

Parris didn't understand the earnest note in the doctor's voice and smiled at the wrong time.

"No, no!" Dr. Tower held up his slim hand. "I mean that—precisely. Man was happy in his place of importance and when it was shaken he was too weak and scared ever really to have a sound sleep again. Later on he found himself pushed away out into the backwater of a vast universe, an unconsidered accident, maybe, of chemistry and weather.

"You see, man had invented heavens, and gods, and universes to make himself happy, and science has taken them away from him. He simply can't stand it. He whimpers around in the shallow safeties and ineffective panaceas of inferior religions, but he isn't having a good time—he isn't having a good time at all. And just there, Parris, is where you will come in someday—you and the men like you."

Parris sat up. "I—I'm afraid I don't—"

"I mean this. Man breaks down under the strain of bewilderment and disappointment and disillusionment. He goes crazy, commits suicide, and all such things. If he thinks, he's in danger. And—it seems to be his incorrigible habit to think.

"The doctors of the future have got to find out somehow where in this infernal organism man really lives. We don't really know where essential man resides. Probably in his nerves, though you can't prove it. More likely in the way his nerves behave."

"I don't—"

"No, of course you don't. I don't either. We're just as far away from anything you can operate on or give a pill to as the medieval medicine man was when something went wrong with what they called the soul.

"They had some good names to cover up and bridge the vast abysses of their ignorance, didn't they? We have, too. We've still got them, and we're still inventing them. The nearest thing to a meaning in any of those great words, Parris, is some hint of the way something acts. When they said something was wrong with a man's soul, they simply meant to describe a way he behaved when he strayed beyond the margins of a known design of action. He'd gotten out of our little circle of light. They couldn't touch him with their finger. But—that's moonshine, too. You'll have to learn in the next half century how to handle moonshine."

Dr. Tower laid aside the book he had been holding. "I wouldn't be such a fool as to prophesy how humanity is going to behave in the next half century, or what factors will enter to complicate, or maybe to simplify, man's estate on this earth. Probably nothing much will change him greatly in so short a time. But the little root of fact I've been talking about is this: man is unhappy because he really has no home in the universe. He knows it now. And he's afraid of the dark.

"You read that new pamphlet I gave you two weeks ago?"

"Yes, sir."

"You see the whole trend of this newer attitude toward hysteria, and the widening inclusiveness of the word itself. Hysteria is a kind of psychic bellyache brought on by worry. The victim runs this way and that to get out from under. He invents escapes. He invents disguises. You've seen the most effective disguise of all. When everything is too bad, he invents a disguise so effective that he doesn't know himself. Then we say the man has gone crazy.

"The general run of difficulties must be much the same in one age and another—only intensified and broadened in actual quantity by the increased—er—what is the word I want?—maybe we might say *density*—rather than intensity—of living."

Dr. Tower was silent for a moment. Parris picked up a copy of the little German pamphlet from the table. Do you think that's the direction that kind of treatment is going to go?"

"How do you mean?"

"Well, sir." Parris spoke hesitatingly. "It seemed to me that according to this, any one of these sort of halfway crazy—"

"Borderline."

"Yes, sir. Borderline cases. It seems that such a person has kind of *fooled* himself—and fooled himself clear out of the world of reality, and that the right way to handle him is to fool him back into it again. Like catching a rabbit that has strayed out of his pen. Get his attention on something else, and he doesn't see the gate. First thing he knows he's back home again."

Dr. Tower leaned back in his chair, and for the first time in their acquaintance laughed aloud.

"That's pretty near hitting the nail on the head. I think even the writer of that little book would like your way of saying 'back home again in the pen.'"

"Well, I mean—"

"Oh, it's all right. It's a good figure of speech. Maybe a lot better than you know." He was all at once quite serious again. "It seems to me that we have lived in the midst of a more violent intellectual revolution than people ever had to face in earlier centuries because of an altered physical universe."

He paused, and tapped softly on the table with first one end of a pencil and then the other.

"What poor mankind is really up against is the easing of his wounded vanity. Wounded! It's lacerated, and shredded! So everybody is busy trying to spot the shining goal toward which we must be tending. If we are evolving, it must be toward something. Just there, my guess is, they are mistaken. We aren't going anywhere at all. It's hard for us to believe that we are simply adjusting. Heaven knows that's a noble enough end, and a perfectly ample excuse and reason for everything. But the whole structure of the human mind is so damned flimsy and weak that it has to have a framework. Since there isn't any, the mind invents one—something to hold on to, to lean on, something to keep itself from spilling all over like milk poured out of a glass. Usually, it invents a cage for itself.

"God! if man were only good at making such a pattern, it would be all right. But it is precisely there that he does his very worst. As soon as he has invented a cage for himself he declares it of divine origin, and pronounces it perfect. The joke is that he intended it as a jail for his neighbor, but he invariably locks himself in.

"That's why your figure of speech about the pen a while ago struck me as being pretty good comedy." He laughed again, but there was a ring of scorn in it this time.

"Do you see, Parris, what I mean about having a point of view appropriate for the work of a physician—particularly a physician who expects to work in that hide-and-seek world of insanity?"

"Yes, sir. I think I do."

"You must try to understand the character of the thinking and feeling— particularly the feeling—of the period you live in. Don't idealize it; don't try to see it according to some preconceived idea. Try to see it as it is. Try to understand it in its own terms. That's not easy."

Dr. Tower straightened suddenly in his chair. "Are you, perhaps, religious?"

Parris answered directly, almost abruptly: "No, sir. Not at all."

"Don't believe in God?"

"No, sir."

"I wonder why."

"I don't suppose I could explain it. I just know it isn't so."

"The men in the middle ages 'just knew' it was so."

"I don't know how to answer that, I guess. Maybe we're, well, maybe we're—"

"I hope you aren't going to say we're more intelligent than they were."

"No, I wasn't going to say that. I don't believe I know how to say just what I do think."

"If you think really, Parris, you can usually say what you think. If you mistake a sort of warmish, mistyish feeling for thought, you can't express it."

"Well—something like this. Maybe we're more advanced."

"How do you arrive at that?" Dr. Tower was manifestly teasing, and Parris grinned a little.

"We're farther along the road."

"Toward the nice shining goal of evolution's perfect end?"

"No. I don't mean that. Maybe we remember the mistakes, and just—just think something else!"

The doctor looked askance at Parris. "You didn't think that. You've been doing some extracurricular reading, I think."

But Parris was in earnest. Color came out on his cheekbones, having the odd effect of lengthening his face. His hair was tousled now, and he leaned forward to speak.

"You remember, Dr. Tower, two or three times you've talked about subconscious observations, and the way we arrive at conclusions without knowing why we do?"

"Yes, I remember, of course. Go on."

"Well—like that. The way we read, and study—the way we are educated, perhaps—couldn't we get some kind of a subconscious result from it that is better than the one we are really meant to get? A—a sort of personal verdict of history."

"Did you read that last phrase somewhere?"

"Which one?"

"Personal verdict of history."

"No; I don't think so. Why?"

"Not bad."

Dr. Tower did not speak again for several minutes. Parris was used to this habit the doctor had of falling silent as though following some half-glimpsed idea down a sideway. He never interrupted the meditations. Just now he wondered more than he ever had about Dr. Tower. He still did not know where the Towers came from—he had not dared, even, to ask Cassie. He did not know why Dr. Tower ever came to Kings Row, or why he stayed on in the face of the chill hostility that was clearly evident on all sides. He wondered why he had never had a practice. Obviously he had purposed practicing medicine when he came. There was the shingle: DR. ALEXANDER Q. TOWER, PHYSICIAN AND SURGEON. It still hung outside the study, the lettering nearly obliterated now. It swung and creaked sometimes in the wind.

"The way the mind acts—" Dr. Tower spoke softly, and Parris came back with an effort, scrambling hastily amid the fragments of his shattered speculations, for a hold on the interrupted train of the discussion.

"—the way the mind acts. That is, as far as we can tell by the most careful observation—there is our only key to the puzzle of the individual personality. And it is only with the utmost care that we can avoid misreading our observations.

"You were referring just a moment ago to our discussions of subconscious observations. Naturally, the value of any such conclusion would rest entirely on the integrity—the elementary and basic logic of the mind of the observer when it is working subconsciously.

"I rather disagree with this man—" Dr. Tower hunted through a stack of pamphlets. "Where is it now? Here—this one. Krätschman. You read him, I think. I disagree with his notion that subconscious man is more likely to run true to some racial form. 'Brothers under our skins,' to paraphrase: I don't believe that. Neither does Marchan-Debroellet. That's where we're really unlike. Each man is a separate and strange equation."

Dr. Tower arose, and Parris stood, too.

"No, no. Sit down. I've not finished. How would you like a cup of coffee?"

Parris was so astonished that he stammered and swallowed before he could answer. "Why, I'd like it, sir, very much."

Dr. Tower lighted a spirit lamp on the table. "This was made just before you came. It'll bear reheating. I think I'm a little tired today. Didn't sleep well. Never do sleep well. Don't take enough exercise, I suppose."

He took some cups from a little cabinet, and sugar. "Will you have it black? There isn't any cream in here."

"Oh, certainly."

"I don't like exercise. Hate it. I suspect I don't really like or admire action too much. Or enough. The spectacle of active man—I must say I find him more tolerable as a thinking animal."

He turned and looked at Parris with a look that was almost shy.

"I believe that's my only special sympathy with India. They created a god that was all mind—that's what all their vague mental meanderings mean in the end—at least *mind* as they understood it."

He poured the coffee. "Here you are. Hope you like it strong."

"Yes, sir. My grandmother likes her coffee very black."

"Um."

The coffee was really inky. Parris did not like it, and drank it slowly. Dr. Tower swung one knee over the arm of his chair—an unprecedented informality.

"... That subconscious observation, now. Intuition, and the like. It's what makes a born physician. It isn't just brilliant guesswork either in the case of the fine diagnostician. It's a kind of certainty which he can't explain. I think all of us are a shade diffident at times in expressing these certainties. We know that it is unwise to tell other people that they *are* intuitions. You'll find out soon enough that you have to present your best intuitive conclusions to more stupid men as some sort of scientific finding. Sometimes you almost have to use the old witch doctor's hocus-pocus to get a perfectly good thing into action."

Again Parris felt a quick surge of curiosity. He was sure that this man was really able and intelligent—probably a very fine doctor. What was the matter? What landed him here in Kings Row with his sole contact these lectures and talks to a medical student?

Parris couldn't quite define his own feeling at this moment. He had experienced on first acquaintance with Dr. Tower a sudden, unquestioning loyalty. This had never changed. It was deeper and stronger. Just now he realized that he was glimpsing a very little more of the nature of the man than he ever had. And he felt a curious sympathy—or more—he felt sorry for Dr. Tower. Even as he thought this, he realized how furious Dr. Tower would be if he knew it. That kind of sympathy was clearly the one tribute that he would never accept from anyone. Further, Parris realized, with a surge of surprise, he was fond of Dr. Tower. He more than liked him. Some sort of affection, not easy to classify or to name, had grown up quietly. His attention wandered around and around these speculations, and surprises. He was not listening. He came back to the moment with a jump.

"... That, I suppose, is the obvious and principal reason why the analysis of personality is so difficult. It changes every minute.

"Each individual is like a sum—a grand total—set at the foot of a long column of figures. Those figures are the symbols of everything that has contributed to the making of the man—his ancestors, the events in his ancestors' lives, the thoughts they had, the thoughts they *tried* to have, the injuries and betrayals, the pain and all—everything, that is, except death. The experience of death is not set down in that long column of figures. Perhaps that is why we persist in feeling or imagining ourselves immortal.

"No two columns of figures which add up into the sum which is the mind and body and personality of a man are ever the same. Nor is it the same for two consecutive instants. Each moment with its event and its unique cargo of emotion changes the total.

"There's too much, you see, for the mind to grasp even in our own case. But it may be that it isn't too much for the subconscious man and his mind. It is out of that experience, maybe, that the subconscious is able to reach conclusions of some validity about others."

Dr. Tower finished his coffee, and set the cup on the table.

"May I fill your cup? No? Well—you see, don't you, what a complex, slippery problem there is for the physician who goes poking about in a mind that is out of order."

Parris sighed. "It sounds pretty discouraging when you put it that way."

"Well, it need not. You're in the same boat with all other doctors in that way."

"I know, but—"

"But what?"

"I started to say maybe it would be more sensible for me just to be a doctor, and not start out to specialize in any sort of way, but—"

"Well?"

"It's just that I think I really *want* to. It sounds a lot more interesting."

"It is. It is a vast field for research. I don't know if the time has come for this kind of study, or not. It may be a hundred years off. It *looks* as if it might come now. There is a stir in Vienna. Whether it's the real thing or not, I fancy no one can say."

"I guess I keep thinking of Mrs. Carr and—"

"Who?"

"Lucy Carr, the—"

"Oh, yes. The insane woman you played to. Oh, yes, yes."

"And Benny Singer."

"You don't feel such people—well, sort of objectionable?"

Parris looked as if he didn't understand what the doctor meant. He shook his head. "No, sir. Never. I liked Mrs. Carr, and I like Benny Singer."

Dr. Tower nodded. "Um. I see."

"But—the problems do sound—just as you said, awfully slippery to get hold of."

"Yes." Dr. Tower half closed his eyes. "I sometimes think the whole thing is a problem for the poet."

"A poet?"

"Yes."

"Because he's a sort of madman, too? Is that what you mean?"

"The madness of poets is simply a larger sanity that comes from a special vision. Good God! I must sound like a professor at Aberdeen College. But, nevertheless, I mean precisely what I say. I suspect poets, and great writers of other kinds—novelists, know more about the way the human mind works, and is likely to work, than all of the psychologists rolled into one."

"You're serious? You aren't joking?"

"Indeed, I am not. Look at Shakespeare—that sounds like your Aberdeen lecturer again! Everybody's been 'looking at Shakespeare' for centuries. But I daresay the old boy knew more about the insides of human skulls, what goes on there, and what is likely to come out of them, than any man that ever lived. Subconscious observation, maybe. I believe he just looked at people and knew what was inside of them."

"I guess he could have been a great doctor."

Dr. Tower looked solemnly at Parris, but his strange overbrilliant eyes sparkled with a friendly humor.

"I daresay he would have. It is fortunate, however, that he chose to be a poet."

Parris would have liked to tell Dr. Tower about Jamie Wakefield, but he dreaded the ironic look that always met any mention of individuals in Kings Row.

"The great poets, and the great novelists," Dr. Tower continued, "knew by some trick of genius what it always takes the ordinary man centuries to find out by—by—well—normal processes. You will profit by an intimate acquaintance with the best of them, and never let anybody laugh you out of that notion. Particularly those Viennese."

Parris looked a question, and Dr. Tower nodded. "Some men of science are poets, too. A lot of them—the general run of them are realists, and a realist is a man who is willfully blind. Or—what is just as lamentable—a man whose senses function only on a low grade of perception."

Dr. Tower stood up. He pushed books and papers about impatiently. "I think you'd better go home. I seem to be in a vein of epigrammatic sententiousness today, and I shouldn't like you to—to carry away that kind of an impression of my way of teaching."

"I've enjoyed this an awful lot, Dr. Tower. I guess perhaps I didn't understand the—er—application of it all, but—"

"Well, I hope you've enjoyed the chat. I did. Now, get on with you, Parris Mitchell. You've got a summer of tough work ahead. I won't fool you about that. We'll get those letters off to Vienna, and then we'll know in a month or so how things stand."

Parris walked slowly down Cherry Street. As he turned into Federal Street toward home he heard a suppressed giggle. He looked about for a full minute before he saw Louise Gordon. She was sitting in the double-seated lawn swing. Drake McHugh sat facing her.

"Parris, I believe you're getting nearsighted."

"Hello, Louise. Oh, hello there, Drake. How are you?"

"Fine. You'd better get some specs." Louise giggled again.

"He'd better take his face out a book now and then. That's what he needs." Drake sounded downright gruff.

"Come in and sit with us a little while, Parris. Nobody ever sees you any more."

Parris thought Louise seemed nervous and scared. Her voice was too high-pitched, although it was evident she tried to keep it down.

"Come on in, Parris. Hop over the fence."

Drake did not second the invitation. He had a cloudy look about him today—a look Parris knew well.

"Thanks a lot, Louise. I've really got to hurry on home. I'll just come in for a minute."

"Are you working this summer? All the classes at Aberdeen are over now, aren't they?"

"Of course. It's just stuff I have to read up on—"

Drake interrupted. "I told you, Louise, that Parris was working with Dr. Tower—reading, or something."

"Oh, yes. Of course. I forgot."

Parris noticed that Louise kept looking toward the house. She was evidently uneasy about something.

"Say, what's the matter with you two? What are you so scared about?" The question blurted itself out. Parris hadn't really meant to ask it.

Louise and Drake exchanged glances. Drake looked away again, and Louise avoided Parris' eye. She half tossed her head. "Oh, nothing much. Papa's just— well, he's just trying to interfere with anything anybody wants to do."

"Well, that's perfectly clear. Excuse me, anyway. I didn't really mean to ask you, but you—both of you just looked so nervous."

Drake kicked at the latticed floor of the swing. "I'm not nervous. I'm just doggoned mad, that's what's the matter with me."

Louise leaned forward and gave him a little pat on the hand. "Oh, nonsense, Drake. Papa's always interfering. He's made me mad ever since I was old enough to realize that he is really—unjust." She hesitated a moment and added: "He's kind of mean to me, Parris."

Parris couldn't think of anything to say. Both Louise and Drake looked so serious and so distressed. They also didn't seem to realize that he didn't know what they were talking about. Louise caught his look of question.

"Parris, it's just that Papa doesn't want me to see Drake."

"*Just—*" Drake jeered angrily.

"Well, Drake, you know perfectly well what I mean when I say 'just.' You know I'm going to see you anyhow—some way."

"You can't."

"Of course I can."

"It's not the same."

"Why not? It shows I want to see you, doesn't it?"

"Well, what's the matter with me, anyway? Ain't I good enough for your old man? If I'm not, then I don't want—"

"Don't want what, Drake?" A tremor of alarm showed in her voice. "Do you mean you don't want to see me—in—in that case?"

"No. I guess I don't mean that, exactly."

"You guess?"

"Well, darn it all, Louise; I'm not going to slip around and meet you on the sly. I—I like you—I love you, and I don't care who knows it. I told Parris so more than a year ago, didn't I, Parris?"

"Certainly. I guess Louise knows that, too."

"Well, what's the old—old geezer got against me? Why can't I come right out in the open and—and go around with you like I want to?"

Louise didn't reply to this. Parris stared at his hands. He was uncomfortable. One thing, he decided, was certain: Louise was really in love with Drake. He had always thought Louise Gordon attractive, but she was almost beautiful today. Her thin, rather hard prettiness had softened. Her glance rested on Drake's face like a caress. She was evidently trying to make up her mind to say something but found it difficult.

"Drake, listen to me a minute."

"Well, all right. What is it?"

"I don't mind saying this before Parris—you know I do love you, don't you?"

"Well, then, why don't you stand up to your old man and tell him—tell him—"

"Tell him what, Drake?"

"What you said, just now."

"That I'm in love with you?"

"Yes."

"I did."

Drake straightened in his seat. "Did you, honest?"

"Of course."

"What did he say to that?"

"Nothing."

"Nothing? He must have said something."

Louise blushed. She put her hands to her face as if to hide the rush of color. Her eyes looked very large and bright, and not quite so shallow, as she kept them anxiously turned toward Drake.

"Drake!"

"Yeh?"

"Will you not be mad if I tell you something?"

"Well, what? I don't know. I'm already mad."

"Oh, Drake. You've got to try and help me work all of this out some way."

"Well, what do you want to tell me?"

"Promise you won't get mad at me?"

"How can I promise that?"

"I won't talk about it then."

"What is it? Go on."

Louise turned to Parris. "I'm glad you're here, Parris. Maybe you can help me keep Drake kind of reasonable."

"Well, good gracious, Louise! I don't more'n half see what's the matter. Your father—"

"Just wants me to stop seeing Drake."

Drake exploded. "*Just!* There's that word again. She talks like it ain't anything much. 'Just wants me to stop seeing Drake!' For time's sake, I can't hurt you seeing you, can I? I'm not trying to—to eat you, am I? What's the matter with him, anyway?"

"All right, Drake, I'll tell you what he said. He—he—well, it's about Poppy Ross."

Drake turned beet-red. Louise looked straight at him. Her own color receded as his deepened, and a sort of fright darkened her eyes.

A painful minute passed. Drake looked out of the sides of his eyes. "Oh," he said, rather weakly. "That!"

"Of course I didn't pay any attention to what he said. I knew you had been taking her out buggy-riding, I—I understand lots of boys do."

Drake flared again, and started to answer. Parris laid his hand quickly on Drake's knee.

Louise went on hurriedly. "Please try to understand how I'm placed, Drake. I—I love you, no matter what you do. I can see it's pretty lonesome for you, and—" She took a handkerchief from her belt and held it against her mouth. Her eyes brimmed, but she did not cry. "I can't see you all the time. If you've got to be with somebody I'd just as soon it would be Poppy Ross as anybody— rather, almost. I know you can't be in love with her. But—but Drake—people are talking about you."

"About me?"

"Of course. Don't you know how people are? They've got to talk."

"Well, let 'em talk. I don't care."

"You care about me, don't you? You said—"

"Of course I do. But if everybody makes my business their business and— and if they think they can stop me doing anything by talking about me behind my back, why I—"

"Don't be silly, Drake. Nobody's trying to stop you from doing anything. You're always telling me that you are your own boss now. Well, I guess you are. You ought to think about me, too."

"So you think your father is right? You're on his side?"

Louise bit her lip hard. Parris felt sorry for her. "Look here, Drake, that wasn't a fair thing to say to Louise."

"Oh, you think she's right!"

"Right about what? That's not the question. She only told you something, that's all. And—and she asked you not to be mad at her. You oughtn't to get mad at Louise for that."

"All right! All right! I'm always wrong. I've always been wrong about everything since I can remember. You all make me sick—just like Uncle Rhodes and Aunt Mamie."

Parris laughed, and Drake's darkened face relaxed a little. He almost smiled. "All right. What do you all want me to do?"

Parris spoke first. "Good heavens, Drake, I'm not in this. I don't want you to do anything."

"Neither do I, Drake," Louise said the words very softly. "I'm not asking you to do anything. I just want you to be patient, and let's not see each other—except once in a while, and it'll all blow over. Papa'll forget about it, and—"

"I bet he don't. I guess he hates me."

"I don't think so. He—he thinks you're too wild."

Drake snorted. "Wild!"

"Please, Drake. We don't have to give up seeing each other altogether."

"But, gee, Louise, I want to see you all the time—any time."

"Do you, Drake?"

"Of course I do."

"Well, don't you think I want to be with you, too?"

Drake answered in a mollified tone. "Gee, what'll I do all the time? I get lonesome."

Louise looked away, and back again quickly. A momentary flash lit her light blue eyes. "You can go buggy-riding with—Poppy Ross. Nobody can stop you. You're your own boss."

Drake stood up. "Come on, Parris, let's go."

Louise held out her hand. "I'm sorry, Drake, I said that. But—" She was about to cry again. "But I've got feelings, too. I guess I can be lonesome as much as anyone. I haven't got a—a Poppy Ross."

Drake was still angry. "Come on, Parris, if you're going with me."

Parris struggled out of the swing. "Stop quarreling, you two. It's silly. Make up now, and let's go."

Louise held out her hand again. "Friends, Drake?"

"Aw—of course. Listen, you write to me, will you?"

She hesitated. "Yes. But you can't write to me. They'd find out."

"They? So your mother is in this, too."

"Mama is always with Papa in everything."

Drake's mouth hardened. "Well, for time's sake!"

"You'd better go on now, Drake. It's about time for Papa to come home, and I—I just can't go through anything more today Good-by."

"'By, Louise. I'll see you somehow."

"All right, Drake. Remember, I do love you."

Parris and Drake walked almost the length of the block without speaking. Parris looked back once. Louise was standing beside the" swing, drooping a little, and biting the corner of her handkerchief. Parris felt sorry for her. She seemed rather helpless in the whole matter. After all, there wasn't much that a girl could do if her parents got set a certain way. She looked forlorn and surprisingly little as she stood there. He sensed somehow that Louise did not have a great deal of strength. Her physical frailty, charming and pretty in itself—like a shallow pink blossom of some kind—was reflected in the look of her light blue eyes. They lacked steadiness as they lacked depth. Strange, Parris thought, as he remembered Mrs. Gordon. She was thin and frail, too, but dry and hard—and steely. And Dr. Gordon—he was like steel, too.

Maybe Louise didn't have a chance to develop either strength or purpose against the united wills of those overwhelming parents. But she was—he supposed *sweet* was the word. That seemed to be about all. You looked at Louise and sort of took her all in at a glance. Parris had an absurd feeling that he knew exactly how Louise would look without any clothes on—pink and white, and thin and soft, and—well, just nothing else.

He thought of Cassie. Even after all of this time and its many intimacies she had something of mystery about her. He threaded his thought carefully: Cassie's very flesh seemed to have a complexity, and a depth. Her eyes were deep, too—bottomless. When you looked into them you felt as if you were looking into shadowy wells. He really couldn't liken Cassie to any one thing. She didn't simplify at all. Louise was like candy.

All of that didn't make much difference at the moment. Louise, he supposed, could be just as unhappy as anyone. Even if she was kind of shallow. Besides, she was Drake's girl. He looked at Drake.

Drake was walking with his head down, his hands in his pockets. He swung absently from side to side and scuffed the walk with his heels, like a small boy. His face, too, was the face of a frowning, sulking child.

Drake gave a sudden vicious thrust with his foot at a crumpled paper lying on the ground. He kicked it ahead of him this way and that until it fell too far to one side to reach easily. He lifted his head and looked bitterly down the long vista that stretched beyond the end of Federal Street.

"For Christ's sake!" he muttered. He stopped and turned squarely toward Parris. "What would you do if you was in my place?"

"Gee, I don't know, Drake."

"That's it! Nobody can ever help you when you're in trouble."

"There's no use talking like that, Drake."

"Like what?"

"As if no one wanted to help. I'd tell you what to do if I knew. But if you can't think what to do yourself, how can you expect anybody else to."

Drake grumbled something under his breath, and Parris continued. "You know more about how you feel than anybody else does."

"Well, it just looks like everybody is against me."

"They're not. You know I'm not. You know Louise isn't."

"Well, why don't she—?"

"I know what you're going to say, and I can see Louise's side of this a little bit."

"I can't."

"I guess it's a whole lot harder for a girl to go against her family than it is for a boy, Drake. You can see that. They're more helpless. Louise is a kind of helpless girl."

"She is, sure enough, ain't she?"

"Yes, and—and—"

"And what?"

"Why don't you just—"

"Go on. What you going to say?"

"You're sure enough in love with her, aren't you?"

"You bet I am."

"Well, she's in love with you all right."

"Honest, do you think she is?"

"Anybody could see that, you fool."

"Well—"

"Listen, Drake."

"Hell, I know that tone of voice. You're going to have some kind of a sensible suggestion. I don't want sensible suggestions. I want you to say something to make me feel better."

"Doggone you, Drake McHugh! I don't ever preach to you, do I?"

"Sometimes you do—a little. I don't care. You're all right, kid. Come on. What was it you wanted to say?"

"I was just going to ask you why you don't marry Louise, right off."

"Well, if you ain't the darndest unexpected person." He laughed with a peculiar half-sniffing sound. "Do you suppose I haven't thought of that?"

"Well, what's the matter with the idea?"

"Everything."

"You're your own boss, as Louise said. You've got enough money—"

"Not to get married."

"What do you mean?"

"I'm not twenty-one yet, Parris. The Farmers Exchange Bank haven't got much to say about what I do, but they don't have to give me a cent more'n they think I need to live on."

"But I thought—"

"I've got a checking account. But it's just about three thousand dollars, it *was*, I mean. I've spent a lot of it. Can you imagine what old Mr. Curley, he's the trustee, would say if I told him I wanted some of my money so I could get married? He's already been after me about spending so much."

"Do you reckon you could get a job?"

"Doing what?"

"I don't know, Drake. Maybe you ought to go on to school and learn to do something."

"Nope. Takes too long. I'm through with school. I don't like to study, Parris, the way you do, and—I guess I'm not very smart anyhow—"

"Rats!"

"Not about books, I ain't. I don't fool myself about that. And, to tell you the truth, I don't really care. I guess I'm not too thickheaded about some things—maybe."

"Could you start in some kind of business, do you think?"

"I've been turning that over and over in my mind. You know I've been talking to Peyton Graves. He's quit school this year and he's got a place in with Breakstone and Clinton. He's going to work in real estate."

"Sure enough. Old Peyton Graves. I didn't know he had any get-up about him."

"He wants to get married, too."

"Peyton? Who to?"

"Some girl down around Miller's Crossing. She's older'n he is. A schoolteacher."

"Well, what do you know about that? Gee—and I've got years of school ahead of me."

"I saw Peyton's girl. Awful plain-looking. But what I was going to tell you. Peyton's got the same idea I had about that tract of land right up there by the public school. He said if I could get my money out and put some in with him—his uncle would let him have some—we could swing in together and make us a lot of money."

Parris looked respectfully at Drake. Drake talked like a man of affairs.

"Are you going to do it?"

"Can't. I just halfway hinted to old Curley something about an investment, and he nearly jumped on me. Not a cent till I'm twenty-one! I'd borrow it against my inheritance, but I don't expect anybody'd let me have it. Curley'd stop anything, I guess."

"That's pretty hard on you, I think. Why don't you talk to Mr. St. George about it? He knows a lot about land. I bet he'd give you good advice. He might even lend you the money."

"I guess you don't know the way people around this town think about me."

"There you go. Imagining things!"

"I'm not. You heard what Louise said. Wild! All the old busybodies in this town sit around and talk about me. Just 'cause I'm out in the open about what I do. If I want to take Poppy Ross out to the country somewhere I ride right out of town with her. I don't hide it. Hell! I don't care. Everybody knows about Poppy and Jinny. I'm not the only one."

"But honest, Drake—you know I think whatever you do is all right—I—"

"Of course. I know you're on my side."

"You bet I am. But—I kind of understand how Louise feels about that, too."

"God-a-mighty! That surprised me! I didn't know she knew anything about it!"

Parris laughed. "You just said everybody—"

"Men, I meant. I guess I had a fool idea nice girls didn't know anything about Poppy Ross."

"You're crazy."

"Well, anyhow. Don't you see what a slim chance I've got to get married, or do anything till I'm twenty-one? I've got to wait and loaf—and then everybody jumps on me for loafing. Hell!"

"I wish you'd come to Europe with me. You could do that, couldn't you?"

"Europe? What for?"

"Well—to be with me, for one thing. We could have a lot of fun."

"I bet we could. But—no—I'm going to stick around where Louise is. She'd forget all about me."

"I don't think so."

"Say—when are you going to Europe? Not soon?"

"In September."

"Why'n't you tell me?"

"I didn't know it until today."

"Say—that's tough! I'll be darned if I know what I'm going to do without you." Drake thwacked Parris resoundingly to lessen the sentiment of the remark.

"I don't know what I'll do without you, either. My grandmother arranged it all with Dr. Tower. He told me. They just move me around like a chair or something. Just to suit themselves."

"You talk like a baby. Get out of that, now. The quicker you get all that Europe stuff over with, the quicker you can be a doctor—and be your own boss."

"Maybe my grandmother could do something to help you, Drake. She likes you."

"Don't you ask her! I—I—well, it's nice of you, but I expect she's got her hands full with you."

"She's sick, too."

"Gosh, I'm sorry, Parris. You think a lot of her, don't you?"

"Everything in the world."

"Gosh!"

They walked on for a few minutes. They reached the corner of Aberdeen campus. "I guess I better go on back, Parris. We won't be walking out here together much longer, will we?"

Parris' face worked a little. He did not reply.

"You'll be in Europe—in Vienna—and seeing a lot of new sights. I guess I'll miss you like hell, Parris. I haven't got anything to do, and Louise won't see me any more." He laughed again—a short, unpleasant laugh. "Well, there's Poppy Ross—and Jinny, if necessary, for variety. And let me tell you something—no more tobacco barns, either. She can come right on up to my house, and I'd like to hear anybody say anything about that!"

Parris knew better than to argue with Drake when he was in such a frame of mind.

"Parris, you and me have been in pretty much the same kind of boat so much of the time. You remember I said that right here at this corner about three years ago. We still are, in lots of ways. My girl can't see me, and won't, and yours can't come out in the open either and go around with you like other girls and their fellows."

"Cassie's not my girl—not in that way exactly, Drake. I've told you that a thousand times, though I wouldn't tell anybody else. Dr. Tower is very peculiar—"

"I should say he is. I think he's kind of crazy—keeping Cassie shut up all the time away from everybody. But Dr. Gordon's not crazy. He just don't like me."

"Things'll work out all right somehow, Drake. They're bound to. You and Louise—"

"Yeh! I wouldn't be one bit surprised if it was all over between Louise and me."

"You talk like a fool."

"You'll see. They'll keep stuffing her with lies about me until she believes them. That's what they want, I guess."

"Drake, you take on like everything was all over. You can get things fixed up all right, but it's like Louise says, you got to have a little patience."

"I haven't got any patience. I don't give a damn whether they're fixed up or not." Drake spoke louder and louder. He was feeding his temper with itself and was beyond listening.

"Now, listen, Drake—"

"Oh, let me alone! You don't know how I feel. I'm going to get my horse and buggy and ride right by the Gordons with Poppy Ross. I'm going to keep Poppy all night at my house. I'll wear out every damn chippy in this town right in front of 'em. I don't care Don't talk to me, Parris, I—I just can't stand any more." He turned quickly and almost ran up Federal Street.

Parris wondered if he should follow him and try to prevent him from carrying out his threats. But Drake was hard to handle when he set his head, and still harder if he felt himself opposed. Perhaps if he were left alone he'd cool off and forget about his rashest intentions.

For the first time Parris drew back a little from Drake to get a better perspective. He realized, as he never had, that Drake could be completely illogical and inconsistent, and then feel terribly hurt because he was misunderstood. He hated to admit it, but he knew that Drake not only didn't think things out, but that he wasn't really capable of thinking when his emotions were involved. He recalled how bitterly stubborn Drake used to become at school, and the curious brute determination that arose in him on such occasions. Drake never cared whom he hurt, or how badly he hurt them when they got in his way.

A new and deep fear for Drake arose like a physical ache in his heart. Drake was the best friend he had, probably the best he would ever have. He must not lose him, and he must not let Drake ruin himself with this kind of childish retaliation. But even as he thought about it he knew that his hopes for Drake had always been uncritical. He had refused to look squarely at a single fault in him. Drake carried the signal of terrible dangers to himself written clearly in his face. The ache inside of Parris hardened to actual pain. That overhandsome face of Drake's was not a thinking face.

The chances of terrible frustration lay deep in Drake's character—chances, even, of disaster.

Just a few days earlier, at the conclusion of one of their long and fruitless discussions, Drake had said: "Things are going to be different from now on." Parris thought of it now, as he watched Drake go out of sight. Yes. Things were going to be different. The changes that were coming, and coming so quickly, were all a part of the way he had felt about time that afternoon he went to the little pond hidden away in the spruces. Everything was moving. Everything was getting under way.

He and Drake were no longer spectators. He groaned a little disconsolately under his breath. Already the days just passed seemed so happy, and spacious, and free. Restraint was falling across his way. It seemed to be coming from every direction. And compulsion. He bit his lip hard as he tried to find his way through the tangle of these new aspects.

Struggle. He had heard that word a thousand times. His grandmother used it, Anna used it, Tom Carr used it—he had heard sermons at church on the subject. It had never really meant anything. Struggle went on—he understood it. He saw it and recognized it. But he had never realized that he would have to take part in it.

He walked slowly down the hill toward home. Once he stopped to look at the landscape, every detail of it familiar as a friend's face. It was radiant and luxuriant in this rising tide of summer, some of it deeply green and shaded, some of it striped and splotched with high lights of sun.

It was hard for him at this moment to believe that he was soon to leave it—to go away from it for years. In September. There was a sudden cold contraction in his stomach. *In September.*

He would have to talk to his grandmother—tonight. He had always supposed that when he went to Vienna he would stay until his studies were finished. Why—his grandmother might not live that long! Surely she must be planning for him to come back on visits, or for her to visit him. He began to walk more quickly. Best talk about it at once and find out.

He walked with his head down. His usually lively interest in everything about him was quenched in a heavy dismay. He was blinded by his dread of these violent changes.

It was hard to understand, when one stopped to think about it, that you couldn't really *see* any of the forces that made disagreeable changes necessary. It was all so abstract. This necessity, and that—this compulsion, and that. Each one an invisible and implacable monitor of some still more remote imperative. Suppose one just paid no attention to any of it, and simply went on in the familiar ways of every day? Like Drake. No. One couldn't do that. The things—whatever they were that compelled him—were like the turning of the earth—imperceptible but certain. You couldn't see them, or touch them, or even deal with them as though they were real.

They were things that had no faces!

He pondered this. He liked the phrase. It helped to dramatize the whole matter. *Things without faces.*

He usually felt better about any problem when he could find a fine, high phrase to describe or characterize it. This time he was not so happy. The thought of things that had no faces was a little bit sinister. He said it aloud… the sound sent a wiggle of cold down the back of his neck.

Parris did not talk to his grandmother about Vienna. She looked very ill now, and remained in bed most of the day. Somehow Vienna came naturally into the conversation and Parris found himself accepting it as a settled question without any discussion having taken place.

The cicadas came early that year. Their dry exasperating call rasped the ear and exacerbated nerves already worn by the persistent hot weather.

Parris worked hard. He read day and night, and for the first time prepared digests of his reading for Dr. Tower. His eyes were often red-rimmed, but no one noticed. Anna, who usually kept a sharp watch over him, looked haggard and drawn from her continuous vigil with Madame.

It was a strange battle the two women were fighting in that upper room of the old stone house—strange because it was so secret and so desperate.

Parris was so overwhelmed with work that many incidents escaped his attention. He was tired and distrait. Once he had heard his grandmother cry out in the night and he had gone quickly to see what was wrong. Anna met him quietly at the door. "Madame was dreaming. She sleeps badly tonight."

There was a conspiracy of silence among Madame's older friends. Most of them knew of Parris' almost fanatical devotion to his grandmother. They looked at him a little pityingly, but said nothing. Even Drake seldom asked about Madame, but he knew. Sometimes he was uneasy and several times was near to telling Parris. Drake was sure that everyone was making a mistake. He feared for Parris if Madame's death should come suddenly and unexpectedly.

Madame von Eln and Anna managed with incredible skill. Parris accepted the fact of Madame's illness so gradually that his fears were never too sharply aroused.

Madame wished to hurry Parris' departure, but Dr. Tower advised against it. A few more weeks and he would be able to pass necessary examinations and get off to a good start. Otherwise he might waste all of a valuable year in Vienna.

"I must live, Anna, until he is gone. It will be hard to see him go, but easier for him. I must live a little longer somehow. Keep me reminded that I have only to live one minute at a time. If I try to think of longer time than that I cannot endure it."

She sat, propped up in bed, white as paper, and incredibly thin. But each day she achieved some kind of toilet and saw Parris for a few minutes. The effort wracked her and left her exhausted for hours.

One minute at a time, she repeated to herself. Anything can be done that way—one minute at a time. But she was not sure, even of this.

She called to her aid every technique of living and clear thinking she had ever known. She needed all of them now.

One by one she felt the supports of character itself threatened by the insistent destruction of pain. Of course Anna was always there, ready with drugs when the fiery claws seemed to reach for the last vestiges of reason. She felt as if Anna with each ministration only drew her up a little, a very little, to higher ground, out of reach, for a short while only, of the steadily encroaching tides of torment. Soon there would be no retreat at all—no higher ground to escape to. She would be engulfed. What then? She could not think of it. She must not think of it. Maybe—one minute at a time. Maybe—a blessed overdose—yes, that perhaps, as soon as Parris was safely in Vienna. There was always that door of escape. She had thought of it long ago—more than three years ago. Then, the question seemed far in the future. Now it was here. Now she stood with her back to that door, with all the furies closing in on her. When necessary she could open the door. Until then—one minute at a time.

Anna looked with wide, dry, wondering eyes at the seemingly unbreakable old woman, so slight and thin now she scarcely dented the heaped-up pillows. Madame insisted each day on having her hair done high on her head and fastened with the tall silver comb. For a few moments she smiled and spoke casually to Parris. Then she gave over to the interminable hours of incredible horror—one minute at a time until tomorrow.

She armored herself at every point. Each day she felt that perhaps this time she held the invasion at bay by the sheer force of determination. But each day, insidiously, like a sliding blade, it was there attacking through some unguarded opening in her mind, moving with a devilish deliberation along her nerves, searing, tearing with white-hot points, until every citadel of resistance collapsed in a weltering chaos of hideous agony.

Even in her extremity of suffering she realized that morphine was failing. What—what in God's name could she do then? The release that narcotics brought was only partial. More and more it brought only a half obliteration, a nightmare of dreams and threats hardly less dreadful than pain itself.

"Listen, Anna. You must listen and promise. I must not lose everything that makes me a human being. I must die with dignity. Surely I can command that much for myself. I must not die like an animal, in a trap. You must see to that. I charge you with that, Anna—solemnly, as—as if it were a dying word. Dear God, what a way to die! ... Anna, I want to die silently....

"Listen, Anna, listen again ... this is getting to be more than I can bear. You must get word to Dr. Tower, tell Dr. Gordon to tell him, or else see him yourself—telephone him—this cannot wait.... Parris must go to Vienna— now—next week—tomorrow!

"Or—perhaps! Anna, you must help me to think now. I can't even think! Is that wrong? Should I perhaps keep him here until—until it is over?"

"Oh, Madame, how can I say? I don't know."

"Perhaps it would be a bad blow for him when he is alone with no friends in a strange place. Perhaps I am wrong. Perhaps I should try—try to die now. It should be easy if I do not fight it any longer—and I cannot fight much longer. Does Parris realize?"

"He isn't blind, Madame. But you know—he is like you that way—he is so secret about himself. He works very hard."

"He will miss me." Madame turned her head and looked out of the window. The tops of the maple trees hung motionless and grayish green in the devastating heat.

"He will miss me," she repeated softly. Tears gathered in her eyes. She cried a little, but not for herself, nor in real regret for the world she was about to leave.

"Anna!"

"Yes, Madame."

"*Ach,* I have been so stupid! You must go with him."

"I—to Vienna?"

"Yes, of course. Stay with him until he is settled and content there. Of course, of course. How foolish I have been. He must stay here—here, with me, until it is over. That will be hard for him, but anything else would be harder. Then you can go with him."

"I will do whatever Parris wishes, Madame."

"Thank you, Anna." She looked up at Anna with a faint gleam of humor. "I can die now—any time I want to! It will be easier to live whatever days are necessary when I know I don't have to hold on by force. *Dieu! Dieu de toute puissance* ... but we are having a bad time, Anna, aren't we? I always could endure anything by saying to myself, 'This will come to an end. Patience, now, hold still, it will end by and by.' Do you think it may be soon, Anna?"

Anna was not crying. With an effort that matched Madame's own miraculous control, Anna kept dry eyes.

"I do not know, Madame."

"What does Dr. Gordon think?"

"No one can say, Madame."

"It must not be too long. Not even sanity can hold up against such things, Anna."

"I am always here, Madame."

During the next two weeks, Dr. Gordon came every day. It was no longer possible to put Parris off with childish answers.

He was eating breakfast absently and gloomily. Anna came downstairs. He looked up quickly. "How is she today, Anna?"

"The same."

"She is terribly ill, isn't she, now?"

"Very ill, yes. But the weather will be cooler soon—it is usually better the last two weeks of August, you know."

Parris looked hard at Anna. He said nothing more. Anna went to the kitchen door and spoke to the new cook: "And give me a cup of coffee, too, please."

Parris went quietly upstairs and into his grandmother's room. She lay on her side, asleep. He could not see her face, but her shoulder showed sharp and thin under the sheet. He went out again and stood for a moment in Madame's little dressing room. The table was covered with medicines. He looked at them absently. Then he started. A hypodermic case was lying open: the needle and piston evidently freshly dried had not been replaced. He picked up the tube of white tablets and read the label.

Just then Anna returned. He pointed at the hypodermic case. Anna blanched a little.

"How long has—has this been necessary, Anna?" His voice shook slightly.

Anna did not answer at once. She carefully closed the door leading into Madame's room.

"Anna!"

"For several weeks, Parris."

He waited as if he could not say the next word. He picked up the shining hypodermic needle and laid it down again.

"Cancer?" He was surprised that he could say it.

Anna answered in the same tone of voice. "Yes, Parris."

"Why wasn't I told? Why have I been kept out of this—like a child?"

"Madame wished it, Parris. She wanted you to finish your work without worry. She insisted, Parris; she made me promise."

"Yes, yes. I guess so. So that's it! But why did she make plans for me to go to Europe in September? Didn't she—doesn't she know?"

"Yes, of course she knows. She—she thought she would live through September."

The last tinge of color left his face. Anna moved instinctively nearer.

"And—she won't. Is that what you mean?"

"It is impossible that she should live more than a few days. I had made up my mind after Dr. Gordon's visit yesterday to tell you."

"A—few—days? Only a—a few days?"

"Yes, Parris."

He turned and left the room without speaking. Anna heard the door of his room close softly. She shook her head. Then she took a long breath and released it jerkily.

"*Barmherziger Gott! Wieder einen Tag überlebt—*" she whispered as she went into Madame's room.

Parris sat down at his table and looked blankly about his book-littered room. He had the curious feeling that he had never seen it before.

"Parris!" Cassie's voice over the telephone sounded hurried and anxious.

"Yes."

"Listen, Parris. I've got to see you."

"Oh, I can't now, Cassie—"

"Parris. This is important."

"Where's your father?"

"He went to Bloomington. He'll be back tomorrow."

"But Cassie—"

"Parris, you've got to listen to me! I wouldn't call you—just now, if it wasn't important. I must see you."

"All right." Cassie sounded almost tender. He warmed toward her a little in spite of his stunned feeling. "All right, Cassie—right after supper?"

"Yes. Listen. I'll meet you at nine o'clock at the corner of the Aberdeen campus. I—I—" She faltered with an embarrassment Parris couldn't quite understand. It had always been agreed that she'd call him when she could. Of course she didn't know what was happening to him just now. He'd have to tell her. Cassie found her voice again. "It's just that I want to tell you something," she finished breathlessly.

"All right, Cassie, I'll be there."

It was a velvety dark night, oppressive from the long-sustained heat. There was no threat of rain but an almost continuous flicker of heat lightning played along the far southwest. From time to time a brighter flash revealed the presence of great thunderheads stretching from north to south. They started from the darkness for a moment—long ranges of spectral peaks—were instantly blacked out, and reappeared in constantly changing aspects as the lightning rose and fell behind them.

Cassie was waiting at the campus gates when Parris arrived.

"Hello, Parris."

"Did I keep you waiting?"

"Just a minute."

"Weren't you scared here in the dark by yourself?"

"A little."

"I'm sorry I was late."

"I was early. I couldn't wait. I had to see you."

"Where let's go?"

"Can't we walk here on the campus?"

"Don't you want to go back to your house?"

"No: I had to get out of the house tonight. I felt like I couldn't stay there."

"What's the matter?"

"Oh, I don't know."

"Say, Cassie, who's staying with you? You're not there by yourself, are you?"

"No. The cook's staying tonight."

"Oh."

She held tight to his arm and they walked slowly up the long avenue of elms. It was black dark, but he could see the outline of her light dress and the shape of her face. He peered down at her.

"You know, Cassie, I never realize how little you are until I walk with you."

"You've just gotten to be awfully tall. Do you remember when I went to public school, I was taller than you?"

"I believe you were."

"It seems a long time ago." She squeezed his arm. He did not reply. It was unusual for Cassie to refer to anything in the past. She never told him anything about herself, and it was by tacit agreement that they spoke only of the immediate present and their own feeling for each other. Parris laid his hand over hers where it rested on his arm, and they walked on in silence.

They reached the main building and stood for a moment. It seemed monstrous as it loomed among the tall trees that grew close to the walls.

"Let's go around. There are some benches on the other walk—along the edge there."

"Yes, I know."

"Ever been up here?"

"With—Papa, yes."

There was a new semicircular seat there—the gift of one of the old graduates—a classic arrangement of marble bench facing an oval of greensward and looking toward a small statue which showed a white blur against a tall hedge.

"It's pretty here—when you can see it." Parris guided her to the bench and they sat down. Almost mechanically she moved close to him, and his arm fell around her shoulder. She leaned her head against him. They sat for some time. The stone seat was still warm from the sun, but a faint breath of cooler air came up from the creek below them. Parris' painful tension relaxed a little. It was sweet to have Cassie close to him. He'd have to tell her presently about his grandmother.

"Parris."

"Yes?"

"You'll be going away pretty soon now?"

"Yes, I guess so."

She leaned harder against him. "I'll miss you."

"Will you—sure enough, Cassie?"

"So much that I don't know what will become of me."

"Why, Cassie—"

"Don't—even now—don't say anything you don't mean. I don't even know just how I feel about you—I never have. I just never think of anybody else but you."

He drew her close and kissed her hair.

"I didn't ask you to come here to say that, though."

"What is it, Cassie? Anything the matter?"

"It's about you."

"Me."

"Yes."

"What are you talking about, Cassie?"

"I don't think they're treating you right, Parris, and I've got to tell you."

"Cassie, I don't know what you're talking about. Who? What?"

She sat up and moved away a little. Then she turned and held his face between her hands. "You know that I wouldn't do anything to hurt you, don't you?"

"Of course."

"You know—well—you love your grandmother terribly much, don't you?"

He nodded, and reached out to draw her close again.

"It's about her, Parris."

"Yes, Cassie."

"Everybody's been trying to keep you from knowing how sick she is."

Parris did not reply. He held quite still. Just in this instant a genuine realization of the terrible truth seemed to strike at him with a new and brutal strength. It had seemed this afternoon a sort of secret that only Anna knew. And that made it seem to be—well, maybe not true at all. But Cassie's words struck through him. *Everybody knew!*

"They should have told you long ago, I think."

Still he did not answer.

"I'm going to tell you because you mean something special to me, and because—but that doesn't make any difference." She took hold of his arms and shook him slightly. "Parris, your grandmother is dying, and they don't tell you!"

She stopped suddenly, terrified now that she had actually said the words. She waited, but he said nothing. He felt a sudden flare of resentment. There they were again—everybody—treating him like a child!"

"Who told *you?*" He asked the question roughly.

"Papa."

"Oh, I see."

"He talked to Dr. Gordon, I guess. You know you're the only person I ever saw Papa be interested in. Your grandmother is dying of cancer. She can't last much longer—and—and I thought you ought to know. I know how you feel about her—and Parris, darling, I was afraid of what the sudden shock might do to you. I guess it's been just as much of a shock the way I've told you...."

"No, it's all right, Cassie. I knew it."

"Did you?"

"Just today. Anna told me. This afternoon."

"Oh."

"But I'm glad you felt like you did about it. I'm glad you wanted to tell me. I guess you're the only person except maybe Anna who has any idea of what my grandmother is to me, and what she always has been. I guess I can't explain it very well."

"I think perhaps I sort of understand it, Parris."

"Perhaps. I don't know. I—I care a lot more about her than other boys seem to care about their mothers, even. You see, I didn't know my mother and so she didn't mean anything at all to me. But she—*Grand'mère*—well, somehow, Cassie, she has always been the world I lived in. I just never could imagine what it would be like to be without her. I don't—I'm not able to imagine it now."

They sat without speaking for a few minutes.

"I—I just won't have anybody at all, Cassie, when—"

She turned her head quickly, started to speak, but changed her mind.

Sometimes the flickering from the west ran into a few seconds of faint but continuous light. Cassie's face showed startlingly white, her wide eyes deep and black. Parris twisted his fingers in her curly hair which she still wore short.

"I forget sometimes how pretty you are, Cassie."

"I don't suppose it makes much difference whether I'm pretty or not."

"Oh, yes, it does. I should think it would be a lovely surprise just to see yourself in the looking glass every morning."

"I think I don't look at myself much."

"You should." He kissed her lightly, then again—and again. Presently she fitted her head into the hollow of his shoulder.

"Look!"

"At what?"

She pointed toward the low levels that stretched along the creek. Thousands of fireflies streaked the dark.

"Oh, yes—lightning bugs. Beautiful, aren't they?"

"I never saw so many. Look, Parris, some of them are green."

"They're all different sizes, too. Some of them make a real light close to them."

"They're lovely."

"Yes. They look like music sounds, don't they?"

"I don't know. Do they?"

"Sort of."

"I don't know much about music. I've never heard much."

"You ought to study."

"I don't think I want to."

"It's fun sometimes. I like it all right."

"Parris."

"Yes?"

"You're going to Europe right away?"

"Oh—I don't know now. It was all arranged for September, but I don't know now—"

"How do you mean?"

"My grandmother being so sick."

"But—oh, Parris, I'm sorry, it seems so hard to say."

"What?"

"She won't live until September! Don't you know that?"

"Anna said that, too—but I guess nobody can be sure—when."

"I'm awfully sorry, really."

"You're sweet to me. I guess I'll go some time this fall."

"Then—"

"Then what?"

"Then *I* won't have anybody, either. It's hard enough to see you just once in a while, but I always know you're here, in Kings Row. When you're gone—"

"Cassie, do you care that much?"

Instantly she seemed to withdraw a little into herself. "I care a lot—of course." Her voice flattened a little—it sounded faintly warning. He wanted to ask a dozen questions that were always troubling him, but he sensed, he was not sure how, that he must not.

She sat up and straightened her dress. When she spoke again her voice sounded almost casual.

"You just said that you'd have nobody at all—after a while. I happened to realize that I wouldn't either when you go away."

"But you've got your father, anyhow."

"Yes."

"Cassie, I never had chance to say much about your mother to you, and you always seemed to kind of head me off whenever I started to say anything."

"Well?"

Parris wished he hadn't brought up the subject. Decidedly, Cassie was being difficult.

"Well, I guess I just wanted to tell you—"

"Let's don't talk about it, please."

"Oh, all right." He sounded offended. Suddenly she put her arms around him and held him tight.

"Don't pay any attention to what I say, Parris." She kissed him hard on the mouth.

"You know, Cassie—you and me—for two kids—we seem awfully alone in the world. Drake McHugh was saying the same thing to me—he's been mentioning it for a long time. He's got no relations either. Seems like all my friends—there's Jamie Wakefield, too. He's got a family but he doesn't like them. I think they don't like him much either. Sometimes it looks like it."

"Do they treat him badly?"

"Just don't understand him."

"Oh. That's nothing. Nobody understands anybody much anyway. Is Jamie a special friend of yours?"

"Well—kind of, I guess. I'm sorry for him, and he hangs on to me."

"Isn't he—kind of queer?"

"Why, how do you mean?"

"You know perfectly well what I mean. I read Papa's books, too."

"Oh, I see. Ye-es, I guess he is."

"He gives me the creeps."

"Why?"

"I don't know."

"Jamie's nice in lots of ways."

"I wish you'd keep away from him."

"I couldn't go back on a friend, Cassie."

"Listen, Parris. I've seen Drake McHugh with Jamie sometimes. Drake's not like that, is he?"

Parris forgot his heaviness and grief for a moment and yelped with laughter. "Drake? Well, I should say not. I guess I'm telling tales, but do you know Poppy and Jinny Ross?"

"There used to be two little Ross girls in school—"

"Same ones, I guess."

"They were dark and had very red cheeks, I remember, and wore ruffly clothes."

"That was Poppy and Jinny."

"I remember they used always to be hanging around with older boys and whispering and laughing. I didn't know then, but I guess—"

"Yes, they learned fast."

Cassie drew her shoulders up in a quick gesture of distaste. "Ugh—how horrid!"

"Well—"

"Being like that—with just anybody!"

"Drake likes them."

"Do you?"

"I don't know them, Cassie."

"Parris, *we're* not like that. I guess there was a time when I'd just have died if—if—"

He kissed her quickly and stopped the words, but she pushed him away. "Maybe you'll understand someday—I don't know."

"Maybe I do."

"No, you don't. Not at all. Let's don't talk about it. Let me sit on your lap."

He shifted his position and she curled tight against him. Her breath was warm and damp against his throat. They sat for a long time again without speaking. The myriad fireflies sparkled orange and green, and a solitary whippoorwill somewhere near repeated his maddening complaint.

"He sounds like an idiot," Cassie murmured.

"What—who?"

"That bird."

"It's a whippoorwill."

"I don't care. He sounds crazy. It could make you nervous, couldn't it?"

"Maybe."

She thrust her arm under his coat and hooked her fingers into the armhole. Her bare arm lay warm against him.

"Sleepy?" Her question itself sounded drowsy.

"No, are you?"

"No. Whenever you want to go—"

"I don't want to go."

"It seems lighter than it was."

"Your eyes just get more and more used to the dark."

"I guess so."

"Besides, the lightning pretty near keeps going all the time."

'Is there going to be a storm?" She lifted her head and looked at the sky.

"I don't think so. Just heat lightning."

"I don't hear any thunder."

"It's too far away."

"Oh."

After a while his leg went to sleep. He wiggled his foot cautiously. He didn't want to disturb her. The warm soft pressure of her weight against him was comforting.

"Am I hurting you?"

"No."

"Maybe I'm too heavy."

"No, my foot's asleep."

"Wiggle it. It'll feel all right then."

He stretched and wiggled.

"Feel better?"

"Yes."

He twisted his neck around and tried to catch a glimpse of the lights at home. Sometimes when there was a breeze and the trees were moving he could see the lights in his grandmother's windows from here. But there was not the slightest stir in the air. It seemed as if the whole world must be standing still— waiting.

All at once he felt unbearably desolate and tears started in his eyes. He held his head carefully to one side, but Cassie felt a drop on her shoulder. She put up her hand to his face.

"Why, Parris, you're crying!"

"Just a little bit. Never mind."

She sat up. "But I do mind. I mind awfully. Why do you have to have things happen to you? Why do *you* have to cry? You never did anything to anybody! You're the nicest, best—why do any of us have to cry? You, or me? What have we done? Oh, I hate it—I hate everything! I'd hate God if I could, but there's just nothing you can reach. Nothing in the whole world cares— cares a damn!"

"Why, Cassie—"

"Don't! Don't! Don't! Don't try to fix it up. I couldn't bear any kind of philosophy. I want you to hate it, too—whatever hurts us! Don't cry, Parris, please don't cry. I just can't stand that!"

She kissed him stormily, and pushed his hair back from his face, and kissed him again. Then she held his head tight against her breast.

"Ouch! Cassie, you're breaking my neck!" He squirmed free of her tight embrace, and she laughed a little hysterically.

"Isn't that like me? I can't even—even show you how I feel without breaking your neck!"

They laughed and rocked together. Cassie found his handkerchief and dried his eyes and her own.

The multitudinous murmur of the night went on around them. The whippoorwill ceased. The night seemed to grow more still as if the turning earth plunged deeper upon a darker and lonelier way.

Parris and Cassandra held to each other. Grief and bewilderment and loneliness and desire mingled oddly in them. Here was the immemorial setting of the familiar way of youth and love. Darkness and solitude, and the hospitality of summer. And as always since the world began, youth and summer and the unmindful stars made familiar clamor in the blood—the claims and rights of life measuring themselves against the claims of death.

"Cassie!" She pressed her head harder against his shoulder.

"Yes."

"I think it must be terribly late."

"Yes, I think it is."

"I haven't got my watch, but it feels different. It always does about three o'clock in the morning. Did you ever notice? You kind of feel night turning into day."

"Do you have to go?"

"Maybe we'd better. Does your cook who's staying with you know you're out of the house?"

"I don't think so. She wouldn't say anything, anyway."

"I see."

"I believe it's getting light, Parris."

"Just a late moon—look back there. A piece of a moon."

She squeezed his arm. "I don't want to look. If you say it's there, I guess it is." She laughed softly. "I'm silly, am I not? I just don't want to go."

"I don't either, really." But he was not telling the truth. He was beginning to be uneasy. The successive blows of the day were just now taking effect. Cassie felt the change.

"Come on, let's go." The misty light fell on her face as she arose.

"You look—" He hesitated.

"How do I look? All mussed up, I suppose."

"No. You look sad."

Cassie wriggled slightly, settling her clothes. She stooped and smoothed her stockings. Then she stood up and looked at him.

"This might be the very last time, Parris."

"Oh, Cassie!"

She laughed. "Come on." She linked her arm in his. The tilt of her head was almost gay. Her burnished hair showed a faint gleam. He stopped and held her close to him and kissed her. "Cassie, darling—"

"Come on, Parris. We must go now."

"All right."

They walked soberly down the long avenue.

"You're not like anybody else, Parris. Do you know that?"

"I don't know. How, Cassie?"

"Of course I don't know anybody. Ever since I can remember I've just lived in our house and yard. I don't ever think much about the time I went to school. I just know people in books, and from seeing them pass on the street. But—I just know you're altogether different. Even Papa says you are."

"Does he? I've wondered what he does think about me. I like him an awful lot, Cassie. He's taught me everything."

"Well, I just feel like in your mind you're 'way ahead of me and other people—young people, I mean, but—"

"What?"

"But—I don't mean this the way it sounds—kind of uncomplimentary—but in other ways you are younger than everybody your age."

"I guess I don't know myself. I don't understand what you say—not very well, but I expect it's so."

"I wouldn't want you to be different. When I think about you, you seem kind of—mysterious, almost. No: I don't really mean mysterious. Just kind of enigmatic. Papa talks about you sometimes—not often. He doesn't talk to me very often about anything except books."

"What does he really say about me, Cassie?"

"Well, he said one day that you were—now, let me see, I want to get it just right. He said you were a very rare personality."

"Oh, gee! That sounds so sort of grand and important, doesn't it?"

"And he said something else, too. He said: 'a dark nature.'"

"What do you suppose he meant by that?"

"I don't know. He said you were going to be a great doctor someday."

"Honest?"

"Yes."

Parris stopped and held her by the arms. "Cassie, do you love me?"

She did not answer.

"Listen, Cassie: I want to be a good doctor—a great one if I can. When I come back—maybe, somehow the time'll pass quickly—when I come back will you marry me?"

She twisted herself free of his grasp.

"Do you love me, Cassie?"

He felt her stiffen. She looked almost as if she shrank into herself and became smaller. Her voice was thin and colorless as she answered.

"I don't know, Parris."

He was suddenly angry, but even in this half-dark he could see the haggard, ravaged look that came into her face, a look so old, so tragically different, that he was immediately contrite.

"Never mind, honey, never mind. If you don't want to say it—but somehow after—after a night like this, I guess I just want you to say the words."

She stood quite still as though his question had somehow taken away her power to move or think. There was, he thought, almost a look of horror on her face.

"Never mind, Cassie darling, I—"

"Please don't say it, Parris. Everything is perfect until we try to talk about it. Don't try to understand me. Just—just take me when you can, and—and forget everything else."

Parris bit his lip in exasperation. This was the utterly baffling side of her he always met when he forced any aspect of their relationship into words. In every other way she acted as if she loved him. She was here, wasn't she? What did it mean if she didn't love him? Perhaps he was foolish to ask.

Back of all the stormy questions that arose against her strange retreat was one small cool question that thrust itself into the heated melee of his resentments. She never permitted him to say that he was in love with her. Just here he was obscurely aware of some justness in her, some intimation of her own that dictated her behavior. He had asked himself many times if he loved Cassie in the way he was so ready to declare. Actually, he was not sure.

She was something to him that escaped clear definition. She was excitement—yes, an excitement that could be, and often was, painful. And she was—he felt for words to shape his thought—she was so darned sweet, he concluded, knowing the word to be lame and inadequate. She bewildered his senses, and certainly befuddled his thinking. All he had to do was to think of her name, and all she was of delight and wonder surged into instant recognition. But always she troubled him. The slightest thought of her—the most casual image of her that drifted into his daydreaming—carried unrest with it. Unrest and something else—something that he had often thought might be a feeling of guilt. Bad conscience in that she was the daughter of the man whom he so much respected—the man to whom he owed so much. But he couldn't really bring such a feeling to realization. He couldn't feel treacherous or that he was betraying the man who helped him, however much he said so to himself. The words fell wingless and dead. Some other emotion effectively blocked them off. No: all that he and Cassie were to each other, all that they had done seemed to have its existence in a separate world—a world of their own in which they were accountable only to each other. It was like—some almost forgotten words came easily to his mind—it was like his and Renée's "secret lake."

"Parris?"

"Yes, Renée?"

"What did you say?"

"When?" He was confused.

"Just now—what did you call me?"

"Me? Call you?"

"Yes. You said—some other name, or word."

"I don't know. I guess I was thinking. What were you going to say?" She stopped again, and laid her hands flat against his chest.

"Listen, Parris."

"Of course, Cassie. I'm listening."

"You're not mad at me, are you?"

"Was that what you were going to say a minute ago?"

"Yes."

"How did you happen to think of saying that?"

"I thought maybe you were mad at me; that's all. Why?"

"Nothing." He seized her and held her tight.

"Oh—"

"Did I hurt you?"

"Sort of squeezed the breath out of me."

"Well, that answers you, doesn't it?"

She nodded. "We'd better hurry."

"All right."

It was still dark when they reached the gate on Cherry Street.

"Good night, Parris."

He kissed her. "Good night—my sweetheart."

She touched his cheeks with her finger tips. "Good night," she whispered.

Parris' heart grew heavier and colder with every step. He did not wish to go home. He felt shut out of it.

The east was light as he went slowly up the terrace steps and to his room. He had been there but a few minutes when Anna knocked and opened the door.

"*Ach,* Parris, you are here!"

"Yes. I just came in. I—I was out."

"I know. I know. I came for you at midnight when Dr. Gordon left."

Parris sprang to his feet.

"She—is she—?"

Anna shook her head. "No. Dr. Gordon came at midnight. He said then he couldn't do anything more. He gave her an injection."

Anna looked out of the window at the coming dawn. "Since then," she went on, "she hasn't known anything. I called for you, but you were not here. I thought maybe—I hoped, Parris, maybe it would be over before you came in." She spoke rather apologetically. Her words came evenly and without emotion. Parris realized that Anna was desperately tired. The long strain showed now, clearly. "I supposed you were with Drake, but I didn't call you."

Parris did not answer. He was not even thinking. He was receiving almost unfeelingly the successive blows of Anna's information. This was the hour. All the long dread and apprehension and terror had led to this dull, leaden center where he felt nothing—seemingly realized nothing. Every nerve was numb.

"Parris, I think maybe you better come now."

"Come—go in—there?" He pointed like a small child toward the door.

Anna nodded. "Yes. Come. I go with you."

She took him by the hand, and side by side the two entered the room.

Madame was propped high on her pillows. Her face was white and expressionless; her eyes were nearly closed and deeply sunken.

"Anna. She is asleep?"

"She is unconscious, Parris. She won't wake again."

Suddenly a low rasping sound grated through the room. Parris started with a kind of terror. He had heard that sound once before.

"Anna!" The whisper was wrenched from him.

"*Ja. Das Todes röcheln.*"

Parris clenched his hands. "Anna—stop it—some way!"

Anna laid her hands on his shoulder. "Listen to me, Parris. That is why I looked for you just now. This could go on for many hours. I think—I think I cannot stand it. Listen to me, my child—if I take the pillows from under her head she—she will die quickly. Think now—it is for you to say."

She stared hard into his face. Her eyes were bloodshot from loss of sleep, and deep circles lay about them.

"It is for you to say," she repeated.

The color left his face. He looked back at Madame and then, very slowly, back to Anna. He nodded slowly.

"Yes," he said. "Quickly."

Very gently Anna removed the pillows and dropped them on the floor. She took one of Madame's thin hands between her own and waited. Parris felt as if screams were trying to tear their way out of his throat, but he made no sound.

Presently a long, hesitant sigh fluttered on Madame's lips, and stopped. Anna released the hand she had been holding, and turned to Parris.

"You go now," she said quietly.

Parris went downstairs and out on the terrace. The first light of the sun was touching the tops of the tall trees. There were the stir and the far slight echoes of an awakening world, but he did not hear them. He felt as if everything had stopped still. He looked with a bewildered curiosity at the familiar surroundings. It appeared to be the same, but he knew it was not. He knew that the heart of the whole world had stopped beating.

The directors' room of the Burton County Bank was a stuffy place. It had a dry, powdery smell—like the contents of an old pocket. The chairs were uncomfortable, and the roughened felt cover of the table was unpleasant to the touch. Two large flies carried on a buzzing duo as they bumped about over the large uncurtained window that looked out on the open hitching space back of the bank.

It was the week after Madame von Eln's funeral, and Patterson Lawes, chairman of the board, was going over figures with Colonel Skeffington and Parris.

Mr. Lawes was as fusty-looking as the room, but there was a resonant quality to his speech that contradicted his generally desiccated appearance. He snapped some rubber bands around the packets of papers, and removed his gold-rimmed glasses.

"And that's the whole story, young man."

"Thank you," Parris murmured uneasily, glancing at Skeffington. Parris looked pale and a little thin. The lines of blue veins on his forehead showed plainly. He leaned his head on his hand and moved some scraps of paper about on the table. His hair fell over his fingers and concealed the look in his eyes. Skeffington and Lawes exchanged glances.

Lawes cleared his throat, and assumed a brisk manner. "I suppose I ought to offer you some words of advice, but I have a feeling you don't need 'em. Hear good reports about you from all sides. Your grandma made the plans. Our business to carry 'em out. I can't say I think going off to a foreign country is what I'd want a boy of mine to do. You know, in that matter, we could use our own judgment in case you'd prefer staying in the United States. Mighty good medical schools in St. Louis and Chicago."

Lawes looked inquiringly at Parris who realized he was expected to reply to this.

"I prefer going to Vienna, sir."

"Very well, very well. That's as you wish. Now you see what you've got and how much you can spend. Of course, if you can get along on less, you'll have that much more to help you out when you get back. It's sufficient for the most expensive kind of training, I should surmise.

"We can go right ahead and arrange sale of the property. That amount, Colonel Skeffington here agrees, should be safely invested for you to set you up in practice when you get back from Europe. We can pay off the mortgage and you'll have a pretty nice little nest egg left."

Parris looked steadily at Mr. Lawes. His overbrilliant gaze disconcerted Mr. Lawes somewhat.

The boy looked overwrought. Looked like he might break up. Amazing to see a youngster take the death of an old woman so hard. Did him credit, though. Even though the grandmother was a sort of foreigner, she'd done a fine job of raising old General Mitchell's grandson. Looked like a gentleman. A little too fine drawn, but—Mr. Lawes looked hard at Parris—looked tough, too, like he could stand a lot. Well, time would tell.

"Skeffington tells me you plan to go pretty quick now."

"Yes, sir, I hope so."

"We'll fix up your letter of credit for—say, five or six hundred dollars. Then we'll arrange through New York for you to draw directly on your account through a Vienna bank. You better talk to Carter—he can make arrangements about your tickets and—and passage, and so forth. We want to look after you right, my boy. We were very fond of your grandma."

"Thank you, sir."

"Well, now, is there anything else?"

Parris sat up. "I'd like you to put some things in safe deposit—my grandmother's jewelry and some things."

"All right. Now, about the sale—"

"I have asked Anna—"

"Is she the German woman who looked after your grandma?"

"Yes, sir. I have asked Anna to take anything she wants from the house."

"That will be all right, if you wish it."

"Why didn't my grandmother leave her anything in the will?"

"Well, son, I reckon because the woman was well paid. She saved her money and is mighty well fixed for anybody in her position. She—"

"I'd like to give her five hundred dollars."

Lawes looked at Skeffington. Parris' tone had a curious ring to it. Lawes wasn't exactly accustomed to that tone of voice. Just possibly there was a shade of command in it. Skeffington clawed his whiskers, and a slight pink showed in his cheeks.

"Well, now, my boy, that's a generous impulse, but hardly necessary. Something, maybe, say fifty, or even a hundred."

"I'd rather it were five hundred, sir."

"Well, after all—"

"May I have a blank check, sir?" Parris' interruption was not impolite. He was merely inattentive.

Lawes was surprised to find himself opening a drawer and handing a check across the table.

"Thank you, sir."

He wrote the check and handed it back to Mr. Lawes. "She keeps her money here, doesn't she?"

"Yes."

"There are two other people I want to do something for, too. Tom Carr, the overseer, and Benny Singer, but I'll do that out of my own expense account, sir."

Skeffington sneezed and made great ado with a handkerchief.

Parris arose. He looked a little shyly at both men. "I can't thank you enough for your kindness. Someday I'll be able to."

Skeffington was touched, and Lawes stared. He was not used to this either. His own grandsons had no such manners, dammit!

"I shan't be staying at home—at the house after tonight. Anna can stay in charge—until the sale. I—I guess I don't have to be at that, do I?"

"No, no. Of course not, if you'd rather not."

"I couldn't, sir."

"Where are you going?"

"I'll stay with Drake McHugh until I leave. He has invited me."

"Drake McHugh?"

"Yes, sir."

"Well, son, do you think that's best?"

Parris looked at Mr. Lawes uncomprehendingly. "Drake is my best friend, sir."

"I see." Lawes glanced sidewise at Skeffington again. He felt he wasn't exactly doing the business of guardianship. Skeffington was busy with his whiskers again and offered no help.

"Good day, sir. Good day, Colonel Skeffington."

"Good day, son. Drop in to see me."

"I will, sir."

Parris walked up Union Street. He had had a note from Dr. Tower and, surprisingly, one from Cassie, but he had not been back to the house on Walnut Street. He felt that he couldn't quite face any expression of sympathy from anyone, yet.

He was unaware of anyone, and walked with his head down. Tomorrow he would come and stay with Drake. Today—

He turned abruptly and crossed to Walnut. The little Catholic church stood in the deep shade of the high trees. It looked as out of the world as he felt. He walked quickly the half block and rather timidly tried the door. It opened, and he went in. He stood for a moment until he could see in the half-dark, then walked down the side aisle and sat down.

The place felt strange. He was grateful for that very strangeness. Just now he was sure he couldn't bear anything familiar—anything that reached back and touched the life from which he was completely severed. Everything, at this moment—everything in all that life seemed to be left far behind, and to be receding at hideous speed. Continents of distance already lay between. He knew he would break down if he stayed at home any longer. He had gone through the funeral, and accepted words of condolence only by subtracting himself from the whole scene and all of its proceedings. Even now he could hardly remember it. It was like something he had heard about, but had not seen.

"Good afternoon."

Parris looked up, so startled that he had difficulty realizing at once where he was.

Father Donovan repeated the greeting. "Good afternoon, my son."

Parris arose. "Good afternoon, sir."

Father Donovan looked very steadily at the white drawn face before him.

"You are Parris Mitchell, are you not?"

"Yes, sir."

"I have seen you on the streets. Sit down, sit down."

Parris looked about him. He wanted to go now, but he was afraid of seeming rude.

"I—I just came in—in."

"That was quite right."

"I hope it isn't an intrusion of any kind."

"Not at all. Sit down."

Father Donovan was so impersonal that Parris obeyed. The priest sat in the next pew.

"You lost your grandmother last week, I hear."

Parris lowered his head and stared at his hands. "Yes, sir."

Father Donovan got slowly to his feet. "Come whenever you wish. I hope you may find some peace and comfort here."

Parris raised his eyes. Father Donovan's face was almost inexpressive. It asked no questions, and presaged no invasion of anyone's thoughts.

To his own surprise, Parris found himself speaking.

"I didn't have any place to go," he said simply.

Father Donovan turned his head sideways a little. "How do you mean?"

Parris was silent for a moment. A trancelike agony froze him to immobility. It seemed to him that he was speaking to someone at a distance.

"My grandmother is dead," he said evenly.

The priest stared hard. He sat down again.

"Your home?" He said the words softly, with just a shade of question.

Parris looked away. "Oh, the house is there."

"Have you no one at all?" The priest spoke a little wonderingly.

"No, sir."

"I am sorry, my son."

"Thank you, sir."

"Do you mind if I ask you what you are going to do?"

"I am going to—to Vienna."

"To relatives, perhaps?"

"I have none. I'm going to study medicine."

"Oh, I see. That is very fine."

"My grandmother arranged it."

"But you wish to go?"

"Yes, sir."

"Vienna is very beautiful."

"You have been there?"

"Once."

They fell silent. Parris did not feel any embarrassment. Father Donovan sat so still, he might have been inanimate. Parris glanced at him obliquely. The man looked very patient, and a little sad. He felt now that somehow he *was* an intruder, and that maybe Father Donovan mistook his reason for coming. He wanted to find some way of saying this, but some words blurted themselves before he could think.

"I don't believe in God."

Not a muscle of Father Donovan's face changed. After a moment he said: "That must be very difficult."

"Difficult?"

"Yes, my son. It must be—pretty hard going sometimes, isn't it?"

"Yes."

"I don't believe I could do it."

Parris stared. He realized that he had wished to strike at something. He was immediately contrite. "I am very sorry that I said that to you, sir. I—I only meant to explain myself."

The priest nodded.

"Grief is heavy. I know. But you realize that you could not even experience grief without love."

Parris did not answer.

Father Donovan continued. "You are experiencing grief only because you loved someone. Without the ennobling thing that love must have been to you, you could not know grief. You could not mourn for someone you did not love." He paused. "Grief is ennobling, too."

Parris relaxed a little. He did not wish to speak.

"It will be no comfort to you now to say that grief and loneliness come to all of us." He drummed with his fingers casually on the back of the pew. "That's why I say it must be difficult not to believe in God. It's so hard to be alone." He waited again, and then he spoke so gently that he seemed scarcely to begin.

"I went to Europe once. I was in Rome, too. I remember all of it. Peter's great church, the windows, the organs, the choirs, and the many people.

"I come in here sometimes and then I can see it all and hear it all again. It's like feeling the pulse in your wrist that tells you you are alive. I come here and I can hear the beating of the great heart of Rome. It makes me feel that I'm a part of something—far away as it seems to be sometimes—but a part of something. Yes: I can understand that it must be very hard not to believe in God."

He smiled, a comradely smile as if they had spoken of some mutual problem.

"Maybe you will believe in God someday. Maybe you will find that you are mistaken. But don't think about it now. Don't worry about it. If—if you are mistaken, God will still be there when you find it out. Stay here as long as you like. Come in whenever you like. Try to be at peace. The measure, as I said, of the heights and breadths and depths of grief is also the measure of the heights and breadths and depths of love."

He said something else that Parris did not understand. Then he went quietly out of the door. Parris saw him striding across the sunburned lawn between the church and the little house where he lived.

Parris remained sitting for half an hour. When he left the little church he walked as fast as he could toward home. Once or twice he reeled a little. He felt dizzy.

At the foot of the terrace steps he lagged. He made each step as if it required a separate effort of will.

He could hear Anna moving about the kitchen and talking to the cook, but every sound seemed to echo. The usual stir of the life of the place came in at the windows, but it seemed to pass on through the house as though it were not there at all. He thought of what Father Donovan had said about the pulse in your wrist that tells you you are alive: the house was pulseless; it was not alive.

He went upstairs and packed a large bag. When he had finished he crossed the hall to the door of Madame von Eln's room. He placed his hand on the knob of the door, but he did not turn it. He stood for a minute or two with his hand resting there. Then he touched the panel of the door with his finger tips and let them slide downward with a gesture like a caress.

Anna called from the foot of the stairs.

"Yes, Anna, I'm coming down."

She looked at the valise, and a queer expression came into her eyes. She nodded toward the heavy bag as Parris dropped it at the foot of the stairs.

"You go—now?"

"Yes. Do you think Benny would mind hitching up and driving me in to Drake's?"

"Of course he wouldn't mind. But supper—you stay for supper?"

He shook his head. "I can't."

Anna put her arms around him and pressed his head hard against her stiff starched dress. "Don't take it so hard. It was better for her to go—so, when the suffering was so bad."

Parris patted Anna's hand, but his face kept its stony look. "That doesn't make sense, Anna. Of course, once she was dying of cancer, it was better to die and—but why did she have to have a cancer? There's just no sense to anything. That's all."

Anna swallowed hard. "You come out again tomorrow, or the next day?"

"No. I'm not coming back. You'll pack up my things and send them on to Drake's, won't you?"

"You do not come back—any more?"

"No, Anna. I'll see you—in town."

"Yes, of course. I'll tell Benny."

"Thank you, Anna. I'll wait for him at the lower drive."

Anna watched him out of the door. Then she put her apron over her face and sat down in the nearest chair, rocking silently as she listened to his steps on the stone stairs.

Parris was sorting and packing books. He sat back on his heels and wiped his face on his sleeve.

"You're sure you won't mind having these boxes around somewhere? I don't know what to do with them, and I think there'll be only a few I need to take along."

Drake waved his hand in a widely inclusive gesture. "There's a whole house here. I'll take care of 'em, kid. If I ever rent the old barn, I'll store 'em away somewhere. Don't worry."

"I'm not worried about them. Just don't feel like throwing them away. I doubt, though, if they'll ever be any good to me."

"Why?"

Parris looked at the stacks of fat volumes and sighed. "Most of that stuff gets out of date pretty quick. It's—er—superseded by something new in no time at all. "

"Gosh, kid. Do you mean you spent these years reading all that stuff and a lot of it's not so?"

Parris smiled slightly. "Not exactly that. It's improved on, or changed—you know, just like anything else. But this is what you've got to know now."

"Gee. You couldn't wait, I guess, until the improvements were made, could you?" Drake grinned. "I'm just trying to save you some work. I'm going to miss you, boy."

Parris leaned over the box and did not reply at once. He joked up presently and smiled at Drake.

"It's been awfully good of you, Drake, to take me in—just now."

"Aw—"

"I haven't been—I guess I can't be any fun to be with."

"I wanted you to stay here. I wish you wouldn't go away at all."

"I half wish so, too, Drake. Or—that you'd come along."

"What would I do over there? Couldn't talk the lingo or—anything."

"You'd get on all right."

"Nope. Guess my place is round here."

"Drake."

"Yep."

"You haven't said anything about Louise."

"Ain't seen her—to talk to her—since that day you came along."

"Drake—that's not fair."

"You bet it ain't."

"I mean it's not fair of you. You're not fair to her."

"How do you figure that out?"

"You ought—oh, I don't know. It's not my business, I guess."

"Go ahead. Hell! Say anything you want to."

"Well, she can't follow you around and try to see you."

"And you can bet your bottom dollar I ain't going to follow her around. Not where I ain't wanted. No, sir! Not me."

"I think she likes you—just as much as you do her."

"Well." Drake grumbled the word in his throat. "I don't know sometimes how much I think of her. Gosh—nice girls, as you call 'em, are funny."

"How?"

"Oh, hell! You just touch 'em or something and you'd think you was pulling their clothes off the way they go on."

Parris nearly laughed. "I can imagine."

Drake was serious. "It's so. Jesus, maybe it wouldn't be any fun to be married to one of that kind. I don't know."

"I guess that would be different."

"I don't know. Can you imagine my Aunt Mamie ever letting down the bars at all? Why, I bet when she was young, even—well. I just can't imagine her and Uncle Rhodes having any kind of good time."

"Does seem unlikely, doesn't it?"

"Sure. You knew Aunt Mamie. Now, if you had Poppy around—that would be different."

"Do you think you'd want to marry Poppy?"

"Well—maybe not Poppy or Jinny. But somebody of that free-and-easy kind. Full of the devil. You know what I mean."

"Yes, I guess I do."

"You look tired, kid. Just leave the books and stuff there on the floor—the ones you don't want to take along, Esther can pack 'em up. You better take things a little easy."

"I feel all right, I guess."

"Darned if you look it."

"All right. I think I will leave them." Parris reached for a pillow and put it under his head. "Gee, I'm too tired to get up from here."

"You've had a pretty big day, kid. Take it easy.... Listen! What's that?"

"What's what?"

"I hear someone running up the drive."

"Somebody cutting through the block, I guess."

"No. Somebody coming here."

Parris sat up. There was a rush of steps on the long side porch, then a quick knock at the door. Drake opened it, and Cassandra Tower came into the room. She was out of breath and a little disheveled. Parris struggled awkwardly to his feet.

"Cassie! What's up?"

"I've got to talk to you a minute."

Drake wheeled a chair forward. "Sit down, Cassie."

She looked at him and nodded but remained standing.

"Well, if you all will excuse me—" Drake began half facetiously.

Cassie put out her hand. "Don't go. I've just got a word to say. You might as well hear it."

"Well—"

"You know all about us, anyway."

Drake's embarrassment showed in his face. Parris stared curiously at Cassandra. She had that look he had seen a few times before—desperate—a sort of shocked desperation.

"Sit down, Cassie. What's the matter?"

Her eyes seemed to come slowly to focus, almost as if she had difficulty in seeing.

"Parris—you remember the other night—the last time?"

"Of course!" His voice was suddenly hoarse.

"You said—when—when you came back—would I marry you."

"Yes, Cassie. I meant it. I'll say it again."

"Parris!"

"Yes, Cassie, what's the matter? You look—"

"How?"

"You look scared."

"Listen."

"All right, Cassie, I'm listening. What's the matter? Is—are you—?"

She looked at him for a moment. "No," she said roughly. "Don't be foolish. You—you *did* mean what you said?"

"Of course I did."

"Then let me go with you—now."

"Now?"

"Yes, now. Oh, I don't care if you marry me or not. Just let me go away with you. I've got to. I'll run away somewhere—let me go with you. I—I can take care of you."

Parris was completely bewildered. "Cassie! You're sure—"

She lifted her head angrily. "There's nothing the matter with me!"

"But Cassie, I don't understand you. I—why. I can't get married now. I've got to get through—all that study first. Why—" He stopped. It seemed an unbelievably absurd proposal. Why—he almost wanted to say he wasn't grown up yet. He hunted confusedly for the right words to say. He was a little embarrassed for her before Drake, but Cassie seemed unaware of Drake's presence. Her eyes, strained and almost staring, never left Parris' face.

Suddenly, every vestige of expression left her features. Her face seemed to go dead.

"Never mind." Her voice, too, seemed utterly lifeless. She turned to go.

Parris was beside her instantly. "Wait a minute, Cassie. Sit down, and—and tell me what's happened."

She looked as if she didn't hear. "Nothing, Parris. Nothing at all. I—I must go."

"Here. I'll take you home."

"No, no! No, you can't. You mustn't. I'm all right, now."

"But, Cassie, you've got to let me talk to you, now."

"Not now, Parris. Excuse me. I've got to go."

Drake picked up his hat. "You'd better let me walk part of the way with you anyhow, Cassie."

"Thank you, Drake. No. Good night."

And before either of them could say another word she had gone. They heard her running again, going back the same way she had come.

Parris stood in the middle of the room, unable to think or to move. He looked up, a little fearful that Drake would laugh, or make some half-jeering remark. Whatever might be the matter, he knew that Cassie was in earnest, and that she was horribly frightened about something.

"Drake, do you suppose Dr. Tower found out?"

"I don't know."

"I think I'd better go over there."

Drake caught him by the arm. "Wait a minute. Better go slow. She said—you heard her. She didn't want you to come along—she looked twice as scared when you suggested it."

"That's just why I think I ought to go over there and see what's the matter."

"But suppose her old man don't know she's been here, or out of the house even."

"Well?"

"You'd give the whole thing away and get her into sure-enough trouble."

"I believe she is in sure-enough trouble."

"You better wait. That's my advice."

"I can't leave her there alone to take it by herself—whatever has happened."

"If that'd been it, she'd have told you."

"What makes you think so?"

"I don't know. Just feel it in my bones. You know what I think?"

"What?"

"I believe she just got to thinking about you going away and just kind of went off her base for a minute. Gee, she's all gone on you, ain't she?"

"It might have been just a—a kind of hysterical outbreak."

"Says Dr. Mitchell!"

Parris did not smile. "Drake, you come with me if you want to, but I'm going to go over there and walk by the house and see if there is anything that looks out of the way."

"Good idea. Come on."

They walked rapidly until the Tower house was in sight. Then they strolled slowly past. The house was half hidden in shrubbery, but they could see Dr. Tower on the front porch. The glow of his cigar moved slowly back and forth.

"See there. Everything's all right. He's sitting on the porch swing."

"Wait a minute, Drake. Go slow."

"Come on. We better keep moving." They walked to the end of the block and back again.

Drake nudged Parris sharply. "Look! There's Cassie herself."

They could see the gleam of the hall light on her bright hair as she came out on the porch. She said something to Dr. Tower and re-entered the house.

"See! Old Cass was just having a fit over you going away. That's all."

"It doesn't seem much like her—somehow. Still, I have seen her have outbreaks once in a while."

Drake quickened his step. He did not quite succeed in concealing his concern, which was somewhat for Cassie but more for Parris.

"I bet you have. All women and girls act like that sometimes. Don't mean anything. Come on and get to bed. You need sleep, kid. Don't let this worry you. You can get word to her somehow tomorrow."

"Maybe." Parris still hung back. "I am wondering what got into her, though."

"Say, Parris—are you sure enough in love with Cassie?"

"Oh, gosh, Drake, I don't know. Sometimes I think I am, and sometimes I think I'm not."

"What do you want to marry her for, then?"

"I guess I ought to."

"Hell! Not unless you want to."

"I think I'd like to marry her. She's kind of wonderful, Drake."

"How so?"

"Smart, and everything."

"'Specially 'everything,' I bet!" Drake flung his arm over Parris' shoulder.

"Don't be funny about it, Drake. This has been going on a long time, you know. I don't know how to say it, exactly, but Cassie is—is just in my blood. When I think about her I get all—"

"Sure! I bet you do! Who wouldn't?"

"You don't understand, Drake, I know you don't."

"Well, I do. You don't think I understand anything, do you, sometimes? Well, I can see into a lot more things than you think I do. Now, take Poppy. When I think about Poppy I remember how soft she is, and how warm she is, and the way she cuddles up to you that makes you sort of crazy. And—she laughs and giggles and romps around with you. She's funny as hell, and she goes to bed with you and her—aw, kid, you don't know!—she has a regular picnic."

"I can imagine."

"And then, there on the other hand—there's Louise. When I think of her she is something altogether different. I can feel all funny and excited about her, too, but, it's just different. We talk—we used to, anyway—about different things from what Poppy and I talk about. So, I can guess, all right, that Cassie Tower is both of them rolled into one as far as you are concerned."

Parris was a little surprised, and a little touched, too. It wasn't like Drake to talk that much about his own feelings. Parris knew that these elaborate and cumbersome explanations were made to convince him of sympathy and understanding.

"I guess it's like that, Drake. But still—first of all, I don't understand Cassie breaking out like that tonight. Gee, Drake! I couldn't get married now. I'm not twenty years old yet."

'That don't make any difference, kid, if you want to."

"But I've got four years in medical school. It might be five."

"Say, you could afford to get married if you want to, couldn't you—as far as money is concerned?"

"I don't know, I guess so. I guess even at that I'd have to have the consent of somebody or other."

"'Cause if you sure enough want to get married and might need some money later on—you know I'll have mine in a little more'n a year now."

"Drake, I can't bear for you always to be doing something for me, I never have done anything for you—"

"Shut up."

"I mean it. But—well you know how I feel. I don't have to tell you. Honestly, I never have thought about getting married for a long time yet. I remember the day you talked to me about Louise I was so astonished I couldn't say anything. I just never had thought about either one of us being old enough to get married."

"You've been old enough to think of some other things for quite some time, now."

"Ye-es, I know. I never have been sorry, either."

"That's the stuff! That's the way to talk. Come on home—you need to go to bed."

"You don't think I ought to try and find out some way about Cassie? For half a cent, I'd just go on in to see Dr. Tower and—"

"And get your pants kicked all the way to the front gate?"

"Well, what is the matter with him, anyway? Cassie's a girl like anybody else."

"Yes, but you know as well as I do that Dr. Tower is a man like nobody else! Ain't he kept her in as strict as if—like she was a prisoner? Once in a while some man acts like that about his daughter, like he was afraid somebody's going to rape her if he let her out of sight. I don't know what's the matter with people like that. But you know darn well ain't anything about the Towers been like anybody else."

"I don't believe it's as mysterious as it looks, Drake. I've been going there all this time, and Dr. Tower seems just like anybody else, except smarter."

"Ever mention Cassie to him?"

"Once or twice."

"What happened?"

"He froze up completely."

"There you are! That's not natural. Seems like he'd 'a' wanted you to marry Cassie. You say he likes you."

"I think something must have happened when they first came here, before we knew anything about things. He's awfully bitter about Kings Row and about pretty near everybody in it."

"Don't Cassie ever explain anything about themselves to you?"

"Never has. Always shies off the subject."

"You don't know anything about them?"

"No more than you do."

"No wonder you're not so anxious to marry Cass!"

"It's not that. I'd marry her in a minute—if it were necessary, I just don't want to marry anybody right now, I think."

"Well, you're the one that's got to know."

"Of course, I think I'm going to be so lonesome I won't know what to do. To go where I don't know anybody."

"Well, kid, I'm not very smart, but I figure something out my own way. I think you got to be natural. You've got to want something—anything—with all of you, mind and body, before it's important enough to lose any sleep over."

"Anyhow, Drake, I see I've got to think this over before I go to Vienna. I almost wish—"

"What, kid? Spit it out."

"I could almost wish I could marry Cassie and stay here, and maybe live out at my own house. Maybe I could learn to run that place myself. Tom Carr could help me, could teach me about it. Maybe—gee, maybe you could come in on it with me!"

"Not on your life! I wouldn't let you do any such damn fool thing, kid. I know you better'n you know your own self. You always have wanted to be a doctor, ever since I can remember that we talked about such things. You never would be happy in this world if you didn't go ahead and do it."

"But—"

"Besides, your grandma wanted you to do it. She fixed everything up so you could. You've got to go through with it. Hell, that nursery out there is just a kind of farm. You ain't a farmer. Can you imagine Cassie Tower being on a farm?"

Parris smiled.

"Besides, kid, I know what got into you this evening. All this time there's been Cassie. You two got together somehow whenever you could. You get tired of slipping around behind people's backs after a while, especially when you feel that maybe you got some right to what you're doing, anyway. You get to thinking about having Cassie around all the time, and about going to bed with her every night and nobody interfering with it—and—and all that looks better than anything in the world. You're just ready to throw up everything else. But, kid, that's just because it's right now."

They were walking slowly now. Drake watched Parris with a deepening concern.

"It's just that I feel so unbearably lonely, Drake, without anybody. You're the best friend I have—the only friend I've got. I wouldn't tell anybody else, but I'm scared."

"Of course you are. Do you think I ain't been scared a lot of times? Other people have been right nice: they seem to understand sometimes when you are a kid and by yourself. Not lately, though. I guess everybody's down on me a little."

Parris suddenly remembered Mr. Lawes' reluctance to have him stay with Drake.

"Why, Drake? Why are they?"

"They think I'm getting tough."

"Why?"

"I have been seen a lot with Poppy and Jinny."

"Do you think, maybe, you could kind of watch out a little?"

"What for?"

"If you're going to live in Kings Row, you've got to get along with the people in Kings Row."

"Never mind, kid. Never mind about me. I'll work it ail out some way. Don't you worry."

"You'll write to me, and tell me how everything is, won't you?"

"Of course. I'm not much on letters, though."

"I'll have to get letters to Cassie, somehow, through you, if—"

"Look out, now!"

"I mean it. If she doesn't go with me."

Both Parris and Drake slept late the next morning. Esther, the tall black maid who kept house now for Drake, was rattling noisily about the kitchen when they awoke.

Drake arose and dressed and went to see about breakfast. Parris dozed again, but in his half-sleep he heard Esther's excited talk and Drake's low-voiced questions. Presently he heard Drake at the telephone but could hear nothing of his conversation. It wasn't usual for Drake to stir about so busily in the morning. Parris drifted off to sleep again.

When he waked, Drake was standing beside the bed with a breakfast tray.

"Wake up, kid, eat your breakfast."

"Hello! What's the idea of all this?" He sat up and rubbed his eyes and yawned. He grinned at Drake, and then he remembered the troublous questions of the preceding evening. He sighed.

"Better eat this, kid."

Drake's manner was so grave that Parris looked up in surprise. Drake was very wide-eyed, and Parris thought he even looked pale.

"Are you all right, Drake? Anything the matter?"

"I'm all right." His gaze never left Parris' face.

"Say! You look awful strange."

"Come on, eat your breakfast."

Parris threw back the covers and swung his feet out of bed. "See here, Drake, you can't fool me. Something's the matter with you."

"I've got something to tell you, but you've got to drink your coffee first."

Parris pushed the tray aside. "What is it. Tell me now."

"It's something about Cassie, Parris."

"What? Quick! Don't keep me waiting, Drake!"

"Something pretty bad has happened."

"Drake—"

"Cassie's dead, Parris."

Parris opened his mouth but he couldn't make a sound.

"She was killed, Parris, early last night. I guess shortly after we passed there."

"W-who?"

"Her father killed her—and committed suicide."

Parris held tight to Drake's arm. "How do you know? Who told you?"

"Esther. Everybody knows by now. I telephoned the *Gazette* office. He left a letter."

"Good God, Drake! It must have been because—it was my fault."

"Don't even think that, Parris." Drake shook him. "Now, you listen to me. You keep your mouth shut. Tight, do you hear?"

Parris tried to pull away.

"Listen to me, Parris. You can ruin everything if you don't watch out. It's not your fault. He must have been crazy."

"He found out, and she came here—and—I sent her back."

"That couldn't have been it. Remember, we saw both of them about ten o'clock last night."

"Drake!"

"Yes."

"How—"

"She was dead in bed from some kind of poison—they don't know yet what it was. But it must have been something quick. They say she's been dead for a good many hours."

"My God, Drake! This is terrible. What are we going to do?"

"You're not going to do anything, if I have to tie you up in the cellar. You sit tight."

Parris tried to dress, but he couldn't.

"Here. You got your pants wrong. Here—"

"I can't think—"

"Dr. Tower shot himself. That must have been a lot later. Nobody heard anything, and they say he hadn't been dead very long when the cook came in and found them."

"You said he left a letter?"

"That's what they said down at the *Gazette* office. I believe they said letters,' I'm not sure."

"What did—what was in them?"

"They said they didn't have any further information. I guess everybody's been telephoning to find out."

"Drake—I've got to go and find out—"

"Oh, no, you don't! You stay right here, and I'll go. But—damn it, kid, don't you see you might be mixed up in this some way? No use you rushing right into any kind of a fix."

"Mixed—up—in—it?"

"Well, you're the only person ever went there. You have been playing around with Cassie, haven't you? And she was here in this house, last night!"

"Well, we've got to tell them. I—"

"We won't tell them anything until they ask us, or until we think we better had. Now, you're going to stay right where you are. I'm going to see what I can find out."

"I'm going with you."

"Not a bit. You'll give something away. Your face'll tell everything."

"Well, what is there to tell? I haven't done anything."

"Listen, you fool. Suppose Cassie's old man just went crazy, or was crazy, or whatever, and just killed her for some other reason than you think. Do you want to tell about everything? I think you've got to protect Cassie that much."

"Protect her! Good God, Drake, I think I killed her, by—"

"Yeh, just say that out loud a few times, and somebody'll believe you. Now shut up, and stay here, and don't telephone and don't answer the telephone. I'm going to see what in hell happened anyway."

"I can't, Drake. I've got to go with you. This is more my business than anybody's, it seems to me."

"I swear, I'll knock your head loose if you don't do what I tell you. Listen—just as a favor to me, let me go downtown, and I'll come right back. If everything looks all right, you can go out yourself. I just don't want you to get talked about unnecessarily. That's all. Now, will you promise me?"

"Yes."

"That's the stuff."

Drake didn't come back until noon. He looked hot and tired.

Parris met him at the door. "Well?"

"Just rest easy. I'll tell you all I know. Esther!"

Esther came ambling slowly from the kitchen. "Yassuh!"

"Fix me some cold lemonade, or something, please."

"Yassuh. Did you heah any mo' 'bout Dr. Towah?"

"No. That was all—what you told me."

"Yassuh." She ambled away.

"Drake—quick!"

"It's all right, kid, as far as you're concerned."

"That's not the question. I mean, did you find out why he killed her?"

"No. His letter—he left a letter on his study table—didn't tell any reason at all. He just explained that he had killed his daughter and was going to kill himself. The rest was just directions that he and Cassie were to be buried here in Kings Row."

"Is that all?"

"Well, that was all I could find out at first. Then I went to see Colonel Skeffington. I thought he might know something more if anybody did."

"Did he?"

"Yes."

"Quick, Drake. You drive me crazy!"

"Well, kid. There's something awful curious about this. You're in for a surprise. I told you it was all right as far as you are concerned."

"What in the world are you—?"

"There was a letter addressed to the bank, and to Colonel Skeffington—a kind of a will."

"Then he did have kinfolks somewhere?"

"No. He left everything he had to you."

"You're crazy!"

"No, I'm not. But I'm damn sure Dr. Tower must have been."

"Left it to me! Why? What for?"

"No explanation at all. Colonel Skeffington asked all sorts of questions. Wondered if you had any inkling of this. But you see it excuses you, all right, from any responsibility in Cassie's death. If that had been what he killed her for, he wouldn't have left you his property."

Parris beat on the table with his fists. "I don't care about that! I don't care about that! It's Cassie! Cassie ... too! What did she do?" He leaned forward and bent his head on his clenched hands. He began to cry, uncontrollably, making small, incoherent sounds.

Drake stood up. "Aw, Jesus Christ, kid, for—aw, Jesus Christ, kid! If this ain't the God-damnedest world I ever heard of!" He seized Parris awkwardly and held him close and hard as one holds a child to ward off danger.

Parris sat through the afternoon, silent and dazed. Drake tried all of the devices he could think of to break the stony look that had settled on his face. Parris only returned such a stricken gaze that Drake gave up after a while. The long hot afternoon passed. Only once did Parris ask a question.

"Drake!"

"Right here, Parris."

"What are they doing over there? Who's looking after them?"

"It's in the hands of the coroner, of course, Parris. I guess they've got charge. If you're thinking of going—"

"But it seems to be my place, somehow."

"You stay out of it. Somebody'll begin to ask you questions, and just like I said, you haven't got any more sense than to tell everything you know."

Parris looked a little blank. "Everything I know?"

"Yes."

"But I don't know anything."

"You know that Cassie came running here last night like something was after her, and wanted you to marry her."

"Well—"

"Can't you imagine what Kings Row would make out of that! Think a little, you numbskull! This town's been talking about the Towers ever since I can remember anything, wondering about 'em, and the like. Sometimes the talk died down a little because the old gossips couldn't think of anything more to say. And the Towers never furnished them any ammunition. I kind of think Kings Row found that harder to get over than anything about the Towers." Drake nodded shrewdly to his own remark. "A town like this just can't get over anybody not working for a living, anyhow. And when Cassie Tower began to grow up and was better-looking than any girl in town there was a lot of people got jealous. I know that. I saw it even in Louise. She never did have a good word to say for Cassie, but she went awful far out of her way to say a lot of bad ones."

"Why, Drake? Why?"

"Just cussed human nature. Sometimes I think you don't know anything about people at all. Lots of people are jealous of you, too."

"Me? For heaven's sake, why?"

"You got money. Your grandma acted stuck-up, they thought. You walk around looking—"

"How? I don't mean to look any kind of way."

"Well, you look just like what you are—superior."

"Stuff."

"'S the truth. Of course, I know you. That's different. Gosh, Parris, I feel the same way sometimes. Uncle Rhodes and Aunt Mamie were awful strict, and hard on me, and they—they weren't very smart in some ways, but they were top layer. Why—their families—"

"Of course, I know."

"Well, I don't take much stock in all that stuff about your ancestors, but when I know people are talking behind my back and some of 'em thinking they're better'n I am because they go to church with a long face, I just remember who some of my ancestors were, and I—aw, you know what I mean. I stick my head up a little higher, too."

"You've got a right to. You're—you're all right." Parris wriggled in his chair, breaking his apathy a little. He couldn't say all he wanted to, but he felt that Drake understood him.

"But, Parris. I've kept my eyes open these last two years. That's the very kind of thing people don't like. Whether you are better'n they are, or not—I mean, don't make any difference whether you know you're better stuff, or whether you think so. They don't want to know it themselves. They just can't get over it. I'm not going to have such an easy time here, and I don't believe you will, either."

"Oh, gosh a'mighty, Drake, you make me feel bad. I never have done anything to anybody—"

"You went your own way, though. You always have. You're old General Mitchell's grandson—"

"Honest, Drake, I never once thought of that in my whole life. I actually don't know much about my grandfather Mitchell—or care."

"Sure, I know. But other people know. And your grandma had—foreign ways."

"She was everything fine and great, Drake."

"I bet she was. But Kings Row didn't know that. They thought she—she was just a foreigner who ran a nursery out there. It's you they'll go gunning for someday, I'm afraid, unless you learn to mix around with 'em."

"Maybe I'll learn."

"Well, the first lesson is keeping out of that business over there on Walnut Street."

"You wouldn't tell me to back out of everything I ought to stand up to, would you?"

"I might even do that. Listen, Parris. I know this sounds hard. But Dr. Tower and Cassie are dead. You can't change that. I don't know why a man could kill his own daughter, and I guess you don't either."

Drake waited a few seconds, but Parris said nothing.

"But you know as well as I do—common sense tells you that he didn't kill her for nothing. As far as we know, the only thing he could have had against her would have been if he found out about you and her—"

Parris stood up.

"Sit down, now, and listen. But, he willed you his house and his money. That don't look like he was mad at you, does it?"

"Drake, for God's sake, why do you suppose he did that?"

"You mean, left you all his stuff?"

"Yes."

"Maybe didn't have anybody else to leave it to. Guess he must have thought a lot of you. Can't see any other reason."

"That tangles everything up, doesn't it?"

"As far as understanding why he killed Cassie, and himself, it certainly does."

"Drake, I've just got to find out something. I'll go crazy just sitting here."

"No, you won't."

"But—"

"I told Colonel Skeffington you was awful upset, and to let me know anything he found out. He said he would. If anybody can find out anything, that old fox can."

Parris sat down again and rested his head between his hands.

"Gee, Drake! Cassie—and she was right here last night!"

"Yes. It's hard to believe. But it's right there you better lay low and keep your mouth shut. If you say anything about Cassie, you're going to give everything away—"

"Everything? Every what?"

"Well, I don't know. But it'll stir up talk, and you'll be mixed up in it to your neck, and you might as well never count on coming back to Kings Row."

"I keep wondering. It just doesn't make any sense."

"Listen, I want to ask you a question. You don't have to answer if you don't want to."

"What?"

"Now, don't get mad. You can just tell me to shut my trap and tend to my own business."

"Go on. What is it?"

"You don't think maybe Cassie was going to have a baby, do you?"

Parris wheeled around in his chair. He was silent a moment.

"I thought of that last night, Drake, first thing when she said something about having to go away."

"Well, what do you think?"

"You heard me ask her."

"No, I didn't!"

"That's what I meant. She understood me. No, Drake, I thought it over this morning. That's not it."

"Sure?"

"Yes."

"'Cause if it was anything like that—"

Parris started up again. "Drake, do you suppose they'll have an autopsy?"

Drake shook his head.

"How do you know?"

"Well, suppose they did—are you afraid of what they'd find out about Cassie?"

"No, Drake. I tell you, I know—soon as I thought it over."

"Well, Colonel Skeffington said there wouldn't be an autopsy, that it wasn't necessary. Dr. Tower's letters, I guess. She was poisoned—"

"You don't suppose she might have taken it herself, do you?"

"N-no. Her father's letters put that out of the question."

"Oh, yes. I forgot the letters for a minute. You said 'letters.' There wasn't one to me, was there?"

"No. One to—to the authorities, and one to the bank—that's the one that was a will, too."

"I wish I could go over to that house, right now—but I don't believe I could bear it."

"Better stay away. We'll have to go to the funeral, though."

Parris paled. "I—hadn't—thought—of that."

"But—"

"Oh, of course. I'd want to anyway. I have such a funny feeling about the whole thing, Drake. I feel somehow that I ought to go and stand by Cassie, and stay close to her until—until—"

"That's easy to understand, kid. But don't let your conscience do things to you, now. You're not to blame. Lord, kid, I was right here, and I know everything that happened. Don't you think if I thought you ought to do anything, I'd have been the first one to tell you so?"

"But I just sat there, like a—dumb fool, and didn't say much of anything one way or the other."

"What could you say? I can see you couldn't think right off what to say. I couldn't have, either. First thing you knew she was running down the driveway and was gone. Then when we saw her at home everything looked natural and all right. Didn't it?"

"Yes."

"Say! That's another thing. It'll be just as well if we don't say anything about being over there on Walnut Street last night. There'd be questions of some kind. What was we doing there, and all. The less questions asked, the better. Now, listen, Parris, you understand I'm doing this for your own sake, don't you."

"Of course, Drake, but I just don't want to be a coward."

"Nothing cowardly about this. I think maybe we'll figure this out some way, but not now. Take it easy, kid. You better eat something."

"I can't—not now."

Parris turned again to the window. Drake watched him for a few minutes, his own warm gray eyes shadowed with a kind of brooding concern.

"Say, Parris!"

Parris looked up without speaking.

"Say—the Towers lived pretty well, didn't they?"

"I guess so. Why?"

"Well—have you forgotten he left you everything?"

Parris frowned, and then looked startled.

"Say, kid—gosh, maybe you're sure enough rich now!"

Parris looked hard at the floor for a moment. Then he resumed his apparently sightless staring out of the window.

"I don't care," he said after a while. "That doesn't make any difference."

The narrow circle of questions began its grinding revolutions again. *Why? What? Why?*

Why did Cassie come last night?

What was she afraid of?

What had happened since the night in Aberdeen campus?

What reason could her father have had for killing her?

What reason could he have had for killing himself?

Why didn't Cassie explain things last night?

Why didn't Dr. Tower leave a letter for him since he was leaving him his property?

Why—and why, why hadn't he ever come right out and asked Cassie about herself?

He couldn't go on always not knowing what lay in the past.

Why—and why—and why? He held his head tight between his hands. There was a stabbing pain in his temples. He felt shaky. Perhaps he was hungry. He believed he was. Yes, he was hungry. But it seemed wrong, somehow, to eat, or to think about food. Cassie.... He kept seeing her as she must be, her singular whiteness even whiter now. What kind of poison was given her? How did her father manage to make her take it? He wondered with a spasm of pain, and something near to fear, if it hurt much. Cassie ... she didn't do anything to ... why? Why would anyone want to kill Cassie? If her father wanted to commit suicide, why couldn't he leave Cassie alone? He thought with a strange complex wave of feeling how simple everything would have been. Then he could have taken Cassie with him.

Parris sat rigid, and Drake waited. Drake's lips quivered ever so little as he watched. Parris' face had altered during these hours. That soft-complexioned look he had always had was gone. The muscles showed through as though they were hard and set. Everything about his face looked harder—and older.

Drake left the room and returned after a while with a tray of food and a glass.

"Here, now, kid. You drink this."

Parris shook his head.

"'Yes, you are. You need it."

"'What is it?"

"'Brandy. Drink it down. You'll feel better. Come on now."

Parris took it.

"All of it now—straight down."

Parris strangled a little and handed the glass to Drake. There was a mute look of accusation in his eye. Drake half grinned.

"Burned like hell, didn't it?"

"Yes."

"Well, that's all right. Now, eat this."

"I don't—"

"Come on. Don't talk."

Parris began to eat slowly. The mere act of opening his mouth relaxed the tense muscles of his face and throat. He felt his control dip a little. It was difficult to chew. He looked appealingly at Drake.

"Eat it, kid. You've got to. I know how you feel. Go on and bawl if you want to. It's all right. God a-mighty, I guess you've got a right to if ever anybody did. Go on there, eat the rest of that."

The late afternoon light began to fail. People were out for their evening drive. The sound of voices drifted in at the windows. Parris could imagine all of Kings Row making the most of a new sensation, driving by the Tower house and eying it curiously—while ... He swallowed audibly. Behind the shabby green shutters ... in that darkened house ... Cassie ... He pounded softly on the arm of the chair with his fists. His long relationship with Cassie had been so tentative, despite its passion and its suppressed intensity. It had been so— so childish. He hadn't ever been really grown-up about it. It had been, even in the beginning, due more to Cassie's initiative than to his. He reflected on this, wondering if it was a kind of disloyalty, or a kind of disrespect, even to remember it.

No: he believed he liked her even better because she had never pretended anything. There were no little modesties, no silly retreats. She had had, with him, a kind of untutored freedom, rather intense sometimes, and a little wild.

He thought cannily back through his recent reading. He wondered if it was because of his life with his grandmother and his whole acceptance of her authority that he had almost made himself subservient to Cassie's imperative nature. But his speculations could not go far. At the slightest veering toward anything that was a calculated consideration of Cassie a great fiery wave of loyalty and resentment against himself swept his thinking into a welter of emotion. Cassie was dead ... *murdered.* He had read of murders, but he always thought of them as something that occurred far away and in the wake of incomprehensible and alien violences. But here ... now. *Cassie!* He realized again that all of Kings Row would gather about its supper tables and that the Tower murder and suicide would be the one topic of talk. They would talk and talk and talk—about Cassie. They would speculate and—perhaps, suggest things—what things? What could anyone suggest, or think of? He found himself back again on the hateful round of questions. Why ... why ... why?

He resented, this talk which was going on at this very minute. Cassie had lived in a mysterious loneliness. She did not seem to dislike it, or even to be aware of it. Maybe she preferred it, as her father evidently did. Now, everybody was talking—about her. She would hate that. He hated it for her. He hated the whole town—nearly. He thought of Father Donovan. But he was also sure he wouldn't want to talk to Father Donovan about this. He shrank from the thought of any discussion with anyone. Almost it seemed that this was his— his—he couldn't find the word at once. His affair, maybe, or his own sorrow, and nobody else's. He would like to go away—far away so he could think about it all alone. He *would* be going soon. There was no reason for delay now. He would go—quickly. A little stab of contrition reminded him of Drake. And yet, he wasn't at all necessary to Drake. Drake was so magnificently self-sufficient. If Drake didn't have what he wanted in the world, he went out and got it.

He started nervously when Drake touched him on the shoulder.

"Listen, kid."

"I'm listening. What?"

"I'm going downtown for a few minutes."

"What for?"

"See what I can find out."

"All right."

"I told Esther to stay around and answer the telephone. She'll just say we're not here. Don't answer."

"I won't."

"We'll have some late supper. Guess you don't want anything more right now, do you?"

"No. I'm dizzy."

"It's the brandy. Why don't you go to sleep?"

"I'd rather sit here."

"Well, maybe you'll doze a little."

"I'll try."

"See you pretty shortly. Take it easy, kid."

He'd have to go to the funeral. That would probably be tomorrow. Everybody would be looking at him. He hoped he wouldn't cry. Yes ... he'd have to go. He wished he didn't—no, he didn't wish that. He did wish to go. He must go with Cassie—somehow help her through all that.

His head was swimming violently now. He supposed he must be a little drunk.

Thinking about this was like trying to fight a way through a brier patch. He couldn't get through to anything. A thousand inconsistencies held him. Recollections snagged and caught—and hurt. He went back—backward and forward through these years he had known Dr. Tower and Cassie. He tried to recall that Dr. Tower had even once appeared to be sinister, or threatening. He could not place a single look or word that suggested any clue. True, he was strange. Strange in small ways. Sudden reticences used to mask his talk. Then he would change the subject abruptly and go on about something else, or sometimes he would be silent for several minutes after such interruptions, as if he had forgotten that he was not alone. Dr. Tower was often bitter, of course, and caustic, but not more so than Colonel Skeffington. Different, maybe, but that was just where the mystery seemed to lie. Different in what way? Dr. Tower was awfully proud of his mind. That was clear. But he had a right to be.

Parris could not remember that Dr. Tower had ever spoken of either Mrs. Tower or Cassie unless he himself mentioned them first. Then Dr. Tower always spoke quickly of something else. None of the small personal concern of the individual ever came into his conversation. It was just as though he lived somewhere else than actually here in Kings Row, eating and sleeping. Parris frowned. Eating and sleeping! Wasn't it curious that he just couldn't think of Dr. Tower going through any of the ordinary acts of living?

... And Cassie. She had always been equally reticent about small things. She would talk about books, and characters in books, but never about people. Of course, she didn't really know anyone. She hadn't been like anyone else he had ever known any more than her father had been. That night when he had gone to her father's study for his notebooks: she had acted simply as if all that followed had been planned, or to be taken for granted. Parris could not permit himself to judge Cassie in any way. Just now as he thought of her it seemed that he must not consider any act of hers as other than right. It was right for her. That's the way she was.

He remembered her comment on Poppy Ross, as she held her shoulders in a long shrug: "We're not like that!"

No: she hadn't been like that. She hadn't been like anyone but herself. Whatever she did seemed natural. It was right—there where she lived in that house which seemed to have no relation to the world about it. The almost casual way she slipped out of her clothes that night ... the frankness and curious absorbed quality of her passion ... her odd concern and care for him as though he were the only consideration. A kind of fury gathered in the foreground of his mind. He felt that he must—*must* have answers to some of the questions that flew at him from every side. If only he had asked! Now it seemed utterly unnatural that he had not asked questions. He felt that he had behaved like a child—a stupid, acquiescent ninny.

Cassie had always seemed older, much older than he felt. Now, with the incredible fact of her death, she appeared in his retroactive imagination more knowing and more mysterious than she had ever been.

Death—sudden and violent death. He rubbed his eyes as though he were driving away the fragments of a bad dream. Death—for old people, or for people he didn't know very well—seemed rather natural. But for death to snatch away someone close—Cassie—it was as though some fearful distinction translated her into a still more extraordinary state of being than had been hers before. That he had been so close to her, that he had held her and loved her and lain side by side with her in the dark, had a kind of terror in it. Whatever was to be her death, he thought shudderingly, had been already in existence. Whatever terrible necessity compelled the tragedy had even then walked close upon her. Dr. Tower must already have been thinking of it. Parris backed away from this image. He couldn't quite make himself realize or even believe that this was an act of normal volition. He could scarcely say to himself that Dr. Tower had done it at all. It was as if something outside of them—something in the house—in the shadows; something hiding in a corner; or something riding on the hot hours of that whole dreadful week that struck horribly and insanely. Nothing about this could be viewed reasonably. Parris shrank, as he always did, from anything suggestive of unreasoning violence. The feeling of something other than the normal mechanisms of living made him shiver. It had gotten quite dark. He arose. The floor tilted a little, but he lighted a lamp, and called Esther.

"Yassuh, Mistah Parris. You ready fuh some suppah?"

"Not yet. But I guess I'd like some coffee."

"Yas*suh*."

Drake came in with a false air of ease. He flung his hat on the couch and flopped in a low wicker chair.

"Gee, it's hot."

"What did you find out?"

"Nothing."

"Nothing?"

"Well, pretty near nothing. Funeral's tomorrow—at four. Colonel Skeffington said he'd come by in his surrey and take us."

"Why is he doing that?"

"Well, one thing, he's your lawyer. Another thing he's a friend of your family—was, when you had a family."

"I still don't see—"

"Oh, dummy, you don't see lots of things. He just kind of wants to go along—you know, so everybody sees that you've got friends, I guess."

"Drake!"

"Yep."

"Will you tell me the truth about something, if I ask you?"

"Yep."

"Are people in town saying anything about me—in connection with—this?"

"No, Parris, they're not. Naturally, they mention your name because you studied with Dr. Tower. You and Dr. Gordon were about the only ones who ever talked to Dr. Tower at all."

"I see."

"Then, of course, the paper today said something about Dr, Tower leaving you his money."

"It did?"

"Yep. Headline."

"Oh gee!"

"You can kind of see, can't you, that Colonel Skeffington is a little anxious. He wants to be sure that nobody says anything about you, or asks any questions. He's just on guard against—contingencies."

"You've been talking to him."

"How do you know?"

"You didn't think of that word by yourself!"

Drake grinned. "Of course I've been talking to him. I told you I had."

"You'll go with me, tomorrow?"

"Of course. I'll be right with you. Say, you know they've been telephoning all day trying to find out if Dr. Tower had any kinfolks."

"They didn't find anybody?"

"The bank—I believe it was in Philadelphia—said there wasn't any. Dr. Tower came from some place in Maryland first."

"It's awful strange, isn't it?"

"Well, it's strange for so many people with no kinfolks to get all mixed up. I haven't got any relatives, much—nobody close—and you haven't either."

Esther came in with a tray.

"What's that, Esther?"

"Coffee for Mistah Parris."

"Coffee? Say, let's have some supper. I'm hungry."

Parris and Drake returned from the double funeral late the next afternoon. It had been more of an ordeal than either of them had anticipated. There was a curious crowd that packed the dim, shabby house. Everyone watched Parris. He had gone a little faint when they seated him near the coffins. A sheaf of flowers hid Cassie's face from him, but he could see her hands. He had been unable to look away. He felt that never again would he be able to forget the terrible, unnatural immobility of those wax-white interlaced fingers.

He did not listen to the minister's talk. The regular clergymen in Kings Row had declined to conduct the services. An awkward, gawky country preacher read long chapters, and talked in a wandering, hardly coherent fashion, evading any reference to the lives or deaths of Dr. Tower and Cassandra.

Parris did not listen, but he caught the end of a sentence. "Those who wish to view the remains may now come forward."

He saw to his horror that everyone was looking at him, and he realized that he was expected to go first. The undertaker signaled to him. He got stiffly to his feet, wondering if he could force himself to walk the four steps to the open coffin.

He clutched the side of the nearest coffin to steady himself, and leaned forward a little. He drew back suddenly. Ever since yesterday he had forgotten to think even of Dr. Tower's body as being any longer present. It was terribly startling to find himself looking into the familiar face, now, all at once so withdrawn and remote. For the first time he saw what he had read about so many times—the oddly enigmatic and slightly mocking smile that rests on the lips of the dead. Dr. Tower seemed to be celebrating some mysterious triumph.

Parris moved immediately to the other coffin. Again he had to steady himself as he looked at Cassie. She lay like a snowdrift under the glass—a faint gleam showed between her not quite closed lids. But there was no smile on her lips. She looked instead like an exhausted child. Only her brilliant, curly hair seemed to sparkle and to fill the narrow coffin space with unquenchable life.

All horror went out of him now. He wished he might touch her, but the glass was closed. A cluster of pale rosebuds lay under her hands. They were slightly withered. Parris thought they looked unreal, as if they too had suffered the violence of change. Together with the frozen beauty of the dead girl they seemed the sharers of a secret.

The undertaker touched him on the arm. He had almost forgotten where he was. He nodded as the man gave him a little push. He heard a quick murmur run through the room, and Drake took tight hold on his arm as he sat down.

"Take it easy, kid—take it easy."

The ceremonies seemed interminable, and the long hot drive that followed was almost worse. There was a garish reality about the whole proceeding. The harsh, unmasked graves, the morbid onlookers. It was like a public execution. No one cared. They were merely following a spectacle. One powerful emotion surged to the front in Parris' breast and drove out all trace of the horror that had pressed him for two days. He felt an overpowering pity for the two who were so exposed to the common interest of utterly vulgar minds. Whatever the mystery might be that lay back of this dark and terrible happening, he felt that Dr. Tower and Cassie belonged to him, and to him alone. For Dr. Tower there was a loyalty—the devotion of a disciple for a brilliant and able master. He owed this man a gratitude that he could not even communicate. But he felt that it would always be there. And Cassie—whatever it was that made up his attachment to her—love, excitement, allure, ecstasy—they were subdued now to a new feeling. It was not easy to define, this feeling, but he knew that whatever it was, it made her inviolably his, his unique possession, and that her secrets, whatever *they* might be, were somehow safe from any possible invasion because of that possession.

Thus, gently and imperceptibly, the first impalpable strands of pity began to fall across his mind and heart—the kind of pity that is a stronger and a far more lasting tyranny than love itself.

In that gradual recrudescence of an emotion which he had not had occasion to experience in a long time, someone else came into the forefront of his consciousness: *Renée*.

It had been a long time since he had thought much about Renée. The picture of her in his mind had worn thin. He thought of her, yes; but he had not been haunted as he once was with the feeling that she was walking with him as she used to, a few steps behind, and just out of sight.

Renée! It seemed to him now that he could really see her again. She assumed three-dimensional depth and substance. She came, gravely, into the strange company of Cassie Tower. She seemed to stand as gravely, as patiently as Cassie herself, and to be waiting.

Lucy, his grandmother, Robert Callicott, Dr. Tower, Cassie, and Renée—no: Renée did not belong there. He had forgotten for the moment that she was alive—somewhere. But there was attached to her as little seeming of life as to the others.

An awful lot of them, he thought, for me.

He realized then that he was dramatizing. Lucy had not been important to him. She hadn't really been a friend. Nor Robert Callicott. Still, he persisted to himself, even three—to lose three people who were a real part of your life, all in one week. He shook his head, recognizing some old symptoms of self-pity.

There was Drake, and Drake wouldn't think as he was thinking. He thrust the mood aside.

Parris waked from a deep, dreamless sleep. He lay very still The place looked strange. He hadn't gotten used to it yet. But, of course—

He was waiting for something, he wasn't quite sure what it was. Then it came, that numbing shock that came every day with full awakening. He struggled for an instant, trying to reach back, trying to throw himself back into the kind absence of realization. He edged lower in the bed as if he might avoid the violence of the blow that hung waiting to fall.

Drake called from the next room. "Say, you awake?"

"Yes."

"Colonel Skeffington wants to know if you can come down to the bank this morning. Ten o'clock."

"Yes. Tell him I'll be there."

Drake relayed the message and came into the room. An immediate release of tension always came with Drake's presence. He was more than reassuring. Some of the aggressive horror of the past days quite simply ceased to exist.

"Gee, Drake."

"What?"

"I don't know what I'm going to do without you."

"Aw, shut up. You'll find somebody—lots of friends. I bet you forget all about me."

"I couldn't."

"Well. I hate to see you go, kid; but I know you got to."

Colonel Skeffington and Patterson Lawes were waiting in the same dingy room when he reached the bank.

"Excuse me. Am I late?"

"No, no, son. It's not quite ten yet. Lawes and I were just sitting here chinning. Sit down, son."

Parris sat down and waited. Lawes fidgeted with his papers. "Well, my boy, you're getting to be a regular inheritor around here."

Skeffington looked down his long sharp nose. Parris hardly heard the inept remark. He looked from Lawes to Skeffington and back again, and waited.

Skeffington spoke first. "This is a sad sort of business, Parris, and a strange one. We've been sending despatches back and forth a good deal. All we can get out of the bank at Philadelphia is what you already know. Dr. Tower's estate is yours. It's perfectly legal, but some kind of unforeseen complications might come up. There might be kin—maybe some of Mrs. Tower's folks. We'll have to have power to act for you if anything comes up until you're twenty-one. Just now, there's nothing but to tell you about it, I guess."

Parris waited. Mr. Lawes rustled papers in his despatch case.

"It seems the house up there on Walnut Street is all clear of encumbrances. The estate—what's in the bank in Philadelphia—isn't as large as one might have supposed. It's been running lower and lower, they report. Dr. Tower left bonds and a few stocks that'll pay between five and six hundred a year. Not much. I guess he was using capital to live on—"

Mr. Lawes interrupted. "D'you reckon that had anything to do with his suicide?"

Skeffington looked doubtful. "He wasn't at the end of his rope, by any means. You can live on fifty dollars a month in Kings Row."

"Yes, that's so. A heap of people live on less."

"He had no rent to pay. Little personal expense of any kind. No: we'll have to look farther if we're going to find out why he—why he murdered his own daughter and shot himself. If we ever find out. I doubt very much if we do find out."

Mr. Lawes looked narrowly at Parris. "Did you have any inkling—any kind of a hint that you might ever be the doctor's heir?"

"Why, no. Of course not."

"Don't be such a fool, Lawes." Skeffington looked unusually short-tempered this morning. "This is just a kind of formality, Parris. This bequest simply comes into your estate, and since we're already in charge of that, this automatically falls under the same jurisdiction."

"Yes, sir."

"Now, I've been thinking all this over. That place is no good to you up there. Needs a lot of repairs. It would cost considerable to fix it up. Best we could do would be to hold it for you as a house—"

Parris shivered slightly. Skeffington looked at him shrewdly. "Wouldn't want that, eh, son?"

"No, sir."

"Can't say I blame you. Or, we could rent it, and that's poor business. The thing to do is offer it for sale and swing on to it till we get a good offer. What do you think?"

"That seems all right, sir."

"Now, here's a question. Is there anything up there you want yourself?"

Parris blinked. He still hadn't realized that Dr. Tower's house and possessions were now his.

"I—I don't—"

"We've been all over the place in process of investigation. The furniture's not worth much. We can sell it easy enough. Then there are certain small personal properties—some jewelry, and young Miss Tower's clothes."

A kind of amazement kept Parris confused. Cassie had always been so unknown to him in small, commonplace, familiar ways that he couldn't easily make himself think of her room, her jewelry, her clothes. That he should have to consider and decide what to do with them—

He came back to the moment. "Could—could we pack up Cassie's things and—keep them somewhere? It doesn't seem just right to sell them, or anything, or give them away."

Skeffington regarded Parris closely. "That could be done," he said in a noncommittal tone. "Now, what about the library? There's a ton of books there—mostly professional. Wouldn't they be of some use to you?"

"I'd like to keep them, sir. Could I do that?"

"Certainly. Seems a good idea. Might save you some money later on—standard stuff, I suppose, a lot of it."

"Yes, sir."

"All right. We'll see to it, eh, Lawes?"

"Oh, yes. Certainly."

"All right. That's all there is to it. All of this does make one important difference to you, my boy. When we sell that place and add the money to the Tower investments, you'll have a neat little figure there. You won't be rich, but you couldn't starve while you're waiting for a practice to come along."

Parris nodded and looked at Mr. Lawes, who, oddly enough, took the hint. "I'll leave you two. You might want to talk over some details."

Skeffington nodded. "Thanks, Patterson."

Mr. Lawes made a noisy and confused exit.

"Now, young man. I want to talk to you a little. Anything you want to say to me?"

"Well—only that I feel very strange about this money and everything coming to me. I can't feel that I've got any right to it at all."

"It is strange. We may hear from someone later on. We've had death notices put in some Eastern papers. But, legally, you're the heir. That's all there is to that."

"I see."

"Listen, son, have you any idea in God's world about all of this, or why it happened?"

"No, sir. I haven't."

"You were in and out there all the time?"

"Two or three times a week—to Dr. Tower's study."

"Never saw anything queer about the house?"

"I never was in the part of the house where they lived until the day of the funeral—not since I went to a birthday party there years ago."

"You don't say so!"

"Yes, sir. Dr. Tower always had me come in the side door to his study. He even asked me to go the back way out by Cherry Street."

"Why?"

"Well, I don't know. Sometimes Mrs. Tower or Cassie would be on the front porch. Maybe he didn't want me to speak to them."

"What about the girl?"

"Sir?"

"Cassandra, what about her?"

"I don't know what you mean."

"How did Dr. Tower seem—seem to be around her?"

"I don't know. She never came into the study, and he never let me see her."

Skeffington whistled. "Then you didn't know her at all?"

Parris waited a moment, then looked straight at Colonel Skeffington. "Yes, sir, I did."

"Oh, ho! Did Dr. Tower know that?"

"No, sir. I didn't see her very often—couldn't."

"I see. I see. Well, well. What did she say about her father, and everything? Her way of having to live in seclusion, for instance?"

"Nothing."

"Nothing?"

"She never mentioned her father. Once she said he was more interested in me than she had ever seen him be in anyone."

"Nothing else?"

"No, sir."

Skeffington pulled spasmodically at his beard. He took off his glasses and thrust them into a battered leather case.

"Were you engaged to Cassandra Tower?" he asked casually.

"No, sir."

"Ever talk about it?"

"I asked her if she'd marry me when I came back from Europe."

"What did she say to that?"

"She said no."

"Why, what in thunder? She did?"

"Yes, sir."

"Well, I'll be—Then her father—no help there, is there, on the whole mystery?"

"No, sir. I thought it all over."

"I've been through all the papers up there. Nothing to help clear it up at all. He had only some professional correspondence with publishers and authors of books, mostly European. He must always have destroyed papers and letters as they came."

"That reminds me, Colonel Skeffington. Dr. Tower was to have some letters from Vienna about my entrances over there. Did you see them?"

"Yes, I did. Meant to bring them along. Forgot them. There are some notebooks of yours, too."

"Yes, I ought to have them. I'll have to have the letters."

"I'll get the keys for you. They're here. You can go by and get them. They're in the upper right-hand desk drawer."

"Couldn't I get someone to get them for me?"

"Oh! Don't fancy going in there, do you? That's natural. Spooky as hell. I've got my horse and buggy out there. I'll drive up with you."

"'You're sure I'm not putting you to too much trouble?"

"Not at all. Not at all. Got nothing important to do this morning. Mrs. Skeffington wants some sweet potatoes for dinner. I'd have to get out and dig 'em if I went home."

The letters from Vienna were in order. There would be some examinations to take, but Dr. Tower had been reassuring about them. Parris placed the letters carefully in his new large billfold. He was about to pack the composition books away when he noticed one, thicker than the others, which looked unfamiliar. He opened it, leafed hurriedly through, read a little, and turned back to the beginning. It was closely written in Dr. Tower's small, difficult handwriting. It didn't appear to be a diary, though the entries were dated, but rather a record—disjointed notes—of thinking along some more or less obscure lines.

Parris stared at it for a moment. He wondered if he had a right to read it. It was clearly a sort of confidential record. He decided that Dr. Tower had either forgotten the book in the onslaught of a sudden and violent impulse, or had been indifferent. Certainly, Parris thought, he, more than anyone else, had some right to know what led up to the tragic outcome of that mysterious night.

He turned the lamp up a little. Drake had gone to bed. Then he began to read.

The short, abruptly worded notes were difficult to understand. At first they seemed to make no sense whatever. Gradually Parris perceived some slight connections, a scarcely perceptible thread that led from one cryptic paragraph to the next. None of the entries referred directly to actual, or concrete happenings, but rather to the way Dr. Tower felt about himself. Occasionally a note pointed to some person, or period, but the effect was one of indirection, a slanting glimpse into a mood—hardly more than an overtone.

Little by little it became less vague. Dr. Tower's familiar elliptical style of utterance was there and the quick, fleeting touches upon widely scattered, but subtly related stations of a subject. Parris was sufficiently familiar with Dr. Tower's manner of expressing himself to read more on the page than was actually written there. But the effect of the whole was a little dizzying. He leaned closely over the book to follow the tortuous script. Once or twice he put the book down partly to rest his eyes, but also to reassure himself of the actuality of the room and his surroundings. Sometimes the sentences rushed along in a kind of steaming fury; sometimes they dripped slowly, precisely, coldly, like clear drops from an icicle.

Again and again Parris found himself obliged to turn back and reread many pages—to puzzle, and wonder, and guess. But it was beginning to make sense. The very psychological study Dr. Tower had made him do, and the severe discipline he had had in following the confused and confusing processes of unsound minds as revealed in their various expressions, made some understanding of these pages possible. For Parris had no doubt that what he was reading sprang from a mind that had long since gone upon dangerous ways. That Dr. Tower's mind had been driven willfully upon such journeys was also apparent.

Parris rubbed his eyes, turned back to the beginning of the book and began again. Here were notes dating back to the days when Dr. Tower first came to Kings Row. Even here an arrogant and intrepid intelligence flared through the pages. Dr. Tower had evidently experienced some sort of setback at the beginning of his stay that hurt his pride and began immediately to turn him in on himself. The words flamed at times with disdainful reference to the "half-simian inhabitants of Kings Row."

Parris wondered why Dr. Tower had remained in Kings Row, but it might well have been a corollary of the same pride that so despised the people about him. He would not be driven out.

One concrete injury appeared. Dr. Tower had at one time hoped for a post at the state asylum. Someone or something had prevented it. From then on the record was that of a man who fed on the bitterness of his own solitude, and who consoled himself with assurances of his own superiority—a sense of intellectual supremacy that seemed to devour the very mind that bred it.

And then the notes broke somewhat. There were passages which seemed to be pure rhapsody—a kind of Dionysiac poetry that quivered precariously on the verge of jargon. Here the writer was much concerned with what he repeatedly called "supersensation," the "beyond-ecstasies of superior organisms tuned to stimuli outside the common receptiveness of ordinary individuals."

Parris grew heavier of heart as he read. This was another man than the one who sat and taught him clearly and methodically. This was the same brain, but functioning in an altogether different manner.

There were a few pages of fragmentary observations which quite eluded Parris. They were made up of unfamiliar references, and with several passages in Greek. Almost immediately following these a new quality came into the writing. It seemed more ordered, more definite, and some of the unmistakable phrases filled Parris with a new horror. There was another change a little later—the tone was colder—and clearly insane.

Parris read rapidly now, it was like following the helpless gyrations of someone disappearing down a narrowing and darkening vortex of roaring waters. He closed the book. His face was wet, and his hands were clammy. He was a little sick.

He sat for some time before Drake came to the door. "Say, kid, what are you doing? Do you know what time it is? Why don't you come to bed?"

"What time is it, Drake?"

"My gosh, it's nearly morning. It's pretty near four o'clock. What's the matter with you, anyway?"

"Come in here, Drake, and sit down. I guess I've got to tell you something. I've got to tell somebody."

"For Jesus' sake, what's up now?"

"I've just read—well, it's a kind of diary of Dr. Tower's."

"Where'd you get it?"

"It was here with the digest books I left there for Dr. Tower to look over. It looked just like mine and got put in the same package when they were looking over papers and things. I—I've just read it."

"Well, what does it say?"

"Drake, you've got to promise me that this will be a secret between us."

"All right, all right, you know me. Go ahead."

"I think I know now—I *know* why Dr. Tower killed Cassie—and himself."

"Sure enough? God a-mighty, why?"

"Well, I have to tell you first that it looks like he'd been going kind of crazy for a long time—"

"I should think so!"

"Well, not the usual kind of crazy. He was so proud of his intelligence that he began to think he was better than anybody else, and beyond any kind of law that—you know—that keeps us all kind of in place."

"Just crazy—plain crazy, if that's so, Parris."

"No, not just *plain* crazy. Then he—I guess wanted to experiment with his own mind—how it would act, and how he would feel under extraordinary circumstances."

"What kind of circumstances?"

"Drake, do you know what incest is?"

"Incest?"

"Yes."

"Gee—do you mean like in the Bible—in the Old Testament?"

Parris managed a wan smile. "I didn't know you ever read the Old Testament!"

"Of course I did, one time. Aunt Mamie made me. You mean father and daughter. Was Dr. Tower—?"

Parris nodded. "Incest was at the bottom of this last phase of the whole business."

"Good God a-mighty. I've heard of things like that happening way off in the country among poor white trash."

"Well, it runs through all history. In this case it was a poison that destroyed Dr. Tower's mind first, and him along with it."

"And Cassie—"

"I believe she was kind of hypnotized or something. The darndest, strangest look used to come into her eyes whenever I mentioned her father— not scared, exactly, but as though she all at once had the breath knocked out of her."

"Well, ain't this the damnedest thing you ever heard of?"

"It's common enough, Drake, but not usually so terribly destructive."

"Say, you talk like a doctor already!"

"I've read a lot about all sorts of sex peculiarities."

"Do you think Cassie was—Jesus, I don't know how to say it!—do you think she was in love with her own old man?"

"N-no, I don't. She was under some kind of powerful influence—compulsion, I guess you'd say, though. I guess she couldn't quite help herself."

"I bet that's why she always shied off saying whether she'd marry you or not!"

"Maybe. Drake—that last night I was with her on Aberdeen campus she wanted to tell me something—said she had something to tell me, and I was so full of my own trouble about my grandmother that I didn't try to make her tell me."

"She must have wanted to tell you a lot of times."

"I don't know."

"I think she did. 'Cause, I'm not a fool all the time, and I know Cassie Tower was head over heels in love with you. She was plumb crazy at times—I could see it. You said once she was a—"

"I know I did—a nymphomaniac. Well, she wasn't. I ought to have known better. That was too strong a word."

"Well, she was in love with you."

"Maybe."

"Did her old man find out about you, and kill her for that?"

"No. I don't think he knew anything about me at all. The last part of this book hardly makes sense."

"Then what—?"

"I think she must have tried at last to break away, or he must have lost his hold on her, or control over her—"

"And that's why she came running over here the other night!"

"I believe that was it, Drake. And the terrible thing about it is that maybe I could have saved her life if I'd have just said all right."

"But, kid, you couldn't know all you know now."

"No, of course. And Drake—there's something else."

"What?"

"It's just hinted, but I think—I think Dr. Tower killed Mrs. Tower to get her out of the way."

"God, Parris, that's awful—then he had Cassie all alone."

"Yes."

"My God—it's a good thing he's dead, I say."

"Drake, remember now, it won't do any good for anybody to know this. I just had to talk to somebody." He clapped his hand to his forehead. "Gee, I was a fool. Drake, you remember that night I came in here 'way along in the morning."

"Of course."

"That was the first time, but—but it wasn't Cassie's first experience. I thought about it at the time—and wondered, because I couldn't think of anybody Cassie had ever known at all. Then I guess I just sort of put it out of my mind, but I never did quite forget."

Drake said nothing to this, and Parris fluttered the pages of Dr. Tower's notebook again.

"That means, Drake, that all of this began 'way back there when Cassie was a little girl."

"Jesus!"

"Listen, let's burn this damned book up, and nobody will ever know but us."

"Come on. We can burn it in the kitchen stove."

Parris stopped at the door and pressed his forehead against the frame. "It makes me sick."

"Me, too. Come on, let's get rid of it."

"Drake, I'm going now as quick as I can."

"Where?"

"I mean to Europe. I—I've had just about as much as I can stand, I think."

"All right, kid. You go whenever you want to. There's nothing holding you now."

"Except you."

"Aw—shucks!"

"I—I'll go around tomorrow and see a few people and say good-by. Tom Carr and Mrs. Skeffington. And I guess I've got to see Jamie Wakefield, too, and Professor Berdorff."

"I'll go with you. We'll get it over with tomorrow." Drake's shoulders drooped a little, but Parris did not notice.

It was almost a week before Parris was ready to go. It took time to arrange steamship passage. During that week Parris lived in a curious limbo of suspension. He felt that he no longer belonged in Kings Row. He almost felt sometimes as if he were not actually there at all. The new life to which he was going was wholly unknown. He could only guess what Vienna might be like. Colonel Skeffington thought he should go at once to begin his work and delay any side trips or sightseeing expeditions until the following year.

Parris could not bear to go back home again, but Anna came to see him. She had gone to the Burton County Bank that morning and asked for Mr. Long.

"Yes, Miss Hauser. What can I do for you today?"

She opened her big leather pocketbook.

"This check, Mr. Long, that the bank sends to me from Mr. Parris."

Mr. Long looked at it. "Yes, I know about it. Just endorse it and we'll put it to your account."

"But I don't want it."

"Eh? Don't want it?"

"No, sir. I have enough money. I want you should put it back with Mr. Parris' money. He'll need it."

Mr. Long smiled. "Just a minute, Miss Hauser." He went to his desk and returned with a slip of paper. "Young Mitchell left this at the bank yesterday."

"What is it? What does it say?"

"Read it."

Anna held the paper off and tilted it to the light. It was just a line in Parris' handwriting.

If Anna Hauser tries to give me back the check for five hundred dollars I gave her, don't take it. Make her *keep* it.

Anna returned the note. She did not respond to Mr. Long's smile.

"But I can do with my money what I want, can't I?"

"Certainly, Miss Hauser."

"Then I put this in Mr. Parris Mitchell's account."

Saying good-by to Anna was pretty hard. She cried so much Parris' own throat ached.

"Where are you going, Anna?"

"I go first to my cousin in St. Louis, and then maybe I go back to Germany."

"To Germany! If you do I can come to see you!"

"Will you, Parris? Maybe by that time you won't want to."

"Anna!"

"Yes, my *Liebchen,* everything changes in time, everything."

"I'll never forget how heavenly good you have been to me."

Anna cried a good deal more, but eventually she got herself away.

Parris and Drake stood on the little station platform. They were stiff and awkward.

"Well, she'll be here now, any minute."

"Yes."

They stood, and waited, and exchanged commonplace remarks. Both of them wished these last minutes were over.

Parris was taking the late afternoon train which connected at Camperville with the main line for St. Louis. There were only a few passengers waiting, and the usual traintime loafers who stood idly about and gazed curiously at anyone who might be starting on a journey.

Drake walked uneasily up and down. Parris waited in that indescribable state of half consciousness that falls upon people waiting for the moment of departure. He could not make himself believe that he was really leaving, that tomorrow he would not be here, nor the next day, nor the next—not for years. Everything would be changed then—everyone he knew would be older. *He* would be older. Everything that he could call a part of his life was passing away—now, in the sluggish moment of these last minutes. It seemed to him that, surely, when the train had passed and these other people had gone away, he would still be here. He would go home and his grandmother would be there, and tomorrow he would have his usual lessons with Dr. Tower, and maybe he would see Cassie.

A girl came through the station door and stood looking about. She was very pretty in a husky, forthright fashion. Her reddish hair was wound about her head in two heavy braids, and her gray-blue eyes looked out with an easy assurance from under her thick curly lashes. She saw Drake and smiled to herself. Her small even teeth gave her smile an impish quality.

"'Lo, Drake McHugh!"

Drake turned. "Well, hello, Randy Monaghan."

"You going away?"

Parris came over to the two. "Hello, Randy. I haven't seen you in an awfully long time." He held out his hand and she took it with a faint lock of surprise.

"It's been a long time, hasn't it?" Her voice had lost its rough boyish huskiness, and had changed to a throaty contralto.

"Parris is going to Europe."

She opened her eyes very wide. "Sure enough? Going to stay long?"

"Four years—maybe five."

"Goodness, that's almost forever."

"Seems so to me just now."

"I heard your grandmother died."

"Yes."

"I'm sorry."

"Thank you."

Drake was looking very steadily at Randy. A slow warmth of color rose under her deep tan. Drake took her by the arm. "Gee, Randy, I bet you're the prettiest girl in the world!"

She laughed—a not very good attempt at her old rough and ready manner. Her color deepened.

"Here she comes!"

There was a bustle and a quite unnecessary hurry about the place as the train of two coaches clanked to a standstill. The passengers climbed the steep little steps, the few trunks were thumped into the baggage compartment of the forward coach, and the wheezy conductor called, "All aboard."

Parris stood on the rear platform and looked back through the thick smudge of acrid train smoke as the station slowly receded. He felt a blinding terror at this moment.

Drake stood with his arm linked through Randy's. They waved until the train disappeared around a sharp curve.

Drake gave a deep sigh.

"Gee!"

"What's the matter?"

"I hate to see that boy going away. He's the best friend I got."

"He's a nice boy, isn't he?"

"The very best. Well—there he goes. Four years! Gosh!" He turned, and his stiffened features achieved something of his old faunlike grin. "Say— my buggy's down here. How about coming for a ride out in the country somewhere?"

Randy looked into his overbright eyes.

"All right," she said, "let's."

Book Four

1

"May I come in, Colonel Skeffington?"

The Colonel looked up from his paper. Tom Carr was standing in the door. His immense shock of white hair and great beard seemed almost to fill the doorway.

"Why, hello, Tom! Come right in. Come right in."

"I just want to speak with you a minute, Colonel."

"Have a seat. Pull up that other chair. Sit down."

"Thank you, Colonel."

"What's up with you today, Tom?"

"Nothing special, sir. I'm going away."

"Is that so? Well, now."

"Yes, sir. There's nothing much for me to do here."

"What about your job at the nursery?"

"Well, they've let everybody go out there. You know the Vandiver Plant and Seed Company bought the place, of course?"

"Oh, yes. Some little time back. Before Christmas, wasn't it?"

"Yes, sir. They're making an experiment station there."

"Well. Seems to me they could have used you."

"No, sir. They thought not. It's going to be scientific. They want college graduates and plant experts. People that know about the chemistry of soils and all that kind of thing."

"I see."

"I've got a pretty good education, Colonel Skeffington, but not that good."

"Not specialized, of course."

"No, sir."

"Well, that's too bad. Madame von Eln would be sorry to know you're leaving the place. She thought a heap of you."

"She was a fine woman. Not many like her."

"No, that's a fact. She had the best qualities of a good woman, and none of the bad ones."

"And it seemed to me that she thought like a man. She did business like a man."

The Colonel smiled. "A rare compliment—from a man."

Tom smiled, too—at least, the Colonel supposed he did. There was an agitation deep in the white forest of his whiskers that appeared to harmonize with the twinkle in his merry eyes.

"Well, Tom. Mighty sorry to see you go. Where are you thinking of going?"

"West."

"Yes, but where?"

"Just out West. I always meant to go on farther out. Just got stuck here. Then Lucy was sick—"

"Yes, I remember."

"So, I just did the best I could. I wasn't lucky, I guess. You know I had enough money when I came in here to get started and do as well as any of them that are old fellows now—like Thurston St. George, for instance—but I just didn't. I think I'll go on out and kind of take a fresh start."

Colonel Skeffington looked keenly at the man before him. "How old are you, Tom?"

"Not as old as you think, Colonel, and I know what you're thinking. You are wondering if I ain't too old to be going on by myself."

"I was thinking that, for a fact, Tom."

Tom Carr busied a huge hand in his beard. "I came here in 1866. I was thirty-three then. I'd been in the war. Everything seemed upset, and it looked like a good time to come out here. They didn't like the Yanks much, though, not in this town. Kind of funny, too, that. I never had anything against the Rebs. Just had to fight, that's all. So I didn't make out so well. You fellows that had been here and the ones that came from Virginia or Tennessee got on better."

"Yes, I guess so."

"Well, you see, I'm just sixty-five. I'm strong and hearty. Haven't got an ailment of any kind. I can do as big a day's work as anybody. I figure I'll find some kind of an opening."

"Things are different, even in the real West, Tom. Pioneer times are over— past and gone."

"I thought I might like Wyoming or maybe Idaho."

"I wish you luck. How are you fixed for the trip?"

"All right, Colonel, all right. I saved some money. I got me a covered wagon—looks like a horse trader's outfit—hitched right out there on the south side of the square—but it's fixed up all right. Got a good little tent, two good horses, and good bedding. I've got the whole summer ahead to travel and kind of look around."

"I guess you've got about the last of the covered wagons, eh, Tom?"

"Maybe, so far as the wagon itself is concerned, but I take it there's always a steady movement west. Always has been. It's natural, somehow Whether it goes on in wagons, or by train, or however. Seems to me you're kind of in line with the will of the Lord when you move west. It's against the grain to go back the other direction."

The Colonel laughed. "Maybe you're right. It's history."

"But that's not what I came here for. I wanted to talk to you about Benny Singer."

"Singer? Oh, yes, that boy Madame took on her place. How'd he make out?"

"All right, Colonel—fine. But he ought to have a job somewhere. I'd like to see him in something before I leave."

"Why don't they keep him out there?"

"They could use him—they need a few handy men around. But they made a complete cleanout. The foreman won't listen to anything."

"That's always the way with a newcomer, isn't it?"

"Yes, sir. Now, Benny's a little weak in the head. Can't remember anything very long; you have to keep telling him. But he's willing, and good-natured. He's got a regular hand with growing things."

"Is that so?"

"Yes, sir."

"Can he handle a horse?"

"Oh, yes. Fine."

"Well, I guess I could use a boy myself. You know I don't like to hoe in my vegetable garden as much as I used to. Getting too old, Tom. Now—"

"He could take care of your place fine, Colonel. Mow the grass, and the like."

"I need a boy to 'tend to my horse, too. I made my back yard into a front yard, and my front yard into a truck garden, so I haven't got any place for a stable. I keep my horse and buggy up at Trent's livery. If this boy could take 'em back and forth, and curry down my horse himself—"

"He'd be just your boy, Colonel. I'd feel a heap easier in my mind if you'd be good enough to take him."

"Tell him to come in to see me."

"I'll do that, and right away. He's waiting in my wagon down there."

"All right, all right. And—the best of luck to you."

"Thank you, sir. By the way, do you know where I can get some of those government maps of the state?"

"Try Duncan's office downstairs. If he hasn't got them—let me see, you going by the capital?"

"Yes, sir. I thought I'd strike out through Hancock County."

"Well, you can get maps at the capitol building. Go in and see Fred Weatherford—state geologist's office—tell him I sent you."

"Thank you, Colonel, and good-by."

"Good-by, Tom. Mighty sorry to see you go. Kings Row can't spare all its good old stock. New lot coming in don't look so good."

"They'll make out, Colonel. They always do."

"Well, you're more optimistic than I am. Look at all the young squirts we're getting in office!"

"Yes, sir, I know. But a lot of old ones in now went in when they were young. Maybe they didn't look so good at the time."

Colonel Skeffington slapped Tom on the back. "Fine way to feel. I hope you're right." He watched Tom down the stairs. He turned back to the window. Tom was shaking hands with Benny Singer, a gangling, towheaded fellow who looked sixteen or so. Must be older than that, however, the Colonel decided.

A small crowd had gathered around Tom's "covered wagon." It was, as Tom had said, indistinguishable from the canvas-covered wagons which were used by that drifting, shiftless class of horse-trading nomads, known in this part of the country as "movers." Tom's horses looked better, though.

There were hearty exchanges, and a good deal of laughter from the men standing around. Everybody knew Tom Carr, and everybody liked him. But no one overly respected him. An old man who owned no property: that was plain evidence of general and thorough failure.

"Fine old fellow. Honest, too. But not much force—no, sir, not much force."

"Well, you take that goodhearted, easygoing kind, and they never do seem to get nowhere much, do they?"

"No. That's a fact."

"You got to be hard in this world."

"And a leetle smarter'n the next one."

"Yeh. Look at Rodney Green. Started as a hand down there in the clay pit. Now he owns it and lives up on Union Street."

"They say his boy's a smart one, too."

"Yeh. Fulmer. He's got a job in the tax collector's office now. Says he's going to run for recorder next fall. Studying law on the side."

"Is he twenty-one?"

"Oh, yeh."

"Bet he gets it, too. Doggone—them young uns that get out and go after it when they're young!"

"He didn't waste no time going to Aberdeen College like most of 'em."

"Hell! That's no good, unless you're going to be a professor or a doctor or something like that."

"You're right."

"It's better for 'em to get out and scratch like their old folks did."

"You bet. Now look at that McHugh boy. Going to have a pile of money when he's twenty-one. He don't do nothing but burn up the roads in that rubber-tired buggy. Out hellin' around ever' night."

"I seen him a dozen times, I bet, 'way out past my place with one or another"—the speaker looked around before he went on—"with one or another of Alec Ross' girls."

"Yeh, I seen him, too. His folks was high-toned, but he sure comes down—"

"Hell. He's no better'n anybody else. I don't take any stock in that kind of talk. Still—I hear Alec's girls are pretty—well, they say all you need is two dollars!"

"I bet you ain't ever had the two dollars!"

A general laugh signaled a touch. Henry Potts, who was doing the talking, never had had two dollars at one time in his life. He laughed good-naturedly in response.

"No, but I'll be dogged if I'd know any better way to spend it."

"Which un would you pick?"

"I like the oldest one. Got more meat on her."

"I like Jinny. Looks like she's got more devil in her."

"I guess Drake McHugh must like 'em both, turn about."

"Well, there you are. Drake McHugh'll run through with his money in no time, then he'll get a job working on the street and be a halfway loafer all the rest of his life like old Frank Greenaway."

"Yeh, Greenaway used to have money, too, didn't he?"

"Sure. He run through with it before he was twenty-five years old."

"That's the way it goes."

"Yep, that's the way it goes."

Tom Carr drove out Federal Street. At this moment he had not a care in the world. With Benny in Colonel Skeffington's employ, he felt that the boy was assured of a certain amount of protection.

What Colonel Skeffington had said about "the last of the covered wagons" pleased him greatly. The phrase aroused a little of the old stir and excitement that he had felt many years ago. He had intended going out West long before the war, but one thing and then another had interfered. He remembered the hullabaloo about California in 1849. He was sixteen then, and his father wouldn't hear of his going out upon so dangerous a venture. Ten years later he had had a great chance—a wealthy neighbor had wanted to send him with a substantial stake, but his mother was seriously ailing at that time. He had been obliged to stay with her. Then came the war. After that was over he married Lucy and with their joint inheritances they had set out riding the crest of a wave of irresponsibility for the "wild and woolly" West. They had not found it wild or woolly. Kings Row had differed but little from his little home town in New York state. And then—somehow he hadn't been lucky. The tragedy of Lucy's mental breakdown had kept him from any kind of enterprise that took him far from her side. After her death he had been able to acquire a little nest egg again. Now, he was free to go on.

At the brow of the hill where Federal Street dipped down across Town Creek and became the road to Camperville, he pulled up his horses and leaned out to one side of his wagon to look back at the town where he had spent the thirty-two-year interruption of his journey west to romance and adventure.

A tenacious winter still contended with an urgent spring. The last of the dingy snow patches which diminished slowly in fence corners and sheltered spots had disappeared. There were sharp little blades of emerald green on the sunny banks to his right, and a blur of mixed red and green on the highest twigs of the trees. The town and the familiar buildings were slightly obscured by the swelling buds thick on every branch. Tom did not really feel regret at leaving Kings Row. He thought of it as a friendly place. He had made a living there. Lucy was buried there. But no matter where he might be he would know it was there. He would be able to see it in his memory. It could never be wholly lost to him. All he needed of it was to remember it. There was no one who would know whether he was there or some other place. Except, perhaps, Benny. Benny—poor Benny—didn't really have enough sense to trouble long. Benny would forget all about him. And Benny was all right now.

He leaned back in the comfortable spring seat, and looked toward the west. Out there—across that distance, and beyond the hill. He could go north or south; he was free. Kansas was out there, and Nebraska, and Wyoming, and, away up that direction, Montana and Idaho. He liked to say the names to himself. They repeated somewhat the legend of all the great adventures he had dreamed of when he was a boy, and hinted at the great saga of America's increasing destiny. It appeared now that people were forgetting the war and were going ahead united.

A great ocean of wind poured eastward—it told of the almost illimitable spaces of the mighty prairies which began at that very rise of land along the horizon. He stood up, leaning forward a little to clear the canvas top. The wind caught at his long hair and beard and whipped it up into a veritable cloud about his head. Once more Colonel Skeffington's phrase came back to mind and touched his imagination. *The last of the covered wagons.* Not a *mover.* Just one man in that endless westward trek that began long ago and would go on, he thought, wave after wave, forever.

He sat down and jerked the reins. "Get up there, boys. We got to get going."

A half mile beyond the Macintosh place he met a trim, shiny buggy spinning into town. He recognized Drake McHugh, and held up his arm. Drake pulled up beside the wagon.

"Why, howdy, Mr. Carr. You're going away, I hear."

"Yes, I am, son."

"Benny Singer told me. Where are you heading for?"

"Somewhere west." The old man glanced at the good-looking girl sitting beside Drake. He didn't know her. Drake saw the look.

"This is Miss Randy Monaghan, Mr. Carr."

Tom inclined his head politely. "Howdy, Miss Randy. I guess I know your pa."

She smiled. It was a frank, easy smile. "I expect you do. Everybody does. He works on the railroad."

"Section boss, ain't he?"

"Yes."

"I know him. I'm very pleased to make your acquaintance. Drake, what do you hear from Parris?"

"Well, sir, Mr. Carr, he doesn't write much. I guess it's been six weeks since I heard from him."

"Getting along all right, is he?"

"Oh, yes."

"He's a smart boy."

"Yep. Parris is all right. He's working hard, he says, and hasn't got any time for anything else."

"Well, when you write to him, give him my best regards. You tell him I sent him my very best."

"I'll do that, Mr. Carr. And good luck to you."

"Thank you. Same to you—both of you."

Drake's restless horse sprang forward at a word. Tom picked up the reins again. "Get up, boys, get on now." The new wagon creaked just a little with its heavy load. It moved slowly up the long slope past the Dickerson place, past the Sansome clay pits, past White Cloud church. The road was straight now all the way to Morgan's store over the county line. Tom figured he'd spend the night there.

"Randy, I want to show you something."

"All right. Show ahead."

Drake looked down good-humoredly into the impudent face that returned a half-affectionate, half-jeering grimace. They reached town and Drake took a short cut across some vacant lots north of the public school. It was really nothing more than pasture land. The buggy bumped and swayed and Randy held on tight.

"What do you think you're doing, Drake? You've jarred my wisdom teeth loose."

"Just want to show you something." He turned sharply and brought his horse to a standstill on the crest of the rise. This was a continuation of the higher ground of Aberdeen campus. Here was the drop to the town creek. Farther along, Jinktown huddled against the steep slope. Farther still, the creek swept in a wide crescent west and the hill followed the curve.

Drake pointed with the buggy whip, and the horse started nervously. "Whoa, there; stand still, fool!"

"Drake, you're always swishing the whip over his head. He doesn't understand when you don't mean it!"

"Kind to animals—and little children, aren't you?"

"But I'm hard on idiots."

"All right. I'll apologize to the horse. But—you see all that—all this long sweep of hillside?"

"Yes, of course. Did you bring me up here in the wind to look at the scenery?"

"In a way, yes. And you see, on top of the hill—like where we are right here, it runs back level."

"Yes."

"All right. This land—all the way around that bend of the creek, as far as Parris' old place—is for sale. Dirt cheap."

"I'm just holding my breath for the big surprise. Have you bought it?"

"No. But I want to."

"What for?"

"Listen, dummy—"

"I could listen better if the wind didn't blow so hard." A sudden gust whipped her skirt over her knees. Drake quickly pinched her bare leg. She slapped his fingers but he held her hand and made an immemorial gesture on the upturned palm.

"Honest, Drake McHugh! Don't you ever think of anything else?"

"Do you know anything better to think of?"

"Go on about your land."

"'Tain't mine yet. I won't get my money till late this summer. But Peyton Graves and I want to do this together."

"I asked you what for."

"And you wouldn't listen while I was talking."

"Take your hands away."

"All right. I'm serious now. Can you imagine what it would be like to have a big house built up here right where we are, with pretty green lawns back of the house running all the way to the street, and terraces and rock steps leading down the hill to the creek?"

"Yes. It would be windy."

"Shut up. It's not windy all the time. Look at the view. And how private it would be. Nice, great big lots, big enough for croquet grounds and tennis courts. I can just see big white houses shining through the trees all the way around this big bend. It's the prettiest land around this town."

"It would be nice," she conceded.

"You bet it would."

"But Drake, wouldn't it cost a lot of money?"

"To buy it?"

"No. I don't mean to buy it in the first place, but to have a place up here—along here, anywhere?"

"Well, they'd be *nice* places."

"Only rich people could build houses like you're talking about and have grounds like that."

"Well, that's all right. We'll sell 'em to rich people."

"But how many rich people are there in Kings Row?"

"Not so many, but enough, I guess."

"And all of 'em have already got houses, on Union Street, of Federal, or even Walnut."

"But people are always building new houses."

"No, they're not."

"Aw, quit throwing cold water on this idea."

"Well, I just think you ought to look into it mighty well before you put all your money in it."

"Peyton Graves thinks just like I do about it, and he's in the real-estate office downtown where he hears talk about real estate all the time."

"I don't care."

"Thunder, Randy! Rich people have children, and they buy places and build new houses."

"Even rich people's children start smaller than—than your idea of a place up here."

"Gee, look how pretty it would be!"

"I'm looking. It's pretty, all right."

"We wouldn't expect to sell all of it right away. We'd hold it."

"What would pay the interest on your loan while you hold it?"

Drake stared.

"I'm supposing," she said, "that you wouldn't pay cash for it, all at once?"

"No." He spoke doubtfully. "No, I guess not. It'd be too much."

"Who does it belong to?"

"Thurston and Macmillan St. George have got a mortgage on it."

"Funny they never thought of developing it. They're right smart about land, and money—those two."

Drake looked sideways at Randy. "Gee, you're smart, aren't you?"

"No. But I hear people talk all the time—mostly kind of poor people, Drake. Once you understand how poor people have to scheme and scrimp and plan to get along you begin to understand something about money. Of course. I'm just a kid—and a girl besides."

"You're doggone smart. That's what I say."

"Well, then, you know what I think would be a good idea?"

"What?"

"You know all that bottom land on the other side of the creek, down below where I live?"

"Ye-es, I guess so."

"It's all grown up in underbrush. There's a lot of big sycamores, and it's kind of cut up in gullies."

"Oh, yes! I know where you mean—southeast of town, down from the asylum?"

"That's the place."

"Well, what about it, Randy? That land's worthless."

"I bet it could be fixed up. Could be cleared and drained. I heard Pa say that—I don't know."

"Well, what in heck could you do with it after you had it, and fixed it up?"

"Drake, there's lots and lots of people who work in Kings Row, people in the tobacco factory, and the stocking mill, and the clay pits and the coal mines, who don't own their own homes."

"Well, gee, kid, they haven't got any money!"

"Not much. But couldn't somebody buy that land down there awful cheap and clean it up and sell little lots pretty cheap? It looks to me like a little profit on a lot of little lots is as good as a bigger profit on just a few big lots."

Drake pursed his lips. He looked a little downcast. Randy saw the look. "Of course, I don't know. You'd have to figure it out. It's just an idea. Just seems to me you could manage a thing like that on less money and not have to make big loans. Poor people like all the foreigners could pay a little at a time. But, like I said, you'd have to figure it out."

"Yes. Of course. It does sound like chicken feed, though—a whole lot of nickels and dimes—"

"Make dollars."

"I'll talk to Peyton about it. Course we can't do anything until I have some cash. Peyton thinks he could borrow some, and—"

"But for all that land down below town—I bet you could buy it for a mighty little bit."

"I wonder who owns it."

Randy grinned. "Thurston St. George."

Drake saw his opening. "Funny he never thought of that himself. He's right smart about—"

"All right, all right. But you think about it. He's less apt to think of a little scheme like that than a big one."

"Maybe you're right."

Drake clucked to the horse. "Let's go, noney." They bumped and swayed back to the street.

"Say, Drake, You mentioned Benny Singer to that Mr. Carr we met. Is that the same boy used to go to school?"

"Yes, of course."

"I haven't seen him for several years. Wasn't he a kind of an idiot, or something?"

"Well, sort of. Parris said it wasn't as bad as that. You know Parris' grandma took Benny to work on her place one time he had some trouble with Fulmer Green."

"I've got a brother that's not quite all right, that way."

"Aw, that's too bad. You mean—"

"He's not an idiot. He's just kind of simple. He's a lot older'n I am. I'm the youngest—guess I was a surprise to Pa and Ma. Ma was pretty old when I came along. Tod—"

"Is that your brother?"

"Yes. Tod. He's got a job on the railroad. Works with Pa. Pa's the section boss."

"Um." Drake was only half listening.

"It's funny how your feelings get wrapped up in somebody like that."

"Yeh. Parris was always talking about Benny. Wanted to find out some way to cure him."

"My brother's awfully good to all of us. He's just got one ambition."

"What's that?"

"He wants to be section boss when Pa quits. The railroad's going to retire Pa someday. He's kind of old now. But I'm afraid Tod won't get it."

"Why not? That ought to be easy."

"No. Tod's simple. He's not smart enough even for that. At least, *they* think so. He just loves the railroad, and he knows every inch of it and what it'll do when the ground thaws in the spring, and when there's heavy rains."

Drake nodded.

"Pa says Tod knows the road better than he does. Why, on Sundays instead of sitting around home and resting, Tod walks down the track—just to look at it."

"That's funny, now."

"I guess when you love something, that's the way you act about it."

"Yeh, I guess so."

Drake swished the tasseled whip above the horse's ears. "Say, honey. Let's ride down and look at that bottom land."

"No, Drake. Not today."

"Why not?"

"'Cause we'd have to pass right by home, and Pa's at home by this time."

"Well, for goodness' sake—"

"Now, Drake—"

"Well, ain't I good enough, even—?"

"Drake! You were just going to say, *even for me!*"

Drake turned bright red. "I wasn't, either."

"Yes, you were."

"No. I was going to say, even for *them*."

Randy smiled a little. "I'll tell you why, Drake."

"Why?" He gave the word a belligerent snap.

"It's not because they think you are not good enough for me, but—" She looked away and set her lips hard.

"But what, Randy?"

She looked back at him. "It's this. They know I'm not good enough for you."

"Well, what in the hell—"

"Now, keep your temper! You belong up on Union Street. Your uncle and your aunt were rich and high-toned. My Pa is a railroad-section boss. We're Irish Catholics, and you know what Kings Row thinks about that."

"I like you—"

"Yes. I think you do. You know I like you, don't you?"

"I guess so."

"You *guess* so?"

"Well—of course!"

"Drake." She settled back in the seat and pressed a little closer to him. "Drake!"

"Yes, honey."

"You never have gone around with girls of your own class."

"Class! Hell! Are you going to talk like that, too?"

"Well, it's so. Class is something that is actually so, I guess."

"I don't know."

"Well, wouldn't you be surprised if I was invited to a party at Mrs. Sansome's?"

Drake flushed again. "Aw—"

"Now. There you are."

"Well."

"Why haven't you ever gone with some of the girls uptown?"

"I was kind of gone on Louise Gordon once, but her old man wouldn't let me come around."

"Why?"

"Thought I was too wild."

"So you came downtown. Anything south of the courthouse!"

"Randy, you know that's not so. You know we met that day Parris went to Europe. I was awful blue and took you riding, and you were so nice, and I just like you."

"Well, thank you, Drake."

"What for?"

"For being that honest. But here's the thing. When a boy from uptown begins to take a girl from the lower end of town out buggy-riding at night, everybody knows it's just for one thing."

"Well, for Jesus' sake, Randy, you talk just like—like—"

"Like who?"

"Well, like Aunt Mamie, or Mrs. Gordon."

A slight shade crossed Randy's open, gamin face. "And I guess they're close to the truth."

"Shoot!"

"No, Drake. We might as well have this out right now. Pa doesn't like me to go with you. I guess Ma wouldn't either if she was still living. But I'm going with you anyhow, whenever you ask me."

"Gee, Randy—"

"Wait now. I know what people are going to say. Maybe they're already saying it."

"I'd like to hear 'em."

"You will, if you wait a little. Drake—you went with both of the Ross kids for a long time!"

Drake reddened slightly. "Well, I never made a secret of it."

"And people thought just one thing."

Drake did not reply.

"People thought just one thing, Drake, and they said it, too."

"Yeh, I guess so."

"Of course they did. I heard it often enough. I know all about Poppy and Jinny."

"Well."

"The point is, Drake, what they said was so. I know that."

"I never denied it, did I?"

"No. I never asked you, either, did I?"

Drake was beginning to go sullen. Randy knew the signs. Presently he would flare.

"Don't you see, Drake, you can't honestly blame people for saying something that's so, can you?"

"I guess not. But nobody will leave me alone."

"You, or anybody else, crazy. Now listen—suppose they say the same thing about me—?"

Drake slashed the horse, and Randy's head jerked with the sudden lunge.

"For goodness' sake, Drake!"

"Well, I'd just like to hear them say it once—to me!"

"But Drake—it's so. How can we expect them not to talk about it?"

"Aw, hell—"

"Just saying 'hell' doesn't clear up anything."

"Well, what's got to be cleared up?"

"Only why Pa doesn't want me to go with you, and why I have to be a little careful. I'm going with you as long as you want me to, but don't get mad when I tell you how things are."

"Well, if I married you—"

Randy shrank away. Instantly her face went blank and cold.

"I wouldn't marry you, Drake."

"Well, why not?"

"Surprised, aren't you?"

"Yes, I am."

"Let's don't talk about it, ever again. I'll go on this way—but no other way, Drake. Will you remember that?"

He did not answer at once. His face, too, was as cold and hard as Randy's.

"Where do you want me to let you out?"

"Right here, Drake."

He hopped out, and helped her over the wheel.

"Good-by, Drake."

He looked hard at her, and a half-smile came to his lips. "'By, honey. When'll I see you?"

"Pretty soon. I got to run now. 'By."

"'By, honey."

Drake took a long way around so that he would not have to pass the Monaghan house. He drove back of the asylum and to a dead-end road that overlooked the bottoms Randy had mentioned.

The thick shrubbery was breaking into leaf, and little dots of brilliant green studded the sycamore branches. He could not tell anything about the area. It was overgrown and apparently crisscrossed with gullies that the heavy summer rains had cut deep.

The wind had fallen now, and a subtle intoxicating warmth came up from the ground. Drake sat for a long time staring dreamily at the scene. His face softened, and a look of boyish gentleness replaced the fighting look Randy's talk had brought out.

He shrugged his shoulders in a gesture he had taken from Parris, and tightened the reins which had fallen slack across the dashboard. He drove as fast as he could back the way he had come. In a few minutes he stopped at the Monaghan house, and hitched his horse to the whitewashed paling fence.

He walked up the short boardwalk to the front door, and knocked.

2

In a few days the west winds slowed, shifted, and warmed, and became a gentle drift from the south. Kings Row responded like an anthill. People came out of their houses and took on new interest in their outdoor world. They spaded and raked and planted in haste to catch up on delayed gardening. Others lingered along the streets and stretched trivial gossip to saga proportions. Old men and women sat in the sun, grateful for the slightest sense of acceleration in their slow blood.

Benny Singer made industrious transformation in the Skeffington vegetable garden. The soil was fine and soft. He stood about in a kind of bewildered waiting while the Colonel and Mrs. Skeffington fought at bitter length over the location of the bean patch, or the best place to sow radishes this year.

Sometimes Mrs. Skeffington—no less peppery than the Colonel—won, and sometimes the Colonel was victorious. Occasionally they referred the question to Benny who nearly burst with importance.

Benny liked making the Skeffington garden. He worked in sight of the street with people passing all day. Neighbors stopped to ask what the Colonel was about this time.

"Going to put his roasting ears over there in that corner? They won't do no good there—too shady." Or, "Tell the Colonel he better drain that lower end down there or he'll kill all his strawberries."

Benny felt that he was a citizen of the town in full and honorable standing.

One day a small boy threw a clod at him, and he playfully threw one back. The boy backed off and looked scared, and presently ran away.

Another day Fulmer Green passed. Fulmer was looking very fine, Benny thought, all dressed up as if it were Sunday.

"Well, if it ain't old crazy Benny!"

Benny grinned, and nodded. He hardly noticed the old nickname.

"Working for Colonel Skeffington, now, eh?"

"Yes. Making his garden."

"Well, well, old Benny working for the Colonel. Good idea, Benny. The Colonel might come in handy keeping you out of jail." Fulmer laughed, and Benny laughed, too. But later in the day when he thought of it, he didn't like Fulmer saying anything about jail. It was Fulmer Green's fault that he got put in jail one time, and it was Colonel Skeffington who got him out. Vaguely he felt a troubling sense of old, old injuries and slights. He had almost forgotten the feeling. Everything had been so pleasant out at the von Eln place. Tom Carr never did anything to make him feel awkward or ashamed. Fulmer, somehow or another, made him feel a little ashamed. He wondered why. Ashamed of what?

Benny knotted his brow and thought hard about that. He concluded that it was just Fulmer's way. He guessed Fulmer didn't mean to make him feel bad. Might be, even, that Fulmer never so much as guessed the effect his words had. Benny worked hard and fast. He tried to forget all about it, but he still felt a kind of spot inside of him where he remembered. He chopped at some old vines and dried weeds with unnecessary violence. It was pretty bad to have Tom Carr go away just now. He didn't have anybody to talk to, or anyone to explain things to him. He guessed he'd just have to think the best he could, and try to figure out all sorts of puzzling things for himself. He liked to have people pass and speak to him and ask questions about the work he was doing, but he hoped Fulmer Green wouldn't come by too often.

Benny shook his head heavily as though he wee trying to clear himself of a cloud of buzzing insects. He wiped his face on his sleeve. Jiminy! He didn't really feel so good today.

3

Every day Drake McHugh drove out of town—sometimes out Federal Street, sometimes out the asylum road, sometimes by a less frequented way—always with Randy Monaghan beside him.

The town talked.

Kings Row had perfectly understood about Poppy and Jinny Ross. The men passed that off lightly. Somebody was always out driving with the Ross girls. The women, deeply scandalized even when they were grateful for delectable subject matter, were disposed to be half lenient about such an escapade. There were any number of women who gossiped about Drake and the way he "carried on" with those Ross girls, who were coolly aware of Drake's desirability as a catch. Drake McHugh, after all, came from "nice people." He belonged to the best. The Ross girls were just nobody at all, and ought not to be mentioned in good company. There were repeated opinions that somebody ought to run them out of town.

It was, as was also often repeated, probably not Drake's fault at all. No doubt they ran after him for what they could get out of him. At present that wasn't anything to worry about because everyone knew exactly how much Drake's allowance was. Mrs. Curley had remarked many times that Mr. Curley was as strict with Drake as he could be, but after all Drake wasn't Mr. Curley's son, and he could only advise. No use bothering too much about Poppy and Jinny Ross. Of course, it was downright curious that he went around with *both* of them. The men made ribald jokes. Mrs. Skeffington, who had much of the Colonel's ribaldry and freedom and an Elizabethan vocabulary to boot, repeated these jests.

But Randy Monaghan was another matter.

Everyone saw how the Gordons handled the question when Drake looked in the direction of Louise. Harriet Gordon was maybe a little on the overstrict side but she was looking out for her own daughter, and no one could blame her for that. That little slap in the face should have taught Drake McHugh something of a lesson. For a while it looked as though it really had. Then all at once it was this Monaghan girl from the lower end of town. Irish Catholics. Railroad people. The menfolks said old Mr. Monaghan was a straight, honest, self-respecting man. He'd probably take a shotgun to anyone who fooled around his girl.

All that made this intimacy look a little too serious. It was agreed that somebody ought to talk to Drake McHugh, if only for Mamie Livingstone's sake. But no one undertook the duty.

One afternoon Drake and Randy flashed out Federal Street at a conspicuous clip.

Mrs. Henry Gordon, sitting in her south bay window, busy with her crocheting, saw them. She leaned forward and watched them. Drake's back was turned her way as he talked, but she caught a glimpse of Randy's face as she made some laughing response. Mrs. Gordon frowned. The girl was really pretty—probably common-looking if you saw her close, but at that distance she was decidedly pretty. Healthy-looking, with that kind of wide-mouthed smile men always seemed to like.

Randy Monaghan certainly looked frank and—happy. Mrs. Gordon conceded that much. And she was certainly out in the open with whatever it was she was about. If it was what she herself was morally sure it was, the girl must have all the brass in the world. On the other hand—Mrs. Gordon shook the thought aside. The girl surely couldn't be setting her cap for Drake McHugh. That kind of a girl to marry into the Union Street crowd—for, no matter how you looked at it, Drake McHugh belonged to that crowd and, moreover, he'd have money. She had to admit she rather liked Drake. She always had. But it had been necessary to teach him a lesson. He must know he couldn't come around Louise and be seen with trashy people at the same time. She supposed he'd get over this kind of thing soon, most boys did, and come back to his own kind of people. But a little teasing unease persisted. There was something in the warm look of confidence on the Monaghan girl's face that didn't promise well. She looked too sure of herself—and too much in love with Drake!

There was another person who had noticed Drake and Randy. That was Louise herself. She had been standing at the open window directly above her mother's sitting room. She drew back a little when the buggy passed, but she, too, had seen the look on Randy Monaghan's face, and had heard the soft, contented laugh that floated back. Louise's appraisal was as keen as her mother's, keener, maybe, and because it was Drake who was involved, she was much more accurate in her conclusions. She knew Drake well enough to know that he wouldn't be out much with any girl without getting what he wanted. She had burned with a fury of jealousy about the Ross affair, but she wasn't afraid of Poppy and Jinny.

Louise, like all of Kings Row, felt that this was different.

She was certain that the intimacy with Randy Monaghan had progressed far. All the way, probably. Randy, very likely, wouldn't be too particular about what she did. But—the way she looked up in Drake's face as they passed, the sound of her laugh, the easy air of possession—Randy was no Poppy Ross to be set aside—nor, she grudgingly agreed with herself, could Randy be won in the same way. Here Louise was clearer than Mrs. Gordon. It was quite possible that Drake might want to marry Randy. It was quite possible that he would. Certainly, he would if he wanted to. Drake had already shown Kings Row that he didn't in the least care what they thought about him in any way. And Randy. Well, of course, Randy Monaghan would jump at the chance to marry Drake. Who wouldn't? He could mighty near pick any girl he wanted and get her. Heaven knows she wanted him herself. More than ever now. If only she had some way of calling him back. She'd pocket a lot of her pride, she'd go more than halfway, but she didn't even have that chance now. He never even looked her way any more. She had written to him, but he had not answered.

She thought of Parris Mitchell. That one afternoon Parris had looked so understanding, and really sympathetic. If Parris were here, she believed she'd try to get him to help straighten things out. Parris could do anything with Drake, it seemed.

She'd never love anybody else, she was sure of that. Drake's touch used to make her shiver and tingle all over. What a goody-goody she had been! It was silly. The whole way she had been reared was silly. It had nothing to do with the strength and urgency—the sheer necessity of one's emotions. She thought again of Drake's impish advances. She clenched her hands. If only it could be once more, now—this minute. Drake could have anything he wanted: she would give him anything—not only to win him and hold him but because she wanted to!

She sat down on the edge of the bed and hunched her thin shoulders as she braced herself against tears.

Downstairs Mrs. Gordon had a sudden intuition. She went quietly to Louise's room and opened the door. Louise was crying now. Small tears, oddly dry-looking tears squeezed from her eyes. Her fists were set hard against her knees, and her arms were stiff and straight. Her throat ached and she made small coughing sounds.

"Louise!"

Louise did not turn. She dropped her head, and was silent.

"Louise!"

"Yes. What do you want?"

"What are you crying about?"

"Does it make any difference?"

Mrs. Gordon's face hardened. She was suddenly angry. She was angry at Drake, and still angrier at Randy Monaghan. Her narrow fierce devotion to her own child took a strange turn in her mind. All the harsh violence of her feeling turned on Louise as if she were to blame.

"Don't answer me like that!"

"Why can't you let me alone?"

"Because I don't want you sitting up here crying like a little fool over nothing."

"Nothing!"

"Oh, I know what you're crying about. I saw Drake McHugh going by with that little—nobody from downtown. Aren't you ashamed of yourself?"

"For what? For letting her take him away from me?"

"Louise! You know what I mean. Haven't you any self-respect?"

"No."

"Well, I almost believe you. If he wants to run around with that kind of trash—"

"Maybe she isn't. What do you know about her?" Louise had a faint half-hopeful feeling her mother might be right, but she also felt she had to defend Drake.

"Of course she's trash."

Louise wiped her eyes. "I don't know anything about her and I don't care anything about her."

"Then stop crying. You know what boys are like. Your father is a doctor, and if you knew all I know—"

"I don't want to hear it."

"Well, you can be sure Drake McHugh's just after one thing when he rides around with a girl like that."

Louise stood up. Her eyes were dry now, and she was trembling. "I wish it was me!"

Mrs. Gordon waited a second. "What did you say?"

Louise turned on her mother. "I'm not a baby. Of course I know what he's after. God knows I'd give it to him in a minute if he asked me!"

Mrs. Gordon dropped her crocheting and struck Louise across the mouth with all her strength.

Louise stood perfectly still. A little streak of blood showed on her lips. Mechanically she wiped it away with the back of her hand. "Mother, don't you ever do that again! Don't you ever touch me again as long as you live!"

Mrs. Gordon was shaken and somewhat abashed by the suddenness of her own rage. But she felt she must keep face.

"And what will you do about it, miss?"

"I'll kill you," Louise said calmly. Then, shouting, she pushed Mrs. Gordon toward the door.

"Get out of here! Get out of here, do you hear? Get out of here."

4

Drake's horse clop-clopped softly along the sandy road. The wheels made scarcely a sound. The buggy top was down and the warm sun glistened on Randy's thick shining hair. The fresh green leaves swayed in the light breeze. Mighty clouds sailed slowly overhead.

"What a day! Whoa, Tom Thumb! Slow up there."

"What do you call him 'Tom Thumb' for, Drake?"

"'Cause he's so big."

"That makes sense!"

"My kind of sense, honey."

"That's what I mean."

They both laughed. Out of their overflowing spirits the slightest sentence assumed meaning and humor. Every word was charged. Drake wound the reins around the whip in its socket, and Tom Thumb obediently assumed a gentle plodding gait.

"Got him trained."

"Yes, I see."

"He knows just what I want him to do."

"Guess he's had plenty of training, too, hasn't he?"

"You mean going on by himself?"

"Yes."

"Sure he has."

"Why?"

Drake's face crinkled. "For *this,* honey." He gathered her in a tight hug, and kissed her on the eyes, and nose, and mouth.

"You bear! You squeeze too hard."

"That's how hard I love you."

"Yeh, I bet."

"Sure enough."

"Don't you ever get tired of saying that?"

"No: do you get tired of hearing it?"

She shook her head. "Haven't yet."

He squeezed her hands. "Honest, you're sweet."

She took a long breath. "Isn't it the prettiest day you ever saw?"

His teasing glance never left her face. "Just about."

They were in the open farm country now, but on one side of the road the pasture land dipped down and away in slopes and small hills to a tiny creek—it was hardly more than a brook—and long stretches of feathery willows.

There was some late plowing, and the fragrance of fresh earth mingled with the warm smell of new leaves, and small hidden flowers, and the heady, intoxicating breath of wild plum.

Randy inhaled deeply and closed her eyes. "Isn't that delicious?"

"Yes. Kind of stirs you up, doesn't it?"

"Yes."

"I mean—"

She opened her eyes and looked at him with a playful, teasing affection, slightly tinged with wonder.

"Yes, honey—I know exactly what you mean."

"Well, doesn't it?"

"Yes, I guess it does. But Drake—"

"You're fixing to yell at me about something."

"No, I wasn't."

"Well, go ahead then."

"I was just kind of wondering."

"What?"

"Most everything 'stirs you up,' as you say, doesn't it?"

"How so?"

"This—" She waved at the landscape. "The smell of wild-plum blossoms, the sunshine, or the moonshine—or morning, or noon, or night—just anything!"

He held both her hands to his face. "But mostly you."

"Aw—"

"Honest!"

"Let's get out and walk down there. It looks so pretty."

"You bet." He laughed his familiar provoking laugh as he helped her out of the buggy.

"Now, Drake—that's not why I said let's walk."

"All right, all right! Anything you say!"

"Drake, you make me awful mad sometimes."

He pretended astonishment and innocent incomprehension. "Why?"

"You always think—"

"What?"

She was embarrassed now. "Well. You know what I mean. You think I think as much about—something as you do."

He threw back his head and laughed. "I think maybe you do."

"Drake McHugh."

"Now, listen, honey. One of the nicest things about you is that you don't pretend anything."

"Well, I don't pretend."

"Well, then, what are we talking about?"

"For instance—right now. I suggested we walk down here."

"All right, What's wrong with that?"

"And you thought right away—"

"What?"

She colored. "I thought maybe we could gather some flowers."

"What kind?"

"Drake McHugh, you're terrible."

"You're sweet."

They went hand in hand, laughing, teasing, stopping to argue and to quarrel, down the long green pasture slopes. The great oak trees were decked out in sprays of young puffy-looking young leaves and streaming tassels. Randy pinned a bunch on each shoulder of his coat.

"You look like a general!"

"Attention!"

She snapped her heels together.

"Right about face! Kiss the general!"

"Look—those tassels shed pollen all over your coat."

"You've got streaks of it on your face."

"Look, Drake—dogwood!"

They had come to a narrow glenlike fold in the hills. The sun light slanted through the high trees and touched the cluster of dogwood trees with a transfiguring light. The blossoms lay against the shadowy background in tilting planes. They looked like butterflies arrested in mid-flight. Overhead the very tops of the trees glinted bright yellow and gold. The brilliant leaves laid a broken pattern above the darker layers underneath. There were furtive rustlings of wings among the branches, but it seemed as if they had come upon a hushed and waiting space in the midst of the murmurous afternoon.

"Gee, Drake, it's beautiful."

"Yes. It is."

She moved close to him, and his arm went around her. She leaned her head against him and looked up through the trees. The light made glittering little movements in her eyes. He kissed her slowly and gently on her parted lips.

She held to him for a moment.

"It feels almost like a church, doesn't it?"

"Does it?"

She nodded.

The dogwood blossoms held the light. Neither twigs nor the beginning leaves showed. They hung there, radiant and still, a miraculous shower of starry white. A curious unreality invested them. They were so serene, so detached, so utterly contained within their own beauty that they seemed almost to mock at human unrest and imperfection.

Randy sighed. "I wish I could keep it."

"What, honey?"

"All of this. The way it looks. This minute, too, with you."

He drew her closer.

"Don't you, Drake? You know—just us, and everything so still, and nothing troubling us at all."

They sat down, and she snuggled her head against him. After a little he tilted her backward and looked in her eyes.

"Oh, Drake—"

"Please! I just can't wait—"

"Somebody might come!"

"Here? On a weekday. No. We're safe."

"I'm a little scared."

"You needn't be."

They were silent for a moment, both of them listening. The woods were as still as the night. Far away they could hear the gurgling whisper of the brook, though it might have been the sound of moving leaves. Still farther away they could just hear a plowman calling to his horses.

"All right?" Drake whispered close to her ear.

"All right." The answer came with a quick trembling sigh of release.

Her cheek burned against his.

The gold-laced canopy stretched over the dark underleaves, and the dark underleaves slanted down branch under branch to the green-and-brown-lit space where the dogwood shimmered. The pale flowers were as motionless as clusters of candle flames in a windless room.

Randy stood up and smoothed her dress.

"Look, I'm all wrinkled up!"

Drake industriously helped her. He pulled at the hem, and brushed vigorously with his hand.

"Oh, it's all right."

"Yeh. Looks all right now."

"Should we go?"

"How about picking those flowers?"

She laughed. "I've been right down this way lots of times, Drake McHugh. There are always lots of Johnny-jump-ups just over the rise. I bet they're in bloom now."

"Let's go see."

They ran down through the glade, now more deeply shaded as the sun dropped low, and up the far side.

She paused at the top of the hill.

"Ooh! Gets your breath."

"Yeh—specially after—"

She put her fingers over his mouth.

"Hush now. Stop talking about it!"

"Sure, honey. Where's the Johnny-jump-ups?"

"All around you, dummy. Look!"

"Gee, sure enough. Well, well, now."

"Come on, help me pick some."

"They're pretty, sure enough, Randy."

"I told you they were here, didn't I?"

Drake sat back on his heels. "Say! Who'd you come with when you came here before?"

Randy laughed, and crinkled her nose at him.

"I came with Pa."

"Sure you did?"

"You don't even have to pretend to be jealous, Drake."

"Why not?"

"You know better."

"How so, I'd like to know?"

He was laughing, the usual teasing look in his eyes, but Randy became serious all at once.

"First of all, you know darn well you're the first."

"*First?*"

"The only one, then."

"Yeh, honey, I know. I was just teasing."

"You remember once you came down to the icehouse one Sunday, and you and Parris Mitchell and I played on the bars and rings?"

"Of course I do!"

"I was an awful little toughie then, wasn't I?"

"No."

"Yes, I was. And you teased me about some boy, or other. You said you had heard—"

"I remember. Gee, you got mad!"

"Yes, I was."

"I didn't mean it."

"What did you say it for?"

"I don't know."

"Just trying me out, I expect."

"I guess so."

"You got an early start, didn't you?"

"Gosh, I was an awful kid, I guess."

"Yes. I think I was mad mostly that day because you said it before Parris."

"Why?"

"I liked him a whole lot better than I did you."

"Say! You did?"

"Then."

"Oh! You're sure?"

"What do you think, dummy, after this afternoon—and all the other times?"

"Aw—of course. I know."

"Listen, Drake, when a girl acts the way I do about you, she means it. It's because I want to, because I like you better than anybody in the world."

Drake nodded gravely. His slow gaze came back to her face. "Someday—" he began.

"Hush. I like everything just the way it is. We're just a couple of kids. I'm happy. I'm having a good time. Let's don't talk about anything else, or any other time."

"But, honey—"

"Please, Drake. Honest, I mean it."

"Gee, you're funny."

"We've got to go."

"Aw—what for?"

"It's getting late. Pa'll be getting home, and he likes me to be there for supper."

"Well, if you want to—"

"Why don't you come home and have supper with us?"

"You want me to?"

"Of course. I think Pa likes you, ever since that time you walked in and asked him right out if you could take me out buggy-riding."

"Sure enough?"

"Yes. I think he was so surprised he couldn't think of anything to say. So he just said yes."

"That was funny, wasn't it? I was kind of mad at you. I thought we'd better have a showdown right then and there."

"I guess it was a good thing."

"Sure it was."

"Well, I guess after that Pa just liked you for yourself."

"Never says anything against me?"

"Never. Not a word. He always says you're all right."

"Gee. That's nice."

They walked slowly through the hazy late afternoon. The sweetness of the fresh spring world increased as the shadows stretched across the newly planted fields.

"Maybe we can drive out some more after supper." Drake was casual.

Randy took his arm and carefully matched her step to his. "All right, if you want to."

5

"Hey, Jamie!"

Drake pulled his horse to a walk. "Jamie!"

"Oh! Hello, Drake. I thought I heard my name. I was thinking hard, I guess."

"Hop in. I'll drive you home."

"Thanks, Drake."

"I bet I can name one thing you were not thinking about."

"That might be easy enough."

"Yeh. But you weren't worrying your mind about your work down at the bank!"

Jamie almost managed a smile. "I forget it as quick as I can when I get outside the door, Drake."

"Don't like it, eh?"

"I hate it!"

"Why, kid? It ought not to be so bad."

"It's hideous."

"Yeh?"

"Yes, it is. Figures! Checks! Statements! And it's all just mechanical. Any fool could do it."

"There's a lot of fellows think you're lucky to have your old man in the bank to get a job for you."

"Yes, I know." Jamie's tone was exceedingly bitter. "I wish they could have the job."

"What would you like to do, Jamie?"

"Just write—poetry."

"Aw—Jamie, that's not work!"

"It's what I want to do."

"Can't you write poetry anyhow?"

"Parris asked me that same question once, Drake. I was surprised."

"Don't understand."

"Well, Drake, I don't mean anything about you, but Parris was a musician and he ought to have understood better."

"But you wouldn't expect me to!" Drake made a good-humored grimace.

"Well, that's nothing against you, Drake. You never have thought about it at all, I'm sure."

"Nope. Never have. You just want to write poetry?"

"Yes."

"All day long?"

Jamie sighed helplessly. "You don't write all day long."

"That's what I thought."

"But, you've got to have some time to—to—oh, I can't explain it!"

"Go ahead. I'm just teasing you, Jamie. For goodness' sake, don't fly off the handle."

"It's kind of like this, Drake. You have to look around, and listen to the world, and think, and dream—and wait."

Drake nodded.

"It takes a long time for a poem to come into any kind of existence at all."

"I guess I can understand that."

"And then maybe it's all cloudy and vague—just a kind of feeling. But you have to wait, and stay on guard for it. And by and bye you get a couple of words, or a line that seems to belong to the feeling. You hold onto that and—wait some more. Someday you feel that the whole thing is ready. You sit down and go after it. And that's where the work begins. You do know what it ought to be like. You know what kind of thing you want, but you have to turn your mind upside down to find it."

"But you do feel you got to do it?"

"Yes, Drake, I do."

"Well go to it! Do the best you can. Don't give it up."

Jamie looked at Drake with sudden amazement. "Do you know, Drake, you're the first person to say that to me since—"

"Parris?"

"No. Parris, even, didn't say that exactly. He was encouraging, but you know Parris kind of attended to his own business and thought about what *he* had to do."

"Yes, I know. He didn't meddle with your business, ever, did he?"

"No. I was going to say since Bob Callicott."

"Oh, yes. Parris told me all about him."

"It just surprised me to hear you say the same thing."

"Well, Jinks—" Drake slapped Jamie on the leg in hearty fashion. "I just think everybody ought to do whatever he wants to do. No matter what it is."

"But I can't."

"They put you in the bank anyhow, eh?"

"Yes."

"Say. Your old man's got enough money to let you go on to college some more and do whatever you want to, hasn't he?"

"I think so, Drake. But there's no use talking to him. He won't listen to anybody."

"Knows it all, eh?"

"Yes. And he hated Bob Callicott. Kept saying, 'See there, that's where that kind of foolishness gets you!'"

"Gosh. People are unreasonable. I guess Callicott didn't die because he wrote poetry."

"No. But he drank a good deal. And they used to talk about the way he ran after women."

"Oh, yes. I remember. Lots of people lifting petticoats don't ever try to write poetry—why don't you tell 'em that?"

"The more I talk the worse fix I get into."

"I'm sorry, Jinks."

"Funny, hearing you use that old nickname."

"Used to call you that at school."

"I haven't heard it since. Parris never called me 'Jinks.'"

"Parris was pretty proper, wasn't he? I guess he'd have said 'correct.'"

Jamie sighed again. "I miss Parris."

"You don't know anything. Pretty near pulled me up by the roots when he went away."

"I get letters from him—oh, just once in a long while. Do you?"

"Yes. Short notes. He's getting along all right, looks like."

"I think people talk more about Parris now than they did when he was here."

"Yeh. He's somebody you don't forget, somehow. But I think this old town's proud of having him over in Europe studying medicine."

"Yes, I think so, too. Like Vera Lichinsky."

"What about her?"

"She's gone to Europe, too."

"You don't say!"

"About two months ago. There was a long piece in the paper about her."

"I never read the papers."

"She's going to be a concert violinist."

"Where'd she go? To Vienna, too?"

"No. To Berlin."

"Want to ride around a little while?"

"Weren't you going any place?"

"Nope. Just riding."

"I'd like to."

They were silent for a little while. Jamie looked almost hungrily at everything they passed. The most ordinary bush or tree seemed to engage his liveliest attention.

"Looks like everybody gets to do what they want to, except me."

Drake gave him a careless thump. "Don't feel sorry for yourself, Jinks. I've tried plenty of that. Don't do you any good."

"I know. But Parris goes off to Europe, and little old Vera Lichinsky goes to Berlin—and everybody does something they like."

"I don't believe many people do. I think you're wrong there."

"Well, anyhow, they're not kept from doing something they're just dying to do."

"That might be."

"It's terrible, and I'd just as soon be dead."

"Aw—"

"Yes, I had, honest, Drake. And I'm so lonesome."

Drake glanced quickly at Jamie's brooding face. He looked sulky and sullen. There were bluish shadows under his eyes. He did look dead-tired, sure enough.

"Why, Jinks?"

"Why what?"

"You said you were so lonesome. Why?"

"I haven't got any friends."

"Why?" Drake was peculiarly persistent.

"I don't know."

Drake did not question further. Once more he gave Jamie a quick, keen, scrutinizing glance. Jamie was much as he had always been. He looked no more than sixteen, Drake decided. His face was as soft of contour and as warm and lovely in coloring as ever. He was incredibly good-looking. Drake thought he looked a good deal like Poppy Ross. Jamie had the same yielding look—the same sensuous roundness, and the same silky-looking mouth.

Drake slapped the horse with the reins, and half-whistled under his breath. He would not have liked for anyone to know just what he was thinking at that moment, or how Jamie actually made him feel.

He set his face a little, and flicked the horse with the whip. They rode for some time without speaking. The swirl of dust back of them changed from powdery gray to a misty cloud of reddish gold as the sun dropped to the horizon.

"Jinks!"

Jamie started. "What?"

"Well, I'd kind of like to talk to you about something, but I don't know how."

"What, Drake?" Jamie's wide lovely eyes looked up with such a frank look of almost childlike wonder that Drake was confused.

"Go ahead, Drake. What do you want to say?"

"Well, you said you haven't got any friends."

"I haven't. Parris, I thought was my friend—he really was, I mean, and—I think you are."

"Sure, sure I am."

"But that's all. Parris is gone, and I don't ever see you. You're always busy with somebody."

"Yeh. I go around a lot."

"You see?"

"Are there any of the fellows around town you like at all?"

Jamie puckered his mouth.

"Honestly, I can't say there are, Drake. They—nobody is interested in the same things I am."

"I'm not either, Jamie. But that doesn't keep us from getting on all right together, does it?"

"N-no."

"See, Jinks. Why don't you be interested in the same things that the other fellows are—just a little, anyhow?"

"I just can't, and I can't pretend, either."

"Well, enough so you'd have some kind of company."

"I—I guess I'd rather be all by myself than try that."

"How about girls. Got a girl?"

A look, near to bewilderment, came into Jamie's troubled eyes—also an oddly withdrawn expression as if he shrank from something acutely disagreeable.

"No, Drake. I don't get on with girls a bit."

"Gee, why? I thought they always wanted to talk about poetry and music—and stuff like that."

"They're the most unpoetic things on earth." Jamie gave the words a syllable-by-syllable emphasis.

Drake laughed. "Got no use for their brains, have you, Jinks?"

"They haven't got any brains, Drake."

"Aw—get out!"

"Honest."

"Well, you don't have to like 'em for their brains. They've got other things."

"What?"

Drake was so astonished by Jamie's utterly innocent look that he gasped. Then he clapped himself on the knee and laughed.

Jamie's face colored darkly. But he did not laugh. "Oh, that!" He spoke with an intense contempt and disgust.

"Say, Jinks. It won't do to talk like that."

"I hate girls."

"Why?"

"I don't know. I just can't stand 'em!"

"You mean you don't even like to look at 'em?"

"Not 'specially."

"Hell, kid, they're the prettiest things on God's green earth!"

"I can't stand them, I tell you."

"I don't see why. God a-mighty, Jinks, you look like a girl yourself. You ought not hate 'em."

Jamie seemed almost to become smaller. He drew to his side of the seat as if he were trying to hide. Slowly the color left his face until it was almost gray.

"Oh, Drake. Please don't say that!"

"Now look here, Jamie. I haven't said anything to hurt you. I'm just saying you're the handsomest—bestlooking boy I ever saw."

Jamie did not answer. His eyes were haggard. Drake continued, but he covertly observed Jamie's face. He was sorry now, but he felt he had to go on.

"You just ought to like girls. It's natural."

"I'm made different, I guess, Drake."

Drake jerked Tom Thumb to a walk. "Now right there, you're wrong, Jinks."

"No. I'm different. I've just told you."

"You just let yourself think that way, that's all."

Jamie shook his head obstinately. "No, no, no!"

"Aw—quit it now. Don't be pigheaded. You listen to me—for your own good. Just because you want to be a poet—"

"I am a poet."

"All right, then. Just because you're a poet, do you have to be different in every other way?"

"I'm not different every other way."

"That way, then. And that's a devil of an important way, let me tell you."

"Drake, it seems to me the least important thing in the whole world."

"You don't mean that. You mean the way I like girls is not important to you."

"Yes."

"But, see here. The way you don't like 'em is mighty bad for you."

"Oh, Drake!" Jamie half turned away and looked stonily out across the fields.

Drake's face darkened a little with anger. He pulled Jamie around again.

"I said I was going to talk to you, and I am."

"Maybe you'd better let me out. I don't want to talk about it."

"You're going to—at least you're going to listen."

Jamie tightened his mouth obstinately.

"Don't be mulish, Jinks!" Drake was a shade conciliatory. "I'm not saying you got to go out every night and raise hell with some little lower-end-of-town chippie, but you got to be natural. When we were kids, of course we fooled around and—kind of experimented, and played little games and all that stuff. That was all right, I guess. Didn't do anybody any harm. But I've read some about this kind of stuff—read a lot, as a matter of fact, in some books Parris had at my house—"

"Did you and Parris talk about me?"

"Not about this, Jamie. Not since we were kids, too. But you know several of us—well, we played along with you. All of us in the same boat. But we got interested in girls—"

"Did Parris—have a girl?"

"Sure, he did—more'n one!"

"Who?"

"None of your business, Jinks. Now—you know darn well that's just kid stuff—the things we used to do—it's just kid stuff." He waited a minute.

"Well?" Jamie's voice was dry.

"Well—Jinks, that's my point. You know as well as I do that since we're grown up we're not going to play like that any more, don't you?"

Jamie did not answer, but the stricken look about his eyes seemed to deepen.

"It's this, Jamie." Drake laid his hand on Jamie's knee. "It's this: you're going to go on with younger and younger kids and—"

"What do you mean, Drake?"

"I'm no fool, Jamie. You got to do something, I guess, though I don't know how in the hell you feel about anything. But you'll get in trouble about young kids. You'll get put in the pen, sure's you're born."

"Drake, I hate all of this talk."

"Of course, you do. So do I."

"Well, let's drop it."

"I hate to drop it here, Jamie, after we've gone this far."

Jamie whipped around suddenly toward Drake. "What do you want me to do?"

Drake was taken by surprise. "Me. I don't want you to do anything!"

"Then what are you talking to me for?"

"Aw—Jamie. You take everything wrong."

"How do you want me to take it?"

"Well, I'd just like to help keep you out of trouble. And this is all the thanks I get."

"I asked you what you want me to do?"

"Well, all right. You've got the wrong kind of ideas in your mind. You've got to get 'em right somehow."

"In the first place, maybe they're not necessarily wrong. What's wrong and what's right, anyhow?"

"That's foolish, Jamie, and you know it. There's one kind of natural sex stuff, and all the rest is—just crazy."

"That's the way you feel about it."

"There's a better argument than that."

"What?"

"One kind gets kids into this world. So that's natural—"

"It's disgusting!"

Drake opened wide, incredulous eyes. "What is?"

"What you're saying."

"How do you know it's disgusting?"

"It is."

"Ever try it?" Drake asked the question slyly, and with enough of his lusty, faunish gusto behind the words to make Jamie smile faintly.

"Of course not!"

"Gosh, what you've missed!"

This time Jamie laughed, and some of their mutual constraint fell away.

"I tell you, Jinks. Any time you change your mind, I'll find you some little cutie will make you think you're Christopher Columbus discovering a new world."

"I do want to say one thing, Drake."

"Shoot! What is it?"

"You accused me of something."

"I did?"

"Yes."

"What?"

"What you said about younger—and younger kids."

"Oh—well, I didn't mean anybody in particular—"

"I know what you meant. Drake, there haven't—I haven't been doing anything."

"Honest, Jamie?"

"I don't lie, Drake."

"No, I don't believe you do."

"I—it's just like I said. I haven't any friends—just nobody at all."

"Boys, or girls, eh?"

"No."

"That's hell, Jamie."

"It *is* hell. *You* don't know."

"Well, you get out and get you somebody."

"I don't know. I just want somebody I can read with, and talk to, and make plans with. Somebody who knows what I'm talking about and likes the same things I do."

"Gee, kid. You sound pretty sad."

"I'm just explaining. Maybe I ought to get used to the feeling. Maybe I ought to say to myself that I'm born to be lonesome like some people are born blind, or something, and just go on the best I can."

"Well, I don't know what to say to that."

"No one does."

"But you know you can count on me for anything I can do. Just yell and I'll come running."

Jamie looked as if he might cry, and that embarrassed Drake acutely.

"We better get back to town. What you say?"

They rode the distance in silence. Drake was already thinking of something else. Having said what he had to say about the subject that had come so unexpectedly into the discussion, he immediately forgot all about it.

Jamie thanked him for the drive and said a moody good night. His mother was waiting for him when he came in.

Mrs. Wakefield was a large gelatinous woman who seemed to be precariously held together by tight clothes and a generous amount of corseting. Even so, she shook so alarmingly that the spectator was likely to gasp if she stooped, or leaned far to the side. It seemed impossible that she should not spill over the edge of her high stays.

"Why, Jamie, where have you been? I was so worried when you didn't come home in time for supper. I telephoned the bank and everywhere I thought you might be."

"What did you do that for?"

"Why, you know Mama worries when she doesn't know where you are."

"You needn't."

"Mama can't help it, darling. Where did you go?"

"Oh, just for a ride out in the country."

"With whom, darling?"

"Drake McHugh."

"Oh!" The tone was most eloquent. "Drake McHugh?"

"Yes. He picked me up at the bank as I was coming out."

"Well, darling, it's all right once in a while, I guess, but I wouldn't make a practice of going riding with Drake McHugh."

"He's all right."

"Yes, I am sure he is. I knew his aunt well. But I don't think Papa would like it."

"Oh, let me alone."

"Mama's just telling you for your own good, son. Come on now, and Mama'll give you some supper. I've kept it nice and warm for you."

"I don't know if I want any supper, or not."

"Oh, you've got to eat your supper. Mama's boy'll be sick if he doesn't eat. Are you tired, dear?"

"Yes."

"Did you work hard today?"

"I work hard every day."

"Mama's awfully proud."

"Well, you needn't be. I don't do anything to be proud of. Anybody could do it."

"Oh, I don't believe that."

"I hate it."

"Now, now. You mustn't say that. What would Papa say if he heard you?"

"I don't care what he'd say. It's so."

"Sh-h! Come on now and eat your supper."

Jamie ate abstractedly. He tried not to listen to the steady patter of nagging questions and sirupy endearment from his mother. As soon as he could escape, he went upstairs. He slipped out of his chair while his mother was in the kitchen, and made his way quickly through the dark hall to his own room. He closed the door, turned the key in the lock, and stood listening. His mother had apparently given up her siege. He leaned back against the door and closed his eyes. His hands were limp at his side for a moment, then he lifted both of them and rubbed his eyes with his fists, like a child.

Presently he struck a match and lighted the squat heavily shaded lamp, and sat down at his table. The ruffled curtains hung straight and still at the windows. The room, which was over the kitchen and looked out on the flat tin roof of the back porch, was hot as an oven.

It was a curious room, neither feminine in its appointments and decorations, nor masculine in any way. It was neat as arithmetic, and as sexless. The table was a discarded dining table, but the wood was pine and Jamie had polished it to a subdued and rich beauty. His papers and pencils were mathematically disposed. A coarse linen square at one side, blocked with heavy embroidery which he had done himself, and a dull orange jar with a lumpy, jagged, Japanese-looking branch of evergreen in it were the only ornaments. A few shallow shelves above the table were filled with small limp-leather volumes of poetry and prose classics. Above them a panel of portraits looked out serenely: Mozart, Shelley, Byron, Keats, and an idealized Burns. The tormented eyes of Edgar Allan Poe had place of honor below the shelves. There was a straw matting on the floor. The bed was covered with an India print. The one easy chair was set so the occupant could look away from the kitchen yard and outhouses toward the green shaded lawn of the Sansomes next door.

Jamie sat down and held his head between his hands. This little space of time before he must go to bed was his own. He drew the papers under the light and looked at the regular lines set in precise order in his rounded childish handwriting.

He read, and reread. Then he folded the papers and, unlocking the drawer, filed them carefully away in a flat cedar box. He sighed heavily, and sank back in the chair. An expression of misery came out on his face as though it had lain in wait for this moment. Jamie drew into himself. He seemed to be trying to escape from something immediate, something actually pressing against him. At this moment he appeared older, a little wilted, and nerveless. He felt of himself—his arms, his legs—trying to stop the absurd trembling that shook him from head to foot. He had not realized how shattering the talk with Drake had been. He wondered why he was always such a fool, so helpless that he couldn't defend or explain himself. What Drake had suggested—he had wanted to say loudly and firmly that it wasn't so. There was no longer anyone—anyone with whom he had—nothing of that kind had happened in a long, long time.

Now, as he thought of it, he half understood how Drake might feel. He was a little shocked himself. It hadn't been very nice, really. Something fastidious in him looked hard the other way. But—*that other—girls*—he shuddered away from the very words themselves. Here Drake was wholly wrong. There was nothing in him that responded to such a suggestion. He did not even ask himself why. It seemed the only natural thing for him. What he loved was beauty—all that world out there that he had so little time to think about, or even to look at—that was what he loved. The humblest weed growing in a ditch was richer in beauty, more wonderful in its shape and design, more a thing to dream over and write somehow into his own story and vision of the earth than all the men and women living. He hated them—nearly all of them. He particularly hated women. Maybe it wasn't hate exactly. It was just that he wished he need never see them or think about them. He quivered as he thought of the way his mother looked, and others—oh, many of them. He particularly hated the smell of them.

The room was still stifling. He looked at the tiny clock in its gilt case. If he went downstairs now his mother would be sure to want him to go to prayer meeting with her. There was still time. He recalled now that the first bell had rung just a few minutes before. He wiped the beads of sweat from his forehead and upper lip. Perhaps he could go out the back way. He arose and washed his face. He emptied the bowl into the jar and replaced the lid cautiously. Then he tiptoed down the back stairs and hurried through the garden to the street.

He decided to go to Aberdeen campus. It was nearly dark, but he could be alone there. He walked with his head down. He hoped he wouldn't meet anyone he knew. He didn't want to talk.

The campus was pretty black by the time he arrived at the corner gates. Jamie wasn't exactly afraid of the dark, but it made him uncomfortable. He had to keep looking behind him, and that always made him a little ashamed of himself.

He took the shortest way to the high ridge back of the chapel. His favorite bench was there. He scuffed rather noisily along the cinder paths. Once or twice he had surprised clandestine lovers along the way, to his extreme embarrassment.

He came out from the thick shade of the elms to the clear space on the brow of the hill. He stopped and took a deep breath. The wide outlook gave him a feeling of freedom from everything back there. He looked back. Houses! People! The bank! His father and, what was far worse, his mother! All of the painful, enchaining things were back there. If only he might walk on out into this great circling space in front of him—on and on and on. But he wouldn't know what to do. He would be frightened, and as badly off with whatever he might find. He was sure that he was a complete weakling. Maybe he didn't deserve any better than what he had.

He sat down on the bench and leaned back. Where the light lingered a little on trees and tilted fields there was a deep watery green. Between lay folds and hollows of velvety black. It was very still. Later in the summer it would be filled with innumerable small sounds and voices. He reflected on that. Each season had its own sounds. Now, in this dampish early summer, all of nature seemed to be silently at work, secretly, deeply engaged on the transforming enterprises of air and earth. Later, it would speak.

How still it was! At rest, but maybe breathing very deeply and mysteriously. The earth's own kind of sleep.

Jamie half closed his eyes. He was forgetting now the swarming horrors of the day—his day. The bitterest thought of all was that no one else's days were like his.

The earth's own sleep. The phrase kept coming back. He had often thought that sleep—just simple, common sleep was probably the most beautiful thing under the sky. It seemed to transform everything, and everybody. The most hateful creature lost something of its worst qualities when it slept. People and animals were a little pathetic. All of them entered into a special magic.

Now he scarcely thought at all. He was half listening, half dreaming, but a small place in his mind burned to a sudden painful awareness. He moved his lips and counted on his fingers. He shook his head impatiently and began again. Then he waked entirely from his reverie. Mechanically, he counted with this thumb on his fingers, He said the words in a hoarse whisper.

It has the beauty of all things that sleep,

Whether—he stammered and hesitated. Then he started again.

It has the beauty of all things that sleep,

Whether they be informed of life or death.

He stumbled to his feet and started home. He walked rapidly, leaning forward and moving into a sort of dogtrot—like a little boy in a hurry.

Jamie slowed as he reached Federal Street. He looked ahead before continuing. He could not bear the thought of meeting anyone just now. People! They stopped him to slap him on the back and to ask about his new job with a false heartiness that filled him with loathing.

He forgot the lines of the poem he had thought about. Parris Mitchell came back to mind. He must write to Parris—tonight. It was marvelous that Parris could do such wonderful things. The opera, and concerts, and ballets—palaces and historic buildings! He wondered if he would ever see an opera, or hear a great orchestra. That was a curious question Drake had asked about his father. Of course his father had rather a lot of money. Someday, a long time from now, it would all come to him—the bank stock and the two stores on Commerce Street, the shares in the cigar factory, and the house on Union Street. He had never really thought much about it. He would have a lot of money someday. And then—what could he do with it? It would probably be too late to do anything. He'd almost be old. It had never occurred to him to be resentful that he had so little of anything. The property belonged to his father, and his father was a silent, unapproachable man. Jamie was sure his father was disappointed in him. He didn't know why, but he was sure of it.

Drake's unexpected question started a new sequence of thought. If all of this money was going to be his someday, why couldn't he have some of it now? Even a little. He could go to Vienna, too. It wouldn't take much. He'd be willing to live in a garret as poets did in stories, and as they actually had so many times. He only wished to be left alone—to be alone, to think, and to try and try to write.

Jamie wasn't exactly resentful now, as he thought on and on. Money, property—these things belonged to his father. He wasn't really fit his mind asking that anything should be given to him. But to work in the bank, to listen every day to the same inane jocularities, the same yokel jests, the same speculative gossip about uninteresting people. It was a nightmare.

He'd have to wait, to hold fast to his hopes with all the strength he could summon from his dreams. He wondered if he could wait. He must save his money—save and save and save. He could at least be sure that his father would approve of *that*. Then—perhaps ...

He returned to the picture of Kings Row itself as he used to see it and think of it. A jumble—yes, a large and bewildering and incomprehensible confusion. Then as he grew up, it clarified. There were parts of it he must consider because these were the people his father and mother knew. He learned early from his mother's constant reiterations which were the "nice" children, and which ones he should ignore. Happily, he had not been forced to follow the pattern when he was in school, or to observe the divisions. He had been free to choose, and to like whom he would.

During all of those years the town of Kings Row was no more to him than a mechanical arrangement of place and people. It was without physiognomy and without any aspect of either friendliness or unfriendliness to him. He had played alone much of the time because his mother wouldn't permit him to be out of her sight. He hadn't minded that much because he liked to play alone, and to go through long imaginative adventures which no other children cared to share. He remembered that he had had a doll once which he kept a secret from everyone. He couldn't recall where it had come from.

Later his mother embarrassed him somewhat by saying to everyone that he was so delicate and refined that he didn't like to play with rough companions. That wasn't true, of course, but he hadn't disputed it. He never disputed anything. His mother taught him to sew and to embroider, but his father had put a stop to that, rather to his regret. He really liked to do fancywork.

Then had come the revelations of adolescence. The at first unbelievable stories the other boys told him, the experiments, the "games," as Drake called them. No one, he supposed, could ever understand the strange, almost unbearable excitement and thrill of those adventures. It had been Val Meacham, really, who taught him a lot of things. Big, handsome Val Meacham, five years older than he was. He had adored Val, and after those first encounters he could hardly bear to be separated from his idol. He used to be so jealous of Val's friends. What a baby he had been!

He supposed all of that was over and done with now. A dull resentment oppressed him for a moment as he thought of Drake. Drake had been mistaken in warning him—almost threatening him. But, that made no difference, really. Drake was all right.

There were no specters of that kind to disturb him. It was Kings Row—the Kings Row which had killed Robert Callicott. He was sure Kings Row had killed Bob.

Jamie felt, as he looked at the houses set back among the trees, that Kings Row was lined up against him. Kings Row was not hospitable to the things he loved—the things which had been the breath and lifeblood of Robert Callicott. It seemed to him that the town had through these recent years set itself in a pattern. It was a subtle, and secret alignment of people and forces. The whole place had fallen into formations, here, and here, and here, and he stood alone, or almost alone. It was all arranged against him. It stood close-ranked, solid and waiting. He could not move against it.

Someday it would move against him.

It seemed so arbitrary, and heartless, and impersonal. Some were included in the approval of the arranged mass, some were left outside. He felt—he could not say to himself just why he felt so—that Drake McHugh was outside. He himself was, certainly. Bob Callicott had been, and the unfortunate Towers. He imagined that Parris might be his only friend against the enemy. Kings Row clearly approved of Parris Mitchell.

Jamie stopped and leaned against the fence at the corner of Judge Lamond's yard, to look at the design of leaves where a maple branch hung between him and the street light. He stood for some time until the Judge himself came along and put on his glasses to see who was loitering in the dark. Jamie started off, stumbling a little on the uneven walk. Judge Lamond frowned, shook his head, and muttered to himself.

Jamie tried to resume his thread of thought, but it was broken now. He thought he might be all wrong. Possibly no one was thinking about him at all. He might just be self-conscious because he hated the bank so. Perhaps Kings Row could turn out to be friendly after all. He decided that he must not allow himself to become morbid and suspicious.

6

The summer came on hot and dry. It reached a burning, nerve-wearing climax and mellowed a little toward the end of August. People said the long hot spell was broken now.

"Of course we can expect some more hot days, but the worst of it is over."

"Yes. It's cooler at nights, so's a body can sleep."

"That's the worst of July and August—the hot nights."

"It's true. You can stand a good deal in the day if you've had some rest at night."

"You know it got so hot in my upstairs rooms that the mattresses were still hot when you went to bed. You could smell the heated varnish from the woodwork all night."

"I noticed that, too."

Much conversation moved about the subject of weather.

"I always look forward to the fall."

"So do I. It's the prettiest season we've got in this part of the country."

Drake McHugh came out of the Farmers Exchange Bank one morning. He was preoccupied and looked cross.

"Hi, Drake!"

Drake looked up absently. "Oh, hello, Peyton. How's everything?"

"Fine and dandy. I was just looking for you."

"Me? What you want?"

"Going anywhere in particular?"

"Not just now."

"Let me drive around with you a little. Want to talk to you."

"Come along."

They rode for a few blocks without speaking. Peyton seemed a little nervous, and observed Drake closely.

"Let's drive out once more and look at all that hill property, Drake."

Drake brightened perceptibly. "Fine. Let's."

"I tell you, let's take the bottom road and go along that side of the creek and see how the whole business looks from below."

There was a road that followed the creek. It led to Jinktown, and curving westward again with the bend of the stream joined the main county road to the northwest.

They passed through Jinktown. Drake had not been there for a long time.

"Funny-looking place. Doggone if everything in it isn't undersized."

"Yeh. They've even got bantam chickens."

"It's the darnedest-looking thing!"

"It's one of the things we'll have to clear out."

"Why?"

"Eyesore. Look, Drake. Stop a minute. Now see—suppose we can develop this proposition the way we want to. All along up there a row of fine houses— right up there on the hill facing out this way—lawns running right down there to the creek."

"Yes."

"Well, don't you see they'd look directly down on Jinktown."

"Don't see anything wrong with it. It's kind of pretty from a little distance."

"All these foreigners, and white trash, and niggers beginning to move in, too!"

"Yeh, I guess I get your point."

"What I'd like to see is this—"

Peyton flung his leg over the side of the buggy seat and pointed to the big square of land bounded by the unused road on two sides and by the county road on the other two. Half of it was meadow with fine trees, the other half was a cornfield.

"See that piece of land?"

"Yeh."

"B'longs to old Mis' Macintosh. She'd sell it cheap."

"What'd you want to do with it?"

"Park!"

"Park?"

"Yes, siree."

"Kings Row's going to keep growing. You watch. Everybody says we're in for boom times. If we could get this for a little city park it would increase the value of that whole row of lots up there on the hill."

"Ye-es. I guess so." Drake was doubtful.

"Of course it would. Bound to. We'd sell to the toniest crowd in Kings Row. They'd be guaranteed a good outlook forever. Remember how the stocking mill just spoiled all those places Mr. Searcy built up there at the end of Porter Street?"

"That's so."

"Now, that's the point. I believe we could get the city to buy this. Sansome's bullheaded because he hasn't got any interests out this way, but I believe we

could put Doc Church and Arch Miller on city council. We could swing it
then against Sansome's opposition."

"What would they get out of it?"

"Miller Construction Company would get to make any improvements,
and Doc Church owns down there on the other side of the road—south. That
would bring his property up."

"How you going to get rid of Jinktown?"

"Get the city to condemn the property. Buy 'em out cheap and clean it out
altogether."

"Gosh—"

"You know I'm trying to work this out myself, but I've had to get Bill Elliot
in the office to help me. He'll keep his mouth shut. Of course Mr. Breakstone
knows about it, but he's getting kind of old and he just says go ahead and see
what I can do about it."

"Did you talk to Mr. St. George?"

Peyton hesitated. "Yes. He's interested. But we've got to get going on it or
someday somebody'll have the same idea, somebody with a little cash could
step in ahead of us."

"Yeh. Of course, that's so."

"When do you get your money, Drake?"

"I'm twenty-one first week in October—the third. It's all turned over to me
without any strings to it."

"What's your money in?"

"*In?* What do you mean? It's in the bank."

Peyton laughed. "Is it stocks, or bonds, or what?"

"Oh! It's all in United States government bonds. That's what Uncle Rhodes
told me, and Mr. Curley explained that's why I got such a low rate of interest."

Peyton whistled.

"Government bonds! Drake—if I get this thing worked out and you can
put up some money we'll be rich."

"You think so?"

"I don't believe we could fail. It's the biggest deal anybody ever tried to put
over in Kings Row real estate."

"You think we could do it ourselves?"

"It's money that talks, Drake. You've got the money. It's ideas can put it
through. I've got the ideas."

"It just worries me where you're going to find that many people with
enough money to buy property like this will be."

"Don't you worry. It's just like something I read a while back on success.
You got to have imagination, and that appeals to the imagination of others—of
other people. You get things going that way."

Drake looked speculatively at Peyton. He was uncertain whether he should
respect all of this new enterprise in Peyton, or put most of it down to Peyton's

own enthusiasm. But Peyton evidently had courage. He had gone ahead and married his schoolteacher sweetheart on faith, and had set up housekeeping on Pine Street in what the *Gazette* called "a beautiful new residence with all modern equipment." Peyton had explained that he hadn't been able to pay much down on it, but it made a good impression everywhere. Even those who knew that the Burton County Bank put up the money decided that young Graves must be good stuff if the bank believed in him.

"Well, what do you think, Drake?"

"It sounds fine, of course, Peyton. But I guess I want some advice from somewhere before I put up all I got."

Peyton looked disappointed. "But it was your idea in the first place, Drake. I'm just handing your own arguments back to you."

"Yes. I know, Peyton, but the way you say it, it sounds like getting in mighty deep."

"You can't lose, Drake."

"Maybe you couldn't, but I could. I'm an unlucky kind—"

"Rats! You're not."

"Well, I'm going to think about it, Peyton. Say, I forgot to ask you—how's your—how's Mrs. Graves?"

Peyton frowned. "Patty's not very well, Drake. She's been going to see Dr. Gordon."

"Gee, is that so? I'm sorry."

"She—she's got some kind of—of female trouble."

"Aw—that's too bad! Well, I hope she'll be all right pretty soon."

"Come around and have supper with us, Drake. Whenever you feel like it—just let me know ahead. Patty's kind of nervous and company gets her all het up. She goes to a lot of trouble to have everything just so."

Drake nodded. He decided that supper with Patty "all het up" about it would be too uncomfortable an undertaking. He had seen Mrs. Graves once or twice since the marriage in June, and he was sure that he wouldn't get on very well with her. She was thin, and stiff and severe. She gave Drake the impression of being starched to the bone. He had talked about her to Randy. "A regular bean pole. She looks like somebody's old-maid aunt."

"What you reckon made Peyton marry her?"

"Randy, I've asked that question a hundred times. I'd just as soon get into bed with a stepladder."

7

Drake walked across the lawn and stopped to straighten a row of sea shells that bordered a rectangular flower bed near the drive. It had been his Aunt Mamie's favorite spot. All of her pet plants flourished here. It was looking a little withered just now, but of course it was late September. He'd get the place fixed up—have the house painted and the low picket fence taken down. There were really many repairs to be made. He noticed that the roof leaked just over Uncle Rhodes' room. Place really looked seedy. Well, in a short time now he'd have his own say-so. No wonder the house didn't rent. He had never looked at it closely before. It was dilapidated, that's what it was—downright dilapidated.

The lawn was as pretty as any on Union Street. Needed reseeding, though.

He heard the telephone ringing. He went slowly and indifferently toward the house. It was Mr. Wakefield, Jamie's father, calling.

"Hello, that you, Drake?"

"Yes, sir."

"Could you come down here for a few minutes?"

"Why, certainly."

"Nothing important. Just want to see you for a second."

"Be right down, sir."

Half an hour later he faced Mr. Wakefield at the cashier's window.

"Oh, good morning, Drake. Step around to the side there—or, better still, come on in."

Drake passed the three windows on the side.

"Hi, Jamie!"

Jamie looked up and blinked as if he found it difficult to see against the light. "Hi, Drake."

Mr. Wakefield came back and unlocked the heavy oak door.

"Come in, come in. How are you this morning?"

"Fine, Mr. Wakefield."

"I just wanted to speak to you a minute about your account."

"Yes, sir."

"It's overdrawn a little, you know."

"Overdrawn?"

"Yes. Let me see, I think about eighty dollars, or so, nothing to speak of."

"But it ought not to be overdrawn."

Mr. Wakefield smiled. "Do you keep your checkbook in order?"

Drake grinned. "Sometimes I forget."

"Well, I guess that's it."

"But—could I speak to Mr. Curley?"

"Mr. Curley's in Texas. Went down on business. I expect him back next week."

"But I thought I had more'n a thousand dollars in my account!" Mr. Wakefield stared a little.

"How could you be that far off?"

"I'm sure I'm not."

Mr. Wakefield smiled again. "Now, Drake—"

"No. Sure enough, Mr. Wakefield. I haven't been spending any money—not much. And on the first of July there must have been about a thousand dollars put in."

"Well—was there?"

"I declare, Mr. Wakefield, I didn't look at my bank statement. I just kind of kept it in my head."

Mr. Wakefield motioned to a chair. "Sit down." Then he called Jamie.

"Yes, sir."

"Son, get Drake's account, will you? See when his regular July deposit was made."

Mr. Wakefield leaned back in his chair.

"Nice weather we're having now."

"Yes, sir. It'll be fine from now on."

"A very pleasant season. We don't get to see much of the seasons down here, though. We're not as lucky as you are, Drake."

"Well, sir, I'm anxious to be getting at something. I'm twenty-one next week, you know."

"That's so, isn't it? Well, you'll have to learn to keep a sharp eye on your property then, my boy, when you won't have Mr. Curley to do it for you."

"I suppose I'll learn when I know I have to do it."

"I'm sure you will, Drake, I'm sure you will. Your Uncle Rhodes had a level head on his shoulders. Well, Jamie?"

"The deposit wasn't made, sir."

Mr. Wakefield frowned. "Wasn't made? What do you mean?"

"The last deposit was made April the second."

"Are you sure?"

"Yes, sir, of course."

"Well, well. I see. Drake, I guess Mr. Curley just overlooked it. But he's usually very punctilious, very punctilious, indeed."

"What about my account? You said it was overdrawn?"

"Well, we'll fix that up. It's just a matter of a few days. I can arrange that myself. You won't require the whole amount, of course?"

"No, certainly not."

"Mr. Curley ought to be back on Tuesday."

"All right, sir. 'By, Jamie."

"'By, Drake."

Mr. Wakefield watched Drake as he left. "That's curious, isn't it? Curley's always clipped coupons the day they fell due."

"Papa!"

"Yes, son."

"Mr. Curley hasn't put any coupons through since last year—I mean, on Drake's account."

Mr. Wakefield was walking away. He stopped and turned halfway, speaking over his shoulder.

"What was that, Jamie?"

Jamie repeated his statement.

"Rubbish, Jamie!"

"No, sir. I know. Mr. Davis and I spoke of it once or twice. He put in Drake's money with his personal check. Then he transferred the allowance to Drake's checking account. Usually he checked the remainder back to himself."

"For reinvestment."

"I suppose so."

"The bonds are in Mr. Curley's own box still, I suppose?"

"I don't know."

"He always kept the estate papers in his box with his own stuff. Well—we'll have to wait until he comes back."

On the way back to his own window, Mr. Wakefield stopped to speak to Percy Davis. They chatted for a moment.

"Mr. Wakefield, I don't think Drake's stuff is in government bonds anymore."

"Why, what do you mean?"

"Mr. Curley spoke of them last winter when he went to New York. He said something about selling them and putting the money in something that would give Drake a little bigger income."

"You don't know if he did that, or not?"

"No, sir. But I happen to know that he did take the bonds to New York. It was just an accident that I knew it—I went in to his office to ask him something, and I saw the packages in his leather case."

"I see. Well, well."

"And then, as Jamie told you, no more coupons went through here."

"Um." Mr. Wakefield grunted noncommittally, but there was a slightly troubled look in his eye. Mr. Curley was a reticent man, but he usually discussed such matters with someone. Mr. Wakefield tried to recall the terms of Rhodes Livingstone's will, but he was pretty sure that Curley had an absolute freedom in managing the estate. Still, knowing how extremely conservative Mr. Livingstone had been, it would have seemed more than likely that Curley would continue the same policy with the estate.

All through the morning Mr. Wakefield was somewhat distrait. He always walked home to midday dinner, leaving the bank exactly at half-past twelve. Today he left fifteen minutes earlier.

"See you at home, Jamie. If I'm late, tell Mama I went on a little errand."

"Yes, sir."

Mr. Wakefield hurried his usual deliberate step. He went up Walnut Street, and then hesitated at the gate of the Curley house. He looked at the neatly clipped grass, a little yellow now, and the gay rows of late flowers along the red-brick walk that led to the deep shaded porch. Yes, he'd better step in and inquire.

A Negro maid answered his ring.

"I want to speak to Mrs. Curley, please, Mary, if she's at leisure."

"Yes, suh, will you just step into the parlor?"

"Tell Mrs. Curley it's nothing important if it's inconvenient for her to come down."

"Oh, she's dressed all right, suh. She be right down, Mr. Wakefield."

Mrs. Curley came downstairs immediately. She was a shy, anxious-looking woman. Her face was much wrinkled as if from some inner collapse. All of her features seemed to go inward. But, ever so slightly, she gave the impression of dignity—unassertive, but nevertheless a fine, personal dignity.

"Good morning, Mr. Wakefield. This is a pleasant surprise."

"Thank you, ma'am. Glad to see you. You're looking well. Just passing on my way to dinner. Thought I'd stop to pass the time of day."

"Sit down. Won't you stay to dinner here?"

"Oh, no, ma'am. I'm expected at home. What do you hear from Mr. Curley?"

"From Mr. Curley?" She looked a little startled.

"Yes. What does he say?"

A somewhat blank look succeeded the surprise on her face. "Why, I haven't heard from Mr. Curley at all."

"You haven't?"

"No, Mr. Wakefield. I was just going to call the bank to see what you've heard."

"We haven't had a word from him." Mr. Wakefield spoke bluntly, and the words brought back Mrs. Curley's startled look.

"He—he said when he left that he'd be very busy and that I'd have news through the bank. He doesn't like to write letters."

"We haven't heard from him." This time Mr. Wakefield's tone was colorless and flat. He continued to look searchingly at Mrs. Curley. He realized that he was disturbing her.

"What is it, Mr. Wakefield? You haven't heard any bad news, have you?"

Mr. Wakefield arose briskly. "Why, no, no, indeed, ma'am. I just happened to be passing. When you hear from Mr. Curley let us know, will you? I expect we'll hear from him ourselves—probably today. His business down there must have taken longer than he expected."

Mrs. Curley fingered the gold-and-black-enamel locket she wore on a heavy chain. "Let me know the minute you hear. I do hope he isn't sick, or something."

"Don't worry, ma'am. We'd have heard in that case."

Mr. Wakefield ate his dinner in silence. He did not hear Mrs. Wakefield's questions or comments. After a while she subsided into a hurt silence and cast appealing looks at Jamie. But Jamie was being inattentive, too. He leaned low over his plate and ate slowly.

"Sit up, Jamie. What are you stooping so for?"

"Gee, I can't see what I'm eating unless I lean over."

"Can't see? Why, you need glasses. That's what's the matter. Herbert, I'm sure Jamie works in a bad light."

Mr. Wakefield looked vague. "What's that?"

"Jamie's eyes! I think he ought to go over to Linden's jewelry store and have Mr. Linden see if he doesn't need glasses."

"He can go any time he wants to. Just go."

"Aw, Mama. I wouldn't want to wear glasses!"

"You do what I say. You wouldn't want to go blind, either, would you?"

"I'm not—"

"Everybody in the bank wears glasses. It's hard on your eyes—that kind of work. And you're always reading and writing, too, at night."

Jamie sighed. "All right, I'll go."

"Well, that's a good boy. You have to take care of your precious eyes, son."

Mr. Wakefield and Jamie walked back to the bank in complete silence. Jamie was grateful for any respite from his father's didactic and platitudinous talk about business and banking, the responsibility of the banker to the community and the excellence of honesty as a policy.

When they reached the bank Jamie resumed the mechanical pursuit of his daily grind. His eyes were really uncomfortable. He faced a strong light from the south—he supposed his mother was right about it, she usually was right. He'd have to wear glasses just as everybody else in the bank did. Doubtless he'd grow more and more like everybody else in the bank until he was exactly like them. He groaned.

Mr. Wakefield waited on several customers. Then he called Percy Davis. Davis was a round-faced elderly man who had been in the Farmers Exchange for many years.

"Yes, sir, Mr. Wakefield."

"Come on back to the vault with me, Percy."

"Yes, sir."

They entered the vault.

"Which is Mr. Curley's box?"

"Right up there, Mr. Wakefield, that brown one."

"Has he another?"

"No, sir. He keeps all of his personal papers in there, and the three—no, four estates he's executor and trustee for."

"I see. Hand it down here to me a minute."

Davis looked his surprise. "Mr. Curley's box, sir?"

"Yes, get it down."

Davis mounted the little two-step ladder used for reaching the higher shelves and safety-deposit boxes.

"Here you are, Mr. Wakefield—why—why—"

"What, man? What's the matter?"

"Why, it seems very light!"

Mr. Wakefield took the box and hefted it.

"It's empty."

Davis stared, his little button mouth making a perfect O.

Mr. Wakefield spoke casually.

"Transferred everything to a safety-deposit box, I suppose."

"No, siree, Mr. Wakefield. Mr. Curley hasn't got a safety-deposit box—not in this bank."

"He might have made use of one without mentioning it—before he went away. Look at the record."

Davis hurried away, panting. He was back in two minutes.

"No, sir."

"All right, put the box back in place."

"Yes, sir. What do you suppose—?"

"Keep your mouth shut. We'll have to find out why he transferred his papers, and where."

"Mr. Wakefield!"

"Yes."

"Is Mr. Curley seeing about that land in Texas he's been talking about buying for Breakstone?"

"Yes." Then he added, "I hope so."

Davis paled slightly, and looked more like a scared hen than ever.

"Why—why, what do you mean, Mr. Wakefield?" Percy Davis was no fool, even if he was acting like one. He had long since followed Mr. Wakefield's growing fear, but he didn't wish to countenance it. He'd have to hear the words pronounced by someone else before he'd so much as admit the existence of the thought.

"Percy."

"Yes, sir. Yes, sir."

"There's no use you and me trying to fool each other. We've got to face this in a few hours, anyhow. Might as well be now."

Percy sat down on the low ladder.

"Yes, sir. I guess so."

"Well. Unless I'm mightily mistaken the president of the Farmers Exchange has skipped out—probably with everything he could lay his hands on!"

"My God! *Mister* Curley!" Davis spoke the name with a kind of utter incredulity.

"Yes. *Mister* Curley!" Wakefield repeated the emphasis with a scornful intensity. "Percy, I'm going over to the telegraph office. I'll have the bank examiner here tomorrow—and—I'll try to see if I can find out where Curley is. He was to see Major Pomfret at Dallas first, and after that he was to go on to Brownsville."

"Right at the border, Brownsville, isn't it?"

Mr. Wakefield looked steadily at Davis. "Yes; right at the Mexican border— if he went that way."

Telegraph messages confirmed Mr. Wakefield's fears. Mr. Curley had not been to Dallas. Major Pomfret had had no word of his coming. He was not in Brownsville, and had not been there, so far as the bank officials there knew.

Mr. Wakefield conferred with Breakstone of the Breakstone and Clinton office. They had authorized Curley to draw on their account in St. Louis. It would be impossible to find out before morning if he had done so.

After supper Mr. Wakefield called on Colonel Skeffington.

"What in hell's up? You look like a scarecrow."

"Feel like one. Something serious, Colonel."

"Come in, come in. Come on back here to my den … sit down. Have a cigar?"

"No, thanks, Colonel. I've come down here to talk to you in someone else's behalf. Maybe you won't want to make it your business, but I wish you would."

"Whose behalf, Ben?"

"Drake McHugh."

"What's that young hellion done now?"

"Nothing. Curley was executor and trustee of Drake's money."

"*Was*? Still is, isn't he?"

"Curley's cleared out with all Drake's estate, and everything else he could lay his hands on. Don't know how much yet."

"Well, I'll be damned!" Colonel Skeffington lit a cigar. "Ben!"

"Yes, Colonel."

"I'm not as surprised as I suppose I ought to be."

"Why not? I thought Curley—"

"Remember we used to go hunting together—all of us?"

"Yes, of course. What's that got to do with—this?"

"Recollect the damned low-life used to shoot birds on the ground?"

Mr. Wakefield nodded gloomily.

"Fact!" Skeffington continued. "Not that alone, though of course I remember it—couldn't forget it—but I never did trust Curley."

"Everybody else did. I did, myself."

"I know. I know. Honest up to now, very likely. But that kind of damned hypocrite will do something like this first good chance he gets. Yes, sir. Every time."

Mr. Wakefield nodded again. Now that Colonel Skeffington said it so bluntly, he began to feel that he hadn't trusted Curley, either. Certainly he had never liked him.

"How hard is the bank hit, Ben?"

"Can't tell fully until tomorrow. It may be that he's just done away with private trusts. If that's so, the Federal government won't be after him."

"Drake McHugh's money! Who else?"

"Mrs. Pettigrew, the Hammond twins—they didn't have much—and old Mrs. Thiemann."

"All private trusts?"

"Every one. He had authorization to buy up some mortgaged property in Texas for Breakstone. He was to draw on their account."

"Suppose he did?"

"We'll know by morning."

"What you want me to do?"

"Look after young McHugh's interests—if there is anything to be done at all. He's got nobody—and no money at all."

"All gone?"

"Every red cent. Curley switched government bonds, or sold 'em, as far as I can find out. Paid Drake's allowance out of his own account. Drake's overdrawn. I let him have a hundred dollars this morning. He owes us that, now. That's how I happened to get on to this."

"How long has Curley been gone?"

"Ten days."

"He's in Central America by now."

"Mrs. Curley hasn't had a word from him."

"Does she know?"

"Not yet."

"He put that house up there in her name six months ago." Mr. Wakefield narrowed his eyes. "Then he was planning it that long ago."

"Was Curley in any kind of financial trouble?"

"No. Not that I know of, and I suppose I would have known."

"What you reckon's back of all this?"

"I don't know, Isaac, I don't know. I can't think."

"No woman you know of?"

"Couldn't have been. He's been too much out in the open every day—impossible."

"Well, I just wondered."

"So did I. There's no woman."

"People do this kind of thing sometimes. Get tired. Want to go somewhere. Want to be free, they think. Worn out with the monotony of their kind of life. God! Curley was always so damned pious and mealymouthed, it's a wonder we never kept an eye on him long ago."

"He was so active in the church." Mr. Wakefield seemed to protest. He wished so to find some argument that would prove the whole matter false.

Skeffington snickered.

"Yes, and he shot birds on the ground!"

"You see, Isaac, Drake McHugh's been a friend of my boy Jamie, and old Mr. Rhodes Livingstone was a lifelong friend of mine. I'd like something done for him. If he needs a lawyer when all this mess comes out, I'd like to feel you were there with him."

"He'll need a job more'n anything. Why don't you take him in the bank?"

"Drake McHugh? Oh, we couldn't do that, Colonel!"

Colonel Skeffington laughed shortly.

"No: I thought you wouldn't. All you damned bankers are alike. Not a teaspoonful of blood in all of you. I'll see what I can do for Drake. Does he know about this?"

"Not yet. Nobody knows. But tomorrow it'll have to break."

"Hope you can catch the skunk. I'd enjoy sending him to the pen."

"We'll try, Colonel, you can depend on that."

"Yes: and you can depend on never laying eyes on Jim Curley again! Mark my words."

"I hope you're wrong, Ike; but I'm afraid you're not."

8

The Farmers Exchange scandal was the prevailing sensation for a month. There were all sorts of stories and rumors. The bald fact remained: James Cuthbert Curley, president of the Farmers Exchange Bank, had stolen money and run away. Presumably he had gone to Central or South America. Efforts were being made to find him but no one was particularly hopeful of success. Certain bank funds were missing. Mrs. Curley turned over the house and other small properties. Stockholders would not lose anything, but the trust funds were gone. Nothing could be done about them. Drake McHugh was penniless. The house on Union Street was his, and Mr. Wakefield arranged a mortgage so that Drake would have some funds to live on for a while.

No one guessed how bewildered Drake was by this ill fortune. He had simply never thought about money at all. He sold his horse and buggy, and began to look for a job. No one wanted him.

Behind his back the talk went on. There were those who were not displeased to see Drake McHugh humbled a little. He had been altogether too carefree and happy to suit those who felt that life should not rest too easily on one. Maybe he'd stop flying around at night with all kinds of shady girls. He would see mighty quick how the Ross girls would have other fish to fry when he had to walk instead of ride. The Monaghan girl, too, would be showing him the front gate.

Kings Row watched. Like any pack of the wild they waited for the victim to falter. But they were at least temporarily disappointed. Drake looked as usual. He whistled as he walked. He was persistent in his search for work. He was offered a job at the livery stable, but he hadn't come to that yet. He stayed on at the house on Union Street. Only when he was inside of it with the doors closed did he show his deep disquiet. He sat sometimes for hours with his head in his hands trying to plan some way out. But everything required capital. He could sell the house, but it would be at a great sacrifice, and then—when that was spent, he would have nothing. His head ached with the unaccustomed effort. When he wearied of thinking, he went on wondering. What—what should he do? Where to begin? What was really going to become of him? He was troubled by sleeplessness. Sometimes he took a small glass of whisky to put himself off to sleep. He was a little jumpy. But, he thought, he'd find some way out.

He made Jamie and Randy promise not to let Parris know. No use troubling Parris. It never occurred to him that Parris had money and he didn't. It was simply that he didn't want Parris bothered about this. Then, of course, he'd get it all fixed up some way pretty soon. When that time came he'd write Parris all about it.

9

But Drake did not "fix things up." The winter passed, and he had no job. He tried for anything he thought he might be able to do. Everywhere the men he talked to were good-humored and jocular—sometimes a shade contemptuous. By spring he was becoming sensitive. He avoided mention of a job unless he was actually making application. He was casual on the outside but watchful and attentive inside. He immediately followed any suggestion he heard of a possible job.

Then he began to pretend he wasn't looking for work.

He left the boardinghouse and cooked his own meals. At first he made a frightful mess of it, but later he improved. When Randy found out about it she came sometimes late in the evening and helped him. She put the rooms in order and taught him something about helping himself. By the end of the summer his cash was running alarmingly low. He supposed he'd have to give a second mortgage on the house. But he wouldn't be able to raise much. He was still afraid to sell.

Now he did his own washing, and dried the clothes in the kitchen so no one would know.

People said Drake McHugh was drinking.

"Yes, sir, I saw him staggering out of Fritz Bachman's lunchroom just last Saturday. Drunk as a fool."

Fritz Bachman's lunchroom, which was patronized by railroad men, was also a convenient "blind tiger."

The temperance organizations had won the local liquor fight and had closed the saloons. The general drinking population—and that was considerable—took to the "blind tigers." The better class of consumers made their purchases through the drugstores. The ladies of the various societies were complacent. They had won a moral victory and cleaned up the town. It was safe for young people, now, they said.

Dodd McLean, who had opened a small grocery store back of the asylum, thrived and prospered beyond the dreams of any small grocer. Dodd was a regular caller now on Ludie Sims. Dodd's esthetic sensibilities were not disturbed by Ludie's horribly disfigured face. With a hat and heavy veil, Ludie still presented a trim and attractive appearance.

Somehow Drake found himself going rather often to Fritz Bachman's place. Sleep came with increasing difficulty. He had made it a habit to stop by the smelly little lunchroom when he left Randy's house at night. It was directly on the way home. He exchanged a few rough jokes with Fritz, gulped a glass of whisky, and went home. Randy knew nothing of this. Drake was always sober when she saw him.

There were others, however, who noticed the changes in Drake. Jamie Wakefield was one of them. Jamie, with his quick, dose observation, was probably one of the first to see the general slackening in Drake's whole make-up. His clothes were often unpressed. Sometimes he forgot to shave.

Jamie tried to be more friendly. He went to see Drake. He invited him repeatedly to supper, but Drake was shy of the homes where he used to be welcome. He was dogged these days by a horrid feeling that everyone knew of his difficulties. He avoided meeting older acquaintances and spent much of his time around the railway station, loafing and talking.

He came and went from home by the back way. He dreaded Union Street.

One day in a kind of desperation he went to see Peyton Graves. Peyton had a new office, better fitted up than any office in town. There was plain gray carpeting on the floor—an unheard-of innovation in a business office, and hangings at the windows. Mrs, Graves had attended to this.

Peyton leaned back in his chair. He did not rise or offer to shake hands.

Drake smiled at the surroundings. "Well, well! You look like a bank president in here, Peyton."

"Rather better than that, don't you think?"

"Well, maybe."

"What can I do for you, Drake?"

"Just dropped in to see how you're getting along, Peyte. Are you busy?"

"Pretty busy, Drake, just now."

"Well, I'll come again."

"No, no. Sit down. What's up?"

"Nothing."

"You've had a lot of bad luck, haven't you?"

"Yeh. Pretty bad. I'll get things straightened out, though. How's your big proposition coming on?"

"You mean the West End Crescent?"

"Is that what you call it?"

"Yes. Well, pretty fine, Drake. I finally got Macmillan St. George interested, and he talked old Thurston into it. They are going to let me put it through. Takes money, though."

"Yeh, I guess so."

"Thurston St. George thinks I ought to build out there myself and make one bang-up place just to show how it would look."

"That would be pretty expensive, wouldn't it?"

"Well, between you and me, Drake, they'd have to put up the money to further their own investment. But I'd live in it, and it would look pretty prosperous. Good idea, what do you think?"

"Sounds fine."

"Patricia is crazy for me to do it. She can't think of anything else. She spends all her time reading these women's magazines on how to fix up houses. She's got wonderful taste. She says, too, if we led the way with the finest house in Kings Row, it would be the best thing we could do for business."

"I see. Sounds right smart, Peyte."

"Yes. She's smart as a whip. Patty's all right. But gosh—" Peyton laughed. "You know, Drake, I just don't know myself at home! Everything so spick and fine I can't put down a paper or anything but she's right on me about it. She fixed up a den for me so I've got a place to lounge and smoke in. Cute as you please."

"I bet." Drake was thinking at that moment of the state of his own rooms. "Yeh. I bet."

Peyton sighed and moved some papers suggestively. "Too bad you lost your money, Drake. That would have been a fine proposition for you and me."

"Well, I was just going to ask you, Peyton, if you don't need some help."

"Help? What kind of help?"

"I mean—me. Couldn't you use me some way? You know we had that idea a long time ago. Maybe I could be of some kind of help."

Peyton flushed. "Gosh, Drake. I haven't got a thing for you to do. You know, of course, this thing's just getting going. I'm working altogether with other people's money—for the time being. La'er—maybe."

"Well, I just thought—"

"I'm awfully sorry, Drake. Wish I did have something."

"So long, Peyte. Good luck."

"Thanks, Drake."

Peyton scratched his head. "Gosh," he said, "my good gosh."

He settled back to his papers and worked for an hour steadily. He tousled his hair and hitched himself about in his chair. He'd have to watch out—Patty was spending too much on the house, particularly if they were going to have to fit up another one right away out on the Crescent. He'd have to talk to her about it. She was so touchy, though, ever since she'd had that operation. He scratched his head again. If she had some kids, she'd feel different about her house. He had to admit that the house was pretty—prettier than any house he'd ever seen in his life, but it wasn't very homelike. Patty made him come around to the side entrance and change to house shoes when he came in so no dust could be tracked over the rugs. He didn't like that much. He didn't feel very manly not using his own front door. But Patty was kind of peculiar. Maybe it was just because she was older than he that she made him feel— doggone it, she *did* make him feel as if she were the boss.

The door opened and Macmillan St. George came in.

"Howdy, Graves."

Peyton arose. "Howdy do, Mr. St. George."

Mr. St. George pulled a chair to one side so he wouldn't face the light. Peyton resumed his seat, rather nervously. Mr. St. George took a plug of tobacco from his pocket, slowly opened a large pocketknife, and cut a slice. He deliberately bit it into three or four pieces, stored it in one cheek where it bulged noticeably, and replaced the plug and knife in his pocket.

Peyton waited, slightly embarrassed.

"There's a meeting of the school board next week, Graves."

"Yes, sir, I know."

"Glad to see some new blood in there."

Peyton made a deprecating gesture.

"Eh. Needed some young men on the board," Mr. St. George continued.

"Well, I'm awful glad, sir—I—"

"Need some young men to help run the town. You'll do—better'n most."

"Thank you a lot, Mr. St. George. I hope I can be of some use to all of you."

"You can. Something I want you to attend to right away."

"Yes, sir."

"Do you know Melissa?"

"Melissa?" Peyton looked blank. "Melissa who?"

"She's the daughter of my housekeeper. Nigger gal—pretty near white."

Peyton tried to fight down the color in his face. He wished to heaven he didn't have this childish habit of blushing. He recalled Melissa now—the pretty little quadroon girl who used to play on Macmillan's front porch. Macmillan's own child.

"Well, she's been off to school. Nigger college. Fanny, that's her mother, wants her to teach school."

"Here—in Kings Row?"

"Yes, of course. Now, Mr. Ashby won't be back here until middle of August. You'll have to take over the applications, read 'em over, and make the recommendations of new teachers to the board. Just a formality. There's two vacancies in the white school. Ashby's already made recommendations. One vacancy in the nigger school—beginning grade—whatever they call it. Melissa'll make application for it. Give it to her."

"All right, Mr. St. George."

"I'll tell her to come up and see you. She can bring her certificate and stuff. Just a formality. Board'll elect her."

"Yes, sir."

"Thanks, Graves. Do something for you in return. Surveyors finished yet out on the creek?"

"Yes, sir. I'm working on the plots now."

"Fine. Good stuff, Graves. If you can hold on long enough, you'll make a pile of money out there."

"I hope so."

"You will. Good day."

Peyton returned to his figures and plans after Macmillan St. George left. He was tired. After a while he pushed the papers together and bundled them into a table drawer. He went to the window and looked out. The courthouse square was almost deserted, but there was, despite the "slack" season and the sleepy hour of the day, a somewhat livelier look about the few people who were passing than—Peyton felt for an expression—a livelier look than the same people had a year ago. Doubtless, he thought, it was only his imagination, but, nevertheless, everyone was saying these days that Kings Row was waking up.

Some people gave Hart Sansome the credit. Sansome had been mayor of Kings Row for a number of years. He was generally popular, and since he was a rich man with an interest in most of Kings Row's enterprises, it was felt that what he had to say had genuine weight and value. Certainly, Hart Sansome had worked day and night for the town. He had been directly responsible for some new projects, and powerfully instrumental in reviving and promoting old ones. A real mayor for an up-and-coming town. Near-by towns spoke of Kings Row with increasing respect.

Most of the ragged old shade trees had been cut from the business streets. That showed up the store fronts, and everybody had been obliged to repair and repaint. There were more and more plate-glass show windows on the Union Street block. Thurston St. George had refused to have the trees cut in front of his old general store in spite of the city council, and no one had pressed the matter too vigorously. Mr. St. George liked to sit out on the sidewalk on summer days chatting with his old friends. A few farmers hitched their wagons to these remaining trees around the St. George store, ignoring the big free hitching lot around the Culbertson blacksmith shop.

But taken altogether—Peyton leaned forward to look up and down the street again—there was great general improvement. Kings Row was beginning to look more and more like a town and less like a country village. All of these changes were pushing real-estate values. Things were moving, no doubt about it. He reflected that whatever changes went into effect in Kings Row were directly beneficial to those who helped most to bring them about. There was Mr. Breakstone, for example. He'd made a pile of money in the building and loan. Before he organized the association he had bought up the whole tract north of the asylum. It was the logical place for a medium-priced development, and the lots went like hot cakes. Now Mr. Breakstone was ready to quit and enjoy himself. Went to Florida last winter, and was off somewhere in Canada right now.

Peyton felt his chest swell with enthusiasm. He was the very one, placed as he now was, to step into Mr. Breakstone's shoes. And it wouldn't be long before those shoes would be empty, either. He'd have to be ready. He'd been lucky past all dreaming hopes in getting the St. Georges to back him. Of course, if he didn't swing everything just right, it would all fall right back in the St. Georges' laps—improvements and all. He had already heard that people were saying the St. George brothers were just using him to work up a big job for them, and that he'd be left out in the cold. That was pure nonsense. The St. Georges were honest beyond any suspicion. All that talk sprang from envy. It would probably be worse when he built that big house out on the Crescent. He turned to get out the plans and look at them once more, but he changed his mind. He knew those plans by heart. He'd gone over them a hundred times with Patty.

He thought with elation of Macmillan St. George's visit this afternoon. It was the first time either of the St. Georges had asked him a favor. He was pleased as could be. He was sure Patty would be tickled when she heard about it. All of those things helped. The older generation who had been in control of Kings Row were dying out. Pretty soon there wouldn't be any of them left. Then the town would belong to *his* crowd. He must be ready to do his part. It had to be a big part—somewhat for Patty's sake, but also for his own. He would be a rich man. After all, the St. Georges made their money here. Those estates would scatter after a while. Macmillan's money, he guessed, would go to Thurston's daughter Hester. Funny about old Thurston marrying as late in life as he did … married a young wife and outlived her. All of that money, and there'd be a lot of it, would go to Hester St. George. Hester must be—yes, she was two years older than he was, but still younger than Patty. A thought crossed his mind—he blocked it loyally. The St. Georges took themselves pretty seriously. Doubtless Hester would marry some "big bug" from St. Louis or Chicago. Well, anyway—he'd make his by himself. He'd plan and watch and look out for every opportunity. People seemed to like him well enough.

That almost surprised him. He had never been noticed much, but since he married—and he had remembered that Patterson Lawes and such people spoke of Patty as "a good sensible girl"—and since he'd been in Breakstone's firm, everyone was cordial. Older men asked for his opinions and listened. Of course he wasn't the kind of rough-and-ready mixer that Fulmer Green had come to be, but he wasn't sure he wanted to be. Fulmer was pretty low-down in a lot of ways. He had taken Fulmer to the house once for supper, and Patty had been pretty chilly. Patty was so doggoned refined that—he tried to block that thought, too, but it came through: he wished Patty would be more cordial to people no matter what their manners were like. Still, maybe she'd give such a high-toned air to the new place out there that he'd be right in with the Sansomes and—he nearly said Curleys, when he remembered that there weren't any Curleys now. Mrs. Curley had gone back to Kentucky to relatives, quite crushed, everybody said.

Kings Row had been badly shaken by old Mr. Curley's runaway. Stealing other people's money, too. Jiminy! He'd never have thought that of Mr. Curley. Hard on Drake McHugh, that mess. Good thing for *him*, though, that he didn't get too much tied up with Drake before it happened. He'd have had Drake on his hands then. But he was sorry for Drake. Gosh—Drake McHugh asking *him* for a job! Things certainly could change fast. A person just had to watch out and see that when the changes came you were on the upgo, instead of the other way. He wished he'd been able to help Drake, but he couldn't. Even if he tried, Patty would be pretty sure to disapprove of it. He always talked everything over with her. She had mighty sound judgment—mighty sound. He guessed he was pretty lucky to have married a girl with sense instead—the word "attractive" hung for a moment and was brushed aside— instead of a flighty somebody who didn't think about anything but clothes and gadding about. A small annoying reservation persisted—an obstinate objection from somewhere: he couldn't define it clearly. But he recalled in this connection that he used to look at Poppy Ross with a good deal of interest— of course, that was before she got a bad name, and before her father just let her run loose. She had been such a warm little—little armful, he thought guiltily. The Rosses had been respectable enough until all that began. Then Drake McHugh ... a stinging small thrust of envy jabbed him ... girls always went overboard for Drake McHugh. Drake McHugh and Poppy Ross: the disturbing pictures of his imagination brought out a shine of perspiration on his face. Good heavens—he couldn't think of things like that: he was married to Patty! Patty was a lady and hated coarseness and sensuality. She had had a good deal to say about men's "lower nature." Sometimes he had been frightfully embarrassed and ashamed.

Peyton looked at his watch and snapped it shut. Five o'clock. He'd done enough for today. He looked around the room and picked up his hat. Then he put it down. He'd forgotten about Melissa. Didn't Macmillan say she'd be around this afternoon? She'd better hurry up. He wasn't going to wait longer for a nigger, that was certain. He drummed impatiently on the table, and his thoughts strayed back into the ways of his early afternoon dreaming. He forgot about Melissa after a while. He sat drawing interlacing circles on his desk pad. He was almost startled when a knock sounded.

"Come in."

The door opened slowly.

"Come," Peyton repeated.

The girl came in rather timidly.

"Are you Mr. Graves?"

"Yes."

"Well, I'm Melissa St. George."

Peyton was surprised to find that he was placing a chair for her. He swallowed once or twice. He had never thought about her last name. *St. George!* Just like that! But of course there were a lot of Negroes named St. George.

"All right, Melissa, all right. Sit down."

"Thank you, sir."

Her voice was low-pitched but distinct. It was—well, he thought a bit breathlessly, it was a well-bred-sounding voice. He supposed they taught them things like that at "nigger colleges."

He looked at her as she leafed through some papers in her purse.

Melissa St. George was almost white. Her skin was light olive and as smooth as satin. A warm red showed in her cheeks and in her full sensitive lips. Her hair, Peyton was quick to note, was a white person's hair, black and glossy, but soft and flowing. Her eyebrows made a sharp arch, almost Gothic, over her large, slow-moving eyes. She wore a white organdy dress and no jewelry. My good God a-mighty, she's a beauty, he thought in astonishment. Looks more like Hester St. George than Hester does herself! He looked at her hands. They were slender, and perfectly kept. Melissa sat without the slightest shade of embarrassment, waiting.

"Well," Peyton smiled more warmly than he meant to when he spoke.

"I guess Mr. Macmillan St. George told you I want to teach in the public school?"

"Yes. He told me today."

"He said there was a vacancy in the first grade and that I should apply. He thought maybe you'd give it to me."

"There is a vacancy, yes." Peyton was observing her remarkably even teeth and her frank, engaging smile. She wasn't the least bit like a—he couldn't make himself say "nigger"—the word seemed to have not the remotest application to Melissa, daughter of Macmillan St. George.

"I brought you the letters of recommendation from my teachers."

"Where did you go to school?"

"I went to Emerson-Lee in Tennessee first."

"And then?"

"I went to Pragmore Institute for two years."

"Pragmore?"

"Yes, sir."

"In New York state?"

"Yes, sir."

"Is that so? But I thought Pragmore was—" he stopped, biting his words off short.

"You thought it was a *white* school. Is that what you were going to say?"

"Well—yes."

"It is, Mr. Graves, but they don't draw a line if—if you're a decent person. And presentable."

Peyton noted the word.

"Well, they certainly couldn't shut you out on that ground, could they?"

Instantly he regretted the familiarity, but Melissa showed no sign of recognizing it.

"It's a very good school. Didn't Mr. Macmillan say I went to school there?"

"No, he just—may I see your letters?"

She handed him the unfolded testimonials. Peyton glanced at them, and then held them lower, bracing his arms against the desk. He must be pretty tired, he thought; his fingers were trembling.

Melissa glanced around the office.

"My, but you've got the prettiest office I ever saw."

Peyton glanced at Melissa, and looked back quickly at the letters. "Yes, my wife fixed it up."

"Miss Patty?"

"Oh, do you know who my wife is?"

"Yes, sir. I used to know Miss Patty when I was a little girl. She was a grown-up young lady then. My aunt used to sew for her mother—and Miss Patty, too. I read it in the Kings Row paper when she was married."

Peyton didn't know what to say. The conversation with Melissa didn't seem to stay in the right track, somehow. He ignored the reference to his marriage.

"Mrs. Graves has very fine taste."

"She must have. This is very nice."

"Glad you like it, Melissa."

"Your flowers are dying, Mr. Graves. I'll put some water in the vase while you're reading the letters." She arose before he could say anything, and laid the flowers out on a newspaper. "Where do you get water?"

"Right in the next room."

She came back in a few minutes. "Got a knife or a pair of scissors, Mr. Graves? I'll cut the stems."

He pointed to a wire basket on the desk. "Scissors in there."

"That other room is prettier than this one, Mr. Graves. Do you stay down here?"

"No, no. It's just fixed up for a—resting place, and for lady clients."

"It's awful nice."

Melissa resumed her seat. Peyton laid the letters on the table. He kept thinking how little she had the air of an applicant. She was mighty sure of herself—just like all of the St. Georges. She sat there as if she were perfectly accustomed to getting what she asked for. Doubtless she did. Doubtless she always had. He had heard that Macmillan St. George gave her a good allowance. Peyton wondered why she wanted to teach school. The question was so strong in his mind that he asked it aloud before he knew it.

"Well, you see, Mr. Graves, my mother is here, and I've got to stay with her as long as she lives."

"I see."

"I've got to do something."

"Of course."

"I guess I wouldn't be obliged to. Mr. St. George gave me a good education, and I'm used to being around—white people. Maybe I might as well get used to being around my own people part of the time."

Peyton was embarrassed now. He wished she would go.

"Don't be bothered by the question, Mr. Graves. I've had to think all that out, and we—all of us—were taught a lot about our place in the world. I mean in school. I don't think I'll always stay this far south, though."

"I can understand that, of course."

She laughed. "I doubt that, Mr. Graves. I don't imagine you've ever thought of it."

"I'm thinking about it right now, Melissa."

"There are all kinds of troublesome sides to the question, Mr. Graves. We—people like me—are in a mighty peculiar situation."

"I suppose so."

"Neither white nor black."

"Oh, you're not—"

"Excuse me for interrupting you, but I—"

She waited a moment.

"What were you going to say, Melissa?"

"Well, since we've got to talking, we might as well go on. I'm not all white."

"I know."

"I mean I'm not all white in my feelings. I'm not all St. George, Mr. Graves."

Peyton batted his eyelids very fast. He didn't know at all what to make of this girl who talked as intelligently and as well as any white girl he knew.

"I'm not all St. George. I'm part Fanny Hanscomb, too. That's my mother. I guess I can feel a good deal like a St. George at times. I've always lived in the same house with Mr. Macmillan, you know, until now."

"Where are you now?"

"Mr. Macmillan gave Ma a house right next to the Colored Baptist church—over on Andrews Street."

"Oh, yes. I know the place."

"But, what I was going to say—more than half the time I feel like Ma does. But I'm not like her, even if she is half white. I've got my troubles, you see."

"Yes. Is that why you want to teach school?"

"No. I don't care about school. I'll probably hate it. Little colored children are not very nice. But I've got to do something. I can't go with white people—I don't suppose I want to, really. If I don't go among the colored people, they'd all be down on me. I thought the school—"

"You're right. That's a smart decision, Melissa."

Peyton settled back in his chair. "Now tell me—"

The talk went on. Peyton tried carefully to maintain the correct differences between them. But he was interested in spite of himself. He wasn't much given to consideration of purely human problems, but he was really a gentlehearted person. Once during the conversation he asked himself clearly if he would be as interested in talk of racial problems if Melissa were Daisy, his cook. But he realized that Daisy, of course, couldn't discuss such problems.

The shadows moved steadily across the square. It was Melissa who noticed the hour.

"Goodness, Mr. Graves, didn't that town clock strike seven?"

Peyton was startled. He glanced out of the window.

"Why, yes, it did."

She stood up and he handed her the letters.

"I didn't notice your certificates in there, Melissa. You took the teachers' examinations, didn't you?"

"Oh, yes. Yes, sir. I thought I had everything there."

"Well, I think I'll have to have them—see them, at least, just for purposes of record."

"Why, of course. I'll bring them in, or send them if you're too busy. Whichever you say."

He pursed his lips and looked away, then back again at the glowing face under the wide straw hat.

"Just bring them by sometime. I only need to see them—then you can take them on back with you."

"Shall I bring them—tomorrow?"

This time he looked very steadily into her eyes.

"Yes—tomorrow."

Melissa looked down at her purse. She turned her handkerchief tightly around her little finger.

"What time, Mr. Graves?"

"How about tomorrow afternoon—late?"

She waited a moment. Then she raised her eyes and looked back frankly. "All right, sir."

"Good afternoon, Melissa."

"Good-by, Mr. Graves."

He heard her go down the bare wooden stairs. He wiped his face, although a cool breeze floated through the open window. He thrust the chair back against the wall and locked his desk.

Dodd McLean was just getting into his delivery wagon as Melissa came out on the street. He gave her a broad wink, but she did not see it. Dodd grunted and looked after her. Then he glanced up at the gilt-lettered signs on the second-story offices. Peyton Graves was closing his window.

Dodd McLean whistled a long, low note of astonishment.

"Well, I'll be doggoned," he muttered. "Right in broad day-light. Ol' Peyte Graves! I wouldn't a-believed it if I hadn't a-seen it with my own eyes."

Peyton hurried home. Patty met him at the side door.

"You're pretty late, aren't you?"

"Yes—busy. Forgot the time."

"Change your shoes and come on in. Supper's waiting." Mrs. Graves looked cool and dry in a sheer blue dress with immaculate edgings of lace at the square-cut neck, and at the elbow-length sleeves. She made a slight grimace as she looked at Peyton. "You look hot, Peyton."

"Of course I'm hot. I hurried home as fast as I could come."

"Well, don't be cross, dear. Maybe you'd better freshen up and change to some white clothes before supper."

"I'm hungry, Patty."

"You'll enjoy your supper more if you're all clean and fresh."

Peyton stamped a little as he went to the bathroom.

Twenty minutes later he reappeared, hunching himself into a white linen coat.

"You know, Patty, I must be getting fat. This suit's tight."

Mrs. Graves arched her brows with a tolerant smile. "Why don't you finish dressing, dear, before you come out of your room?"

Peyton looked mystified. "I am dressed."

"You are now." She smiled as one smiles at a small child. "Come on in to supper."

"Gee, that's a pretty table, Patty!"

She nodded. "Isn't it?"

"What we got to eat? Aw—Patty!"

"What's the matter?"

"Is this all we got?"

"Why, yes, dear. What's the matter with it?"

"No meat?"

She shook her head playfully. "Not so good for you in hot weather, Peyton. I know what you ought to have."

"Well, I'm hungry. Aren't there any chops out there you could have Daisy fry up for me?"

"No, dear. Eat your supper. You'll like it, and you'll feel fine afterward."

He did feel pretty good after the fourth glass of iced tea. He absently scraped at the bottom of the tall glass with a spoon for the sugary residue until Patty took it away from him.

"Peyton, you're like a child."

"Eh? Oh—I always did go after the sugar that was left in my tea glass."

"Your mother spoiled you."

"I guess so. Gosh, she's a good cook!"

Patty arose. "Come on, Peyton. Let's sit on the porch."

He put his arm around her, but she somehow slipped out of the embrace.

10

Young Peyton Graves' new house was the subject of much discussion. Of course, everybody knew that the St. Georges were back of Graves, but it did show what an enterprising young man could do in Kings Row. There was a boy now came up from the river-bottom country. Family put him in Kings Row to go to school. Quiet, respectable farm people, everyone heard, though no one knew them. Seldom came to town. But Peyton was a good boy. Went to see them regularly once a month. Mrs. Graves was all right, too, it was decided. Nice, sensible woman, a little on the "persnickety" side, but a good wife for a young man starting up in the world. You could keep your eye on young Graves. He'd go pretty far—pretty far: you could bank on it.

The new house, now being built on the knoll just above the public school, was a new kind of house to Kings Row. Peyton Graves was going "whole hog" on it. Mrs. Graves used such unfamiliar terms as *master bedrooms, dressing rooms, sun parlor,* and *breakfast room.* Kings Row didn't quite know what to make of it, though most of the women read the same magazines Mrs. Graves read. They just somehow hadn't taken those new things too seriously, or literally. A good deal of all this writing in women's periodicals they regarded as a sort of semifiction. Everybody knew Patty, and where she came from, and how she had always lived at home. Therefore it was a little startling to hear her smooth and easy talk about the modern features of her new house as though they were simply a matter of course. *Dressing rooms!* One dressed in one's bedroom. And *breakfast room!* Well, Kings Row ate breakfast in the dining room—usually. Even the Sansomes were likely to have breakfast in the big, roomy kitchen on cold winter mornings.

Once Mrs. Pearson, who had as comfortable a house as you'd find anywhere around, reported that Patty Graves was talking about a *playroom*. But Mrs. Pearson was hard of hearing and was doubtless mistaken.

Secretly, all but the most fossilized of Kings Row housewives took a fresh look at their own homes. If possible, they made capital in their own minds of certain fine, solid features of the old orders of living. But in most places there was an uneasy and persistent feeling that things had been allowed to "rock along," and that no one had really noticed how old-fashioned they had become.

Mrs. Peyton Graves was swiftly becoming an arbiter in all matters of decoration and furnishing as well as in certain intellectual affairs. The old Century Club, made up mostly of wives of Aberdeen faculty members, had absorbed the earlier Browning Club, but still confined its studies and talks to the assured classics. Mrs. Graves organized the Contemporary Literature Club made up of younger women. The club met on Wednesdays at the astounding hour of eleven in the morning. Hitherto no woman of Kings Row would have dreamed of leaving her household before three in the afternoon. Mrs. Graves was establishing an easy leadership by the simple device of courageously doing the unheard of.

Peyton drove out to the Crescent every morning and every afternoon through the late summer and early fall to superintend the work. He was pushing construction rather anxiously. The place should be finished before the cold weather. Next spring he'd have everything looking shipshape and be able to start an intensive sales campaign. Also he was eager to have the actual building finished before Patty could think of anything new to add. The cost of the house had already exceeded his estimates because of alterations in the original plans.

The brilliant, heady October days filled him with a delight in living he had never known in his life before. The clatter and buzz of the carpentering was music to him. He looked at the rising house with amazement. Sometimes he was a little frightened, but the tremor passed quickly. Everybody was praising his business sense these days. Back of him stood the solid money of the St. Georges. He reassured himself and his chest rose, though he kept a modest bearing. No other young man of his age that he knew had a house like this, or even dreamed of one.

He walked slowly around the place, conferring gravely with Mr. Harry, the contracting carpenter. Peyton was pleased at the new deference older men were showing him.

He left the house presently, and strolled back to the long grassy slope. It would have to be seeded this fall. There weren't as many trees on this lot as on some others, but that would permit a finer lawn. He visualized the sweep of emerald from the brick terrace which would be built here, on down to the water's edge. The stony little creek wasn't much of a body of water, but—he snapped his fingers. Say! That was an idea, now! If they could get a dam built down below Aberdeen there'd be a long stretch here where—why, you could have little stone steps and canoes. He stood, staring, but he was not seeing the actual landscape: he was seeing something that looked like a stretch of the Thames which he had seen pictured in one of Patty's books on gardening. He snapped his fingers again, softly. The things a fellow might be able to do in this town if he had the vision and the nerve to go at it!

Hills and lowland, sky and stream, swam back into focus again. The leaves were just beginning to turn. Late this year. The Spanish nettle swept the wide tilted fields toward the west and southwest like a prairie fire. Their intense color fairly crackled against the vision. The buckeye trees were a roughish, rusty red, and the hickories were turning pure gold on the sunny side. The immense sky was as soft as May—just a slight shade of smokiness in its lucent blue proclaimed the season.

Peyton wasn't seeing this exactly as it was. The extravagant beauty of the day did not speak to him in terms of itself. He was transforming it, rearranging it, making it into a setting for another vision of his own. All of these untidy fields, and shaggy growths of shrubs and trees, were to be shaped into a well-parked order, the proper enhancement of fine houses, all shiny with fresh paint, and approached by winding, bordered walks. He sighed with impatience.

He walked down the slope and along the creek, absently slapping his trouser leg with a smooth switch he had picked up. At the curve of the creek he looked back. The frame of his new house stood out boldly against the sky. He had picked a perfect location for it. He surveyed the westward bend of the stream. It was rocky and irregular. Here and there were deep pools washed by spring freshets, crumbling banks, and long bars of sand and gravel all very rough and countrylike, but not impossible. A careful straightening of the channel, and ...

Peyton sighed again, and retraced his steps.

There was another person who stood looking at this same spectacle of October burning across the landscape. That was Father Donovan.

He, too, sighed.

The clatter of hammers and the rasp of saws made him hunch his shoulders. He glanced at the new Graves house and frowned. This was a favorite walk of his, through the scattered grove, down the hill and along the creek. He had read in the paper of the plans for "developing" the Crescent, but he had forgotten about it shortly afterward. He hadn't realized that it was going to spoil one of his pleasantest walks.

Well, well—he'd have to go farther out in the country now.

Father Donovan plunged down the hill, stumbling awkwardly from time to time as the buckberry bushes snared his feet. He hopped down the creek bank and began walking along the gravel beds, following the stream, crossing and recrossing the water again and again. He liked the hard going, the feel of stony gravel under foot, the whole sense of being upon his own way along an untrodden route. He stopped often to pick up flat stones worn to smooth contours by the passing of innumerable waters.

He knew very little of geology or mineralogy. Perhaps he should have some books on these subjects. He wasn't sure, though, that he wanted to be confused with irrelevant scientific information. Just the look of things was always sufficient to set his imagination going. Then he could seize upon the smallest of objects and see them as exponents of the mighty forces of the universe. This little stone—a humble witness of creation, a patient subject of all the titanic convulsions and catastrophes of the earth's making—shaped now to outlines of conformity. He would speak of this next Sunday. "Sermons in stones"—it pleased him mightily to think that it was so.

Father Donovan was changing in appearance. During the past few years he had read and studied much. He had made his long, lonely walks every day. He had thought, and pondered, mused and considered, to the very best of his mental powers. The result showed in his face. The bony foundation was more prominent: the features were thinned and chiseled now rather than molded. He was paler, too, and the look in his eyes was more faraway than ever. He had, altogether, the spiritualized appearance of a man who had been tried, though not beyond his basic powers of endurance.

Like many of his blood, he had a fondness—a weakness he admitted—for large, cosmic thinking. He liked to dwell on the ideas of the vastness of the universe, the infinity of space, the endlessness of time. Anything that had to do with incalculable numbers fascinated him. He was practical enough, he told himself, to indulge a little in such flights—to try his mental and spiritual wings in rarefied airs. It kept him from becoming prosaic and earthbound.

To watch the stars pour across a clear sky, to look at a field of swaying clover, to dwell upon the inexhaustible variety of snow crystals—these things and a kind of dreaming contemplation of them brought him to the verge of ecstasy. He felt that here was his field of growth. These were indeed the furnitures of God's great house.

Preaching to his little congregation, and visiting with them, did not bring him the satisfaction and the returns that he would have liked to know and feel. Preaching, he held, was a fine exercise of his office and a noble practice of the elements and faculties of priesthood, but the sound of it upon his own ears, and the reaction of it upon his own mind, was most of its reward. He knew that the attendance in his little church was halfhearted. It disturbed him somewhat, but he was learning to be patient. How long it took for the rocky upheaval of a mountain range to wear to rounded contour and the softness of soil where trees might grow!

He knew all of this, recognized the fact and the necessity, and was resigned to it. But, he could be sore at heart at the same time. It was the terrible loneliness that shook him so badly. Without the blessed out-of-doors, and his daily excursions into the comfort of half-thinking, half-feeling, he would have been a desolate man indeed.

Father Donovan was sure that he was learning a little. He had made some steps. He had made journeys of the mind, and achieved experiences of the heart which, he was sure, were valuable. He most earnestly wished to communicate them to someone capable of understanding them.

There had been a time not so long ago when he had felt that a man, even though he was a priest with all of the refuges and consolations of that hallowed privilege, must yet have human consideration. *Consideration*. Yes: he had thought a great deal about that at one time; and he had suffered much because of the lack of it. Now, it was something else. It was the need of communication. He was pressed with the need of saying to someone these things which had become the rarest treasures of his life. It was an ache within him.

He had walked today along his favorite way. Up the creek for a mile, then through the woods, and out where the hayfields and slanting meadows were ablaze now with late fall flowers. The Spanish nettle, rich gold of a lingering summer, was fading. The goldenrod plumes waved handsomely. The stately joe-pye held its rose-purple plumes high in every corner. Father Donovan stood leaning against an old rail fence. He plucked sprays of Indian paintbrush and stroked his fingers with the silky clusters. A breeze set the whole field of yellow blossoms to running madly. How gay they were! A world of little people in festival. Father Donovan wished he could raise his hands and give them a blessing.

They were happy and good—these flowers. And when you looked closely they were all different. Each one had its own face. He smiled down into the crowd of them about his knees. Some of them had a comic look, some were serious, but none of them was sad.

He raised his head, and shaded his eyes with his hand as he gazed for a long time at the roofs of Kings Row, just showing here and there through the trees. If one could see all of the people of the town gathered together like this they would look alike, too, just as the black-eyed nettle flowers did. But, like these wild-blooming things, they too were different when you looked close. Each one different—some gay, some thoughtful, but, alas! a great many of them sad.

He wished this were his country, his town, and all of these his people as countrysides and towns were the pastoral property of priests in European countries. So that he could know every one of them, share with them, and be father to them. He had seen French country priests go out to bless the fields and the crops, and down to the sea to bless the fishing boats. This seemed to Father Donovan both beautiful and proper. How warm he would feel if he were called on to bless this land about him!

He shook his head. It might be that this was the insidious tempter sowing unrest in his heart. It might be the terrible sin of ambition presented to him under this noble guise. He lowered his head and his lips moved. This was his place, this was his task, his privilege. One could not serve the many who could not serve the few. He must not fail the modest little place that was his own.

He raised his head, happy again. He hummed a phrase or two. The mellow October sun was kind and warm and comforting. The vast illimitable ocean of it pouring upon the earth—the very mercy of God visible to the eye.

Each year in this part of the country the January weather repeated a familiar cycle. Hard, bright cold after New Year. Then, in mid-month a few days—sometimes a week—of warm, springlike airs. Immediately afterward roaring winds came from the northwest whirling sleet and snow, and freezing the ground until it was hard as iron. Dark weather. It would continue so through February.

The usual week of soft, almost balmy days had passed. The sky was lead-colored and heavy. It was getting colder hour by hour.

Drake McHugh looked out of the window. The tall maples around the Presbyterian Church were whipping violently in the wind. He tilted the bottle of whisky he was holding and emptied it into a glass. He drank it quickly and shivered a little. He took his heaviest coat from the closet and fumbled for a red woolen muffler. It had fallen on the floor and it took him some time to find it. He closed the damper in the front of the stove with his foot, and looked around to see if he had forgotten anything. Maybe he'd better wear arctics ... he decided against them. Too difficult to fasten. Wouldn't be gone long, anyway. Needed some fresh air. Got heavyheaded lying around the house all day like this. He went out and slammed the door, neglecting to lock it. It was cold: cold as hell. He turned up the wide collar of his ulster and snuggled his head into it as deeply as he could.

Drake walked west on a narrow street that dodged in a zigzag way across town. He was walking straight into the wind. Better to face it going than coming. He'd have it behind him on his way home.

Not many people out today, he thought, as he went along the narrow flagstoned sidewalk. People who had any sense stuck close to their firesides. Took a fool to go out for a walk on a day like this. Had to get out, though. Couldn't stand another minute of that empty, dreary house.

He had had a letter from Parris that morning—a longish letter this time. Parris said he was terribly busy, working harder than ever, but now that his stay was certainly more than half over, he had begun to think about his return. He had hoped he could come back in the fall of this year, but it would likely take him another full year. He couldn't hope now to start back to America before September of 1902. He had been in correspondence with Dr. Nolan, the medical head of the state asylum, and that situation looked encouraging.

They couldn't of course commit themselves right now, but it was a reasonable expectation that they would add him to the staff as soon as he got back. Much of his work would be in hospital this coming year. How was everybody, and why didn't somebody write him all the news? Just notes from Jamie Wakefield and half yearly reports from Mr. Patterson Lawes, that was all he ever heard of Kings Row. Why didn't Drake write? What was he doing? Had he really ever started that real-estate venture? And how about Louise? Had Kings Row heard about Vera? Vera had come to Vienna, and played with the Royal Philharmonic. She'd made a real success. He had intended writing to tell Herr Professor Berdorff about it, but he supposed the Lichinskys would see to that. Vera had developed amazingly in every way. Musically, of course, but did Drake remember what a funny-looking little washed-out thing she had always been? Well, she was positively glowing. Success certainly improved her. He had been glad to see her, and had dined with her, gone to the opera, and so on in spite of all the engagements of one kind and another which filled her time. But she hadn't had much news of Kings Row either. Sometimes he almost wondered if there was such a place any more. Vera thought of staying in Europe permanently. She was wild about Germany. But, of course, any kind of life must seem wonderful to her after all the years she had lived cooped up in those narrow rooms above the Lichinsky jewelry store.

Drake kept his head down as he walked. There was a fine needle-sharp sleet in the wind. Little, drab-colored Vera Lichinsky—he noticed that Parris wrote it Lichinska. He couldn't imagine Vera standing up in a big concert hall playing to a brilliant foreign audience. Those people over there knew a lot about music, too. Vera must be pretty good. He simply couldn't imagine it. But then he couldn't imagine what anything must be like over there. Parris' letters didn't really picture any of it to him. Parris seemed to feel himself very much at home in Vienna. Vienna, when he tried to think about it with Parris living there, became as vague as a story out of a book, as unreal, and as far away. As far away as the days when he used to drive about Kings Row in his shining new buggy. God, that was just three years ago! It felt ages and ages removed—just something that happened once, and now all but forgotten.

... Almost two more years before Parris would return. Almost as long as the time he had been absent. And that had seemed an eternity. He had never told anyone how much he missed Parris, not even Randy. He couldn't explain that to anyone. It was hard for him to understand it himself. He had never felt that way about anyone. He remembered how Parris used to seem so much younger, and how he listened to advice. Advice—and from him! That was something to laugh about now. Now Parris seemed to him to be wise, and steady, and older. If only Parris were here a lot of things would surely straighten themselves out right away. He wouldn't drink if Parris were here: he wouldn't want to. He'd have somebody to talk to—somebody who understood everything— everything.

Drake's thoughts mulled around and around, taking shape and feeling from his recollections, and from the discomfort of the moment. The cold was beginning to get through even this heavy coat. He continued to muse on the thought of Parris. He was scarcely thinking now. It was just a vague feeling. He was wishing for Parris. He knew everything would somehow be all right if Parris were here. It was characteristic of him that even in these troubled days Drake never really thought about Parris' money. That his own present misfortunes could be contrasted with Parris' better luck on the basis of money never clearly occurred to him. He had tried so hard, with his limited capacities for thought, to resolve his troubles and find some satisfactory way out of them, that he was tired of the oft-repeated process. He didn't see any use in trying to think about it any more. His thoughts went the same way every time. The conclusion—no, there was no conclusion. He simply came back to the beginning again. If old Mr. Curley hadn't stolen his money....

He was distracted by a greater roaring of the wind. He looked up. At first he scarcely knew where he was.

He had walked all the way across town and had come out on the edge of the drop toward the creek. This was the Crescent, Peyton Graves' big project. It had been his project, too, once. But old Peyte had seemed to make a go of it. That was his house down there farther along the—the Crescent! He hadn't seen it before—hadn't even been over in this part of town since he used to drive out here with Randy. He walked toward the new house. It certainly was a whopper. Peyte was doing himself proud!

Drake turned aside to avoid going near the new house. Didn't want to see anybody today. Didn't want to talk, either.

... There was the public school—high school, now. The grades were housed in a new building up on the north edge of town. On beyond Aberdeen. Everything made him remember today. School—when he was a kid ... Aberdeen campus—talks with Parris and—and Jamie. Jamie! He hadn't seen Jamie for some time. He wondered if Jamie were still up to his old tricks. He was sorry for Jamie. Nice kid, even if he did do some funny things. Aberdeen campus—and Poppy Ross. Damn Poppy Ross! ... It was colder. The wind was leveling out into a steady cutting blast. He'd have to get in somewhere. Darned if he wasn't half frozen....

Drake made a wide arc about the lower end of town. Part of the way along narrow streets of "nigger-town." It was hard going sometimes—rough as a field. Puddles had frozen so quickly and so hard that the ice had buckled and humped, showing circles of blue-white cracks patterned like a spider web. He came presently to the railroad and followed it to Fritz Bachman's place. He fumbled the doorknob with numb fingers. A steaming cloud enveloped him as the cold met the overheated air inside. He stamped his feet and stretched his hands close to the red-hot stove.

"Give me a drink, Fritz."

"Coffee?" Fritz winked at the two customers seated at an oilcloth-covered table. They grinned at this brilliancy.

"Hell, no." Drake's words came indistinctly—his face was stiff.

"Hey, there, Drake. You go out and rub a piece of ice on your face—you got two frozen spots on your cheeks—end of your nose, too."

"Sure enough, Fritz? It's too damned cold for any of your jokes today."

"No, sure enough. I'm telling you the truth. Get away from that stove."

Drake stumbled out and returned presently with his face fiery red.

"All right now, Fritz?"

"Yes—the white spots are gone. But I wouldn't set too close to that fire for a while."

"Where's my drink?"

"Better step into the back room, Drake. I bring it."

Drake dropped into a chair at a small table in Fritz's back room. He felt as heavy and cold inside as that gray-blue ice blocking the creek. He couldn't think, and he couldn't even shape his feelings into any kind of order.

Fritz placed a bottle, a glass, and a pitcher of water on the table.

"Pour me a glass, Fritz; my fingers are stiff as pokers. Here—fill it full. I need it."

Sam Winters finished up a cup of coffee, and stood up. He walked over to the stove and toasted his fingers before putting on his leather-and-wool gloves. He glanced toward the back room.

"Who you got in there, Fritz?"

Fritz looked up from his account book. "Back room? Oh, it's that McHugh feller."

"Drunk?"

"Yeh. Dead to the world for the last two hours. Don't know what to do with him, neither. I ain't a-going to take him home, not tonight."

"Well, you can't turn him out. He'll freeze, sure as hell."

Fritz grumbled a little. "What I do, then? I want to close up and go home now pretty soon."

Sam walked to the door and looked in. Drake was sitting with his head resting on the table. His arms were hanging at his sides. He was, as Fritz said, dead to the world.

Fritz came to the door and regarded his customer with a mixture of irritation and curiosity. "I ain't a-goin' to leave him here by himself, either. Somethin' might happen, and then I'd get the blame."

"Well, you sold him the likker, didn't you?"

"Sure. Good stuff, too."

"Yeh, I know. Rot-gut! You goddam Dutchmen are all alike."

"What you mean?"

Sam looked straight at Fritz. "You'd turn that boy out, wouldn't you?"

"I got to go home."

"Well, I tell you what I'll do. I can't git him home no way when he's as drunk as that. You help me and I'll take him to the calaboose for the night so's he won't git froze somewhere. I got a couple of niggers locked up, have to stay there anyhow. He'll be safe till mornin'."

"All right, I help you."

The town lockup was only a block or two away, but it was hard to support Drake that distance.

Fritz slipped and puffed. "Hell, what are we botherin' for?"

"Shut your mouth, and hold him up there."

"All right. An' the next time he comes in my place, I throw him out."

"You do, and I'll kick your backside from here to McGowan's Crossing. Hold him up, I told you!"

Randy Monaghan's father opened the door of the kitchen stove and laid several sticks of wood on the coals. It was Sunday morning, and he had had breakfast two hours earlier. But he didn't really know what to do with himself on Sunday. Tod had gone out, and Randy was upstairs. He could hear her moving overhead. Straightening up Tod's room, he supposed. Laura, the fat Negro cook, was at home with toothache.

He used to like Sundays when his wife was living. He used to sit in the kitchen while she fixed the big Sunday dinner. He still missed her, but he accepted the bereavement with a kind of unthinking stoicism. The house never had seemed much like home since she died, though. He guessed it never would. He washed the coffeepot, put in fresh water, and dumped in a cupful of ground coffee.

Mr. Monaghan scraped the frost from one of the small panes of glass in the window. Blue cold. A good day to stay in the house. He filled his pipe, lighted it, and sat down to wait for the coffee to boil.

He lifted his head and listened. Someone coming up the path from the back way. Tod, maybe.

There was a slow, undecided knock on the door. Mr. Monaghan opened it, first kicking out of the way a piece of rag carpet laid to keep the cold air from coming in the wide crack at the threshold.

"Good morning, Mr. Monaghan."

"Why, good morning, Drake. Come in, come in."

Mr. Monaghan stared hard at Drake. The boy looked like a tramp. He wasn't shaved, his hair was tousled, and his shirt was unfastened at the throat.

"What's up, Drake?"

"I want to talk to you a little while, Mr. Monaghan. Is Randy here?"

"She's upstairs."

"I don't want her to see me this morning, looking like this. I just want to talk to you."

"How about a cup of coffee?"

"No, thank you. Sam Winters gave me some coffee."

"Sam Winters?"

"Yes. I was locked up in the calaboose last night, Mr. Monaghan."

Mr. Monaghan set the coffeepot down with a clatter. "What for?"

"I got drunk at Fritz Bachman's, and Sam Winters happened to come along about the time Fritz wanted to close up. Sam took me to the calaboose so I wouldn't freeze somewhere."

Mr. Monaghan grunted.

"I guess Fritz Bachman would have kicked me out when he got ready to go home."

"Goddam low-life skunk!"

"Well, I didn't have to go there and get drunk."

"No, you didn't. To tell the truth, Drake, I've been meaning to give you a talking-to."

"You won't need to, Mr. Monaghan. I gave myself a talking-to this morning when I woke up in jail with three niggers."

Mr. Monaghan shook his head. "It won't do, Drake. You'll be good for nothing, first thing you know."

"I want a job, Mr. Monaghan!"

"Can't you get one?"

"I've tried everywhere. Since Mr. Curley ran away with my money I—I've just not been wanted anywhere."

"Well?"

"Could you get me a job on the railroad?"

The weather-beaten old man looked keenly at Drake. "You're not strong enough to do the work, son."

"I'd get strong doing it, maybe."

"Got no place on the section, Drake."

Drake slumped in his chair. "I guess I will have a cup of coffee, please."

Mr. Monaghan gave it to him. "Tell you what I think I can do."

"Yes?"

"I'll talk to Mr. Turner tomorrow. I believe he'd give you a job in the yards—switchman, or flagman, or something. Sure you'd be willing to take that kind of a job, Drake?"

The cup shook in Drake's unsteady hand. "I've tried everybody in town. I'm not trained for anything. Nobody wants me because they believe I think I'm too good for a poor job, and they know I'm not good enough for a good job." He set the cup and saucer on the table. "Look at me, Mr. Monaghan, I look like a tramp. I'll be a bum if somebody doesn't give me a job."

"Turner'll give you a job, if you'll take it."

"I'll take it."

"It means being out in all kinds of weather. 'Twon't break your back, but it's work and no mistake."

"I'd be happy to get it."

"What are all your tony friends up on Union Street going to say?"

Drake laughed. Mr. Monaghan was unable to sense the bitterness and humiliation and scorn in the sound. "I've got no friends, and besides I don't give a damn what anybody says. I've got to have a job."

"I'll get you a job, Drake. You can depend on me."

"Thank you—sir."

Drake arose. "I'm going home." He turned at the door. "If I get a job down here, I'm going to sell the place uptown. It's already mortgaged. Then I'll have a little bit of money anyhow. I'm going to come down here somewhere to live."

"We could let you have a room, Drake."

"No, sir. Thank you. You've done enough when you get me a job. None of my 'tony friends,' as you call 'em, would do it. No, sir. I'm coming down here somewhere to live where my real friends are. I can get a room over at Mrs. Blake's boardinghouse."

"Pretty rough over there, Drake."

"It'll be all right. Good enough for me."

"And say—"

"Yes, sir?"

"You'll have to cut out likker."

"I won't drink any more. I promise."

"All right, son. We'll see how you do."

"Why, Drake! What are you doing here?" Randy came cheerfully into the room.

Drake flushed darkly. "Aw, Randy—"

"What's the matter, Drake? You look, why—"

"Yes, I know how I look, Randy. I was in the calaboose last night."

"Drake! What did you do?"

"Drunk. I wasn't arrested. Sam Winters just—just locked me up so I wouldn't freeze."

"Oh, Drake!"

"It won't happen again, Randy. Your pa's going to get me a job of some kind."

Randy's glance veiled a little. It was a strange look—Drake didn't understand it. It was a faraway look, almost impersonal, but steady as a lamp set on stone.

"I'm going on up home now and clean up. I guess the house is an awful mess, too."

Randy laid both hands on his arm, "You stay here."

"But—"

· "Go up to Tod's room. I'll bring you some hot water. You wash and shave, and I'll fix you something to eat. Then you're going to bed and get some sleep."

"Aw—"

"Do as I say. I've got to talk to you."

Drake went heavily up the stairs. Mr. Monaghan knocked the ashes from his pipe. He had never quite known what to make of his tomboy daughter, but at this moment he felt that he understood her better. She looked exactly like her mother as she stood watching Drake.

Mr. Monaghan kept his word, and Drake kept his. Mat Turner, an old acquaintance of Drake's Uncle Rhodes, was reluctant at first. He didn't believe too much in the earnestness and sincerity of Drake's resolution, but Monaghan persuaded him. Drake was given a nondescript job as switchman, and general helper around the freight office. He never set foot in Fritz Bachman's lunchroom again, or took another drink.

The bank sold the Livingstone house, and Drake paid his debts. There wasn't much left but Drake put it in the bank and managed to live on his wages. He had a room at Mrs. Blake's railroad boardinghouse. It was, as Randy's father had said, rather rough, but Drake spent as much time with Randy as possible.

Kings Row almost forgot Drake McHugh in the next few months. He had gotten a job of some kind, people heard, on the railroad. Enough to make Colonel Rhodes Livingstone turn over in his grave. It was a mercy that he didn't live to see one of his family turn into a common laborer. The lack of logic in this remark never seemed to be recognized. There was some talk, too, about that common little girl he used to fly around with. But even this talk died soon. No one saw Drake. He never came uptown any more.

Drake lost his casual, laughing manner, and a part of his good looks was lost with it. He wasn't happy, and showed it. But he was healthier-looking. He had browned and reddened quickly into that lean, leathery, weathered appearance that railroad men always have, and which is peculiar to them.

He and Randy walked a good deal when spring came, and sat sometimes for half an afternoon without speaking.

Drake was moody and brooding much of the time. She never intruded on these moods. She kept pace with his long-legged stride. He accepted her presence without much comment, but he was anxious and miserable when he was alone. Randy followed his changing humors with a quick adaptiveness, but she watched him closely, almost nervously at times. Her feeling for him was a curiously mixed one. The old glamorous romance of their relationship was gone. In its place was a confusion of two attitudes, one of pitying affection, and one of almost fierce solicitude. She knew that she loved Drake—that was what all of this added up to—and she knew he loved her in his mercurial fashion. She remembered once or twice that Drake used to talk about marriage, half banteringly, and that she had refused the discussion. Now it rarely occurred to her. She had Drake as completely for her own as she wanted him. She actually appeared to be far more content than he. She was not at all sure that she wished any change in the way everything was now. Certainly, Drake never seemed to think about it at all.

Randy was correct in her guess. Drake quite simply accepted Randy as the partner of his free time. Drake was trying hard to think of some way to get on now to a better job and better living. He had begun to realize that it would be difficult, and that it would depend entirely on his own efforts. Parallel to this groping and awkward effort at thinking was an increasing resentment against the circumstances which had helped to bring about his present state. He was ready to take his share of blame, but there was that old scoundrel Curley to blame, and back of Curley all of Kings Row, which had been ready to blame him more than the direct causes of his misfortune.

He had never seen Louise Gordon again. The thought of her crossed his mind once in a while—a tingling anger mixed with a faint desire.

Drake was not ashamed of his job, or of the necessity that drove him to it, but he hated the thought of the talk which he was sure went on about him. He hated traintime because he hated to see anyone out of his former existence. Several times he had decided to write and tell Parris the whole story, now that the worst of it was over, but he put it off each time. He wasn't sure that the worst of it *was* really over. As soon as he arranged something else, and felt that he was on his feet a bit more securely—then he would write. It would amuse Parris, he was sure, to think of him really going to work. It would be a happy day when Parris returned. Lord, they'd have a lot to talk over! It would be wonderful to hear Parris tell all about Europe. He wondered, the least bit uneasily, if Parris would want to come down here and talk to him and Randy. He wasn't sure how Parris might feel about Randy now that they were all grown up, but he put that doubt quickly aside. It was a disloyal thought. Parris wasn't made out of the shoddy stuff of Kings Row.

He smiled happily to himself, slapped himself lightly on the thigh, and gave his head a sideways jerk. Just a little more than a year now and old Parris would be back! He almost wished he hadn't sold the house. Parris might have come to live with him if he'd kept it.

Colonel Skeffington climbed the stairs to his office. He paused at the top of the long, steep flight to recover his breath. His face was very red, and the net of veins stood out on his brow in thin hard ridges. His heart was pounding uncomfortably.

He stood waiting for all the inner turmoil to subside before he ventured farther. Might as well face the fact that he was an old man, he decided. Only this morning he had remarked to Mrs. Skeffington that he wouldn't really mind being old if it didn't hurt so damned bad. His knee troubled him all the time now. He couldn't make the stairs easily. It was becoming more and more difficult to sleep. Might as well be dead.

He unlocked his door, pushed the sagging leather chair to the south window, and let himself down carefully.

Yes: might as well be dead as to have to think about yourself all of the time.

The Colonel's heart subsided a little, and the red in his face faded. He straightened his left leg cautiously, and laid his thick hickory cane across the arms of the chair so that he could rest his hands on it. He looked out of the window and nodded. Fine day, fine day. Early summer was always an exciting season in this part of the country. Rich-feeling weather, sense of quick growth everywhere, magnificent clouds. Beautiful country, beautiful. Nothing finer this side of Virginia. He loved it—always had. Loved it when he first saw it sixty years ago. It was like home then—like the lovely Shenandoah Valley, but wilder, and that wildness had appealed to him then. It had held up a challenge. The people—the first ones he had known as he really grew up and got into the practice of law—had been like the country. A little rough, but fine stuff. Independent, self-respecting. Stood on their own feet. Made a state, a real state, out of a raw territory. Made sensible laws. When they slipped and made foolish laws, they broke 'em. Didn't always have time to wait on process of legislation. Hell, it was their own country, wasn't it? And their own laws?

It had been like that. He had admired it, because he was already out of patience with the rapidly hardening forms of life in the East. He dreamed then. All young men, he imagined, dreamed similar dreams. The great names were still echoing—Jefferson, Adams, Franklin. You felt that the living force of the colonial Americans still moved. All of those things were history now—cold, dead history.

People talked of the greatness of America then. They looked out to faraway horizons. There was breadth to everything.

He hated to think that he was an old man with whitened whiskers sitting here thinking how much better the old times had been. But they *had* been better. Not so comfortable: no, but spacious. Plenty of rascals and scalawags then, too. Fortune hunters. People came West to better themselves. No use being sentimental about that. No disgrace to go somewhere to better one's self, was it? The other day that fiddling, piddling Sansome had rather belittled not only the original pioneer spirit, but the spirit and the motives of that great second wave—the men who brought a culture, notions of order, the men, like his own father, who built academies and seminaries. What did Sansome know of the ferment, and the abiding dreams of such men? There had been enough of them to make a civilization, to set up a way of life free of the small annoyances of Eastern custom which had "set" too hard, but free with obligations of discipline and control.

It had been easy to be expansive, and to work with an enthusiastic sense of accomplishment.

Now—well—

The keen lines of cynicism smoothed away from the Colonel's eyes. The surface mask of brittle inuredness vanished. Colonel Skeffington looked sad. Few people had ever seen this look.

It wasn't, he told himself, that he expected this country to turn into a kind of utopia. Not at all. He knew human nature too well to expect miracles. But—what he had liked so much in those years was the largeness of outlook, the generous acceptance of what seemed good, and the simple, unrancorous rejection of the unworthy. It had not been a trivial kind of life.

The men who developed this region—and he had been one of them—had been of bigger caliber—that was it. The very breadth of all their activities saved them from the ultimate degradation of triviality.

The Colonel's old face sagged a little. He was disappointed in the whole damned state. They had lost sight of the thing that brought the best here in the first place. The unimportant people seemed to be conquering through sheer numbers. But even that might have aspects of hope if one saw anywhere among the young anything of those earlier qualities. They were little, they were downright picayune, they talked about money as if there were nothing else under God's heaven worth while. Their language was undignified and mean. They were not gentlemen. Out of the whole lot of youngsters just grown up he couldn't think of but one who thought of saying "sir" to older men—that young devil McHugh everybody was so down on, and, yes, young Mitchell.

Well—he shifted in his chair, settling himself deeper—he mustn't be too pessimistic. The poor qualities of the human race were always in evidence. One might as well believe in the enduring persistence of a few good qualities, too. These problems were no longer his. Others would have to cope with them—but that was just the trouble—no one was coping. A new cheapness—a shoddy, sleazy social fabric was being accepted.

But ... a shy feeling came from deep hiding in the heart of the old man ... he loved this part of the country. He felt that it had been his country. He had helped it to grow. He wanted to see it do well.

Under his closed lids fragments of recollections drifted uncertainly... stretches of young woods in the fresh dress of spring, moonlight silvering the plain world on a summer night ... brightest moonlight you could imagine— here in this very country ... fishing trips ... new farms pushing the woods aside ... his own house—better even than his grandfather's house in Virginia— with its quiet, shaded lawn ...

The sun beat through the tall uncurtained window, shining full in the Colonel's face. A slight wind stirred the reddish-white locks of hair still thick above the high forehead. The slim bony hands, with fingers interlaced, rested on the heavy cane.

A young man came into the office and spoke. There was no answer. He crossed the room and looked at the thin figure in the chair. Then he lowered the shade, crossed the room, and rang the telephone.

"Number twenty-four, please … yes … Dr. Gordon. … Well, tell him to come down to the courthouse right away. Colonel Skeffington is dead."

Book Five

1

"The twentieth century" was beginning to be a familiar phrase. At first it had a fabulous sound, like a connotation of some fantastic futurity. But one became a little accustomed to it as one learned to write 1900 and 1901 without too much hesitation. Now while it was pleasantly familiar to the ear, it still suggested a happy sense of progress and advancement. There was a tingle of excitement in it—*the twentieth century!* The newspapers—especially those picturesque inside pages of papers from the large cities—dwelt upon the present wonders of civilization, and predicted greater wonders to come.

In all of these prophecies and forecasts there was more stress laid upon new things than upon new ideas. Of course that was in large measure the real charm of the whole outlook—the same comfortable, well-tried, familiar thoughts and habits in a shining setting of modernity. The enchantment which usually invests the past or the far future was surprisingly and delightfully shed upon the present, giving it at once the air and quality of something desirable and actually within reach. The unusual aspect of the new excitement was a corollary of the first attitude toward the new century, but few suspected it of being just that: everyone felt, and was sure, that the whole of the just past century was rather pathetically old-fashioned and not much of a credit to those who lived in it.

The promises of the new century did not have the usually diaphanous and uncertain seeming of things to come: they had, on the contrary, an amazing appearance of solidity, as of matters roundly accomplished.

From time to time Miles Jackson discoursed editorially on the new century. He stressed the artificial nature of man's divisions of time. He reminded his readers that the same airs blew through the new year and the new century, and that the cantankerous qualities of human beings had a way of following them wherever they went. But, he continued, these arbitrary divisions of time had advantages. They furnished excuses for stocktaking and house cleaning. It was wise, he said, to remember and to deliberate when we engage upon such mental, moral, political, and civic house cleaning that we do not behave as too many energetic housewives do in such seasons of upheaval and furniture moving. Often in such a frenzy of household reform the housekeeper throws away too much. It would be better to evaluate carefully anything we are about to discard. If we could sort out from the clutter our senseless prejudices, our unhappy procrastinations, and our destructive hatreds, we could indeed look toward a brighter hundred years to come.

Miles Jackson wrote in homely vein, but sometimes he was eloquent. Sometimes he took to fine flights in the newspaper tradition which still flourished in privately owned papers.

Kings Row read and smiled. They liked Miles Jackson and rather admired his caustic wit. But of course he was, well, a little, a very little, old-fashioned in his views. Maybe it was all right to have someone in an influential position who spoke loudly and often for the preservation of the old. It was a fine counterbalance. Kept progress from running away with itself. Anyway, his "pieces" in the *Gazette* made good reading.

Perhaps the world always enjoys a good-natured opposition to the inevitable. Certainly that was what Miles Jackson represented. He was not bitter, and he was not despairing. He stood gallantly against certain new movements. He called names in the fine old manner of political and civic battle, but he seemed resigned to what was surely coming.

The outward changes in Kings Row, taking place gradually as they did, were not too violent to disturb even conservative people much. Of course, if one stopped to think about it, a lot of things had happened. Trees gone from the courthouse square, and from Union Street as far as the Methodist church. Lots of bright new paint and plate-glass store windows. Surprising, too, how many of the old houses had come down to be replaced with one-story "bungalows."

"A smart little city," Hart Sansome said, "As neat and bright as a pin."

"Looks like every town its size from Ohio to Kansas," Miles Jackson said. "You can't tell by looking around if you're in Indiana or Iowa. Looks like any town—and just as ugly."

"Neat and bright as a pin," Sansome repeated.

"New and raw as a pine board," Jackson insisted.

But everyone noticed that since the death of his old crony, Colonel Skeffington, Miles Jackson was less acid, less violent. He had less to say about the "vanishing qualities of our pioneer forefathers." His objections to the town council's innovations were less vituperative and less sustained.

"He's gradually coming around to the new ways." Sansome said this in the privacy of official meetings. "All of these old mossbacks have to come around. If they don't—Kings Row and other progressive towns just go on without them."

On such occasions Sansome would lean forward at the council table and speak in a rich confidential tone. "It seems a hard thing to say, gentlemen, and I say it only here when the affairs of our little city are entrusted to our guidance, *but*, the reactionaries must not deter us from our clear and certain duty. We owe such service to those who place us here, and to those who will come after us.

"I regret—I deeply regret the passing of our sturdy old citizens, but it is only by such means that we grow. I remember hearing old Dr. McCants— gentlemen, you recall Dr. McCants, I'm sure, fine old Scotch Presbyterian—I remember hearing him say that the giant trees fall only to provide soil for the growth of the new monarchs of the forest. It is like that. We have to be realistic about such matters. Kings Row must go on. It must not be second to any city of its size or kind. Gentlemen, I'm not satisfied even to say 'as good as any.' We must be first. We must be better. We can show the way."

The city fathers were always impressed by Hart Sansome's eloquence, and most of all by his evident earnestness. They knew he meant every word he said.

Wonderful, they agreed, how as big a man as Sansome was willing just to work for the town like this. Why, he could go anywhere. He was smart, "well-posted"—he had the presence and the magnetism for bigger things. If he'd go out for the governorship, he'd get it—sure as shot. Well, he was certainly a fine example to everyone.

It had been decided this year to abandon the annual county fair with its stock show and horse racing and general rural festivity. The grandstand on the old fairgrounds was a little shaky anyhow, and the Fair Association wasn't disposed to spend a lot of money fixing it up. There was something new. A lot of towns had tried it out. That was the Street Fair.

Hart Sansome had gone all the way to some town in Ohio, at his own expense, to see one and be sure how it worked out. He was enthusiastic.

There would be a new Fair Association, made up mostly of the merchants. "Booths" were to be built around the square and along one block of Federal Street west of the square. These were to be decorated gaily and appropriately with flags and bunting and would serve for displays. The usual exhibits of farm products, canned goods, fancy cooking, and needlework. It combined the best qualities, Sansome said, of a street carnival, a circus, and the old-fashioned fair. It kept the county visitors right in town at the store doors, encouraged them to eat at the hotel and restaurants, and in every way looked toward making the whole undertaking profitable.

There would be band concerts. A platform would be built across the courthouse colonnade, and vaudeville acts, brought from Chicago, would be put on free. The last day would be the big day—a floral parade with prizes generous enough to encourage a lot of people to go to the trouble of decorating their phaetons and carriages with artificial flowers. The merchants were to have "floats"—symbolical and allegorical of their several kinds of business.

Someone suggested an outdoor dancing pavilion, but the new ministerial association brought its influence sternly against the idea. Father Donovan, who had been reluctantly invited into this organization after much debate, was the only one who favored the dancing. His attitude, and his remarks on the subject, proved pretty conclusively that admitting him to the association had been a mistake. You just couldn't mix Catholic and Protestant. It wouldn't work.

The Street Fair was a pretty good illustration of the changes and the new ways of life that were coming to the progressive towns of this and the near-by states. Nearly everyone agreed on this.

Miles Jackson gave generous space in the *Gazette* to advance publicity, and undoubtedly he reached the country people as no one else, or nothing else, could. But, editorially, he was rather reticent, and the city council noticed it. The real credit for boosting the Street Fair for all it was worth must go to the new daily paper, *The Evening Chronicle*, and its alert young editor, Wardlaw White. Of course a town daily didn't reach the country readers at all, but in town the influence of the bright, new paper was beyond question. And this was something else to thank Hart Sansome for. The paper had a good deal of backing from the merchants because, as Sansome said, the stores didn't have an advertising medium to put their daily offerings before Kings Row shoppers. No one seemed to realize that there were few daily changes in sales offerings, but it nevertheless seemed a fine progressive idea. *The Evening Chronicle* was practically subsidized.

Some people thought that the *Gazette* had suffered because of its new rival, but Miles Jackson seemed as unperturbed as ever, and gave the first issue of *The Evening Chronicle* a rousing editorial send-off in the *Gazette*.

Hart Sansome said he thought that was as fine a civic gesture as Miles Jackson had ever made. He called personally at the *Gazette* office to thank Jackson, and often made a point of mentioning the incident as typical of the new pull-together spirit that was necessary for genuine civic progress.

The Street Fair was pronounced a success. The crowds in Kings Row on the last day were estimated to have been the largest in the town's history.

Some members of the new Fair Association were doubtful if this success could be repeated annually, and a few merchants were uncertain of the profits they had derived; but, in general, there was high praise from all quarters. Even the country people had felt it to be a citified performance. They had gotten a little tired, too, of the sameness of the old county fair.

"Sansome luck" had held all through Fair Week. The weather had been of Indian summer's best. The whole celebration, in the careful words of *The Evening Chronicle*, "had been marred by one untoward incident." Benny Singer had gotten into a fight with some half-grown boys from Daltonville and had thrown a brickbat which crashed through Dorset and Gay's show window.

Hart Sansome had been quite indignant in the city court, and Judge Holloway fined Benny one hundred dollars and costs, which Mrs. Skeffington paid while she delivered herself at the same time of remarks about yokels and hoodlums in the best manner of her late husband. Judge Holloway's gavel and a threat of contempt didn't stay Sarah Skeffington's tongue until she had said all that was in her mind. That was a good deal, and even the urbane mayor was pretty red of face before she left the courtroom with Benny in tow.

Shortly after Fair Week there was a sudden onslaught of bad weather. Cold rains and sharp winds stripped the trees of leaves overnight. There was not another day of the fine fall weather usual in October and early

November. Snow was skimming the hard frozen ground by Thanksgiving, and everybody said the winter was going to be a hard one. Hunters noticed that the rabbits had unusually heavy coats this year—a sure sign of long cold months ahead.

December was a black month.

In mid-January the usual thaw set in. The mercury went up and everybody complained. There would certainly be a lot of sickness if this kept up. February was always an unhealthy month, anyhow.

Drake McHugh developed a bad cold and laid off from work for nearly a week. He spent most of the time with Randy.

One evening after supper he was on his way back to his boardinghouse. He took the short cut through the freight yards as usual. Bill Hockinson was running the switch engine, shifting boxcars for the early freight train the next day. Drake stepped off the track as Bill passed with a dozen empty flats. He waved and Bill shouted something that could not be heard above the rattle and clash of wheels rolling over the switches. He saw Bill waving frantically, and grinned. Some rowdy joke that wouldn't wait....

Harley Davis, brakeman on the regular freight run to Camperville, slammed the door of the freight office open. Arnold Schultz, the freight agent, grabbed his blowing papers. "Say! What in the hell—"

"Quick, Schultz, get a doctor down here! There's been a hell of an accident out there. Get Dr. Gordon, quick as you can!"

Arnold moved slowly toward the telephone.

"Quick, you clodhopping Dutchman; be quick, can't you?"

"What happened, Harley?"

"Drake McHugh's been run over."

"Run over?"

"Get the doctor, damn you!"

"Sure, sure. Right away." He rang the telephone and asked the central office to locate Dr. Gordon and send him right away to the freight depot.

"Come on, Schultz, get a long plank or something so we can move him."

"Is he cut up much, Harley?"

"Can't tell. Looks to me like he's all mashed to hell."

"That's awful."

"Terrible. We got him out but he's unconscious, or dead—I don't know which."

"How about this old door? Think we could carry him on this?"

"The very thing. Come on."

"How in the world did such a thing happen, Harley?"

"A damn funny accident, Schultz. You know that wagonload of tile that's been standing up there on the edge of the cut for a week?"

"Sure, yes, belongs to the tile works. They're waiting for orders to ship it."

"Well, the bank thawed and the whole wagon fell down—"

"On Drake?"

"It hit him and pushed him under them cars Bill Hockinson's been shunting around."

"Run right over him, eh?"

"No. It was just lucky Bill saw what happened. He was going slow. It just caught Drake as he came to a stop. Mashed him. Otherwise it would have cut him right in two."

"My God, that's awful!"

"Here—right around the other side of this car."

Dr. Gordon looked up from the table where Drake lay in the freight office. "I'll have to have some help."

"What you going to do, Doc?"

Dr. Gordon didn't answer. "Someone—you, Davis, get me some blankets and a half-dozen sheets—anywhere here in the neighborhood, and be quick. Can you heat some more water on that stove, Schultz?"

"Yes, sir."

"I'll help, Doc. Tell me what you want." Sam Winters stepped into the cone of light that fell from the tin-shaded lamp hanging over the table.

"All right, Sam. I'll need somebody steady. Everybody else get out now. Quick."

"What you want me to do first?" Sam took off his coat and turned up his sleeves.

"Cut these clothes off of him."

Dr. Gordon turned toward the door. "Will somebody stand at this door and keep everybody out?"

"I'll do that, sir." Tod Monaghan moved toward the door. "I'll keep 'em out, and when you've finished we'll take him over to my house. Just a few steps."

"Good. Now, Sam, let me see." Dr. Gordon proceeded with his examination.

"What'll have to be done, Doc?"

"Amputation."

"His leg? Which one?"

"Both. Close to the hips. There's a chance."

For nearly three hours both men worked under the crude light of the oil lamps. Then Dr. Gordon folded the blankets about Drake and stepped to the door.

"You—what's your name?"

"Tod Monaghan."

"Oh, yes, of course. Well, you and Davis can take him home, I think. Careful, and easy now. I'll be back at midnight. Just put him in bed and leave the blankets wrapped around him till I get there."

"Yes, sir."

"You'll clean up, Sam?"

"Yes, sir."

"I have to hurry. Got a pneumonia case. I'll be back as soon as possible."

"All right, sir. I'll clean up and go up to the Monaghan house. See if there's anything I can do."

"Very good, Sam. You were quite a help. Thank you."

"You're welcome, Doc."

A few minutes later Bill Hockinson put his head in the door, "Doctor gone?"

"Yep. Come in."

"Good God!" Bill paled until his weather-beaten face looked like dirty-white oilcloth. "Good God! It looks like a slaughterhouse."

"Yeh. Damnedest piece of work I ever seen in my life. Quick, too."

"What's—" Bill pointed at a freight truck pulled up beside the table. "Say, Sam, what's that?"

"Under them papers?"

"Yeh!"

"It's that feller's legs—both of 'em."

Hockinson stumbled to the door, jerked it open and slammed it quickly behind him.

Sam proceeded quietly with his work.

Dr. Gordon sat in his living room with a tray before him. He ate slowly, almost absently.

The door opened so slowly and so silently that he did not notice Louise's entrance.

"Father!"

He looked up, and nodded. "You're up late, aren't you, Louise?"

"Father!" Louise spoke in a curious flat, colorless voice.

"What's the matter?"

"I—I heard about Drake McHugh."

"Oh, I see."

"I heard he'd been hurt—"

"How did you hear that?"

"Mother told me the call came here."

"Um." The doctor turned his attention to his food.

Louise seized his arm and jerked it away from the tray.

"Louise!"

"I stood it as long as I could, then I went down to the—railroad."

"You had no business there."

"You had just left. They had carried Drake away somewhere. A terrible old man was—was cleaning up the depot room where—"

"That will do, Louise. It was most unbecoming of you to go about parading your feelings—whatever they happen to be."

"Father!" Louise stared stony-faced at Dr. Gordon.

"What do you want to say, Louise?"

The girl shook now so violently she could scarcely stand. She leaned on the table and thrust her head forward.

"You monster!"

"Louise!"

"You fiend!"

Dr. Gordon arose, laid his napkin on the table, and with the utmost deliberation struck her. She staggered and slumped to the floor. Very slowly she laid hold of a chair and struggled to her feet. She spoke with difficulty.

"I'll let the world know what you are, if it's the only thing I ever do in this world. Tomorrow—tomorrow—I'll tell everyone. I know what you are. I know all about you—and your operations."

Dr. Gordon took her by both arms. "You are going to bed—at once."

"I will not—I—I'm going to tell—"

"Louise."

She turned automatically.

"Listen. I cannot permit my daughter to make an hysterical spectacle of herself. Go to your room and do not come out of it again until you have my permission."

"I will tell. I will tell. I will tell—" Louise began a sort of singsong chant that rose suddenly to a shriek.

Dr. Gordon struck her again, a sharp, stinging slap that cut her screams short.

She shook her head slowly like a dazed animal. "I'll tell them—"

"Louise—this is enough of your willful tantrum now. If you persist, there is one thing I shall have to do—"

He waited. She stared at him, half listening, then suddenly alert.

"What?" she whispered.

"If you utter one more word of the kind of nonsense I've heard from you I shall—commit you to the insane asylum."

Louise backed away. "You wouldn't dare!"

"I have only to call Dr. Nolan on that telephone there in the hall, and have you in a cell—behind bars—in one hour. Now, can you get that through your head?"

"I'm not crazy, and you know it."

"I do not know anything of the sort."

"You mean—actually—that you think—you really think—?"

"I could think nothing else when you make these insane accusations."

Louise swallowed hard.

"I—I'll go," she said.

"That's better. And stay in your room until I say you can come out."

Louise nodded her head like a small child who only half understands what is being said. She backed toward the door.

"Yes—sir."

For three days Randy scarcely slept. She felt that she dared not leave Drake. She knew that she had to be with him when he found out what had happened.

Her face was thin and white and harsh with the effort she made for control. She felt that she must not let herself go for an instant. She must not even look in the direction of any release of her own grief. She was fearful that she might never gain control of herself again. She had not been able really to realize that this unspeakable horror had occurred.

It was late afternoon. She had made some coffee. Her head ached.

Tod came softly down the back stairs.

"Randy!"

"Yes—what—"

"He's waking up, I think. Did the doctor say give him another injection this afternoon?"

"No."

"Well, I think he's waking up now pretty soon."

"I'll go to him, Tod. There's some fresh coffee, if you want some."

Randy set her foot on the first step, and paused. It was all she could do to re-enter that room. She stood for several minutes leaning her head against the door frame. It was then that the dreadful sound came from that upper room. Randy knew even in that terrifying instant that she would never forget the sound of Drake's voice. It was a hoarse scream—almost a yell in which there was horror, and pain, and something worse—sheer animal terror.

She tore up the narrow staircase and flung the door open.

"Drake!"

Drake's eyes were rolling and his face worked violently as if the very bone structure had been shattered. Randy saw with a sick horror that his hands were groping frantically under the blankets.

She almost leapt across the room and seized his hands. *"Drake! Drake!"*

"Randy!"

"Yes, I'm here, Drake. I'm here with you."

"Randy!"

"Yes, dear. I'm here."

"Randy—where—where's the rest of me?" His voice rose to a sharp wail.

"Hush, Drake. I'm here with you. You'll get well, now."

He held hard to her shoulders. Little by little he quieted.

"Randy!"

"Yes, Drake."

"It was that accident?"

"Yes, Drake. But don't try to talk about it yet. You'll get well now."

His grasp loosened. She looked fearfully at him. He was quieter now. Very slowly he turned his face to the wall. He did not make another sound.

2

Randy turned away from the window where she had been standing. The frost-rimmed squares of glass gave a distorted vision of the still cold day. She felt that her mind was like that wavy glass. She had no true pictures of anything. She couldn't think.

It was only three o'clock, but there was already a twilight look about the day. She turned to the window again and rubbed a clear dry spot in a pane with her handkerchief. The two thick cedar trees in the small front yard were as still and stiff-looking as stone. The whole snowy landscape was blue. She leaned her forehead against the biting cold glass. It made a throbbing ache as she felt the cold reach through to the bone. She was grateful for the pain. It held her wild thoughts at one spot for a moment. If she could only think—or stop trying to think.

Randy tried to take a deep breath, but her tight breast refused the relief.

She dropped the stiff-starched curtains and mechanically straightened them. She looked around the room. This was her mother's "front room," the best room reserved for very special company, or funerals. It was stuffy and hot now. The base-burner glowed and hummed. But even the warmth and the soft rosy light shining through the isinglass panels of the brightly polished stove failed to make the room friendly or familiar.

There were the religious pictures on the wall—unreal and inhuman figures representing ideas and feelings she could not remotely apprehend. The chairs stood inhospitably against the wall. The flowered red carpet looked new and unused, although it had covered this floor since Randy was a child. Randy realized that this room and its contents bore no relation to anything that had made up the actual existence of the warmhearted, practical woman who had been her mother. It was some kind of a convention—a mere assemblage....

Her mother had made it and closed the door on it. For this moment Randy realized that the room with its comfortless furniture was a symbol of everything that had made her own life up to now. All she had been, all she had thought, and the way of her daily progress had been an assemblage—something made by someone else, or something outside of her.

There was not one object in this room to which she could turn for an association, or a suggestion of comfort. She tried to think about her mother whom she had loved, but she achieved nothing but a rather blurred image. Her mother had laughed a great deal, and joked in her warm Irish brogue. She had always been busy with her housekeeping. Baking, cleaning, washing, and

ironing. She wondered a little just what her mother had had. And her father—
he had, as well as she could remember, been gayer while her mother lived. He
was more silent now. He seldom expressed an opinion and seemed to spend
his leisure time smoking, and remembering. Perhaps her mother had been
religious, or maybe she had accepted religion as she did so many other things,
unthinkingly, as a convention—like this room.

Randy drew her shoulders together a little. Her mother must have created
this soulless room for some reason. Was it just because other people had a
best room? Because it was respectable to have such a room as an evidence of
prosperity and proper living? Randy doubted that. Her mother had been too
free for mere custom to have exerted much pressure. Her mother, whether she
herself knew it and understood it or not, had some other reason.

It must have been some sort of a shield, or some sort of barricade. Randy
tried again to breathe deeply, but the contraction in her chest held tight. No:
there was no answer in this room to any of the terrible questions pressing
against her consciousness.

She thrust her fingers into her hair to lift the heavy braids wound coronet
fashion above her broad white brow. Her face worked a little but she did not
cry. She had not cried since that first terrible day in January when they had
brought Drake home. That had been two weeks ago. He was out of danger
now but....

Yes: Drake would live. It was just here that all of the savage questions arose
against her—arose and stood like an impassable barrier across her way.

Randy laid both hands on the soft chenille cover that lay diagonally on the
ornate center table. It was as though she tried to steady either the room, or
herself. She held fast to the table. She tried to seize something—anything—in
the moving bewilderment of her mind. She must think, and she must find
some place to begin. She closed her eyes for a minute. The whole of her
consciousness seemed a world without direction, and without dimensions.
It had no up or down to it, no here or there. It was strange, all of it. She was
strange herself.

First, she thought, first she must identify herself. That was it—*identify
herself*. She must find some place to stand. She must go out now from this
room. This room! Two weeks ago she had built a fire here and had kept it going
night and day. This room had always been kept for extraordinary occasions.
Perhaps that was why she had instinctively opened it and made it ready for
use. The extraordinary occasion. The familiar simple remaining rooms in the
house had somehow been places from which she must escape. They had been
invaded by impossible horrors. For one day this threshold had been a boundary
of safety. Across it, into the room and the door closed behind her, she had felt
that she was out of reach of everything just back of her, everything that was
clawing at her very sanity. It was so no longer. The room was merely a sort of
limbo where action and actual feeling had no place. She knew she couldn't

escape anything—not now. She knew also that she didn't want to escape. The whole circle of questions leaping at her throat had to be answered and answered from within herself.

She went to the window and lowered the shade. Then she closed the lower damper in the stove. The fire could burn itself out now.

She went out of the room and closed the door.

Randy put on her heaviest coat and wrapped a knitted muffler around her head.

She went into the kitchen. Her father had come in and had taken off his shoes to warm his feet at the oven door.

"Going somewhere, Randy?"

"Yes, I've got to get out for a while."

"It's mighty cold."

"I know it, but I can't stay in any longer."

"Watch out you don't freeze your hands or feet. It's eighteen below zero, and getting colder all the time."

"I'll be careful. It's not windy, is it?"

"No, it's a still cold. Kind o' fools you. It's colder than it feels at first."

"I won't be gone long."

"Is Drake asleep?"

"I don't know. The nurse is up there."

"How long is she going to stay?"

"Dr. Gordon said Drake wouldn't have to have her after next Monday."

"How's he going to make out then?"

Randy stood quite still with her hand on the doorknob. Her father looked at her with heavy eyes.

The sound of her father's words cleared something in Randy's brain. A mass of confusion broke and fell away to either side, like the parting of troubled waters. Her face cleared, too. The quivering uncertainty disappeared. A simple resolution replaced it. She began to unwind the muffler from her head. Her bright hair, slightly disarranged, stood out and caught the dim light from the window.

"What's the matter, Randy? Change your mind?"

"Yes. I don't need to go out now."

"What's that? What did you say?"

"I said I don't need to go now. I know now." She spoke the last phrase half to herself.

"What is it, daughter? What's on your mind?"

"Drake's been on my mind—until now."

"I guess I don't understand you, honey."

"I didn't know what to do. I know now what I'm going to do."

Mr. Monaghan kept his eyes down. He didn't want her to see how much he pitied her.

"Listen, honey."

"Yes." Randy answered absently.

"Listen, honey. I want you to hear what I got to say."

"I'm listening. Go ahead."

Mr. Monaghan stood up. His gaunt, bony figure towered above her. His shaggy white hair almost touched the low kitchen ceiling.

"Randy, you want to keep Drake here, don't you?"

Randy lifted her hand to her throat and held it as though to stop whatever was struggling for utterance.

"That's what you want, ain't it, Randy?"

Very slowly her eyes filled with tears. Very slowly her hand relaxed. She let her hands hang straight beside her. She did not make a sound but let herself sway and lean against her father's breast as he reached out and put his arms around her.

He held her for a while, then he patted her shoulder.

"Come on, now, and set down. How we going to fix it up, you reckon?"

She shook her head. She was not able to speak.

"Randy, honey, has Drake got any money at all?"

She blew her nose and wiped her eyes. She had found her place to stand.

"He's got about eight hundred dollars in the bank."

"You know, of course, he can't get any compensation or damages from the railroad?"

"Yes. He knows that, too. It wasn't anybody's fault."

"That's right."

There was a loud stamping on the porch outside, and Tod came in.

Mr. Monaghan nodded. "Hello, Tod."

"Hello. We had to lay off. Too cold."

"Clear that ice this side of the bridge?"

"Yes."

Tod removed his coat and sat down on the other side of the stove. Mr. Monaghan resumed his place.

"We're just talking about Drake, Randy and me."

Tod looked at Randy. His almost lineless face took on as much of a look of tenderness as it was capable of.

"Too bad, too bad." He shook his head in somber fashion. "I like Drake fine."

"Randy wants to keep Drake here."

Tod smiled. "That's fine. Got to have somebody to look after him."

Randy began to cry again.

"Aw, Randy. Why, what's the matter, sis?"

She quieted again with an effort. "Listen, Tod. Drake hasn't got any money. Almost none, anyway."

Tod looked puzzled.

"Money?"

"Yes. He's got just a few dollars."

"Well. He don't need any, does he?"

Randy arose and laid her hands on Tod's head. Very gently she let them slip down across his chapped and roughened cheeks.

Tod squirmed. "Aw—Randy!"

Blind with tears, she returned to the front room. She closed the door behind her and leaned against it. She did not know what to do. She wanted to do something or say something. For a moment she had a recollection of her old grandmother, her father's mother, sitting by the fire with the beads of the rosary moving one by one between her fingers. She had not thought of the old woman in a long time. She died so many years ago. But that—maybe that was what brought her back to this room. Some instinct to pray, to speak, to answer the crazy despair she had known here but a few minutes ago.

But Randy could not pray, nor did she wish to—not, certainly, as her grandmother prayed, nor as Father Donovan said one should pray. No: there was no sense to that. If there had been a power for good, for benevolence in the universe, it would have saved Drake from a senseless accident. No: she could not pray. But she could recognize and be grateful to an understanding and to a simple goodness such as her father had shown, such as Tod had shown this day. Drake's world had turned its back on him. She used to look a little wistfully, a little yearningly at that world and wish she were in it, and of it. She recalled Drake's aunt, Mrs. Livingstone. She had seemed to Randy the very peak of elegance and charm. But what of all of those people who should have helped Drake when he needed it?

And now: her father, hard and knotty from years of hard work, and Tod who would never and could never know anything else....

Randy reopened the damper of the stove. A quick hum began in the stovepipe. She returned to the kitchen.

"How would you like some hot coffee and some doughnuts before supper?"

"That'd be fine, Randy." Mr. Monaghan reached for his shoes. "I'll help you."

"No. You and Tod go on into the front room and wait. I'll warm the doughnuts and bring them in there."

Tod opened his eyes very wide. "The *front* room, Randy?"

She smiled. "Yes. The front room, Tod."

Tod and Mr. Monaghan sat rather stiffly in the company room, and drank their coffee.

"Randy." Tod spoke a little hesitatingly.

"Yes."

"You know, one time I saw a fellow over at the Vandalia Fair what had both legs cut off."

Randy winced and drew herself together.

"Yes."

"He had a little wagon."

"What? A wagon?"

"Yeh. He had a boy pull him around."

Randy placed her cup on the table. Her hand shook so violently she could not hold it.

"Tod!"

"Yeh."

"Listen, Tod. Don't you ever mention that to Drake, never in this world, do you hear?"

"Why not? I thought—"

"I know what you thought. Never mind. Just forget you ever saw that man at Vandalia. Not a word of it to Drake."

"Well, all right, I just thought—"

"Never mind."

"Well, anyhow, I bet we can take care of Drake good as anybody."

"Yes. I think we can. We'll do something, somehow. We'll find some way."

Mr. Monaghan got up and put his cup beside Randy's.

"Now you listen to me, daughter."

"All right."

"I never said anything to you about Drake when he began coming around here. I—I just didn't know what to think. I feel awful bad that everything's turned out this way, but we got to take everything as it comes. Now, like I asked you a while ago, how we going to fix this up?"

"I guess I know what you mean. I'm going to marry Drake."

The old man looked searchingly at her. The underlid of his eyes sagged a little.

"Is that the way you want to do it?"

"Yes."

"All right."

"I'll have a time with Drake, though. He won't want to, now."

"I expect that's so."

"I've got to convince him, someway. I'll think it out."

"Randy, you're a good girl."

"I'm just doing what I want to."

"Now look here. There's one thing. There's just me and Tod. I kinder guess Tod won't ever get married."

Tod grinned sheepishly.

"So this house is yours, anyhow. I saved a little money. Tod has, too. Ain't any of us going to starve."

Randy waited a moment. She could not speak at once. "D-Drake won't take charity, I know that."

"We got to fix it up someway, among us."

"I'll think of something. First of all, I'm going to send a cable to Parris Mitchell. There's been enough of this foolishness."

"Parris Mitchell. Oh, yes. I know who you mean."

"He's Drake's best friend, and Drake has never even let him know he lost his money."

"Well, my goodness, ain't that Mitchell fellow got a lot of money?"

"He has some money. But that's not it."

"Why ain't he ever told him?"

"Just some kind of pride, I guess. Didn't want to complain, I suppose."

"You ought to let Mitchell know, I think."

"I'm going to—right today. Is the telegraph office open this late?"

Tod looked at his thick silver watch. "Half an hour yet. Want me to send it?"

"No, I'll do it myself. I have to get the address from someone. I guess I know where I can get it."

Randy dressed again and went out. It was horribly cold, but she scarcely noticed it. She was excited, and terrified, too. How Drake could be managed was the real question. He'd be mad, no doubt, about letting Parris know, but she was certain that she should.

The telegraph office was in the railway station. The wicket was closed, but Randy knocked. Sidney Mills, the telegraph agent, opened the door to one side.

"Oh, hello, Randy."

"Howdy, Sid. I want to use the telephone to get an address."

"Sure. Come in. You're looking fine, Randy. How's Drake?"

"Better."

"Going to be all right, is he?"

"Yes."

"Gosh, it's a wonder he's alive after—"

"Yes, it is. But he's really pretty well."

"I'm sure glad. Drake's all right."

"I want to call the Farmers Exchange Bank."

"It's number sixty-six."

Randy rang and asked for Jamie Wakefield.

"Hello. Hello, is this Jamie? ... Listen, Jamie, this is Randy Monaghan ... yes, thank you, all right ... he's better ... yes, he'll be able to see you any time—at least pretty soon ... listen, Jamie, do you know Parris Mitchell's address ... yes ... wait till I get a pencil. I can't remember all that...."

Sidney held the paper against the wall for her, and slowly she wrote out the long strange address, checking it letter by letter.

"Thank you, Jamie ... you didn't write Parris about Drake's accident, did you? No? Well, that was right ... yes, that's exactly the way he *did* feel about it. Thank you ... yes, I'll let you know."

"Here, Randy, set down at the table. Here's the cable blanks. Is that what you want?"

"Yes."

She wrote carefully, crossing out words, and finally rewrote the whole message. It was a succinct but full account of the loss of Drake's money, and the accident. She bit the eraser in the pencil for a moment or two, and added: I MUST KEEP HIM WITH ME SOMEHOW.

The next afternoon Mr. Patterson Lawes at the Burton County Bank carefully polished his glasses and reread the cablegram that had been handed to him.

"Look here, Tyson. Read this."

The cashier looked through the message. He raised his eyebrows. "Curious, isn't it?"

"Curious? It's crazy—it's foolish—it's quixotic! Does he think he's got money to throw away?"

"Well, that's his business, I suppose."

"I'll cable him right back."

Mr. Carter, the assistant cashier, came out of the vault. "What's up?"

"That young Mitchell—trying to be a fool."

"Yes?"

"Cabled orders to turn over that—you know, the Tower estate that was left to him, to Drake McHugh."

"Well, well! Very nice for McHugh."

"Thunderation. It's half of what Mitchell's got left."

Carter nodded. "I imagine he knows that."

"Well, I ain't a-going to do it!"

Carter picked up the blue sheet and read it carefully. "He seems quite clear."

"Well, I'm going to send him a cablegram, first, before I do anything."

But Mr. Lawes was not comforted the next day. A second cablegram from Vienna read: INSTRUCTIONS IN FIRST CABLEGRAM TO BE CARRIED OUT FULLY AND AT ONCE.

Mr. Lawes slapped it on the desk. "Well, of all the damned foolishness I ever heard of!"

Randy adjusted the window shade, poked the fire, and made small rustling noises.

Drake spoke finally. "It's no use Randy, you've got to talk to me sooner or later. Might as well be now."

She came across the room and sat down beside him. "All right. What do you want to say?"

"Same things I said to you yesterday."

"Go ahead."

"I still wish you hadn't told Parris."

"I had to."

"Why?"

"How would you like it if something happened to Parris and he didn't let you know?"

Drake hesitated. "I don't know. I hadn't thought of it."

"Well, it's the same thing. Drake, he's your best friend."

"Excepting you!"

"Maybe."

"Go on with your wobbly, weak-kneed explanations!"

"That sounds more like you. You see, Drake, from Parris' cablegram how bad he feels that you didn't let him know sooner—about everything."

"Yeh. Maybe that *was* wrong."

"Well, then."

Drake picked up the message from the counterpane. He had almost worn it out since yesterday reading and rereading it. He looked at it and his mouth quivered a little.

"Gee, he's a great friend, Randy."

"Of course."

"But—"

"But what, now? What?"

Drake waited. He seemed unable to speak.

"What, Drake?"

'This last sentence."

"Yes, I know. What about it?"

"'You and Randy stick together till I get there. We'll work everything out.'"

"I know it by heart," she said softly.

"Of course he doesn't understand."

"Doesn't understand what? What are you driving at, Drake?"

"Well—Randy. Hell! I haven't got any money."

"I know that."

"Just a few hundred dollars."

"Yes. You told me that once."

"Well, I've got a few things I've got to pay up. I won't have more'n five hundred left."

"Yes." She kept her glance anxiously on his face.

"Well, doggone it, Randy, I can't ever earn any more. So I thought—"

She waited. He did not notice how pale she had become.

"I tell you, Randy, I—I remembered that if you had just a little money there—" His voice faded. He rallied with an effort and tried to speak briskly. "I've heard there was *homes* you could get into—maybe."

She did not speak.

"You know Randy—kind of poorhouses, I guess you'd call them."

Randy's voice broke harshly against his last word. "Drake McHugh!"

"Why, what?"

"Would you—would you deliberately treat me that way, and Parris, too?"

"I—I don't—"

"Yes, you do understand!"

Randy remembered the long cablegram she had had from Parris yesterday. She was trying to recall its directions and follow them carefully. But she could not manage herself. She began to cry.

"Oh, Randy, don't do that. I—I guess I'll be all right, somehow."

"You—you bet you will, and I'm going to see to it. Listen, Drake—I didn't ask you to come into my life, did I?"

"Why, no, of course not."

"All right, then you owe me something."

"My God, Randy—don't talk like that!"

"You owe me yourself."

"What do you mean, honey? I don't understand you. What can I do—or be—I'm just—"

"Hush!"

Drake was looking at Randy with an expression half desperate with his own emotion, and half a puzzled concern for her.

"Drake!"

"Yes, Randy."

"Would you do something for me?"

"Me—something for you? Of course."

"Then listen carefully."

Whatever you say, or however you feel—it's you and me hereafter—together—somehow."

The expression went out of Drake's face. A curious emptiness remained. The look frightened Randy.

"Drake!"

"Yes."

"Are you all right?"

"Yes, Randy."

"Did you hear what I said?"

"Yes. But—I guess I just don't get it through my head what you want."

"It's simple."

"What is?"

"What I want. I want you to trust yourself entirely to me for a while until you are well and—" She bit her lip sharply. Almost she had said "up and around again."

Drake half smiled.

"But you see, honey—I can't ever be 'well,' as you say."

"Drake. What has happened is terrible. But you are alive."

"That's a lot of good."

"It is to me."

"Oh, Randy. Don't talk to me about—well, I don't know what you're talking about. But, Jesus, try to think how I feel lying here—no legs! I can't walk."

"You are alive, and I love you."

Drake turned his face to the wall. It was an old habit from his childhood, but Randy did not know that. She almost held her breath until he turned back again and looked at her. His usually warm gray eyes were like winter.

"Drake, I'm going to tell you something, and I want you to listen until I have finished. Then you can talk if you want to. But I want my say first. It's first of all about what Parris said there in that cablegram: 'You and Randy stick together till I get there.' We're going to do that. But I made up my own mind about that long before this—happened. Then after you got hurt I just had to think of how—that was all. This is my house, my home, Drake. It's all I've got, and you are all I've got, though I guess I oughtn't to say that. I never knew what was inside of my father and Tod until the other day. I guess I oughtn't even to have been surprised. It's just that they think like I do. Do you remember one time you said something about marrying me? Well, I made fun of the idea because I guess I'd been a little hurt. I knew you never had thought about it until just then. I shouldn't have blamed you even that much because you never thought much about anything those days—until you had to. But later on when you came down here—remember the morning you came to ask Pa to help you get a job? I made up my mind that day that I'd marry you as soon as the right time came around. I guess I was convinced inside by that time that you did want to marry me. I knew I wanted to marry you—"

"Oh, for God's sake, Randy—how can you—?"

"Hush. You were to listen. So, now the right time has come."

Drake flung his arms across his face, but Randy went on evenly.

"We'll get married, any time now, and then we'll work out someway what we'll do afterward."

"Randy—"

"I won't listen, Drake. Other men have been hurt as bad as you have and still made a living for their family—someway. We'll work that out—later."

Drake raised his arms and clutched the head of the bed. Then he turned his face to the wall again, but one hand reached out for hers. He held it so tight she winced, but she held perfectly still.

It seemed to Randy that all of the balances of life were slowly turning in the singing silence of the little room.

Three days later Randy hurried about her housekeeping. Old Ruth, black and mountainous, helped as best she could. She had been the Monaghan's cook ever since Randy's mother died, but her efforts at housekeeping were not of the best.

"Somebody knockin' at de front do', Miss Randy."

"See who it is."

Ruth returned to the kitchen in a moment. "Some gemman what want to see Mistah McHugh. He's got a satchel wid him."

"I'll see him."

"I set him in de front room, Miss Randy."

"All right."

Mr. Lawes arose and bowed when Randy came in.

"Good morning, miss."

"Good morning."

"I am Patterson Lawes. I believe Mr. Drake McHugh is here at present."

"Yes, he is. Won't you sit down?"

"Thank you. My business is with him. How is he progressing?"

"Pretty well. It will take time, of course."

"Of course, of course! Lamentable accident. Can I see Mr. McHugh?"

"I am afraid not, Mr. Lawes. Dr. Gordon thought he shouldn't see anyone just yet."

"Um, I see."

"Dr. Gordon thinks he will need to—to sort of adjust himself somewhat before—"

"I see. Well, I have a little matter of business to talk over with him."

"Perhaps I can do it for him. What is it?"

"Well, I suppose one would say it is a private and personal matter."

"I think Drake would want me to deal with it—whatever it is."

Mr. Lawes reached for his leather despatch case. "I hardly think so. Miss—er—"

"I am Mrs. Drake McHugh, Mr. Lawes."

"What!"

"Drake McHugh is my husband."

"I hadn't been advised of that, Mrs. McHugh." He arose and bowed slightly. "I didn't know Drake was married."

"We were married yesterday."

"Eh!"

"Yesterday."

"But—God bless me, the boy hasn't any legs!"

"I didn't marry Drake because of his legs, Mr. Lawes. Suppose we hear about the business now?"

"Well, of course. Excuse me. I'm just very surprised. I think it's extremely—well, *noble* of you."

Randy flushed bright red. "I guess I'd like you and any other of Drake's friends to know I didn't marry him because I'm sorry for him. I wouldn't be that mean to Drake. I married him because I love him. We'll make out somehow, Mr. Lawes."

"Well, I'm sure I hope so, Mrs. McHugh." Patterson Lawes was not sure what to make of this young woman who talked up to him as if he were a book agent.

"Well—I have here, Mrs. McHugh, a communication that should be of great interest to both of you. I suppose it will help solve some problems—if you have any," he added hastily.

"What is it?"

He looked at her sharply. A glint of suspicion showed in his narrow gaze.

"Were you expecting a communication from Mr. Parris Mitchell in Vienna?"

"I expect a letter soon, I had a cable from him. Drake had one also."

"Indeed. Did he know of Drake's condition?"

"I cabled him about it Tuesday."

"I see. Did he say anything about his intentions?"

"Intentions? To do what?"

"Could I see his message, I wonder?"

"Why, of course. It's right here."

Mr. Lawes read the lengthy cable and handed it back with a puzzled air.

"I see. Now, Mrs. McHugh—" He laid the papers on the table and explained briefly their purport. Randy listened with an increasing dismay.

"I shall leave these with you, er—Mrs. McHugh. We require signatures for receipt, and so forth. You understand these, now?"

"Yes. Yes, I understand."

"I hope this news will contribute to Drake's peace of mind and hasten his recovery."

Randy shook her head. "I don't know how Drake is going to take this."

"Why, what do you mean?"

"I'm so afraid he may think I asked Parris for help."

"You didn't?"

"Certainly not! Drake and I could have managed without help."

Mr. Lawes rubbed the back of his head. He was completely perplexed. He did not understand a single phase of this whole crazy proceeding.

"I wish you good day, ma'am—and good luck—my good wishes to Drake, please."

"Certainly. I'll tell him."

"Good day, ma'am."

"Good day, Mr. Lawes."

Randy went through the house. She stopped at the foot of the stairs.

"You got bad news, Miss Randy?"

"I don't know, Ruth. I don't know yet."

She went heavily up the narrow stairs.

3

"I don't know, Randy, I just don't know what to say." Spots of high color stood out on Drake's thin cheeks. Randy was disturbed by his agitation.

"Well, we can talk about it tomorrow, Drake. Let it drop now."

"No: I think we should settle the question. Gee, Randy, I can't lie here and just think and think. I've got to feel that—"

"What, Drake?"

"I guess I—oh, I don't know. What do you think about it?"

The discussion of Parris' offer had proved less troublesome than Randy had anticipated. Drake was not violent about it, but he was not easily convinced that he should accept it. She remembered a warning line in a second cablegram she had had from Parris: AS SOON AS HE IS WELL ENOUGH MAKE HIM DECIDE THINGS STOP GIVE HIM FULL SENSE OF INDEPENDENCE.

"I don't know what to say, Drake. Of course Parris wants you to use the money. We've got to look at it as a loan, not as a gift."

"That's just it. Parris means to give it to me. I can't let him do that. It's too much—well, it's just charity."

"I'm certain Parris thinks too much of you to mean it like that. I'd hate for you to hurt his feelings."

"Hurt Parris' feelings?"

"Yes. If you wanted to do something for him, you'd like him to see it the way you meant it, wouldn't you?"

"Ye-es, of course."

"Well, I just think we have to be careful. You've got to decide this yourself."

"But what do you think I ought to do?"

"I don't know, Drake. After all, women haven't got much sense about money. You're a man and you know better than I do what's right."

"It's such a lot of money, Randy!"

"Yes, it is. But you don't have to use it all. It isn't as though you were going out tomorrow and spend it, is it?"

"No."

"Do you suppose Parris would let us consider it as a loan?"

"But how are we ever going to pay it back, Randy?"

"Well, out of whatever we make someday. As soon as you are able we've got to make some plans about what we'll do."

"Jesus, Randy, what can I ever do?"

"You've got your brains, Drake. No—don't turn your face to the wall, Drake! Look here at me. There are two of us. If you can't walk, I can. If I can't think things out, you can. Together—"

"Oh, gee, Randy!"

"You see, Drake, that's all there is to it."

"You think we ought just to take the money, then?"

"You have to say that yourself."

Drake closed his eyes and his chest sank with a sigh of weariness.

"You don't have to think about it now—"

"Yes I do, Randy. We've got to cable Parris. Say, for goodness' sake, don't all these cablegrams cost an awful lot?"

"That's all right. We've got to straighten things out."

"All right, Randy. We'll take it. When Parris comes home maybe we can give most of it back."

"Maybe so."

"Then we'll take it, eh?"

"Whatever you say."

"I guess we'd better."

"Just as you think best, darling."

"I believe it's the right thing. Like you say we've got to think some way out." Drake managed a smile. "I feel better. You reckon I could learn to do fancywork, honey?"

Randy did not respond to the smile. She bit her lip hard to keep back tears.

"What's the matter, honey?"

"Listen, Drake. Don't ever joke like that. You're a man, and above everything else you're *my* man. I've loved you for a long time, but now I'm going to be proud of you."

Drake looked away for a moment and then back at her. The serious look deepened, then he smiled again.

"You don't mean we can't ever laugh and joke any more, do you honey?"

"We'll laugh more than ever, Drake."

"I just can't keep up with things, Randy, A month ago I felt pretty low. I couldn't seem to save any money. I felt terrible. Then I—I got cut in two, and—it would have been the end of the world if it hadn't been for you. Now look at us! We've got each other and a lot of money."

"It does sound like a storybook, the way things are turning out."

"But I feel awful about you—getting you into all this."

"Drake, dear, it does all sound wonderful, but we've just begun. We're just two young married people starting out—and we're starting out on borrowed money. Our hard work, maybe our real hard times, are all ahead of us. We've got to think sharp, and quick. Or, *you* do. I'll help, but—"

"You'll send that cablegram off to Parris right away?"

"Yes, this very evening. You realize he doesn't know we're married!"

"Wonder what he'll say!"

"He'll be pleased—if you are."

"Oh, Lord, Randy. I'll never get finished thanking you—being grateful—"

"Oh, hush. I can't stand that kind of talk."

"I've got to say it once in a while, Randy, just to keep square with myself."

"I'm going on now and send this message."

"Hurry back!"

4

Randy spread out the sheets of Parris' letter on the kitchen table. The letter had come two days ago, and she had read it a dozen times, but she returned to it again and again for the warmth and comfort, the sense of security and safety that she derived from it.

She had scarcely known Parris Mitchell, but here he was, on paper, closer than if she had known him all her life, closer than her brother or her father. She scanned the opening lines of the difficult writing. Parris' pen seemed to have leapt across the page, stabbing and slashing as it crossed the curious quadrilled paper.

… Of course, Randy, it is a ghastly and terrible tragedy, particularly so to have happened to Drake. It will be harder for him than for most people because he was so free and independent. And now, I want you to note carefully my advices. Drake lived by that same freedom and independence. He will feel—probably already feels—that he has lost both. It will be your problem to restore them to him, that is if you really purpose taking care of him as you suggest in your cabled message.

The first thing that you must realize about him is that he is all at once living in another world, totally different from the one he has always known and inhabited. A different world, but he has only the old equipment that he had and used in a world that no longer exists for him.

(You'll excuse me if I sound didactic and professional in all of this, but it is the only way I know how to say these things.)

It is all precisely as if he had suddenly been transplanted to another planet—new surroundings, new habits, new sensations, and new thoughts that result from the changes and from the violence of the changes.

The repairs to the body can so often be made in a short space of time. The injury to the mind, to the self, to the deeply buried ego, to what is called the psyche—this takes longer. And that injury is far more severe probably in Drake's case than it would be with an ordinary person. These psychic injuries strike at his pride, his self-respect, his independence and self-reliance, at his initiative, and at every phase of what is the real life of the personality. We shall have to save all of these if we are to save Drake.

I don't know what Drake means to you. He has written me so little during these years. But Drake McHugh is still my best and dearest friend. I feel that I understand him pretty well, because I have known everything that went to make him a particular kind of person as he grew up. I love Drake, and he is almost my only tie to the town there where I was born and to which I expect to return. I shall guess that Drake means in some way a lot to you. I hope so, because in that one little glimpse I had of you at the depot years ago, and from what I feel of you in your cablegrams, I am sure that you can be and must be important to him.

The first thing that you will have to do to aid in the reorientation of so seriously disrupted a life is to assume that the same forces which operated in and on his life before the crisis are still in normal operation. By this I don't mean you are simply to say so. You have to act so.

Of course I can't tell you how deeply distressed, and hurt, too, I was to find that Drake had been needing money. I am sure that in like circumstances I should have behaved differently. I should have come running to him for help. But, since he was making a living he must later on be allowed to feel that of course he will go on making a living. It sounds heartless, I know, but it is not only important, it is essential. That is why I was in such haste to cable you the initial instructions. (You'll think I'm a conceited young doctor who thinks he knows everything, but I have to say that I fear the general practitioner in Kings Row may be unaware of some of these psychological problems that medicine is just now becoming aware of.)

I am sure that you have already made Drake feel that he is needed and wanted in the world. I am writing him in this same post that he is certainly needed and important in my life. Like a baby, Drake has to be made welcome. Do you understand what I mean? There must be no feeling possible in him that he is a burden. The "helpless invalid" complex must be avoided, and that can only be done in his case by so arranging his thought for him, and so leading him that he will assume responsibility. As soon as he feels useful, and important, and necessary, our problem is solved. We can't give him his legs, but we can keep his mind and personality, and soul, if you wish to call it that, whole and well.

I know you are going to ask me how all of this is to be done. I wish I were there this minute. I shall be back in Kings Row earlier than I had planned. I can cut short my stay in Germany. But in the meantime I shall be able to make some practical suggestions, and I will write you as often as anything occurs to me. By all means write me as fully as you can, and use the cable whenever necessary.

I recalled last night that a long time ago Drake talked of real-estate projects of some kind, I don't remember just what the ideas were. But it occurs to me that in any small town that is growing at all, there must be place for several real-estate businesses. Of course I don't know what's happened in Kings Row. That may be an overcrowded field. Now I suppose the bank has turned over the small Tower estate to Drake as I directed them to do. It isn't much, but I wonder if it wouldn't do for some kind of a small beginning—something to think about, whether you do anything about it now or not. The main point is to get his mind and imagination going on something definitely constructive.

It isn't important whether the project is real estate or raising chickens, but it must be something in which you can make him feel that he is the chief and moving force—whether he is or not.

If you can start in this direction, the first essential stages can be covered in no time at all.

And this—don't try to avoid mentioning the loss of his legs. Simply speak of it when necessary. He mustn't be permitted to think of it as an unmentionable affliction. This is most important.

... Your cablegram has just come telling me that you two are married. My dear Randy, I can't tell you what I feel. I know you must love Drake greatly, and I know you don't and can't think of this marriage as any kind of sacrifice on your part—but I think it is simply one of the most courageous and admirable acts I ever heard of.

If I could command every happiness in the world for you, I would; but I think you have done what is even better: I think you have created an infinite happiness of the deepest kind for yourself. The nature you must have, and the very nature of this move carried inside of itself greater and finer things than anything the world could ever give you.

Selfishly, for the sake of my friend, I am overwhelmingly happy and grateful. I feel that I don't have to be happy for you—you have more than anyone can wish for you, I know that.

Drake has been more than a brother to me, and from this moment on you are more than my sister. In you two I feel that I have more than a professional reason for coming back to Kings Row. You know, of course, that I have always hoped for an appointment at the State Hospital for the Insane. Naturally, I have no assurance that I shall get it. I have kept Dr. Nolan informed of my progress. He has promised to recommend my appointment when I have finished my work here in Vienna. I don't know if his recommendation has full weight, or not. Formerly, I believe it did, but so often politics play parts in these state appointments. In case I do not find a place at the hospital in Kings Row

I shall have to look elsewhere. There is no place in private practice for
my special training. I'm destined to be an institutional man whether I
want to be or not.

My best love to both of you. Not so many weeks now, and I shall
be able to say directly to you both what I find it too difficult to say on
paper. (Actually, I find that at present I write English a little stiffly—I
have to stop and think. I am almost a foreigner now, sure enough.
Remember that the kids at school used to call me a foreigner?)

Randy folded the thin sheets of paper carefully. It was strange, she thought,
how well she knew Parris Mitchell.

5

Gradually, as the weeks went by, Randy pressed the suggestions Parris had
made in his first letter. She was amazed to see how Drake fell more and more
easily into the pattern she so carefully planned.

Drake's convalescence was slow at first. He was so still and so white and so
unreal a great deal of the time that again and again Randy called Dr. Gordon
for advice and reassurance. He would rally for an hour or perhaps for a whole
afternoon, and then slip back again. He was like a ghost at such times.

It seemed to Randy as she remembered those weeks that she had not
slept at all. She had drowsed, but her senses were constantly alert for a sound
or a murmur from his room. Parris was sure, writing in response to her
detailed letters, that her marriage to Drake had given him the first grasp on a
redetermination.

The whole period now seemed to have been a half-waking fantasy. Perhaps,
she thought, it was really because she had slept so little that she could not recall
much of it clearly. She felt drugged.

One day, following her carefully disguised leads, Drake recalled the old
project for reclaiming the creek-bottom lands near by. He alighted upon it
with joy. He had begun from that day to move toward a normal life. He was
still white, and his face was thin. Sometimes, as Randy studied the sharp-cut
profile, it seemed as though this catastrophe had burned Drake clear of every
trait that had been a little careless and coarse. She was not sure that she knew
this new Drake very well. Drake spoke differently. He was actually careful of
his speech and his accent. Randy recognized something that she associated with
Drake's aunt, Mrs. Livingstone, and the life of Union Street as she had always
imagined it. It made her a little shy sometimes.

What Randy did not notice was the sudden and deep change in herself. The
tomboy look was gone. The rounded look of rough-and-ready rowdiness that
had always characterized her had slipped away like a mask.

"Randy!"

"Yes, Drake."

"You aren't pretty any more."

"I'm sorry," she answered absently as she pounded his pillows into shape.

"No: you're beautiful now."

"Oh, get out."

But Drake was right. He was probably the only person who thought so. People who knew Randy remarked on how bad she looked. She seldom smiled.

"I'm going out for a while, Drake."

"Yes. You ought to. It's really spring, isn't it?"

There was something more than wistful in his voice. Her heart seemed suddenly cold and heavy.

"I'll stay with you if you want me to."

"Don't be silly, Randy. You've got to get out."

"I'm going to move you downstairs next week, Drake."

He frowned. "Where?"

"The front room. It just stands idle. That's going to be our living room, and the little room off to the side that never has been anything but a storeroom will be our bedroom."

He thought a moment. "It sounds pleasant. It's funny, but do you know I can't remember exactly what the view is out of those windows!"

"There is just one front window. It looks into the front yard. There's a big cedar tree outside, and across the road you can see around Harper's Hill on out into the country. It's quieter, too. You don't hear the switch engines as you do back here."

Drake's face contracted suddenly. "I'll be glad to get where I don't hear them so plain. Sometimes I dream—I guess I'll always have dreams like that."

"I don't think so, Drake." Randy spoke very calmly, but her chest was tight. "You'll have a lot of other things to think about."

"I can't see down to the creek-bottom lots, can I, from downstairs?"

"No. I think not quite." She controlled her voice with extreme care as she went on. The suggestion, she knew, must sound casual. "You could have a wheel chair, of course."

"Randy!"

Drake's voice cracked and shivered.

"Yes, honey. What's the matter?"

He reached for her hand and held it with all of his strength.

"Listen!"

"Yes, Drake. What is it?"

He swallowed hard. The look in his eyes was strained and agonized.

"Listen, Randy, there's just one more thing I want you to promise me."

"I'll promise you anything. You know that."

"I want you to promise me that I'll never have to go out of this house until—until I'm dead."

"Why Drake, how foolish!"

"Promise me!"

"Well, of course, I'll promise you if you want me to. But you won't always want to hold me to it. Likely as not we'll build us another house someday."

"That would be different. I could be moved at night."

Randy sat down beside him and held his head against her. "Now, darling, you listen to me."

"All right." Drake's breath came in short, quick gasps. Randy knew all at once where the great injury lay, and by some half conscious instinct what she must say, and what she must avoid saying.

"I'm listening, Randy."

"Remember this always. You've had a terrible accident and all that, but you're just Drake McHugh. You're no different. You can arrange your life anyway you want to. I'm here to see that it's done the way you want it, but—you are Drake, and I love you. Do I have to tell you that every day?"

"Yes."

"Then I will."

"And now you're going out."

"If you say so."

Tod came into Drake's room just as Randy was preparing to go out. He laid a stereoscope and bundles of photographs on the bed. "I thought you'd like to look at them."

"Why, thank you Tod. Gee—you know we used to have one of these things at home when I was a kid! I wonder what became of it. But we had just a few pictures."

Tod smiled happily. "I've got a lot more pictures when you get through looking at these."

"Tod's been collecting them for years."

Tod nodded vigorously and shuffled a little with embarrassment. He slipped out quickly when Drake reached for the pictures.

"That was kind of Tod to think of me." Drake made a funny face. "You know, Randy, I *will* enjoy these, sure enough."

"Tod's goodhearted. He'll do anything for you if he likes you."

Drake nodded and fixed a picture in place. "How do you work this slide, Randy?"

"Turn that little brass knob underneath, first."

"Oh, I see. Say, Randy, how old is Tod?"

"Tod? Let me see. Tod's about fifty, I guess."

Drake whistled. "Long way between you, isn't there?"

"Yes. I guess I was a surprise."

"You said Tod wanted to be section boss?"

"It's the only ambition he has ever had in his life. Pa put him to work, or maybe just let him go to work when he was about fifteen or sixteen, and he's been there ever since. He loves the railroad. You'd think it belonged to him. He works six days a week and on Sundays walks for miles up or down the track just to look at it."

"I used to always like railroads." Drake spoke in a low smothered voice.

Randy noticed the tone, but ignored it. "I suppose all kids like cars and engines. I always did myself."

"Say, this is a bully picture of the Mammoth Cave—do you remember it?"

"Drake, I know all Tod's pictures by heart. I used to think it was like traveling, just to look at them."

"They are kind of nice. I'm glad Tod brought them in."

"Well, I'll run out now for a while. Anything you want before I go?"

"No. I'm all right."

It was really spring, as Drake had said, but it wasn't warm or leafy. The buds were mere dots of bright moist green. There was a wind today, a wind that roared in the treetops but seemed to lie altogether on high levels. It was almost quiet under the tall sycamores that bordered the creek. Randy stood still for a while at the foot of Harper's Hill and listened. The wind came across the hill and swept through the high trees with the sound of a great waterfall. She closed her eyes. It was easy to imagine herself standing by a giant cataract. It was exciting to try to make a picture to go with the sound.

She opened her eyes again. The world, the familiar landscape, seemed to slip back into place. She looked down the shallow valley toward the open country. She would have liked to go out that way today, but it was too wet and muddy. She would have to walk along the railroad track. Of late she had almost confined her walks to the tracks. The crossties were too close together to step on each one, and too far apart to take two at a step comfortably. She found that she had to think how she was walking. That prevented her from thinking of anything else. There was a kind of hypnotic quality in the monotonous procession of wooden ties under her feet. It tired her legs, but it released the tension in her head.

From time to time she stopped to look at the fields. Everything was brown, or gray-green. Down below her, the bushes on the sunny side of the fills looked as if they had been dusted with bright green powder. There was a heady smell of damp earth, now and then a dizzying breath from a stretch of fresh-plowed land.

She walked on and on, crossing the long trestle over Paisley's Branch, and coming out just beyond to the wide view that reached toward the high level country named James' Prairie. She was tired now. The wind had a straight thrust at her but it was rather pleasant. She sat down on some heavy timbers piled beside the track and took off her hat. Her hair was heavy and pressed hard upon her temples. She unwound the plaits, loosened the ends, making what Tod used to call mule tails of them—poor Tod!—and gave her head a childish shake. The wind felt like a stream of water against her forehead. She ran her fingers over her face as though she were washing it in the cool air.

A sense of vibrant awakening arose from the earth, but Randy responded to it with only a vague feeling of dismay. She had never felt like this before. She tried to understand herself, but her mind was unwilling to follow any thought at all. Perhaps she was just awfully tired. She dwelt on that for a moment. No: there was no use trying to fool herself. She was tired, of course. Taking care of Drake had been an arduous and exacting process, but that alone was only part of her weariness. She had had to sustain his beginnings of readjustment with all her strength. She felt that she might like to cry, but she had not cried much since Drake's accident. What was inside of her could not be released through tears. Tears—a girl's crying spells—these seemed too trivial to consider.

She had always been so happy—thoughtlessly happy, of course; and there had been nothing to prepare her for this. All those rather tomboy play years at school. Her freedom with boys. She supposed there might have been people in Kings Row who thought she was a bad girl just because she played with boys and exchanged rough banter with them. Even the two years of tightly restricted life in the convent at St. Louis where her father sent her after she finished high school were pleasant enough. There had been at least one of the nuns she liked. Sister Seraphina. She began to remember Sister Seraphina's counsels. Yes: she would have need of those counsels now.

A sudden contrition thrust her thinking into other channels. What was this she was saying to herself? As if she were sad or regretful on her own account. That, certainly, was not true. Her sorrow—and that sorrow lay deep and dark and bitter within her—was wholly for Drake.

She had never loved anyone else. Even in school she never had "crushes" on boys. She liked them, or didn't. They said naughty things to her, but that was all. Otherwise boys had treated her as one of themselves. Once she had thought she liked Parris better than anyone. She *liked* him; that was all.

The day Drake McHugh met her at the station and took her riding was the beginning of a wholly new state of being. He went simply and directly to a place in her heart that had been waiting for him. He fitted there as completely and perfectly as if it had always been his own. Drake—tall, and laughing, going about, even in his bad days, with his head up in that gay and fearless fashion— she covered her face with both hands and shook, but she could not cry.

She straightened up again and her eyes stared blindly at the woolly clouds scurrying along the sky. She had to answer something that came up in her like a question. Yes: she had loved Drake wholly. Her frank adoration of him had been like a quick flashing stream, rushing—

The catastrophe—what had it done to her, exactly? It seemed, now as she tried hard to think of it, as if that stream had been suddenly checked, its headlong rush thrown back on itself—as if it itself drowned in the weight and power of its own volume.

She drew her shoulders up stiffly. She had to face something—now. She had to ask a question, and answer it.

The effort to force the brutality of the question into the light of consciousness exhausted her. But she had to. She wanted to ask herself what she felt for Drake now. What was the change that threw her back on herself like this?

Yes—yes—yes: she could say into the very face of heaven that she had loved Drake, had loved him utterly. She had given him everything with gladness. There had never been anything solemn or tragic about that. But even the recollection of that passion shook her again with its savage force. There was her question—there, suddenly before her with its stark demand. How about that now? What was left of it? How did she love Drake? Could she even think of the many times they had laughed together, lying in the tall summer grass, laughed and loved and been silent again as the great August moon came up over the trees?

Randy clenched her hands and sat very still. She had to think this through now. The answer was not simple, she could sense that much. It had, somehow, less to do with her than it did with Drake. A door had closed on an episode of youth and fun. That, now, was one step. Yes: *an episode*. She could say the word and know it was true. It had less to do with her than with Drake, this rearing question: she said it quietly over again to herself.

Something from one of Parris' letters came back: "*Not only does he have to live in a new world, as I wrote you before, but he has to live in this new world with a new set of feelings, new impulses, and new wishes. Even where old phases of his old self survive, they survive only in a new and changed relation to each other, and naturally in new relations to you and me and the whole external world.*"

Randy was not sure that she understood that very well. She said the words over and over. An intuitive feeling that she almost understood came to her after a while. Now she made another step toward answering. She did not love Drake today in the same way she had loved him a few months ago. And—she groped again in the snarl and tangle of thought and feeling, lit now and again with halfgleams of understanding—and—*it was because of some overwhelming new feeling she had for Drake*. The attitude did not have to do with herself. The happy-go-lucky boy she had loved—*he* no longer existed. He was gone, and with him, she felt, had gone all of the demands and urgencies of the flesh—forever.

And this new feeling for Drake? Some kind of tenderness, some kind of pity, some kind of protectiveness. If she could only hold him close and keep anyone from ever looking at him so he wouldn't have to remember. All the passion and the wild possessiveness for that other Drake—those feelings would be an injury and a betrayal of the shattered boy with the thin, purified face who lay so patiently in Tod's room at home. Now, she believed, she was clear about one thing at least. She had been half fearful, deep in her, that she might love Drake less—that some accursed physiological instinct might turn her partially away from him. She was relieved. She knew better now, and she could face herself once more without shame. The deep change that had come over her was for his sake, for his protection. She knew that she loved Drake, not as before, but more deeply, and that this strangely compounded love could never loose its hold.

For what remained of her perplexities—she was merely tired.

She remembered that one time her father had showed her some machinery in the tile factory. He had explained the working of the gears attached to the carrying belts. High gear for a light load, low gear for a heavy one. Something like that had happened to her. She was geared differently now. There was no use in denying that the load might be heavy. So be it.

She arose and buttoned her coat about her throat. Her heart was less heavy than it had been at any time during these past weeks. There was one burden, at least, she would never have to bear again. She had been so afraid of her own self, her own nature. She had been secretly afraid that she might have to live in shame of her own heart. But it was not so. She had met her own test. She was not afraid, now; she was not afraid of anything in the whole world.

Randy looked about her. She must learn to observe things better. She must tell Drake everything about the day and the way it looked when she got back.

She walked rapidly, smiling at the little steps she had to take if she stepped on every crosstie, breaking impatiently into a long jumping stride as she took the ties two at a time.

6

The late-afternoon train clanked and rattled its smoky, grimy way from Camperville toward Kings Row.

The passengers sat in the antiquated coach, avoiding, as much as possible, the touch of the gritty, red-plush seats. They wore a look of patient misery—all but one. He was a young man who had stepped from the Chicago express just in time to catch the Kings Row local. He attracted some attention as he attended to the transfer of considerable luggage, all of it tagged and bespotted with foreign labels. Now he sat watching the sun-dried landscape with a curious eagerness. A ragged and exhausted air invested the entire country, but his gaze rested upon it with a lively interest. He scarcely turned from his window during the next two hours. When the brakeman passed through the coach, roaring "Kings Row—all out for Kings Row," the stranger aroused himself as if he were coming out of a dream.

At the station he looked with some surprise at the new brick building. The old one had been of wood, painted a hideous smoke gray. He glanced about him, half expecting to see some familiar faces.

"Hack, sir?"

"Yes. Yes, please."

"Dese yo' valises, suh?"

"Yes. Put those—the two big ones in the hack. Where's—I want to see a baggageman." He spoke slowly as if he had to select words carefully."

"Transfer man? Yes, suh. Hyah! Mist' Howe! Baggage checks, suh."

"All right. Your checks, sir? Where to?"

"Why—the Central Hotel. There is still a Central Hotel, I suppose?"

"Yes, sirree. Only one, in fact. All these?"

"Yes. I suppose I can store them at the hotel, can't I?"

"Oh, yes. Let me see. Seven trunks. Is that right?"

"Yes."

"And four grips?"

"Yes."

"That'll be two dollars and a quarter. Thank you. They'll be there in an hour or two."

"All right."

"Dis way, suh."

The rather decrepit hack swung around the corner and clattered along lower Union Street. The black driver turned in his seat.

"Stranger hyah, suh?"

"I haven't been here in a long time. Things look different."

"Changed, eh?"

"Very much."

"Yes, suh, I bet effen you ain't seen Kings Row in along time you ain't hardly know it. Sho do change fast now."

At the hotel desk, a thin mousy-looking clerk bowed with an imitation of briskness.

"Room, sir?"

"I'd like a suite, please."

"Suite?"

"Yes. Sitting room, bedroom, bath."

"Well—we haven't exactly got that kind of an arrangement. I could throw two rooms together for you."

"Just give me a large, comfortable room for the present, then."

"Yes, sir." He turned to the key rack. "Be here long?"

"I don't know. Permanently, maybe."

"Oh, I see. Register, sir."

He watched as the newcomer wrote: "Dr. Parris Mitchell, Vienna."

The clerk turned the register around, wrote a number opposite the name, and then held out his hand. "You don't remember me, do you?"

Parris batted his eyes rapidly. "Ye-es, I do. You're—you're Miller Jones, aren't you?"

"Yes, sir, that's who I am. Well, I'm mighty glad to see you again, er, Dr. Mitchell." He glanced back at the register. "Vienna? Over in Europe all this time?"

"Five years, Miller. You were just a kid when I left."

"Yeh. Sure, sure. Five years is a long time. Here, boy, take Dr. Mitchell's baggage to two-seventeen. Going to go into practice here, Doc?"

"At the State Hospital."

"Sure enough! Doctor at the asylum, eh? Well, well. All ready to jump right into it, I guess."

"I suppose so."

"Well, that's fine. Glad to have you back home, Doctor. The boy's ready to take you up."

"Send the baggage up. I'm going out first to—to look around. There'll be a lot of trunks and stuff coming along. Can you store them temporarily?"

"Sure, sure. We'll take care of it for you."

Out on the sidewalk Parris stopped and slowly drew on his gloves. Two men sitting in split-bottom rocking chairs just outside the hotel door stared and glanced at each other. When Parris walked away, one of them spoke slowly. "Say, did you see that fellow, putting on gloves?"

"I sure did. Hey, Miller! Come here a minute."

Miller Jones sauntered to the door. "What you want, Pop?"

"See that fellow crossing the square?"

"Yes. He just registered, he's—"

"He was wearing gloves—in August!"

"Yeh? Well, he's Dr. Mitchell. Used to live here. Parris Mitchell. Used to know him in school."

"What's he wearing gloves for?"

"He's been living over in. Europe—in Vienna, for years. Maybe that's the style over there."

"Doctor, you say?"

"Yes. Going to be a doctor over at the asylum."

"Well, now! Government job to start off on?"

"Yep."

Parris walked across the square. At the corner he paused and thought a moment. Yes, Cedar Street, that was the shortest way to Randy's house. He walked slowly, as if some reluctance stayed his feet.

He had thought so often of coming home. Now he was here. This was Kings Row. He looked east and west on the cross street. This shabby, dingy-looking street, this—village. A strange heaviness settled on his heart, and with it came a quick, keen wave of homesickness for Vienna. There had been a place once—a town where he had been a child—but all of that was something which had nothing to do with this reality—this crass, harsh reality confronting him

at this moment. And down there—just down this little street he would find—
Drake. He felt that he could not go on. Better if he had never come back at
all. Better if he had stayed in Vienna. Vienna had meant friends, a comfortable
something that was almost home—Vienna was—he shook himself free of the
thoughts. That was being maudlin, and worse, it was being afraid. He walked
quickly down the street.

"Parris!"

"Randy—my dear!"

"Oh, Parris, I'm so glad to see you. But we weren't expecting you for
another week."

"I had planned to stay over in New York longer. But it wasn't necessary, and
here I am. And Drake?"

Randy had just started out when she met Parris. She swung the white-painted
gate open again. "Come on in. Drake will be crazy, he'll be so glad to see you."

"How is he?" Parris caught her arm and held back as they came to the door.
"How is he really?"

Randy looked away, then back again. Her eyes dimmed a little. "I don't
really know, Parris. I don't really know. He seems—more like himself lately. But
I can't tell."

She pushed the door open, and Parris entered. He dropped his hat and
gloves on a chair. She pointed to a door. "In there," she whispered.
"Come along with me."

Randy opened the door.

"Drake!"

"Yes, honey."

"Look! Look who is here!"

Drake shrank back a little into his pillow, and with an instinctive gesture he
pulled the sheet up under his chin.

"Drake!"

Parris held tight to Drake's hand and looked down into the deeply
shadowed eyes.

"Drake."

Drake moved his lips, but no word came. His face was like a mask of thin
stone. He shifted a little like an embarrassed child and turned his face away.
Randy, who knew this habit of his, now felt that she could not bear the gesture.

Parris sat down on the edge of the bed and laid his cheek hard against
Drake's.

Randy backed out of the door and closed it behind her. She went to the
kitchen and sat down in a low chair behind the stove.

"Mary, blessed Mother of God! Mary, blessed Mother of God! Mary, blessed
Mother of God!" She repeated the words over and over again, neither hearing
the sound of them, nor thinking of their meaning.

7

Parris slipped quietly into the work of the hospital. The place seemed at once familiar and a refuge. Kings Row had terrified him at first. Through the years of his absence he had remembered it with a sort of filial affection. He recalled the pleasant corners he had liked, the views, the small special places which had been the scenes of his thinking and growth. He had enhanced them in every way in his mind. It had been a shock, a most unsettling shock to come without any preparation whatever upon the actual truth. Somehow he had allowed the neatly arranged landscape of Europe to slip into the places of recollection, and to usurp his memory of Kings Row. The ragged, uncared-for countryside was not pleasant. He felt at first that it had become so during his absence. When he actually realized that of course this was not so, his depression deepened. He felt that his most treasured memories had betrayed him.

Inside the great asylum all of this feeling left him. This was known territory. He was rather astonished at first to see how superior all American equipment was. The scrupulous hygiene, the smooth efficiency in all mechanical and material phases of administration, were a professional delight after the poverty and sometimes almost impossible working conditions of comparable institutions he had seen abroad.

Dr. Nolan had welcomed him so warmly that he had almost a sense of home-coming. Dr. Nolan, he found, was intelligent and progressive. The general staff was not well enough trained. Parris saw at once the evil hand of politics. But he thought little of this at the time. He found himself happier than he could have believed possible. For the first time in years he sensed security. Here was his post, and his work. He could give the best he had—all he had, without other consideration.

Outside the "asylum," as Kings Row continued to call the State Hospital, he was less happy. He had no points of contact with old acquaintances. They became shy when they met him, and he fell silent. His return to Kings Row was so quiet that only a few people knew of his presence. The changes in five years had been deeper than Kings Row suspected.

Drake had been his real concern. Parris saw him three or four times a week. Without Drake suspecting it in the least, he had begun the application of all that he knew to a restoration of personality. So far everything went well. Drake was at times almost like the impudent, half-jeering lad who had said good-by to him at the station more than five years before.

Drake was now definitely started in business. Randy's own project for the reclaiming of the old neglected creek bottoms had been put into effect. Parris had been enthusiastic about the whole idea, and Drake sat up every day with huge sheets of paper on which the surveyors' plottings were inscribed. Randy was to do the actual outside work. Drake was made to feel that the entire administration of the undertaking was his own.

Snow was flying over the hard-frozen earth before Parris began to feel that he was really settling into his own place. He had not yet gone out to see his old home. He had been told of the changes and rearrangements, and while he felt just now little of any kind of emotion concerning it, he was unaccountably unwilling to go.

The few people in town who saw Parris, and who knew him at all, talked quietly to each other about him. He was, they agreed, all that anyone could have hoped. His deep seriousness was particularly impressive. But no one went further than that. No one remarked that young Dr. Mitchell made one a little uncomfortable. It was hard to say just how, but the impression remained.

"He is the most perfectly poised person I ever met." Dr. McFee, one of the hospital staff, was talking about him. "I don't think I ever saw anybody, particularly a young person, who held so still."

"Or who could listen longer without batting an eye," Dr. Nolan added.

But they were wrong about his poise. He "held so still" because he was shy. Parris himself knew that in his own field his mind worked rapidly and rather surely. But in ordinary social relations he had lost something. It puzzled him, and made constant question in his mind. He had always been at ease in Kings Row. He had certainly been at ease in Vienna. Yes: he had been more than at ease there; he had been happy there. But here, back among the people whose ways he had known for so long a time, he felt that he had lost the knack of following their thoughts. He was often tongue-tied and miserable. He couldn't talk to them.

His acquaintances guessed nothing of this. They continued to admire the good-looking young doctor with his interesting foreign ways, and they never stopped to think that they didn't really like him very much because they were not at ease with him.

Patterson Lawes often sat just inside the big plate-glass window of the Burton County Bank and watched the town go by. Gradually he had been joined by friends and acquaintances. This morning gathering had rather taken the place of Colonel Skeffington's old courthouse crowd. But it was more exclusive than the Colonel's circle had been.

Parris was passing one morning when Mr. Lawes motioned him in.

"Dr. Mitchell, I want to introduce you to the Reverend Cole—our new Presbyterian minister. You know these other gentlemen, I believe."

Parris bowed. The Reverend Cole arose and shook hands.

There were general greetings. Parris dragged a chair from the corner. Dr. Cole leaned forward, his bony, rather shiny face assured and a shade arrogant.

"I hope I may see you up at our church sometime, Doctor."

Parris bowed again. "As a matter of fact, I believe it's my church, too."

"Oh! Is that so?"

"Yes. I joined when I was a small boy."

"That's fine."

Parris' eyelids drooped a little. He instinctively and instantly disliked Dr. Cole.

"Yes. There was a whole bench full of boys at a revival, and we were stampeded somehow. Everyone followed the leader."

Patterson Lawes laughed heartily, but Dr. Cole did not. "I hope you were the leader."

"No. I rather recall that I dreaded being left alone. I was the small end of the procession."

"I see, I see."

"Sit down, Doctor, sit down."

"Mr. Lawes tells me you are doing a great work among the unfortunate people in the State Hospital."

"That is kind of Mr. Lawes. I'm just a staff physician."

Dr. Cole put his finger tips together. "I have always felt that it must be like being in another world to live among diseased minds. Isn't it, Dr. Mitchell?"

"No. Not exactly."

"But to move among the wild dreams and hallucinations of the insane—"

Parris cut him short. "Insanity is tragic, of course, but it doesn't seem so at close range."

"Really? How is that?"

"It mostly seems merely silly."

"I'm afraid I'm rather shocked to hear you say that, Dr. Mitchell."

Parris knew he was going to be really angry with this fool in a few minutes. He had been so pent up all of these weeks that he welcomed the sensation of anger. He encouraged it.

"Naturally, Dr. Cole, there are times when we are touched by wrecked humanity. But a physician may not indulge the luxury of emotion. He is confronted only by a problem. The actual spectacle of insanity, as I said, is in most cases merely silly."

"I think that sounds singularly unfeeling, sir."

"A doctor who went about being sentimental would be a very bad doctor."

"I had another impression of the nobility of medicine."

"It's probably noble enough, but again, naturally the physician doesn't think about it. Working with a case is just like mending anything else that's out of order. You try to find out what the trouble is, and then try to do something about it. It is, in some respects, no more romantic than plumbing."

Patterson Lawes grinned and covered his mouth with his hand.

"I should think, Dr. Mitchell, you would *have* to think of your calling out there in that great institution as the working of an angel of mercy."

"Why?"

"Well, sir, because it is, God's work."

"But man's job, Dr. Cole."

"God had set it there—"

"Excuse me, Dr. Cole. I'm afraid you are about to say that God in his wisdom has seen fit to afflict these his children—and so forth."

Dr. Cole stared, and an ugly mottled flush darkened his face.

"I was indeed about to say something like that. Do you find fault with those words?"

"Has it occurred to you that if God in his wisdom has driven three thousand of our fellow citizens crazy for some secret purpose of his own that it might be sacrilege for us to interfere, and try to thwart his purpose? Or do you think it happened just to make the world more difficult for us?"

"I don't suppose you are denying the hand of God in human affairs, are you?" Dr. Cole looked about at his listeners. He was not sure that he was coming off well in this encounter, nor was he sure of the sympathy of his listeners. He, too, was thoroughly angry.

Parris leaned back in his chair. "I certainly don't overlook the hand of man in either the fate of his body or his mind."

"What do you mean?"

"If you eat too much cucumber salad, and die of acute indigestion tonight, it seems beside the question for some brother minister of yours to stand up tomorrow and talk about the wisdom of God when it was gluttony that killed you."

"It would be the hand of God—"

"Yes, yes—moving in a mysterious way. Forcing you to make a pig out of yourself in order to call you before the throne? Fortunately, Dr. Cole, I have a more dignified conception of what Deity should be, and how Deity should work."

"We seem to be getting off the subject."

"Yes, we are. You were talking about patients in the hospital. There are human, very human, causes for the plight of most of them. We don't have to blame God."

"Well, doubtless, man's ignorance of God's laws—"

"Man's stupidity, his neglect of decency, his cruelty. It is unwise, Dr. Cole, to talk to a scientist, however humble a scientist, about the causes of human misery. Somehow, I don't understand quite how you arrive at it, most of you are proud of the State Hospital. It is maybe a monument to our pity and our good will, but that particular hospital is also a monument to the three thousand failures of civilization to do the right things by its citizens, and also a monument of the failure of man to withstand the pressures of the civilization he has himself created.

"No, Dr. Cole, it would be very simple if we could shift the blame of our troubles to God, but if we could, it seems to me that we might also look to the same quarter for help. Doesn't it seem to you that a deity such as you have described this morning might be a bad neighbor?"

"Scripture says—"

Parris arose. "Pardon me. I must go. Sorry, Mr. Lawes, to spoil your party in here. You looked so peaceful when I came in!"

"Not at all, my boy. I love an argument. I'd like to hear more from you sometime."

Parris turned to Dr. Cole. "You were about to quote Scripture. I've read the Bible—in four languages. I suspect there are deeper truths in the great history of the Jews than the average ecclesiastical reader apprehends."

Parris came out of the bank and walked rapidly back toward the State Hospital. How on earth, he asked himself, did this happen? It was hard to understand how he and the minister had come so quickly at each other's throats. He had been wrong, that he knew. There was no kind of discussion so fruitless as this. He had been guilty of distinctly unprofessional behavior. Moreover, he decided, he had acted young—and smarty. But, he had to admit, he also felt better after getting a certain amount of impatience and rancor out of his system. He concluded, a little ashamedly, that he was certain Dr. Nolan would have handled such a situation with tact. For a young doctor to have a religious argument with a preacher—it had been an incredible folly. It had been a lesson, too, but Parris wondered if he would have to learn all of the lessons of adjustment to Kings Row as painfully as this one.

Less than a week later Dr. Henry Gordon died. Parris was surprised to find himself one of the honorary pallbearers.

It was the largest funeral Kings Row had ever seen. The Presbyterian church was crowded to the last seat of the high gallery. Parris endured the penance of hearing the Reverend Cole preach a lengthy sermon on "a great physician who was also a humble man of God."

"He never in his long career of service to the sick and the afflicted allowed the petty and uncertain science of man to cloud his vision of Almighty God.

"He saw the scourge of God fall upon the guilty shoulders of sinful humanity. With unfailing faith and certain humility he addressed himself to his divinely appointed task of binding up the wounds which man's transgressions of God's law inflicted upon him. He never questioned the justice of the punishment, but always used the occasion to bring home to the soul the great lesson of suffering without which mere man is an unbearable example of pride and self-sufficiency."

There was much in this vein, and Parris was certain that most of it was directed at his own head. His attention wandered after a while. He had noticed that Louise was not present. He wondered a little about it, but supposed that she might be ill. He could scarcely suppose her too grief-stricken to be present. He thought she had never cared very deeply for her father, and then he wondered why he thought so.

"… He is gone, and we shall not soon see his like again. A great tree is fallen, and there is an empty place against the sky. What young man trained in the arts of healing will have sufficient humility of spirit, sufficient faith in the justice of Almighty God, to take his place? We do not see such an one. May God, in his mercy, send him speedily."

Parris wanted to smile. What a fool, he thought, and what a hideous advantage a fool takes of his position! He hoped he would not have to see or hear much of the Reverend Edmund Brewster Cole.

After the funeral Parris left the cemetery on foot. It was a stony-cold day, and the afternoon was darkening rapidly. The walks were covered with ice and sleet. Sometimes he had to hold to the picket fences to keep his footing.

He stopped before the little German parsonage. He could see the warm, steady lamplight and the flicker of firelight, too, through the stiff lace curtains. He rang, and Herr Berdorff himself answered.

"*Ach,* I am glad to see you today. What are you doing out in such weather?"

"Funeral."

"*Ach,* yes. Dr. Gordon. Let me hang your coat here. Come into my study now and have a cup of hot coffee. I always read how people die catching cold at other people's funerals."

"You're a cheerful prophet, Professor. But I'd love the coffee."

"Kätchen will bring it. Come in and sit down. One minute and I am back again. Pull close your chair to the fire."

Parris sank gratefully into the deep chair before the open fire.

There was a thick haze of tobacco smoke in the room, and several heavy books lay open on the low table beside Herr Berdorff's chair. It was peaceful, and quiet, and comfortable—oddly withdrawn and Old World here in this little town far from all of the traditions and ideas which made the life of this scholarly, obscure German preacher.

Herr Berdorff came back. Parris wondered why he used to be so awed. The Professor was like thousands of professional men in Germany or Austria. Stern, yes, but—

Herr Berdorff sat down. "We talk German, yes?"

"*Natürlich.*"

"Good. So you have been to Dr. Gordon's funeral?"

"Yes. And I think most of the sermon was about me."

"You?"

"Yes."

Parris told the story of his meeting with Mr. Cole. Herr Berdorff nodded his head.

"Yes, yes. I know. The work of the church is sometimes—how shall I say? Perhaps just that *der lieber Gott* sometimes has to make use of improbable instruments. It is hard to judge, but very hard not to, is it not?"

"I think the man is terrible."

"Yes. It seems so. It is hard to judge, as I say." Herr Berdorff lighted his huge calabash pipe.

"It is like this sometimes, Parris: the preacher who has much hard work to do becomes perhaps too zealous, he believes too much in himself, he thinks of himself as the emissary of God—and naturally he thinks who is there to question God?—and he too becomes impatient. He merely wishes you to listen while he tells you!"

Parris laughed.

Herr Berdorff shook a little and blew clouds of smoke through his thick black whiskers.

"It is an ecclesiastical sin." He laughed again. "It's also a peculiarly German trait, though I believe your Mr. Cole is Scotch. I know of this tendency myself. But I am not saying what I began. I wished to say that too often the preacher feels that he must explain everything, reconcile everything, and justify God in the sight of man."

The old man had trouble with his pipe. After it was going again, he nodded as if affirming his own words.

"Nowhere else must a man be expected to justify the sources and elements of his work. You do not understand all of the mysteries of the human body. You do not know why a drug behaves so with one patient, and differently with another. No one demands that you should know.

"You are young, Parris, but you were long my pupil. You will pardon me, I know, if I advise sometimes a little. You have not said so to me, but I suspect that you do not believe in God."

Parris started to speak, but Herr Berdorff checked him.

"You have not said so, ever, to me because you fear to hurt my feelings—maybe you think it could insult my calling. This is foolishness. God does not belong to me. I did not make Him. As I said, you are young. It is common not to believe in God when one is young. I, myself—" He waved aside the recollection with a gesture.

"It is most possible that in twenty-five years, in forty years you will be less sure about the hand of God in the affairs of man. There is so much that otherwise is intolerable—impossible to think about.

"Mind you, I do not preach—not to you, and not today. I preach on Sunday—to those who come for the purpose of listening to me. *Ach,* Kätchen, the coffee."

The becapped maid curtsied to Parris.

"Good day, Kätchen. I remember your coffee and your coffee-cake."

Kätchen blushed.

"There is coffeecake today—see, and fresh butter."

"Wonderful."

Herr Berdorff laid his pipe aside. "And it is all for you, Parris. Coffeecake? *Nein!* It is neither cake nor bread!"

"The bread and butter is for you, Herr Berdorff." Kätchen poured the coffee.
"Good. Now. So. Thank you, Kätchen."

Parris drank the coffee and ate the cake absently.

Herr Berdorff took up his pipe again after a while.

"The position of a preacher becomes steadily more difficult, particularly if he is a man of integrity. Science strikes at the root of so much which he must preach and teach. The higher criticism in Germany, which you may scarcely mention, attacks the very text itself. But I think all of this is really nothing. Of course religion leaves much unexplained. But science leaves still more without explanation. Very early in my studies a great scientist remarked that so far science had explained nothing—it had merely found names for phenomena. But the antagonist of religion rushes at us again and again demanding that we explain, and reconcile each new word of science in relation to the Bible. The Bible, which is only a simple story compared to what each of us must sometimes know in his heart."

"I don't understand you, Professor, when you begin to talk about revelation, or become mystical."

"I myself, Parris, do not understand the simplest emotion, or aspiration of my own heart. I do not understand most things. Any theory of the universe leaves so many things out in the cold. Science does not account for music—it cannot very well account for the religious emotion. No! No! Do not tell me of primitive beginnings. I understand these childish things, of course—but the aspiration that remains, the *necessity* for this aspiration when all else is swept away—that I do not understand."

The professor raked the coals forward in the fireplace and laid some logs on the andirons.

"You will stay for supper tonight? Kätchen expects it, I could see. Can you, from your work, today?"

"Yes. Thank you, I'll be happy to stay. Shall I run out and tell Kätchen?"

"I can tell from the great alarms she makes out there among the pans that she expects you. Rest quietly. She will call us when all is ready."

Parris lay back in the chair and closed his eyes.

"This is very nice, Parris. I have not seen you often enough since you came back."

"I've been working hard. But I'm settled into it now, and into as much of a schedule as a doctor ever has."

"Tell me, you like this work?"

"Very much."

"You do not regret the music?"

"I practiced all the time I was in Vienna."

Herr Berdorff sat up. His eyes were shining.

"You don't say so? You did not tell me this. You practice now, too?"

"I've begun again."

"You have a good piano out there?"

"I bought a Bechstein in Germany."

"*Ach,* so?"

"I'll be coming around for you to hear me, and help me again."

"Maybe you do not need me now."

"Just as always."

Professor Berdorff was immensely pleased.

"I miss you, you and the little Lichinsky."

"Haven't you some interesting pupils now?"

"No. No more. Dunderheads."

"You know I saw Vera several times."

"You wrote me in your letters. And her concerts were good?"

"Very good. In fact she's pretty well known everywhere now, but—"

"Yes? What?"

"A rather peculiar thing happened shortly before I left."

"To Vera? I have heard nothing."

"Well, she was slated for an appearance at the Mannheim festival during the summer. She came to see me and seemed to be very much upset about something. She never told me what about. But she canceled her date there, and one or two others. She tried to talk to me about it but she was rather incoherent. I thought she was on the very edge of a breakdown—she'd been playing a lot—and I sent her to a doctor. She came once more, but I was in the thick of examinations, and preparations to come home, too, and I didn't talk to her much. She looked a little wild-eyed, and said something about not playing this year. She went off to the Tyrol shortly afterward."

"And you have not heard more?"

"I went to see her father. He said she was having a rest, that she had overworked."

"It is too bad."

"Yes. She's pretty serious. Doesn't know how to let down, I'd guess."

"She has really no brains, the little Lichinsky."

"Oh, now—"

"No. Not really. Musical she is, yes, very—talented. And a kind of blind genius for work, but I never found that she could think."

"Well, anyway, she's made a genuine success, there's nothing uncertain about that. She plays magnificently, really."

"I have had fears of her career, always."

"Why?"

"I do not know."

"I believe they may be groundless. She's already made a place in the best concert ranks."

"It is interesting. I must go by the jewelry shop to see her father. He has maybe late news."

"I fancy she just needed a rest."

"Yes. She would not know very well how to do that. And you—you practiced! That is fine. That is fine."

"Had some lessons, too."

"You found the time?"

"I made it. You'd never guess whom I had lessons with."

"Now, who?"

"Leschetizky!"

"Lesche—oh, yes. One hears of him much now, since Paderewski."

"Well, he didn't think I could be a concert pianist, and wasn't much interested when I told him I didn't want to be. But we talked, and he was pleased with the way I played—credit to you, there!—and I really had a few private lessons with him. Went to his classes. The old man was pretty nice to me. He's peppery, though. A genius at teaching."

"How so?"

"Like this—" The discussion went on until Kätchen called them to supper. Afterward it was continued at the piano.

Herr Berdorff nodded vigorously at each step of Parris' explanations.

"Yes, I can see that. It is good. It works, eh?"

"Made a lot of things easier. Makes good tone, I think."

"Yes. I can see the reason for that. Good. I learn something today. That does not happen to me often—not now. Please come often. I want to hear about your special work, too. I have been reading—this new stuff, all of it. I'd like you to tell me."

"I'll be delighted. I'll do the best I can. Some of it will shock you."

"Me? I do not shock easily."

"Well—we'll see. It's really a new psychology, Professor, and so far as my work is concerned, it's a start in the direction of a new technique. It's, in a way, judging the mind by the apparent way the mind itself behaves. And—and devising new tricks to catch the mind unawares."

"I do not understand this at all. You will have to begin at the beginning with me, I imagine. Have you some books I could read?"

"Tons of them!"

"Good. I will begin. Isn't it exciting to think of a new field, and of learning maybe a new way of thinking about something?"

"It is, exactly, Professor. But I'm afraid there aren't many like you."

"Nonsense."

"I'm serious. Mostly people don't want to be disturbed in what they already think, or they're like our Mr. Cole—they know everything now."

Herr Berdorff laughed. "You have also the youthful pessimism. But now, I want to play something for you. It is a nice set of variations. I have composed them this summer. No one has heard them."

"A *première!*"

"Sure enough! I have waited to have you listen. *Wozu hat man Freunde wenn er sie nicht rupft?* The theme is a little folk song. I remember it from my childhood. Twelve variations and a nice double fugue."

"How did you find time?"

"Time? *Ach,* it was a hot summer! One must be occupied."

Herr Berdorff moved piles of books and music from the top of the piano. He smiled. "I open her up a little. It comes out better, the music."

Parris realized that the Professor was excited. It amused him a little to see his giant old teacher being a bit fluttery. It flattered him also, and touched him.

"I'll help you."

"*Ach,* no! Sit. One minute now."

Parris moved to a corner of the sofa so that he could view the keyboard. Herr Berdorff looked astonishingly like a famous lithograph of Johannes Brahms as he sat down and ran his fingers briskly up and down the keyboard. He adjusted his seat once more and thundered out a series of mighty chords as if commanding the silence and attention of a great audience. He breathed heavily through his nose and waggled his head at Parris.

"We go now, *hein?*"

The first notes of a familiar little folk song, simply harmonized, came like pure crystal from the piano.

All at once the harshness of mood that had possessed Parris for weeks melted and fell away. He relaxed and rested his head on his hand. The Professor played the little tune with such simplicity and such artlessness that Parris had to make some effort to keep back tears. The music suggested and brought back to him so many details of the past five years: Christmas trees, little blue-eyed girls with taffy-candy smooth plaits of hair bound about their heads, the good smell of cinnamon cookies, and a hundred naïve ways of life that he had already half-forgotten. He set these tiny colored vignettes of recollection against the hard and uncompromising background of his present, and something close to rebellion stirred in him. Perhaps he was wrong to be here. Perhaps it had been a mistake to return. A brief reprise of the theme in minor, a tiny wistful four-measure coda, blurred across his attention like rain across a windowpane.

Herr Berdorff ended unexpectedly in the major key. He nodded again to Parris.

The theme was repeated—scarcely changed, but with a subtle filling of the harmonies and occasional chromatic changes. The theme had been like a child's face. The variation was like seeing the same face grown older, a little wiser of look, but not sad.

The pianist leaned lower over the keyboard. It was really fine playing, Parris realized. Unaffected, capable, and in distinguished taste.

The variations that followed were like so many scenes of childhood. They were rollicking, gay, dreaming, and then suddenly there was a group shot through with uncertain, wavering lights. Bits of the theme and the simple harmonies of the beginning showed through like glimpses of lighted windows caught through windy trees and storm,

Parris listened with an increasing astonishment. This was not just *made* music of a literate musician. Now and then obvious, now and then a shade banal, it still had a shy poetry and a quality of sure inspiration.

The music became more serious. There were troubled variations, the familiar German *Sturm und Drang*, and then an odd repetition of the theme that Parris could not quite grasp: it sounded like an inversion of the theme played against itself, as though one saw a cherished face in a distorting mirror.

Herr Berdorff's "nice double fugue" was a good solid German fugue, learned, didactic, disproportionately heavy, but with a sterling shine of honesty about it. He finished. Parris looked up and smiled. Herr Berdorff smiled, too. Both of them made little approving German-fashion gestures with their heads. They did not have to talk. Herr Berdorff fussed about and brought out the manuscript. Parris looked through it, pointing out passages he had particularly liked.

"It is difficult, isn't it?"

"It is not easy, but for you—if you should ever care to practice it maybe a little, it is not too much."

"Of course I want to learn it. It's good, Professor, it's real music."

"You think so?"

"Of course it is."

It was, Parris realized, a rather amazingly realistic bit of autobiography set out in musical notation. The innocence and sweetness, the solid integrity and stern self-searching of the old preacher musician, were as clear as day. These qualities, taken together, summed up something that was clearly nobility. Nobility of character, nobility of mind, and a noble search for authentic beauty.

Nobility! Parris thought how strange the word seemed as it came to consciousness. It's very strangeness was a sort of commentary. One had almost forgotten the word because one so seldom saw the quality itself. He wondered if he were being "young" again. This new pessimism and cynicism came so easily. Where had it come from? It was new in his own experience, but he felt, now as he weighed the sentiment, that it had always lain deep like a bitter salt stream beneath his thinking.

With the thought came a kind of shame. He turned the pages of the beautifully written manuscript, noting again and again the neat felicity of the counterpoint, the almost modern touches of harmony. This man, burdened with the dull job of shepherding a thickheaded and cranky flock, was able to turn with a clear and childlike freshness of vision to a graceful exercise of an exacting art. "*One must be occupied!*"

The music was, Parris realized again, not merely autobiography, but a naïve kind of credo. Here, in inhospitable surroundings, this man did not forget to practice a gospel that more than anything Parris could think of might have within itself the power to save one's soul.

Drake and Randy prospered during the next year. Parris watched over Drake with an anxiety that was not apparent to anyone except Randy. Often she sat observing the two as they laughed and talked and planned. One thing she noticed particularly: Parris always led Drake away from reminiscence by appearing uninterested. More and more she saw Drake live in the present, and look with something like eagerness and faith to the future. She was often aware of the tension underlying Parris' professional scrutiny of Drake's manner and appearance.

It was more than a year after his return from Europe that she detected signs of relief and assurance in his face as he talked with Drake.

One evening as he was leaving he stopped at the door and looked quizzically at Randy.

"Do you suppose you'd hate to give me a cup of coffee? It's pretty cold out there."

"Why, of course I won't hate it, silly. Come on out with me while I make it."

In the kitchen Parris laid his hand on her arm. "Don't bother to make it. Is there some left from supper?"

"Yes, but—"

"I just wanted to talk to you for a minute, anyhow."

Her eyes darkened a little. "What's the matter, Parris? Is Drake—"

"He's all right. I just wanted to say that I think we've won in a very ticklish fight. I didn't know a year ago whether we could bring Drake back or not. I think we have."

"Bring him back? I don't understand, quite, Parris. Was he—?"

"Drake was more shattered in—not in his mind exactly—I guess I have to say in his soul than he was in body. Our job has been to bring him back to himself. You've done the biggest share of it yourself."

"I did just what you told me—as nearly as I could."

"You've been pretty wonderful, Randy. Drake was lucky. He's all right. He's just Drake, now. He's like anyone else. As normal as anybody can be expected to be. We can go on from here now treating him pretty much like anyone."

Randy began to cry, softly.

"Parris, you—"

"Drake was and is my best friend, Randy. Drake was just as necessary to me when I came back as, maybe, I have been to him."

"You—I can't tell you—I can't say it!"

"Don't try. By the way, isn't that coffee boiling?"

"Oh, dear, yes. Wait. I will make some more. This would be terrible."

"Never mind. I don't really need it."

"Please, I'd like to."

"All right. Go ahead."

Parris shoved a chair toward the kitchen table and sat down. Randy stood for a moment looking at him.

"What's the matter, Randy?"

"You said just now that you considered Drake all right—just as he always was. What about you?"

Parris looked puzzled.

Randy finished the preparations for coffee. "Yes, Parris, you."

"Why—why—I think—well, what do you mean?"

"I've known ever since you got back here to Kings Row that you're not happy. I don't mean to meddle with your business in any way, but—I just wondered if there is anything I can do for you."

"You're a sweet kid to think about me. I guess I'm not exactly hilarious, but it's just a matter of readjustment. I—I didn't like Kings Row when I came back."

"I know that. I could see it."

"Well—Drake kept me here."

"I guessed that, too."

"He was not only my good friend in trouble, but he was a sort of professional job."

"And now you want to go away."

"Go away?"

"Yes. Don't you?"

"You were never more mistaken in your life. I've got my job—it's work I like and want to do."

"I'm glad, Parris. I'd hate to see you go away."

"I never expect to. It's a little hard to explain, but in some way that lies considerably beyond the ordinary meaning of the word, this is home. I guess I'd say I grew out of this place. I was pretty suddenly and violently uprooted, and when I came back there didn't seem to be anything here that I thought *was* here. My friendship with Drake was about all that was left of parent soil—do you understand what I mean?"

"I think so."

"Drake, and old Professor Berdorff. Funny, I always thought of him as old, because of his big black beard, I suppose. I was surprised to death not long ago to find that he's just fifty-five. Well—it took me a while to put down roots again. The hospital is new ground, of course."

Randy nodded. She was afraid to speak. She understood that Parris needed to talk about himself a little.

"Randy, do you know what mysticism is?"

"No—yes!"

"Well, which? No? Yes?"

"I kind of know, I guess. Belief in something that is behind something else that isn't there."

Parris laughed, and Randy set cups on the table. For the first time Parris saw in her face the impish look she used to have as a little girl.

"Well, that'll do as a starting point! I hate mysticism, as I hate everything that isn't clear. And that's ridiculous, too, because just about all of my work is concerned with chasing spooks that aren't there. I have to try to keep myself and my ideas realistic, but hallucinations—I'm getting off the track. I started out to say something else. I'm not exactly in love with Kings Row, nor with the town, or the way it looks, nor any places in the town, nor the people that live here. But I'm attracted to all of the stages of being I went through right here. Maybe I like the place where the town is—because I honestly think the town itself is pretty awful—and the place happens to be the scene of all my memories. I guess I'm not being very explicit."

"I understand something of what you mean. Go on."

Randy poured the coffee and sat down on the opposite side of the table.

"I thought and felt certain things here. I went through certain experiences here. Now a lot of people carry their spiritual homes around with them—either inside of them, or, well, maybe the way a snail carries his shell on his back: I can't do that. I have to have a place. And, strangely enough, this is my place. I hate it sometimes. I haven't found any life here outside of the hospital except you and Drake and Herr Berdorff, but I know in some sort of way that I've got to be here. I used to love to walk about the country and—just look at it. I loved every leaf and stick of it. I have to learn to do that again."

He stirred his coffee vigorously, and drank rather absently.

"I used to walk a lot around Vienna."

"Was it beautiful?"

"Very."

"Are you homesick for Europe?"

"I guess I was for a while, but—it's curious, Randy. I'm in some ways more European than American, but I don't much like Europeans—not deeply. They're older and more cynical, and that very cynicism—no, it's more like fatalism—acts like a frost. I used to long for the youthful dreams of my own country. We're incorrigible dreamers, really, and we are full of projects, like little boys. Somebody says, 'Let's do this or that,' and then we actually do it! We don't know as much as the Europeans, but—oh, and Kings Row is downright backwoods, really—but we've got something that can grow into something else. The Europeans don't seem to me to have that. They are already what they are—a finished product."

"Another cup, Parris?"

"Yes—" Parris laughed. "You know I don't remember drinking it! I'm talking too much."

"It's your own medicine, Doctor."

"What?"

"You know—talking it out. You've explained it to me—"

"Maybe. How did this get started, anyway?"

"You needed to talk to someone, that's all."

"Well, I know I'm going home—that's the first time I've said 'home' since I landed here!"

"Maybe you ought to get married, Parris."

He looked at her thoughtfully. "No, Randy, I don't think so. There doesn't seem to be any room anywhere for that kind of—an arrangement." He stood up.

"Well, good night, Parris. Hope the coffee doesn't keep you awake."

"Good night, Randy."

There was a special-delivery letter lying under the lamp on his table when he reached his apartment. It was postmarked Kings Row. He opened it and read:

Dear Dr. Mitchell:

I haven't had the pleasure of meeting you since your return from abroad, and I regret that my first communication with you is somewhat professional rather than social.

I shall be grateful if you will call as soon as convenient. I should like, also, to have you keep this in strict confidence.

Very truly,

HARRIET GORDON

(Mrs. Henry Gordon)

P.S. It would be more convenient if you could call some evening after supper, instead of during the day.

H. G.

Parris frowned. Mrs. Henry Gordon! Strange ...

He shrugged, tore the letter into small pieces, and dropped the shreds on the dying coals in the fireplace.

The paper blazed up for a moment. He watched it until the ashy fragments grayed against the fire beneath them. He turned and looked around the apartment. The door stood open into his study. Beyond he could see a dim light burning in the bedroom. He had called this "home." Without thinking.

It was a small apartment on the fifth floor of the central administrative building of the hospital, identical with those assigned to all bachelor staff members. It was comfortable, and the view from the windows through the tops of the tall elm trees and across the town was fine at all seasons. The many books, his writing table in the next room, his, big Bechstein piano—Parris sighed a little and shrugged his shoulders again, rather as if he were shaking off something that oppressed him.

Randy's suggestion that he marry found no response in him, nor did it disturb him in any way. There was no one ... But something else did disturb him. Just two words she had spoken in her friendly fashion: "*And you?*"

He had said Drake was "all right," and then she had asked that disconcerting question. He wondered why she had asked it at all. He was "all right." He was well, and busy, and—yes, he was happy enough. He supposed he had always been serious, more or less. He wasn't a kid any more to go hopping about. Once more there was an almost imperceptible flick of his eyebrows and the beginning of a gesture that might have moved into his characteristic, French-looking shrug of dismissal.

He supposed maybe he had been taking himself pretty seriously. He had been trying to live up to the praise and the good opinion of Dr. Nolan and the staff. Perhaps he had been overgrave. Young doctors were likely to assume a look of heavy responsibility.

It seemed to Parris that he had never at any time since his return from Vienna really had a moment to think about himself. He had come back to Kings Row quite as he might have come to a strange town. He had made almost no effort to see anyone, except Drake, and the men at the bank who were directly concerned in his affairs. His anxiety for Drake had been an absorbing matter. He had called at the Farmers Exchange Bank twice to see Jamie Wakefield, but that had been a dismal experience. Jamie had aged peculiarly. He was dry and bankerish, and clearly was rather reluctant to take up an old friendship where it had been dropped. Parris wondered if Jamie had come to know more about himself and shrank, consequently, from association with a physician. He had observed closely to determine Jamie's standing in the bank and in the town. So far as he could tell, no one seemed to sense that Jamie was anything but a shy and reserved young man whose tastes kept him at home during his leisure time. A few people called him "Miss Nancy," but no one seemed to imply much by the nickname.

It would have been pleasant, Parris thought, to have talked with Jamie about poetry, and nature, and such things. Jamie had had a genuinely poetic streak, he decided. But there was no time to urge and pursue a friendship that did not seem to be welcomed. Parris sighed again. He somehow regretted that he couldn't be grieved about Jamie. Jamie was now completely turned in on himself, and like all of his kind must go on living in the strange limbo of an increasing detachment and isolation.

Parris knew that it was not the fault of the town that he felt himself so much a stranger. His own detachment followed certainly on an attitude of his own, and his isolation, outside of his actual work, was greater than Jamie's.

And you?

Oh, damn the teasing question! He went into the bedroom and began to undress. He switched on lights and made a good deal of clatter moving about.

The lights in the white-tiled bathroom were dazzling, and he avoided the blinding glare for a moment. He turned the spigots, but the water ran slowly on this top floor. He threw a towel over an enameled bench and sat down to wait for the bath to fill. The bluish, greenish ripples chased back and forth in the deep tub which stood high on claw feet. Something about the patterns in the water made him think of the little pools and shallows of the creek where he used to play with Renée.

He leaned against the wall, but the tiles were icy against his back, and he straightened up again. Renée ... and Cassie ... and somehow Jamie moving through the drift of recollections. Events stood out with flaming clarity against the half haze of the surrounding time. Events, distinct and painful. It was not easy to summon back a sure feeling of just how deep the pain had been. That it had been real, he had no doubt. That much he could say. But—he felt his way cautiously as one moves in a half light along almost forgotten paths—Renée ... Cassie ...

He wondered with a slight stir of uneasiness, if all that these experiences had meant was really safely sealed away, or if deep in his subconscious they still exerted pressures he was not aware of. It might be, as he thought cautiously along prescribed lines, that he remembered too well, too clearly, and had remembered too often for those crises of the past to have established complexes of any kind. In a way which he perfectly understood now, he had loved Renée with the pure clear fire that belongs to such a period. All that followed was no fault of his own. It left a deep and agonizing wound at the time. Scars of old wounds like these may ache at times. Certainly this one could. It was an ache that came quickly at the faintest adumbration of recollection.

Cassie. That had been different. But again it was the tragic conclusion for which he was not to blame, that laid the haunting shadow on the time and on his memory of it.

He had little enough in the recollections of his boyhood life in Kings Row to be happy about. The nature of his bereavements and his griefs had been too dark, and too severe for a boy. And now that he was living again in the scene of their happening there must be at times some unconscious associations; some spectral presences ...

A splash on his foot aroused him. The tub was running over. He hastily cut off the water, released the drain—and went absently back to his study. He had completely forgotten his bath.

A week passed before Parris was free to call on Mrs. Gordon. She answered his ring herself and greeted him in a restrained half voice which gave him an uncomfortable feeling at once. She ushered him into the parlor where a bright fire was burning in an old-fashioned open-front stove. The room had a musty smell, and a slight chill hung in the air. The fire had evidently been kindled for his visit.

"Sit down, Dr. Mitchell."

"Thank you, Mrs. Gordon."

"It's been a long time since I've seen you. Of course I've heard—Louise was always speaking of Parris Mitchell."

"How is Louise? I haven't seen her since I came back."

"No. I fancy not. I want to talk to you about Louise. But first tell me about yourself. Could I offer you a cup of hot chocolate? They tell me it's very cold out."

"Nothing, thank you."

Mrs. Gordon was nervous and fluttery. Parris wondered what brought Mrs. Gordon to summon him on what she had said was a "rather professional" call. He was not a general practitioner, nor did he have patients of any kind outside of the hospital. Mrs. Gordon must know that. In any case it would have been natural for her to call one of Dr. Gordon's older colleagues. He listened to her fragmentary small talk and made mechanical answers.

Mrs. Gordon sat, very stiff and straight, in an incongruous Roman chair. She was much thinner than she used to be, and the bone structure of her face stood out with rather uncomfortable distinctness. Her hair, a surprisingly even dark chestnut, waved evenly and was fastened high with a comb. The comb reminded him of his grandmother. He wandered a little ...

"... after Dr. Gordon passed away."

"I beg your pardon."

Mrs. Gordon looked sharply at him. "I said, that I have been going through a very trying experience since my husband passed away."

"Oh, I'm sorry to hear that."

"Dr. Mitchell, I'm sure you were surprised to hear from me. I wrote you, as I said, in strictest confidence. I don't want any talk of any kind to get started. Somehow I felt that I could trust your discretion since you used to be a friend of Louise."

Parris waited without replying. Mrs. Gordon moved forward in her chair. "I have called you to speak about Louise."

"Yes."

"I am at a loss what to do. Indeed, I don't know quite where to begin, but—"

"Is Louise ill?"

"I don't know."

Mrs. Gordon twisted the ends of her black-lace scarf. "Dr. Mitchell, I've been afraid Louise's mind has been affected."

She waited. Parris nodded slowly. "Do you wish me to see her?"

"Presently, Dr. Mitchell. First let me explain a little. You may remember that some time ago Louise had a most unfortunate attachment for one of the most undesirable boys in this town."

"You are speaking of Drake McHugh."

"Yes—a very sad case. His aunt was one of my friends, but she knew nothing of rearing children. I suppose I was lax in my care of Louise, but before I could guess what might happen she imagined she was in love with him."

"Yes, Mrs. Gordon. I know all of those circumstances. You might just tell me what happened later."

"Dr. Mitchell, Louise hated her father!"

"Really? Why?"

"I could never guess. Dr. Gordon was a saint." The woman's face was suddenly transformed. A look that was curiously still and white gave her an appearance of—Parris almost said "exaltation." It might have been nearly such an appearance if it had not been at the same time so hard, and so—yes, it was a cruel look. Every line of Mrs. Gordon's expression was fanatic.

"I could never guess. She hated him, maybe because her own nature was so different. She was always rebellious and—difficult to discipline. When— when—," Mrs. Gordon struggled for composure. Parris saw that her agitation was deep and genuine. He felt a little creepy. He decidedly did not like this interview. He was on the point of suggesting that it might be advisable to speak to someone else when she read his thought. She held up her hand.

"No, Dr. Mitchell, I must speak to *you*. I feel that you will understand this—that you will understand Louise and help me in some way."

"Very well. But I think I should see Louise and—"

"I must prepare you a little for what you will find."

Mrs. Gordon laid her hand on her heart and closed her eyes for a second.

"Listen, Doctor. After Drake McHugh met with his accident Louise had a terrible scene with Dr. Gordon. Then, a few days later we heard the strange report that he had actually married a—a—"

"A Miss Monaghan, whom I know quite well, and who has taken marvelous care of Drake, Mrs. Gordon."

"Really? It seems remarkable, doesn't it? But from that day on Louise refused to leave her room. We could do nothing with her—nothing. Dr. Gordon was not really well at the time—he was frightfully overworked—and the burden of trying to manage her fell on me."

"Manage her?"

"I don't mean that she was violent. She wouldn't speak. She did nothing but sit in her room. Then Dr. Gordon passed away. And now I have to tell you a terrible thing."

Mrs. Gordon held a handkerchief to her mouth. She was shaking.

"When—when my dear husband was lying—here—in this room, Louise came downstairs. I followed her after a few minutes, and found her—"

"Yes, Mrs. Gordon. Try to tell me—quietly."

"I—I found her—striking her dead father in the face, and—and cursing him!"

Parris caught his breath with surprise. He waited a moment before speaking.

"I see. What did she say?"

"Nothing, to me. I managed to get her upstairs without anyone knowing about—the incident. I locked her in her room. That's why she was not at the funeral."

"And afterward?"

"She kept silent. She showed no inclination to leave her room, and I decided it might be better to keep her door locked. No one knows but the two servants. They have been with me for years, but I am sure that there is talk. Have you heard anything at all?"

"Not a word. This is the first."

"She used to say terrible things about her father, and accuse him of unspeakable things. Dr. Mitchell, I am a desperate mother. I want you to see Louise now and tell me what I should do. I—I cannot bear that my daughter should be insane, or that she should so defame the memory of a great man."

Parris arose quickly.

"Where is she?"

"I'll go with you. Then I'll leave you to talk to her."

Mrs. Gordon led the way to a rear room upstairs. She unlocked the door. The room was stuffy and overheated. The only light came from a hanging lamp that appeared to be out of reach.

Louise was lying on the bed with her arms crossed over her face.

"Daughter, listen to me. I've brought an old friend to see you."

Louise almost leapt from the bed. She looked wildly at Parris and sat down weakly.

"It's Parris Mitchell, daughter. Dr. Mitchell now, and he's come to see you."

Parris held out his hand. "Hello, Louise."

She looked at him for a full minute. Then she held out her hand. "Parris?"

"Yes."

"Parris Mitchell. Sit down."

"I'm awfully glad to see you, Louise. It's been a long time."

"Yes." She repeated the words mechanically. "It's been a long time."

She kept her gaze fixed on his face. After a moment she turned toward her mother. "Go away."

Mrs. Gordon half sobbed, as she left the room.

Louise continued to stare. Her face was flushed, but it might have been from the overheated room. Her hair was untidy and hung about her shoulders.

She wore a silk robe over a crumpled nightgown. Her feet were bare, and she sat childlike with one foot resting on the other. She was very thin, but her fragile prettiness remained.

She took a deep breath.

"You are Dr. Mitchell now?"

"Yes, Louise."

"I'm not crazy, Parris."

He smiled. "Of course not."

"She thinks I am."

"Does she?"

"Yes. It's a wonder I'm not, but I'm not."

"I know that, Louise."

"Have you seen Drake?"

"Yes."

"How is he?"

"As well as he can be."

"She married him!"

"Yes."

"She was a whore. But that was what he liked. He never went with any other kind."

"She takes good care of him, Louise. He had to have care, you understand."

"My father cut his legs off, Parris."

"Yes, I know."

"I was there."

Parris was startled. "You were where?"

"Down at some kind of a depot. I saw the—I saw—"

"You saw the operation?"

"No. I was too late."

"What do you mean, Louise?"

"If I'd have known, I could have called Dr. Saunders or somebody, maybe. I saw—"

"Yes." Parris laid his hand over hers, and she seized it with both of hers. "I saw what was left—*on a table!*"

Louise bit her lips hard.

"I'm not crazy, Parris."

"I know, Louise."

"You must find out. There was a man who helped my father. Maybe he'd know."

"Yes, Louise. Know what?"

"I don't believe it was necessary. He cut off Drake's legs on my account."

Parris started in spite of himself and, before he could think, drew back a little.

"You see! You think I'm crazy, too."

"Not at all. You surprised me." He spoke very quietly.

"That was one reason—the other was that he was a butcher. Oh, I read about things like that. He was cold as ice. He liked to butcher people. He was—oh, I knew the word once, I read it—Parris, you know—he was a sadist."

Parris held very still and kept his eyes on her face.

"Listen, Parris. This is my one chance. You've got to believe me. You've got to listen. I kept lists—he always talked about his operations. Other doctors don't do that. And nearly always he said the patient's heart was too weak for chloroform. Remember that now. But their hearts were not too weak to be cut to pieces. I tell you, Parris, he liked to hear them scream."

She watched Parris as she talked. At that moment Parris was remembering something—a bright, sunny day, Renée, Willie Macintosh, and the appalling howls and screams of a man in utter agony. A slight moisture came out on his brow.

"Parris!" Louise shook his arm.

"You think I'm crazy."

"No, Louise."

"I want you to begin quietly. I want you to gather all the evidence. I want—"

"But your father is dead, Louise. It's all over and done with."

"*I want to destroy his memory!*"

Parris leaned back in his chair and waited. She leaned forward and looked under the bed.

"What is it, Louise?"

"I was just looking for my slippers. This is a terrible way to receive you."

"There they are, by the stove. I'll get them."

She smiled, ever so slightly, and held out her feet stiffly. He slipped on the satin house shoes for her. She pushed her hair back from her face.

"That's better." He smiled at her.

"Parris, will you help me?"

"Yes."

"You'll keep it a secret, until—"

"We'll keep it a secret."

"What shall I do first?"

"Get up tomorrow and dress and go out."

She shrank away from him.

"You'll do that for me, won't you?"

The fright in her eyes subsided a little. "Yes, Parris."

"Fine. Now—"

Dr. Thaddeus Nolan regarded Parris with scarcely concealed concern. Dr. Nolan had the face of a wise man, and a kind one. Several weeks earlier

Parris had told him in detail the story of Louise Gordon. Since then they had discussed it a number of times. Parris had been overmuch excited about the case at the beginning, Dr. Nolan felt. Later on he was less sure. Parris had made no direct effort to check any of Louise's accusations, but Dr. Nolan was able to recall an incredible number of instances which fitted perfectly into a purely hypothetical speculation as Dr. Nolan persisted in calling it.

"How do you find Louise, Mitchell? Any change?"

"No. She goes about a great deal now. But I detect a slyness about her now that doesn't look well at all. She's not following any suggestions of mine for the right reason. She's got plans of some kind. It's a simple case, really, and runs exactly true to form. Of course, every once in a while, I'm thrown off the track a little and wonder if I'm all wrong."

"That's regular, too, isn't it?" Dr. Nolan smiled.

"Yes, of course."

"I suppose there are as many kinds of hysteria, varieties, I mean, as there are human beings suffering from it. There is no other form of mental derangement that exhibits such a wide range of—of oscillation, so to speak, from what we like to think is the norm of the disease. We always have to base our whole finding on the environment, the exciting causes, and—what would seem to be factors outside of the case."

"Yes."

Dr. Nolan swung halfway around in his chair, and looked out of the window. He tapped his front teeth with his pince-nez.

"I knew Gordon for more than thirty years." The remark seemed detached—apropos of nothing. But Parris knew that Dr. Nolan did not make remarks apropos of nothing. He edged forward, and laid his arms on the desk.

"Dr. Nolan."

"Yes, Mitchell."

"I've never asked you one question, because I scarcely asked it of myself."

"I fancy I could guess it."

"Well, sir. I just tried to remember that I was dealing with the workings of an unhinged mind, and—"

"Well, go on."

"I'd like to ask if you think there could be the slightest possible ground for Louise's charges against her father."

Dr. Nolan brought his chair back again. He faced Parris.

"Yes," he said quietly.

The answer was so unexpected that Parris gasped.

"You don't mean it."

"Certainly I mean it. Sadistic surgeons are not unknown in medical history. After all, Mitchell, you are familiar with the extent and what people outside of our special branch of medicine would call unbelievable kinds of psychopathia that exist and always have existed."

"Well, yes. But, heavens—"

"Mind you, I don't say we *know* anything about such a phase of Gordon, really. I knew him, as I said, for more than thirty years. I knew that he was a fine diagnostician and an able surgeon. I never liked him, and in some ways I never trusted him. I don't suppose I ever asked myself why. Now, you're a little startled because you hear of some strange case that might have existed right here in Kings Row. It is the proximity of this kind of thing to our regular and normal experience that is shocking. If you had read of such a case existing in some remote town of Hungary, or Rumania, would you have been surprised, or shocked? Not at all. Your journals are filled with such reports. The psychiatrist in Budapest would have no difficulty in believing such a story of the remote North American town of Kings Row."

Parris smiled. "Yes, of course. I know, but—"

Dr. Nolan pulled at his short gray beard. "I said I wouldn't be surprised if there were grounds for Louise's belief. What she gathered, or imagined, or saw, or *knew,* is the cause of her trouble, not a result of it. Now, what exaggerations or transformations have followed, it is difficult to say. You have ascertained that Gordon did actually beat her rather often. That's something to go on. You don't hear of fathers in Gordon's kind of society beating their daughters—or finding it necessary. I never could say whether Gordon had a cruel face, or merely a cold face. Many surgeons have that kind of detachment that is so easily mistaken for lack of feeling."

"But, my lord, if it were true—"

"What?"

Parris flushed. His feelings were running away with him.

"Mitchell!"

"Yes, sir."

"You had better understand your own feeling in this matter. Were you ever interested at all in Dr. Gordon's daughter?"

"Oh, no. Never. Not in the least."

"I see. Then it's just because a remote possibility touches your friend, Drake McHugh."

"Yes, sir. I'm fully aware of that. I've been trying to keep an even keel."

"Pretty hard, sometimes. Now, see here. Suppose we knew for a fact that Dr. Gordon was all of the evil things Louise believes him to have been."

"Yes, sir."

"Where would you be? Any better off?"

"Well—"

"You'd know, that's all. But Gordon is dead. Whatever damage he may have done is done, and can't be undone. You can't do anything to him. Louise wants a post-mortem hate to be aroused. No end is served in this way."

"When I think of even a remote possibility that Drake McHugh—"

"I know, son. You might as well stop thinking about it. You never have sounded out Sam Winters, have you, to see if he thought anything unusual about that amputation?"

"No. Dr. Nolan, I know why I haven't. I'm afraid of what I might find out. That a man—a doctor—"

"Son. Men have often killed other men who were after their daughters. Stop to think of that."

"Murder, yes."

"Mitchell, I want to get you free of this Gordon case in some way. I don't like it. It isn't good for you, and it isn't good for the hospital—for us to be involved in just this way. If Mrs. Gordon wants an ordinary, routine examination of Louise to determine her sanity, why that's our business, but these half-social, *sub rosa* tactics—it's not a good idea."

"Oh, she's convinced that Louise is practically herself again."

"Louise is fooling her, and she's trying to fool us for her own purposes."

"I know that. She's determined to damage her father's memory in some way."

"There's another danger you haven't thought of—the obvious one. I'm surprised that you haven't thought of it."

"What is that?"

"Louise's attachment to you."

"What?"

"Why, it's plain as day. Just ordinary transference."

Parris sank back in his chair.

"Oh, my goodness."

"You see if she should come to feel that you're not co-operating with her any more against the memory of her father, she'd turn on you right away."

Parris nodded. "Of course."

"So, my boy, I guess we'd better begin watching out a little. Let's ease it off. I think if you could persuade Mrs. Gordon to take Louise away for a while— wouldn't do Louise a particle of good, but it might be pretty lucky for you."

Dr. Nolan continued to look speculatively and perhaps a little absently at Parris. Parris had more than fulfilled Dr. Nolan's hopes, even in this short time. The young doctor's winning trick of deference to the age and experience of his colleagues had endeared him to the whole staff. Dr. Nolan was pleased.

Kings Row, too, was beginning to hear highly favorable things about Dr. Mitchell, but the more they heard, the less they saw of him. He went out very little, but it was said that he was quite shy socially. Mrs. Cornfeldt, who knew a good deal about music, said that he was a fine pianist. Everyone had heard more or less about his devotion to the unfortunate Drake McHugh. It was thought very fine of Dr. Mitchell to maintain a loyal friendship for a boyhood acquaintance.

Just lately there had been a bit of gossip about Louise Gordon. Kings Row knew that Louise had had a very bad nervous breakdown. Mrs. Gordon had made it quite clear after a while that Dr. Mitchell had been consulted professionally, but later she was more reticent. Dr. Mitchell frequently walked in the late afternoon with Louise, and it was noticeable that Louise had "come out" amazingly. She was really a very pretty girl.

Parris was probably the only person who realized the brittle state of nerves that lay beneath Louise's apparent improvement. His concern had been greatly increased by Dr. Nolan's shrewd long-distance diagnosis. He realized that he would have to see less of Louise. It was going to be difficult to manage. Louise was abnormally quick at recognizing the motives behind any action taken for her benefit.

She had talked herself out rather thoroughly about her father. At present she seemed more released from that particular tension, but Parris knew that she was still snarled and tangled with various complexes about both of her parents.

One startling piece of information emerged from her chatter. It concerned the Towers. It puzzled Parris a little that Louise should be able to recall so much of what her mother had said years ago of other people. He brrought himself quickly to attention at the first mention of Dr. Tower and Cassie. Then gradually he pieced together the casual fragments. He was unable to recall precisely the words of Dr. Tower's diary at this point, but he was certain now that the mysterious person or persons who had blocked his purpose of working at the asylum had been the Gordons.

Parris was careful to ask Louise no direct questions, but again and again he brought the conversations around to easy reach of the subject. Finally, he was reasonably certain. Mrs. Gordon had apparently been a whisperer all of her life. It had really been Mrs. Gordon who had somehow prevented Dr. Tower's appointment to the asylum staff.

Parris discussed this with Dr. Nolan, but the events must have occurred prior to Dr. Nolan's appointment. Parris regretted having destroyed the Tower diary. There had been much of it which he did not understand at the time which doubtless would be clear today. One thing was obvious now. He must break off with the Gordons. First of all he recognized dangers—the obvious ones which Dr. Nolan had pointed out, and also obscurer ones that he sensed.

He wished he could talk to Drake, but so far he had been careful not to mention the name of Louise Gordon. He had no guess, even, what Drake's reaction might be. He wondered several times if Randy knew that he had been seeing Louise, but, again with her, it seemed a forbidden topic.

In the fall Louise had an attack of bronchitis, and Dr. Saunders, one of Kings Row's older doctors, was called. Dr. Saunders happily ended Parris' worries about Louise. He advised Mrs. Gordon to take Louise to Florida for the winter, and when his own advices were added, Mrs. Gordon agreed.

Parris shrugged the whole matter aside as best he could. Increasing burdens of work left him very little time for thought about anything outside of professional duties. Dr. Nolan had suggested that he write a series of studies for a newly founded journal of psychiatry, and he was spending as much time as he could on the preparation of these.

Winter was breaking into a wet, disagreeable early spring. Parris discovered suddenly that he was tired. He had not realized it until Dr. Nolan ordered a reorganization of his schedule. He had been playing the piano one day just after lunch. The afternoon was free, and he wondered what he should do with it. The playing was pretty bad, he decided. He had no time for satisfactory practice. He did not particularly wish to see Drake and Randy. There were times when he felt too much outside of the life in the little white house. Drake and Randy seemed to be really quite happy. They had made a go of their business. Drake was talking about repaying the Tower money that Parris had turned over to him. Parris had urged Drake to continue to use whatever profits came in for the enlargement of the business. Randy agreed that this was a good idea, but Drake still talked of some kind of formal business arrangement—a silent partnership, or something.

Parris walked to the mantel and looked at himself. Yes, he did look tired. He'd better go out, he decided. He'd drop in to see Drake and then take a long walk.

He was in sight of the Monaghan house when he heard Randy calling to him. She was half a block behind him, and he turned back to meet her.

"I'm awfully glad you came down today."

"'Specially?"

"Yes."

"Anything wrong, Randy?"

"N-no."

"Drake all right?"

"Yes. He's fine."

Randy's frank face was a little clouded.

"What's troubling you, Randy?"

"I'd like to talk to you a little while, Parris."

"Fine. I need talk today."

Randy lowered her head and walked a little distance before she spoke again.

"Let's go somewhere where we won't be interrupted, Parris."

"Why—of course. Where?"

"Well—let's just walk—on out this way." She pointed west.

It was a little-used back street that led toward the lower end of Aberdeen campus.

"Certainly. Now, hadn't you better tell me what's up?"

"In a minute. I don't—I'm not sure how to begin."

Parris frowned. It was most unlike Randy's usual behavior. She had never been mysterious before.

The street turned, following the low bank of the creek.

"There's the Old Cemetery. It looks a bit sunny. Couldn't we go in there and sit—and talk?" Randy actually choked a little.

"Child, what is the matter with you? I never saw you so excited."

"I'm not excited."

"Something's the matter."

"I'm a little worried, maybe."

"Oh."

"No, not worried, either. That's not the right word. I'm just a little troubled maybe, if that's different from being worried."

"Drake?"

"No: I'll tell you in a minute."

They crossed the stone stile and stood for a moment. Parris had been here two or three times to look after his grandmother's grave, but he hadn't walked about much since he used to come here with Jamie. The Old South Cemetery had always been one of Jamie's favorite spots.

"I want to go down this way, Randy, just a minute. Come along. Do you mind?"

"No. Not at all."

The narrow walk was hedged with tall shrubbery, some sort of aromatic-smelling evergreen. It suddenly reminded Parris of the evergreen thickets where he used to play with Renée.

They came presently to a small square enclosed with the same evergreen. The severe granite slabs had only names and dates: ALEXANDER Q. TOWER, AND CASSANDRA TOWER.

Parris looked at the plot with surprise. It was carefully tended, and some sort of shiny-leafed vine covered the ground and twined across the slabs.

He looked at Randy. She colored and looked a little embarrassed.

"I've been taking care of these graves, Parris. Drake told me that Cassie and her father meant a lot to you. I thought you'd like to have the place looked after."

"Well, bless your heart! Of course I'm glad you did it, but—I think the cemetery association, or whatever it is, is paid to look after this place for me."

"Oh, old Sam Winters just does a little."

"Well—thank you, Randy. I—I never have been able to make myself come here before."

Randy looked up suddenly.

"I hadn't realized, Parris—Drake didn't tell me much. I didn't know Cassie was—"

"I was devoted to both Dr. Tower and Cassie."

Parris was relieved that apparently Drake had told Randy so little. It was not the kind of memory that he could share with anyone. Just now he was hoping that Randy could not see how deeply shaken he was. He felt cold.

"Thank you, Randy. Let's go now."

They went back through the little green alley and across the cemetery to the slope where the sunshine was warmest.

They sat for a while on a painted wooden bench that faced the big Sansome plot.

"Well, Randy."

"I don't know how to begin, Parris."

"Just start."

"It's about you."

"Me?"

"Yes. I've been hearing some stories that I don't understand—so, I thought I'd better let you know."

Parris felt a curious chill of apprehension. He spoke a shade thickly.

"Well, go ahead."

It surprised him to discover that he was apprehensive of what Randy was about to tell him. He cleared his throat and repeated the words.

"Go ahead. What in the world could there be to make a story about me?"

"Well, I'll tell you as straight as I can, Parris. I've been hearing just fragments—stray bits of gossip—for several months—all winter in fact. At first I didn't pay any attention to anything."

"Why didn't you or Drake say something to me about—whatever you are talking about?"

"Drake doesn't know a word of it."

"I see."

"I first began to—say, do you know Mrs. Robert Orr?"

"Orr? No. Never heard of her." Parris laughed. "Is there a dark mysterious woman in the case?"

Randy did not smile.

"Mrs. Orr is a terrible gossip. You must know her. She lives on Bailey Street, in the old Whitmire house."

"I know the house."

"Well, I know her pretty well, because I see her often at Donneley's. She began asking questions about you—and Louise Gordon last summer."

"Louise Gordon. Oh—I see."

"Well, it seems that talk sort of runs around and around and takes on first one meaning, then another. When I first heard Louise's name mentioned, they said you were 'going with' Louise."

Parris nodded. He remembered his talk with Dr. Nolan. It had been too late, even then, he guessed.

"I heard that Louise had been pretty sick after her father's death. There was some awfully queer talk just then. The first I heard of that was from old Mariah Shane—the janitress up at the church. Louise said some awful things about Dr. Gordon."

"Yes. I can imagine. Louise had a bad breakdown."

"I never mentioned the talk about Louise in any way, because of Drake." Parris looked his question.

"Oh, I knew that Drake was wild about Louise once. When I first knew him he talked about her a lot."

Randy swallowed hard.

"He was really all over that long before I went to Europe, Randy."

"You may be wrong about that, Parris." She quirked her lips into a half-smile. "Also, you may be lying."

"No. Honest."

"It doesn't matter. I was only fearful that if you were in love with Louise that it might do something to the friendship between you and Drake."

"I see."

"Then came the old stories again."

"Just—what were the old stories, Randy?"

"I suspect that you know. Stories of her father's operations."

"What did you hear, exactly?"

"It was said that Louise said her father performed unnecessary operations just—well, just because he liked to, and that he did too many of them without chloroform."

"Um." Parris nodded again. He was watching Randy closely. "Where do I come in on that?"

"Well, Parris, I hate to tell you. But the story that's been going on this winter is that Louise told you about all of this, and that you've been investigating it."

"Good Lord!"

"Yes. And I'm afraid the feeling is that—no, there are two kinds of feelings."

"What do you mean?"

"Some people think you are trying to ruin the reputation of a great doctor like Dr. Gordon."

"Why does anyone suppose I would do that?"

"To try and make yourself important."

"It's rather silly, isn't it? And the other feeling?"

"The other is that you and Louise together somehow or other stumbled on a truth. People began to remember. You ought to hear the long lists of operations Dr. Gordon did without an anesthetic! It's always the same story. The patient's heart was weak."

"Strange!" Parris spoke half to himself.

"But Parris—have you ever counted up the number of terribly disfigured people he left behind him?"

Parris looked at Randy again. She had gone deathly white.

"Randy!"

"Yes, Parris." She was looking away from him.

"What's the matter?"

"Don't you know what's the matter?"

He waited for a moment. "No," he said finally.

"You don't know what I'm thinking about?"

"No."

She reached out and held his hand while she peered into his face. A look of bitter fear was in her eyes.

"Drake!" she whispered. "Drake!"

Parris held perfectly still. Randy continued to search his face. She shook his arm violently.

"Parris!"

"Yes, Randy. What is it?"

"You've got to tell me!"

He shook his head.

"What do you mean, Parris?"

"Nothing."

"Do you mean that you don't know, or that you won't tell me?"

"I mean that—*l don't know*, Randy."

"Then the stories are true?"

"Partly."

"What about Louise?"

"It was Louise who began—everything. I was called in by her mother—professionally. I've not been interested in her in any other way. She said these things about her father. Mrs. Gordon knew she was saying them. That's why she sent for me. Louise told me. At first I thought it was symptomatic of her general nervous and hysterical condition. Then—I wasn't so sure. She knew something. The total of what she knew was—stupefying. I talked to Dr. Nolan. We agreed to try and silence Louise. It wouldn't do any good to find out the truth about Dr. Gordon—not now."

"Parris—you were afraid!"

"How do you mean, Randy?"

"You were afraid you'd find out about Drake!"

"I didn't think about Drake at first, Randy. I just didn't connect Drake's accident and the amputation with Dr. Gordon at all."

"But you think something about it!"

"No, I don't. Listen, Randy: there are strange cases in medical history—like this. But it doesn't follow that every operation Dr. Gordon performed was or could have been unnecessary. Do you know any of the details of Drake's injury?"

"He wasn't run over, if that's what you mean."

"*He wasn't?*"

"No. Did you think so?"

"That's what you cabled me."

"Well—he was caught by the train—some cars were being switched. A wagon tumbled off the edge of the cut and knocked him under the train which was just coming to a stop. He was under the car—between two of them. As near as I know he was sort of—I guess you'd have to say pinched by a wheel that didn't pass over him. The cars sort of reversed and he was caught in the same way On the other side. But he wasn't run over."

"Strange. I thought he was. He never talked to me about it."

"He doesn't know. He was knocked unconscious when the wagonload of tiles struck him."

"I see."

"Parris. I've got something else to tell you. I got Tod to make some inquiries for me—after I heard those terrible stories this winter. I thought Tod could in his simple way get some information that I couldn't. Tod was at the station that night. He came back here for sheets and blankets. Sam Winters helped Dr. Gordon. They—the amputation was done in the freight depot."

"Yes, I know."

"So I got Tod to get Sam Winters to talking about it. He said—"

Randy stopped and twisted her hands together.

"Go on, Randy. You have to get it said."

"Sam Winters said Dr. Gordon was a wonderful doctor and must have seen something he himself—Sam, I mean—couldn't understand."

"What did he mean by that?"

"He said it looked to him like Drake was just badly bruised."

"Oh, Randy! I can't quite believe that!"

"Sam was sure of one thing—"

"Yes?" Parris said the one questioning word with difficulty. He didn't wish to hear any more. He didn't wish to hear Randy's answer.

"Sam was positive that there were no bones broken!"

Parris drew his gloves thoughtfully through his fingers.

Randy never took her anxious gaze from Parris' face. She spoke with difficulty, but desperately, as if she knew she had to go through with it.

"He said—" She choked up again.

"What, Randy? Go on."

"He said—these are his exact words: 'I looked good at them legs. The bones in neither one of 'em was cracked up one bit.'"

Parris straightened himself, and took Randy's hands in his.

"Now, listen. You've got to listen carefully. Sam Winter's testimony doesn't mean a thing."

Randy waited a few moments before attempting to speak. Her voice when it came uncertainly sounded like the voice of a small child.

"Are you telling me the truth, Parris?"

"Yes, Randy. Absolutely. The injury may have been extensive, must have been, considering the nature of the accident. Now listen again."

"All right."

"Dr. Gordon must have done a crack job, or Drake wouldn't have lived. We have Drake, and Drake is in a way adjusted. Human beings adjust themselves to amazingly difficult conditions. It's all over and done with. Dr. Gordon is dead. We've got to forget it."

"But these stories, Parris!"

"Yes. These stories. Of course, you can't ever catch up with a rumor, especially if it's one that people want to believe."

"What might it do to you, Parris?"

"To me? Oh, I don't know. Nothing much, maybe. I'm thinking about Drake."

"I guess I don't understand you. Drake?"

"Yes. When I came back and began with you to make Drake over—well, that isn't quite the right phrase. When I saw Drake and talked to him I realized that we really did have a difficult job ahead of us. Drake was always a free soul. He valued his independence above everything else, I fancy. All at once everything had been taken away from him. Of course, he had lost immeasurably before the accident. Much of his freedom went with the loss of his money. He couldn't even come and go freely in the little world where he played. Then—when everything was gone—well, Randy, there simply wasn't anything of Drake McHugh left. Your marriage to him was a wonderful thing for him. I have never asked what it meant to you—what it may have cost—"

"Parris!"

"Yes, Randy. What?"

"I think that wondering about it should be put out of your mind right now. I loved Drake—better than anything in the world. I didn't marry Drake out of pity. But the way I loved Drake afterward was something different—it was something that went 'way beyond anything I had ever felt for him before. You know, of course, that I was—*everything* to Drake and had been for a long time?"

"No. I didn't know. If I had thought about it at all, I suppose I might have guessed. Drake was hardly the kind of person to wait for anything he wanted."

"Well—I just wanted you to know. He is—always will be—the only man in my world."

"I'm glad, Randy—for both your sakes. I was going to say that beginning to restore Drake was a peculiar task because literally we had just half a man to go to work on."

Randy shrank deeper into the corner of the bench.

"You have to excuse the way I put things, Randy. That's just the exact fact. Now, I'm coming to the point of this. It would be just like some meddlesome fool to drop some hint of this story about Dr. Gordon to him someday."

"I know, Parris. I've thought of that. I wake up cold and shivering sometimes thinking about that very possibility."

"It must never happen. Just as I said: we have brought Drake back to himself and to ourselves—but he is not quite the same Drake. He's built on an artificial foundation that we, the two of us, have supplied. If it should ever enter his mind that his whole catastrophe was anything but an accident—"

"What would happen?"

"I think the whole structure would topple down again, and that time we couldn't rebuild it. He'd be gone."

Parris thought for a few minutes. He continued to slap his knee with his gloves.

"You see, Randy, how important it is that it shouldn't ever happen?"

"Of course. But Parris—"

"Yes?"

"I've got to know something. What do you think—honestly?"

"About what?"

"About Dr. Gordon."

Parris hesitated. "I don't know, Randy—quite."

"But you suspect?"

He faced her squarely. "Randy, there's some sort of foundation for all of this story—fantastic and horrible as it seems to us. The places of the human mind are full of strange shadows—of course, that sounds like a romantic novelist, but it's sober, scientific truth. I haven't one shred of actual proof of any of this, not one. But the very existence of the story, and the unaccountable number of cases that point to some sort of malpractice—it all suggests something out of the ordinary. There is no possible purpose in finding out—if we could, and I don't think we can. It's strange, though—" Parris' voice faded out as he looked away. His eyelids dropped a little. Randy knew this sign of a sudden turn in his thinking.

"What's strange, Parris? You can talk to me, you know."

"Yes, I know, Randy. I was about to say that it's strange, or curious, or something, that wherever there is a ghastly or a grotesque tragedy in this town, you'll find Dr. Gordon somewhere in the story."

"You do believe—"

"Hush! Neither you nor I can ever know about Drake. There's no possible way. It's better we don't know. I've got to believe that it was a necessary amputation. So must you. We must, Randy. Don't you see that? He had no reason—"

"Yes, he did! Louise!"

"He had separated them, anyhow. That was over."

"Are you sure?"

"I saw the end of it long before Drake and you became friends."

"You're not lying to me, Parris?"

"On my honor."

Randy stood up. "Let's go. I feel better, somehow."

"Tell Drake we went for a walk—I'll see him tomorrow."

Parris crossed the cemetery and came up on the steep south slope of Aberdeen campus. The sunshine dimmed, and a thick scurry of clouds was blowing up from the west. The campus was deserted.

He crossed behind the buildings and kept to the "Sunset Walk." He came presently to the little sunken garden with its marble bench and statue. It had been enclosed with a hedge of evergreens. From inside of it the view was cut off in every direction. The marble seat was already weather-stained, and marked with the patterns of clinging wet leaves that blew down from the tall oaks. Some sort of formal planting had been done in the oval enclosure, but the beds were filled with dead stalks that had been broken and beaten down by snow and winter storms. It was bleak and forbidding.

Parris drew his heavy coat close about him and settled into a half-dry corner of the curved seat. He was surprised to find how poignantly he was moved by the place. It was difficult to define his emotions exactly, but he realized that beneath the seeming calm exterior maturity had built about him lay the whole of those earlier tragic experiences, fearfully, terrifyingly alive.

He had been wholly unprepared for the sudden onslaught of feeling when he came to Cassie's grave. He had been equally unprepared for the impact of the present moment.

For one brief instant he was almost glad to find himself so much alive.

The obscuring effects of the past half-dozen years fled like wisps of smoke. He rubbed his eyes and looked about him. The moment was like an awakening. He was grateful just now for the tall, thick hedge. There in that direction he would be able to see his grandmother's house. He did not wish to see it. Not today. He must connect himself gradually now with those years. He thought hard for a few moments, and arose briskly, and took the long diagonal walk toward Federal Street. He had gone down this very way with Cassie on that last night.

He walked rapidly. It was like running a gauntlet with the thrusts of emotions coming from every side.

When he came out on Federal Street, he composed himself. He felt that something inside that had been a dark confusion was now placed in order. He drew on his gloves and buttoned his coat. It was getting colder.

"Hey, Parris!"

Parris stopped and waited. Someone was crossing the street.

"That you, Parris?"

"Yes. Well, hello, Peyton! How are you?"

"Fine, fine. What you doing?"

"Not a thing."

"Why don't you come on home with me for supper? Patty's been after me for the longest time to corral you. She's been wanting to have you out ever since she met you two years ago."

Parris hesitated. "Why—I'll be delighted. But are you sure I'll be welcome—coming without warning like this?"

"Oh, sure, sure. Patty's always ready for company. She'll be tickled to death. She's talked about you a lot. Admires you. Says you're the only cosmopolitan in Kings Row."

"Nonsense."

"Fact. She's always saying that."

"Well, I'm a long way from being anything of the sort. Just a hard-working doctor in a country town."

"Say, our office wouldn't like to hear you call Kings Row a country town!"

"What do you call it, Peyte?"

Peyton laughed. A little, a very little of his old boyish charm came back with it.

"Well, we're used to saying 'our enterprising young city,' or something like that."

Parris laughed, too, and linked arms with Peyton. "Actually I rather think Kings Row has a kind of dry rot, old boy. You don't have to take that as a professional affront, though."

"Kings Row, Parris? You're mighty mistaken, if you think that."

"Oh, come on, Peyte. You don't have to sell me anything. I'm not buying."

"Say—you're not down on Kings Row in any way, are you?"

"Peyton, for heaven's sake! I was born in Kings Row. I don't have to have old friends like you tell me about it. All small towns are much alike. Kings Row is all right, I suppose, but it's just Kings Row. I don't think you do any place much good trying to call it something it isn't, do you?"

Peyton shook his head. "You have to keep boosting."

"Well, well. Maybe you do. I don't know anything about business. I just see the old town as it is. You've got a special vision, maybe."

They turned into the wide-parked grounds of Peyton's place.

"How you like the looks of this, Parris?" Peyton's tone was proud and possessive.

"It's fine, Peyte. Very handsome."

"Wait till you see the inside of it!"

Patty Graves welcomed Parris with an easy hospitality that was, he thought, distinctly unlike the Kings Row custom. It was several minutes before he realized that she was following some sort of mental formula. There was a curious artificial brittle quality about her speech and action that was logical but not spontaneous. Her whole manner reminded him of a multiplication table. Start her at any given point and she would go smoothly through to the end.

Parris listened a little absently as she talked evenly of the new books, and of some concerts she had heard the past winter in St. Louis. He was not giving much attention to the subjects or the words, but his ear was keenly attentive to her voice. It was dry and a shade hollow, like the voice of an old woman that occasionally takes on a half-masculine timbre. He glanced at her several times with quick professional observation. He was trying to remember something— something that was pertinent to the moment, but it eluded him.

Dinner—Peyton noticed that Mrs. Graves did not say "supper"—was not comfortable. Parris had the feeling that some difficult game, of which he did not know the rules, was being played around him. He noticed that the maid kept an anxious eye on Mrs. Graves. Once when something was being served to him he noticed the girl's brown hands were trembling slightly.

Afterward in the living room when coffee was served, Peyton spoke up with a kind of false heartiness.

"Smoke, Parris? Cigar, or a cigarette?"

"No thanks, Peyton."

"Don't you ever smoke?"

"I smoked a little in Vienna, perhaps because all students did, but I stopped. Never really liked it, I guess."

"Um, that so?"

Parris sensed that Peyton was childishly disappointed. "Don't let that stop *you,* Peyton." He intercepted a quick look from Mrs. Graves. All at once he understood Peyton's concern. Mrs. Graves didn't permit smoking in her rooms. He had heard funny stories about her meticulous care of the house. She made Peyton come in a side door when he came home from the office and all that sort of thing. He glanced about the rooms again. It was a strange house. The furniture and decorations were all in a key of understatement. Subdued because somebody had been afraid of a breach of taste.. The curtains hung in small, neat, accurate folds like carvings. The pictures were carefully lined. All of them were quiet prints of unimportant subjects. The rugs were good Orientals, but tended toward olive and ocher tints. Every object in this house had been chosen for its relation to other objects. Not one was there because of any relation to a person. The whole of the three rooms opening into each other constituted an exhibit of the standards of the current women's magazines. It was the negation of personal taste, and at the same time the negation of feeling, emotional choice, and personal concern. It was sterile-looking. Parris' attention caught on the word as on a hook. Sterile. Why—of course. He recalled now what had been teasing back of his memory all evening. Peyton had once mentioned an operation that Patty had to have. "Some sort of female trouble," he had said.

Dr. Gordon! Again!

Parris looked steadily at Patty Graves for a few seconds. She was thin and rather dry-looking. Her hair was lusterless and combed back in severe lines. There was more than a suspicion of blond down on her chin. Her light-blue eyes were opaque and slow-moving. She looked like a rather ugly china doll.

Now Parris recalled something else he had heard shortly after his return. Someone, he couldn't recall who it was, had told him that Peyton Graves had a mistress—Melissa St. George, a teacher in the Negro school. Parris remembered Melissa. Everyone had known her.

He looked at Peyton as the conversation ran mechanically along conventional ways. Peyton was only a year or two older than he was, but he was getting fat. There were worry wrinkles across his brow. He had a furtive and unhappy look.

Parris fidgeted in his deep chair. He felt that he was just under a trap that might spring at any moment. Peyton was pitiable, now, as Parris saw him. His glance wandered back to Patty again. She was as cold as a corpse. He had no doubt she had always been a ruthless and unscrupulous woman, but her inherent traits had probably been greatly intensified. His own words of this afternoon came back to him: "*Wherever there is a ghastly or a grotesque tragedy in this town, you'll find Dr. Gordon somewhere in the story.*"

He wanted to go home. Certainly he wouldn't want to return to this house again. Not if he could help it.

Twice he wanted to ask Peyton about business—the Crescent—but both times he shied from the subject. He had heard recently that things were not going so well with the Crescent. No one had enough money to build and maintain places on such a scale. So far Peyton had refused to break the property into smaller plots. A few options had been taken, and Dr. Ferris, a newcomer, had built a bungalow far along the curve. It was hidden in the woods, and was not, according to Peyton, much of an asset to the Crescent as a whole.

So far Peyton's house stood up in solitary state. It seemed an empty and uncommunicative display that curiously existed for itself alone. It appeared to be, in some way, a symbol of the whole undertaking.

As soon as he could, Parris said good night. He had spent a miserable evening.

When Parris reached home he found a letter waiting for him. He opened it hastily and read:

My Dear Dr. Mitchell:

I am writing in order to make a rather melancholy report on Louise. Her general condition did not improve here and I called in the doctor recommended to me by Dr. Saunders. He, in turn, consulted with two alienists, both of whom have a considerable local reputation. They corroborated and supported your own diagnosis, but in much plainer terms and with far greater emphasis. I realize now how much you must have tried to spare my feelings, and I wish to express my belated appreciation.

It has seemed best, in their judgment, to keep Louise under close observation for an indefinite period of time, and we have accordingly removed her for the present to a private sanitarium where she can have the best of care. I sincerely hope the changed surroundings may help her to forget her unfortunate and distressing delusions concerning her sainted father. You can imagine, I am sure, my own great personal suffering when I saw my own child attempt to besmirch the memory of a great man and a great physician. I labored through many years by his side and I know better than anyone how great were his sacrifices, and how pure were his devotions to the healing of infirmities. My husband was not only a healer of the body, Dr. Mitchell; he was equally a minister to the mind and soul of sinful humanity. I think he realized more acutely than most medical men do, how close was the relationship between moral and physical health.

In the light of this, the collapse of Louise's reason—I cannot call it by a kinder name, or a lesser one—is all the more inexplicable.

I was well informed before leaving Kings Row that Louise had set in circulation certain of those rumors and accusations. This she seems to have managed despite my extreme vigilance. I suppose such cunning is a symptom of her disorder.

Knowing, therefore, that something of this witless talk of hers must have fallen on the fertile ground of public gossip, I feel that it is only justice to the memory of my late husband that Kings Row should understand the unreliability of the source of the slanders. Dr. Mitchell, my heart is deeply torn between devotion to my unfortunate child and an even holier devotion to the memory of her father. I feel that I shall have, in some measure, to sacrifice the former to the latter.

It is my wish that Kings Row should know fully that Louise is in no way responsible for whatever stories she may have told about Dr. Gordon, and that she has been *confined* in safekeeping. I have sent a note to Miles Jackson which I have worded discreetly, but clearly. I have also written to certain friends and acquaintances who will, I am sure, make mention of these late sad events and thus, in some measure, set wild tales at rest.

I heard, within the last few days, that Louise had in some slight degree involved you in these stories. I am sure you will know how to handle any such aspects of the matter, if, indeed, they exist.

Let me assure you again of my gratitude for your efforts in behalf of my poor child. For the rest I can only trust in the Maker of all things who holds us all in the hollow of His hand.

Very truly yours,

HARRIET GORDON

(Mrs. Henry Gordon)

Parris turned back and read the letter a second time, carefully. His face clouded darkly. The word "*confined*" stood out on the page as if written in red. He could guess a large part of what had happened in Florida. It could not have been difficult for Mrs. Gordon to drive Louise to violence. That Mrs. Gordon could deliberately make use of this event as she was now using it filled him with horror. Too many dread possibilities lay back of this sequence of happenings.

He leaned his head on his hand and began slowly to piece together all the fragmentary accusations he had heard Louise make. These, coupled with stories of her own personal encounters with Dr. Gordon, began to fit into a pattern.

It was pretty clear that Mrs. Gordon was touched with religious fanaticism and, with it, carried a conviction that the correction of many evils, and the rectifying of many wrongs, was her own personal duty. It was this that had turned her against the Tower family. She could not actually have known anything against Dr. Tower at the time. If Louise's stories could be depended upon—and Parris was sure that they could be—Dr. Gordon told his wife many things which should have been professional confidences. He, too, had had more than a trace of the same fanaticism. The two of them must have worked up some sort of misdirected fervor against what they considered evil-doing.

Parris tried desperately to direct his own attention away from certain dawning convictions. Sadism was common enough in many forms, but sadism coupled with religious fanaticism was particularly dangerous. Such a person with a surgeon's knife in his hands—

Suddenly Parris remembered Ludie Sims. A pretty, flighty, quasi prostitute—a subject of town talk. And then suddenly a disfiguring operation. Facial paralysis. What kind of an operation had that been, he wondered, and for what?

He bowed his head over the table and groaned. *Drake!* Drake McHugh— the certain object of Dr. Gordon's disapproval and dislike. The unbearable thought was fortified unexpectedly from another quarter. Parris was sure now that Dr. Gordon's cruelty to Louise had another familiar aspect, that of sex jealousy. Louise had been deeply in love with Drake....

Parris pushed himself away from the table and went to the window. He pressed his forehead hard against the cold pane. He must not, *must not* think this through. Even at this moment he realized how ordinary the whole case might be—were it true. Psychopathology abounded in case histories of unbelievable horror. He had read them and studied them coolly and with unwavering detachment. But this!—*Drake!* He could not put out of his mind the many pictures of Drake, laughing, gay, inconsequential, hurting no one but himself, but even at that, generous, uncritical, and kind.

Above all he must keep Randy from guessing what he—he stopped and looked squarely at the question. Yes: it was true! Of course it was true.

There was no use in trying to deceive himself. Now as he recalled Dr. Gordon's face, he was all the more convinced. Every feature of the man and every detail of his odd manner proclaimed him for what he was. Those china-blue eyes with a slight rim of white showing all around the iris. The unblinking gaze and—he summoned the recollection with a shiver—the peculiar intake of breath that was Dr. Gordon's way of laughing.

How in the world had this man managed to go through a whole career in Kings Row without ever being called into question? Parris realized that Dr. Gordon had been a really skillful surgeon. Even Dr. Tower had said Gordon was a capable man.

What had Dr. Tower known? Something. Yes: certainly. Parris remembered that Dr. Tower had questioned him closely about Dr. Gordon's conduct of Madame von Eln's case. Thank God, there was no question there!

Dr. Tower had been noncommittal sometimes, but Parris had set it down to the usual professional reticence. He was certain that there had been more behind Dr. Tower's omissions than he could have guessed at the time.

He sighed heavily and shook himself a little. He decided that he would have to show the letter to Dr. Nolan, but hereafter he would not discuss any phase of the matter with anyone. He felt that already he knew more than he was willing to accept. More would come, he knew. Missing pieces of the puzzle—if it could still be called a puzzle—would drop into place. He wanted to close his memory on the dark chapter and, if possible, seal it away.

Secondary aspects of the whole affair troubled him very little. He realized, however, with a kind of bleak certainty, that Louise's talk might have started a slow poison in the mind of the town. How slowly, or how swiftly it might work, or if it would work at all, he could not even guess. He was not quite sure that he cared much.

Parris was acutely surprised to find an entirely new and strange feeling about Kings Row. New, at least, to his consciousness, and strange because it had been unsuspected up to this moment. He had been just a bit astonished at his instant resentment when Peyton had leapt so absurdly to the defense of the town. Now, without any doubt at all, he knew that he didn't like Kings Row. He stopped his flow of thought to make immediate amendment. What he didn't like was the visible Kings Row. Maybe that was a little difficult to clarify even to himself. He considered the factors and points one by one.

He didn't like the visible Kings Row. Not now. Not any more. He didn't like the changes that had been made by his own contemporaries. He didn't much like the people who controlled opinion and governed the town.

Kings Row had been the expression of a certain way of life, of a kind of thinking, and a kind of being. It was still that—exactly that. But the new thinking and being, the new ways of life, he felt were insincere, blatantly exhibitionistic, and false.

What held him here? The hospital? There were other hospitals. Was it Drake and Randy? Was it Dr. Nolan? Was it his memories of his grandmother, of Renée and Tom Carr, and Cassie, and of people like Colonel Skeffington? No: he was clearly convinced that it was no one of these things, or even all of them. It was something less easy of access, less tangible maybe, something that had to do with the early making of him which, as parent soil, held him fast.

He stopped at the window again. The clouds were scudding across a wildly rocking moon. The heavily budded elms surged and tossed. It was weather quite typical of this region, and this season, but tonight his fancy filled the skies with portent. He felt obscurely deep in his being some gathering storm. He shrugged this away, and returned to his thought of the town.

He had had exceptional training, and his equipment and the quality of his work here could open many places to him if he cared to go away. He knew perfectly that he did not wish to go away. He was loyal, first of all, deeply loyal to Dr. Nolan who was, Parris was sure, a really great man in his position. The hospital was a rich field for his own work, and he had complete liberty of action.

No: the professional aspects of his life had nothing to do with a kind of animal obstinacy that he felt rise in him when he thought of leaving this place. The feeling went deeper, farther back than anything he could readily remember.

His grandmother had found herself here under most unfavorable circumstances. But she had stayed. He had once heard another old woman tell tales of early days when civil factions had tried to drive her and her father away. He remembered her laconic remark: "But we stayed on."

They had stayed on, those who were here before him. Herr Berdorff, lonely, perhaps homesick at times for the idyllic Germany he remembered; Isaac Skeffington, talking of the civilized charm of country life in his Virginia; his own great-grandfather Mitchell bred in the fastidious and exacting life of a great family tradition—all of them. *They stayed on.*

Why? Was it nothing more than the human unwillingness to retreat? Or did man's endless march across the world set his foot upon strange places and by that act transform them into a mystical home from which he could not turn back and save his soul? Maybe that was it.

He had had a bad time in Kings Row. Tragedy and disaster came too early.
He had been like a field of young wheat blown down by spring storms. He had
straightened but slowly. But somehow he knew that he was rooted.

He used to think of Kings Row when he was studying in Vienna. He had
not been homesick, not precisely, but he had never ceased to feel the tie and
the pull of the bond. Turning home at the end of the long five years had been
like a release. A natural gravity would have brought him back had there been
no practical reason for his return. In those days whenever he thought of Kings
Row he saw the vast arch of sky filled with enormous clouds. He saw the green
surrounding country. He recalled with an amazing accuracy tens of thousands
of details of the physical appearance of the place. He remembered plants—
weeds and wild flowers, trees—and the honey-colored creek bottom in the late
days of summer. But he had not often thought of people.

That picture, or rather that succession of pictures of Kings Row he
remembered when he was half a world away was what he thought of and
what he saw now as he tried to seize upon something as a secure place for his
homeless fancy.

He had heard Tom Carr say that people make a place. A home maybe, or
a household, yes, but not a town in the sense that he was now seeing the place
of Kings Row. People were something that moved in it and passed through it.
But there was something else here, more important than the unlikable human
beings who passed daily before his eyes.

Parris pulled himself up on that thought. It was only the color of an
untoward day that was at work on his vision. Surely he possessed more
humanity than to permit himself this kind of sweeping judgment. Dr. Tower
had once said: "Mankind, for all of its dislikable traits, is greater and more
important than any one man's thought of it."

A sharp impatience with himself scattered his efforts to think. He felt
himself such a child in experience of men. He did not know people save
through the teaching of a special science. He had had only glimpses of larger
philosophies. He did not know what to make of them or how to handle them.
Dr. Tower and Isaac Skeffington and Dr. Nolan—these men had in some
way made a useful and effective implement from the world's long experience
of itself. They had a refuge and a defense. They had certainly found life
tolerable—more than tolerable—even in Kings Row.

Kings Row! He *must* clarify himself on that trivial point. Kings Row had
nothing to do with the chief problem of setting oneself in harmony with a
surrounding. And yet—there was a persistent feeling that in Kings Row itself
he had sometime to meet a special adversary. He had said half facetiously to
Peyton that Kings Row had the dry rot. Now, what did he really mean by that?
It was more than a mere figure of speech. He was sure of that.

A town, he supposed, could be young and vigorous, raw in newness, and
lusty with the conditions that brought it into existence. A town could grow

older as a person grows into a mellower life, take on graces, prosper, and assume a character that must represent the sum of its best thought in its best moments. Individuals could be rich and fine, deep and spiritual, or they could be mean and spiteful, material and cruel.

Parris tried to picture from all he had heard old people say of the town what it must have been like in other times. He thought of the simpler economic features of Kings Row's beginning and of the forces that were now operative.

Kings Row had been unfortunate in one major respect. The great trunk lines built across the continent in the latter half of the nineteenth century had passed it by. They were thirty miles away, one to the north, another to the south. Other towns had profited and grown. Kings Row had been drained of prosperity and, in a similar degree, of vitality. Colonel Skeffington had often remarked, and so had Thurston St. George, that there were "no chances" for a young man in Kings Row now. Now as Parris ran over the names of the promising younger people he realized that they had gone away. They had not found places for themselves in Kings Row. The town could lose more and more of its blood until it became as empty and dry as a locust shell. So many things, people—individuals and organizations—retain their form long after life itself has withdrawn.

Some old people were good, some were bad. Perhaps some old towns were good, while some were bad.

Society in its crystallizations could of course exert the cruelest and most senseless of pressures. In such cases conformity seemed to be the only course of safety. Conformity—yes, and mediocrity. It was the way of the wilderness. To run with the pack one must not wear spots and streaks differently at the risk of being torn to pieces. One must be, in such case, stronger than the others. Be weak and you die. Be different and you must face the snarling circle that closes in on you without mercy. Parris remembered, even in school, how these ancient laws of the jungle operated.

That was what Miles Jackson was talking about when he spoke at Bob Callicott's funeral. And then Parris remembered some sentences from that bewildering talk, sentences he had not understood at the time.

"... *In the midst of continuous hurricane of destruction and death there are born from time to time men who resolve this disorder. They create another vision from the fire and dust of disaster, They are poets, and musicians, and artists. That is their answer to the ugliness of the world ...*"

The answer to ugliness, and disorder, and disaster. Yes: Miles Jackson had been right. It was amazing that this vision and understanding existed here— here in Kings Row.

Of course, and of course, and of course, this was the simple answer to all of these worrying questions. There was one answer for ugliness and disaster, one answer for the senseless and implacable rule of all primitive instinct—and the same answer for Kings Row. Beauty could be stronger than all of these things combined.

He thought of Herr Berdorff and his variations and their "nice double fugue" for conclusion. He thought of Bob Callicott's lyrics, and Jamie's sonnets....

Fidelity, and faith, and order, and creation. He said the words over carefully, thinking of each one....

He believed he knew now why he was in Kings Row, and why he must remain.

One afternoon in the late summer Herr Berdorff called Parris on the telephone.

"Dr. Mitchell, Parris, I have something iss important for you to do."

"Certainly, what is it?" Parris could hear his old friend breathing heavily and excitedly.

"It iss the little Lichinskal."

"Vera? You have heard from her?"

"She iss here."

"Vera in Kings Row? Well, well. When did she come back—and what for?"

"That iss it. I think maybe it iss better I see you. I can talk *besser*—better, not on the telephone." Herr Berdorff's English suffered in excitement. Parris smiled a little, but he knew that whatever it was that was disturbing Herr Berdorff, it must be serious.

"I can see you any time this afternoon, Professor. Let's see—why don't I come to see *you?* Then we can talk quietly."

"That would be nice, Parris. I think you can help. You know the little Lichinska. I wait, then."

"Be right over."

Parris found Herr Berdorff walking up and down his little side porch.

"*Ach!* You come! Sit down. I tell you right away."

"Yes. What's happened?"

"The little Lichinska she comes home without warning. Her papa he comes to see me at once. He says she iss—crazy."

"Vera? Oh, nonsense."

"She canceled all of her engagements. She says she cannot play any more."

"But why—what's up?"

"She says she does not understand her playing. She must study herself, she says. Mr. Lichinsky iss—well, *he* iss crazy! He pulls his hair, Parris, you can imagine, this excitable Polish-Jewish papa of a great violinist who cancels all of her good engagements and comes home to sit down and say she cannot play. Cannot play! What iss this?"

"Should I go to see her?"

"That iss why Mr. Lichinsky came to see me—to ask you. If you will be so good."

"Well, of course. H'm—do you recall Vera had a breakdown of some sort when I was in Vienna? She canceled some engagements then, but I noticed since that she's been playing all over—with great success."

"Maybe she has been working too much."

"Maybe. I'll see."

"You will let me know?"

"Of course."

"It surely cannot be serious. I have been happy to think that I was the first teacher of the Lichinska."

"Her best teacher, too, Herr Berdorff. You made her."

"*Ach!* You go now?"

"Yes. I'll telephone you."

"Please!"

Parris sat in the little living room above the jewelry shop where the Lichinskys had lived ever since Parris had first known of them. Vera leaned back in the low rocking chair, and Parris faced her. It was hard to believe that this poised, lovely young woman was the colorless little Vera who used to stump awkwardly along the street with her violin case under her arm. She was smartly dressed, and carried an air of—Parris bit his lip: here was Patty Graves' cosmopolitan. Vera's fine strong hands lay rather inertly in her lap. She looked well, save for her eyes. She looked as if she were controlling some desperate fear with the greatest of difficulty.

"Parris!" Her voice was steady and warm. It fitted her personality. "Parris, you have to promise me that you'll try to understand me."

"Of course."

"You must let me talk through this—tell you the whole story."

"First off, Vera, the whole story of what?"

"I canceled my tours. I came home. I couldn't play."

"Couldn't play?"

"No. It stopped—of itself."

"Go ahead. Tell me about it."

"You remember, in Vienna, I was rather fearful of that concert in Mannheim?"

"Yes. You were nervous about it, I recall."

"More than nervous. Afraid."

"Of what?"

"Afraid I couldn't play—at all. I canceled that concert. Then, after a while, I played again, better than ever. All of the critics said so. I was a great violinist, they said."

"*Are* a great violinist."

"*Was.* Let me tell you."

"All right. Tell me what happened first."

Vera looked out of the window for several minutes. The color left her face gradually. When she turned back again to Parris she looked thin and old.

"I had a concert—not very important—scheduled for the second of May. I was rehearsing a few days before with a pianist, the Brahms Concerto. It went, not too well, and next I began to practice alone. All at once—this, perhaps, is what I cannot make clear to you—all at once I seemed to hear myself as if—as if I had never heard myself before. I lowered my violin and thought a moment. I asked myself a question—and I couldn't answer it—and, then, I couldn't play any more."

"Yes?"

Vera struggled for composure.

"What then, Vera?"

"I—I couldn't play!"

"What was the question you couldn't answer?"

"Parris, you are a doctor, a nerve specialist, or something like that. You must be able to understand me. You used to be so nice to me when I was—just a wet-nosed little girl! You will not think me silly."

"I'm a doctor, Vera, and I don't think things are silly when they're important to someone else. What was the question?"

"I—I simply asked myself why I played a passage just the way I did."

Her voice broke, and she held tight to the arms of her chair. "You see, Parris, I had just heard myself—as I said—as if I had heard for the first time in my life. It sounded a—a certain way. I knew by some sort of intuition that that was right, but I wanted to know why I knew it, and how I ever had come to know it. I couldn't answer."

Parris waited quietly. "And then?"

"I tried to play again, and I couldn't."

"How do you mean, you couldn't?"

"It wouldn't go any way at all. It sounded suddenly like a child—a beginner—no meaning."

"I see."

"I canceled the concert. The manager was very cross. I had to cancel all of the summer-festival series—there were many concerts and recitals. I had to have a physician certify that I couldn't play. I had to get that in Vienna."

"Who was the doctor?"

"Dr. Seiss."

"Oh, yes. He was one of my professors."

"He told me. We spoke of you. He seemed to understand—somewhat. He gave me the certificate saying that I must rest. The manager was furious. Then I went away to a little place and tried to think. Then I came home."

"What did Dr. Seiss say about it? Any theory, or suggestion?"

"No. Not clearly. I saw him when I came back through Vienna. He said he would write you. You have not heard from him?"

"No, but I did hear that he is ill."

"It must have been sudden. He seemed well when I saw him. I suppose he will write later. But, Parris, I think I have figured out much for myself."

"That would be the best information, maybe, we could have."

"Well. I guess I was a kind of prodigy."

"Yes. You were."

"Not one of the spectacular kind. Thanks to Berdorff. But I played by intuition—wholly, do you understand?"

Parris unconsciously leaned forward in his chair a little.

"Yes. Of course."

"Parris, I never had any real education. I found out later that I couldn't use my mind very well. I began to read, and go to lectures, I went to the theater and to exhibitions of pictures. I was hurrying desperately to supply for myself all of the background which I had discovered a great artist must have. I understood a lot of things. I felt very rich in all of this, but I knew that much of what I read about, and heard in plays had something to do with my music. But I couldn't determine what. Books and plays talked of love, and pain, and grief. I did not really know what those things meant."

"Well, Vera. You are still young. What about—well, there was no one you fell in love with?"

She looked at him almost uncomprehendingly, as if the very words were without meaning. She shook her head.

"I have never loved anyone. I have never felt sorrow, or grief. I have been frightened—much, and often. That is all."

"Frightened of what?"

She slumped a little and let her head rest against the back of the chair.

"When I was a very little girl I was afraid of Kings Row."

"The town—here?"

"Yes."

"Why?"

"I knew when I was the littlest sort of a girl that we—the Lichinskys—were different. It was a long time before I knew that it was because we were Jews."

"Vera, you may be mistaken about that. Not because you were Jews. Maybe because you were 'foreigners.' You know I felt that very much as a child because I could speak French and German."

Vera shook her head. "No, it was because we were Jews. It scared my brother Amos, too. It's in our blood, I guess—we remember, perhaps. Look at Amos. He—he's so *over*polite to everyone because he's afraid."

"Did anyone ever really say anything to you as a child to establish the feeling?"

"No, I can't remember that anyone did, except my own family."

Parris nodded.

"My father was always saying that I must work hard—harder—harder, or what would Kings Row say? I can hear the sentences. I never forgot them—it seems to me that I heard them day and night. '*What will Kings Row say?*' He only wished me to do well. I know that, now. But I didn't know it then. I thought somehow that I had to justify my existence, to earn a right to live. I wondered for a while what would happen if I didn't do well, and then one day while I was still a very small child I thought I understood. I was out driving with my father and we passed the asylum. I don't remember exactly, but I think we must have driven through the grounds, because I remember the barred windows. I remember them vividly. I asked my father what the place was, and he said it was a place where they put crazy people and kept them locked up. I said, 'Away from their mamas and papas?' And he said yes. 'Forever?' I asked. He said yes, forever. Then I said, 'What are crazy people? What is crazy?' He said, 'They ain't smart no more.' I thought about it all the afternoon, and I decided that I knew then why my father was so afraid that I wouldn't be 'smart,' and do well with my fiddle. He had always stressed the fiddle, you see: 'Practice hard and be smart, and you'll see what Kings Row will say!' Do you see, Parris—it's simple in a way, isn't it?"

"Ye-es. That was a childish fear. But you learned soon enough, I imagine, what 'crazy' meant. Wasn't the fear gone then?"

"No. It never went. I was always afraid of that asylum—of being locked away forever. Long after I understood what words meant."

"Did you tell Dr. Seiss all of this?"

"Most of it. He seemed to understand. He thought—at least I believe he thought—that I should come back here for a while and, assure myself that there was nothing frightening here."

"Yes. I can understand that suggestion."

"But, Parris—the things I suddenly feared are not here—not in Kings Row, but here—*here,* inside of my own head!"

"Well. Go on. Let's get back to that day you thought you couldn't play."

"I stood there, Parris, for hours, trying to work, trying to understand what I was doing, trying to play consciously."

"Why did you feel that you had to play consciously?"

"Because I couldn't play any other way, either. I couldn't turn back and just let go—let my fingers and bow fly of their own accord. You see, Parris, there were always the technical phases of playing which I did and accomplished in an ordinary, orthodox way. I knew what I was doing technically. But when I had mastered a work something new came into it—something beyond technique, but I never knew where it came from, or what it was. Critics talked of depth, of understanding, of feeling, and interpretations. I swear to you I did not know what they meant. When I had learned a composition I—I just let myself go, and it played itself. Now, I couldn't play either way—intuitively, or consciously.

It went dead—in one moment. I had broken a connection between my fingers and some hidden source of music which was what had been called my talent. I could not regain it. Outside of that hidden source I was a simple, ordinary girl. I cannot play."

"Do you want to play?"

A bleak, opaque look came into her eyes. It was as though a windowpane had suddenly frozen over.

"Yes." She spoke the word out of an immeasurable despair.

"Then I think you can. You'll have to rest, then begin again, quietly, simply, like a child. Creep up on it—so to speak." He smiled at her, but she shook her head.

"You speak the exact words of Dr. Seiss. I have not told you why I was so suddenly frightened. That morning when I found that I could not play, the first thought that flashed across my mind was that I was going crazy—that, perhaps, I was already crazy. I saw the asylum, I saw those barred windows. I thought of my father's words from away back there in my childhood—I seemed actually to hear him. *'Locked up. Forever. They ain't smart!'* I tried to reason with that fear. It was curious, Parris, what I seemed to be most afraid of was this asylum here in Kings Row."

"Did you tell Dr. Seiss that, too?"

"No. Maybe I hadn't thought that much out clearly at that time. I don't remember, but I'm sure I didn't mention that to him. I would find myself almost frantic sometimes. Then when he said I should come back here to see that there was nothing to be afraid of, I thought I'd have to come, and look straight at the asylum."

Parris smiled genially, as if all of this were the most natural thing in the world. "And you did that?"

"Yes."

"And so?"

"I have money, you know, Parris. I made a lot of money."

"That's pleasant."

"I have rented a room to be by myself."

"Well—you shouldn't make a point of being alone too much. There are plenty of people who want to see you—your friends—you'll have a lot of new ones."

She seemed not to hear him. "I rented a room on Carrier Street."

"Carrier Street? Why, that's way over—"

"Yes, it faces the north wing of the asylum. I've got a room on the front of a house, upstairs. I can look right out at the asylum all of the time. I come here, of course, to see the family, but I spend most of my time there. I've been back more than a week. Every night I stand at my window and look at the asylum until the lights are out. I've got to stare it down. I can't let it get the better of me, Parris!"

Parris was disappointed in his efforts to aid Vera Lichinska. The family refused to consider Vera a "case." They were certain that some more understandable and more commonplace cause lay back of her unwillingness to go on with her career. This phrase "unwillingness to go on" perfectly expressed their attitude. Vera's father was sure that a man was concerned, somehow, in his daughter's breakdown. Her mother, her brother Amos, and even her aged grandmother united in a kind of inquisitorial persecution. It was not long before Vera shut herself up for good in the little upper room in Carrier Street. She was sure that she understood herself perfectly. In a way, Parris had to admit, she really did. She was able to define and name the conditions which brought about the sudden collapse of her playing, but she had read just enough of the literature of psychiatry to make her wary. She recognized any approach to a cure, and defeated it at the outset. Since no one could force her to any kind of course, she placed herself beyond help. Within the year she began to avoid Parris altogether. He saw her occasionally, and once in a while passing the house he heard her at practice, slow painful practice. It sounded like the effort of a child.

Parris explained to Herr Berdorff. The old man shook his head.

"It seems to me a nonsense. Never have I heard of something like this." He spread his hands with a gesture expressive of question and incredulity. "One day she iss a great violinist; the next day she cannot play! I do not understand."

Parris was patient.

"It's rather simple, really, Professor. You have to forget certain ideas you have always had about the way the mind works. The human mind works as a whole—it moves all at once, the whole machine, like an engine on rails."

"Well?"

"At different times, under different conditions—different pressures, the mind works differently. Sometimes when the person develops, changes, the operations of the mind make a gradual adjustment and change along with the conditions."

"What, for example, iss such a condition?"

"Well, the most common transformation is puberty."

"Ach, yes. Of course. I see something now. Go on."

"Vera played the violin largely by a kind of musical intuition."

"What? She was taught, wasn't she, soundly? I myself—"

"I'm not talking about technique. I'm talking about the farther reaches of music—"

"Yes, yes. Excuse. I see."

"There was nothing in her personal experience to tell her what the great composers meant by their deepest and greatest writing, Was there?"

"N-no."

"That she grasped by intuition. Talent—genius, whatever you choose to call it. But, on the side, she was growing up, maturing intellectually. You see? But she failed gradually to connect her growth and maturity with her playing. That went on by itself for a long time—the old intuition process."

"Parris—well, I guess I will call you Dr. Mitchell now! I believe I begin already. Yes, yes!"

"Of course you do. Then one day this mature girl turned her attention on her intuitive performance and couldn't make the connection. She had really built a kind of intellectual support for her intuitive act, but—well, it was just as if she had built this support off to one side. It wasn't properly under the other. Her violin playing was up in the air—it rested on nothing."

Herr Berdorff frowned. "I still wonder why she cannot pick up her violin— and just play!"

Parris laughed. "We're back at the beginning. She can't do that because all at once she ceased to function intuitively. She had begun to function consciously. And just because the two processes were not welded together skillfully, the one is lost. As a matter of fact, Herr Berdorff, Vera Lichinska who sits up there in that room on Carrier Street is a very ordinary girl with a very ordinary mind. She is actually incapable of understanding the other girl who played the violin."

"That is tragic. An artiste!"

"Of course it's tragic. It's no fault of her own. She was always afraid of something. That—that damned family drove her, and drove her with silly threats of what Kings Row would think if she did this or that—it's infuriating."

Herr Berdorff stuffed his pipe. His big face had no look of the masterful, severe, ascetic that was usually there. He looked like a bewildered child who had been hurt from an unexpected and trusted quarter.

"I told you what she told me at first about being afraid of being locked up?" The old man nodded. "Yes. So childish, so unnecessary!"

"It's strange, isn't it, that, in a way, it happened? Exactly what she feared. Vera Lichinska—the *little* Vera—is locked up, tight and fast. I am afraid, unless something unexpected or entirely unforeseen happens, that it is forever."

The two men talked, each somewhat surprised after years of acquaintance at what he found in the other. Herr Berdorff was surprised to find his old pupil so deeply serious, so much older in philosophy than his experience warranted. He was a little distressed, too, though he gave no sign of it, to find in Parris a strain of something that seemed at times not quite bitter, but perhaps verging near it. Something a shade disillusioned, doubtful, and doubting, maybe. He wanted to talk about it. He wanted to say that there are many refuges for the human spirit—fidelity, faith—but he kept waiting for some fortunate opening in the conversation.

Parris, thinking half idly of this good man he had come to love so much, was a little startled to find that Herr Berdorff was at times dismayed and discouraged by the same problems which dismayed and discouraged him. It somehow left him feeling a little lonelier than before. He had to travel too often by the uncertain light of his own unsteady self.

"Parris, my boy."

"Yes, Professor."

"I have a piece of news for you. I have hesitated to say it, but the time has come. I must tell you now. I hope, I very much hope that you will feel it iss bad news."

"What's that? You 'hope' it's bad news?"

"I hope you will think it is. It is that I am going away from Kings Row."

"Why—what for? Where are you going?"

"I am going back to Germany. I have always been homesick, of course, for my own Bavaria, but this alone would not send me away."

"What then—?"

"It iss my own people here—my little congregation—that does not wish to have me any longer."

Parris was stunned. He kept silent for a full minute. "I can't believe it. Are you sure?"

"They have told me so. It was a great surprise. I did not guess."

"But what's the matter? What's the reason? What did they say?

"They want someone who iss more a pastor than I have been, who will visit more in their homes. They are right. I have neglected them, perhaps. It iss my fault. I have forgotten too much my first duties here. There was so much to do. The study to make good sermons, the school in the summer, the music lessons, the choir which must be trained, the Sunday school which must be kept going. It was much. To rest me a little from it I practice the piano and the organ and make a little music—like my variations. They—they do not like that I do this."

"It's the most outrageous thing I ever heard of in my life! The stupid, silly—"

"No, no! You must not say that. They are right. I am not too old to learn a lesson."

"But—is it all settled?"

Herr Berdorff nodded. "They have talked it all over among themselves. Yes: it iss settled. I go now very soon."

Parris leaned forward in his chair. "Listen, Professor! Why don't you stay and teach? I happen to know that the chair of German at Aberdeen is going to be vacant—"

"Parris!" Herr Berdorff's voice was stern. "I am a preacher."

"Yes, but—"

"Teaching! Yes, on the side, for some help to someone, and for pleasure. But my work—my real work, that is for God. I could not do something else—never."

"I see."

The old man was gentle again. "You see why I hoped it was bad news to you?"

"The worst news I have had in a long time—the very worst."

"I am glad it iss so. For me it iss also bad news. I am distressed that I have failed."

"You! Listen again, Professor; you have been—*ach!* You have been wonderful for all of us that knew you. You gave me a whole world."

"But as a pas*tor* I have failed. I am sad to leave my work. I am not sad to leave Kings Row. I am very sad to leave you—you are the only one."

Parris stood up. "I have to go. I can't talk now. I'll cry—like—I'll see you tomorrow."

"So. There is yet time for some good talks."

"Good night."

Parris hurried away. He felt his face burn. At the gate of the parsonage he stopped and looked out across the lower part of town where most of the Professor's people lived. He shut his teeth tight. "Fools, fools—thickheaded—*destructive* fools!"

He pulled his hat down over his eyes. He didn't want to see anybody, or have anyone speak to him.

Parris watched the yellow leaves flying from the trees. The tops of the highest elms were already bare, and the brown twigs stood up stiffly against a gray-blue October sky. It was chilly in his apartment today. The black boy who took care of the rooms had kindled a small fire in the grate. It had crackled gaily for a while, the room had warmed, and the quick-burning logs were already dropping to a bed of embers.

The telephone rang. Parris groaned a little. He had had a difficult week, and he was dog-tired. He hesitated. It was probably Randy. He felt that he couldn't see anyone this evening. Herr Berdorff had left two days ago, and Parris burned with a wearisome mixture of resentment and regret. The telephone repeated its ring.

"Hello."

"Dr. Mitchell?"

"Yes."

"This is Cary Whitehead speaking."

"I don't believe I—"

"No, Dr. Mitchell, I'm sure you don't know who I am, but I am calling you at the suggestion of Mrs. Skeffington. She is a friend of mine—"

"Yes, of course. I know Mrs. Skeffington."

"Well, Doctor, I want to see you and talk about something that happened today. Mrs. Skeffington thought maybe you could help."

"What is it? Glad to do anything I can for Mrs. Skeffington."

"I suppose you heard about the Singer boy?"

"Benny Singer? No. What's happened?"

"Well, Doctor, he's in serious trouble. Seems that a gang—I can't call them anything else—of half-grown kids up around Jinktown have been nagging him, playing jokes and the like for a long time. This afternoon, right after dinnertime, they were at it again, and this Singer fellow got a gun and shot into the gang—just outside of his gate."

"Any of them seriously hurt?"

"He killed two of them, Dr. Mitchell."

"Good Lord! Where's Benny now?"

"In the town calaboose, but there's been some pretty ugly talk already, and I believe they're going to move him over to the county jail—just to be on the safe side."

"I'm not surprised, much, at all this, Mr.—er—"

"Whitehead, Dr. Mitchell."

"I'm sorry. I didn't quite catch your name at first. Are you a lawyer?"

"Yes, sir. I'm with Carter and Price—it's Colonel Skeffington's old firm, you know."

"Oh, I see. Are you going to look out for Benny?"

"Mrs. Skeffington asked me to."

"Good. I'll back that up. Don't worry about your fee."

"I'm not, Doctor. But I think I ought to see you."

"All right. Will you come here, or shall I come over to see you? Where's your office?"

"I'll come to see you. I can be there in a few minutes if you are free."

"Come right ahead."

Mr. Whitehead arrived in less than half an hour. Parris was favorably impressed. The young lawyer was intelligent-looking quick, and sympathetic.

"Strange I haven't met you, Mr. Whitehead. Have you been here long?"

"Only six months. I haven't gotten around much. Don't know many people. Kings Row seems to be cautious about newcomers."

"Yes. I daresay. Well, I don't get around at all. Born here but I know only the old-timers. One stays pretty close to my kind of job. I'm walled in, almost as much so as the patients. But tell me about Benny. I went to school with him."

"Mrs. Skeffington thought he worked for you once."

"For my grandmother. I'm sorry to say I'd sort of lost track of him. I've had a lot on my hands. How did all this happen?"

"It's pretty much a familiar kind of story, Doctor. Sad story. Town idiot—"

"Benny's not an idiot."

"Well—whatever. He's feeble-minded, or something. You'd know the exact definition better than I do."

"Pardon me. Go ahead."

"Just young hoodlums. Found somebody to pick on. It happens over and over. Wore him to a frazzle, I expect. He tried to get rid of them today. They hung around his place, and—he shot them. That's all."

"Looks bad."

"It is bad. Hard to convince a jury that he isn't much to blame. It's understandable."

"Benny's been picked on all of his life. Society gave him no aid and no protection. But—" Parris sighed, and turned a paper cutter over and over on the table. "This kind of thing seldom turns out the way it ought to. What do you want me to do?"

"Well, first of all, I guess the court will appoint a commission."

"Yes, that's the procedure. Three doctors and three laymen. The doctors in such instances are no more understanding or helpful than the laymen—they're worse than useless."

"Well, what Mrs. Skeffington thought right away was that maybe we could get you on that commission so that there'd be someone who had the background of the case. Mrs. Skeffington is pretty much wrought up about it. The boy—he's really a man, but he looks like a boy in his teens—has been with her since before the Colonel died, and she's taken this on herself pretty much. In fact, she retained me for his defense."

"Fine. I'll do what I can. In the meantime it might be best if I don't see Benny. But will you tell him—something or other from me, some kind of message. It's a shame. Benny's not crazy—"

"Sorry to hear you say that, Doctor."

"Why, what—?"

"It'll be our only chance. He'll swing if he isn't crazy."

Parris clapped his hand to his brow. "I meant to say—I was thinking in technical terms, really—I meant to say that these moronic cases, and he's above the usual moron type, could be made into useful and self-sustaining people with the right conditions. Benny was on the way—I almost feel as if that were partly my fault. He was doing a piece of work that would have set him up all right. I meant to say that Benny is not insane in our definition. He might very well have been crazed by this persecution, in a legal sense."

"That's our line, Dr. Mitchell."

"I see. I see."

The commission appointed to examine Benny Singer and pass on his responsibility for his acts consisted, to Parris' extreme dismay, of Dr. Alton Ferris, instantly and openly antagonistic to Parris but for no apparent reason; Dr. Saunders, elderly and pompous, deaf to any voice but his own; Emory Feelan, a law partner of Fulmer Green, the new prosecuting attorney; Professor Campbell, elderly substitute professor of psychology at Aberdeen; and the Reverend Mr. Cole of the Presbyterian church.

Parris controlled himself with the greatest difficulty throughout the proceedings that took place nearly six weeks later.

Dr. Ferris and Dr. Saunders took time to express their general disapproval of the new theories of medical psychology. They were supported by Professor Campbell.

Parris, acting chairman, finally interrupted this symposium.

"May I point out, gentlemen, that opinions of the newer theories of medical psychology have nothing at this moment to do with the case of Benny Singer? Our sole purpose here is to determine the degree of his responsibility. May we proceed on that notion?"

Dr. Saunders glared, and Dr. Ferris smiled covertly.

"It is my opinion," said Professor Campbell with an air of finality, "that this man has a perfectly clear comprehension of right and wrong. He answered my questions with greater intelligence than I had been led to expect. He is, I am perfectly sure, entirely responsible to society for his actions."

The discussion wore on. It was personal, vindictive, unintelligent, and stubborn.

The Reverend Dr. Cole hunched obstinately in his chair. Two dull red spots burned angrily in his cheeks. His eyes glittered. He was surprisingly influential in this meeting, and he was well aware of it.

Parris explained his own point of view with extreme care, and with caution. He knew that his only hope to win was to conciliate these inexplicably prejudiced men. He elaborated his thesis of temporary insanity, and based his arguments on Benny's life as he had known it from the days in primary school. He put forward the plea that Benny could be sent here to the hospital instead of to prison or to the gallows, that he could to a large extent be restored and rehabilitated. He could at least serve the state here as a laborer in the gardens. He begged that the senseless cruelty of a conviction on other grounds should be considered as a confession of failure on the part of society to do its duty by its responsibilities to the weak and deficient.

Dr. Cole kept his mouth shut in a tight straight line until Parris had finished.

"I should feel myself derelict to my duties as a citizen if I condoned in any degree such an open and brutal crime. The two young men, who are mourned today in homes which could ill afford to spare them as breadwinners, were probably nothing more than playful. I find nothing in their record to prove them vicious in intent. On the other hand, Singer has on several occasions shown indications of a violent and uncontrollable nature. I am in full accord with Dr. Campbell here, whom we cannot hold ignorant of the workings of the human mind. As I have said, I feel my own responsibility to society—I feel it keenly. I feel that the laws of our country must be honored. It is our duty to hand this murderer over to the arm of the law, and beyond that to trust in the mercy of the Lord Jesus Christ."

Parris fought quietly with every weapon of reason at his command, but the commission was solidly against him. He arose, and bowed slightly. The men reached for their hats and coats. Dr. Cole shook hands with the others, and bowed to Parris. "I am sorry," he said, "that I could not support you in the defense of your friend, but my duty—"

A cold fury swept Parris from head to foot. He was astonished to find his knees quaking under him, but he managed his voice. His words came evenly and quietly.

"I am still unimpressed, Dr. Cole, with your feeling of responsibility to society, but I cannot tell you how immeasurably shocked I am to hear the name of the Saviour of men on your lips in such a connection."

"Why—why! What do you mean, sir?"

"You have helped this afternoon to hand a helpless man over to legal murder. I seem to recall that another judge in circumstances not entirely dissimilar first washed his hands. I doubt, Dr. Cole, that such a simple procedure would serve to cleanse your own."

The color faded partly from the infuriated minister's face, leaving it mottled and streaked. He half choked over his words as he faced Parris.

"Do you realize that you are actually likening this idiot murderer to Christ in—in this ridiculous and insulting comparison?"

Parris regained his temper instantly.

"Dr. Cole, some of the simple people of this world—simple but deep and rich in wisdom—always speak of the mentally deficient as 'God's children.' You may remember that the man whose name you use rather recklessly said: 'In as much as ye did it not to one of the least of these, ye did it not to me.' Remember?"

He turned to the staring group of men. "Good afternoon, gentlemen. I trust that all of you may be able to sleep well tonight."

Parris elbowed his way out of the crowded courtroom. There was a hubbub of conversation on every side. There were many expressions of approval and some laughter. He came out on the west portico of the courthouse, nodded absently to a few greetings, and buttoned his overcoat up about his throat. It was a bitterly cold February day, and the wind came from the northwest with a vicious whip.

He walked rapidly south. Drake and Randy would be waiting to hear details.

The snow crunched under his feet. It was packed hard as ice on the short boardwalk leading to Randy's front porch.

He knocked, and Randy opened the door.

"Hello, Randy."

"Oh, Parris. I can tell you have bad news! Drake has been on pins and needles, all afternoon."

"Yes, the news is bad, Randy."

"Guilty?"

"Yes."

"And the sentence? Did they give that poor boy life?"

He looked at her and shook his head.

"Parris! You don't mean—they aren't going to hang him?"

"I'm afraid so. That's the sentence."

"Come on in to Drake's room."

The room seemed close and overheated. Drake had a lapboard across the bed. It was covered with papers. He held out his hand.

"I heard what you said, from the hall. Gosh, Parris, that's a damned shame!"

"Well, there are appeals. Whitehead will do the best he can, but he's got no public back of him. I don't believe there are one dozen people in this town in any way sympathetic to Benny."

"He'll move for an appeal?"

"Oh, yes. Right away. Poor chance, I'm afraid."

"Poor old Benny!"

"Yes. You know, Drake, I don't believe Benny really realizes altogether what's happening. He actually smiled and looked interested through the whole day. If the jury had just looked at him one time they should have been able to see—oh, it makes me wild! Fulmer Green, ranting up and down, actually making jokes about the evidence, clowning, playing for the death of a human being. He had the jury and the whole court laughing. *Laughing!*"

"He always was rotten, Parris."

"Yes, I know."

"Remember how he used to be after Benny all the time? Fulmer and his gang? Always deviling Benny, trying to get him to fight."

"Yes, I remember, of course. Well, he's still at it. He had his gang behind him today, too."

"Eh?"

"I mean Kings Row—all of Kings Row. The pack—closing in for the last time."

"God, I hope we can do something!"

"I don't expect much from appeals. Of course there is the Governor—as a last resort. But he's not going to do anything against public opinion."

"No. I suppose not. Any chance of commutation?"

"I don't believe so. I tell you the town has been made into a legal mob. Fulmer Green is a perfect rabble-rouser. They've got to kill Benny. They won't be satisfied with anything less."

"I kept hoping they'd call you for expert testimony."

"I think Whitehead didn't dare. That senseless flare-up of mine at the committee did poor old Benny a bad turn."

Drake bit his lip. He wanted to say something, but evidently was hesitating.

"Well, Drake, what is it?"

Drake flushed slightly. "It's just—well, Randy tells me that Presbyterian preacher's been doing a lot of talking about you. Seems he's got a good deal of feeling worked up against you here and there. Not that it means anything, I guess."

"It doesn't mean anything to me—myself, Drake. I don't care. I believe he's the only human being I ever hated—maybe until today. There's Fulmer Green—though I feel more a terrific disgust and contempt in that quarter. I don't care, Drake, I don't care what any of them think about me—I know when I'm right and when I'm wrong. I know that most of them are wild animals who have a thin coating of civil behavior—that's all. But there are those they prey on, abuse, tyrannize over, stultify. Drake, I hate a particular kind of tyranny—it's a tyranny that is laid on the *mind* of man. It's the most deeply dangerous kind. Cole does it through religion and cant. Fulmer Green does it with the familiar demagogic methods that are as old as the world. Somebody has to stand up and call these things by their right names once in a while."

"Could this little stir-up about you have any effect on your position?"

"At the hospital, you mean?"

"Yes."

"Oh, I don't know. Maybe not. Dr. Nolan thinks I'm good at my job."

"There's always been politics in behind everything out at the asylum, though."

"I know. I know. Well, we won't bother about that."

"No. I know we don't need to. Benny's the question right now."

"Drake, don't fool yourself. They're going to hang Benny."

Drake thrust his papers to one side. "Fulmer Green—the lowdown—"

"Save your breath, Drake. We'll do what we can."

Drake subsided, and Randy came in with coffee.

Parris pressed his fingers tight against his eyes. "Let's don't talk about it any more today."

Randy looked anxiously at him. A small blue vein in his temple throbbed visibly. He took the cup of coffee and stirred it slowly,

"I feel so much to blame. Benny was doing well out at the place. I should have kept inquiring, and have seen to it that he kept a job out in the country, away from the town and hoodlums. And then this fool preacher—I don't know why I allow him to upset me. First time I ever saw him I—well, I really laced into him. It was unpardonable. I made an enemy for Benny. But I rather thought that he had a good place with the Skeffingtons."

"You'll stay to supper, Parris?"

"No, I can't. Thanks, Randy. Wish I could. What time is it?"

"After five."

"Good Lord, I'm late. I'll see you—let's see, on Tuesday. Right?"

"Fine. Try not to blame yourself, Parris. Maybe it'll work out some way."

"I'm afraid it won't. Thanks, Randy. 'By, both of you."

Randy watched Parris as he went out of the gate and trudged through the snow.

"Poor old Parris. He's taking this hard, isn't he?"

"Yes. He's a strange fellow, Parris is."

"Strange?"

"Yes. Long as I've known him, I know that I don't understand the first thing that goes on inside of his head."

"Parris is all right."

"He's the best ever, but I don't understand him."

"He's lonely."

Randy picked up the tray and left the room. Drake slipped a rubber band over a sheaf of papers. He pushed a pillow aside and sank back. A lock of hair fell across his brow, giving him suddenly the look of a tired child. He winced and bit his lip as he tried to find a comfortable position.

Parris was correct in his prophecies. Parris, Mrs. Skeffington, and Cary Whitehead made every possible effort to save Benny Singer, but all failed.

One balmy afternoon in early May Sam Winters and two assistant carpenters were noisily putting the finishing touches to the gallows in the stone-paved jail yard. Sam surveyed his preparations and chewed a toothpick.

"Well, I guess that's about all. You boys carry that sandbag up there. I got to test out the rope and we'll be all set for tomorrow morning."

A jail attendant opened a small green-painted iron door and called to Sam.

"Reporter to see you, Sam!"

"A what?"

"Reporter from the newspaper."

"What's he want?"

"Wants to talk to you."

"What for?"

"Guess he wants to put a piece in the paper about you maybe."

"Tell him to come on out here."

A tall, lanky young man stooped and came through the low, narrow door. Sam squinted at him.

"Howdy."

"Are you Mr. Winters?"

"I'm Sam Winters, yes."

"I'd like to ask you a few questions about tomorrow's execution."

"For the newspaper?"

"Yes, sir. The *Chronicle.*"

"Don't see what you want that kind of stuff in a newspaper for."

"People want to know, I guess." The reporter looked up at the gallows and at the sinister loop of rope that swung lightly in the breeze. "Gosh!" he said, and gulped audibly.

"Never see one of them things before?"

"A gallows? No. Never before."

"I've built about twenty of 'em in my time."

"I believe you've executed quite a number, haven't you?"

"Yep. A lot of 'em. One woman among 'em. Come on up here with me, and I'll show you how it works."

Sam led the way and talked as casually as if he were discussing any commonplace matter. The reporter made a few notes, but looked uncomfortable.

"The drop's just about nine feet."

The reporter looked down through the trap which hung open. He stepped back and gulped again.

"About right to top 'em."

"Top them? What's that?"

Sam smiled. "Break their necks. Of course that depends some on a man's weight. Too heavy and they're likely to break the rope. Too light and they don't give enough snap at the end of the drop." Sam rolled the toothpick between his gold teeth. "I'd say a hundred and eighty's about the ideal weight."

"The ideal—yes, yes, I see."

Sam lowered his voice a little. "Now this boy we got in here's a leetle light."

"Yes—er, of course you expect everything to go off all right?"

"Yes, siree. Done a careful job here. It'll go off smooth as satin. You going to be here?"

"Well, er—I think I was to be, but I rather think Mr. Wardlaw will come himself."

"Um—"

"Thanks, Mr. Winters."

"Not at all. Not at all."

"Mr. Winters!"

The attendant came to the door again.

"Yep. What you want, Ned?"

"Somebody to see you."

"Send 'em out."

"Well, I think you'd better come in here."

"All right."

An old woman was waiting in the sheriff's office. Sam saw her through the hall. "Who's that in there, Ned?"

"It's Mis' Singer."

"His ma, eh?"

"Yes."

"Guess she wants to see him. It's all right."

"No, sir. She said she wanted to see you."

"What for? I can't talk to her."

"She said she's just got to see you."

Sam set his face a little. This wasn't much to his liking, but if it had to be gone through with, why, it had to. That's all there was to it.

He took off his hat and stepped into the little office.

"Good day, ma'am."

Mrs. Singer got slowly to her feet.

"You're him?"

"Who, ma'am? I'm Sam Winters."

"You're the one what's going to do it?"

Sam looked hard at her. She swayed a little. He reached out to catch her arm, but she stepped back.

"I'm all right," she said shortly. She lowered her head but kept her gaze on his face as if looking for something there. She moved her lips once or twice but no word came. She held out a cardboard box.

"Take it to him, will you? Tell him I sent it."

"What is it, ma'am?"

"It's a clean shirt. I washed and ironed it today."

"You want to see him, ma'am?"

She shook her head. "I can't—any more."

The old woman turned and walked steadily toward the door. She did not look back.

Sam opened the box, looked at the neatly folded white shirt inside, and replaced the lid.

"Ned!"

"Yes, sir."

"Give this to Ben in the morning when you take his breakfast in to him."

"All right, Mr. Winters. Sure."

"And listen."

"Yes, sir."

"I ain't seeing anybody else this afternoon, you hear?"

"Yes, sir. Of course."

Mrs. Singer stopped at the corner. She looked up the sloping street toward the town. Then she turned and went down toward the creek. At the bridge she walked along the water's edge. It was muddy and the lush grass was high. A little farther along she came to a thicket of shrubbery. She plunged into it and made her way through, thrusting at the branches which tore her hands and arms until they bled. She kept her way along the bank, now and then ankle deep in mud, but she looked fearfully at each crossing as if she dreaded seeing anyone. She followed the stream, hiding in the bushes, and fighting her way through the thick growth. She was out of breath and her heart pounded. She stopped for a moment in sight of her own house to rest. Her hands bent the branches aside and stripped off the leaves.

A small boy raced along past the little Singer house and around to the back porch of the house next door.

"Ma!"

"What you want? Stop hollering so loud!"

"I seen Mis' Singer!"

"Well, what of it? Where?"

"She's just a-standin' in them willow bushes down there."

"What's she doing down there, the poor woman?"

"She's just a-standin' there and when I come by she seen me and she kinder *mooed* at me and tore off a lot of them leaves and throwed 'em on the ground and stomped on 'em. I got scared, and I run home."

The woman turned from her washtub and dried her hands on her apron.

"I'll go down there and see if I can get her home. I guess she's near crazy."

"You reckon she's crazy, Ma?"

"I don't know. I wouldn't be one bit surprised."

"Will they lock her up in the asylum if she's crazy, Ma?"

"Shut up!" She gave the boy a resounding slap on the ear. "Go in the house and shut up, an' don't you come out of there, you hear me?"

Benny Singer walked slowly from the narrow iron door across the flagged yard. Dr. Malcolm Fletcher, the county health officer, was on one side of him, and Parris on the other. Parris held to Benny's arm and talked quietly. Benny did not see the gallows until he stood at the foot of the steps. He looked up suddenly and then quickly back at Parris. For the first time something like a bewildered fear came into his eyes. He stopped and pulled back a little.

"You come—you come up there with me—will you, Parris?"

"Of course, Benny, of course."

The jail yard was filled with witnesses. A small crowd had gathered on the roof of Hoxey's feed store overlooking the enclosure,

Benny looked down at the group of upturned faces. A little of the bewildered look came back to his eyes, and then he smiled—a childish, almost welcoming smile.

"Hello, everybody," he said. His voice wavered on the last word and went out like a light. Sam Winters stepped in front of him.

The early morning sun fell level across the treetops; a fresh, flowery breath of air sprang up. Parris turned quickly, descended the steps, and went back through the building, and out into the street. No one saw him go.

The circle of watchers never took their eyes from the proceedings on the scaffold.

One man leaned against the stone wall for support and looked away. Sam Winters' careful preparations did not carry through as he had planned: Benny

Singer was slowly strangling to death in the bright sunshine of this spring morning.

Dr. Nolan knocked the ashes from his pipe and leaned back in the creaking swivel chair. He had been talking rather absently but he had been watching Parris closely. Parris had been aware of the scrutiny.

"Well, Dr. Nolan, what's the diagnosis?"

Dr. Nolan smiled. "Too simple to talk about. You take things too hard. You've let this Benny Singer business flatten you out."

"Yes, I know. It has—somewhat. But, heavens—"

Dr. Nolan held up his hand. "I know everything you're going to say. I agree with you. But you are the question at the moment. You're useful around here, Dr. Mitchell."

"You mean I was."

"You'll have to take some time off. Take six months."

"It sounds as if I were being fired."

Dr. Nolan stood up and gave Parris a passing thwack on the back. "You are. You're fired for six months."

"I think I'll go to Europe, sir."

"Good idea. Where?"

"Switzerland."

Dr. Nolan looked sharply at Parris. "More work?"

"In a way. But different. I'd like to see what they're doing at Zurich. You—"

"Yes, yes. Interesting enough. But you need rest. Of course, if that's what you want to do, go ahead. Anything to take your mind off of all this for a while. You haven't taken enough small vacations. You know as well as I do that you can't stay in this atmosphere on too long a stretch."

"All right, sir. Could Carruthers take over for me?"

"Yes. That would be my idea."

Parris sighed, but it did not sound like relief or relaxation.

"I'd like to go right away."

"Of course. How long will it take you to get ready?"

"I can make over to Carruthers in a few days."

"Nothing else to delay you?"

Parris looked surprised. "Why, no, sir."

Dr. Nolan nodded, and half smiled. "Free as that?" But he looked gravely after Parris as the door closed. He had been struck from the beginning by the peculiar solitariness of his young assistant. Dr. Mitchell had made friends with the staff and had kept their consideration. He corrected himself: the newcomer had not really made friends. No one knew him very well, and no one made any special effort to know him. He had worked as hard as any man on the staff, harder at times, but he seemed always to enclose himself, as if—as if he were just passing on his way to some pressing concern elsewhere. Dr.

Nolan picked up his pipe again and reached for the tobacco jar. Fellow needed to get married, for one thing. Something to take up his mind when he was off duty.

Parris went up to his apartment. He walked back and forth for a few minutes, opened the closets, took some suitcases from a high shelf. He wondered where the big collapsible one was. Must be down in storage. He'd have it up tomorrow. He'd travel light, he decided. He tried to stir an excitement in his mind about the trip. There were a lot of things he'd like to see. He'd make short trips to Italy, see the French cathedrals, walk some in Switzerland. Perhaps he should go to Diisseldorf to look up Anna. She was still living there. And Herr Berdorff, settled now in a small Bavarian town. He could do anything he wanted to! But he felt, for the first time, a little depressed about it. He could do exactly as he pleased because it didn't make any difference to anyone. Randy and Drake would be interested and excited, even. He thought about Drake, and the thin, new lines across his forehead deepened. If he could induce Drake to leave that house, to live somewhere with a wide outlook, and maybe a large lawn. But Drake was violently obstinate about that. He wouldn't be moved and he wouldn't go out of doors. It was a pathological phase, of course, of the whole case, but so far he had not been able to do anything about it. Yes, Drake and Randy would make some ado about his going, but even to them it meant only the absence of a friend for a while. He thought of Dr. Nolan's fatherly kindliness and was touched. This fine, intelligent humanitarian was the nearest to an understanding acquaintance he had.

He opened the wide front window in his study and leaned out. The warm air of early summer was sweet and kind. There was a full moon, he knew, not only by the quicksilver light that washed the extensive grounds, but by the noise from the wards. On moonlit nights the great buildings seemed not to sleep at all. They were murmurous with a steady, quivering sound that was thrust through again and again by sudden screams and shouts. These disturbing sounds came and went like heat lightning on a heavy night. Tonight the sounds touched his nerves like the flick of a whip. He closed the window, picked up his hat, and went out.

Drake and Randy were surprised to see him. He seldom came late. Drake had his lapboard across the bed. Both the bed and the wide table beside it were covered with papers.

"Business this time of night?"

Drake nodded. "A kind of half-year straightening up. Say, Parris, do you know we're getting rich?"

"I'm glad, Drake. That's fine."

"I mean all of us. You, too."

Parris looked a bit mystified. "Me?"

"Yep. We've kept on putting profits back—"

"Are you still talking about that old Tower money?"

Drake subsided. He looked a little hurt. Parris realized his mistake instantly. "I just mean—oh, thunder, Drake. I don't want you to do anything about that."

Randy tapped on the table with a pencil. She looked a little anxiously from Drake to Parris.

"It's this, Parris. Drake and I could never have done this without your help. So let's don't be silly about it. You say it wasn't much—and that's a silly remark, too. That much is a lot of money anywhere, any time. We've been unbelievably lucky. The sales have been awfully good. Now here's the way it is. We've finished selling out the Sheeley tract entirely."

"The whole thing?"

"Yes. Isn't that wonderful? Do you know how much it was? A hundred and ten lots. All of them little, of course, and cheap, but they were a good bargain. Mostly the clay-pit workers took them. Now we've figured up—" She took up some long strips of paper, and handed one to Parris. "That's how we stand today."

He whistled, and Drake grinned.

"How's that, Parris, for a girl that didn't know anything about business and an old cripple piled up in bed?"

Parris' heart jumped at the phrase. It was the first time Drake had ever spoken of himself like that.

"It's marvelous! You kids! I'm as pleased as can be."

Randy continued, her eyes and voice serious. "We've made up our minds now about what we want to do next. Half of this is yours, of course."

"Are you beginning that again?"

"Yes, and I'll likely keep on with the subject. That's business, sir, and I'd like to keep it that way."

"No friendship comes in, I guess."

"Oh, Parris!" She came hurriedly around the table and kissed him. "Please. It's just that Drake and I want to hold up our half of the friendship, that's all."

He reached up and patted her flushed face. "All right. All right. Whatever you say."

"But I don't want to give you the money."

Parris laughed.

"At least not yet, Parris. Drake and I want to start a building-and-loan association, and we want you in—your money, rather. You don't have to do anything, but we want it fixed up properly—legally."

Parris pushed his chair back from the table. "I don't understand the first thing about business of any kind. Fix it any way you want to. You're going to be nasty old rich people, I can see that. I came down here tonight to talk about myself."

"What's the matter, Parris?" Drake spoke quickly.

"Nothing serious. I'm tired—at least Dr. Nolan thinks so. I haven't really had any kind of letup. I'm going to Europe." Out of the corner of his eye Parris saw Drake slump slightly into his pillows.

"Aw, gee—but that's fine. You need it, I bet."

"Maybe, I don't know. I'm going to do some work."

"Work?"

"Study—and observation. Very important new things being tried out over there."

"Are you going to be away long?" Drake's voice came a shade hesitatingly, as if he were controlling a stammer.

"Dr. Nolan says six months. I think I'll be back in four."

"Oh! I was afraid you were going to say a year."

"Nothing like that."

"Gee, I'm glad."

Parris looked curiously at Drake, and then at Randy. He wanted very much to know how much it mattered to them whether he went or stayed. He was moved somehow by Drake's quick apprehension. He would have liked to talk about it, to have them say that they needed him, or would miss him. He felt certain at this one moment that they felt just that, but he could not make himself say anything more. They talked on of the trip, and back again to the plans for the business venture. It was late when Parris left, and the bright round moon was hanging in a clear deep sky. He walked toward the hospital through deserted streets. Kings Row went to bed early, even in summer.

At the gate he turned and circled the grounds. He had seen a light that caught his attention. He followed the tall iron fence, walking quietly in the damp grass. He came out on Carrier Street. The branches of the maples hung low and almost canopied the side walk. A block farther on he stopped and looked at the house opposite. In the second-story room there was a bright light. The upper half of the window was lowered and Vera Lichinska stood there, resting her arms on the sash. He watched her for several minutes. She was as still as an image. The moonlight fell full on her face and whitened it to a stony pallor. She was staring fixedly at the huge building facing her—the huge, gloomy building that seemed even to Parris to crouch among the tall trees, and to wait.

Book Six

1

Parris looked at Kings Row with a heavy heart. He had remained in Europe for the whole of his six months' leave of absence, and had returned just in time to meet the early winter. It had begun this year with an onslaught of particularly disagreeable weather. The town was drab and shabby-looking. The features of it which were not shabby were worse. The juxtaposition of the dilapidated older parts of town and the raw and tasteless newer parts only accentuated the uglier aspects of both. The trees were bare, and all of the unpainted outhouses and fences were rain-soaked and gray.

He shuddered with distaste as he viewed it. He had been shocked on his first return to Kings Row after an absence of five years, but this time he was pained. It wasn't, he said to himself, because it was a small town without imposing buildings and monuments. He cared little enough for such things. Nor was it because the town was poor. Kings Row was far from being poor. It was ugly in a negative and neglected fashion. Ugly because no one had happened to think of beauty or charm. Ugly because it was the outward expression of a way of thinking that was without such factors as made life and living itself an act of grace. It was, he thought wryly, ugly on purpose.

Of course Kings Row wasn't always ugly. There were seasons, he amended, when it was lovely with sun and leaves—yes, sun and leaves, but the work of Kings Row itself was a clumsy, shoddy, cheap utilitarianism. He had found on this journey that he was more European than he had ever guessed. European in tastes, but not in thinking. There he had been dismayed by the ancient crystallizations of thought and habit, by the mechanical repetitions of senseless ways of doing and being, and by the utter indifference of one class toward the misfortunes and miseries of another. He realized that Dr. Seiss had been at least partially right in pronouncing Europe old and diseased. Parris felt it even when he could not say that he saw evidences of it. And he had sincerely turned away from the mellow old towns and the glorious cathedrals and the enchanting countryside where peasants toiled blindly. He turned away with a new vision toward the youth and hopefulness of his own country. Perhaps it had been just that attitude which darkened his mood to melancholy now that he was here seeing it in its reality.

There was something here, yes, that was lacking in Europe, but its fulfillment seemed a discouragingly long way off.

He had returned to find his work waiting. The hospital was the same. He was glad to be back. Glad to take up the troublous details of the daily routine. The hospital was terribly crowded, and the entire staff was rejoicing over the state's appropriation for extensive new buildings. A huge tract of land belonging to the estate of the late Thurston St. George had been bought for a farm and vegetable garden. It meant ease and expansion in many ways.

This was the first news that greeted him. Dr. Nolan was full of plans.

Parris had seen Drake and Randy only once in these three days. Randy was quiet and sober. Her father had died in August, and she had been deeply grieved. Parris had respected the sturdy old man, and understood her grief.

"I suppose they'll make Tod section boss now, won't they, Randy? You told me once that had been his whole life's ambition."

Her face clouded. "I don't know, Parris. Tod could handle the job, of course, but you know how Tod is. They may not want to. For the present a man named Shaughnessy is acting boss."

"I see. Well, I hope Tod gets what he wants. He's a good soul."

"Yes, he is, Parris."

They had met in the post office and stood chatting in the door.

"I'll have to hurry on, Parris. Can you come down tomorrow night? We've got a big piece of news for you. Saved it up. Just couldn't tell you Monday because of one or two details still hanging there."

"What is it—the building-and-loan thing?"

She shook her head. "Better than that. You wait."

"All right. I'll try to see you Friday evening, after supper. Is that convenient for you?"

"You know all evenings are the same. Any time."

"Friday evening, then."

"Fine."

A week passed and Parris had still not found time for his visit with Drake and Randy. He was dressing one evening when Arty, his Negro houseboy, came in and laid a copy of *The Evening Chronicle* on the table. Parris glanced at it and saw a heavy, black headline. He unfolded the paper and switched on the table light. ASYLUM DOCTOR MAKES FORTUNE OUT OF ASYLUM DEAL.

He rubbed his eyes. The second headline, scarcely smaller than the first, said I*t Pays to Be on the Inside.*

"What in the world! Who—" And then his eye caught his own name.

Dr. Parris Mitchell, staff physician at the State Hospital for the Insane, and the silent partner of Drake McHugh, real-estate dealer, realized a cool one hundred thousand dollars on the purchase of the old St. George tract recently acquired by the state for the improvement of hospital facilities. It appears that this plan for expansion of the hospital has been afoot for some time. In the early summer Dr. Mitchell went abroad for a rest, it was said, and during his absence the real-estate firm, as it now appears to be, acquired this land. When the hospital was ready to buy it paid the price of the real-estate dealers' foresight.

Mr. Fulmer Green, elected this past November to the legislature has promised that an investigation will be made.

There was a good deal more, all in the same outspoken vein.

Parris went to the telephone. He would have to call Randy and find out what this was about. He hesitated and came back to the table. He thought for a moment and then picked up the house telephone.

"Can you get Dr. Nolan for me, Miss Stevenson?"

"He's in his apartment, sir."

"Call him, please."

"... Dr. Nolan? May I see you right away, please?..."

"Yes. I'll be right down ..."

Parris laid the paper before his chief. "Have you seen this, sir?"

"Yes, I have."

"Had you heard anything about this before?"

"Not a word."

"There's no truth in this, Dr. Nolan. I mean—if Drake McHugh put this through it was entirely without my knowledge."

"How do you happen to be in business on the outside?" Dr. Nolan looked grave.

"I'll have to tell you the whole story, sir."

"Very well. Sit down."

Parris related in detail the story of his friendship with Drake, the gift or loan of the Tower money, the slow rehabilitation of Drake through being made to feel and to be successful, and then his conversation with Drake and Randy just before he left for Europe.

"I signed some sort of papers, power of attorney among them. I had never heard of the proposed purchase of this land before I left, and I know that they—I suppose I have to say 'we'—that we didn't own it when I left."

Dr. Nolan sat very still in his chair until Parris had finished.

"I knew all of that, Dr. Mitchell."

"You knew it?"

"Certainly. I mean I knew when I read this paper an hour ago that you knew nothing about it. I didn't know that you hadn't heard of it yet."

"I saw the McHughs only once. Randy told me a week ago that she had a big piece of news for me."

"This was it. Sorry you got it this way. Here's the story, Dr. Mitchell. The suggestion that we attempt this purchase and expansion was made by Senator Depass of Poplar Grove. He came to see me in the latter part of June. You were already in Europe—had been there for a month or more. Of course we'd talked often of the need of spreading out. I inquired right away about this property.

We had actually talked once or twice to the St. George brothers long ago about this purchase, but they wanted too much money. I knew the state legislature would never do it, and I felt that the St. Georges were holding us up a little. Thurston might have let it go at a reasonable figure but Macmillan held out. After both of them died and the estate was being settled I thought of it again, but I never mentioned it to anyone. Senator Depass acted on his own initiative.

"Then I found out, to my surprise, that a new real-estate company had bought it, paid a good bit, and that the Burton County Bank held a mortgage. But your friend Drake McHugh, through his wife, bought the place up even before Senator Depass came to see me."

"What about the price?"

"It wasn't too high. It was appraised and the price found reasonable. My real surprise came when we concluded the purchase, and I found you were a sort of partner in the business. There's nothing illegal about you, making some money on the side. I just didn't know you were in on that."

"Neither did I."

"As I found out right away. I had no intention of making any comment on the matter. I know better than you do how sensitive public feeling is about public money. There's something behind this, of course. Has anybody on that paper got a grudge against you for anything at all?"

"Not that I know of. I haven't many friends, that's a fact, but I thought I had no enemies at all."

"You're evidently mistaken. Well, we'll see after a while what's hidden in the woodpile."

"Shouldn't I make a forthright denial, right away?"

"No."

"No?"

"For this reason. Let's find out who's after you, and why."

"It gives me a very strange feeling, Dr. Nolan, to think that anyone is 'after' me."

"Yes, yes. That's natural. You'll get used to it the longer you remain in the service of the state."

The undertone of irony and bitterness was strange and surprising coming from Dr. Nolan. Parris raised his eyebrows inquiringly.

Dr. Nolan continued. "They 'honor' you with a state appointment. The work is harder than private work; the pay is far less. Then they sit back and watch for the first chance to get something on you."

Parris started to speak, but Dr. Nolan interrupted. "Fact. They always speak of these 'soft state jobs' with 'good state money.' Well, I suppose it's a point of view. The doctors, even in a town with a state institution, are not very kind toward the staff doctors. Institutional work has advantages, of course, from a professional angle, but from any worldly consideration we have poor jobs, and we have to prove our rights to hold them after they're given to us. Now that's one side of the picture.

"The first reaction to this—this mess here in the paper—will be that you are using your position here to take advantage of the state, and secondly that you *must* be borrowing state time to conduct outside business. You know this—this, what's his name?—Fulmer Green?"

"Oh, yes. Since childhood."

"What's he like?"

"Braggart, bully, coward, and liar. He made a circus out of the Singer trial and hanged the boy to enhance his position as prosecuting attorney."

"Were you called for testimony?"

"No. I was on the committee—"

"Yes, yes! I recall. You collided with Cole!"

"Yes. That was too bad. Second time, too. I was wrong the first time."

"Green got anything against you?"

"Not that I know of. Couldn't imagine anything from that quarter."

"Queer, isn't it?"

"Yes, it is. It troubles me more than I can say—but—"

"But what?"

"Just for your sake."

"Mine?"

"Yes, Dr. Nolan. You gave me my post here—pretty much on faith. You've made it an interesting one for me—I hate to make any kind of trouble for you."

"Stuff. Gave you your post because we had a first-rate report on you from Seiss in Vienna. You're a good man at your job. Trouble! Fiddlesticks. If I never have anything more serious than this to deal with!"

"What shall we do?"

"Nothing."

"Nothing?"

"Not a thing. Wait. They'll call you from the paper. Say you have nothing to say at present."

"What about this investigation?"

"Isn't it—wouldn't it be a joke on them to find out just what you've told me?"

"Well—but in the meantime?"

"Son, I think this hospital, and its staff, and you, and me, and the great commonwealth that supports us, can stand up under the thunders of *The Evening Chronicle* for a while."

"But I am so sorry—I'm so happy in my work here."

"That's good. Go on as before. I've got some influence in the board and in the legislature."

"You think it'll come to that?"

"To what?"

"To your having to use that influence."

"It might. What of it?"

"I don't like publicity."

"Well, you're not the kind that'll go through this world without it. You might as well get used to the idea."

"I don't understand you."

"You're sort of conspicuous, in a quiet way!"

Dr. Nolan laughed, and Parris smiled slightly.

"Listen, son. That money is legitimately yours. I don't need to tell you what I think of the way you've lived up to your friendship with Drake McHugh—I knew his uncle, by the way—or the magnificent job you and Mrs. McHugh must have done restoring him to some sort of adjustment."

Parris waved his hand and shrugged.

"And, furthermore, Dr. Mitchell, if it comes to that, I'll take pleasure in telling whatever powers may happen to inquire into it."

"I don't know how to thank you for this, Dr. Nolan. I—I was thunderstruck when I picked up the paper today."

"I can imagine. Well, well, if you don't mind, I'll just use you for bait for a while. I want to know what's behind this. There's something. Might be just a little community stir of ill will about anybody making some money. God knows everybody tries to soak the state for whatever they can! Why, we can't buy a load of sand and get it hauled out of the creek down there for the same price that anybody else can get it for. That's one reason why I want a big farm here. As I say, though, there may be just someone trying to make use of the incident. I think Wardlaw, who runs this paper, is a skunk. You'll see that Miles Jackson will write a very different piece about it. Might just be that your old chum Mr. Green doesn't overlook anything that'll make him appear to the voters as a watchful public servant. They make me sick, these one-horse politicians! Go on and get a good night's sleep. Don't bother your head about it."

"Thank you, sir."

"Fiddle-faddle. Don't mention it. And don't talk to the staff, either. We'll all keep our ears open, though. There are times when this whole staff can unite against the outside enemy!"

"Good night, sir."

"Good night, Mitchell, good night to you."

Parris returned to his apartment and called Randy. Her voice was tense. He thought she had been crying.

"Oh, Parris, I've been trying to get you all evening, ever since the paper came out. Drake's crazy with worry. I'm so sorry, Parris, We thought we were doing such a fine thing."

"Wait a minute. Let me get in a word, will you? It's all right."

"All right? What do you mean? You read the paper, didn't you?"

"That's nothing. I talked to Dr. Nolan. He knew all about it."

"He did?"

"Yes. I had to tell him, though, how I happened to be in this with you."

"Well, of course."

"Now listen. Tell Drake to—to dry up, or whatever is necessary. And don't you worry. It's all right."

"It can't—it won't affect your place, or—or your career, will it?"

"No. Anyway, I'm rich, aren't I?"

"Oh, Parris! We were so proud of making so much money, and Drake just couldn't wait until you got here to tell you himself. We never imagined it would make trouble."

"It doesn't make a bit of difference. I was troubled for a minute about Dr. Nolan but as long as it doesn't affect him, and it doesn't, and since he feels all right about it, why, there's nothing to it. *I'm famous.*"

A half-choked laugh came over the wire. "Oh, Parris, you're so—so—"

"Go to sleep. I'll be down to thank you."

"For what—for trouble? Drake said just now we'd never been anything but trouble to you."

"You're my friends, and my only friends, Randy. Trouble? The paper said a hundred thousand dollars. Call that trouble?"

"It won't be that much—Drake said when he read that that the whole damn county wasn't worth a hundred thousand dollars. But it *will* be a lot—if that's any comfort to you."

"Good night. Don't worry, and give Drake my love."

"Good night, Parris."

Parris turned away from the telephone and pressed his fingers to his temples. His head ached, and he felt cold and empty. He remembered once when he was a little boy that someone had thrown a dirty snowball at him which spattered a new overcoat. He didn't know who threw it, and he wondered why they had wanted to. He felt the same way now. It hadn't occurred to him that anyone was thinking about him at all, and to discover that there was someone willing to make this senseless attack depressed him greatly. He was hurt. It was a childish feeling, he realized, but that didn't lessen the confusion and distress in his mind.

This feeling was considerably modified during the next two days. Various members of the staff, some of whom he had not thought of as being particularly friendly, had come to him with some jocular or sympathetic comment. Parris did not know how much of this was spontaneous and how much of it might have been inspired by Dr. Nolan.

Dr. Maughs, the oldest physician in the hospital, stopped him outside one of the wards. He was an able man but quiet and unassertive. In conferences he had always seemed a bit acid.

He threw a long bony arm over Parris' shoulder.

"Mitchell, don't pay any attention to this mudslinging. The best men in this place have come in for it one way and another in my time. Some of them were ousted, too. I know nothing of the sort'll happen to you. Nolan told me something about the facts in this affair. You have to learn to stand up under it when you are an officer of the state. Damned if I know why they're always after us about one thing or another."

He patted Parris awkwardly.

"Thank you a lot, Dr. Maughs. All of you have made me feel a lot better today."

"You're doing a good job here, Mitchell. Interesting, too. Wish I had a new slant of some kind to work on. Job gets pretty monotonous sometimes."

"Well, I'm still excited about it."

"Yes, of course. What I wanted to say was something like this. I'm glad you got hold of a little money on the side. There's a lot of poppycock written and talked about the nobility of a doctor's work. You hear that mostly from somebody who's not practicing medicine, and never did. It's monotonous and most times commonplace. Same things—bad colds, stomach-aches, constipation, and the like. Seldom interesting. Here in state institutions they don't exactly burden you with recompense. When you get old you get a kick in the pants. Foolish not to salt a little something away. Don't know what I'd have to look forward to if my wife's people hadn't left us something. They can throw me out whenever they get ready. I'm going to raise bees."

Parris laughed. "You'll die in harness, and it'll be a long time off, too. It's the kind of thing you said just now, Dr. Maughs, that makes the whole work show up as noble as it really is. Stomachache and constipation—but you do something about it, day after day. That's really what I take my hat off to, sir."

The old physician looked at Parris for a minute. His clear fine eyes showed no sign of what he might be thinking. He gave Parris another thump with his big hand and was off down the long hall.

During the day Parris had a call from Mrs. Skeffington—a peremptory invitation to tea.

The old-fashioned parlor in the Skeffington house had not changed since Parris had seen it as a small boy. A huge-flowered carpet covered the floor to the baseboards. Heavy red draperies crowded the windows, and stiff lace curtains billowed out into a wide fan on the floor.

Mrs. Skeffington sat near the fire which glowed behind an elaborate apparatus of brass fender, andirons, and screen.

Parris bowed over the long skinny hands.

"I'm awfully glad to see you."

"Glad to see you, too. I hear you've been skinning the state out of a hundred thousand dollars. How'd you do it?"

"I didn't."

"Piffle. Of course you did. Doggone smart trick. Congratulate you."

Parris laughed. Mrs. Skeffington began to fuss with tea things. "I'm sorry the Colonel didn't live to see it. He always said you never could get enough money out of the state to run the asylum. He was on the state board, or commission, or whatever they called it then. Hundred thousand! God bless me!"

Parris sobered.

"Really—"

"All right, all right. How'll you have your tea? Then you can spout your story."

"One lump."

"Cream?"

"No."

"Humph! Here you are. Now then. Did that fellow, Drake McHugh, actually have anything to do with this?"

"Everything. I was in Europe."

"So I heard. Smart. Didn't think Drake had that much gumption."

"Well, his wife Randy—"

"Oh ho! So that's it. Little gal's got the brains, eh?"

"She is smart. She's a fine girl, Mrs. Skeffington."

"I dare say, I dare say. Peculiar though—whole business. Man's legs cut off. Girl marries him. What for?"

Parris would have resented this from anyone else, but he understood Mrs. Skeffington. It was Mrs. Skeffington who tried to save Benny, and it was Mrs. Skeffington who joined with him in providing for Mrs. Singer after Benny's execution.

"Bet you no man would marry a woman without legs!" Her old eyes sparkled with malice. Since the Colonel's death she had no one to talk to. No one with whom she could be free. She felt a greater liberty with Parris Mitchell than with anyone else. Maybe because he was a doctor, though there were few things or people that could check her tongue once it was started.

"Fond of those two, aren't you?"

"Drake and Randy? Yes."

"Loyalty's scarce nowadays. Dying out, along with most everything else worth talking about. How'd they come to put this over while you were gallivanting around Europe? Did you have a good time?"

"Fine."

"Bet you did."

"I'll tell you about this real-estate business if you really want to know."

"Of course I do. That's why I sent for you today."

"It isn't. You sent for me because you wanted to see me and because you know I love to see you."

"Go on, now. Soft soap's no good. Want to know how you jingoed the state out of a hundred thousand. A hundred thousand dollars! My word!"

"I'm going to tell you, but you've got to believe me."

"Maybe I will."

"I think you will. Well, this really began when Drake's accident happened. Randy wrote me, or cabled me...."

Parris explained that Drake had to have something to keep his grasp on the world and ordinary sanity.

"Where'd he get the money to start on?"

Again Parris looked at her for a moment before answering. "I gave it to him—lent it, that's the way he considered it. It was the money Dr. Tower left to me."

"I see. I see. By the way, money just comes to you, doesn't it? Just from anywhere. Must be a pleasant talent to possess."

"My talent for friendship with sharp-tongued old ladies is worth much more to me."

"Get on with the story."

Parris continued. When he came to the end she peered sharply through her gold-rimmed glasses.

"That's all?"

"Absolutely."

"I believe you."

"Thanks." His tone was dry, but he smiled.

"Well, you needn't be persnickety about it. I doubt if anybody else will."

"I don't think I care much."

"I hope you don't. The Colonel—well, you know how the Colonel would have reacted to all this. What you going to do about that dirty little newspaper?"

"Nothing."

"Well, I don't know. I think a horsewhip would help a lot."

"That's old-fashioned, Mrs. Skeffington."

"A good licking is never out of date. Low-down scalawag."

"Now, see here—no word of this."

"Hiding your light under a bushel, or whatever the saying is, eh?"

"No, it's not that. All that's happened between Drake and me is—well, not for Kings Row. He was kicked around, Mrs. Skeffington, you know that."

"I expect he behaved a good deal like a blackguard, now, didn't he?"

"I don't think so."

"What about the Gordon girl?"

"Dr. Gordon put a stop to it."

"Huh! The idea of any boy taking that. Took to a little—well, that little Ross girl. You know what she was."

"She was pretty."

"So! You knew her, too?"

"I did not. But if I had—"

"None of my business, eh?"

"I didn't say it."

"Thought it, though. So you think Drake's really a pretty good fellow, do you?"

"He's a very close and very dear friend. I love him more than anybody in the world, Mrs. Skeffington."

"H'm. Want to bring—what's her name?"

"Randy. Name really is Miranda."

"Want to bring her up to see me someday? I guess I'd better know your friends if you are going to have them."

"I won't let you patronize her."

"Do you think I haven't any manners, Parris Mitchell?"

"I've seen people in your world and in your circumstances forget that they had manners."

Mrs. Skeffington glared. "Stand your ground, don't you? I like that. Bring her up to see me. I'll behave."

"I'll be delighted, and thank you."

"Parris."

"Yes, ma'am."

She laughed. "You sound so old-fashioned when you say that! I knew your grandmother, not very well, but well enough to know she was a lady."

"Yes."

"I want to give you some advice."

"All right."

"Get out of this town."

"Why?"

"It'll never let you alone. It was a better town once."

"Are you sure?"

"You're going to tell me I'm like all old people. No such thing. I remember also what was raw and crude about it. But there were a few people—like the Colonel, like Macmillan St. George, like your grandmother—they leavened the lump. Yes—and I was one of them, too. They're gone. Something's gone with 'em. Place is finished."

"Oh, now—"

"Let me talk. A town can be the temporary camp of a tradition, of a good way of life. It can be an outpost for a long time. Sometimes the thing that made it live moves on—goes somewhere else. Leaves a shell. Keeps the form of life but the juice is gone out of it. It can bind you until you can't move a finger. And a town like this—the way it is now—is common to the marrow. It'll go after you. It's begun already. It'll go after you because you're better."

"You'd advise running away—you?"

"Yes! But it is common sense. It's left high and dry, this place. The best of the town gets out, goes somewhere where life is still on the move. I tell you some towns die."

"But Kings Row isn't dead. It has five thousand people living in it."

"Five thousand goats!"

"But, Mrs. Skeffington, Kings Row isn't really my principal concern. It's the hospital, my work there. The patients out at the end of Federal Street are just as important as patients in Baltimore, or Boston, or Zurich, or Vienna. They're people. Same cases, and the same work. There are—I haven't said this even to myself—"

"Go on."

"There are plenty of specialists in my field in the important cities, and in the famous clinics. But I'm the only one here, at present. I believe I'm useful. I'm doing what I set out to do when I was a kid. It's very different from what I thought it would be, different even from what I expected when I began, but it's my work. It might as well be here. This is home."

"I think you may be a fool."

"Maybe. I told you what Herr Berdorff said when I suggested he take a professorship at Aberdeen and let his stupid little congregation go to thunder."

"What did he say? I forget."

"He said: '*Parris, I am a preacher.*' I'll never forget the setback I got that time."

"You're telling me the same thing, I see."

"No, not really. You are kind to think of me. Colonel Skeffington was heavenly good to my grandmother. You're just like him. But the Colonel stayed on in Kings Row, too!"

"He was tough. So am I."

"Then I'll be tough."

2

Events and circumstances of the winter brought surprises to Parris. First of all he was surprised to discover that he cared what the people of Kings Row thought of him. He had lived a curiously detached life for the past few years. This had not been from choice—not quite; but he had thought of himself as detached, and so unconsciously accepted the town's unconscious attitude toward him. Then when an actual newspaper attack opened on him, he found that he was hurt, and that he had perhaps quite secretly hoped for a kind of general esteem. He was ashamed, even though he was entirely guiltless. For the sake of Drake and Randy he had to appear indifferent. It was a complex state of mind.

The second surprise came when he sensed the real attitude of Kings Row. There were perhaps, here and there, a few people who were envious of any good fortune that came to others, but the town as a whole regarded him with respect. Money, to most people, represented superior cleverness. There were probably not a dozen people in the whole town who did not believe that Dr. Mitchell and Drake McHugh had quietly swindled the state out of a lot of money. There were even fewer who disapproved of the transaction. It seemed odd to Parris that people thought of the state—their own state—as a sort of legitimate prey. He recalled what Dr. Nolan had said about the price of a load of sand when the state bought it.

People he didn't know stopped him in the street with a friendly handshake.

Kings Row also rediscovered Drake McHugh. He was, after all, the nephew of old Major Livingstone. He'd had some hard luck, and all that—married out of his class—but Kings Row was ready to open its heart, and arms, and doors to a returned prodigal. Old neighbors on Union Street made inquiries. Mrs. Sansome was heard to say that Mrs. McHugh was said to be really quite acceptable. Undoubtedly she had taken on a good deal from Drake, and, as to her cleverness, there was talk among businessmen that it was really Randy who swung the entire deal—of course, on information from Parris Mitchell.

Drake knew nothing of this. If Randy knew it, or heard of it, she never mentioned it.

It was observed, however, that old Mrs. Skeffington saw Mrs. McHugh rather often. Whenever anyone asked Sarah Skeffington about the girl from the lower end of town, she merely chuckled, as though she knew the best joke in the world. This didn't increase the comfort of the questioner, but it greatly enhanced the reputation of Randy McHugh.

Sarah Skeffington clapped her hands together like a convert at a camp meeting when she talked to Parris about it.

"I guess maybe I was wrong once. Thought Kings Row'd get on your trail and yelp along after you for years. Might have known better, long as I've lived here. But they respect just one thing: that's money. They say you're smart. It's just like cracking a whip at a pack of dogs. A hundred thousand dollars is something they can understand!"

"I told you I didn't make that much money." Parris was bewildered, and Sarah Skeffington didn't clear matters up much. "Besides, I don't want to be respected for being a crook!"

"Listen, son—you don't mind if I call you that, do you?—if you've got a vicious animal snapping at you, do you care what he respects you for as long as you can make him crawl?"

"I don't want to make anything or anybody crawl."

"Sometimes I think you're a fool, Parris Mitchell."

"I'm sure of it."

"Parris, democracy is a fine thing. At least I imagine it is. But it only operates among equals!"

Parris laughed. "Among people like you and the Colonel, and a few chosen ones, I suppose?"

"Of course."

"But you're really a stiff-necked old aristocrat."

"I hope to God I am. So are you."

"I don't think so."

"Then there are the fine old virtues of brotherly love, sympathy, understanding. They never seem to work except on a small scale. When you think of any wide application of these things—well, you just make a dunce of yourself if you try anything like that. Sow's ears, you know."

"I'm ashamed of your philosophy. I don't know anybody who goes farther out of the way to do something for—"

"Ever hear of *noblesse oblige?*"

"Yes, and—"

"You listen to me. Some of us practice such a thing because we know we're superior. It's based on a kind of contempt of people who need it!"

"You don't believe a word you're saying."

"I believe most of it. I feel a lot of it is really true—the rest—oh, well, it seems to be logical, and I have great respect for logic."

"I suppose you expect me to believe that you believe we should just crack the whip, and throw a crust from time to time."

She smiled. "Until a different order prevails in this world—maybe."

"And that you and I are privileged to do just that?"

"If we're really superior. You know what I mean by that—*thinking* in a superior way, having a vision of—" She let her voice trail off, as if she were thinking of something else.

"And that 'different order' you're talking about?"

"A time when all of us will be aristocrats—of spirit."

"We're talking about the same thing. We just happen to begin at different ends."

"We were talking about you and Kings Row. You made this nice little pile of money honestly, didn't you?"

"Yes."

"Inadvertently, at that?"

"Yes."

"You know that, don't you?"

"Yes."

"Then what are you worrying about? You can look anybody in the eye, can't you?"

"Yes. But I don't want them to think I'm dishonest. And above everything else I don't want people to admire me for being dishonest."

"Well, in this case, if you tried, for instance, to get rid of the money, then everybody'd know you stole it."

"I wasn't really thinking of getting rid of it."

"Go on about your business, then. Kings Row'll either admire you for a smart swindler, or despise you for a fool. Spend your money, and enjoy yourself."

"You're a fine, helpful friend."

"You bet I am. I'm talking sense. Learned a lot of it from the Colonel. Born with some of it, though."

Mrs. Skeffington smoothed the heavy silk dress across her knees.

"Wish you'd play a piece for me before you go."

"When are you going to get that old music box of yours tuned?"

"Tuned?"

"Yes. I told you a month ago."

"Does it need it?"

"It's frightful!"

"Well, well. Glad I'm not so persnickety about the way my piano sounds. Sit down and play something—something loud."

Spring came. A boisterous, shrewish, coltish kind of spring with rowdy winds and a damp, clinging cold. The leaves came out and hung crinkled and half open, shaking in the rain. The season broke very gradually. By and by the courthouse group of idle talkers gathered on the sunny side of the building. The crowd changed from year to year. A few old ones died and were replaced by others whom life had thrust out of the passing action. They talked of the weather, discussed crop prospects, and recalled bad years when it had snowed as late as the first of May. One old man said his father had once seen ice in August, but everyone regarded that as a probable fiction. They remarked the annual changes in Kings Row, and embalmed the characters of those who had died. The town legends were fixed here, and passed into permanent forms of reference.

The talk was fitful and timid like the sunshine on this day in mid-April. Old man Capers and Bill Paisley reverted to childhood and played hully-gull with a handful of polished pebbles picked from the trough where the drip from the high eaves had worn through the soil.

"There goes that Catholic priest."

"Passes by here every day 'bout the same time."

"Always walks out toward the lower end of town, don't he?"

"All them foreigner Catholics live down that way."

"He ain't going to see them, though."

"Might be going to see the womenfolks while the menfolks is at work."

"Yeh, that's so. Never thought of that."

"He's got somebody with him today."

"Looks like that young doctor from the asylum."

"Doc Mitchell?"

"Yeh."

"I think it is."

"What's he doing going around with a Catholic priest? He ain't a Catholic, is he?"

"No, I don't think so."

"Funny, ain't it?"

"They say he's a smart feller."

"Yeh. I heard he's one of the finest doctors for crazy people there is in this part of the country."

"He learned to be a doctor somewhere in one of the old countries."

"They say the best medical schools in the world are over there."

"It's a fact."

"He was over there again last year."

"Yeh. You know they say a doctor can stay just so long 'mongst crazy people, then he's got to git out for a while."

"Goes off a little, eh?"

"Yes sir. They say some of them doctors out to the asylum is pretty near as crazy as the patients."

"I've heard that, too."

"Some says you have to be a little crazy to understand the lunatics."

"Well, I've heard that a lot of them highly educated doctors is a little off."

"Yes. I guess studying so hard does that."

"Well, you all recollect this here Dr. Mitchell ain't so crazy he couldn't slip a whole fortune of state's money into his own pocket."

"Yeh. I ain't heard much about that lately."

"Newspapers seem to kinder quieted down about it."

"Guess he bought 'em off, maybe. Paid 'em to let up on him."

"Like as not."

"Well, you remember the *Gazette* never did have much to say about it. It was the *Chronicle*."

"Yes, that's so."

"They say that Wardlaw is smart as all get out."

"Looks to me like Doc Mitchell's the smart one."

"Whole thing was pulled off while he was in the old country over there."

"Yeh. That was just a blind. He knowed what was going on, I bet you."

"Well, of course. But it was that crippled fellow, McHugh, and his wife put it through."

Old man Capers spoke up. He had won all of Bill Paisley's pebbles by clairvoyant guessing. "I heard a whole different story about that deal over at the asylum. They tell me the asylum tried for years to get that big tract of land from the St. Georges, and they held out for a great big pile. The state couldn't pay it. Had to wait for 'em to die, both of 'em. I believe myself Thurston St. George would have sold reasonable, but Macmillan wouldn't come to no agreement.

That's where this here Mitchell fellow comes in. He got it for the asylum—they tell me for a whole lot less'n they would have had to pay in any other way."

"I bet he made a pile out of it, though."

"Who?"

"Dr. Mitchell."

"Well, he's a smart fellow. I guess he had a right to his share of the profits."

"Maybe so. Maybe so. Seems like you can hear anything you want to in this town. Just wait long enough and the story you want to believe'll come around."

"Well, this was told to me for a fact."

"That McHugh feller and his wife sure have done a sight of selling round here."

"They've worked up the biggest business in half a dozen counties, they tell me."

"It's so, too. Began selling lots to them bohunks and Polacks, and even to the niggers. First thing anybody knowed they branched out and went after bigger things. Of course, this asylum sale made 'em rich."

"McHugh himself never goes out of the house. Does the whole thing on paper."

"His wife gets around, though."

"She's smart as a whip."

"Besides, she knows how to talk to them people they sell to."

"She ought to know how. Lived down in the lower end of town all her life. She's one of 'em. Her daddy was a section man on the railroad till he died."

"Her brother works on the road yet."

"I guess all that kinder put a crimp in these other real-estate offices."

"You can bet your life. Particularly Peyton Graves."

"Yes. Well, well. That kind of highfalutin stuff he tried on Kings Row just couldn't go. Thunderation, his kind of plans might work in St. Louis or some place like that where there's scads of money, but not in Kings Row."

"I been hearing some talk about him not getting on so good since the St. Georges died."

"Stands to reason. Thurston St. George was always for whatever would improve Kings Row, but you can bet the estate ain't got any such ideas. I expect they put the clamps on the way Graves was spending money improving all that Crescent Hill property."

"He'll have to sell that out in small parcels. Gosh, nobody wants one of them big places. Why, they're regular ess-tates."

"Plenty might want 'em, but ain't nobody got the money to pay for 'em, much less build on 'em and keep 'em up."

"Is Graves still got that nigger schoolteacher on the string?"

"Yeh. She comes to his office regular."

"Bold as brass, ain't it?"

"I guess Miz Graves don't care, long as he lets her alone."

"Must be right easy to let Mrs. Graves alone."

"Why?"

"Ain't you ever seen her?"

"Not that I recollect. What's the matter with her?"

"Looks like a dried-up old woman."

"Honest?"

"Sure she does."

"What'd Peyton Graves marry her for? It's just a few years back."

"She must 'a' had money."

"Maybe; I don't know. All I know is that yeller schoolteacher comes down to his office. Regular, like I said."

"She's good-looking, too."

"For a nigger, yes."

"Well, she ought to be. She's a St. George."

"She's a nigger just the same."

Father Donovan and Parris walked on through the narrow little streets, crossed the railroad tracks, and tramped through the open pastures of the small farms that lay between the town and the much larger farms which spread out in the high level country to the southwest.

Some of the trees were in full leaf, others were still a pale yellow-green, and some were only past the stage of half-open buds. The air warmed as the afternoon advanced, and a softening lassitude of body disposed the mind to gentleness.

Neither Father Donovan nor Parris was quite at ease with the other. Their more intimate acquaintance was a recent happening. The priest came often to the hospital to visit relatives of his parishioners, and Parris had met him several times before they reached the point of conversation.

The priest was shy, and he was too happy to have an occasional companion on his long walks to risk much talk. He was fearful of missteps. He knew so little of the easy, social habits of other men. He was afraid he might estrange his new friend by some awkwardness or ineptness. He watched Parris almost anxiously for signs of the progress of their friendship. Parris was not entirely unaware of this, but he was preoccupied much of the time. Besides, he did not quite know how to put Father Donovan at his ease.

It was seldom that Parris could be away from his work for daylight walks, but on such lucky days he and Father Donovan were likely to walk for miles without speaking. At times they forgot each other and at times they were uneasily aware of the mutual shyness that kept both of them silent.

They stopped to rest where a mighty billow of land rose and leveled out to the west. A silvery-gray zigzag fence divided two fields. Father Donovan sat on the top tail with his heels resting on a lower one. His hunched-over attitude bespoke generations of land-loving men behind him. Just so farmers sit to look

over the fields and to mark the growth of crops. The priest broke the stem of
a dry weed to even lengths, matched them together and absently tossed them
into the breeze.

"Father Donovan."

"Yes, Dr. Mitchell."

"I've been wanting to say something to you for a long time."

Father Donovan colored a little. It was a sign of pleasure and excitement.
He scented talk, and he longed for talk with every corner of his lonely mind.

"What is it, Doctor?"

"Do you remember one time I came into your church when I was just a
boy, and you came in and talked to me?"

"Oh, yes; certainly. I have never forgotten it. In fact, I thought of you often
afterward."

"I was very rude to you that day."

"Were you?"

"Yes. Very."

"I don't remember that."

"I was in your church, and you came to speak to me—politely. I blurted
out that I didn't believe in God."

"Yes: I remember that."

"It must have seemed a—a gratuitously insulting remark."

"I didn't consider it so."

"How did you consider it?"

"I saw that you were in great distress of mind. I—I thought of it then, as I
do now—as a sort of cry."

"It really wasn't that. Not exactly."

"Wasn't it?"

"No. I just felt that I might leave the wrong impression."

"How so, my son?"

Parris noticed the address. It was the first time Father Donovan had ever
said "my son" to him.

"I was afraid you might think I had come there because I was religious, or
for religious consolation, or something of the sort."

"I see." There was ever so faint an inflection of sadness in Father Donovan's
voice.

"It was a kind of effort to put myself honestly before you."

"I see. Yes, of course."

"I didn't want to be there under false colors. But I did want to be there."

"Why?"

"I didn't have any place to go. I really had no friends, except one boy. There
was nothing left of my home. It was an instinct to hide from a loneliness and a
grief that seemed overwhelming."

"Of course." Father Donovan reached for another piece of the dry weed, and carefully broke it into halves, then quarters.

"It was overwhelming. In a way I never really got over it."

"May I ask you a question?"

"Of course."

"I don't want to be misunderstood, Dr. Mitchell. Of course my charge in the world is to keep watch for the souls of men—any men who come my way. I'm not intruding on you in any such fashion. I recognize your own intellectual responsibility too clearly for that."

"What is your question?"

"Have you ever come to believe in God?"

"No."

"I'm very sorry."

"Why?"

"Well—I'd be glad for your sake, because I believe, of course, that the salvation of one's soul lies that way, and that way only—but for other reasons."

"Yes."

"I'd be glad to see you a happier man than I think you are, and—please don't think that impertinent."

"I don't. And—what?"

"Well, that's all really. I'd be glad to see you a happier man." He smiled, a flick of a disarming smile—the smile of a naïveté which knows itself to be naive. "I'm really puzzled by people who don't believe in God. I wonder what they do with their souls, just as I'd wonder how a man would use his eyes if he didn't believe in light."

"It's not so simple as that, Father Donovan."

"It is to me."

"You're fortunate."

"You would resent it if I said you were unfortunate."

"Right. I beg your pardon."

Parris leaned both elbows on the fence back of him. Presently he lifted himself up and sat down by Father Donovan. He took off his hat and ran his fingers through his thick black hair. The priest looked sideways at Parris. A few threads of gray showed in the doctor's tousled hair. His brow was very white, but fine lines lay across it. The eyes, deep and shadowy, had a curious remoteness about their expression. It was a mixed expression, Father Donovan thought, as if mind and heart showed clearly separate there, the one cold and detached—the look of a watchful physician, the other shy and warm—a look that turned inward. A fine, noble face, the priest concluded. One had to look close to see what was there, and then, well, it was not a face that one could read in a glance, no, nor in a day. It was a handsome face, too, he added inconsequentially.

"May I ask you another question—just out of friendly curiosity?" He laid his large pliant hand on Parris' arm. A warm hand, with strong, patient-looking fingers.

"Of course, Father Donovan."

"Every man has to have a refuge. I've noticed something about you lately—after all, my son, I'm a priest and I'm watchful, just as you are a doctor and observant in your own way. I've noticed something that makes me a little sorrowful."

Parris smiled at Father Donovan, a little as one smiles at a child, but Father Donovan ignored it.

"The thing that happens so often to a young man in his first full collision with the world and its intricate ways. It's a kind of recoil from the world that comes to every man about your time of life."

Parris was a bit startled. "*Recoil from the world!*" The phrase was an acute one, and cannily accurate.

Father Donovan matched his little sticks together in twos and threes and built a tiny blockhouse of them on his broad knee.

"It's a natural enough reaction, as you know when you stop to think of it, and it's likely to recur. When that happens, a man has to have a refuge. What is the refuge and the retreat of a man who has no faith in God? I'm curious. And, as I said, it's not meant to be too personal a question. I read that some men turn to an art or to the grave problems of a great science, or to some trivial occupation as an anodyne. What is your refuge?"

Parris waited for a moment. He too reached for a branch of the tall dry weed, and broke it into even lengths.

"I'm not sure that I can answer you—fully. I'm not sure that it's a problem with me. There are, maybe—a few things—phenomena—in the world that engage me. I—I rather think you might not understand me if I told you the first answer that comes into my mind."

"Well, I'll try."

"It's *design*."

The priest looked keenly at Parris. "Design?"

"Yes."

"Maybe I have a glimmer of what you mean, maybe not."

"I'll have to feel my way to a definition. Do you mind if I think aloud for a minute?"

"Please." Father Donovan dropped his gaze to his preoccupied fingers. He wished to hide the eagerness in his mind. He felt a new and unfamiliar warmth at his heart. It had been a long time, if ever, since anyone had talked like this with him, as man to man. He knew, too, that he had come to have a deep affection for this young doctor whose science seemed so new and strange and exciting. He recognized in Dr. Mitchell something of the same consecration and devotion that are demanded of a priest. The man seemed to be working for something over and far beyond the ordinary returns and rewards of his profession. Both of them, he felt, were working in remote regions, outside the familiar outposts of human experience. Out there somewhere lay the mysterious regions where mind and soul appeared to fuse inextricably. There were times, he thought, when a priest becomes a physician, and there were now an increasing number of times when a physician became a priest. The mystic in Father Donovan answered easily to the mystic in Parris Mitchell.

"Well, Father Donovan, you see a large part of my training has been along esthetic lines. I have studied music all of my life, and I listen to it with, I think, an increasing understanding. Deep down in it, buried with its origins, is some sort of relationship with the transcendental *order* of mathematics. Sometimes, I imagine that there are hidden qualities in the greatest music which speak a language which is understood by very deep and remote qualities in our own minds, and that there is also a transcendental recognition of transcendental qualities."

"Yes, yes." Father Donovan felt himself on familiar ground.

"That kind of order appeals to my imagination. I start from there, so to speak. It's—well," Parris laughed deprecatingly. "It's a commonplace word, but there's something soothing in the thought. It probably goes no deeper than that. It's probably no more important, and no deeper than a table of logarithms."

"You said 'design.'"

"Well, that's one kind of design. There are others, in nature, that are staggering in their implication. For instance, take this weed we have been picking at." Parris tugged at it, and the long straight stem with its spearhead root came up easily. "Horseweed," he said absently. "We used to use them for spears when we played Indians." He stripped the branches from the smooth, almost polished shaft. "Look at these joints, where the leaves grow out. See?"

Father Donovan nodded.

"You see that they come out, two on opposite sides, then a little farther along two more at right angles, and so on. The distance between these pairs is less each time, and that is according to a precise mathematical formula."

"I seem to remember something of this."

"Oh, yes. It's old knowledge, really. If you take this staff with these sections and bend it around in a spiral you have the geometric curve of some sea shells—the nautilus, I think—and the designs of some seed pods. I wish I knew enough about mathematics to tell you exactly. But for my purpose of musing on it I don't need more than to know that the formula is there."

"Is all of this the 'design' you were talking about?"

"Yes. And the formation of snow crystals, and mineral crystals, and the like."

"You like to think about them, and they mean something to you—of spiritual value?"

"I'm sure I'm not being one bit clear. But it's the same thing—I mean, when I think about such phenomena, I am terribly stirred. It's almost emotional. I started to say it's the same feeling I have gotten on a few occasions in great cathedrals. It's a kind of humility of spirit, along with a curbing of the pride of mind, that seems to be good for one. But—somehow I feel when I—I suppose I have to say when I dream over these things—I feel that there is a power of order that I can fall back on. The sheer esthetic aspects of these problems are as exciting and moving as music, or great poetry."

"Or astronomy."

"I have thought very little about astronomy."

"All of this is very strange, my son."

"Why so?"

"You believe in all of the attributes of God."

Parris looked his inquiry.

"Yes—one by one, justice, goodness, mercy, love, faith, hope, charity—and then the order which is the manifest word of God in the material universe."

Parris shrugged.

"Don't be contemptuous of the findings of your own heart, and don't think too critically of the intuitions of a simple priest. I have looked often on the order of the universe. I have had need to do so after looking so deeply as I must from time to time into the seeming dark and chaos of the human heart. You and I need not be doctrinal. I think we stand, now and then, on common ground."

Father Donovan extracted his big silver watch. "I have to go. I have some small duties that must be attended to this very day. Do you mind if I leave you here—with your mathematical weed stalk?"

"Not at all. I think I'll go this way. Thank you, Father, for everything."

"Thank *you*. I don't know when I'll have a day off again, but when I do, I'll let you know."

"Fine. Good-by."

Father Donovan waved, and set off at a long-paced walk.

Parris hefted the "mathematical weed stalk," balanced it like a spear, and sent it sailing through the air toward a slender cedar growing in a fence corner. His aim was accurate, and the gray, shiny shaft slipped through the cedar and disappeared.

"Dead Indian," he said aloud.

Parris crossed the field. It was damp and yielding under foot, but the tall grass was dry and yellow. Underneath, threading through the matted stems, was the multitudinous thrust of new green. He climbed the high wire fence—a new one running from the old rail fence where he had been sitting with Father Donovan—and walked up the slope where the maples were already shadowy with buds and leaves. He felt a rising excitement in his breast. Once he paused and considered turning back, then he went on again. The grove came to an abrupt clearing, bounded by a low stone wall.

The view spread out wide and clear before him. There, circled by the shining band of the creek, the whole of it slanting in the sun, lay his old home. His feet had led him almost unconsciously to this place. There it was! And he had lived in dread of seeing it again!

Somehow he had been sure of great changes, but from here they appeared slight. The lowlands were plowed and marked off in small squares. He thought he could discern some faint lines of green breaking the even rich brown of the fresh-plowed soil. There were some new greenhouses—extensive ones blazing in the light. Beyond in the rise toward the north the evergreen plantings still stood, noticeably larger and fuller, the metallic blue of the spruces contrasted with the deep green of cedars and arborvitae. In the midst of the picture was the house—just as it stood when he had last seen it. The huge maples, a little later of leaf than these here on the hill, arose like misty clouds of pale green, and yellow, and pink, giving even to the old stone walls an illusion of moving color.

He stepped up on the wall and looked at the scene for a long time. He could see the flower beds in their neat patterns on the long terrace, the thickly bordered rosewalk back of the house, and the chickens sauntering about in their casual fashion. It was lovelier than he had remembered it to be. The exotic charm of the foreign landscaping and the commonplace features of a small country place blended oddly.

He did not hesitate any longer.

As he almost ran down the wide sloping fields toward the road he felt as if the whole spring day ran with him—the puffy white clouds in the brilliant sky, the wind, and the shimmering leaves. Spring was overhead, sweeping eastward and northward like a vast continental tide. He perceived it underfoot in the sweet, poignant, earthy smells that arose. He felt it all about him, the sun on his back, the faint murmurous hint of voices—a murmur that might be wind, or water, or birds, or all of them together.

Father Donovan's phrase returned: "*Recoil from the world.*" Yes: there had been justification for that astute observation. Recoil from the world and recoil from life. Aspects of life and living had loomed dark enough, and there had been little ahead to make an antidote of cheer. Was it just the passing of the last illusion of youth? He wondered. Somehow that seemed an inadequate explanation. A good many veils had been torn away a long time ago—too soon, perhaps, but torn away, nevertheless.

The water was surprisingly low in the creek. It seemed to him much narrower here than it used to be. The rocky bed seemed higher, but they were the same brown and yellow rocks. He recognized them. He stooped and laid both palms down on a rounded one where he had sat many times to paddle his bare feet in the pools. The surface of the water-worn stone was warm from the sun, but one felt the cold beneath. He had sat here with Renée. Just there, around the bend of the road was the house where she had lived. He dipped his hands in the water and dried them on his handkerchief.

The high, ornamental wooden gates between stone pillars were the same, but there was a new fastening. He opened the small wicket and walked slowly up the avenue toward the house. At the foot of the stone steps leading up to the terrace he felt that this was just like any other day when he came home late in the afternoon. There would be his grandmother, and Anna, and presently there would be cakes, and tea, or coffee.

He ran lightly up the curving stair. A wave of memory struck him—a thousand complex memories compounded in one instant. He caught his breath. Then all at once the frenzied attack passed. He saw the gentle old house, the flagged walks, the traceries of maple shadows on the mellow stone walls. A curious peace was in the light.

"Good afternoon, sir."

Parris jumped.

"Oh, I didn't mean to frighten you!" The girl laughed a little. She was young, and slight. He saw that her hair was a very pale gold, more silver than gold, that her eyes were a smoky blue, the iris darkly marked, that her mouth was singularly red, and that she was dressed in something which exactly matched her eyes. She appeared to be tanned; her complexion was strangely golden for her hair and eyes.

"Your name isn't Renée, is it?"

The smile faded from her face. She looked startled, and drew back a little.

"No," she said unsteadily.

"I do beg your pardon. Of course your name isn't Renée."

"My name is Elise."

"And mine is Mitchell, Parris Mitchell."

"Are you Dr. Mitchell?"

"Yes."

"The one that plays the piano?"

Parris laughed, and walked over to the terrace wall. "No one ever identified me that way before. How on earth did you happen to know that I played the piano—or hear of me at all?"

"Herr Dr. Berdorff often spoke of you."

He noticed now that she had ever so slight an accent. It showed in the precision of her speech.

"Are you German?"

She shook her head. "Viennese."

"Oh, really? I studied medicine in Vienna."

"Yes, I know."

"Oh, you do?"

"Herr Berdorff told me much about you."

"He never mentioned you to me."

"Why should he?"

"Well—I can think of some reasons why he should."

"I was very sorry he had to go."

"Yes. It was terrible. I miss him still. I saw him, though, in Germany, last summer."

"Oh, did you? And how is he?"

"Well. He has a church, and he has married."

"No! It is impossible! He seemed—"

"What?"

"So old."

"It was the big beard."

"Maybe. What is she like, his wife?"

"Quiet little German *Hausfrau* who will mend his socks, and sew on buttons."

"And listen to his variations?"

"Oh, you know the variations. Yes: she will listen and say, '*Wunderschön, Maxel.*'"

"Imagine anyone calling him 'Maxel.'"

"That's exactly what she did call him. But she spoke *of* him as the *Herr Pastor.*"

"Of course. The old darling."

"And you know the variations?"

"Yes, but I could not play them. They were still too difficult for me."

"You studied piano with him?"

"Yes."

"But he told me he had only dunderheads!"

"I was a dunderhead."

"I don't believe it."

"How could you know? He said you were a genius."

"That I was not. Have you been here all of this time, here in this house?"

"My father is the chief of this experimental farm. You know it used to be a government station."

"Why, I thought it still was."

"Oh, no. The government gave it up two years ago. It was bought by the Liberty Plant and Seed Company—you know, the big company in Philadelphia. They continue to experiment, and kept my father here as chief. He is really a famous horticulturist—more of a scientist, but that's what he calls himself."

"I didn't know any of this. And I never saw you anywhere."

"I was away for two years. I have just now come back. You see I'm a little awkward with English, until I get used to it again."

"Were you in Vienna?"

"Yes. I have distant relatives there. My mother was an American."

"Was—?"

"Yes. She died when I was a little girl."

"I'm sorry."

A sudden silence dropped over them. It seemed to envelop them for a moment.

"I was in Vienna myself, last year."

"I know it."

"You know everything, don't you?"

"Some people get talked about!" She smiled, and then was suddenly grave.

"What do you mean, exactly, by that, Miss—"

"Sandor."

"Sandor? That's a strange name for an Austrian."

"Yes, it sounds Hungarian, but it used to be Schöndorff. Sandor is what is left of the original."

"But—let me see, what was I saying? Oh, yes. You said some people get talked about. You heard stories—probably that I robbed the state of immense sums of money."

"Yes. But I don't believe that now."

"Why not?"

"You couldn't do that."

"Thank you, Miss Sandor."

"Everyone calls me Elise. I am not used to 'Miss,' yet."

"How old are you? Do you mind?"

"Nineteen."

"Oh, you're just a baby."

"I don't think so."

"Probably not."

"Did you think you were a baby when you were nineteen?"

Parris was silent for a moment. His face clouded. "No, I suppose not."

"Will you sit down, Dr. Mitchell? My father should be here any moment now."

"I didn't come to see your father."

"Oh."

"No. I told you I didn't know anything about the place, now."

"Oh, yes. So you did." She stopped on a rising inflection.

"You want to ask what I do want, don't you?"

"No. Do I seem so bad-mannered?"

"I came to see the place."

"This place. Yes?"

"I used to live here."

"Oh, no! Really? Here? How nice! Why have you never been here before?"

"I couldn't bear to come back."

"Did you live here a long time?"

"Ever since I can remember, until I went to Europe."

"Was Madame von Eln, who used to own the place, your mother?"

"She was my grandmother."

"Oh."

"I had no parents. I never remembered them. My grandmother was everything."

"I can imagine. But my father—wait till you see him! He is a great darling."

"I can imagine that."

"I think you mean a compliment, but I do not know why. I am not used to compliments."

"Well, I am going to acquaint you with some compliments. You might as well get used to them. Did anyone tell you, ever, that you are as lovely as a spring day?"

"No."

"Or that you probably have the prettiest eyes in North America?"

She laughed. Her teeth were small and even.

"Or that you are perfectly sweet?"

She shook her head, and her short curls flew like sunlight about her head.

"I think you should have some coffee. Or should it be tea?"

"Coffee."

"Good. Coffee is better, isn't it?"

"Yes. You don't mean there will be coffeecake with it, do you?"

"What else?"

"I bet you have a maid named Anna, or Maria."

"No. She has a funny name—for a woman. She is named Fritzel."

"Why?"

"*Gott weiss!*"

"Let's look at—everything a moment, before we go in, may we?"

"Of course. I have been out here all afternoon. I saw you coming from away over there. See? Over there where that wall is."

"Yes. I stood there looking at it. It's the very first glimpse I've had of the house since I left it—it seems a lifetime ago."

"Did you love it so much?"

"It is the only home I ever had."

"Where do you live now?"

"In the asylum."

"What?"

"All the doctors live there—in the big center wing that stands out in front. Have you never been over there?"

"Never. It must be terrible to live in such a place."

"No. One gets used to it. The grounds are beautiful."

"Oh, yes. I have seen that much in passing."

Parris followed Elise into the house. He prepared himself for some sort of shock, but none came. It was different now, it did not seem to be the same place. It seemed smaller, of course; he was prepared to find that difference. It was pleasantly furnished. A small grand piano stood before the west window where his grandmother's desk used to be.

Elise's father came in presently. He was an amiable giant, with eyes like Elise—the same youthful blue. He had a great beard that spread over his chest. Parris noticed that his enormous hands moved as lightly as a feather among the cups and coffee things. There was something elementally good-humored about him, and gentle. Once he crossed the room to fetch his pipe. He walked as if he went on velvet tiptoes.

"And so this used to be your home?"

"Yes."

"You must come often, if my child is not tiresome."

"Elise?"

"She is a little lonely sometimes, and talks too much when she finds someone to listen."

Parris laughed.

"You will stay to supper, Dr. Mitchell?"

"I had hoped you would ask me."

"What would you like?"

"Let's leave it to Fritzel."

Mr. Sandor arose. "Please be welcome, and comfortable. Smoke, or play the piano, or walk. Elise will go with you if you like."

"Thank you."

After supper Elise played. Parris listened critically. She had been well schooled. It was good playing.

"Did you study in Vienna, too?"

"Oh, yes. A little."

"With Leschetizky?"

"Oh, my goodness, no! With a good, simple teacher."

"You're not a dunderhead."

"Surely?"

"Surely. Some things you don't do in the right way. May I show you?"

"Would you really? Oh, you are very good. But this is a visit. The next time you come."

"No, no. Let's get at it now. I'm not a teacher, but I can show you some things, I think." He drew back with mock seriousness. "Will you practice?"

"Six hours a day, if you say."

"Heavens, no! But now—where's that sonata? No, the first one. Here, now. Let's look at the slow movement. Your tone is thin …"

"My child, it's eleven o'clock! I had no idea. Please forgive me." Mr. Sandor, looming through heavy strata of tobacco smoke, laughed warmly.

"It is good to have company, Dr. Mitchell. I hope you will come many times."

Elise broke in eagerly. "Yes, you must feel that it is a little your home again—if you will."

"You're awfully good. That goes to my heart, Elise."

"She means it, Doctor. So do I. For that matter, there is always room here—you know the house—won't you feel that you can come sometimes to rest, to stay over Sunday? Whenever you will."

"Which was your room, Doctor?"

"The northwest corner room."

"Oh, that's my room now. I love it. I have my bed under the big window."

"So did I. And now, good night. This has been a wonderful day—and evening. I'll never forget."

"You'll come—often?" Elise held her hands clasped together like a child.

"Yes. You may be sure."

3

Parris was surprised one evening by a visit from Peyton Graves. Peyton sat for a while, smoked, fidgeted, and made aimless comments on the weather. Parris observed him closely. It was easily evident that he was under some severe strain. There were deep, sagging discolorations under his eyes—dark, almost, as bruises. His hands were unsteady, and a thin shine of perspiration showed on his upper lip.

He crushed out another' half-smoked cigarette. "Parris, how's old Drake getting along?"

Parris raised his eyes slowly and looked straight at Peyton, who flushed uncomfortably. Parris resented the tone of half-familiarity.

"Drake McHugh? Well, I suppose you mean in his business. I should think you'd know about that."

Peyton's color deepened so painfully that Parris almost regretted the thrust.

"Drake is pretty well," he went on without seeming to notice Peyton's embarrassment. "As well as a man can hope to be in his circumstances. Better, really. His health stays fair. I think be is happy, too."

"Well, that's fine. That's just fine. Gee, what a pity to have a thing like that happen!"

"Yes. Bad." Parris' tone of voice was extremely dry. He didn't want to talk about Drake.

"You know, I just never did get down to see him. You know how it is."

"How what is, Peyton?"

"Why, w-why," Peyton stammered and looked exceedingly miserable. "I—I mean, you think at first you'll go and see a person as soon as it's convenient—for them, I mean, and then time slips away, and—"

"You forget all about it."

"Yes—well, no, but—somehow it just never happens."

"I noticed that. All of Drake's old friends seemed to find it difficult to see him."

Peyton shook his head. "Tch! Tch!"

"Do you know, Peyton," Parris spoke evenly with a kind of relentlessness, "not a single one of Drake's old acquaintances ever went to see him at all—not one."

"Aw—why, that's terrible!"

"I thought so."

"Well, you certainly stood by him."

"Drake and I were friends."

"Yes, yes, of course. As a matter of fact, Parris, Drake kind of dropped out of everything after you left."

"So I have heard. Understandable, too."

Peyton wasn't sure just what Parris meant, so he said, "Yes, of course."

Parris wasn't making it easy for Peyton to go on, though it was clear there was something Peyton wanted to say.

"I hear you are, well, sort of in business with him, Parris."

"Did you read that in the *Chronicle*, Peyte?"

"Aw—that! No, no, I didn't—I wasn't referring to that stuff." Peyton laughed uneasily, but Parris did not respond.

"No, Parris, I know you've got a lot of money tied up along with Drake's schemes."

"'Schemes'?"

"Yes—er, plans, I mean. I hear Drake's going to branch out quite a bit."

"Is that so?"

"Don't you know it?"

"I'm a doctor."

"Well, but your money's invested there. Don't you know what's going on?"

"No."

"Well—*well*—"

"I trust Drake and Mrs. McHugh. But my time, and my thought, Peyton, are all used up here in the hospital."

"Well, of course, I can understand that. They tell me you're a tiptop doctor, Parris."

"I'm glad somebody thinks so."

"Everybody's glad, Parris. You've got a lot of friends and well-wishers in Kings Row."

"That's news to me, Peyte."

"It oughtn't to be. It's a fact." Peyton was eager to relay good news. He watched Parris' face anxiously. All at once Parris was sorry for him. Peyton was evidently in distress. Parris decided that Peyton had been punished enough for the moment.

"What's on your mind, Peyte?"

"Me? On my mind?"

"Yes. You're in trouble."

"Gosh, Parris! How did you know it?"

"Anybody could see that."

"Do I show it that plain?"

"Yes. At least it's mighty plain to me."

"Yes; I'm in trouble."

"What's the matter?"

"Business."

"No go with that Crescent Hill project?"

"No."

"Weren't you told long ago you'd have to change your ideas?"

"Yes. But I believed it would go after a while. Patty kept telling me to hold on. She thought it was a kind of an ideal."

"Fiddlesticks!"

"Yes. You're right. Business is no place for ideals."

"That's not so, either. But it is a place for common sense."

"If Thurston St. George had lived—"

"But he's dead. You had the executors to deal with. What did they say?"

"They wanted me to break up this end of the Crescent—up there close to me, into small lots, with cross streets."

"Why didn't you do it?"

"Well, Patty, first of all—"

"What about Patty?"

"She didn't want all those dinky little houses close around our place."

"Oh."

"She wanted me to try breaking up the other end of the Crescent first. But that was really too far out. You never could get the city to put water and lights out there first."

"Well, why don't you sell out? Let it go, and try something else—I mean developing somewhere else around town."

"I can't let go."

"Why?"

"I've used a lot of money that the St. Georges let me have for improvement."

"Peyton!"

"Yes, I did. I'm in a hell of a fix."

"What did you do with it?"

"Spent it on the house. New things all the time! Costly things—rugs, pictures! Patty—"

"Patty again!"

"Yes. She wouldn't let up on me."

"Why?"

"Well, maybe because she had something on me."

"What—Melissa?"

"Jesus, Parris! Do you know about Melissa?"

"Are you crazy, Peyton? There isn't anyone in Kings Row that doesn't know about her."

Peyton seemed stunned.

"God a-mighty! I didn't know people knew."

"You're a fool!"

"Yes. I know that—now. Still, if Patty had left me and—and raised a stink about it, I'd have been ruined."

"And as it is?"

"I'm in a hole, but maybe there's a way out. Parris—" Peyton paled a little. He looked as if he were about to cry.

"What is it? Say whatever you want to."

"I had to have Melissa."

"Well. That's all right. I don't imagine the town has much to say about it."

"Patty wouldn't—" He stopped and stared helplessly at Parris.

"I know, Peyton. Patty wouldn't live with you—as your wife."

"Well, for God's sake!"

"Patty had an operation about the time you were married?"

"Just before."

"Dr. Gordon do it?"

"Yes."

"Ever know exactly what it was for?"

"Some kind of female trouble—that's all Patty ever said. She never would talk about it."

"Um. She was sterilized by that operation."

"How do you know that?"

"Anyone can see that. It makes changes in a person." Parris began to feel actively sorry for Peyton. He looked exactly as he used to look when his teachers at school involved him in unanswerable questions.

"And that's why—"

"That's why she didn't want to live with you. She just couldn't want to, Peyton. You'll have to understand that, and not judge her."

"What did she marry me for, then?"

"I don't know. Probably liked you."

"I don't believe she ever did."

"Why do you stay together?"

Peyton was silent for a few moments. "She loves that goddam house. She'd live with the devil to keep it."

"I see. I think you've hit the nail on the head."

"I had to have Melissa." He repeated the words stubbornly.

"Of course you did. Now try to get this through your head. I'm a doctor, and I understand all of that easily enough. I'm not blaming you. It was a common-sense thing to do."

"Gee, Parris, do you mean you honestly think that way?"

"Of course."

"But I never could feel right about it. I felt dirty. I could see in Patty's eyes that she thought so, too."

"That's where you're wrong, Peyte. You'd no business allowing yourself to care what Patty thought. You gave her what she wanted."

"But, Parris, I've been sleeping with a nigger all these years!"

"What of it?"

Peyton leaned his head on the table. He began to cry.

"Don't be a damned fool, Peyton, You're not even being fair to Melissa!"

"Melissa?"

"Yes. I remember Melissa when she was a kid sitting on Macmillan's front porch. I've seen her around town. You are unfair and unjust, and ungrateful when you say the word 'nigger.'"

"Ungrateful? What do you mean, Parris?"

"Why do you suppose Melissa carries on this affair with you?"

"'Cause she wants to, I suppose."

"But why does she want to?"

"Gosh-a-mighty, Parris, you're not hinting a nigger girl's in love with me?"

"Peyton, you don't deserve sympathy or anything else."

"I don't understand you."

"No, I guess not. May I ask you a question?"

"Of course."

"Do you pay Melissa?"

"No. She never would take anything. I tried to give her money. I gave her some presents, though."

"I see."

"But this isn't getting us anywhere. I'm in trouble—"

"Yes, I see. What do you want me to do?"

"I thought maybe you'd speak to Drake for me?"

"To Drake?"

"Yes. His business is piling up. I ought to be good on the selling end. Maybe I could handle some of his business for him on a commission—through my office, of course. I wouldn't want to—to just be hired in another office. That would finish me up, sure enough."

"What about this money you've misappropriated?"

"I thought maybe if Drake would swing some deals my way, I could make it up."

"Is your own house clear?"

"Lord, no! It's mortgaged to the limit. Patty doesn't know that, though. She's been after me to give her title to it, to protect it in case anything happened, but I couldn't do that, of course."

"Why don't you go to see Drake yourself?"

"I—I can't, Parris."

"Why?"

"Well, it sounds pretty bad, but one time, I guess this was while you were in Europe—yes, I know it was—he came to see me."

"Yes?" Parris' voice took on an icy edge.

"He asked me for a job!"

"In your office?"

"Yes. I was just beginning."

"What did you say?"

"I had to turn him down. I hated to do it."

"Why did you turn him down?"

"I just had to."

"Why?"

"Well, Parris, at that time, Drake was drinking a lot. He—he looked pretty seedy and all that."

"Did you have a job of any kind you could have given him?"

"If he'd straightened out and behaved himself. I needed somebody to—"

"But you didn't give him a chance to 'straighten out and behave himself,' as you put it?"

"I tell you I was just beginning, and I had to keep up appearances."

"That sounds as if Patty had her fine hand in your business along about then."

"She did advise me a lot—fixed up my office and all that kind of stuff."

"Now you want a job from Drake?"

"Yes. It's eating crow, I know, but—"

"But you haven't the ordinary decency or courage to go to see Drake and ask him yourself?"

"Well, can't you understand me a little bit, Parris?"

"I understand you a whole lot better than you'd ever guess, Peyton."

"God, you sound hard!"

"I feel hard. I don't think you're worth the shot it would take to kill you, but—I'll speak to Drake."

"Will you, honest?"

"Tomorrow."

"God, Parris, I'll never—"

"I don't expect thanks, or gratitude, or even understanding from you, Peyton, but I'm going to give you some advice. Go home and tell Patty the business has gone to hell, that you stole some money, and that you've got to get rid of that expensive house. See if she can be decent enough to start over on a modest scale."

"It'll kill her!"

"No it won't. Her kind doesn't die easily."

"The disgrace!"

"I suppose you'd rather be branded a thief. How about the penitentiary?"

"Good God, Parris, don't say that! I've been thinking about it."

"Who are the executors of the St. George estates?"

"White and Robinson."

"Dave Robinson?"

"Yes."

"He's a humane sort of a fellow. He might not be hard on you if you came to him with this."

"I just don't think I could."

"Oh, yes, you could."

"Here's the thing that scares me. Just lately Fulmer Green has had something to do with the St. George properties."

"What?"

"I can't find out exactly. I think he might be trying to buy up a lot. He's got an eye on the real-estate business around here, too."

"Well, God pity you if Fulmer Green gets on your trail."

"I know. I know."

"I tell you what I'll do, Peyton. I'll speak to Drake tomorrow. I'll go farther than that. I'll suggest that you come in with us."

"As a partner?"

"No. I'll be frank. I wouldn't trust you that far. But we can make it look like that. You ought to be good with the farmers—working at that end of things. Drake's been thinking of listing farms and the like."

"I could do that. I get on with country people. They like me. I came from down toward the river, you know."

"Yes. I remember."

"Gee, Parris—"

"How much do you owe the St. George estate?"

"Do you mean altogether?"

"No. How much did you use that didn't belong to you?"

"Not so much."

"How much?"

"About eighteen thousand."

"Suppose Drake and I fixed that up—lent you that much on account—could we depend on you?"

Peyton stood up.

"Yes."

"I'll talk to Drake. I think we can do it. Now understand, this depends entirely on what Drake and his wife say. I won't do anything, or urge anything without their consent. It'll be a plain business arrangement. But you've got to set Patty down hard and talk sense to her."

"I'll try."

"You've got to."

"All right. Now I want to tell you something. I got on to it in a roundabout way."

"What now?"

"About that attack on you in the *Chronicle*."

"What do you know about it?"

"Fulmer Green was behind it."

"How do you know?"

"I know."

"All right. Go on."

"He had advance information about the project, or proposal to buy, and he tried to get an option on the place himself."

"I see." Parris spoke evenly, but he was turning cold inside. He hated the sensation because it was the forerunner of a fury that he dreaded.

"Then he found out you and Drake owned it."

"Of course, but how did he get the *Chronicle* to—"

"He really owns a controlling interest in the *Chronicle*, but nobody knows it. I know it, but I can't tell you how. He backed Wardlaw before Wardlaw ever came to Kings Row, so he'd have a paper behind his political career."

"You're sure?"

"As there is a God above."

"Who could prove it?"

"A lawyer in St. Louis, named R. R. Rosebro."

"What's the address?"

"You won't mix me up in this?"

"No." Parris spoke shortly.

"Rosebro has an office in the Mississippi Trust Building."

"Thanks, Peyton."

"It was worked out through the Merchants Bank in Holly."

"Holly?"

"Yes. Holly, county seat of Pilcher County."

"Away down there."

"The president of that bank is a relative of Rosebro's."

"You ought to be a detective."

"I thought I might have to protect myself."

"Well—I think you've already done that."

"Now, don't get me mixed up in this. There's no telling what Fulmer Green would do."

"Don't worry. You'll hear from me tomorrow night."

"God, I don't know how to thank you enough."

"Never mind."

"Good night, Parris."

Parris waited for a few minutes, and then he leafed through the telephone book.

He picked up the receiver of his desk telephone.

"Number 362, please, Miss Stevenson. Hello, hello. I want to speak to Fulmer Green. Oh, that you, Fulmer? This is Parris Mitchell. I want to talk to you right away—no, I won't come over there. *No!* Tomorrow won't do. I want to talk to you, and it's going to be right now. Be over here at the hospital in half an hour—don't make it longer. Half an hour. Don't talk. Come on over here."

Parris clicked the receiver into place. He glanced at the clock and sat down.

Peyton walked blindly down the long avenue from the main building of the hospital to the tall gates. He scarcely knew where he was going. Once or twice he found himself stepping on the flower beds that bordered the walk. He was terribly confused. The confusion was part relief, and part apprehension and unease. Most of what he had told Parris was the truth. He was willing to work for somebody else. He'd be glad to work for Drake. It would be a relief to have the responsibility belong to someone else. He wouldn't mind if he could just make enough to live on. That would be fine—if it were not for Patty. His throat thickened. He almost choked. Patty! His surge of feeling was half rage, half fear. He hated her. She had deceived him, deceived him about her feelings. She had engineered everything for herself, and that house. She didn't have any principles. She didn't care what happened to him. She didn't care if he did have an affair with a nigger wench, just so she could have what she wanted, and so he left *her* alone. He hated her—hated her completely. But still he was afraid. He felt that somehow she had always undermined his self-respect. She had taken his confidence away from him. She made him feel like a small boy. It was that damned teacher manner that she had never lost. Whenever he was the least bit at fault about anything, he'd find himself stammering and getting red in the face. Damn her, damn her, damn her!

He'd hate like the devil to have the other businessmen in town saying things behind his back, remarking that now he was working for Drake McHugh. God! Drake McHugh whom he had turned out of his office once. He hoped Drake didn't hold it too much against him. He seemed to recall that Drake had been a little drunk that day. Maybe he wouldn't remember. He needed that job and that connection. Drake McHugh, crippled and married to a little nobody, living in a little house down there in the lower end of town with all kinds of foreigners, and railroad hands all around him. Niggers, too, probably. He hadn't been down that little side street in a long time. He might have to go pretty often now—to see his boss. His boss! Mrs. McHugh might try to put on airs with him, too. But—it was either these bitter pills, or others still worse.

Parris had been pretty severe with him. He supposed he deserved it. After all, not many people would do what Parris proposed doing. Not many? Not any, really. Not a single person in Kings Row who would lift a finger to keep him out of the penitentiary. He'd better walk a chalk line, and be glad of the chance. He thought again of Fulmer Green, and a quick perspiration dampened his face.

He reached his office, and paused for an instant. A dim light showed under the door. Melissa! of course. He'd forgotten. A warm, tingly feeling swept over him—a feeling of anticipatory ecstasy that was all mixed up with shame and embarrassment. Parris had said everyone knew. All right, then, let them know. Let them say whatever they liked. And Parris—Parris had been so queer about Melissa. Didn't seem to think anything about it. Actually talked as if it was all right. Maybe that was just because he was a doctor. Doctors didn't always look at such things in the way other people did. Then, too, Parris had always been kind of foreign. French, or something. Everybody said French people didn't have any morals at all.

He unlocked the door and went in.

Peyton didn't know how he had happened to tell Melissa all about it. He had never mentioned his business, or his home, and certainly never Patty, to her before. But she had sensed right away that he was in trouble. Melissa's eyes were so clear and brown and kind. He found himself telling her all about it, his money troubles, the misappropriation of the St. George funds, and of his interview with Parris. She had listened without comment.

"Well, it seems to me like you are all fixed up, now. There isn't anything more to worry about."

"That's the way you see it. But when I think of it, right now as I'm telling it, I'm sure I can't go through with it."

"Go through with what?"

"Telling my wife, and working for another man when I've been my own boss so long, and having people laugh at me behind my back."

"Nobody's going to laugh at you. Plenty of people have setbacks in their business and have to start over."

"I just don't see how I can do it."

A look came into Melissa's face that Peyton had never seen there before. It was warm and tender, and sort of strange, as if she had thought of something for the first time. Peyton watched the look deepen. It startled him—*it was a white woman's look,* he said to himself.

"Listen, Mr. Peyton." Melissa leaned forward in the low chair. "Listen to me a minute."

"All right, Melissa."

"Mr. Peyton, I've got money."

"You have money?"

"Yes. I've got a lot of money."

"Well, that's good, Melissa. It's good sense to save your salary."

"I'm not talking about my salary. That's nothing. I'm talking about the money my pa left me."

"Your—"

"My pa, yes. Mr. St. George."

"Oh, oh, yes."

Melissa was surprised and a little mystified to see that Peyton was actually embarrassed by her mention of Macmillan St. George.

"You know he was my pa. Everybody has always known that. He gave me seventy-five thousand dollars before he died."

"Seventy-five thousand dollars!" A slow light kindled in Peyton's eyes. A deep and sudden relief broke through his stiff and troubled look. His face seemed to melt.

"Seventy-five thousand dollars! Melissa, that's a fortune!"

"Yes, I know that. He gave it to me before he died so he wouldn't have to put it in his will. He thought it would be enough to take care of me all my life. He gave Ma enough to take care of her—not that much, though."

"Where is this money?"

"It's in a Chicago bank. It's a trust. I can't touch it—not the principal—till I'm fifty years old."

"Oh."

Melissa did not notice the dismay in his voice.

"I've been living on my school salary. There's nothing here for me to spend money on. The income has just been piling up."

"I see. Is—is there a good deal of that?"

"It's close to twenty thousand dollars."

"Twenty thousand dollars." He continued to look unwinkingly at her. He was waiting for her to say something. "And you stay here and teach school!"

A dark flush came up under her creamy skin. "What do you think I stayed in Kings Row for, Mr. Peyton?"

There was no archness in her question, no coquetry. It was so simply said that Peyton missed its meaning.

"Well, your mother, and your people—"

She shook her head impatiently. "I'm fond of Ma, of course. But I've been educated and trained, Mr. Peyton. I have no people in the way you mean."

He looked at her a little absently. "Then—"

"I stayed in Kings Row because of you."

She said it so quietly that it was several seconds reaching Peyton's consciousness. When he did understand, he paled slightly, and an incredulous expression made his face look almost blank.

Again, Melissa was so intent on what she was saying that she did not see the change in his face.

"I stayed in Kings Row because I had you—these nights here in your office—that and nothing else. You can't be altogether blind, Mr. Peyton. I've got a heart just like anybody. I'm more white than black, and in some ways I'm altogether white. I've got white ways, and I know it. I love you just as any woman loves her man. And we've been together so long I've just got you in my blood. I hate everything in this world that keeps us apart. I don't know how you feel about me, but from the way—well, I believe I must mean something to you, too."

Peyton sat stone still. His face had stiffened to an immobile mask. His eyes, glittering under his pale lashes, seemed fearfully and intensely alive.

"So now that trouble has come like this, it seems to me it's our chance. I knew Miss Patty couldn't be treating you right. Now listen: there are a lot of places in this world where it doesn't make any difference if you *are* colored. Some of the Central American countries, some of the West Indies—I've read up on all of that. Then there's Europe, France especially. Nobody would hold it against me. We'd have plenty of money to live in perfect comfort. We'd have it all our lives. We could be together all the time, and go anywhere we wanted to. And you wouldn't ever have to do a lick of work again as long as you live. You—you could go away tomorrow. I could meet you in New York, or anywhere you say; I could even wait to meet you in Europe."

He was still silent.

"What do you say, Mr. Peyton? God, I'd be so glad if I could do all that for you."

"Wait, Melissa." His voice was hoarse and strange. She arose.

"Are you sick?"

"No: I'm all right. Thank you, Melissa. Will you go away now—right away. I've got to think."

She put on her hat, picked up her gloves and handbag, and laid her smooth, plump hand on his head.

"Can I come down here again tomorrow night? We can settle it then, can't we?"

"Yes."

"Good night, Mr. Peyton."

"Good night, Melissa."

He waited a few minutes until he was sure she was gone, then he locked the door. He returned to the desk. His lips were shut in a tight, straight line. The *nigger!*

He sat down and buried his face in his hands. Here was what this kind of thing led to in the end! He had had to sit and take it without saying a word. Of all the goddam nerve!—His glance fell on a long envelope on his desk. It was a special-delivery letter. The janitor must have put it there after he left this afternoon. He hadn't seen it before.

He felt a chill down his spine as he saw that it was from Fulmer Green. He ripped it open and read the three short paragraphs almost at a glance. He had really known what was in the letter before he opened it. His knees gave way and he sat down. He thought hard for a few minutes, looking quickly to right and left as if he were trying to find a way out. Then he tore the letter into strips and set a match to it. He tamped the smoldering ashes in a metal ash tray, and emptied them into the wastebasket. He scrawled a note and laid it on the desk. Then he nodded. All right ... all right. Kings Row wouldn't talk behind his back again. He opened the lowest desk drawer and took out a revolver. He lifted it, then he looked at the neat unspotted gray rug Patty had selected for this room. He arose and went into the lavatory and closed the door.

Fulmer Green sat opposite Parris. His face was wet with perspiration.

"I don't know where you got all of this, unless it was from that stinking Peyton Graves, but if you think you can scare me—"

"You *are* scared."

Fulmer tried to laugh, but his mouth was dry, and his lips stuck to his teeth.

"You *are* scared, Fulmer. People like you always are scared whenever they are found out. You were a nasty, cowardly boy when you were in school. You were afraid to jump on anybody until you had a gang behind you. Your kind never changes. Society always has a few like you. They are recurrent, like squash bugs, and as hard to get rid of. The squash bug hides on the underside of the leaves, you remember.

"I don't for a minute think that this little situation will stop you. It'll take something bigger, but that'll come someday. It's in the nature of things, Fulmer."

"I don't know what you're talking about."

"Of course you don't. I don't expect you to. But here are some things you are going to do."

"Eh? Me?"

"Yes. You. First, *The Evening Chronicle* will publish a full retraction of that accusation of last year. I'll furnish you with the correct data. You can save your face to the extent of saying that you have just now come into possession of it."

"*I'll* say?"

"Yes. The retraction won't be editorial. It will be over your signature."

"I won't do it. You're a fool, Parris Mitchell."

"Would you rather Miles Jackson published it in his paper?"

"The *Gazette*—you mean—"

"Of course. Do you think I'll let you do this to me, and do nothing about it? Incidentally, I had a little talk with the Governor last week. He was here for the State Board meeting, you know. He seems an honest sort of man."

"Well—"

"I want to see that retraction before it's printed. It must be in tomorrow's paper."

Fulmer was red as fire, but he said nothing for a moment.

"All right, but—"

"There aren't any 'buts.' Just write it and have it in my hands tomorrow after breakfast. You'll get it back in time for the paper."

"In a hurry, ain't you?"

"Yes. One more thing I advise. I'd get rid of that newspaper, if I were you. People like you can't be trusted with a newspaper."

The telephone rang; its faint leisurely tinkle contrasted with the tense atmosphere of the room. Parris answered.

"Hello ... Yes ... What? ... When? ... I see ... Yes, I'll come on down.... Oh, a note ... to me? ... What does it say? ... Is that all? ... All right, I'll be along in five minutes."

He replaced the receiver.

"Fulmer!"

"Yeh."

"Peyton Graves shot himself a few minutes ago."

Fulmer's eyes stretched wide.

"Is that what they told you, just now?"

"Yes. Listen, Fulmer."

"Well, what?"

"Did you have anything to do with this?"

"What in hell you mean?"

"Peyton was afraid about something."

"I haven't done anything to Peyte Graves."

"I hope you are telling the truth. Come on, you'd better go with me."

"Where to?"

"To Peyton's office."

"Is that where he did it?"

"Yes. Shut himself up in the lavatory and blew his brains out."

"Good God!"

Fulmer looked anxiously at Parris, but Parris' face was set and expressionless. Fulmer followed him rather meekly.

4

Parris sat in the office living room with Drake and Randy. It was a midsummer day, close and sultry. The dry rustle of the big sycamore at one side of the house sounded curiously like rain. Parris and Drake were listening to Randy's account of the sale of Crescent Hill.

"That's really all there was to it, It narrowed down to just three bidders. I was sure the Thompson brothers didn't have the money to swing the deal—they were just hoping the whole thing would go at some ridiculous figure—but I wasn't so sure about Mr. Elliot. Well—anyway, that's it, and we've got Crescent Hill on our hands, the whole thing. Now, the big job is ahead."

"Gee, that's swell!" Drake snapped his fingers joyously. "We'll cut it up in decent-sized lots. Parris, remember when we were kids I used to talk about this whole scheme."

"Yes, Drake, I remember perfectly. I remember that I was a little envious of such magnificent daring. I thought you were pretty wonderful to think it up. I still do, for that matter."

"And now, here it is. And you're a partner. Doesn't that seem strange?"

"Yes, it does. But I haven't got much to do with it. I'd be lost in two minutes in the complexities of any such undertaking. It's you who are taking me along with you."

Randy laughed. "Always try to make yourself out poorly, don't you? But we've got one immediate question to be settled. That's the house."

"The house. Oh, yes, of course, the Graves house." Drake spoke a bit absently. He seemed to be thinking hard about something. "Oh, yes—I remember that house."

Parris glanced quickly at Randy. Drake seldom referred to anything he had seen, or ever known, before his disastrous accident.

"I remember that house," he repeated.

Parris straightened up in his chair. "Why don't you and Randy move in there?"

"What?" Drake pushed himself back into his pillows as he always did when any especially unpleasant factor entered conversation.

"Yes. Why not? It's big and could be made pleasant. There's a sun parlor in the back, almost all glass, that looks out over the whole country. You could use that for an office."

Drake looked at Randy. "Would you want to do that, Randy?"

"What about you, Drake? What do you think?"

"I never want to leave this house, as long as I live." He looked so white and miserable, so deeply shaken by the suggestion, that Parris said no more.

"Why don't you take it, Parris?" Randy kept her glance on Drake.

"Yeah! Why not, Parris?"

"Me? That house? You couldn't give it to me!"

"There you are!" Drake laughed. "You just now tried to give it to me."

"But you've got a home and a business. I have to live at the hospital."

"Do you have to stay there?"

"Well, there's no rule about it, I think. It's just convenient. The medical staff lives in a perpetual state of emergency."

"I see. Then you don't want the house, either?"

"No, siree."

"Well." Randy poured another glass of lemonade. She gestured toward Parris' glass. "More?"

"No, thanks."

"I've already got a half offer on that house."

"Who?"

"Aberdeen wants to use it for a boardinghouse for students. Not a dormitory plan, exactly. Just lease it to someone to run."

Parris shook his head. "But you just bought the place this morning!"

"I don't let grass grow under my feet. I knew we didn't want to use it. You couldn't rent that big a place. I think it would be a good idea to move it down nearer the street, and maybe build in back of it."

"Wouldn't Patty Graves scream if she heard you!" Drake grinned lightheartedly. Then he sobered, and said, "Poor old Peyte."

"Yes," Parris replied rather dryly. "What's become of Patty? Have you heard?"

Randy looked up. "Yes. Someone said she was going to write on homemaking—a sort of department on a St. Louis paper."

"Homemaking?"

"Yes."

"That's appropriate." Parris did not smile.

Drake looked at him curiously. "You've got something against Peyte's wife, haven't you?"

"I didn't like her."

"Well, poor thing, she's gone on to St. Louis. Left several weeks ago." Randy crunched a piece of ice.

Drake wriggled. "Don't do that, Randy!" He spoke sharply.

"Oh, excuse me, Drake."

Parris glanced up quickly. It wasn't like Drake to be cross with Randy. He stood up. "I have to go."

"Oh, Parris. Can't stay to supper?"

"Lord, no. I seldom get away lately at all."

"Are you working too hard?"

"No. Just hard."

Randy followed him to the front porch.

"Walk down to the corner with me, Randy. Want to talk with you a minute."

"Why, of course. Anything wrong?"

"No. I want to ask you about Drake."

"Drake?"

"He seems unusually cross and irritable."

"Yes, he does."

"Has Doctor McNeill been down to see him lately?"

"Last week."

"Say anything special?"

"N-no, I believe not."

"He keeps a pretty close watch on Drake's general condition, doesn't he?"

"Oh, yes. I suppose he's been here at least twice every month since—oh, ever since Doctor Gordon died."

"Maybe it's the heat."

"Might be. I almost wish Drake could be persuaded to move from here. I'd even take the Graves house, though I don't really like it."

"It would be good for him if he'd be willing. But he has a terrific feeling about staying on here. You see, Randy, it was his first refuge after the accident, and it represents protection to him. That strikes pretty deep in his case. It wouldn't be easy to do anything about it—not without a long process. We have to recognize that Drake isn't perfectly normal, and that no one in his circumstances ever regains complete normality. We'd better be glad we've done as well with him as we have. After all, he's not bad off where he is, but it's close quarters for you, isn't it?"

"No. I'm used to the place. It's home."

"But you *could* live anywhere."

"It makes not the slightest difference to me, Parris, where I am. You know I don't want to cultivate Kings Row, don't you?"

"I wasn't thinking of that. I was simply thinking of a wider horizon—I mean an actual, physical horizon. You're pretty well shut in down here."

"It's all right. If it shelters Drake, it suits me."

"All right, Randy. I was just wondering about Drake. He doesn't look quite as well to me. I'll call up McNeill tonight."

"I wish you would. You make me uneasy, now."

"Oh, I don't mean to do that. There can't be anything serious, you know. But we have to watch constantly."

"Of course. There's nothing you want to suggest?"

"No, no. Drake's on my mind a great deal. I see him making a little progress here and there. Did you notice the other day that he asked about something on Union Street? First time the name has crossed his lips. In a way, naturally, all of that is a dead world to him. We see the town, he doesn't."

"Well, I always talk of everything and everybody I see just as if he were going about like anyone else."

"That's quite right. But, lately, he has referred several times to the past. Something or other that he remembers."

"Just as he did today."

"Yes. That's a good sign. We must always accept these references naturally, but don't urge them on him. He's growing outward a little. But the beginning of that growth is extremely sensitive."

"Thank you again, Parris, for everything. You've been our good angel— from the very beginning."

"Ah—don't begin that now."

"I never forget it for a moment. Neither does Drake."

"I've got to run, Randy. 'By."

"Good-by, Parris."

Randy watched him out of sight. It was a good deal as Drake had said once: you couldn't know much about Parris. Randy felt, however, that Parris was lonelier than he himself knew. You can't live forever with just ideas, she thought.

She turned back. It was terribly hot. There was a low murmur of thunder from the west, and a gathering darkness along the horizon. Randy looked up at the tall poplar trees. Not even the topmost leaf moved. It was really terribly close. A good rain would lighten this heaviness. She rather dreaded storms, though, on Drake's account. He was extremely nervous during heavy thunder and lightning. She quickened her step a little as a sudden flare of yellow leapt up from the still distant clouds.

The summer wore itself out. September was still hot, and the shrubs and weeds along the roads were gray with dust. The cicadas kept up an almost incessant whir which was a very counterpart in sound of the prickly discomfort of the weather.

Randy busied herself with the new project, and Drake reported to Parris that they were all going to "kill a big one" with this deal.

"It's a little different from what I planned all those years ago, Parris, but it's going to pay a whole lot bigger than I ever dreamed it could."

"I guess business isn't as bad in Kings Row as I've been hearing."

"In some ways it is, Parris. But the way we've put this on, it's cheaper for a lot of people to own a place than to pay rent."

"Then somebody's going to have some vacant houses in hand?"

"There's a lot of old stuff needs to be pulled down. So Randy tells me. There'll be changes."

"I see."

Parris spent much of his free time with the Sandors. He had begun to feel that the comfortable, mellow, old house was home again. There were always good food, good talk, and some music. Mr. Sandor sat and smoked and listened to the easy quiet talk of Elise and Parris. Occasionally he joined in the discussion. The man was really a thorough scientist, but he scoffed at the appellation.

"I'm a practical horticulturist. Now your scientists—these wizards—I do not do anything like that. You understand, Dr. Mitchell, to grow a bean pod a foot long, to make a turnip as big as a plate! First of all, that is not my job."

"What is your job, exactly?"

"To improve the common breed."

Parris considered this, and repeated the phrase slowly as if each word had some quite ulterior meaning for him. "'To—improve—the—common—breed.'"

"Yes. Exactly. But you understand—like this: to make an improvement on all fronts of advancement at once."

"No. I don't understand you at all."

"Like this. I work with a species of—of bean, let us say. I work to make a few more pods, each pod a little larger, to make fewer leaves maybe, to adapt the plant to a particular climate, to make it a little hardier, maybe a little quicker to flower—many points like that. It is not my job to make a giant or a freak which might quickly revert. Just practical improvement of vegetables, that's all. There is just a beginning made for this region: soil study—much chemistry study, yet. The friendly bacteria, the change of crops—so many factors. But, as I said, just a little at a time on all fronts of advancement, si-mul-ta-ne-ous-ly. My, but that is a hard word!"

"To improve the common breed!" Parris said the words again, rather dreamily.

"Yes. It would be good if somebody would do this for the human beings. They need it."

"I was thinking just that."

Elise broke in eagerly. "But isn't that just what doctors do—are doing now?"

Parris nodded slightly, but doubtfully. "It's slow business when—when your bean plant has legs and is always running into mischief. My own job, of course, is pretty different—it's taking care of the accidents, I suppose you have to call them that."

Mr. Sandor wagged his head vigorously. "I have some plants like that! I will show you. Plants go crazy, too, sometimes, when you put a strain on them. They turn out—act—*monsters* sometimes. I shut my eyes at them!"

Parris laughed. "Imagine a lunatic squash on the rampage!"

Sandor looked solemn. "You'd be surprised, Doctor!"

Sometimes Parris plodded about the familiar fields and slopes with Sandor. Sometimes they talked, but more often these excursions were silent. Sandor was intent on his subjects. He talked to them in his broad Viennese dialect, muttered and quarreled as if with articulate adversaries. Parris dreamed, or remembered. Out of all of his new association with every familiar corner of the old place something was coming back to him. Piece by piece, little by little, a reconstruction was taking place.

He had broken away from this scene so violently after his grandmother's death. The very suddenness of the act and the completeness of his transplantation had built up a completely new life for him, new events to remember and to measure by, new experience, and a new background of reference. Now it was a little as if a light were beginning to glow again in that which had been dark. The old came slowly into the range of perception, joined itself to the new, and seemed to make continuous two parts of his life which he had thought were forever disparate. And with the union came some quality of youth which had been prematurely quenched. Until lately he had actually felt as if he were a contemporary of Dr. Nolan and Dr. Meacham. He smiled a little at his own over-solemn demeanor.

Perhaps Parris was not clearly aware of the most powerful influence which flowed again full against him as the barriers between his past and his present thinned and gave way. That was the sum of the qualities which made up the unique and effective personality of his grandmother.

He thought of her often. He recalled her now with the wistfulness and tenderness that come to invest such a memory. He was able to look directly at these memories. From them there came to him something of buoyancy, of quizzical wisdom and insouciance, something of lightness, and something also that was the keen, unafraid integrity and intellectual honesty that had made up her mind and character.

His thinking altered from the ponderous gravity imposed upon it by his teachers and his work itself. Something of the eternal patience of the universe itself, which often appears lighthearted and indifferent, played across his mind. He began to gain a perspective he had not had.

In his attitude and in his adjustment to his own increasing world, and even in the external manifestations of his personality, the intentions and purposes of Marie von Eln came gradually to their full fruition.

Once in a while Parris talked about his grandmother to Elise. They walked much across the hills, and through the yellow autumn fields. Elise did not share his love of the small details of nature. She liked the great curve of a hill, the color of a distant horizon, or the wild passage of clouds before a storm, but she had less interest in single features of the out of doors.

"I like a flower better if I do not know what it is. Then I can amuse myself by guessing that it is all sorts of things. When father, for instance, tells me all about—about the insides of a flower, I don't like it so much. You know, Doctor Mitchell, I do really love everything—everything out here, but it is better if it is a little mysterious."

Parris listened, amused and a little absent. He told her how he had always supposed a certain plant was the Solomon's-seal, but had never been sure.

"Which one is that?"

"Come up the hill. It grows about those rocks."

They strolled across the slope to the outcropping ledge.

"There, that one!"

"Oh. Yes. I have seen it. And what is it, really?"

"I don't know."

"You mean you never found out?"

"Never."

"You didn't ask anyone?"

"No. For all I know it may actually be Solomon's-seal, but I think Jamie Wakefield said it wasn't."

Elise laughed. "But that is like me! I could not have believed you so foolish."

He watched her as she talked. The half-stately phrases of her careful English had a special charm. It reminded him of his grandmother's speech. There was an odd flavor, almost exotic, about her utterance of the simplest commonplace. Sometimes they spoke German. Elise preferred English, or French, which she spoke only passably well.

"Let's don't tell father!"

"About what?"

"About this vine. He'd tell us all about it, and then that would be the end of the interest."

"You don't talk much like the daughter of a botanist."

They wandered on, aimlessly, talking casually, sometimes drawing together a little as they considered some view they thought particularly lovely.

"Dr. Mitchell, I must ask you a question."

"All right."

"The first time you came here, when you came up on the terrace, you asked me if my name was Renée. Why did you think that might be my name?"

"I think I was startled by the way you looked."

"Like someone named Renée?"

"A little like someone, yes."

"Was she—a—a—?"

"She was a little girl I used to play with."

She looked up quickly. "Your sweetheart?"

"Yes."

"Long ago?"

"I was a small boy. She lived on the place—in the overseer's house."

"What became of her?"

A look, like a sudden shadow, crossed his face, but it went quickly. Elise had seen the expression before.

"She went away. The family left."

"Oh. You never saw her again?"

"No." Parris pointed at the little pond which was just visible through the trees. "We used to go swimming there. We were just babies, but we knew we ought not to. We called it our 'secret lake.'"

Elise considered this for a moment. Then her eyes lighted. She laughed. "You mean—oh, you naughty children!"

"It was long ago." The shadow lay on his face again, and Elise said no more. They turned and walked up the long slopes through the narrow avenues behind the evergreens. They climbed a barbed-wire fence, and Elise tore her skirt. He had helped her over the fence, and still held her hand. They walked on through the tall dry grass of an open field.

5

That winter Parris set about organizing his notes and his published articles into a book. The work proved more difficult than he had expected, and as a consequence he saw very little of Randy and Drake or of the Sandors. A Viennese publishing house had prepared an ambitious scheme of monographs on phases of contemporary psychiatry, and Parris' work appeared to fit into the plan. It had to be written in German, and that took more time than if it had been in English. In February it was arranged to publish simultaneously in French. Parris immediately set about preparing his own version of the French text. It was not until the beginning of April that he reached the end of the task. He planned to go to Vienna in May for final consultation with the board of editors. It was to be a hurried trip. He would be back in America by the middle of June.

One evening Randy called him rather late.

"I want to see you, Parris. Could you come down?"

"Yes, of course. What's up? You sound worried."

"I am."

"Drake?"

"Yes."

"I'll be there in half an hour."

Randy met him at the corner. "Drake's sick, Parris."

"What's wrong?"

"He's in a great deal of pain."

"Where? Did you call McNeill?"

"The pain is in his hip. He's been complaining some all winter. But I thought it was fatigue. He stayed propped up too long at a time. That's what Doctor McNeill thought, too."

"When did McNeill see him?"

"This morning. He had to go to Springfield today, so he won't be back until Thursday."

"What did he say?"

"Not much. But he frightened me."

"Quick, Randy! What are you talking about?"

"He—he didn't say anything, exactly, but I gathered that something *might* be wrong with the bone."

Parris drew breath sharply. "Why didn't he call me?"

"He said he'd talk to you Thursday."

"Does Drake—did he tell Drake anything?"

"No. But he left a sedative. Drake's easier just now."

Parris found Drake half asleep, but tossing restlessly. He sat and talked with Randy until late. He felt extremely depressed when he left the house. He knew that he should hold his apprehensions in check until he talked to Doctor McNeill, but he was unable to shake off a grave premonition.

His interview with Doctor McNeill on Thursday confirmed his fears.

"Of course, Dr. Mitchell, there must be a consultation. I suggest we get Mercer down from Chicago, or Drecher from St. Louis. Both of them, if you think best. But, you see, there was no real indication of anything more than Mr. McHugh's usual discomfort, though perhaps more aggravated. But I'm fairly sure."

"It's not—?" Parris choked a little and cleared his throat. Doctor McNeill sensed the question.

"An operation would be useless. The pelvic structure is involved, and there are certain indications of further spread."

Parris found himself asking the question that so many anxious and stricken people ask a physician.

"How long?"

Doctor McNeill shrugged doubtfully. "I don't give him more than six months—maybe less."

"And in the meantime, of course—"

"Opiates. That's all we can do."

Parris talked to Randy the same day. He tried to veil the pronouncement, and to hold out hopes from the consultation. Randy sat perfectly still. Little by little the color and the expression left her face.

"Don't try to shield *me*, Parris. It's not generous, or even fair to me. Let's think about Drake. What will he have to go through with before the end?"

"God knows, Randy. I've thought of that."

"We have to do something. We can't let Drake endure too much. It would break down everything he has won for himself. We've all fought together to save Drake's sanity and make him the man he was meant to be in the first place. He must not die feeling that he has lost it. He must die while he's himself."

Parris said nothing.

"Do you hear me, Parris?"

"Yes, Randy. You pose an old question. There's nothing any of us can do. There's nothing any honorable physician could do."

"I'm not a physician. I love Drake."

"Don't cross bridges yet, Randy. There's the consultation."

"Nonsense. You know what they'll say. So do I. I know it, I don't know how."

"There are always unpredictable factors—"

"You talk like a doctor. Listen, Parris. I've got to know something."

"Well?"

"Could Drake's—could the amputation have had anything to do with this?"

Parris waited a moment. His eyes darkened. "I can't answer that question, Randy."

"Can't, or won't?"

"I mean I can't. I don't know."

"Could it have had anything to do with it—could it be the faraway cause?"

"Possibly."

"Probably?"

"I don't know, Randy."

"Do you think, *probably?*"

"I can't say. I have already thought of it. Randy, my dear, you are pretty stouthearted. I wouldn't keep a fact from you if it would in any way help you to bear—what we shall have to bear. But I am telling you the truth when I say I don't know. I thought of Dr. Gordon right away—as I always do whenever a case comes up that he has had anything to do with. But I couldn't even in my own mind answer that question. Many people have cancer that attacks bone structure. We don't know causes. Does that answer your question?"

"Partly. If I thought this was a direct result—I'd dig up Gordon's bones and scatter them to the dogs!"

"Oh, Randy! There's no use—"

"I know. I've shut away old tormenting questions about this awful amputation, deep in my mind, but now—"

"Don't cry."

"I'm not crying. I'm cursing. I'm cursing everything there is in this town, everything in the world, everything in heaven, or hell! Parris, I could stand anything for myself—but, Drake! My God, hasn't he had enough?"

"I wish I knew one word to say, Randy. I'm here—to do anything I can for you and Drake—"

"The time will come when you'll have to do something for him. The time will be here soon enough."

About the middle of May Parris consulted Dr. McNeill again.

"I have this fairly important appointment in Vienna, but if there is any immediate danger, I won't go. What do you think?"

"I should say you can go quite safely. Actually, Mr. McHugh has seemed about the same now for the past month."

"He seemed fairly comfortable yesterday, I thought."

"Some days are better than others. The nurses, as you know, have instructions to see that he does not suffer too much. Naturally, there's the time ahead when opiates fail. You know yourself."

"Yes."

"How long do you plan to stay abroad, Dr. Mitchell?"

"A month—I mean, I expect now to be absent only a month."

"Can you make it that quickly?"

"Yes. I have tentative bookings on the *Lusitania*—five-day boat, a week in Vienna, and two or three days in Paris."

"I think you may plan to go ahead. I'll cable you as often as you'd like me to."

"I'll be glad if you will do that."

Exactly a month later Parris stepped on the grimy little local train at Camperville. The reports from Dr. McNeill had been disquieting. Parris was worn from the journey, and nervous.

The train rattled along through the lush warm landscape. Parris stared out of the window, but he was not seeing the fields that ran by, or the long corn rows that seemed to move like the spokes of a giant wheel.

"Hello, Doctor."

"Oh, hello, Brooks."

Tom Brooks had been the conductor on this branch ever since Parris could remember. He was fat and red-faced. His white hair contrasted with his weathered and rather sooty face.

"Been away, Doc?"

"I've been to Europe, Tom."

"Why! That so? Thought I saw you—didn't you ride over to Camperville just a couple of weeks ago?"

"Four weeks ago exactly."

"Been all the way over to the old country and back in that time? Didn't know you could make it that quick."

"Business trip. Had to hurry."

"I see. I see. Well, this'll be about your last ride on this road, Doctor."

"How's that, Tom?"

"Going to cut off the branch first of August."

"You don't say so? Why?"

"Business slack. The Wabash put down a spur from Fielding to Eastport."

"Eastport—that little crossroad place?"

"Yep. Don't know what they plan to work out, but it's draining all our business. You see they can truck freight into Kings Row, and they've already got a bus line for passengers. You must a-heard about the Wabash spur along in, let me see, last fall they began it."

"I guess maybe I did hear about it. I stay pretty close to the hospital, though."

"Well, that's the way it is. We shut down business the first of August."

"You've been on a long time, haven't you?"

"Forty-two years, next November. I'm glad to quit. Guess I'll miss it at first. I got a little farm over close to Monticello."

"Well, good luck, Tom."

"Thanks, Doc."

Tom Brooks moved on. "Tickets, please." In a moment he came back.

"Say, Doc. I hear that McHugh feller's dying."

Parris stiffened. "He's pretty sick, Tom."

"I heard it all come from that old smashup he had in the yards. Is that so?"

"No one could say that for sure."

"It's a cancer, they tell me. I heard the other day that he's just all et up with it."

"He won't live long, Tom. That's the real reason I've hurried back."

"You and him have been great friends, ain't you?"

"Yes."

"Partners, too?"

"Well, yes, in a way. Drake and his wife run that real-estate business."

"Ain't she an up-and-comer! Smart as a whip, that girl. Little Randy Monaghan! Known her ever since she used to hang over her back fence and wave to the train every time it passed. She had a fine daddy, too. Too bad he didn't live to enjoy some of the money she made."

"Yes. Yes, that's so, Tom. He was a fine man."

"None finer. She'll have nobody but Tod, now, to look after. God a-mighty—it's funny the way life turns out for some people, ain't it now? Give her my regards when you see her. Him, too, if you can."

"Thanks, Tom, I'll do that."

It seemed to Parris that the days and weeks and months that followed stood still. Hour by hour, almost minute by minute, Dr. McNeill, Parris, Randy, and the nurse fought back the horror of pain. It was like a demon, an ever-watchful, unrelenting monster that held Drake in a relentless fury.

Consciousness was not allowed to come to Drake very often. He moaned and called, and while it was nerve-racking to hear, he actually did not know much that was happening.

Parris and Dr. McNeill watched Randy with increasing anxiety. It was a miracle that she did not break under the long strain.

Toward the end of August it seemed that Drake could not possibly last from one day to another. Randy came again and again to Parris.

"Please, Parris, for God's sake! You love Drake. You're his friend! How can you let this go on any longer?"

Parris quieted her as best he could. He himself was haggard from loss of sleep and the incessant anxiety.

One morning it seemed to Parris that Drake's mind emerged a little. Increased doses of morphia at lessening intervals were no longer able to hold back the legions of torture. They seemed to be breaking through the last defenses of science itself.

Drake looked with a kind of dazed wonder at Parris, and then at Dr. McNeill. Then he turned his head slowly toward Parris. The cloudy look in his eyes cleared for a few seconds, but in those few seconds something passed between the two men. Dr. McNeill was aware of the communication. He stood looking curiously at Parris.

"It's a matter of hours, Dr. Mitchell," he said evenly.

Drake twisted his head to one side, and clenched his teeth over his lips. A line of blood ran down his chin. Then the fog of an unutterable agony blurred his eyes again, and a long hoarse howl broke from his throat.

Parris sat, white and still. He scarcely breathed.

"It's for you to say, Dr. Mitchell."

Parris started at the sound of the words. He saw another room, and heard another voice say those same words: "*It's for you to say.*" He bent his head a moment. Then he looked up at Dr. McNeill.

"Do you think a normal injection, at shorter intervals—"

Dr. McNeill turned without a word and prepared a hypodermic syringe at the little table. The nurse came in.

"You'd better snatch a little rest before the afternoon. Miss Cooper. I'll call you."

The sound of Dr. McNeill's steps receded. Parris heard the gate latch click. He arose and closed the door leading into the hall. Then he sat down on the edge of the bed and took Drake's hand. He laid his fingers on the thready pulse, and waited.

He sat motionless. He could hear the tiny ticking sound of the nurse's watch on the table behind him.

The sun crept in at the front windows.

Parris laid Drake's hand on the quiet sheet, and folded the other one over it.

He stood for a moment looking down at the blue-white face on the pillow. A sudden breeze swung the curtains inward, and blew a lock of hair across Drake's brow. It gave him a boyish look.

Parris went out and closed the door softly behind him.

6

The days and weeks following Drake's death seemed to Parris to descend to a curious level of monotony. He was as devoid of feeling as the days seemed empty of event. He went about his work mechanically, he made a few visits, he went on long walks alone, and he sat up far into the night trying to read. He seemed incapable of attaching his attention to any of its accustomed points of interest. The whole world was slippery, incorporeal, and kaleidoscopic.

Just before Christmas he saw Randy at Cary Whitehead's office. He had seen her frequently, and he was surprised each time to see how quickly she had regained her calm. The lines of agonized worry had smoothed away. Some sort of deep inner resignation was evident in her rather detached placidity. She spoke of business matters with less enthusiasm.

"It used to be fun, you know, Parris. Drake"—she managed the name with a little difficulty—"was always so excited about anything new that we undertook. Now, I sort of wonder why I bother about it. I have enough money—I don't need too much, you know. There's just Tod and me."

"How is Tod?"

"Not so well. Poorly in spirit, I'd say."

"Now that the railroad no longer exists—"

"That's just it. Poor old Tod. He asked just one simple thing of life—a childish ambition, I guess, but it was his only one. He wanted to be section boss."

"Too bad."

"Yes. It is. It's ironic, too, Parris. They were going to make him boss, just to please him, for a while, but they discontinued the branch before the order ever went through."

"I suppose he wouldn't want to go anywhere else."

"He couldn't. Tod's really an old man—all at once. He was—he adored Drake, you know."

"Yes. I know."

"The railroad company gave him a gold watch. He's pleased about that, but he just mopes."

"We'll have to find something to interest him."

"I wish we could. But—that's not what I called you to talk about. Do you know Dan Gilbert?"

"Yes. Slightly."

"He's in the Elliot Real Estate Company. He's fallen heir to a little money, and wants to come in with us."

"Wouldn't that be a help to you?"

"Yes."

"Is he—competent, and just what you want?"

"He's recommended by everyone. Elliot would hate to lose him, I think."

"Well, Randy, I've been wanting to talk to you about the business. I'd like to get out."

"Would you? Why?"

"For one thing, I've got enough money. I think it would be better in every way if I were not connected even as indirectly as this with any outside business."

"Perhaps you're right."

"I just want to think about my work. Now, I don't want to leave you in the lurch in any way."

"It wouldn't be. Parris, I'd like to quit, too. I believe Dan Gilbert and Elliot would buy us out."

"Do you think so? But what would you do? I think you ought to have something."

"I've got Tod to look after. I'm tired, Parris."

"Yes. I can understand that. All of these years—"

"Parris, it seems like a dream now. I remember the afternoon you left for Europe, and I ran into you and Drake at the depot. I can remember all of that as if it were yesterday. I was awfully happy, I realize now that I was, until real troubles came. It's strange, but I don't seem to be able to recall right now all those years as well as I can the beginning."

"It's rather natural, Randy. You'll have to slowly forget the terrible things—"

"I don't want to forget anything, Parris. Every hour of my life is precious. I'll feel differently about some of it, by and by—I already do feel that I can endure to think it all through. It's all right, Parris. I used to think a great deal about the future. I always dreaded Drake's growing old. It was frightful that he had to die as he did, but … poor Drake!" Randy's eyes dimmed, but she did not cry. "I'll be able to make sense out of it all sometime, I hope. It doesn't seem to make sense now. We mustn't lose sight of each other, Parris. You have been so good—so good."

"You two were my only friends, you know."

"Parris, I'm just thirty-two years old—will be thirty-two on my next birthday, and I feel as though I had lived half a dozen lives."

"I can understand that, too."

"I wonder where Cary is—he said half-past three."

"Well, I can't wait. Can you?"

"Oh, yes."

"Why don't you have him talk to Dan Gilbert and see if we can't get rid of the whole thing, if that's the way you want it."

"I think I do. This would be a slower business than any we have ever undertaken. The project of little lots and little homes is finished, I think. Everything has been moving slower in Kings Row the last year or two. We caught the small real-estate business just at the right minute."

"I'm glad Drake saw that through."

"So am I. He felt that he'd done a man's work, Parris, after all, and *that* really restored him to his full self."

"I think it did. But don't forget that I know how much you had to do with that. You were his good angel."

"Whatever was done, Parris, we did together, you and I—the only two people who really loved him." She looked up quickly. "Do you hear anything about Louise Gordon?"

"Not a word. At least, not in the last year. I did hear that her condition was worse and that there seemed little hope of her recovery."

"Parris, all of that seems a mighty strange, dark business to me. I feel that there are worse things about it than we know."

"I'm afraid so."

Parris walked back toward the hospital. It was a blustery, cold day, and the early dark was thickening when he reached home. He switched on the lights and sat down before the fire. He thought of what Randy had said about her age. Thirty-two. His own age, as well. He didn't, of course, feel old, as Randy did, and as she must after these years of exhausting emotions and intense effort. But he had a disagreeable letdown feeling, as if many things, many courses were suddenly finished. He, too, had lived through experiences that had been too violent. A feeling of havoc and disaster seemed to invest the whole of his existence up to now.

Mrs. Skeffington's denunciations of Kings Row came back to his mind. They mingled in singular accord with his mood. And yet, a clear, cool thread of reason that spun like a thread of crystal through his weaving thought and fancy told him the feeling was wrong. Kings Row. He had simply made the mistake of thinking of Kings Row as a place, complete and circumscribed in itself. Kings Row was only a link in a moving chain. Kings Row was only a small unit in a diverse and fluctuating world. His discontents had grown out of imagining that his work had anything to do with Kings Row. It was only an infinitesimal part of the world's work. He, he—Parris Mitchell—was not Parris Mitchell of Kings Row, but Parris Mitchell of the world. So stationed, there was nothing in Kings Row that could ever reach through to touch him. He had only to think of the vast, interweaving effort of men in all places, and in all times, who strove to connect and link up the scattered labors of the world into a beneficial whole, to have sense of his own destiny.

He remembered now something Father Donovan had said, years ago that afternoon in the dim little church on Walnut Street: "*I come in here sometimes, and then I can hear it all and see it all. It's like feeling the pulse in your wrist that tells you you are alive. I come here, and I can hear the beating of the great heart of Rome....*"

Yes ... yes ... Parris felt uneasily along the ways of a new feeling. He could hear again the slightly mocking voice of Dr. Tower reminding him to be cautious, to be honest, to be shy of sentimentalizing. He could hear, also, the sharp, acid comment of Dr. Seiss, cutting away the emotional debris of decisions, stripping them to their mechanistic and deterministic essentials. The fire died down. Parris went on with his careful process of assorting and arranging the many pieces that were just now falling into some sort of design.

His precise thinking crossed the path of Father Donovan's veiled mysticism, and went on its own way. Father Donovan went into his little church and listened for the life beat that linked him to all great Rome spread out across the world.

He—he had but to lay his finger on the pulse of his own work and so unite himself with a wider world than Rome.

Sarah Skeffington was wrong. Good and bad—they did not come in waves as she thought. The generations of man might seem to come wavelike across the improvised pattern of time, but good and evil ran always in parallel streams. Sometimes they crossed, sometimes the murk of the one obscured the clarity of the other, but in time—yes, all streams run clear at last.

Even Kings Row ...

Late in the spring Parris crossed the Aberdeen campus one afternoon just as the public school across the way was being dismissed for the day. He heard the mixed chatter of the released prisoners, as clash upon clash of soprano dissonances chopped the air. He had come almost to the high wooden fence, which still enclosed the campus, before he saw Father Donovan. The priest was resting both arms on the top board. He was half smiling as he watched the groups of boys and girls ray cut, and cross, form in knots, and break away. He heard Parris' step and turned. He nodded and smiled and shook hands.

"I was watching them go," he said with a wide sweep of his arm. "It's the new world—the next Kings Row." He looked timidly at Parris. "I want to tell you something. You won't be laughing at me?"

"Maybe I will."

"It's this—and I know you won't laugh. I never in my life stand up above any part of the town like this and look down on either men or children upon their way that I don't almost have a vision. I know 'tis a vision of my own making, but it's like this. I see above them a concourse of angels—" He waited a moment and glanced anxiously at Parris. "Yes, sir. Angels. A dance—like of angels on everlasting guard over the people of this world. Good angels, and evil angels, too, contending with them for dominion. I like to think of it and think I can almost see them—each man on his way, and each one with his angel."

Parris did not reply. He watched the crowd of children thin and go away. Just a few years ago he had been one of them, he and Drake, Cassie, Randy, Vera, Peyton, and all the others ... *"Each with his angel—evil angels, too, contending...."*

He looked across the schoolyard, down across the hill, beyond the wide sweep of the creek with its plumy willows. He could see the soft-leafed grove of maples where his old home stood, where Elise lived.

He bade the priest good afternoon, and walked on. Father Donovan watched him with a curious tenderness on his face.

Parris followed the road, past the Macintoshes, across the bridge, along the sandy avenue just threaded with the scant shadows of the birches. He stopped at the gates. They stood open, but he unfastened the narrow wicket and passed through. Now, at last, he lifted his eyes toward the house. Elise was standing on the terrace. She raised her arm straight above her head and waved, a gay, happy, childish gesture. Then she ran down the terrace steps on her way to meet him.

Parris quickened his step.

CPSIA information can be obtained
at www.ICGtesting.com
Printed in the USA
LVHW101547240322
714308LV00009B/1486